'THE FLOWER S
LOP-SIDED. IF S
PETAL, IT MIGH

She stripped the petals one by one. He loves me
. . . he loves me not. As the pills dissolved she
weighed them against the child upstairs. In the
end she spat the fatal flower into the glass and
carried it through to the sink.

In the bedroom she stepped out of her clothes.
They used to tumble into bed, tired out, and lie
there, legs meeting, until a new lease of life ran
through the touching limbs. Still naked she
crossed to the drawers and took out her black
nightdress, "the wicked one" David had called it
. . . She took up a lipstick and drew a scarlet
rictus on the white face. "I look like a whore,"
she thought. It was the first time she had used
that word, even to herself . . . Perhaps madness
began like this . . . The black nightie slipped to
the floor and she left it lying like a wreath.'

DENISE ROBERTSON

The Land of Lost Content

A SIGNET BOOK

SIGNET BOOKS

Published by the Penguin Group
Penguin Books Ltd, 27 Wrights Lane, London W8 5TZ, England
Penguin Books USA Inc., 375 Hudson Street, New York, New York 10014, USA
Penguin Books Australia Ltd, Ringwood, Victoria, Australia
Penguin Books Canada Ltd, 10 Alcorn Avenue, Toronto, Ontario, Canada M4V 3B2
Penguin Books (NZ) Ltd, 182–190 Wairau Road, Auckland 10, New Zealand

Penguin Books Ltd, Registered Offices: Harmondsworth, Middlesex, England

The Land of Lost Content, part I of this trilogy, first published by Constable 1985
A Year of Winter first published by Constable 1986
Blue Remembered Hills first published by Constable 1987
This trilogy, under the title *The Land of Lost Content*, first published by
Penguin Books 1988
Published in Signet 1993
3 5 7 9 10 8 6 4

Printed in England by Clays Ltd, St Ives plc
Filmset in Ehrhardt (Linotron 202)

Remember before God the Durham Miners who have given
their lives in the pits of this county and those who
work in darkness and danger in those pits today.

Miners' Memorial, Durham Cathedral

Part I

The Land of Lost Content

❦❦❦❦❦

1

Thursday, 16 June 1983

She must have been holding her breath, for the words, when they came, gushed out like air from a faulty tyre. 'Would anyone like a cup of tea?' She saw heads swivel, eyes flash. 'Tea!' the eyes said, 'she wants tea? *Tea! Now?*'

She always wanted tea at times of stress. The night before Martin was born her waters had broken, throwing David into a panic. She lay, huge in the bed, and demanded tea, and he'd brought it to her on a tray.

'There won't be time, Fran.' Harold was speaking firmly but she could sense the fear behind his words. He was afraid she would stand her ground, get out cups, throw a teaspoon in the works.

'It'll only take a moment,' she said, feeling a vicious pleasure at scaring him. Scaring them all. It was funny, really, because she used to like them once.

She looked round the room. Harold and Eve, and Dennis and Min. Best friends usually, but alien today. Next to them the general manager and two of the men from the works, uneasy in their Sunday best. Some old friends of David's family, whose names she couldn't remember; and Mrs Bethel in her fur hat. Grey hairs straggled wetly beneath it and her brow was red and angry where the band rested. Someone should've told her it was summer.

Bethel was wearing her bra, in honour of the occasion. Her breasts bulged above and below, hillocks and foothills, a heaving Pennine chain. David would laugh when she told him. Except that David was dead, decomposing quietly in the next room. She switched her mind back to Mrs Bethel's bra. Amusement skipped down the corridors of her mind but she was careful not to let it show. If she laughed aloud they would call it hysteria, and none of them could cope with that.

On Tuesday she had stood outside the door and listened. 'She can't be left alone.' That was Harold, sweating slightly in his business suit but taking the lead as usual. Min had been the first to answer. 'I'd do it like a shot if it wasn't for the kids. And Dennis is tied up at the shop.' There were understanding murmurs and then, 'Well, we can't just go!' with desperation in Eve's voice.

'It's not as though she had a family.' Dennis made her lack of relatives sound faintly shameful, and she had leaned her head against the door-jamb as they continued. They all had children to rear, profits to make, burdens to tote. On the other hand, she couldn't be left on her own. 'You never know how they'll take it,' Harold said gloomily, as though from vast experience. 'We don't want something nasty to happen.'

A cry had formed inside her head: '*Get out all of you. For God's sake leave me alone!*' She waited until she could speak calmly before going into the room. 'Look, I'd rather be on my own. Honestly. Just the two of us. You've been so good, all of you, but I think we've done everything that needs to be done. For today.'

She had almost smiled as they struggled to maintain solicitous expressions. 'Are you sure? Really sure? You're sure you're sure?' They reminded her of children unexpectedly set free from school as they gambolled over the step. When they were gone she had bolted the door and leaned against it in relief.

That had been Tuesday. Now they sat in the Thursday room, dressed in sombre clothes and borrowed hats. Eve wore black stockings and Min had pinned up her neck with a cameo brooch. Sackcloth and ashes circa '83. She looked down at her own grey flannel suit and hoped it would do.

It was strange to sit here with them like this. Usually they met at parties – christenings and housewarmings, because they were still at the breeding stage and all going up in the world. It was stranger still to be without the children but they had been tidied away, even Martin who most belonged here.

At breakfast he had been small and crushed and inclined to tears. She'd given him an apple for playtime and pulled up his socks. 'See you at lunch.' His answering nod was uncertain and she'd had to propel him into the hall. The door to the front room was shut but she'd held her breath until they were past.

They had all been against it. 'You can't bring him back to the

house, Fran, nobody does it nowadays. It's lovely in the Chapel
of Rest. Really good taste. Besides, it's not fair to the child. You
must think of the child, Fran.' That was their weapon and they
used it freely. 'You must think of him . . . what if he saw . . .' A
vision of coffins rose up in her mind, and then she'd remembered
whose house it was. David's house. So she had brought him
home and shut him in the front room behind closed doors.

Suddenly she realized she was rocking backwards and forwards
on her chair. They had noticed too and their unease rose in the
air like smoke. Harold's hands fidgeted on the arms of his chair,
ready to propel him forward. He was trying to take everything on
his shoulders and leave her free; and, freed from responsibility,
she floated. Like an astronaut on a spacewalk, longing for
someone to reel her in and give her something to do.

She smiled at him to convey that all was well and cast about
for an anchoring thought. She must think! From the moment
they had told her David would die she had been aware of the
black hole. It was huge and amorphous and filled with ear-
splitting pain. Once in, she would be devoured. Its edges moved
inward a fraction at a time and could only be held at bay by hard
thinking.

She marshalled the facts of her life and reviewed them. *Frances
Drummond* née *Harvey. Born 16 February 1951. O levels in English
Language, English Literature, Art and Religious Knowledge. A levels
in English and RK. Occupation, Housewife*. No, correction! *Occupation, widow*. She underlined it and felt a new and delicious
pain: '*widow*' – weeds and veils and deadly spiders. She poked it
for a moment like a crevice in a tooth, and then continued. She
had brown hair and hazel eyes and weighed ten stone four
pounds. She had a mole on her left thigh and suffered from
dysmenorrhoea. Suddenly she thought of her own body, white
and naked, locked with David's. That was where she had felt
safe . . . ever since that first time in the back of his father's car,
both of them scared but determined. By the time they married
they'd been lovers for five years, ever since school. She had
never known another man. Never would, now.

She thought of the men outside the door, four bearers in navy
gabardine standing among carnations and roses twisted on wire.

David had brought her flowers every week, and once a single orchid in a jar.

She lurched away from dangerous thoughts and tried to concentrate. There was the faint beginning of a shine on Harold's suit and a powdering of dandruff on his shoulders. But he must be prospering. According to David, accountants always came out on the right side.

She turned her head and caught Eve's eyes watching her watching Harold. Eve was always watchful. David used to laugh about it after parties, when they were alone together in the car speeding home. Fran knew where this train of thought would lead but she couldn't stop. After parties! Speeding home! Kicking off shoes, letting the party finery lie where it fell, reaching for each other ... The train rocketed to its predicted destination and she cried.

For the first time in days she had got the timing right. The undertaker reappeared, the careful faces converged, they led her, weeping, into the hall and out to the waiting cars. Ridiculously, she thought of weddings ... the scent of flowers, limousines, everyone deferring to her, the curious faces of the passers-by. Nothing like a Rolls for drawing the eye! She might have been a bride, except for her mourning face.

Eve and Min climbed in beside her, then Harold and Dennis in the tip-up seats. She wondered about the following cars but dared not turn her head. How did they work out order of preference? Sense of loss, or age, or social status? She closed her eyes on a picture of the undertaker nipping in and out, sheepdog like, picking out socio-economic group threes for one car, group fours for another. Laughter bubbled up and escaped, and she had to turn it into a moan. They wouldn't understand; she hardly understood herself. But she understood their need for a proper grief and she was trying to oblige. How much simpler if she could've changed colour like litmus paper and shown the dying inside.

She turned her face to the window as the cars drew away and tried to stop hating them. They meant well and they were her best friends. As long as they were out of the house when Martin came home! Another smile threatened at the memory of Mrs

Bethel's outraged face when she'd found there would be no funeral feast. No ham, no pease pudding, none of the traditional meringues.

'You can't turn people away without bite or sup!' Oh, but she could. She could do anything she liked now. For the first time in her life there was no need to consult. Yesterday she had nodded gravely while the general manager of David's factory had outlined her rights. No one had ever talked money with her before. 'There's no pension, I'm afraid. If it had been an industrial accident . . . but of course you'll have an entitlement under the National Insurance scheme and there is an ex-gratia payment from the firm. Fifteen hundred pounds.'

His eyes had been anxious, begging for release. 'That's very generous,' she'd said, and watched his face relax. Alive, David had been a company asset; dead, he was a liability, something to be set against tax. Leaving, the general manager had mouthed the usual remark – the twentieth one to say it. 'If there's anything, anything at all . . . you only have to ask.'

Harold's hand was on her elbow, pinching with nerves like her father's hand at her wedding. *'Dearly beloved, we are gathered . . .'* Today, though, it was something about this corruption putting on incorruption. She squeezed her eyes tight and blew her nose in the shelter of a faltering hymn. The perfume on her hanky was sharp and spicy. This morning she had held the bottle in her hand . . . perfume and earrings . . . she wore those things for David. In the end she'd sprinkled it on her hanky, as her mother had done all her days.

The vicar was determinedly cheerful. 'Let us give thanks for the life of David Drummond.' His eyes flicked from face to face, never resting in case of challenge. If he locked gaze, someone might contradict! *'We are here to protest the death of David Drummond. He was only thirty-two years old!'* – she might have shouted that, except that she hung on the ceremony, rising and falling to order. There was no alternative route.

The sunlight struck fierce on her swollen eyes when they came out of church, and she closed them against the light. 'Nearly over.' That was Harold, lying in his teeth. They both knew it was just beginning.

The grave was decently veiled with artificial grass, green shroud for a new-born grave. She watched the vicar's face as he hurried through the committal. His eyes were glazed like the windows of an empty house . . . and then they met hers, and hurt sprang up in them like a candle behind a pane. He did care after all! She wanted to console him but tears trickled into her mouth and the words ran at the edges.

She entered the car clumsily, like Andy Pandy climbing into his basket. Time to go home. Once there she walked proudly, shaking off hands. If she wavered they would stay, and it was quarter to twelve. They stood uncertain. 'If you're sure? We'll ring after lunch . . . tonight . . . tomorrow . . . are you sure? You're sure you're sure?' She armed the last of them over the step and shut the door.

The hall smelled of flowers, and wet petals clung to the carpet. She gathered them carefully one by one and held them in her hand. Pink, white, yellow . . . browning at the edges. Putting on corruption. She carried them through to the kitchen and flushed them down the plughole one by one.

When Martin came through the door his face was wary. 'Fish fingers,' she said calmly, 'and chips.' He put his blazer on a chair. 'I'll come with you when you go back,' Frances said. 'I feel like a walk.' He slipped on to the kitchen bench and slid to his space in the bay window. He moved along, trying to fill his father's place, but he was too small and there was no comforting muddle of legs underneath the table.

She watched the food disappear, slowly at first, then quickly as he settled down. At first she was relieved at his appetite, and then affronted. She wanted to say, 'Have you forgotten Daddy is dead?' The face would crumple then, the eyes well up and dissolve. Repentant, she squeezed him to her, feeling the bones telescope in the small frame. After a moment he pulled away and she lit a cigarette.

The walk through the hall was easier this time, past the open door of the front room. She pushed it wider to proclaim All Clear, but the smell of death lingered and the carpet was imprinted by the coffin trestles. She scooped up the last damp petal and carried it all the way to school.

Without Martin the journey home ran through crocodile-infested waters. They moved towards her and then swam backwards from her hostile face. She couldn't bear it if they sympathized. Much worse, they might ignore it. When David had died, at the moment of his death, she had heard a bus in the street outside. '*No one has told them*,' she thought. '*They're still moving because they don't know*.'

In the distance she could see the outline of the factory, David's factory. She could even hear the faint thud of machinery. It was the factory that had brought them to Belgate. 'Production Manager' – she had teased David about that in order to hide her pride. He had been a good engineer. Now he was dead, but the factory continued to clang and judder and produce.

She saw one of the Malone boys coming towards her and changed direction. The cemetery was afternoon-quiet, a place of stones. A gardener leaned on his hoe, incurious. She closed her eyes at the laurel bushes. Once past them she would see the grave.

When she opened her eyes Mrs Bethel was there. She straightened from examination of the wreaths, grotesque breasts still threatening to escape. Frances waited for laughter to rise but it didn't come. The unaccustomed brassière was more meaningful than flowers.

'Very nice,' Mrs Bethel said at last, a sweep of her arm taking in the flowers. 'But nowt more than he deserved.' She had always got on well with David. 'At least he died in his bed,' she said as they passed through the gates. 'My man went in a fall of stone.' Beside the pit, seagulls showed white on the stockpiled coal. How terrible to lose your man in a fall of stone.

Today Bethel was strangely gentle, talking of little things as she mashed the tea. She moved the pot round against her chest to warm it. Frances remembered her mother doing that and it comforted her. She couldn't afford a char any more, but today was not the time to say so.

It was funny really, the way Bethel had come with the house. 'You couldn't do better than keep on our cleaner,' the vendors had said. 'She's a treasure. Knows her own mind, but a treasure just the same.' So they'd acquired Bethel along with the fixtures and fittings, and taken her for granted in much the same way. Now she seemed to have increased in stature and the set of her chin was firmer. 'Get that down you,' she said, pushing forward a steaming cup, and gratefully Fran raised it to her lips. At four o'clock she shrugged into her coat. 'The lad'll be back directly,' she said, and Frances knew she understood how much that meant.

As Frances moved to get cups and saucers she decided she could get by, working from mealtime to mealtime. When Martin was safely inside, she slid home the bolts. Four o'clock on a summer afternoon, and she wanted the door locked.

They watched *Blue Peter* together. 'See,' their eyes said, 'some things remain.' Halfway through she took the phone off the hook. Bathtime, bedtime. The phone clicked urgently and at eight o'clock she put it back – if they couldn't get through they might drive over. 'It's a pity you live out here,' Harold had said yesterday. He was already planning a move: she saw it in his eyes as his accountant's brain totted up the mileage. Sunderland to Belgate, eight miles each way. Thirty miles to the gallon and petrol a scandalous price!

Twice she mounted the stairs to check on Martin. Each time she was summoned from his bed to answer the phone. The last call came at eight thirty. It was Harold, with Eve at his elbow. 'Get a good night's sleep,' he said, 'and go easy on the pills.'

She made herself watch television, American cops and robbers, safe as houses. Mindful of the neighbours she kept the volume down. Perhaps there were rules, a recognized scale for grieving. After one week you could televise, two weeks smile, three weeks laugh. A month to wear red, six weeks to run in the street. She would find out tomorrow. Bethel would know.

The cringing houseplants caught her eye and guilt carried her through to the kitchen. As the tap gushed a thought formed ... who would water her, now that David was gone? She doubled over the sink. 'Mam,' she called, 'Mam!' No one answered, and she carried the dripping jug back to the streets of San Francisco. No one could hurt her there.

She tried to concentrate on the screen but her mind wandered. She was thirty-two years old. Forty more years to live; four hundred and eighty months. She couldn't manage it on her own! Suddenly the pain of her mother's death came back. David had sat up in bed all night, holding her in his arms. She crossed her arms over her chest, wanting someone to hold her! For a moment she thought of waking Martin, but he would turn to her instead, make demands.

Her hands were shaking and she spread them on the arms of the chair. She mustn't be afraid. She was young and healthy and lived in a Welfare State. Someone would tell her what to do as soon as she felt up to it. She shook her pills on to the coffee table and prodded them into shape. A flower emerged, five petals around a centre. 'Take two if you're pushed,' the doctor had said. She placed one on her tongue but it stuck in her throat and she reached for whisky.

The flower stared up at her, lop-sided. If she took another petal, it might balance. She stripped the petals one by one. He loves me . . . he loves me not. As the pills dissolved she weighed them against the child upstairs. In the end she spat the fatal flower into the glass and carried it through to the sink.

In the bedroom she stepped out of her clothes. They used to tumble into bed, tired out, and lie there, legs meeting, until a new lease of life ran through the touching limbs. Still naked she crossed to the drawers and took out her black nightdress, 'the wicked one' David had called it. The bathroom light was beating as though they had taken away the shade and she looked ghastly above the black chiffon. She took up a lipstick and drew a scarlet rictus on the white face. 'I look like a whore,' she thought. It was the first time she had used that word, even to herself. 'Whore.' She said it aloud to the avocado suite. What a word to choose! Her mind was splitting open like a disseminating seed pod, spewing out filth.

Perhaps madness began like this. 'Poor Fran,' they would say, and would meet downstairs to consign her to Bedlam. She drew the face-cloth hard across her mouth and scrubbed it clean. The black nightie slipped to the floor and she left it lying like a wreath.

It was better in the lamplit bedroom. She climbed into bed, spreading herself until her head slipped into the valley between the pillows. What had she done last night? She couldn't remember, but she had survived – so this night, too, would pass. It was only time, to be reeled in and coiled away. Seven hours; four hundred and twenty minutes. The seconds defeated her. She never could do maths.

What *could* she do? She'd have to get a job of some sort! The lamp winked reproachfully, reminding her that lamplight cost money. She reached out and switched it off. The room was as dark as the grave, a new-dug grave sculpted by spades. Her eyes grew accustomed to the dark and shapes reappeared, but it was too late!

Martin lay with his face to the window. Searching for a resemblance she tried to remember David's face, but it was useless. She kissed the child's forehead, turning her face so that the whisky on her breath did not contaminate his nose and mouth, then she lifted the covers and slipped in beside him.

2

Saturday, 16 July 1983

Saturday morning. No need to get up! The ceiling was flaking in a corner by the window; a tiny piece detached itself and dropped, winnowing, to the floor. She had never thought of the upkeep of a house. Now it seemed to be falling apart. Yesterday she had noticed the jamb of the back door warping and twisting. She knew the cause – anyone who lived in a colliery area knew about subsidence. She had lived in Belgate for three years, and had never really thought about the pit. In spite of once going down with David, seeing it for herself. Now it seemed to yawn beneath her feet, alive . . . threatening the very fabric of the house.

She couldn't cope with a house. Houses were men's work. She started to cry and then remembered how sore it made her eyes. Sitting up in bed, hugging her knees, she wailed, dry-eyed, into the quilt. At the back of her mind problems lined up to file their claim. Today she must think everything out, get organized,

make decisions. It was a battle now, every minute of every day.
She was shoring up a straining dyke, behind it all the black water
in the world.

It was a relief to hear the band, jaunty music growing louder
by the minute. She got out of bed and crossed to the window. It
must be Gala Day, the Miners' Big Meeting. They always held
it in June or July. She drew back the curtain on men marching
six abreast behind Keir Hardie on a crimson field. There was a
wind from the sea and the lodge officials wore gabardine
raincoats. They looked serious and worthy, and she viewed them
with respect.

Their first year in Belgate David had woken her to see them
pass. They had stood in the window, arms entwined. 'They
march all the way to Durham,' David had said, awestruck; and
grimaced in disappointment when she pointed out the waiting
bus. The second year the banner had been draped in black to
mark a death in the pit, and her throat had constricted at the
thought of someone dead in the darkness beneath her feet. Now
it convulsed again, but this time the ache was for herself. The
last marcher passed from sight and she let the curtain slip into
place.

She was bathing her eyes when she heard Martin tapping on
the bathroom door. 'I won't be long.' There was irritation in her
voice and she hated herself for it. His shape was distorted by the
beaten glass but she could see his fingertips whiten as they
pressed against the pane. It didn't really matter if he stood there
a moment . . . except that he was only nine years old and had lost
his father.

There seemed to be always a two-way conversation in her
head now. '*These feelings are understandable. You've had a shock.*'
The other voice, sharp, '*Bitch, bitch, bitch . . . he's only a baby.*'
When she came downstairs she held out her arms, and the
sweetness of him was unbelievable. She was going mad . . .
riding a terrible switchback into Bedlam . . . so there was no
need to be ashamed, because none of it was her fault.

She made him a cooked breakfast, cutting off rind and
chopping up sausage to let out the heat. 'Go on now . . . eat it all
up.' She sat beside him while he ate, holding a cup of yellowing

tea in her hands. The kitchen looked neglected – there was ash around the boiler and a fan of coke dust where she had dropped the hod. She dropped a lot of things now . . . or burned them . . . or watched them go to waste. The fridge was full of milk, but she couldn't bring herself to write the note that would cancel David's pint. Yesterday she had picked up a grapefruit and felt her thumb sink into pulp. Corruption! The warning bell clanged, and she opened her mouth. 'We can go out somewhere later on.'

Martin chewed for a moment before replying, 'The Big Meeting's on.' Fran nodded. 'Everyone at school's going,' he said hopefully.

She put down her cup. 'Durham'll be too crowded, darling. There's no fun when it's like that. Besides, it's all political speeches and things. You wouldn't like it. We could go to the Cleves?'

They had always loved the Cleveland Hills, the space and the height and the clean air. She could lie on the grass and work everything out, and Martin could run about and play. She thought of other days, the ball pounding back and forth, father to son, son to father. Martin didn't look at her when she cried, but he ceased to swallow and sat chewing the same mouthful until she lit herself a cigarette.

An hour later they were ready to go. David always used to get the car out for her and leave it at the door. Now she held her breath until the engine caught and it inched forward. She put on the handbrake and got out to close the garage doors. The back end wasn't far enough forward! She restarted and went forward in a series of jumps. She felt tired already, and they hadn't left the house. She wanted to rest her head on the wheel, but she could feel the tension in the child beside her. He was waiting to see if she could cope.

She drove carefully down Belgate's main street, conscious of hastily averted eyes. 'Poor lass,' they would be saying to themselves. 'Poor bairn.' They were acquainted with grief, the people of Belgate. The car climbed the sliproad to the A19 and she looked back at Belgate, laid out like Toytown between road and sea. Narrow streets of colliery houses beside the pit, and the newly built council estate a red-roofed blur.

It had been a revelation, that first visit to Belgate when David came for his interview. She'd sat in the car, crossing everything, knowing how much the job meant to him. 'It's what I want, Fran ... middle management ... making decisions, taking responsibility.' While she waited she'd looked out at narrow streets of colliery houses, the hulk of the pit, the Fuji-yamas of stockpiled coal. She had lived a few miles from this place all her life, and it had never been more than a name on a map. Her world had been a neat suburban semi, laburnum trees in spring. Michaelmas daisies in autumn, a bus-ride into Sunderland town centre along a tree-lined carriageway. And all the time Belgate had been here, living on coal. She'd watched a whippet lift its leg to a lamp post, a little girl clack by in her mother's high-heeled shoes, and had wondered how she would manage to live with so much grime. And then she'd seen David's triumphant face and had known she could fit in anywhere, as long as he was there.

Since then she had come to know Belgate, a pit village with the North Sea nibbling at its edge, leaving coal dust at the tide line like the black edge of a mourning card. They had looked at colliery houses sold off by the NCB and sprouting new bathrooms and indoor loos. In the end they'd bought a house built long ago for a doctor, in a street running down to a railway that shuddered with shunting coal trucks. 'It's a lovely house,' she'd said when David raised doubtful eyebrows, and so it had been until today, when she saw the first break in its fabric and knew it was crumbling about her ears.

Her spirits lifted when they passed Peterlee and the smoky blur of Middlesbrough appeared in the distance. David had always driven the difficult bits, negotiated traffic. She was afraid of traffic, but Middlesbrough had a flyover that carried them safe to open ground. Crathorne, Kirklemington, County of North Yorkshire. The hills tall to the east, low and rounded to the west like the breasts of a girl ... all gentled by that strange northern sunlight that filters between layers of cloud.

'There's a castle at Helmsley,' she said, forgetting Martin knew. Suddenly and ridiculously she wondered what they could do at Christmas. If no one offered, they could come up here. Bring a feast. Anything but home. It was July now. Six months to

Christmas. Twenty-four weeks, one hundred and sixty-eight days. 'I'll buy you an ice cream in Helmsley,' she said and touched his knee. It was cold and bony and small, and it made her sad. He was little and she was not much use to him.

'*I am burned out, solitary, bereft.*' It was odd how words popped into her mind. The night before last it had been 'whore', today 'bereft'. It was as though new areas of her mind had been ripped open. There was one parking space left in the market square and she took it gratefully. Long after she switched off the engine she could feel it throbbing in her thighs.

When they had come here with David, Helmsley had seemed vast, a warren of shops and alleys and always something left unexplored. Today she plumbed it in an hour. They wound up in a tiny café eating cottage pie from Pyrex plates. There was a funny feeling in her throat, a sore lump that blocked attempts to swallow. It seemed to increase with each forkful until she put up a hand, sure she would find an Adam's apple growing. In the end she gave up eating and lit a cigarette.

'I need a lavatory, Mam.' They were back in the market square. She nodded and watched him scamper away to the public toilet. While she waited she took out her compact. Her irises were a brilliant green inside red rims. She pressed powder on her nose but it dropped from the pink and shining skin. She had been crying now for weeks. In time she might damage her sight and be led around with a stick.

She closed her eyes and tried to imagine darkness, but her eyeballs singed and threw up flashes of colour. It was like November 5th. Her eyes were still closed when she realized Martin had been gone too long. How long did men take?

She moved towards the lavatory, her mouth suddenly full of saliva. There were always psychopaths in public toilets, lurking there waiting for little boys. She started to cry, a thin theatrical cry that somehow eased the pain.

The lavatory was white-tiled, branching off to the right so that all she could see was the facing wall. She halted in the doorway, pinned by a thousand years of convention. She couldn't go in there. She might meet a man zipping his flies!

'Martin!' She threw the name into the tiled depths and heard it echoing from the walls. '*Martin!*' If he'd been alive he would've answered. He was lying there mutilated. They always mutilated their victims. She tried to move forward but her feet refused to carry her. The place smelled and she moved back. She realized she was wringing her hands: she had never believed people did that, but it was true.

A man was approaching, intent on relief. His eyes flicked nervously towards her and then away. 'Please,' she said, shaking her head violently from side to side, 'please . . . my little boy . . .' He disappeared into the labyrinth and reappeared, holding Martin by the shoulder.

Martin had a hanky to his nose. 'It's only a nosebleed,' the man said soothingly. Frances wanted to lie down; her legs trembled and the backs of her knees ached. They were yards away before she remembered to thank the man, and by then he had disappeared.

They sat in the car until the bleeding stopped. Martin's face was white and there were blue shadows under his eyes. She would have to take better care of him. When she was sure the bleeding was over she took out her handkerchief and spread it over her fingers. 'Lick this,' she said.

His tongue was still bloody when he put it out and she drew the hanky away. 'You'll have to have mammy's spit.' She cleaned his face gently then stroked it with her fingertips. 'I love you,' she said. He wriggled in his seat and she knew she had gone too far. He was trying to meet her needs, but some things were too much.

They locked up the car and set off for the castle. There was a seat set into the wall and she settled there. 'I'll just climb these steps, Mam.' He ran about, vanishing and reappearing between the ancient stones. 'Don't go too far,' she called. She couldn't stand another crisis. She closed her eyes against the sun but brilliant colours sprang up behind her lids. She fished out her sunglasses and turned her head to the side. That was better. It was almost nice to sit here in the middle of history. They could do this every weekend. Except that winter would come, and she couldn't afford to keep the car, and she might have to work on Saturdays.

She'd probably wind up in a shop. She couldn't go back to the
bank. She'd have hated the bank if she hadn't simply been
marking time. 'You'll be all right in the bank,' her father had
said. 'It's the nearest thing he can find to a nunnery,' David
joked, and made her laugh. It was true, her father had always
wanted to protect her. And then he had died ... sitting in his
chair, slipper falling from his foot, pipe grown cold in his
clenched fingers. 'I'm here now,' David had said, fresh off the
train from college. 'I'm here now.' She had looked into his face
and seen her father, and known that was why she had chosen
him. 'We'll get married as soon as I get my degree,' he'd
promised, and dried her tears with his handkerchief.

In the end he stayed on for more qualifications, and Harold
and Eve were married before them. Frances had stood in the
church and thought, 'My turn next,' and David had grinned to
show he was thinking it too. They made love that night, and
thought of Harold and Eve in their Harrogate hotel. 'They
must've done it before,' she said, and David shook his head. 'Not
Harold,' he said, 'he's as cautious as they come.'

Harold was then articled to an accountant, and Dennis had
gone into his father's furniture business. Frances had never
known why Eve was so set on Harold; he was a bit dry and
precise, even then. Min was easier to understand; she was after
money. But with Eve it must've been love.

She opened her eyes and looked for Martin. He had given up
climbing and was sitting on the wall, swinging his legs in
boredom. 'We'll come back here,' she said as they went through
the turnstile. 'You can get a pass from the National Trust that
lets you into every ancient monument.' She thought of the future,
a long line of ruined castles. 'It's nothing,' she said when Martin
asked why she was laughing. 'I just thought of something funny,
that's all.'

They drove out of Helmsley and up into the hills. She could
see the smoke of Middlesbrough twenty miles away. At home-
time they would soar over the flyover and back to the empty
house. She couldn't get out of it once Martin went to bed – a
child left alone played with matches and set the house on fire.

They carried the flask and sandwiches halfway down the hill

and settled in a hollow. There was a double-fronted white house on the opposite hillside, a doll's house made in Hong Kong. Any moment now Mrs Fine or Mr Wet would emerge and trundle around on their wooden stand. The doctor had had a wooden face. A round and smooth and pink-cheeked face. 'I'm sorry, Mrs Drummond, but the operation has failed to relieve the pressure.'

If it had been a male doctor she could have leaned her head on his chest and his arms would've come round her. But the woman's eyes were on a level with her own and there was no refuge of arms. The cotton jumper under her white coat was strawberry pink and there was a thin gold chain at her neck. David had died from a cerebral aneurysm, and the doctor's Christian name was Joyce. The certificate said so.

She rummaged for the flask. It seemed all right. Once a flask had broken and the metal case grew hot in her hand. After that David had attended to them. Today she had managed to do it herself.

'We could play with the ball after tea,' she said but Martin shook his head.

'The grass is too lumpy.' He said it crossly and she realized he was bored. He needed a man. A man to chase after him, a man to carry him home when he was tired, a man to explain his body to him when it changed. What would she do when he needed to shave?

The panic was fierce until she remembered Boots. She would go into Boots and buy one of everything and read the instructions. Or she could turn him over to Harold. The thought of Harold in pinstripes lathering a brush was so exquisite that she let out a squeal of delight. 'What's wrong?' Martin said, his eyes already beginning to enjoy the joke.

'I just thought of something,' she said dismissively and then, as his face fell, 'What lies on the ocean floor and trembles?' He looked at her expectantly. 'A nervous wreck,' she said. His laughter was polite and she felt her own laughter turning to tears. She was such a drip! He didn't deserve such a wet for a mother.

'You could go in the woods for a bit,' she said. The woods were on the other side of the road, behind the car. He waited while an orange Volkswagen whizzed past. At least he was careful on roads. He vanished among the trees and she turned back to the valley. It was nearly time to go home and she hadn't thought anything out. There were hundreds of things to attend to, and all sorts of unnameable things would happen if she didn't. She would have to make a list. She liked making lists. Every Thursday she made a list for the supermarket. *Half pound PG Tips, one pound Lurpak, four grapefruit.* She always started with those three items.

There was no one to eat the grapefruit now, but she couldn't take them off the list. It would be like crossing off David. She would have to buy them every week for the rest of her life. Four every week, two hundred and eight a year. They would rot and corrupt and slither under the pantry door in a torrent of slime. She sat up sharply and began to gather up the things.

She started to shout for Martin long before she reached the car. He came out of the wood and she bundled him into his seat. They would be safe in the car with the door locked. Even in lightning you were safe in a car: David had told her that once when she was frightened.

The seat at her back was a comfort, the glass and metal a shield. She was safe in the womb with the heartbeat of the engine for comfort. As they came down from the hills she knew she would have to keep the car somehow. One way or another. Whatever Harold might say.

3

Friday, 22 July 1983

She decided to begin with a bath. It was the only place she felt safe nowadays. Still, it was nice to be getting ready for something. She tipped in bubble-bath and the smell of freesia drifted back. She put in an extra dollop. Some of it clung to her fingers and she sniffed it appreciatively. It was too good to waste, so she stroked it behind her ears.

She mustn't cry tonight. The lining of her eyes felt paper-thin, as though she had cried the goodness out of it. Anyway, it was supposed to be a night out. 'We'll have a girls' night,' Min had said, 'just us and a few others. No reminiscing. I'll ask Sally, she's always good for a laugh . . . and we'll stuff like pigs. No diets allowed.'

Fran had smiled when she put down the phone. Any excuse to show off the house, the well-stocked freezer. Min would never take affluence for granted. 'No way.' She realized she had spoken aloud to the steamed mirror and turned away in confusion.

Lying in the scented water she thought about her mind. It was located in the cerebellum . . . well, somewhere like that. Cerebellum, cortex, clavicle – no, that was a bone. She thought of biology and Miss Davison waxing enthusiastic over everything except reproduction. The one important thing, and they left it out or did it with the rabbit.

There had been sex lessons, special lessons in the Chem. Lab. with the air shimmering above the Bunsen burners, but they'd been queer affairs. One girl had felt she must faint to show her sensibilities and afterwards they'd all felt slightly ashamed.

At least it had been clear about the rabbit. She had never sorted out birds: they courted and mated, but did they actually do it? She raised a knee from the water and saw a pattern of suds upon the skin. Perhaps birds were like frogs, spraying everything in sight. She pictured a harassed cock bird firing hopefully at impenetrable shells. It was funny. Funny and lovely.

Nowadays part of her was always on the lookout for a laugh. Everything was funny, if you thought about it. And everything was sad. Life was a raw and squirming mass of unbearable fun. She winced, knowing that terrible thoughts were about to begin, then she stood up and pulled out the plug.

The mirror was running with condensation. She wiped it clean and stood, arms at sides, seeing her breasts like pockets on her chest, the dark buttons of her nipples holding them closed. Her hips spread above the dark V of hair. She stood until the mirror clouded again, imagining herself a toy soldier at attention. When she relaxed she realized she had controlled her mind, brought down shutters on things she couldn't bear. That was good.

She would have to be careful tonight if Eve asked her about the will. It was crazy really. She had gone to the solicitor with the fixed intention of naming Harold as guardian, for her only blood relation now was Aunt Em in Hastings whom she hardly saw from one decade to another. And Harold would be so good with money. 'Who's to be the guardian?' The solicitor's pen had hesitated over the pad, and she'd heard herself say, 'Bethel, Sarah Mary Bethel.' And then it had been typed and too late to take it back, even if she'd wanted to.

While she painted her nails she thought of all the things they would say if they knew. Eve would be slighted for Harold's sake, and Min would say Fran had gone, predictably, to the dogs. If she didn't tell them, they would never know – unless she died, and then there would be bugger-all they could do about it. The oath made her jump so that the brush skated off her nail and halfway down her thumb. While she was cleaning the polish from her skin she realized it had been enjoyable to swear. She must do it more often.

She felt funny sitting there in her slip . . . daring almost . . . and she couldn't work out why. She had done it a thousand times before with David hammering on the door for his turn. She weighed again the possibility that she was losing her reason. Her mind was like a balloon, huge and gas-filled and tugging at its moorings. Any moment it might break free and rocket off to God knew where. She decided to worry about it tomorrow. Tonight there was the knotty problem of choosing a dress. Mustn't be glamorous, mustn't be gay. Correction, gay wasn't gay any more. Mustn't be cheerful.

She had chosen natural nail polish instead of her favourite Iced Ginger. Now she threw the reject dresses on to the bed. Too low. Too bright. Too thick. Too dressy. She was almost down to skirts and jumpers when she found the green moygashel. Dark green was all right. She sat down to put in her pearl studs, but they looked tarty. She would never wear earrings again. The dark dress drained her cheeks and made her lips look blue, like watered milk. She outlined them with a cheap lip-gloss that could be wiped away until it hardly showed.

Surveying the finished effect, she wondered what she was

afraid of. Let people talk! In the end, though, it was not her own reputation she cared for, but David's. She must be seen to suffer so that the hole he had left in the world would show.

She looked in on Martin. 'I won't be late home and Uncle Dennis will be downstairs if you need him.' He nodded, 'I know.' His brow was cool to her lips and she had to wipe a pink smear from his skin. 'I'm messing you up,' she said and kissed him again. She wanted to hold him until his bones creaked, but it wouldn't do. She called goodnight three times on her way downstairs and halted each time to catch his reply.

She was ready too soon. She checked the casserole for Dennis's supper, poured herself a drink, walked from room to room, and still there was time left over. She wound up at the kitchen window.

Like most of the houses in Belgate, a garden was at the front and a yard behind. A mouse crossed the concrete and vanished beneath the garage door. She could hardly believe her eyes! The crack under the door was just that – a crack – and yet the mouse had flowed under it like water.

'Perhaps you might think in terms of a smaller house?' the solicitor had said. 'Property's at a premium in colliery areas, now that our mining colleagues are so affluent. If you sell you should do well, and you could get something here in town quite cheaply.'

She would have to think about selling. She would have to think about that mouse. But not tonight. She would not think about anything tonight except enjoying herself. Food and drink and a good laugh . . . except that she mustn't laugh too much.

Thinking of food reminded her that she hadn't eaten all day. If she wasn't careful her tummy would rumble. 'You sound like an inter-city drain,' David used to say. He was so clever with words. She ate half a carton of cottage cheese, chomping for a long while until it could be swallowed. She stood with her back against the fridge, holding the carton away from her in case it dripped.

Selling the house hadn't been the solicitor's only suggestion. 'I'd think in terms of some training, if I were you. There are some excellent schemes . . . you'd probably get a grant, and something for the boy. How is he taking things?'

If she knew the answer to that, she'd feel better. A month ago he'd been a small, warm boy who made demands and hung about her neck. Now he was visibly taller, thinner . . . he weighed his words and turned his head away if she probed. 'I know how much you loved dad,' she'd said to him yesterday, and a wooden look had come over his face.

There was a sharp ring at the bell and she heard Dennis in the hall. 'It's only me.' He had a bottle under his arm and a large plastic box in his hand. 'Goodies,' he said in explanation.

'But I've made you a casserole . . .' She felt hurt enough to cry.

'You know Min,' he said apologetically, lifting the lid. There was a chicken leg, three overflowing vol-au-vents, sandwiches in tortured shapes with exotic fillings, a wedge of gâteau and a piece of Brie. Frances turned off the oven.

She tried to feel grateful to Min for letting Dennis babysit. It was more than Eve would've done. She'd suggested asking Bethel but Min wouldn't hear of it. 'Why on earth pay someone, when Dennis is willing?' The main trouble was that Min did nothing for nothing – Fran could hear her at coffee mornings, 'Poor Fran . . . well, I've done what I could . . . not that it's ever enough, but one does one's best.'

Shit! The word shocked her so much she had to put her hands on the sink to steady herself. She had seldom heard that word, let alone used it. When she could pluck up courage she turned to look at Dennis, terrified that she had spoken aloud; but he was drawing the cork from his bottle.

All the way to Min's she wondered about the mouse. She had stamped her feet in the doorway and then tramped noisily towards the car. Nothing had moved. It was probably miles away by now. Anyway, the house was impregnable, David had seen to that. 'I'd die if we got mice, darling. I couldn't stand it.'

The up-and-over doors of the double garage were open to show Min's new Capri, and the flower arrangement in the hall would not have disgraced a cathedral. 'There's no one here,' Min said, drawing her through to the lounge. 'Just us and Sally and Vivienne . . . and Marjorie . . . and Joan . . .' The names reeled on, all of them patting her arm. 'I know, I know,' one or two of them murmured. She wanted to say, '*The hell you do!*' – but she was not John Wayne and this was not Colorado.

'And you know Lilian, of course?' She knew the woman on the settee – Lilian Sparks, the golfer. 'Lilian's been through it all – haven't you, Lilian? – and she wanted to come tonight and tell you she knows how you feel.' Fran smiled politely, wondering if she should say thank you.

'We'll have a nice talk,' Lilian said. Her fingers were covered with rings. Opals, diamonds, a single amethyst, a gold signet ring on her little finger. How did she make a fist?

Min put a glass in her hand and drew a wine table to the side of her chair. She felt a body against her shoulder. It was Vivienne. 'We came to the church, Fran, but we didn't intrude.' Fran felt like a beggar receiving alms. If they all came up to whisper condolences, she would be reduced to a screaming wreck.

Why didn't someone mention TV, or the possibility of a by-election? If she said, 'What do you think of Margaret Thatcher?' would anyone take her up on it? '*I can still talk, you know. And listen. I'm not an invalid.*' The dialogue started up in her head again. '*Come off it, Frances. If they behaved as if nothing had happened you'd resent it like hell.*'

Lilian Sparks leaned forward and touched her knee. 'Give it time,' she said soothingly. 'You'll be your old self in no time. Just sit quietly. No one will mind.' Fran smiled and wondered how best to murder Lilian. And Min. And Vivienne.

'*You are becoming a bitch*,' she told herself. She took a large sip of her drink and then let some of it flow back into the glass. If she sat there knocking back Martinis she would pass out. 'Did you see her?' they would say. 'Paralytic. It takes some of them like that.' She leaned her head against the chair. They couldn't all be bad. Why was she being so critical? Perhaps this was bitterness. She hadn't expected to be bitter, but perhaps she was.

She looked up to find Eve's eyes on her. 'OK?' Eve said and Fran nodded.

At school Eve had been the leader, simply because she wanted the job and Fran and Min were indifferent. They had been an odd trio, Min already ambitious, Eve staid beyond her years, and Fran – what had she been? Nothing really . . . until David. And now she had resumed the status quo. She tried to switch her mind back to the girls. They'd been so different . . . chalk and cheese and Christmas trees. Don't think about Christmas, think about friendships. They'd been different as could be, and yet they'd giggled together and swapped clothes and shared their innermost thoughts. Until David. After that she hadn't wanted anything but him, not even friends.

Min had taken up a pose in the doorway. The black hair was exquisitely cut and the pants suit must have cost a cool £80. How would she buy clothes on a state pension? The first time she had pushed the long, thin pension book under the grille the man had looked up and smiled, and her knees had buckled with relief.

Someone moved from the settee and Lilian Sparks patted the vacant space. Fran moved obediently and tried to concentrate. 'Of course you know what saved me?' One lifted eyebrow demanded an answer. Fran shook her head. 'Golf, golf, and more golf.' Lilian must be at least fifty. There were tiny indents running down from the corners of her mouth and a dewlap of skin beneath her chin. She waved a be-ringed hand. 'But then it doesn't suit everyone. You play bridge, of course?' Fran shook her head apologetically. 'What about gardening? You must have interests!'

Min had joined them. 'She's right, Fran. That's what you must do now . . . fill your life with other things.'

Fran felt her lip prickle. She wanted to say something cutting but couldn't think of anything cutting enough. 'I'm not sure I want other things,' she said at last.

Min smiled sympathetically. 'You won't at first but later on you will.'

Lilian lit a cigarette from a black enamel lighter and blew smoke into the air. 'You have to sublimate . . . God, the books I've read . . . you have to sublimate your natural feelings. Find another outlet.' A hush had fallen on the room.

'Do you mean masturbation?' Fran heard the words quite clearly in her head and wondered if she had said them aloud. Obviously not, for no one was registering shock.

'We'll help you.' That was Eve, backed by a chorus of

agreement. 'We'll have a night together every week . . . different houses . . . no men . . . just us girls.'

Lilian's 'Marvellous!' sounded smoky and somehow suggestive. Looking at them, Frances was surprised at how much she hated them. Tarted-up bitches nodding their heads in sympathy and not understanding a bloody thing! '*How dare you!*' she wanted to shout. '*How bloody dare you!*' Her mouth filled with saliva and the room was shimmering before her eyes. Min was moving towards her, long thighs rippling beneath black silk trousers. She had a lovely figure. Pity she was such a cow!

When Fran got back from the bathroom they had moved into the kitchen. Food was piled all over and Min was pouring wine into glasses. They'd obviously had a conference while she was out of the room for no one looked sympathetic or concerned and everyone was determinedly gay, as though nothing had happened. Lilian was hovering over the eats, picking a vol-au-vent here, a canapé there. 'I shouldn't,' she kept saying, 'I really shouldn't.'

Frances managed to get by without eating. As long as she took things no one bothered to make sure she ate them. She broke them up on her plate and later abandoned it and took another. A girl with upswept hair, whose name Fran couldn't remember, helped her to trifle and then took a generous dollop herself. 'I'll have to starve for a week after this,' she said. 'Geoff can't bear it if I get a few pounds over. It turns him right off!'

Suddenly she tensed, realizing who was her neighbour. Their eyes met and Fran could see panic. '*It's all right*,' she wanted to say. '*You can mention husbands. I won't scream or take a strunt.*' But speaking would have made it worse, so she smiled and moved away. 'I felt awful,' she heard the girl say to Eve. 'I never thought.' So this was how it was going to be . . . no men, no mention of men, just us girls. And she didn't even like girls!

She wound up on the settee, flanked by Eve and Lilian. Everyone was drinking still, some of them burping gently. 'What did you think of *Dallas*?' someone said, and conversation blossomed. What had people talked about before the telly? 'There's never anything on about the North-east and if there is it gives the wrong picture. Cobblestones are out!'

Everyone was nodding agreement. 'We don't call each other "pet" and stand on street corners any more!'

Fran thought of Belgate, every street corner a talking shop. She could open her mouth and tell them, but the desire for argument had left her.

'But that's my point, darling.' Lilian was leaning forward, emphasizing her words with a jerk of her cigarette. 'We're not all the same up here ... not all Geordies gannen along the Scotswood Road. We're different types ... races almost. We're not all pit yackers. Some of us are civilized!'

There was a ripple of laughter. Fran looked at them, lying back in their chairs, comfortably tipsy, falling over themselves to disclaim their heritage. 'We all felt sorry for you, Fran,' Eve said, 'having to live in a pit village, away from town and everything. And you never complained.'

Min was passing round the after-dinner mints, striking a pose at each chair while her guests helped themselves. 'It wasn't Fran I was worried about – adults can keep themselves to themselves, but it was bound to have an effect on Martin. Home influences can only do so much ... still, at least you can get away now.'

She moved to Fran and proffered the dish. Fran shook her head but Min's bangled wrist jerked angrily, demanding obedience. 'Take one, they're only small. The first thing you should do is move ... back here to Sunderland, where we can keep an eye on you. After all, this is your home town ...'

The mint was nauseatingly sweet. 'I never minded Belgate,' she said when she'd swallowed. 'Actually, I liked it being a pit village.' There was a moment's silence and she knew what they were thinking. *'There's no point in arguing, she doesn't know what she's saying. No wonder, poor thing.'* She could have borne an argument more easily than she could bear being tolerated.

'Well, of course that was the right attitude,' Lilian said at last. 'You've got to go where your husband's bread and butter is. All the same it's different now.'

'Are you sure you'll be all right?' Min said, when it was time to go. 'You've such a lonely journey. If Dennis was here he'd insist on running you home.' That was for Eve's benefit, but it fell on deaf ears. Harold was in the next street and there, if Eve had her way, he would stay. Fran felt a terrible smile growing inside her: they were so funny, so transparent, so awful.

It was a relief to be out on the road but the car felt big, a powerful steed that threatened to run away with her. She made an effort to relax her leg muscles, take her foot off the clutch. David was always chiding her for riding the clutch. The street lights raced towards her with alarming speed and she tried to slow down. She was drunk, that was the trouble, unable to judge distance or speed. She wound down the window and breathed deeply.

As she drove she thought of the party débris left behind. In a little while Dennis would flash home in his Mercedes and stride into the house. 'Leave this lot till morning,' he would say and put his arms round Min. She started to cry, little howls escalating to open-mouthed anguish. It was as though someone had opened a valve, relieved the pressure. She watched the needle creep up ... 70 ... 80 ... 90. There was a fierce wobble in the wheel and the blue P of a parking area came into her headlights.

It was quiet in the car park. There was a faint glow to the north ... the lights of Sunderland ... and to the left the wheel of Belgate pit against the sky. Lights shone in the colliery buildings. Lamp cabin, engine-room ... she felt a small glow of pride at her knowledge ... hewer, putter, shot firer, deputy, she knew more words if she put her mind to it. David had taught her. Most of his workforce were ex-miners, and he had enjoyed a pint with them in the club at weekends.

She had loved weekends. No need to set the alarm, no need to sleep too soon ... it was awful the way she kept thinking about sex. And strange, because there was no element of desire in it. They had all talked such tripe tonight. Whatever her problems might be, sexual frustration wouldn't be one of them. Each time the conversation had got too daring Eve had made shut-up eyes at them, as though the mention of sex was no longer seemly in her presence. 'They've put me out of the union,' she thought. 'Taken away my card.' It would be funny if they weren't so pathetic. She started up the engine and drove slowly back on to the road.

'Not at all. Not at all.' Dennis fended off her thanks with a

wave of his hand. 'I'd do anything for you, Fran. You know that.'
For some reason she felt embarrassed. Why didn't he go? He put
an arm round her shoulders and she struggled to smile. 'All
right?' His breath smelled of wine and she turned her head away.

After he'd gone she poured herself a drink and sat in David's
chair. She couldn't make up her mind whether Dennis had been
friendly or fresh, but she had wanted to turn in his arms and
press herself against him. It hadn't been a sexual thing. If he had
been an old man, or better still an old woman, she would have
felt the same. She'd wanted to be embraced, that was all.

She refilled her glass and lifted the lid of the record player.
The six singles were carefully chosen, every one guaranteed a
tear-jerker. She had tried the formula before and it never failed.
She started to cry with Roberta Flack. *'The first time ever I lay
with you and felt your heart beat so close to mine . . .'*

When the music ended she looked at herself in the mirror.
Mascara streaked from her eyes and a river of mucus ran from
nose to mouth. The feeling of self-disgust was a necessary
ending, a proper part of the process.

She climbed into Martin's bed for a special treat. It was a
haven, the best place she knew. After tonight, though, she
wouldn't do it again. That sort of thing could warp a boy.
Terrible thoughts of Freud threatened and she shut them away.
You could do that easily when you were drunk. Every day she
learned something like that. Useful things like that.

4

Wednesday, 27 July 1983

She reversed the car out of the garage into the back street before
she set about cleaning it. 'Give it a good clean,' Harold had said,
'it definitely gets you a better price.' There was a jumble of maps
and old AA books in the glove compartment, a broken whistle of
Martin's, her sun specs and David's winter gloves. They were
huge and shabby and had taken the shape of his hands so that

the fingers curled upwards in supplication. She sat with them in her lap while tears came, and went, then she put them carefully aside and got on with the job. She had expected to be a bit weepy but the main emotion she felt was defeat.

The car had been a possession. Real leather seats, a walnut dash and electric windows. 'And only nine thousand on the clock!' Remembering David's elation as he'd said that she almost cried again, but not quite.

At first Harold had ruled out a car altogether. 'It costs thirty quid a week, Fran. Honestly. Maintenance and insurance, tax, MOT, depreciation . . . and that's before petrol.'

She had tried to stay calm but there had been that funny prickly feeling along her upper lip that always presaged trouble. 'I need it, Harold. I can't go backwards and forwards if I don't have a car.'

His answer was swift. 'Leave Belgate . . . come back to Sunderland. You'll get a good price for this house and you'll be nearer the college, near to us. You won't need a car.'

'You must see he's right, Fran.' That was Eve, unable to keep silent any longer. 'I mean, it's hard enough to run a car on a good salary these days.' Her tone implied that Fran would be hard put to it to buy shoes, let alone wheels. In the end Fran won the day by promising to give up the house as soon as she felt well enough to cope with a move, and exchanging the car for a smaller one in the meantime.

She must keep the car! If she had to walk she couldn't avoid meeting people, seeing apprehension dawn in their eyes as they wondered what to say. It was the same for her. If she said 'Lovely day,' she would be labelled callous; if she beat her breast they would call her a misery; if she said something wild and inconsequential like 'Noses are funny,' they would scurry away to spread news of her dementia. There should be a password. 'Who goes there? Widow. Advance widow and be recognized.'

She finished the washing and began to dry the car with an old towel. When it was done she went inside for a cigarette. She hadn't told Martin about the car because she didn't know how to broach the subject. She would simply turn up at the school at four driving a brand-new Mini, as though it were a triumph instead of a defeat. She drew in a mouthful of smoke and gasped as she tried to inhale. Coughing, she wondered why inhaling was so important. She wouldn't be able to afford cigs much longer, so there was no point in turning them into an endurance test.

She couldn't afford petrol to go to Sunderland for groceries either . . . not every week . . . so she braved the Belgate corner shop for almost the first time. Fancy living on top of a shop for almost three years, and passing it by – that was what she had done. It had been hard to push open the door, wince at the jangling bell, see the husband and wife behind the counter start at her appearance and then compose their faces. 'Poor lass,' they would be saying, 'poor lass.' They'd cut her cheese to an exact amount and humoured her over brands of tea, and she hadn't missed the supermarket at all. Except that she would go back to it next week for reasons she could not understand.

She was beginning to realize how bad she was at managing money. Since yesterday she was the breadwinner, and still she didn't feel capable. She lit another cigarette and thought about that interview. She had tried to look brave and grief-stricken and radiate competency at the same time. 'I see from your application that you're widowed?' He had looked sympathetic. '*Yes, but I shan't allow my personal circumstances to intrude upon my work*' – she could feel the funny little answers forming in her head, but her lips stayed closed. He went on reading, occasionally looking to her for a nod of assent.

'And you think teaching is what you really want to do?' She nodded vigorously. Useless to say it was the only thing she could do and still be home in time for Martin. 'How about studying? It's some time since you engaged in formal study?' She was beginning to dislike him. The suit and tie matched too well, the fingernails were a centimetre too long. He was good-looking and he knew it. She hated men like that.

Her voice came out high and childlike. 'I've always read a great deal, and I'll have a lot of time on my hands . . .'

He was smiling, superior pig! 'With a nine-year-old to look after?'

She sought for the right reply. If she said 'yes', he would mark her a neglectful mother. If she said 'no', he wouldn't give her a place. Always the Devil and the deep blue sea. She was slipping into the waves when he had slammed the folder shut.

'I think we can take you.'

On the way home she had felt afraid. She'd only understood half of what he said and she wouldn't understand the grant forms when they came. There were fresh forms by each post ... pensions, supplementary benefits, pension rights ... all written by Oxford dons for other Oxford dons to read. She couldn't understand a simple form, let alone teach. She liked children – it was just that she hadn't expected them to take her. But they had taken her, and she started in September. Until then there was no point in worrying. She was adept at postponing things. The back of her mind was elastic, endlessly accommodating. She kept tucking things away there but the available space never diminished.

She stubbed out her cigarette and went out to wax the car. She was getting braver, no doubt about it. Yesterday she had managed the week's shopping without buying grapefruit. She had wanted to but they could no longer be afforded. Harold had allowed her £16 for food and cleaning materials. 'You'll have to get rid of your woman, I'm afraid ...'

Frances had cast around for good reasons why Mrs Bethel must stay, and Eve had entered the fray. 'You'll have much more time, Fran ... I mean ...' Her tone became uneasy. 'Now there's just the two of you ... well, you won't have your hands so full.' Frances thought of her college course, a voracious beast bearing down on her, but there seemed no point in mentioning it.

It was a relief when Harold granted her a week or two's grace. 'Perhaps you'll need her to help with the move ... you'd have to let her go then, anyway.' Frances had nodded agreement and stayed silent while he allotted the rest of her income. 'Two pounds a week for clothes ... It's not a lot but we'll see if we can increase it when your grant comes through ...'

She turned, hearing footsteps behind her. It was the Malone boy from the other side of the back street, trousers flapping above his Dr Martens, a spray of studs on his denim jacket. Usually when she saw him he was trudging home from the pit, but today his step was jaunty. 'You've come too late, Brian . . . I could've done with a strong arm on this lot.'

A puppy's head emerged from his jacket as he looked towards the car. 'I wish you'd said, Mrs Drummond. I'd've done it and nee trouble.' Fran smiled her thanks and put out a hand to the puppy.

He disentangled it from his shirt and put it, black and white and squirming, into her arms. It was warm and soft with an endless tongue reaching enthusiastically for her cheek. She held it a moment then gave it back. 'How old?' she said.

He let it chew on a black-rimmed fingernail and scratched behind its ear with his other hand. 'Six weeks. Me mam'll go leet when I take it home, but they said it was for the chop.' Their eyes met in total agreement. Giving the chop to so much life would be unthinkable.

He put the puppy back inside his jacket. 'Remember what I said if you need owt done.' He was yards away when his fervent 'Bloody hell!' drifted back. He turned and opened his jacket, grinning at the steam rising from the wet patch on his shirt. As he walked on, Fran realized how well he had played it. He had never mentioned death or loss, and yet she had been conscious of his sympathy from start to finish.

She ran upstairs to switch off the immersion heater. The boiler had been abandoned after her fifth attempt at keeping it alight. She was stoking it and cleaning out the ash but clinker kept forming and dousing the flame. She would have to master it or they would freeze, but for now she had hot water at the flick of a switch. Harold had suggested lowering the setting on the thermostat, and she had agreed. If she ever found where the thermostat was she might put his suggestion into practice.

She had Martin's lunch on a tray when he came through the door. One sock drooped as usual and there was a red mark where the elastic had been. She gave him his tray and carried her own tea into the living room. 'No,' she said as he moved towards the television set. 'Not at lunch-time. Besides, I've got something to tell you. The Malones have got a dog. A puppy.'

He chewed for a moment. 'What kind?'

She shrugged. 'No particular kind. It's a nice puppy, though.'

She had thought of telling him it was a Heinz, but that might lead to questions on breeding and she wouldn't know what to say.

She went to the door to wave him goodbye and went on standing there long after he had disappeared, like someone watching the sky to glimpse a departing plane. The sight of the gleaming Rover was a knife thrust. Everything was going, would go. Someone had pulled out the keystone and the arch would tumble bit by bit.

Harold was waiting when she arrived. He leaped about, waving her into a parking space, and she had to bend over the dash to hide her smile. She really was becoming a bitch! He was dashing about to do her a favour, and all she could do was laugh. She felt the muscles of her face twitch and suddenly realized it wasn't laughter at all.

'Let me do the talking, Fran. Actually, I know this bloke . . . I've outlined your circumstances and he'll give you the best deal he can. He's not a bad bloke, actually; bit of a spiv but all car salesmen are. We have his accounts so he'll see me all right.'

'It's awfully kind of you, Harold. I do appreciate it.' She felt the word 'actually' form on her lips and sucked it back. She was becoming a mocking bitch and an ingrate into the bargain. As he led her through lines of cars she pondered 'ingrate'. Another word liberated from some subterranean vocabulary.

She liked the car salesman on sight. He was shabby, which always endeared people to her. There was a tiny fringe along his cuff but his fingernails were short and clean. He reminded her of her father, and her feelings of distrust evaporated. 'What did you have in mind?' he said and she lifted her shoulders to demonstrate doubt.

Harold was in his element. 'Economy first . . . petrol consumption . . . low mileage . . . two years old . . . three at the most.' He was halfway down the showroom when he remembered who was paying. 'That's right, isn't it, Frances? You don't want anything flashy?'

She held her breath while the man inspected the Rover. She knew how these things were done. In a moment he would straighten up and purse his lips. '*I can't give you much, I'm afraid*

... look at the state of the body, and that wheel looks a bit dodgy.'
Even as she watched, it seemed blobs appeared on the paintwork
and fly-blown spots on the chrome. If he criticized David's car
she would die!

In the event he patted the body gently. 'Nice motor. I can see
it's been appreciated.'

When they left Harold was driving an almost new red Mini.
She had refused to get behind the wheel in the showroom and
Harold had been happy to oblige. She had a cheque for £50 in
her bag and an uneasy feeling that she had been an object of
charity. Beside her Harold chuntered on, patting himself on the
back for his influential acquaintances. Sometimes the car man
had looked directly at Frances while Harold was talking and she
could have sworn his eyes twinkled.

'You'll have no worries with this one,' he'd said when they
exchanged documents. 'That's what you need, something
trouble-free. I've been on my own now for two years, so I know
the snags.'

Fran had felt a surge of fellow-feeling. 'Do you have children?'

He nodded, tapping the documents on the desk to bring them
into line. 'Two. They're with my wife. It seemed the best.'

It was time to hand over the keys. The salesman twisted the
car key off the bunch before handing the others back. It was the
first time she had really looked at the keys. The door keys, the
key to the bureau, some office keys . . . David's life in a jangling
circle. Her lip prickled and Harold patted her arm. 'Come on,
Frances, it's only a car.'

Now they were threading through the traffic lights. 'I'm not
making you late, I hope?' Harold changed gear with a flourish. 'I
said I'd be back by four. Actually, we might have time for a cup
of tea in Dunns.' They parked in the rooftop car park and she
remembered to lower her head when she climbed out of the car.

Harold suggested cream cakes. Fran shook her head and
settled for a pot of tea. He fussed over cups and stirred the tea
bags with a spoon. 'He's enjoying this,' she thought. 'Wheeling
and dealing, and protecting me into the bargain.'

'I don't know how to say thanks, Harold. I must tell Eve how
good you've been.'

The resultant glow was less than she expected: a new thought had entered his mind. 'Actually, Eve says I don't take her out enough, so we better keep this to ourselves. Not that she'd mind . . .' Poor Harold, holding a tiger by the tail!

He came back with her to the car park and insisted on naming everything on the dashboard. The car bucked once or twice while she grew accustomed to the strange clutch and then she was gliding down the ramp. She was out on the coast road before she realized that this was the first car she had owned.

When Martin came through the school door he glanced unseeing at the Mini and she had to wind down the window and call his name. He slipped self-consciously on to the seat and said, 'Whose is it?'

She tried to sound triumphant. 'Ours. Yours and mine.'

There was a tremor about his mouth. 'Where's *our* car?' He emphasized the 'our' as though to disown the Mini.

'I sold it,' she said, and switched on the engine.

She felt like a traitor as she drove home. Inside the kitchen he said, 'My whistle was in that car.'

Relief made her salivate. 'I've got it. I kept it for you.' He was only half-mollified, but it was better than nothing. Clutching the broken whistle he went through to the living room and she went upstairs, holding David's gloves against her cheek.

When she came back into the kitchen she was met by the indescribable smell of new-baked bread. A round cake lay on the table, covered by a clean tea towel. 'I've brought you a stotty,' said Mrs Bethel.

Fran knew better than to gush. 'Martin loves your bread. We'll have it at tea time.' She had never heard of stotties until she came to Belgate. Now she recognized the flat white bread-cakes as a delicacy.

She brewed a pot of tea and they sat at the table. Mrs Bethel held her cup in both hands. Her arms were muscled and firm. 'She's strong,' Fran thought. 'She's twice my age but she's stronger than me.' The older woman produced a packet of Embassy, took out two cigarettes and handed one to Fran. They leaned their arms on the table and sent up twin trails of smoke.

'I baked some bread once,' Fran said. Mrs Bethel raised an

eyebrow. 'Cannon-balls,' Fran said. 'I made buns and they had a crust like a Sherman tank. You couldn't've got through it with a windy pick.' She looked to see if her grasp of pit jargon had been appreciated.

Mrs Bethel stubbed out her butt. 'I mind when they only had windy picks down the pit and a hewer earned his money. They're nowt but a pack of button-pushers now.'

Fran wanted to keep the conversation going. 'I've been down the pit. Just after we came here. They laid it on for David, and I went too.' She thought of the dark corridors, the light slung from her helmet, the heavy weight of the battery dragging at her belt. 'You don't have to come,' David had said, but she'd vowed she wouldn't miss it for worlds. They had stood together at the coal-face, earth rocking beneath their feet, roof trembling above, while a huge machine sliced coal like cake. 'I couldn't get rid of the dust. It was coming out of my shoes for weeks.' David had been so proud of her, telling everyone of her bravery until she'd had to beg him to hush.

'Well,' Mrs Bethel said, 'I'm sitting here as though I had corn growing.'

Fran didn't want her to go. 'You said your husband died in the pit?'

'Aye, caught in a roof fall. He was twenty-nine.'

Fran made calculations. Husbands were always older than wives. She must be sixty-four now or sixty-five. 'And you've never . . .' The words wouldn't come out. It was a cheek to ask.

'No. I never met his match. And we had no bairns, so I could manage. It was the end of war and there was plenty of work.'

Fran grappled with a desire to put her head on the flowered pinny, feel the strong arms enfold her. As if she understood, the older woman spoke. 'You'll be all right. Just take a day at a time. That's about all you can manage.'

Fran made scrambled egg for Martin's tea and carried it through. It was wrong for him to eat all his meals in front of the telly but cruel to make him eat at the table alone. There was slapstick on TV, a clown with collapsible trousers and a grin like the mouth of a tunnel. Frances had always seen something sinister in a clown's make-up, savage wisdom in the painted eyes.

Beside her Martin squirmed with delight, and she found herself joining in. She was laughing heartily when she remembered David. She would never have believed she could be so uncaring.

The programme changed and Martin's attention wandered. It seemed an opportunity. 'You'll like the new car when you get used to it. It's just the right size for you and me.' His face was wooden, and she knew he had made his mind up. She raised her cup and found herself biting the china edge. Damn him, making her feel bad.

She sought desperately for something else to say. 'Did I tell you about that puppy of Brian Malone's?' He nodded. 'You could go and see it sometimes.' She smiled ingratiatingly, hoping to get back into his good books.

'Could we have one?' he said.

She made a fuss of putting down her cup. Mustn't make him insecure, but he had to face facts. 'We can't afford it at the moment.'

His brows came down. 'They don't cost much.'

She tried to sound reasonable. 'They don't cost anything sometimes, not mongrels . . . but it's the upkeep. Food and the dog licence and injections and things.' He looked baffled. 'Some time . . . when I get a job . . . we'll think about it.' She could have coped with an argument but his air of resignation stung.

She went up to turn on the immersion heater and looked at her face in the mirror. Her nose was definitely swollen: she had noticed it the last few days. She spread her fingers and regarded them. There was a disease that swelled and distorted your features and limbs. Years ago she knew a man who wore gloves and stumped around on elephantine feet. She remembered his nose, huge beneath pleading eyes. She felt the pains of childhood acutely nowadays. They floated up like jetsam to add to her present misery.

Martin was watching *The Incredible Hulk* when she went down, and she sat beside him again. 'Tired, darling?' He shook his head but his eyes remained on the screen. She reached for her cigarettes. Why didn't he talk? Tell her about school? Even if he complained it would be conversation. She felt a surge of dislike and then the inevitable guilt.

She went back upstairs and turned on the tap. Soaping her hands, she felt the water grow hot and then hotter still. She wanted to withdraw her hands but she couldn't. She held them in the full flow until her ears rang with pain. A feeling of peace grew inside her as the agony increased. Eventually, satisfied, she turned off the tap, gripping it gingerly between finger and thumb.

She sat on the edge of the bath. Her legs were shaking and the pain in her hands seemed worse now they were out of the water. She crossed her arms over her breast and put the wounded hands in her armpits. She had seen a boy caned once, seen him flinch as the cane descended. The teacher's spectacles had glinted like mirror glass and foam gathered in the corners of her mouth. Afterwards the boy sucked his throbbing fingers and then enfolded them as she was doing now.

When she was making Martin's cocoa she remembered the stotty cake. It was soft and yielding. New bread. She cut a wedge and buttered it and then a smaller wedge for herself. Martin's brows lifted in pleasure. 'Bethel's bread?'

Fran nodded. 'She made it for your tea and I forgot.' He smiled forgiveness and tucked in. She ate her own piece slowly. It was rich and doughy with a pattern of holes that made her think of cheese. Dusting off the crumbs, she realized her hands were pink and puffy. She had done some stupid things, but that was the worst. She was vowing never to do it again when she went upstairs to vomit the bread.

When Martin was safely in bed she ran warm water into the sink and added detergent. The carrier bag was under the stairs. It had been thrust into her hand as she left the ward that last day, and must be attended to now. David's shaving gear was on top, taken in hopefully and never used. Two towels, and soap wrapped in a stiffening face-cloth, leather slippers, striped dressing gown and then the pyjamas.

She held them for a few seconds before she realized they were damp. When people died, the moment they died, they wet themselves. She had read it, heard it, somewhere, some time. She looked around for somewhere to dump the pyjamas. They were blue paisley. The dark-blue collar had always been crumpled around his face in the morning. One side up and one side

down and his hair tousled from sleep. In the last seconds of his
life they had wrapped him round. She lifted them gently and
buried her face in the damp folds. Later on, after they had
tumbled in the dryer she ironed them. It was the last thing she
would do for him and she did it with exquisite care.

It was nine o'clock when she carried her coffee through to the
living room. Before she sat down she collected pen and paper,
her wallet of stamps, and the bundle of sympathy letters. *'Dear
Frances, what can I say? Words mean so little at a time like this.'*
Seven of them said that.

She took refuge in statistics. Fourteen biblical quotations,
seven with a crucifix on the front, and four of a crucifix lit by
sunbursts. She poured a stiff drink to oil her pen. The raw spirit
took her breath and left her gasping. When she'd got back her
breath, she packed away the letters for another night. Who said
they had to be answered anyway? Perhaps the writers would
rather not be reminded of their condolences. Today, whenever
she had mentioned David, Harold had changed the subject . . .
with the delicacy of a brain surgeon in sheepskin mitts. Other
people did that too. So the letters could wait.

Tomorrow she would pay some bills. She had been putting it
off, afraid to diminish her nest egg. Now she had the cheque for
the car safely in her handbag. The car man had been kind,
almost fatherly. If Harold hadn't been there he might have put
his arms around her and held her gently, there in the middle of
all those cars.

She took out the cheque and examined the signature. A big S
in a flourish and then 'Carter' written quite plainly. Stanley
Carter? Or Sidney? Or Stephen? They had a lot in common,
both of them burdened by kids. She would've liked to go out into
the quiet street now and walk. Just walk. But the papers were full
of women who'd left for a moment and returned to find their
children incinerated. If Martin had not existed she could've gone
anywhere. It wasn't fair.

Suddenly self-pity turned to self-disgust. What was going on
in her head? Not only did she love her first-born child, she had
struggled to have more, spending long afternoons in the Infertility
Clinic. She was due to go back in September. She started to

laugh, bubbling with fun. '*Dear Gynaecologist, I find I have no further need of your services. My womb has become redundant and I have decided to dispose of it.*'

She replaced the bottle in the cabinet and carried the empty glass to the kitchen. There were seven pints of milk on the draining board and the fridge was full. She peeled off a silver top and up-ended the bottle. The contents chugged thickly into the sink and the sharp smell of sour milk assailed her nostrils. She turned on the tap to swill away the curds then she sat down at the table. '*Please cancel one pint per day till further notice.*'

Her feeling of relief at something done lasted all the way upstairs. When she was ready for bed she put a hand to the lamp and plunged the room into darkness. She would have to learn to sleep without a light, and this was as good a night as any to start.

5

Wednesday, 10 August 1983

Fran hated the waiting room. She couldn't bear the smell, the sniffles, the groans. She couldn't think what had possessed her to make the appointment, but once made it had to be kept. If you didn't turn up they labelled you unreliable. When the bell tinkled she jumped like a Pavlov dog and rushed to obey.

The doctor sat in weary resignation while she listed her complaints. A lump in her throat, a pain in her arm, sleeping pills that worked in reverse and kept her awake till daybreak. He prodded her arm and then suggested she untensed her hand. 'That's all it is . . . tension.'

She gestured towards her mouth. 'It's inside.' He peered down. She knew without asking that she was the fourteenth lump in the throat of the day.

He scribbled on a pad. 'I've given you a mild tranquillizer for day-time . . . watch what you're doing with the car. And you can take two of the Dorminox at night. Just adjust the dose to your needs.' She felt a fraud, a massive drain on the Welfare State.

She was halfway to the door when he spoke. 'Give it time. You're doing very well.'

When she got home she made coffee and carried it through to the living room. The long brown envelope lay on the coffee table: £283; £90 for cars, £120 for a coffin, the rest for flowers and notices and disbursements to drivers. It was written in copper-plate on thick and shiny paper. She took out the new chequebook and wrote out cheque and counterfoil. She had £1,274 left and the letter confirming her grant stood on the mantelpiece.

When she went through to the kitchen Mrs Bethel was hanging up her coat. 'Tea?' Frances said and filled the kettle.

'Carter's lass's gone again.' Mrs Bethel passed on the news with satisfaction. She had been prophesying Carter's lass's departure for weeks. They passed on to the doings of the Malone family. 'By, I pity that dog!' Mrs Bethel's tone implied volumes.

'The puppy?' Frances said. 'I'm sure they're good to it.'

Mrs Bethel nodded grimly. 'They're good to it, all right. Its belly's trailing the ground, they've fed it that much ket! Sweets, crisps . . . I catched one of the bairns feeding it chewy yesterday. I told her she'd clog its innards but all I got was a mouthful of impidence.'

Frances leaned forward, concerned. 'What about Brian? Can't he stop them?'

Mrs Bethel's eyes rose heavenwards. 'If he could stop that lot, he could plait sawdust. The bairns is daft and she's dafter.' Dimly Frances remembered a back-street fracas: Bethel *v.* Malone and someone's washing smoked by someone else's bonfire. Obviously it rankled still.

Mrs Bethel rose and began to gather the cups. 'It'll be down the Welfare next.' Frances knew what that meant. There was a pound next to the Welfare where unclaimed dogs were given a week's grace. And then the chop! She wondered how Martin would take it. He had been to see the puppy several times and taken it round the block on a lead. She filed the problem for attention later. She couldn't worry about everything.

'Them flowers in the front room . . .' Mrs Bethel was trying to be delicate.

'I know. They'll have to go. I'll do them now.' She carried the vases through to the kitchen and began to remove the cards. '*We are thinking of you. Aunt Em and Mary R.*' '*A small token of our sympathy. Design office.*' She had never had so many flowers as in the weeks since David's death. There had been none this week, so presumably the wave of sympathy was over.

She lifted the sagging blooms and their trails of slime. Corruption. Everything rotted from the moment of birth. The water smelled rank and made her think of cloakrooms. School cloakrooms, and Frances the flower monitor. '*Strip the leaves . . . no, silly girl, not like that.*' Jam jars of Michaelmas daisies and everyone vying to bring the biggest blooms. '*My dad's asters are bigger than your dad's.*' '*Call them chrysanths? They're like bachelor's buttons.*' She hated the job, loathed the smell of the green water. At last, tired of her ineptitude, they had made her blackboard monitor and she'd had to cope with the feel of chalk. Life was a treadmill. She washed the vases in soapy water and put them safely away.

She went upstairs and started on Martin's room. The broken whistle lay on the chest of drawers. The Rover would be sold by now. It was a lovely car, someone would've snapped it up. Still, the car man wouldn't sell it to someone nasty. She remembered his hand caressing the bonnet, a nice hand with long fingers. His hands had been gentle when they touched her. Confused, she locked her own hands together. He had never touched her! And yet she could remember. She had put her face in the fold of his neck and felt his body bear down on hers. Shutting out the world. Keeping her safe!

The dream came flooding back and she felt weak with relief. It had never happened, it was just a figment of sleep, not even remembered on waking. It wasn't anything to get upset about. She was bound to have dreams. If you didn't dream you went crazy. She had read that somewhere, or David had told her. The car man was just a symbol . . . someone thrown up to fill the vacuum. He wasn't special. '*But he's alive,*' her other voice said, and filled her with shame.

When Mrs Bethel had gone she checked the freezer for something special for Martin's lunch. It was his birthday. This day last year the kitchen had smelled of baking. Queen cakes and cup cakes and individual apple pies. She had cut sandwiches into triangles and made sausage rolls by the dozen. David had come home early to lend a hand, and the house rocked with high spirits. They would have to be careful today, using Eve's house. 'I can manage,' Fran had said, but their faces were implacable. 'It's too soon, Fran,' Eve had urged. 'We want to help ... we really do.'

Min had joined in. 'Be sensible, Fran. You need time ...' Her tone suggested a thirty-year term, but there was a grain of truth in what they said and Fran had given in. So Martin's party was to be held at Eve's house, and Martin could bring along four of his own school friends.

'Surely he can do without them for one day?' Min had said, but Eve saw the storm warnings on Fran's face and stepped in. 'How about one or two?' she said placatingly, and they'd settled for four.

Frances was dishing up when he came in. 'It's all ready,' she said. 'We've got to be quick today so you'll have time to get changed.'

He shuffled into his place. 'Are we going to Aunty Eve's?'

Fran felt a wild and irrational anger. He bloody knew they were going to Eve's! 'Yes, you know we are.'

He pushed his fork along the plate until it squeaked. 'Why can't we have it here?'

Frances felt her anger fizzle out. Poor little devil, adrift in a world where nothing remained the same, not even birthdays.

'It's just this once. I know it would be nice to have it here and we always will after this. But Aunty Eve worries about us and so does Aunty Min. It'll make them happy if they think they've done something nice for us, so you'll have to try.'

She was glad when it was time to get him ready. 'I'll pick you up at home-time. Have the others told their mams?' He nodded. She pulled the clean T-shirt over his head and kissed his forehead when it reappeared. His skin had the texture of a cool and fleshy petal. She held his chin in one hand while she wielded the hairbrush. She had been afraid to brush his hair when he was small, fearing the fontanelle. And now he was ten years old and fully formed. She gave a final flourish and turned him towards the mirror. 'Very smart!'

She had been forbidden to bake anything for the party, but she took a chocolate cake from the freezer. She must do something. Martin's present was hidden behind the settee, a complicated football game with finger-flicking players. It would please him, and it was just what David would've chosen.

She looked at the clock and couldn't believe it was only ten past two. If they had left well alone she would have been busy now, counting down until the kids erupted through the door. She sat back and closed her eyes. Something was happening to her, some strange mutation of character that made her grateful for nothing, resentful of everything. They were her friends and they were kind. Kind, kind, kind. She switched on the radio and gave herself up to *Woman's Hour* until it was time to leave the house.

Mrs Bethel had called the Malone house 'a proper tagareen shop', and it was. A wheel-less motorbike under the tarpaulin, broken-down rabbit hutches, a forgotten spade standing upright in the soil. The Malones had nine children and the house looked as though it was bursting at the seams. Gary Malone had turned up to reconnoitre the day they'd moved in. Martin had looked at him with respect and Gary adopted a swagger. 'Got any glass alleys?' he'd said, and pulled out a handful. She had watched Martin squat in the gutter to fire the alleys, and known it was going to be all right. Now she put out a hand to their door and smelled the mingled odours of drying clothes and proving bread.

'You'll have to excuse the mess,' Mrs Malone was large and red-headed, a youthful face on a shapeless body. Frances followed her into the kitchen and took the proffered chair. Each wall held a crucifix or a picture of the Sacred Heart. Every surface was covered with bric-a-brac, tins, boxes, paperback books, bobbins of thread stuck with needles and brown official envelopes. An inventory would take a thousand years.

The puppy was shut in the cupboard beside the fire: Fran could hear it whining and scratching. Mrs Malone unsnecked the door and the puppy tumbled out. 'Mind, it's a handful that one and no mistake. I've told our Brian it'll have to go, but he's

that soft. I had to put it in there to stop it tormenting the cat.'
She gestured at a battered black tom sitting on the windowsill.

Fran put down a hand to be licked. 'I came to make sure you
knew about tea-time. I'll make sure Gary gets back safely.' Ten
minutes later they parted on the step, Mrs Malone holding the
quivering puppy in her arms. 'We'll be back about seven.' Mrs
Malone nodded her understanding.

Martin was first out of school, an aura of importance about
him, four acolytes behind. She held the seat while the guests
clambered in, the Hepplewhite twins and the boy from the fish
shop and Gary Malone, washed and polished until he shone.
Martin got in beside her and fastened his seat belt. 'OK,' he said
and she let in the clutch.

They were quiet behind for the first few miles and then the
giggling began. Martin twisted in his seat and Frances heard the
sounds of a scuffle. Please God don't let them fight at Eve's! If
they did she would tell them to stop, and if they didn't stop she'd
bundle them into the car and drive them home. She looked
sideways and found Martin's eyes on her. She smiled but his
eyes were steady. Almost hostile. Why didn't he say what he was
thinking?

'They're quite well dressed.' Min's tone expressed surprise.
What did she expect? Bare feet and rags? Frances shepherded
the silent children into the hall and through to the lounge. Eve
was regarding everybody with a bright smile and handing out
crisps, and the other children were ranged round the fireplace,
the place of vantage. Min's Althea, Peter and James, Eve's Fiona
and Elaine. 'This is nice,' Eve said and Fran could have laughed
at the note of terror in her voice.

In the end it worked. The children came together slowly, like
water surmounting a causeway. By half-past six they were one,
shrieking and dishevelled. 'One more game,' Min said firmly and
there was a roar of 'Statues!' Min operated the cassette player,
turning off the music to take them unavares. Any child who did
not immediately turn to stone was out. 'It's been a success,'
Frances thought, watching the quivering figures trying desperately to be still.

Only once had she felt strained. 'We've told the children not to mention Martin's daddy to him,' Min said confidentially before they served tea. Frances had started to smile one of the pretend smiles she was bringing to perfection, and then changed her mind. 'I know you mean well but, afterwards, could you tell them that they *should* mention him?' She wouldn't have him dismissed, erased. The calmness of her voice surprised her and she managed to keep smiling even when Min pressed her hand and said, 'My God, you're brave!'

'The tea was super,' she said gratefully when it was time to go. She had used the take-and-leave technique herself but the children had loved it . . . sausages on sticks, chocolate crispies, the lot.

'Well, we did try,' Eve and Min said together, and she could detect no note of smugness in the combined voices.

The kids were loaded into the car along with presents and paper hats. Fran said her thanks again, and meant them. The children who were remaining behind hung on to the doors and the bonnet and had to be detached by force. Martin sat beside her holding the football game. 'Like it?' she said, and glowed at his enthusiastic nod.

They were halfway home when she heard the familiar tones behind. 'It's *horr–ibly* sticky. Oh dear, you've spilled it . . . how *aw–fully* naughty.' It was Min, captured by the smaller Hepplewhite. She caught Martin's eye and laughed. He had looked uncertain, fearing to be disloyal. Now he joined in. '*Aw–fully*, *aw–fully* naughty,' he said, and shook a wrist of imaginary bangles.

They dropped off the children one by one. 'See you,' Martin said happily as each one said, 'Tarra!' There was only Gary Malone left, and Frances stopped at his back door. 'Stay here,' she said to Martin.

Brian was waiting on the step in his stocking feet. 'Me mam says you're takkin' it?' His relief was almost comical. Fran looked at Gary for signs of distress, but his face was as cheerful as ever. 'You can come and see it whenever you want to,' she said, and he nodded.

She carried the puppy down to the car, along with the bowl and the bright new collar. 'You might as well take the gear,'

Brian had said, piling it into her arms. Martin wound down the window. 'Hallo, dog,' he said. His eyelids were beginning to droop. Frances walked round the car and put the puppy on his knee. 'See yer termorrer,' Gary said equably, but Martin's eyes were fixed on his mother's face.

She nodded. 'We have a dog.'

She followed him up the stairs to bed. 'He can come up this once because it's a birthday, but after this bedrooms are out.'

She held the dog while he climbed into bed. 'Has he got a name?'

Frances held up the dog and regarded him. 'I forgot to ask. Anyway, we'll rechristen him. What shall we call him?'

Martin snuggled down. 'What kind is he?' The puppy looked at them with world-weary eyes.

'He's a flophound,' Frances said. She felt excited and clever. She was giving him what he wanted. She was managing. 'He's definitely a flophound.' She looked at Martin to see if he was appreciating the joke. 'He's a Japanese flophound, and his name is Nee-wan.' She savoured the joke for a moment before she shared it. 'I asked Mrs Malone what kind of dog he was and she said, 'Nee-wan knaas, hinny.'

She left him rolling with laughter and carried the puppy downstairs. Its belly was warm and fleshy and free from hair. She sat down on the bottom stair. The day had gone well – except that all hell would break loose when Harold found out about the puppy. There wouldn't be a thing she could say either. It *was* daft. Another mouth to feed. She fished in her pocket for cigarettes, and remembered she'd run out at the party. 'Come on, my Nipponese friend,' she said. 'Let's see what you're like at sniffing out tab ends.'

6

Monday, 26 September 1983

At twelve o'clock they flooded into the corridors. Frances waited until the rush was over, gathering up the various forms and looking in her bag to make sure the precious cheque was safe. The woman in front turned and looked at her sympathetically. 'Found it all a bit much?'

Frances nodded. 'They all seem so capable.'

The woman smiled. 'It's their youth, I suppose . . . we matures had better stick together. I'm Gwen Franklin.' She held out a plump hand.

Fran had noticed her earlier. Late thirties, overweight, very proud of her hands with their bright red nails. They left the classroom and walked down the corridor.

'Are you lunching here?'

Fran hadn't thought about lunch except to wonder how Martin would enjoy his school dinner. 'Can we?'

Gwen's eyebrows shot up. 'You mean you haven't seen the refectory? I did my last A level here at nights, so I'm fairly *au fait*.' She launched into menus and prices.

Gwen had gammon and chips and a plate of sponge pudding. She eyed Frances's egg mayonnaise and black coffee. 'You're the disciplined type who counts calories.'

She sounded like a naughty baby caught at the syrup jar and Fran laughed. 'Anything but . . . I'm just not hungry today.'

'What did you do before?' Gwen said between mouthfuls. If she told the truth she would reap sympathy and wind up in tears. If she told a lie she'd be stuck with it. 'I worked in a bank . . . but that was years ago.'

Gwen listed her fourteen jobs, sixteen if you counted marriage and motherhood. 'And then I suddenly realized I liked the little beasts. I mean, they're quite interesting if you hold them at arm's length. So here I am.'

'She's funny,' Fran thought. 'Funny and harmless, and I like her.' She pushed the food around her plate.

'You weren't kidding about not being hungry, were you?' Gwen said, but to Fran's relief she left it there. They were on to their coffee when a man appeared, holding a tray.

'May I join you?' Fran shuffled along to make room. 'I'm Edward Pattison, and you're . . .?' They gave their names. 'What did you think of the morning?'

Frances left the conversation to Gwen. The morning had been a blur. Listening for the first miner's footfall in the street, up at five when she could lie no longer, sitting alone at the kitchen table grateful for bird noises and the rattle of bottles on the step. She had made three pots of tea before it was time to wake Martin. As he tucked into Weetabix she wondered if she dared take a Valium. Agitation was using her ribs as a climbing frame, but she couldn't turn up like a zombie, not on the first day. And then it was time to drop Martin at school and drive slowly into town.

She had pictured sitting straight down at a desk, but the reality was different. She'd queued for an hour in a huge gymnasium to be grilled by two formidable ladies. When she left she was clutching a cheque, and someone had shepherded her towards tea and biscuits. 'We're in,' a cheerful girl with a pigtail said and dunked her biscuit.

Now she looked up to find her companions' eyes on her. 'Sorry . . . I didn't catch what you said.'

Gwen wiped the corners of her mouth with a scarlet fingertip. 'We wondered what you thought of the grant?'

What should she say? 'It's adequate, I suppose.'

Edward was offering cigarettes and she took one gratefully. 'It's OK for the kids,' he said, 'the school-leavers. It'll be their first income. I was surprised to find them in with us. I thought we'd be a sort of veteran corps.' The class was a mix of boys and girls fresh out of school and men and women in their thirties and forties. The kids seemed bright-eyed and confident.

'Brash,' Gwen said, when Fran mentioned it.

'They'll learn,' Edward said, 'they'll learn.'

They spent the last ten minutes discussing the course. There were two separate regimes, two sets of tutors. 'Subjects are *what* you teach and Education is *how*,' Gwen explained when Frances looked puzzled. Edward launched into a dissertation on psychology and sociology. 'It's learning what makes them tick,' Gwen said when he'd finished, 'and if they stop ticking you give them a good clout to start them off again.'

They left the refectory together. Frances followed, marvelling at their sureness. Edward noticed her anxious face and waved his timetable at her. 'Don't look so worried. You've got one of these and it's all down. Kenton Building, Room Four, 1.30 p.m.'

They sat in Room Four while yet another lecturer handed out reams of paper and gave a pep talk. 'If I've got a piece of advice it's this: Ask. *Ask.* ASK. Make a bloody nuisance of yourself, but don't sit there uncomprehending.'

Gwen and Edward had found spaces in the car park, and Gwen gave Frances a lift to the town outskirts where the Mini was parked. 'Come right in, tomorrow,' she said. 'You've as much right there as anybody else.'

While she waited for the school bell she imagined the scene. Martin would come out disconsolate . . . even tearful. He wasn't expecting her till five, and there was the long trudge home to an empty house. She had hung a key under his shirt. 'That was Daddy's key, so don't lose it.' She'd wanted to explain that losing David's key would be treachery but you couldn't burden a child. Well, you could – but you mustn't. In the end she'd slipped David's key off the chain and substituted her own.

She went back to her scenario. Martin would trudge over the school step, a pitiful sight, and turn for home, dejection in every step. She would toot her horn and he would turn, face lighting up as he ran. '*You're here, Mum. You're here!*' A tiny laugh was growing somewhere inside her chest. 'Mum' was a deodorant; Martin said 'Mam' like the rest of the kids in Belgate. She was struggling to keep a straight face when the bell clanged out home-time.

He came over the step jauntily, one arm round Gary Malone. She tooted the horn but there was no slow spread of delight and his steps were hardly eager. 'I thought you weren't coming back till after.' It was almost an accusation.

'They let me out early today,' she said apologetically, 'but it's just for today.' She looked at Gary. 'Want a lift?' He climbed into the back, too.

'Can he come to ours for tea?' Martin asked, and she nodded.

'School dinners were OK,' he volunteered. 'And the playground was great after.'

Gary came forward to lean on the back of the seat. 'We let him in our gang. I said it'd be OK.' He said it as though he were conferring a Fellowship of Trinity, and Frances nodded with suitable awe. 'He doesn't need me,' she thought as the children dashed into the house.

Spreading bread for sandwiches she tried to draw comfort from the situation. If he'd clung it would've been a bad sign. That was what motherhood was all about. If you did it properly they grew away from you; only the damaged ones clung to mother. But ten was a bit young for independence and it was all happening too quickly . . . as though he sensed there was nothing to come from her and he'd better look elsewhere.

She drank her tea in the kitchen, elbows on table, evening paper propped against the teapot. They were happy in the living room, feeling for their mouths without taking their eyes off the screen. She would have to put a brake on TV. When she was sorted out. Nee-wan had stayed with the children until he realized there would be no high-jinks. Now he lay in his basket, one ear flopped over the rim, watching her hopefully through half-closed eyes. In the end she capitulated and reached for his lead. 'I'm taking the dog for a walk,' she called, half-hoping they might join her, but all she got was a muttered 'OK'.

The park was on the turn, full of bright flowers that were browning travesties when you got up close. The summer was over and the leaves ready to fall. Another month, and they would be crisped in piles, ready to scatter at the first gust. She felt peaceful here in the park. Unpressured. If they left her alone she would be all right.

The voices broke in. *'Don't lie! You feel neglected when they don't call. You delude yourself.'* This last was said with contempt, and she found she was wrinkling her face to emphasize the point. She looked at the houses beyond the park perimeter. There was sure to be someone there with a telescope watching a madwoman grimacing into space. She whistled up the dog and made for the gate.

She was laying out Martin's clothes for the morning when she heard the car. Eve was wearing a cream suit and her hair had the careful look of a professional set. Fran led them into the front room and offered a sherry. 'Too early,' Harold said. 'Anyway, we can't stay long. We're . . .' He stopped in mid-sentence at a glance from Eve. 'Laser beams,' Fran thought, 'she uses laser beams.' They were obviously going somewhere special and Eve didn't want her to know. Fair enough. Her mules were scuffed and she tried to tuck them under the chair.

'How was college?' Eve said.

'Fine.' Fran would have amplified her answer but their eyes had already moved on.

'Actually, we came for a reason.' That was Harold. 'A nice reason. Well, we think it's nice. We've been keeping it quiet because there was some doubt at the beginning . . . but we wanted you to be the first to know.' Fran felt her face stiffen. Something was coming.

'I'm pregnant.' Eve looked at Harold, and they exchanged a smile.

Fran fought to control her face while she made rapid calculations. David had been dead for three months. If they had made love at the time of his death . . . in the aftermath . . . she would be sick. Here, in front of them. Puke! Puke! Puke! 'That's marvellous. When's it due?'

The baby was due in early March, so it had been conceived in early June. It wasn't their fault because they couldn't have known. 'You must have a drink now,' she said. 'To celebrate.' If they still said no, she would pour one for herself and to hell with them.

'We knew you'd be pleased,' Harold was saying. 'We felt . . . once we were sure it was OK . . . well, Eve felt, actually . . . that a baby coming would be just what you needed at the moment.' Fran gripped the stem of her glass and wondered about the breaking strain. She'd seen it done on the telly but maybe they were trick glasses. If he said anything about one life replacing another – anything remotely like that – she would press on the stem and shatter it.

'I'm so pleased for you both,' she said and raised her glass.

When they'd gone she carried her glass through to the kitchen and sat alone in the dusk. Last night she had prayed, '*Please God, let tomorrow go well.*' So much for prayer! 'I'm jealous.' She said it aloud, one ear cocked for the children. 'I'm a jealous, infertile bitch.' She couldn't bear the words aloud in the empty room. She would have to shut up. '*We felt that a baby coming would be just what you needed.*' How could they be so bloodily, screamingly, wrong?

She went through to the living room. 'Time to go home, Gary.' Martin looked mutinous but Gary put down the Action Man and scrambled to his feet. She wondered once more at his good humour. The Malone house had no order, no system, it was over-crowded and under-cleaned; and it produced children who were straight-limbed and content. There was no justice. Martin was condemned to a one-parent upbringing, and that one parent was leaking at the seams.

She left him to bath himself and went downstairs to make cocoa. Having cocoa together had to be good. They did it in adverts. He leaped into bed when she came into his bedroom and thrust his pyjama bottoms under the covers to put them on. The beginnings of modesty.

'Was that Aunty Eve?' he said as they sipped. Fran nodded. 'Did she see Nee-wan?' His eyes were glittering at the prospect of fun.

'Not tonight. But she saw him the other day.' She anticipated his next question. 'She liked him.' Better not tell him of Eve's disapproval, Min's contempt. '*It's a Heinz. Honestly, Fran, if you had to have a dog . . .*'

She decided to make a joke for him. 'She thinks he really is Japanese. A Japanese flophound. I said they were hunting dogs in Japan, and when they found game they flopped down.'

The cocoa tilted alarmingly as he wriggled with delight. 'Like pointers?'

She nodded. 'Yes, like pointers.'

Going downstairs she decided he was quite intelligent.

Knowing about pointers was intelligent. David must have told him. If David had lived he would've brought Martin on, widened his horizons. It would be up to the school now.

She took down the washing from the pulley and sorted it into piles. Must be ironed; should be ironed; needn't be ironed. 'Diminution of standards.' The full-grown phrase popped up in her mind from God knew where. She would iron it all tomorrow. Every single piece. She put it all back and went in search of a drink.

It had been a funny day. College. Eve's bombshell. Gwen, with the painted fingernails and bulging boobs. Strangely feminine Edward who fancied ladies. The idea that he might fancy her was weird. Invigorating. She would wear something nice tomorrow, and maybe earrings. 'Here come the whorish thoughts.' She forced herself not to think until her hands were under the tap and the bathroom was full of steam.

Back in the living room she collected pad and pencil. She needed some notes. Her nails hurt if she pressed them and the pads of her fingers were tense. Her fingers were scalded. Sterile, but scalded. She started her list. '*Buy some baby wool. Tell Mrs B no more work . . . no more money. See about stone for cemetery.*' How long did wood last, keeping out seeping rain? *Buy Vit.C for Martin.*' After a moment she crossed out *Vit.C* and substituted *Multivitamins*. Better be on the safe side.

Her hands were hurting and she put them in her armpits. No more punishment. When the water got hotter the pain escalated, ran up the machine, and rang the bell at the top. No more. She got to her feet and switched on the TV. *News at Ten.* Pickets and Salvadorean guerrillas. The real world. Peace at last. Out of the corner of her eye she saw a flicker of movement at the skirting board, but when she looked properly there was nothing there.

She contemplated a bath and decided against it. If she fell asleep and drowned they might ask for the grant back. Nee-wan waddled in and she lifted him on to her knee. Eve had looked smug tonight: perhaps they'd been trying for ages? She tried to remember Eve's pregnancies. She'd always wanted a boy and got a girl instead, but otherwise they'd been OK. Not as good as

Min, though. Min gave birth like someone shelling peas for Birds Eye, and the next moment she was back in shape and floating around like Bianca Jagger.

A small pain blossomed down in her groin. The curse was due on the 30th. She resented menstruation now. It was a nuisance, the superfluous outpouring of a redundant organ. She would never again give birth, receive a thrusting penis. She put down the dog and rose to her feet. She was too weary for randy thoughts.

She stood at the front door while the dog snuffled around the garden. 'Hurry up, Nee-wan.' He sidled past her, eyes averted. That meant a puddle in the morning. 'Try again!' She lifted him back over the step, her fingers sinking into the warmth of his belly. He cocked a leg by the hydrangea and she uttered a fervent 'Good boy'.

She lurched slightly as she went upstairs. She was tired. That was good. She would try to do without pills. The nights were better after 4 a.m. when the first footfalls sounded in the street. Men going to the pit. Fore shift . . . or back shift? She could never remember. But she was grateful.

7

Friday, 30 September 1983

She sat on the side of the bath, allowing the conditioner to soak into her hair. Washing her hair had been crazy . . . it was six o'clock and she had to leave at seven. She'd have to use the heated rollers. Her hair-dryer had been broken for months and tucked away on top of the wardrobe.

Tonight was a mistake, a monumental error, but at least she could come home early: 'I'll have to get back to my little boy.' The perfect excuse. She carried the rollers downstairs and plugged them in on the draining board. The tea things were piled there for washing and she had to make room. There wasn't a sound from the living room, and then she heard the rattle of the football game. She smiled, thinking how it would end. Martin would win and Gary would say, 'I couldn't be bothered to win . . . I could've if I'd wanted.' She put her hands on the rollers to see if they were warm enough. One was missing and her hand touched the bare element. She recoiled at the heat and sent a cup crashing to the ground followed by the rollers. There was a blue flash and a bang and the smell of hot plastic.

A cold rivulet ran down her neck as she kneeled to assess the damage. She knew she had smashed the rollers . . . they were already cooling. She looked at the clock. Five past six. There was only one thing to do and she did it, sitting at the kitchen table to cry.

Martin's face was deadpan, Gary's inquiring. 'I've fused the rollers,' she said, wiping her nose. 'I needed them for my hair and I've smashed them.'

Gary's eyes narrowed as he took in the broken china. 'You could mend them.'

Frances shook her head. 'I don't understand electricity.'

Gary gave a weary sigh. '*Women!*' it said, and she smiled in spite of herself. She began to gather up the broken cup, carefully in case bits got into Nee-wan's pads, and the children filed out of the kitchen.

She had just finished when there was a rap of knuckles on the back door. It was Brian Malone. 'Our kid says you've got trouble?'

She pointed at the rollers. 'I knocked them off the draining board and they went up in a flash. I suppose it's the fuse, but I haven't a spare.' She didn't say that, even if she had, she wouldn't know exactly what to do with it.

He was already at work on the plug, twirling the screws with the point of a kitchen knife. His hands were clean but the nails were black-rimmed and there were small blue marks here and there on the skin. David had explained them once: 'They get cuts all the time they're hewing . . . and dust gets in while they're healing and leaves that mark.'

The fuse was small and brown and potent . . . or rather impotent. 'That's it, all right.'

She put up a hand to her hair. It was starting to dry, curling around her face, taking on a life of its own. 'It doesn't matter. I'll manage without them.'

He glanced round the kitchen. 'Got any chocolate biscuits?' She moved to the biscuit tin, startled at his request. He chose a Kit-Kat, pulled off the band and unwrapped the silver paper. 'This'll do.' He tore off a strip of silver and fiddled with the plug. 'That's it.' He plugged in the rollers and put a hand on them. 'They're away.'

Frances felt for herself. 'Is it safe?'

He nodded paternally. 'Why aye, man. Safe as houses.'

When Brian had gone, after an ecstatic reunion with Nee-wan, she dampened her hair and wound it on the rollers, holding them gingerly by the plastic part. She was going to wear her grey suit, but the band of the skirt was loose. She contemplated a safety pin and decided against it. Tomorrow she would take it in.

Downstairs she checked the oven. Bacon, onions and potatoes ... pannacalty. 'I won't take money ... just a bit of supper,' Bethel had said. 'And no need to rush back.' She's giving me *carte blanche*, Fran thought, and winced at the idea.

When Mrs Bethel arrived she fixed Gary with a baleful eye. 'Time you were off home. Her tone brooked no argument.

'I'll see him home,' Fran said. 'I'm taking the dog round the block before I go.' Martin came too. The puppy sniffed reflectively at the Malone gate post and Martin tugged its lead. 'You don't live there any more, dafty. You're ours now.'

'Are you glad we got him?' she said, when Gary had gone in. For once he forgot to be guarded and his 'Yes' was fervent. Frances felt a surge of satisfaction. They could go to hell with their budgets and priorities and common-sense moves. Go to hell and sod off! She had to school her face to hide her satisfaction. It would never do for Martin to know she swore.

She had almost forgotten Edward and the evening ahead, but now it was time to go. It was just a drink and a meal between colleagues. And he was nearly old enough to be her father. Still, he might expect something in return for the meal. Men did. She would just have to be evasive, like she was with Dennis. She always kept one move ahead of Dennis now, that vital centimetre out of trouble. Her mother had told her some women brought out the worst in men, so it must be her fault. With David gone she was showing her true colours.

She parked on the outskirts. Even at night she couldn't face the one-way system. If she had accepted Edward's offer to pick her up it would've saved all the hassle but she had jibbed at the idea. The voices sprang up in her head: '*Why shouldn't you* . . . how can you? . . . *it's harmless* . . . it's disgusting!' Well, she was here now and had to go through with it. In two hours she would be on her way home and would never get into this situation again.

In her mind's eye she had seen them at a corner table beyond the lights and every other table filled with strangers, but the first person she saw as she came through the revolving doors of the hotel was Lilian Sparks. She was standing at the reception desk, shuffling through brochures. Fran saw a door to her left and pushed at it with both hands. If she got through quickly Lilian wouldn't see her. It seemed hours before she realized the doors opened outwards not inwards, and got through. Edward wasn't there and every moment she expected to feel Lilian's hand on her shoulder!

A handful of men were scattered along the bar and the girl behind it devoted herself to them, ignoring the pound note in Fran's outstretched hand. Once she started to give her order . . . 'A small sherry, please' . . . but the girl appeared not to hear.

Eventually she came back. 'Sweet or dry?' Her tone was contemptuous.

'Medium,' Fran said.

The girl surveyed the bottles. 'We haven't got medium,' she said but there was a grudging respect in her voice.

'I'll have to have sweet then.' She had wanted sweet all along, so it was a double victory.

Sitting by herself with her back to the wall, her satisfaction evaporated. What if he didn't come? She couldn't go back to college, that was certain. She was trying to remember his exact words in case it had all been a joke, when the doors swung open and he came into the bar. As he walked towards her she thought how old he looked. Nice . . . kindly . . . but old.

'I thought we said the cocktail bar . . . this is the lounge bar.

Anyway, never mind, I've found you.' Fran snuggled into her chair. It was all right now. He was there, between her and the outside world.

They tossed subject options around and agreed they had both chosen unwisely. Fran had chosen English and History, subjects demanding a lot of study, and Edward was taking Geography. 'I've plumped for Music as a second option . . . it's all I really care about but I don't suppose it will count for much when we're actually in school.' He reeled off his own musical preference and asked for hers.

'I don't really know much about it . . . I like tunes, something you can remember.'

He laughed delightedly. 'Pop classics.' She knew she had pleased him but couldn't understand why.

'What did you do before?' she asked.

'I was a draughtsman. My father was in the shipyards so I wound up there, too. Another?' She nodded. She was drinking too fast, but sweet sherry was like lemonade – one sip and you wanted more.

He set down the drinks and took up the conversation. 'I never liked it. It wasn't so bad when the yards were thriving but latterly it's been hand-to-mouth and lucky if you laid a keel a year.' Fran had never thought about the shipyards. Now she recalled all the headlines. Boilermakers, caulkers, platers . . . laid waste in their hundreds. 'I took voluntary redundancy . . . the old golden handshake . . . and here I am. I couldn't have done it if I hadn't been single . . . well, you must find the grant paltry, but I've no one to consider but myself.'

He must be forty . . . perhaps forty-five. The hair at his temples was grizzled and the skin under his chin sagged. Her hand crept up to her own chin and came away satisfied. 'I know about your trouble.' Fran looked at him blankly. 'Losing your husband. One of the lecturers mentioned it. No details . . . just that you were recently widowed and had a child. It's a boy, isn't it?'

Frances nodded. 'He's ten.'

Edward patted her arm. 'We'll talk about it later . . . if you want to. Now, where do we eat?'

She sat while he outlined the possibilities. 'The Moti Bahal do a good Biriani . . . what's your palate like?'

She felt a moment of terror. He was going to make her choose! 'I like Chinese but I don't know much about it.'

He rose to his feet. 'Chinese it is.' She realized that once again her lack of knowledge had won her a bonus point.

When they were safely out in the street she let out her breath. No sign of Lilian. Thank God. She kept her right hand in her pocket in case he took her arm. She didn't know him well enough. Mercifully he left her alone until they reached the traffic lights. The green man showed and he gripped her elbow. 'Now,' he said.

Swallowed up in the Chinese darkness, she relaxed. 'Choose for me,' she said grandly, and watched the smile blossom on his face. The dishes were on the table when she realized she would have to eat. She hadn't thought about that. As he spooned the rice on to her plate she felt her throat constrict. 'That's enough, thank you.'

He raised an eyebrow. 'Tummy trouble?'

She was filled with gratitude. 'Yes.'

He scooped away some of the rice. 'Well, we won't overdo it tonight.'

She felt safer with every moment, slipping back into childhood, letting him take the reins. He trickled sauce on to her food and stirred. Her father had done that with her Red Riding Hood plate. 'There now, eat it up like a good girl.' She took a mouthful. It was going to be all right.

She ate with a fork, using only her right hand. She'd never done it before but it seemed American and posh and she could hold the fork in the air while she talked. She'd been at it for a while, asking questions and widening her eyes at his answers, before she realized she was flirting. They were in a little bubble of light and the other diners were miles away and blind. She had never flirted before and she liked it. It was like fishing, feeling the line tug and the senses quicken. Once she had seen a picture of the Queen Mother, casting for trout. She had wondered at a nice royal lady up to her knees in cold and swirling water. Now she knew why.

She moved a forkful of rice around her mouth and felt it grow, bulge. She was obscene, sitting here fancying herself a tease. As if he sensed her change of mood, Edward took charge. 'How did it happen . . . your husband, I mean? He can't have been very old.' When she'd finished he signalled for coffee. 'He sounds nice. Does your son resemble him?'

She felt consumed with gratitude. They were talking about David and he wasn't trying to shut her up. 'I think so. He's fair, and tall for his age.'

He gave her hand a pat. 'We must do a concert soon. I'll watch for something with a "good tune".' They both laughed.

'You must think I'm a Philistine,' she said.

He was covering the bill with notes. 'I shall educate you . . . that's my next "educational assignment".'

She wondered if he would kiss her goodnight and was glad when he didn't. He stood back from the car while she inserted the key. She didn't feel nervous. If the car stalled he would simply smile and fix it for her. She drew smoothly away from the kerb and looked in the mirror to see if he was pleased.

The lights of town fell away. She had eaten sparingly but she felt bloated. When the blue P of the car park came into view she drove in. The sea was calm and she could see the lights of a ship far out. She walked towards the cliff, where the grass was long, and stuck a finger into her throat. When she had vomited, she fished in her bag for tissues to wipe her face. Back in the car she lit a cigarette. If it could always be like tonight . . . no one knowing and no funny business . . . it could go on for a bit. She would have to pay her share in case he wanted anything in return. But as long as it was like tonight, it would be all right. She threw away the cigarette in a long, curving arc of light and switched on the engine. Time to go home.

8

Wednesday, 5 October 1983

The hall had that curious smell of school . . . chalk, body odour, polish, poster paint . . . and something indefinable. Each minute the buzz from the waiting children grew. She watched them squirming in their seats, jumping up to wave at incoming parents, turning round again to show off.

Martin had waited to see where she was sitting and then turned resolutely away. If she craned her neck she could see his down-bent head and the quivering ponytail of the little girl next to him. The teachers seemed amazingly relaxed, gathering in groups to chat. Everything must be under control . . . only the heartbeat of the curtains betrayed activity. She caught the eye of Martin's teacher and smiled. She was afraid of teachers. Better keep them sweet.

It was a few moments before she remembered she would be a teacher herself in time. It seemed ludicrous. She wasn't neat or precise or an expert in punctuation. Still, it would be years before she qualified. Plenty of time to change.

The curtains drew back in a series of jerks, revealing a row of seats and a table piled with books. The prizes. Once she had won a book token and swapped it, wickedly, for a movie-star annual.

There was a stir at the end of the row. Gary Malone was squeezing past the assembled knees. She leaned towards him and caught his piercing whisper. 'He's getten a one!'

She knew it was something good from the light in his eye. 'Who has? What?'

He eased himself into a space between knees. 'Your Martin . . . he's getten a one.' She felt the old familiar too-good-to-be-true feeling and then there was a buzz as the platform party appeared. Gary wriggled back along the row until he was seized by an irate young man with a Zapata moustache and hurled towards the front of the hall.

As the headmaster rose to speak she thanked God she had got

here, and winced at how touch-and-go it had been. At first her tutor had stonewalled. 'If you feel you must . . .' They didn't like you if you made demands. That's what they held against women, that they used their children as an excuse to skive.

In the end it was Gwen who had tipped the scales. 'Of course you're going. It's only community studies and philosophy. I'll take your notes with a carbon.' Gwen's notes were better than her own, so nothing was lost.

Suddenly she became aware of the headmaster's words: 'At this school we care about the child, the whole child. And that child can only succeed in so far as we provide the opportunity for success. He or she needs the guidance of teachers and the loving care of parents . . . both parents. That is why I am so glad to see so many fathers here this afternoon.'

There was a sea of people between her and the door so the pain must be borne. Reel it in, coil it away. Tidy. Tidy. But the pain effervesces, the coil erupts and there are not enough fingers to stop up the gaps. When something upset her at school she used to wait until Chemistry and sneak a drop of mercury on to the bench. Round smooth mercury, splitting and reforming. Round, round, smooth, smooth: think about mercury. You can think about fathers tomorrow.

The headmaster resumed his seat and the prize-giving began. Little ones first, toiling up steps and reaching up to shake hands. Each child was clapped and sometimes cheered. Suppose no one clapped Martin? Terror ran riot and then subsided. There was her and Gary Malone: they could hold the bridge.

'Martin Drummond. Class 3. For Attainment.' If David had been there she would have squeezed his hand, glanced sideways to gauge the depth of his pride. Now there was nothing to do but watch the small figure till it was lost to view and applause rolled up for the next winner. The ceremony ended with the school choir singing 'Any Dream Will Do'. *Joseph's Amazing Technicolor Dreamcoat.* Clever music by clever young men, filling children's mouths with song.

When the final words had been sung the room erupted with homing children and seeking parents. She stood by the door till Martin found her. He had a copy of *Treasure Island* under his arm and Gary in close attendance. 'I told you he was getten a one.' She put out her hand and touched Gary's head. He was a good friend.

There was a slight frown between Martin's brows. She knew its meaning . . . 'Don't gush and let's get out of here.' The wind struck chill after the warmth of the hall and the sky to the east was lowering. Winter. She had always liked the smell of a new season with its impulse to plan ahead. Now she was not so sure.

Gary plumbed the depth of *Treasure Island* in a rapid leaf-through as they crossed the playground, and leisurely walks home were not his style. He swooped away, yelling, stepping in and out of the gutter with scant regard for traffic. 'Daddy would have been proud of you today, Martin.' She tried to say it without emotion, for fear of embarrassing him.

His swift reply took her by surprise. 'I expect he is.' His words were certain, their implications endless.

They were almost home when she heard the car horn. A three-wheeled invalid car wobbled past and she glimpsed the ferocious face inside. 'It's Walter Raeburn, Mrs Bethel's friend,' she said.

'It's not a proper car?' Martin's tone was inquiring and she launched into an explanation of invalid tricycles.

'He can't use his legs, you see. He had an accident in the pit. So the government gives him a car to drive about in.'

She would have been glad to talk if Walter had stopped but his manner might have scared Martin. He had growled at Fran when they first met, as if to say, 'Like me if you dare.' Mrs Bethel had felt bound to comment. 'That's how you are today, then, Walter . . . eating nails and spitting rust. As long as we know.'

It was nice to find everything in order when they got home. More and more she looked forward to Bethel's days, in spite of guilt. She had tried to explain her circumstances but Bethel had shushed her impatiently. 'You needn't go on . . . I know how you're held. But you'll need someone now you're out all day. You can't keep that dog penned up till tea time . . . not unless you want your carpets ruined. I'll just pop in and out when it suits, and we'll settle up for the hours.'

The hours to pay had dwindled in direct relationship to the increased spit and polish. 'She's taken over,' Fran thought, looking at the snow-white dishcloth draped across the taps. Soon she would tackle Mrs Bethel, tell her she couldn't go on taking advantage ... but for the moment she would accept it, even wallow in it. She took the last cream sponge from the freezer and sliced it with abandon. There was a lot to celebrate.

After tea they sat together by the fire, the dog at their feet. There was a quiz on the telly and they vied with each other to shout out the answers. She looked at the clock from time to time, measuring the peace that was left. He wouldn't come before half-past eight, she had stressed the impossibility of an earlier arrival. In the meantime, there was her knitting. She was halfway up the side of a matinée jacket. The trouble was, it was meant for a girl and Eve was set on a boy. On impulse she pulled it from the needle. She would start again, this time a boy's pattern.

Martin had risen to his feet to shriek at a tongue-tied contestant. If he was going to be clever she would have to get help. 'Ask Daddy' – that had always been her get-out. Now he would stand expectantly and she would long to say, 'Ask someone else.' Except that there was no one else. She gave herself over to plain and purl.

At seven o'clock she carried out the tea things. Tonight was a mistake. At first it had seemed a good idea: smuggle him in under cover of darkness, repay his kindness, and let him out discreetly at ten thirty. No need to stand in bars or walk through lighted streets. That was the theory. At close quarters, it seemed less sensible. Someone might be passing the door as she let him in – quite apart from his car, left outside like a commercial for goings-on. And once in, where would she put him?

The question sent her scurrying to the living room. Martin was lying on the rug chortling at a comic and she had to dig at his legs to move him. She seized the arms of the chair and began to manhandle it out of the way. David's chair. Edward's arms on David's chair! No! She didn't stop until she had angled it out of use.

At least she'd been honest about the meal. 'I think I've forgotten how to cook. I can do it all, but bringing it together at the right time is beyond me.' He had smiled tolerantly and offered to bring Chinese, and she had agreed as long as it was at her expense. She had several pound notes ready and a purseful of change. Money, money, money. When it got to be less than four figures in the bank she would call a halt. Already she shopped more carefully, but if Harold found out she was buying sherry at the supermarket the sky would fall!

Martin went obediently to bed as though he knew she wanted him out of the way. Back in the living room she poured herself a sherry and sat down. The room looked odd now, unbalanced. She put down her drink and tugged the other chair into line. If she left it looking odd Edward would set about putting it right, fussing. He was always fussing. Perhaps that was why he'd never married. Most people were married by his age. Whatever his age was. 'We'll have to cut through his legs and count the rings,' Gwen had said when he proved cagey.

There wasn't a soul about when he came and the face above the greasy carrier bag was oddly touching. 'How much do I owe you?' she said firmly, and refused to take out the steaming cartons until he'd settled up. There was a bottle of wine and a variety of dishes, and he opened them with the air of a conjuror revealing the dove. Once a container almost fell and his muttered 'Whoops' made her think of Tommy Cooper. She often found him comic but there was a funny little thread of menace in his absurdity, like Lurex running through wool.

When they were settled with trays before the fire she felt awkward. On their evenings out she had felt unreal, like an actress playing a part, but here, in her own home, there could be no pretence. David had been dead for four months, and here she was, sitting knee by knee with a stranger, eating strange food. In a moment he would wipe his mouth, satisfied, and sit back like a husband. She cast around for ways of preventing it, forgetting the sweet and sour congealing on her plate.

When he leaned forward for a second helping he noticed her untouched plate. He put aside his tray. 'Come on now, this won't do.' She was back in the high chair, drumming her heels, turning her head to refuse the white of an egg. He scooped up a spoonful of food, picking here and there to get variety, and she opened her mouth obediently. 'That's a good girl.' She was Alice at the Mad Hatter's tea party, and anything could be expected.

Later on in the kitchen, listening to the grumbling percolator, she wondered about Edward's background. Something had shaped him . . . or someone. But, like his age, it was a military secret.

Over coffee they talked about college. She agreed when he said women lecturers were mostly ambitious and cold: privately she thought them vague and woolly-minded, but anything for peace. She was sincere in her agreement that light-hearted lecturers were good entertainment but didn't teach you much, and that the mad scramble in the library at lunchtime was unfair to everyone. At ten they switched on the news and watched the Third World bleeding to death. How could she tell him she wanted him out of her house? The fire dropped in the grate and she deliberately neglected to build it up.

Perhaps if she let her eyelids droop? A wild desire to leap up and undress possessed her. Gentle hints were lost on Edward. If she put on her nightie, rolled up her hair, took out her teeth, hung up her wooden leg . . . she fought back looming hysteria by deciding to check on Martin. That would break the spell.

Her relief was short-lived. 'I'll come up with you.' He saw her look of horror and smiled. 'The bathroom *is* upstairs?'

She sagged with relief. 'I'm sorry . . . I should've told you.' They parted on the landing and she went into Martin's room.

He lay half out of the blankets, pyjama jacket unbuttoned and twisted to one side. She stood for a moment looking down at him. 'Martin Drummond. Attainer.' He was going to be all right. She was pulling his jacket together to fasten it when she heard the door.

'OK, is he?' Edward was looking benevolently at the bed.

'Oh yes, he's sound.' She eased past him in the doorway. If she went he would have to follow. Mayday! Mayday!

When she had seen him out to his car she felt a fool. Naturally he was interested in Martin, a fatherless ten-year-old boy. If it had been *her* bedroom he wouldn't have intruded. The more she thought about it the surer she was. He was always proper.

Possessive, paternalistic, but proper. She would have to stop being such a neurotic fool.

She poured the last of the wine and kicked off her shoes. The room smelled of soy sauce. She would never eat Chinese again. Not with Edward anyway. Next time he would tie her napkin around her like a bib and catch her dribbles with his spoon. She put out a toe to Nee-wan and rubbed his tummy. 'He didn't care too much for you, did he?' The dog rolled over and squirmed for more. 'Didn't appreciate your oriental ancestry, that's the trouble.'

Tomorrow she would discuss the whole Edward thing with Gwen and come to a logical conclusion. Tomorrow she would make a list, join a club, take up embroidery. She sat by the dying fire and knitted alternate rows of plain and purl until the bright dot of the TV swelled and receded, and it was time to climb the stairs.

9

Friday, 7 October 1983

There was a faint streak of pink in the west as she drove towards town. It would soon be time to put the clocks forward. Or back? She would worry about that tomorrow. There were other things to think about ... like her slingback shoes which were not designed for driving. She could feel her unprotected heel rubbing the floor every time she depressed the clutch. There would be a black mark there now, to be removed with a wet fingertip when she got to Min's.

She was glad to be going out, even to a hen party. When Min had asked her she'd wanted to say, 'Not another ghastly girls' night.' Mercifully her vocal chords had failed and all that came out was a grunt which Min took to be appreciation.

The railway bridge loomed up with its awkward bend. 'Hold on, Stirling Moss,' David used to say if she took a bend too fast. David. David. Important David. They had looked at her today at the factory as if he had never existed. Even the door of his office had abandoned him: now it said 'W. TURNS. Production Manager' and the old inscription was gone, as though it had been written on water.

She had stammered out her request. 'My husband's pen . . . and his antique inkstand . . . I'd like to have them back, for sentimental reasons.' They were valuable, but she mustn't say that. Mustn't seem greedy. The girl looked blank and then embarrassed. 'They must have been put somewhere, Mrs Drummond. I'll try and find out.' But the pen and the inkstand had gone. Forget. Forget! It's a night out after all – might as well enjoy.

'Don't get a sitter, I'll send Dennis over.' Min should have married a Bendy toy. Perhaps she had! Perhaps tall, thin Dennis with the extra hands was really india-rubber.

'Thanks a lot, Min, it's very kind . . . but Mrs Bethel's already promised.'

She had left Martin angelic in clean pyjamas under Bethel's eye. Earlier he had careered up and down the stairs with Neewan, dragging the carpet away from the clips and ignoring her cries of protest. She had wanted to slap him hard on the legs but he was too quick for her. And then she had wanted to cause him remorse. '*Why are you doing this to me? I'm tired. I work all day at college. I shouldn't have to put up with this when I come home.*' She had wanted to say it, but she hadn't dared. The whole of the last psychology lecture had been given over to the effects of rebuke, and she was worried enough. He was already a latch-key kid: the least she could do was keep her mouth shut.

The green belt ebbed and the houses began. Hives of activity. Lift the lid and watch them wriggle. Laugh, cry, love, argue, copulate, bring forth, and die. The gateway of Min's house sprang up and her wheels ground into the gravel drive.

'Come in . . . we thought you'd got lost.' Min wore pleated chiffon and Fran blessed her own decision to dress up. There was something about high heels . . . they might throw your innards out of true but they did wonders for your morale.

'We're all in here.' They were scattered around the upholstery like a Miss World line-up, with Eve in the place of honour. You were always Queen Bee if you were pregnant. Fran shook her head slightly in the hope that envy could be dispersed by physical action and sat down where Eve had made room.

'How was college today?' It was a determined effort to show interest, and Fran wanted to say 'Search me'. But you couldn't display lack of interest, not when you were in receipt of a grant. She took a breath and launched into a blow-by-blow description. Her spirits rose as she ended her account with a sense of duty done. Min refilled her glass and she drained it at a gulp.

As the conversation washed over her, she watched them. She had become a compulsive watcher. They were all extremely well groomed. Smooth legs, and feet, where they showed, baby-soft to match their hands. Their nails were oval with cuticles neat as selvedges. Her own cuticles were in a permanent state of unravelment. Tomorrow she would buy an emery board and some cuticle remover. Tomorrow she would buy a notebook and write 'SELF-IMPROVEMENT PLAN' on the cover.

She had never needed to worry about her looks before. She had been loved, and that was enough. Now she would have to keep up. There were two ways you could get away with being a slob . . . being extra clever and therefore 'eccentric', or belonging to the lowest, lowest social order. And she fitted neither category.

'He doesn't come up to her shoulder, even!' That was the trifle girl with the upswept hair, only tonight it hung loose. 'I mean, can you imagine? He'll need a ladder!'

Everyone was laughing and curiosity overcame her. 'I'm sorry, I've lost the thread . . . who are we talking about?'

There was an immediate chorus. 'Lilian. Lilian Sparks.' Across the room Sally was into her Mike Yarwood act . . . 'Remarry? Me? Replace Frank? Never!'

Fran sensed unrest beside her. Eve was getting ready to emit one of her beams and seal their lips. She leaned forward, anxious to intercept the ray and keep the conversation going. 'What about Lilian?' Chatter was petering out. She fixed Sally with a glare and repeated the question. Sally cast a hunted look in Eve's direction and then gave defiant voice.

'She's got a boyfriend . . . an oriental gentleman.' Eve sat back as though to dissociate herself.

'He's Chinese or Malaysian or something,' the trifle girl said.

'He's a doctor though,' someone added, as though that cancelled out his foreign blood.

Soon it was clear. The Chinese-Malaysian-something doctor was a) small, b) old, c) green as grass to be taken in by Lilian, and d) probably an illegal immigrant. Lilian was suffering from a) nymphomania, b) softening of the brain, c) night starvation and d) an overdose of Phyllosan.

'Well I don't blame her,' the trifle girl said at last. 'I couldn't live alone. I tell you that now, and you can make what you like of it.'

Everyone tried to look noncommittal until they saw the tide of public opinion. 'Personally, I think she's gone mad,' Eve said at last. There was a murmur of agreement.

'Doctors make at least thirty thou' a year . . .' Min said, 'she's not so mad.' Inside Min there was a computer winking away. Totting, totting.

Sally put down the stuffed dates. 'Well, I don't know how she can. It's nothing racial . . . as far as I'm concerned we're all equal . . . but I mean, Frank was a decent chap. Oh, I know he liked his booze, but fundamentally he was all right. Ask anyone in Rotary. And now she's just wiping him out. If you ask me . . .'

They never got a chance to ask her. Eve rose to her feet and clasped her hands the way she used to do before important pronouncements when she was head girl. '*Parents, teachers and fellow pupils* . . .' For once Frances and Min were of one mind. 'All right, Eve, we'll change the subject. What about eating?' Min said.

As they moved into the kitchen, Fran reflected that she learned more about the human condition in one girls' night than she was likely to do in a year with the Psychology tutor. Tonight's lesson could be sub-titled 'The Widowed Situation'. Point I: once widowed you're supposed to stay widowed. If you attempt to escape, your character will be assassinated forthwith. Point 2: attend every social gathering and never leave the room. This is the one way to ensure someone else is done over instead of you. Point 3: if you are foolish enough to have a relationship, keep it quiet.

She blessed her own reluctance to mention Edward. Now they never need know. Lilian's carcase had been picked clean and put aside for broth, and they were on to the food. Food was safe. She worked her way from left to right of the table, carrying the dismembered bits to the side table in the lounge before she abandoned them.

The system was working well when Valerie singled her out. 'How are you, Fran? I've been dying to ask all night.' Her expression implied she was ready to bear the worst.

'Oh, not too bad. You know . . .' Fran found her own tone of cheery fortitude nauseating.

Valerie put out a consoling hand. 'I know . . . and Martin, poor little thing. It's just as well you were only left with one.'

Fran took a moment to break the cream-filled brandy snap and mangle it upon her plate. 'I expect I'd have managed.' If she'd had more of David's children they would have filled the house, all shapes and sizes and a baby with a wobbly neck. You laid them on your knee to sprinkle them with powder and your fingers could meet quite easily around their arms and legs.

'Fran! Fran!' Min was signalling from the hearthrug. 'I'm telling them about your dog . . . the Chinese tripehound . . . they all think you're mad!'

Sally shook her head in rueful agreement. 'They're terribly tying, Fran . . . although of course you don't go out much – on account of Martin, I mean,' she added hastily.

'What kind is it?' the trifle girl asked. 'You weren't serious about it being Chinese?' There was a burst of laughter when someone said, 'Better not let Lilian see it . . .' and then Min was leaning back against the pouffe, crossing her sandalled feet. 'If you had to get a dog, why didn't you get a proper dog?'

Eve put down her glass. 'Mongrels are very hardy. You can have trouble with highly bred dogs.' Fran tried to feel grateful for Eve's intervention but it wasn't easy.

Min was refilling glasses and passing round sweetmeats. Turkish delight this time, and stuffed dates and pistachio nuts. Fran had never tasted them before and had to ask their name. The shells were tasty but the contents were disappointing. That was life.

They had started to talk about sex. She had always been amazed that they were ready to discuss their love-lives at the drop of a hat, but lots of women were the same. Once, at Family Planning before she was married, she had sat beside two women, strangers to one another. They had introduced themselves and then fallen to discussing their husbands' techniques. Within seconds! Fran had sat in unwed superiority vowing never to do that, and she never had.

The air was thick with daring expressions in spite of Eve's disapproval. 'At it like knives' and 'missionary position' and 'I said he'd had his lot for one night'. It had been years before she worked out what missionary position meant. She hadn't even been able to ask David, for fear of where it might lead. There was only one position for her ... on her back, with David above her, a bastion against the world. Sometimes he had reached for her in the night and it was sweet to come up from a well of sleep and meet his lips.

'All right, Fran?' Eve's face was peering anxiously into hers.

'Of course ... sorry ... I just remembered something I have to do tomorrow.' Evidently Eve had signalled a change of conversation. The trifle girl was describing her yoga class, and the only position under discussion was the lotus. They ran through their various hobbies and then turned to their children's progress. Another minefield, Fran thought, and was relieved when they moved on to the lack of anything decent to wear in the shops.

'Fran? Fran?' All eyes were on her. 'We're waiting to hear about college!'

For the second time that night she began a dutiful recitation. 'We have lectures morning and afternoon. Subject lectures, and education lectures – that's technique and understanding the teaching process. And we do community studies in addition to our major and minor subjects.' She saw their eyes glaze. Perhaps she should tell the truth? *'I sit with my knees tight together, trying to get one word in three and understand one word in ten. And when I get home I try to make sense of my notes. And I'm tired all the time and I can never remember which room we're supposed to be in and the*

PE lessons make my legs ache.' Mercifully Min was rising to her feet, and the truth remained untold.

'What about some records? We could have a dance.'

Fran sat down beside Eve. The music was Abba, which track she couldn't be sure. Sometimes she thought Abba put all their notes back in the bag and shook them out for the next release, but the beat was good. Each girl had a style of her own, a foot-pointing, hand-waving, hip-jerking style, and a rapt expression. Fran felt her foot move in rhythm. She had always loved to dance. Beside her Eve clucked, 'I don't like this business of dancing around by yourself, I think you need a man . . .' The words trailed away. She felt Eve's hand on her skirt. 'Sit down, Fran . . . I didn't mean anything . . .'

That was the trouble: no one meant anything. Nothing meant anything. Not anything meant nothing any more. She stumbled off one of her heels and decided to abandon shoes. Barefoot, she let her hips jerk to the music and pushed up her sleeves. It was nice to stroke her arms, feel the fine hairs come erect. She raised her arms above her head and began to gyrate. One by one the others fell away, clapping rhythmically, urging her on.

She felt strong, as though she could go on for ever. If she had this much energy she should use some of it for Martin. They could go ten-pin bowling. The clapping was dying away but their eyes remained on her. She turned and saw Eve, her face strained and anxious. She shut her eyes but the image of Eve remained on her closed lids. If she could remember Eve's face, why not David's?

She would've ended it there but the thought of facing them kept her going. Nothing to do but wait for the music to end. Tonight she had gone for a tea towel and seen the dark seeds of mice-dirt scattered through the drawer. She had closed her mind to the horror of it until now. *'Wee sleekit cowrin' timrous beastie.'* She shut her eyes tighter and switched channels. Tomorrow she must see about a stone. *'Here lies David Drummond who died too soon. And his beloved wife, Frances, who dropped dead of disco-dancing at 10.15 on the night of 7 October.'* She was filled with a desperate need to go home, but the beat went on. She kept her arms aloft,

her hips gyrating, while her mind made its goodbyes and carried
her safely over the step and on to the Belgate road.

10

Saturday, 22 October 1983

She stood with her hands on the boiler top, hoping to feel heat.
Sometimes it seemed the metal grew warm to her touch, but
when she moved her hand to another part of the enamelled
surface the cold struck through again. She had cleaned the flue
and emptied the grate; paper, firelighters, sticks, coal . . . a good
blaze, and then add the coke piece by piece. It had to work if you
did it like that. The knees of her jeans were grey with ash . . . it
must be all over the floor. No use leaving it for Bethel. Today
was Saturday and she didn't come in on Saturdays.

She needed trouble with the boiler like she needed a hole in
the head. The prospect of seeing Edward tonight was daunting
enough. 'Just be firm,' Gwen had said. 'Tell him you need a
breather.' She got down on her knees again and started to riddle
the boiler. It wouldn't be as easy as Gwen made out; all the
same, it had to be done. The gifts to Martin were becoming an
embarrassment . . . last week a kite and a torch, yesterday a
Puffin paperback.

Martin was a funny kid. Enigmatic. When he was a baby she
had known his innermost thoughts. Now he kept himself to
himself. If she made time to do things with him it would be all
right. She felt anguish rising and fell to attacking the boiler again.
The least she could do was keep him warm.

She was still at it when Bethel arrived. She stood in the
doorway wrinkling her nose. 'This place is full of stythe.' Her
eyes took in the piled draining board, the basket of ironing, the
fan of ash before the boiler. 'Howay, let the dog see the rabbit.'
She armed Frances to one side but her tone was kind. 'If you
want to be useful, get yoursel' cleaned up and make a pot of tea.'

It was a relief to run up the stairs, unzipping her jeans and pulling the dirty T-shirt over her head. If Mrs B. got the boiler away she would have a bath, an up-to-the-chin bath with Edward and the thermostat the last things in her mind.

By one the boiler had ceased to smoke and gave forth a steady murmur. 'You'll stay and have some lunch?' she pleaded, and Bethel gave a grudging nod: 'I might as well.' Fran opened tins with abandon and fried a mountain of chips. She might even have one or two herself. They ate at the kitchen table, Martin between them, and when he left to walk the dog they sat in a companionable haze of smoke to rehash the neighbourhood news.

Fran tried not to look at the clock. If Bethel didn't notice the time, she might stay. She cast round for topics of conversation to bait the hook. 'Have you always lived in Belgate?' Mrs Bethel settled back and Fran felt a flood of relief. It was going to be all right.

'I was born here ... Clanny Street ... I went into service down London when I left school. I was eldest of five and the only girl, so I reckoned I might as well be paid for running after folks as do it for nothing. Many a young 'un from Belgate wound up down there.' Fran kept her expression rapt. Anything not to break the spell. 'Some houses weren't too bad. But some ... there was one in Chelsea ... straight off she said, "I can't have a maid called Sally. You'll have to be Jane." They were shouting "Jane" all round the house and I never budged. I let on I was daft and they gave in.' She took out her Players and offered them.

'They used to have a joint like a house-end on Sundays. That big!' Matches went to one side, unlit cigarette to the other. 'Lapping over the dish. Solid beef. They had it on Sunday, and we had it for the rest of the week. Hot, cold, minced ... it was ready to walk off the plate by Friday.'

Fran tried to visualize the girl she must have been: rosy-cheeked, probably, and fair. Setting her face against alien names and left-overs. 'You had to hearthstone the steps, none of your red wax polish. But it was all top show. Bonny entrance, and the back end dropping to bits. I got Thursday afternoons off and every other Sunday. And eleven shillings a week.'

Fran made a little sound of protest. 'There was nowt wrong with that. I was better off in them days. Money was money. It all went with the war, mind. Girls was going down to Birmingham for the munitions and running after Yanks. That's when I came back to get wed.'

The kitchen was growing dark and Fran wondered if she dared suggest a move. If she disturbed the mood Bethel might leave. At last she said, 'Let's go next door ... wrestling'll be on the telly shortly.' She knew Bethel loved wrestling, and the gamble paid off. 'This is the happiest I have been for a long time,' Fran thought as she reached for her knitting. Martin was sprawled on his stomach with a book and the dog slumbered beside him. If they could stay like this for ever it would be all right.

From time to time Bethel leaned forward to cheer on a favourite. 'That's right, Jackie lad. Pin 'im down. No, not like that, man ... pin 'im down.' She saved her worst invective for the referee. 'He's paid, you know ... paid to turn a blind eye. Don't tell me he didn't miss that deliberate ... if he did he needs glasses. By, I wish I was there ...' Fran put out a hand and touched the warm radiator. If Bethel were there, she'd fettle them!

She stuck the needles in the wool and rose to her feet. 'I'm going to make some tea ... now, don't argue. Just a cup of tea and then you can go and see to your fire.' The fire was always Bethel's excuse for going home even though it was banked with slack and burned for ever like the Eternal Flame.

Fran ran through the cupboards. The freezer yielded a packet of teacakes and she sawed them through and put them under the grill. Toasted teacakes and chocolate biscuits: that would do. Tomorrow she would stock up again, put a few things by.

The spell had to be broken sooner or later. 'I'll slip over home and see to the fire. Eight o'clock you're going, isn't it?' Fran nodded. 'I'm going to take the dog round the block and then have a lovely bath.' She injected as much gratitude into her voice as she could, and saw satisfaction spring up in Bethel's eyes.

Martin came with her and they waited at every lamp post while Nee-Wan made the ritual anointing. 'He does a lot of wees,'

Martin said with pride. They turned at the corner and took the road to the allotments. Space there for a boy and a dog, and no fear of traffic. Dusk had softened the ramshackle huts, the down-at-heel fences made up of everything under the sun. The dog snuffled at tempting piles of rubbish and once started up a small creature from the grass.

The track was rutted clay and they had to pick their way, skirting old baths and listing wheelbarrows. She put out a hand to Martin and he took it. Typical man . . . always more forthcoming in the dark. 'We'll come back tomorrow when it's light. Maybe there'll be someone here and we can buy some chrysanths.' Her father used to take her walking on Sundays, down to the gardens where a shilling bought a bunch of marguerites. She felt an almost tangible pain for those days of childhood. If you could only go back, right back into the safety zone.

She was careful with the bubble bath. Only a time or two left, and there was no way she could justify another bottle. Not to herself, let alone Harold. '*Please sir, I want some more bubble bath.*' Oliver Twist in a towelling robe, and Harold in the Beadle's hat. 'Bubble bath? *Bubble bath! Are you asking for more bubble bath, Twist?*' Anyway, now that she didn't have to use the immersion heater she was saving electricity. Coke was hardly cheap but it was paid for when she got it and didn't creep up behind her with the bill.

Up to her neck in foam, she thought about money. Her best thinking was done in the bath. Bed thinking was depressing and thinking on the hoof apt to be disjointed. In the bath she could think like Confucius . . . or that chap who'd discovered something under the foam and leapt out shrieking. If she made stringent economies she might avoid having to sell the house. In her heart she knew a move was inevitable. Living in Belgate now made no sense. But giving Martin time to adjust before uprooting him made all the sense in the world.

Besides, she didn't want to move! There was safety in standing still. Like kids when the music stopped. If you moved, you were out! The water was lapping her lower lip and she contemplated opening her mouth and vanishing beneath the foam. If she died before the end of term, though, they might want the grant back and her only legacy to Martin would be a deficit. She spluttered upright and began to loofah her legs.

She was rubbing her heels with pumice when she heard the scream. Ear-piercing and blood-curdling and full of righteous fury. She stepped from the water and reached for a towel. Martin stood in the hall, mouth open in disbelief, eyes alight with glee. In the kitchen Mrs Bethel was banging about like a woman possessed. Fran pushed open the door and beheld her, hat over one eye, coat hanging open, wielding a long-handled brush like a flail. 'You bugger. You impident little bugger! Come out, you impident little sod! I'll best you. I never could stand mice and I'm not starting now. Come out of it, before I kill you.'

Fran left her rattling behind the cooker and tiptoed back to Martin. 'You shouldn't laugh. It's given her a shock.'

He grinned. 'It was on the draining board when she put the light on. I heard her shout.'

Fran made her way back upstairs. It didn't seem funny any more. Mice were dirty and attracted to dirty houses. Tomorrow, first thing, she would buy traps, poison, get a cat. She tried to convince herself it was only a field mouse. It might have run away . . . and if it had any sense it would have! It was probably miles away by now.

When she came out on to the landing she could feel the heat rising from below, solid and soothing and as expensive as hell. There was nothing to beat a warm house. Somehow she must make some money. She could get another mouse and breed them for table. Or sell their pelts for fun furs. Or train a troupe to perform in public! She decided to pull herself together. It wasn't funny, and an hour from now she had Edward to face. '*Now look here, Edward, let's get this straight* . . .' Thank heaven it was half-term. If she handled things well tonight it would be nine days before she had to face him again.

Bethel's plans for punitive expeditions against the mice followed her over the step. Martin was engrossed in TV and simply mumbled goodbye. She would have to ration TV. They would have a nice holiday, and then start a new regime.

Edward was waiting at a corner table. He rose at the sight of her and came forward, smiling. She sipped her sherry, beset by second thoughts: if she didn't give him the chop she could unburden herself about the mice. Mice were men's work. No, that was shirking: if she didn't do it tonight she would have to go through the whole thing again later on. She made an effort to relax and listen to what he was saying.

'I think I've made a mistake with my subject options.' He didn't look like a man who'd made a mistake. He looked satisfied. Smug. 'Quite frankly, I don't think he knows what he's talking about. I'd skip his lectures, but that's opting out, isn't it?' He took her agreement for granted and went on. 'The trouble with these lecturer chappies is that they've never lived in the outside world. It should be compulsory for them to take a job when they qualify. A proper job. Get among men. They get a few letters after their name, and they're straight in front of a class and everyone kow-towing. No wonder it goes to their heads.'

'They can't have an easy job though, Edward. I mean, we're a pretty motley bunch.' They started to dissect their fellow pupils. Safe ground. Nigel was thick as two short planks, and Gwen sharp as a tack. Stanley was all right when he didn't trot out his left-wing views, and Maggie would make a good teacher if she got through the exams.

'Teaching practice will be my downfall,' Fran said ruefully.

Edward patted her hand. 'You'll be all right. We all worry . . . we'd be queer mortals if we didn't . . . but it works out in the end.'

She declined another drink and they came out into the lighted street. A fine rain was falling and Edward took her arm. 'Let's run.' She put up her collar and held it around her face as they splashed along the pavements. Their stride was uneven and she tried to retrieve her arm but he pulled her closer. 'Relax, Fran . . . let me make the pace.'

When they reached the restaurant she was seething. He had hardly allowed her feet to touch the ground. Imposing his will! She kept her anger alight through Kashmiri chicken and poppadums, and told him over coffee. 'It's not that I don't enjoy coming out with you, Edward . . .' His eyes were the eyes of the ox in the abbatoir. Perhaps if she thought among her friends she could find him a girl? She would think about it tomorrow. Or even tonight . . . once she was safe in the car.

11

Saturday, 29 October 1983

The land was every shade of grey from pearl to charcoal. That was what she loved about the north, that it wore its colours gravely. She halted at the junction and turned south for Durham. 'Get yersel' out,' Bethel had said. 'Put the bairn in the car and get away out.' She looked at Martin but he was intent on the view. To the west the Pennines, to the east the sea. Here and there a colliery wheel. She loved each mucky little colliery village with its Methodist church and Welfare hall. Not to mention its Chinese takeaway! Her laughter made Martin turn.

'What's funny?'

She shook her head. 'I don't know. I'm just glad to be out of the house, I suppose.'

The minute she said it she was sorry. What if he asked why? She could hardly say she was running away from Edward, that would plant all sorts of macabre ideas in his mind. The truth was, she was sorry for Edward and if she took another phone call she would probably give way . . . which wouldn't be kind in the end. Anyway, enough of Edward. She had come out to forget him.

There were still lots of fields left. Breathing spaces. One of the reasons she avoided science fiction was that everyone always lived in tunnels. Aluminium and anchored in space, but tunnels all the same. And everything came out of tubes. Suddenly the cathedral sprang up in the distance, higher than the castle. God before man. There was a blistering of advance factories at the side of the road. Sprats to catch the fat southern mackerel . . . who came, took the subsidies, and exited.

'What are we going to do when we get there?' she asked and took his answering shrug in good part. She must have more patience with him. They came out of the car park and walked up the slope to the market square. As soon as she got in among the buildings she felt safer. A medieval market square with narrow exits and entrances. A womb!

'What are we going to do?' she said again. Why couldn't he decide? Help? David had always known where they should go. They settled for Woolworth's. Good old Woolies! Except that it wasn't old any more, or particularly good, and there was nothing you could buy for sixpence, not even a paper bag. 'I'm just going out for a cigarette. I'll wait in the square. Will you be all right?' He nodded, eyes on the model counter, and she slipped away.

She found a seat near the Londonderry statue – the shako'd third marquess on a tongueless horse. Her father had lifted her up to see into the empty mouth: she could remember his hands firm on her bare legs. *'You're all right. Daddy's got you.'*

She'd have given her eye-teeth for a drink, but to go alone into a pub without someone to meet her was impossible. Nice women didn't do things like that. Her feet were cold and she stamped them gently. If Martin didn't come in a moment she'd get up and walk around. She couldn't lose him here. If it weren't so cold they could stay here till nightfall. In the old grey city, safe. In a hundred years it would still be here, but she would be gone. The span of a life was less than a second in the whole of time. Less than a second of a second. She stood up and threw her cigarette to the ground.

She was grinding it with her toe when someone spoke. 'How's the Mini going?' It was the car salesman! She wondered if the gush of blood to her face would empty her limbs, deprive them of substance so that she would fall to the ground in a heap.

'It's fine, thank you, no bother at all.' She searched his face for signs that he knew about her dreams, but there was no trace there of carnal knowledge.

'Once or twice I've almost picked up the phone to ask how it was running. I like to keep my customers happy.'

She felt fourteen again, coming out of school, hoping her hero wouldn't notice her ankle socks or the pen and pencil in her blazer pocket. 'You should have.' They fell into step and walked on. She wanted to ask about the Rover but feared his answer. As if he read her thoughts he spoke. 'I've still got the Rover. I could've sold it again and again ... nice car. But, I don't know ... I like her.'

They had reached the edge of the market square. 'I must go back ... my son's waiting.'

He nodded. 'Perhaps we could have a drink together some time?' The lines on his face were deep. Lines of good humour. And when she fondled his neck the hair at the nape was thick and soft.

She struggled to sift fact from fantasy and make a proper reply. 'That would be nice. Thank you.'

Still he hesitated, as though unwilling to move away. 'Are you still at the same number? I thought Harry mentioned you were moving?'

She felt saliva fill her mouth. 'I don't know where he got that from. I'm still in the same house.'

As she retraced her steps she fumed. Presumptuous bloody Harold. Shit, shit, shit! But she knew the real reason for her anger: it was reaction to the meeting. Be angry with Harold and you needn't be anything else. Not puzzled or afraid or tremulous or excited – just angry. She could cope with that.

Martin was waiting outside Woolworth's and they went in search of a café. 'Could we have beefburgers?' It was lovely to nod and see him smile.

'What are we going to do after this?' she said, fumbling for her lighter.

To her relief he had a suggestion. 'Can we go round the castle?' They had been round the castle twice before but at least he had made a decision. The doors to the kitchen swung open and she caught a glimpse of clutter. It didn't do to peer into café kitchens: just eat up, and leave it at that.

Last night she'd opened the pantry door and a mouse had stared at her from the shelf. Eyeball to eyeball and still as death. He was small and brown and pretty scared. She'd closed the pantry door and gone to unspring the traps. If she found him impaled in the morning it would be like the death of a friend. She had tried to coax Nee-wan to chase the mice away, but to no avail. As a protector Nee-wan was Nee-use.

They were coming out of the café when she heard the voice. 'Frances? It is Frances? Yes, of course it is!' Valerie's mother. Shit, shit, shit! 'How are you, Frances?' One good thing, they never expected answers. She was peering into Martin's face. 'And what about this big boy then? Are you looking after Mummy? You must be a man now, mustn't you?'

If he spat in the woman's eye there was no way she would smack him. It was a bloody silly question. How could he be a man? He was ten years old, and bereft. 'So nice to see you, Mrs Pearson. Say bye-bye, Martin.' They toiled over the cobbles to the Palace Green and neither of them spoke until the bank was accomplished and the cathedral lay before them, a thousand shades of beige.

They turned towards the castle. Martin was tugging at her arm and she turned to the noticeboard. '*The following still owe for the Boat Club Dinner.*' Fancy having your debts pinned up for all the world to see. Still, if you were in the Boat Club you must have cash.

Once she had sat with David on the river bank and watched the boat crew come down to practise. Brown legs, white shorts and the air of kings. Two boys in jeans had thrown stones in the water and shouted insults at the rowers ... 'Bloody puffs.' At last they had shambled off. 'To carve their names on a monument or smash a window or two,' David had said and they'd sat in silence, dumbfounded by the inequalities of life.

The castle guide bustled up, female and unbelievably young. She had the air of a sheepdog, nippy and tenacious. No chance to slip behind an arras and escape that clear blue eye. They came to the corridor where the students lodged but there was no evidence of occupation save for a dirty coffee mug placed in a mullioned window. It would be nice if Martin came here one day, took a degree. He was clever enough, and David would have died with pride to have a son at Durham. Incongruous remark, she thought. Incontrovertibly incongruous.

The tattered standards above her head had shredded till they resembled spiders' webs. One vandal touch, and they would disintegrate. The guide was rattling off names, a young head full of information. She had a sapphire ring on her ring finger. Fran touched her own ring and was reassured. Still there. And she wasn't going to cry about it. Yesterday Bethel had said, 'Your bladder's too near your eyes,' and her tone was caustic.

She had a comfortable feeling of duty done as they crossed the Green. Castle for Martin, cathedral for her. She explained the sanctuary knocker. 'And once they touched it no one could hurt them anymore.' The massive head was fierce.

'You mean no one could get them once they'd knocked?'

She nodded. 'And then the monks let them in and took care of them.'

Martin was looking dubiously at the leonine head. 'Did they get out again?'

She had never inquired about that. Enough to get in and be safe.

'You have to say a prayer.' He bowed his head and she kneeled beside him. The pillars were grey and massive and patterned differently. Perhaps they'd competed, raced to the top: 'You do herringbone, I'll do diamonds.' There might have been kangaroo courts for the over-eager, and a group of brothers to pronounce sentence. She realized she was grinning irreverently and shut her eyes.

'*Our father which art in heaven* ...' The inside of her lids ceased to sparkle and she tried to picture David's face. His upper lip had been firm, the central indentation sharp. She tried to will the face above it, but it wouldn't come.

Instead she opened her eyes and fixed them on the altar window. A brilliant flower of glass, holy blue and red and gold. '*Please God, let everything be all right. Let Martin be all right ... and college ... and do something about the mice. Nothing cruel. And take care of everyone.*' Comprehensive cover. Did God hear? Did he exist? The prospect of profound thought terrified her. Out into deep water and no comforting shingle beneath your feet. She turned in mid-stroke and made her way hurriedly back to shore. If there was a God – or anything like a God – it would keep.

They walked down the right-hand aisle and halted at the Miners' Memorial. '*Remember before God the Durham Miners who have given their lives in the pits of this county and those who work in*

darkness and danger in those pits today.' The first time she had seen
the memorial she had been disappointed. It should have been
massive and hewn from coal; instead it was made of seventeenth-
century woodcarving, fat cupids and fruit-bearing vines. A nice
touch . . . the fruit of the earth. The top was a pelmet of faces,
tiny distorted bodies, hands holding tools. 'See how many you
can pick out, Martin?' He identified pincers and wedges, a ladder
and drills. But no windy pick. There was a lamp in a garland.
Her lamp had been fastened to her helmet and the battery had
dragged from a belt around her waist. She had trudged behind
David through the velvet dust and known no fear.

She looked at the text above the plinth: '*He breaketh open a
shaft away from where men sojourn. They are forgotten of the foot that
passeth by.*' It was true. Miners were labouring beneath the earth
now. Sweaty and grimy, clad in old underpants or chopped-off
jeans, a neckerchief to catch the sweat, white eyes and teeth in
black faces. Going up in the cage, packed among men coming
off shift, she had reached for David's hand. 'This is the only bit
I don't like,' she had whispered, and had heard a weary voice
pipe up behind, 'Eeeh, missus, it's the only bit I *do* like.'

Martin was reading the inscription '. . . *and those who work in
darkness and danger in those pits today.*' He looked up at her. 'Is
that Brian?'

Frances nodded. 'Yes, that's Brian.' And once it had been
Walter Raeburn, who would spit in your eye as soon as look at
you. Yesterday he had tooted his horn at the door but by the
time Bethel got there he had started up and was halfway down
the street. Seeing Fran's alarm Bethel had been quick to
reassure. 'Don't let it worry you, he's always acting himself like
that. "Come when I toot, or else!" I'll toot him the next time I
see him.' Even in the cathedral she had to laugh at the memory
of Bethel's face.

Martin's eyes demanded explanation. 'And did he really drive
off before she got there?'

Fran nodded, and smiled as he said, 'By, I bet she was mad!'

They passed beneath the window of Oswald, King of Northumbria to the shabby tomb of Bede, father of English learning.
Her school had been named after Bede. She had sat on the tip-

up seats in assembly, her greatest worry merely the cut of her tunic, with a hundred teachers to carry the strain. And then, in the fourth year, she was searching for David's head in front, straining to pick out his voice in the hymns. She concentrated on the tomb. '*Hac Sunt in Oss Baedae Venerabilis Ossa*': here lie the bones of Bede.

There were glass markers in the walls to show settlement. David had pointed them out – 'If the building settles, they break and the engineer picks it up.' David, David. Clever David.

Before they left the cathedral she gave Martin a fifty-pence piece to put in the offertory box. It would keep the fabric intact for a moment of time. She put out a hand to the massive door and felt its grateful pressure in return. There was nothing in religion, she knew that. Except that you couldn't live without it.

Outside, the sky was mauve and salmon pink with long grey flecks of cloud and the last rays of the sun striking the castle walls. It must be nearly five. Time to go home. They hurried down to the market square past students so confident and oddly dressed that they startled her. She was a student, but as ordinary as air.

As she drove north she could see the twinkling lights of Chester-le-Street, and the red lamps round the roundabout looked like jewels hung from a Christmas tree. God save them both from Christmas. Eight weeks. Fifty six days. The sky to the west was pearly, like the inside of a shell. Martin was peaceful inside his seat belt and the vibes were good. A nice day, and now they were speeding through a fairyland of lights. She had deliberately suppressed any thought of her meeting with the car man until now. He had been as nice as she remembered – nicer even. Still, no need for palpitations. He was just an ordinary bloke. If it hadn't been for the dreams, she wouldn't have felt anything ... well, hardly anything. So why did she feel so exaltant? Exaltant? Exultant? What a difference a letter made. She searched the sky for the Christmas Star and, finding none, decided it had been too much to hope for anyway.

12

Wednesday, 2 November 1983

It cost fifty pence each to get in and thirty pence a pair for bowling shoes. Gary's face was rapt as he tied the fancy laces, and Fran wondered if she should tell him they had to be given back on leaving. She decided it would be patronizing, and contented herself with squeezing the toes to make sure they fitted. Martin was struggling with his laces and she kneeled to help. 'Do they fit?' He nodded impatiently and twisted his foot away. She must try not to fuss.

There were only one or two alleys in action but they gave off a mighty rumble. She wasn't sure she could stick it for an hour, not on top of piped music. '*When I need you I hold out my hand and I touch love . . .*' Leo Sayer. She looked at the numbered disc in her hand. 'We're number eight,' she said. They ran, whooping and jumping in the unaccustomed shoes, and grabbed for bowls.

She showed Gary how to fit finger and thumb into the bowl and then selected her own. It was heavy as lead and she had to cradle it with her other hand. When she let go she would be carried with it to crash into the pins and be scooped up by the reaper. Beside her, Gary was hefting his ball with ease. His mother had probably never even heard of a balanced diet, but he was as strong as an ox. Beside him Martin was frail!

Her first ball swerved halfway and ended up in the gutter. There was a hoot of triumph from Gary and a pitying look from Martin. 'I'll just keep score,' she said and relegated herself to the bench. She had dreaded the noise, but it was soothing – great walls of noise shutting out the world. She tapped her feet to the music, relishing the spongy soles of the borrowed shoes. Never mind verrucae, they couldn't get you through socks. If they were going to come here often she would buy shoes, a pair for Gary even. It would be worth it. He was not David, but he filled the gap.

The gap. The vacuum. Nature abhorred a vacuum. Which explained her dreams about the car man. Always she was passing her hand down his back, feeling the scapula, the hollow of his waist, the buttock round and smooth and muscled. Her face fitted his neck, his body was round and about her. He touched her, and his touch was kind. Their bodies mingled but she had never worked out the details. Please God she never would.

She put a hand to her eyes in confusion. It was too late for mental breakdown. At the beginning she had felt the first frost of madness, but it had receded. She had managed, gone out and got a job . . . well, gone out. She was coping. If she did break down, where would it end? The madhouse? Shapeless cotton frocks and slops for tea? She considered the possibility that her dreams were wish-fulfilment and decided against it. If she wanted sex, it wouldn't be with a stranger. Unless it were Paul Newman. She gave a determined laugh and got to her feet. 'I'll show you how to bowl,' she said.

This time she took a line on the pins and weighed the camber of the track. She felt competent, in charge. They were having a good day out. She launched the ball. It wobbled once then made its way unerringly to the centre of the pins.

'A strike! A strike!' Martin's face was glowing.

'I'm in,' Fran thought ruefully. 'If I can keep getting ten at one blow, I'm in.'

Now that she had entered into the game she found she was enjoying it. She felt tall and lithe, thin now as the proverbial rake. The top button of her shirt had come undone. She still had good boobs although she was down to seven stone and the muscles of her face stood out like cords.

Three balls later she had another strike. Martin was more blasé by now, but there was a whoop of encouragement from the next alley. Fran looked across to smile her thanks and dropped eyes as she saw the players. Lads, twenty-year-old lads! Mayday! Mayday!

She turned away and concentrated on finding a suitable ball, weighing them carefully as though she were a connoisseur. The music was beaty . . . '*Karma Karma Karma Karma Karma Kameleon*'. She was conscious of her body, her limbs suffused with life. She let go a ball and stood, hands on hips, to watch its progress, aware of her out-thrust breasts, the jut of her pelvis.

Aware and ashamed and incapable of change. She could feel
eyes on her, and she liked it. The ball struck, claimed its victims
and vanished, and she moved aside to make way for Gary. There
was a word for what she was doing . . . a terrible word – but the
beat was in her blood, the hunt . . . the eternal hunt . . . was in
full swing. Yesterday she had reached for a grapefruit in the
supermarket and drawn back her hand when she remembered.
In the instant that she put out her hand she had forgotten David
was dead, wiped out the last five months as though expunging
scribble from a slate.

She looked up as the denimed figure of a man came into view
and a thin brown hand extended a packet of cigarettes. 'Smoke?'

She tried to sound mature. 'Thank you . . . but I don't think
we're supposed to smoke.'

His hair was long and the bracelet round his wrist was gold.
'There's no one to see . . . they're all in the snack bar drowning
their grief.' She raised her brows in question and accepted a
cigarette. 'It's closing . . . hadn't you heard?' So much for her
plans for weekly bowling and the healthy life!

When he bent forward to light her cigarette he smelled of
aftershave and soap and she could see the curled hairs on his
chest. There was a gold St Christopher around his neck and a
small gold stud in his ear. Jewellery! David wouldn't even wear a
signet ring on his little finger.

'Your kids?' He was looking at the boys.

'One of them . . . the fair one . . . the thin, fair one.'

He smiled and hitched a hip on to the rail. 'You don't look old
enough.'

His eyes were bleak; programmed eyes. 'He's done all this
before,' Fran thought. His jeans were tight, the strength of his
thighs terrifying. She wondered what degree of rudeness would
make him go away. 'Tell that to my husband,' she said lightly,
and noted the tiny flicker in his pupils. 'He pushed us in here
while he did some business. I can't think where he's got to . . .'
If Martin heard her he would know her for a liar – or suspect
her reason.

The cigarette trembled in her fingers as the boy unhooked his
hip and turned on his heel. 'OK,' he said. He hadn't believed

her but he was going just the same. He wouldn't waste time on anything less than a cert. She turned back and saw the light go out on the number eight alley. It was over. Who said God didn't answer prayers?

They made their way out and handed in their bowling shoes. The assistant was bored and listless, seventeen years old and already fed up with life. The maroon polish on her fingernails was chipped and there were heavy nicotine stains on her fingers. A middle-aged man came past and said, 'How's choo-choo face then?' The assistant was hunting for Gary's shoes and gave no sign of recognition except to say 'Sod off' in flat and unemotional tones.

Gary's shoes, when they came to light, were scuffed and shabby, the resin soles worn thin so that they bulged and blistered like the bottom of a crumpet. Last week the sociology tutor had made a pronouncement: 'If you want to know what sort of home a child comes from look at the state of its shoes.' Fran kneeled to help him and saw the hole in his sock with the big toe showing through. 'You've got a *pomme de terre* in your sock,' she said cheerfully.

Martin's brows came down and she could see his mind clicking. 'She means tatie,' he said at last and there was a wealth of contempt in his tone.

She followed them into the cafeteria and bought fizzy oranges and coffee. 'Do you want biscuits?'

Martin's answer was brief. 'Penguins, please.'

They found a table by the window and she scanned the cars below in the car park. A lot of them had older registrations than the Mini and this cheered her. The Mini was all right, really. A safe house on wheels. There was a flurry of activity below: the boys who had had the next alley were leaving. Lithe young men with stomachs flat as boards. In women the chin went first; in men it was the belly. She turned her head from the window in case he looked up and met her eyes.

She had asked for trouble. Some primitive instinct had impelled her into a courting display, and for the life of her she didn't know why. The thought of the boy, young and thin and scented, was nauseating. His only virtue would be speed. Wham, bam, thank you ma'am. No thanks!

The children were locked in conversation as she cast an indulgent ear. 'You haven't got a nana either, have you?' That was Gary and his tone was pitying.

Martin shook his head. 'I did have. I had two . . . my mam's mam and my dad's mam. But they died before I was born.'

Gary drew a last abortive breath through his empty straw. 'When my nana died we had a party. Meat . . . not just gravy . . . git lumps of meat. And cream cakes. You could eat as much as you liked and the priest gave us all tenpence. I've still got one nana left.'

Fran turned away to hide her smile. One nana down, one more to go. Roll on the wake!

They must come here again before it closed. Martin's face was positively rosy. Like it had been last night at the Welfare swimming pool. 'Please Mam, I haven't been for ages . . . not since . . . anyway, can we?'

She had been struggling to hold him on the training belt, and then a man had risen, dripping, from the pool and wrested it from her. 'Mind out, pet . . . he'll have you tip over heels in a minute.' Frances had sat back gratefully and watched Martin find his confidence . . . now that a man was in charge again.

'Thank you very much,' she said to the man when it was over.

'Any time, pet. Any time.' He was hairy and wet, and his shoulders and back were traced with blue. He'd dived into the pool and swum away from her gratitude.

Now she stubbed out her cigarette and thought about the evening ahead. She hated the house once Martin was asleep. She would walk from room to room, knowing she should settle to some study but desperate to get out. Well, tonight would be different. She would have a lovely hot bath. She would have to speak to Bethel about the boiler though – she was stoking it like Humphrey Bogart fuelling the *African Queen*. She was living in the past when coke was 7s 6d a bag.

Anyway, to get back to tonight. She would have a drink. She was trying not to, but there had to be exceptions to every rule. She'd cut out weekend drinks since last week when she'd offered

Bethel a sherry and been withered for her pains. 'Hardly out of your bed, and boozing. You can please yourself but don't pour me one.'

They were playing 'Long and Winding Road' as she came through the foyer: 1963 and Beatlemania, and safe at home with Mam and Dad. She switched on her sidelights as they drove out of town. She would be glad when Christmas came, and with it the shortest day. If she survived to the spring she'd make it. They'd be moved by then – Harold was becoming insistent – and she could tackle the new garden. Plant and prune and cultivate. The boy from the bowling alley didn't matter . . . he was a denimed irrelevance. She liked the phrase and repeated it. She was still discovering the anodyne effect of words. Lexicon with her father, and his pride when she'd made a word. And afterwards Scrabble with David. I LOVE YOU. I WANT YOU. SHALL WE GO TO BED. She had placed YES on the board and he had given her bonus points. The darkness clamped down entirely and she switched on the headlights to illumine the road.

13

Saturday, 5 November 1983

While she washed up the tea things she thought about Eve and Min. Chagrined, that was the word. Or, to put it succinctly, choked! 'We're having this do for Guy Fawkes . . . at my place because it's larger . . . but Eve's helping. Bonfire and jacket potatoes and goodies for the kids, and then we'll pack them off home and the grown-ups can get round the trough. We realize you'll probably want to go home with Martin, so don't think we'll be put out . . .'

She had swilled her coffee twice round her mouth to savour the full glory of her reply before she made it. 'Well, actually, Martin's tied up that night with some other Guy Fawkes thing, but I'd love to come to the grown-ups' do.' And bugger you, darlings! Their eyes had met and signalled, and then Eve had

spoken. 'It'll be lovely if you can come . . . if you're sure?' Then
Min, 'As long as you're sure? I mean, we understand . . .' If
many more people offered to understand her, she'd be up for
GBH! She hung up the tea towel and went upstairs to get ready.

While she was in the bathroom Martin shouted his goodbyes.
He'd be OK with Brian Malone. She was free. No one to tap on
the door, or whinge, or race the dog round the front room and
threaten the Doulton figurine. The firework display was being
laid on by the Miners' Welfare. 'We're allowed one each, and
me dad's taking Gary, so your Martin can come with me.' He
had stood on her step in his NCB jacket, eyes black-rimmed in a
white face, and she'd wanted to embrace him to show her
gratitude. 'That's git marvellous,' Martin had said, and done it
for her. She would have to tell him 'git' was not a word, but that
had not been the time.

She fastened her robe and went downstairs for a drink. The
house was funny without Martin. That was the bloody thing
about life: you got what you wanted and it wasn't what you
wanted after all. Like struggling to climb the fence to the greener
grass, and finding when you got there that it had been napalmed.

She tried to find a blessing to count, and came up with the
mice. It had been so simple once she confided in Gwen. 'Get in
the Council,' Gwen had said. The Council man was small and
quiet, a bit of a wee sleekit beastie himself. 'You don't do
anything cruel, do you?' she'd asked him. He'd looked at Bethel
and Bethel at him and she saw mutual recognition of the
problem! *'This one's not quite twelve pennies to the shilling.'*

He liked mice, he assured her . . . positively liked them . . .
would take them all home with him given the chance. He would
just come and go, and she could leave it all to him and the 'good
lady'. All she needed to do was watch the dog at all times. Bethel
brightened visibly at being called a 'good lady' and Fran retired.
The mice crawled away to die in agony but it was nothing to do
with her. The comings and goings had taken all the mice with
them and 'all points of entry had been stopped'. There was
something to be said for only being eleven pennies to the shilling:
it got you out of the dirty work.

Fran decided on her turquoise crêpe dress with the halter

neck. It hid her bony chest, and bony shoulder-blades didn't seem so bad. Looking at herself, she panicked. Please God let Min phone to say it's off. Or let Bethel decide I look peaky and put me to bed. But God never answered panic prayers; you had to put in your request in triplicate and submit it through the proper channels.

She was nearly ready when Bethel arrived. 'I've put your supper in and there's a fresh teacake in the bread bin if you want it.' She hurried to cover her shoulders with a shawl but Bethel seemed not to notice.

'Is the bairn back?'

Fran shook her head. 'Not yet.'

Bethel snorted. 'I hope he's all right with that lot.'

Her snort demanded reply. 'The Malones are all right . . . they're good-hearted.' She didn't want to fall out with Bethel but she wouldn't have the Malones run down.

She had begun to enjoy the drive into town now that she was more confident of her driving. Tonight the moonlight on the sea was quite spectacular – long paths of light leading to the dark horizon. And tiny winking ships making for port, coal ships for Seaham and Sunderland, bigger ships for the Tyne. David had always wanted to take a trip on the Bergen line, Newcastle to Norway. Now they would never go. She tried hard to remember his face, summon up the features one by one, but it was useless.

The bonfire was dying on the patio when she got to Min's, and there was the smell of cordite in the air. They spilled over every room, men in sweaters and jeans because it was a bonfire party and women dressed to the nines. Now that she was here she felt naked in the bare-shouldered dress, in spite of the shawl, and manoeuvred to get her back to the wall. One or two were looking at her as though she had risen from the dead, and in a way she had . . . slipped down from the funeral pyre and refused incineration. She saw Dennis weaving towards her with bottle and glass, and tilted her chin in welcome.

After that the ice was broken. The glass in her hand was a wand. Abracadabra and tonic. 'How are you . . . you do look well . . . lovely to see you, Fran.' The women looked faintly disapproving, the men relieved. They could cope with uplifted boobs in turquoise crêpe better than downcast eyes in widow's weeds.

Min materialized at her side. 'All right?' Her tone was anxious. Yesterday she had got down to doing something about David's clothes, packing them up for the Oxfam shop because that was what he'd have liked. She had started to cry at his socks, holding them against her mouth and sobbing. When the doorbell had rung she'd stood transfixed until she was forced downstairs by the rattling of the letter box. Min was standing on the step. 'I knew you were in because I saw the car.' And then, as she took in the tears . . . 'What on earth's the matter?' As though there was no good reason why Fran should cry.

Now she looked at Min and smiled. 'I'm fine.'

As Min moved away, Fran felt an arm around her waist. It was Geoff Turner, Valerie's husband, the habitual cigar stuck between his teeth. 'You know how we all feel, Fran. I mean, we couldn't take it in at first . . . not old Davo . . . but at the same time he'd've been the first to say life goes on.'

Desperate to bring it to an end she squeezed his hand. 'I know, Geoff. I know. I must go and help Min, but I know how you feel.' She had hated their inadequate 'I knows'; now she was doing it herself.

She found a haven in the hall. The people either side were strange and drew her into their conversation. She decided to enjoy it while she could. Soon someone would fill them in and constraint would fall upon them like a shroud. Perhaps she should say, 'I'm a widow . . . don't worry. There's a lot of it about but it's not catching.'

Min reappeared, a tall, dark man in tow. 'This is Richard Hindson-Evans' – and then, in a stage whisper, 'He's a surgeon!' Min was looking for signs of awe, and the man himself stood waiting for homage. Fran had a crazy desire to say 'Sod off', like the girl in the bowling alley, but when she opened her mouth the words that came out were perfectly *comme il faut*. 'Are you here on a visit, or do you work here?'

His voice was filtered through marbles. 'I'm at the Royal . . . I'm in Orthopaedics.'

Min was looking expectantly from face to face. 'Richard's in Round Table with Dennis, aren't you Richard?'

He held out his hand for Fran's glass. 'Can I get you a refill?' Min accepted her dismissal meekly and turned away. Fran followed. He could put the refill where the monkey put the nuts.

She was drying glasses in the kitchen when Dennis appeared. A Yogi Bear mask hung round his neck and his hair was rumpled. 'Are you OK, Fran?' She would be if he'd just shift. His breath smelled of booze and tobacco. Funny how you could tolerate such odours in your lover and loathe them in every other man. His lips came down on her face, missing her mouth and sliding.

'For God's sake, Dennis!' She struck his chest with her clenched fist. Afterwards she wished she had handled it better, and merely wishing that made her angry. He was the transgressor and she was the one with the guilt problem!

Out in the hall she heard Margaret Thatcher's name mentioned. Politics are safe. She put her back against the banister and eased the weight on her feet. 'They don't see it as a kitty,' one man was saying. 'They take out but they don't put in.'

'The whole country's riddled with scroungers.' That was Stuart Gray, the sweet wholesaler.

'Well, personally, I'd scrub floors before I'd take social security.' The speaker had inch-long fingernails and wouldn't know a scrubbing brush from a mating hedgehog. Fran moved away as the surge for supper began.

They were piling their plates with food, shovelling it into their mouths. She saw Eve in a corner and made towards her. 'Can I get you something, Eve?' Better pay homage.

'Thanks, Fran . . . Harold's already gone.'

Harold appeared bearing two plates and thrust the second one at Fran. 'You have this . . . I'll get another.' When he came back he got straight down to business. 'They're building some nice maisonettes at the bottom of Greenway, Fran. Two-bedroom jobs. Twenty-two thou', and you'd clear about thirty for your place.'

Eve licked in a stray bit of coleslaw. 'You want to get away from the pit, Fran.'

Harold nodded. 'And we'd help with the move. Actually, it would be nice if you got it over before Eve gets too preggers.'

Fran swallowed. 'Shall I start packing tonight?' She meant to be biting, but it came out as mildly sarcastic and they both laughed.

Harold was nodding rhythmically as he chewed. 'Leave it to me, Fran . . . I know a bit about property.' Fran smiled politely. He knew a bit about everything. What had David said once? 'If I told Harold I'd discovered a band of urban guerrillas drilling in the Civic Centre he'd say, "Known about it for weeks, old chap . . . couldn't let on before."'

Min had joined them and they were tackling plates of lemon mousse when Eve's eyes flashed warning. Lilian Sparks stood in the doorway. The man by her side was small and elegant, skin sallow, eyes dark as prunes and strangely luminous. 'She's come then . . .' Min was rushing to demolish her mousse. 'Isn't he weird?'

Fran demurred. 'I think he looks rather nice.'

Min closed her eyes in exasperation. 'Honestly, Fran, you'd stick up for Dracula!' The next moment she was wafting towards the newcomers, arms outstretched in greeting.

It was a relief to Fran when she was out in the car. Harold came with her and closed the door carefully on her turquoise skirts. 'Think over what I said about the Greenway flats . . . you could do worse.'

Once she was on the road, her relief vanished. What had she gained by going on her own? If she was making a statement no one had heard it. Dennis had made a pass and another man had stroked her bottom. Well, she had asked for it . . . widowed five months, and baring her shoulders. The Victorians had had the right idea, covering themselves with black crêpe and keeping out of trouble. Now there was no recognized code of behaviour for dealing with the bereaved, no comforting tramlines to follow. She had avoided widows herself, crossed them off her list – not out of lack of compassion, but out of confusion. But it was simple really. They didn't want sex, they wanted love.

14

Wednesday, 16 November 1983

She found the pub without much difficulty. A fine drizzle was falling and she wondered about her suit, brand new and the first size eight she had worn. A quick dash, or wait for a lull? If she'd played her cards right she'd have been miles away by now, dining in style with a virgin surgeon. 'This is Richard Hindson-Evans . . . we met the other night.' She'd heard him out and then said no. 'I'm up to my eyes in work at the moment . . . I believe Min told you I was doing teacher training.' Her satisfaction had lasted for at least an hour. That would bring him down a peg or two.

She ran the few yards to the door, trying not to splash her tights. The pub smelled of beer and pine disinfectant and was painted a delicate shade of grot. The advert had jumped at her the night after Min's party. *'Lonely? The Three Rivers Social Club meets in the Duke of Connaught each Wednesday at 8 p.m. Divorced, widowed, single parents etc. welcome.'* If her old friends were out, perhaps she should find new?

She could still go home. Warm. Safe. Nice telly with any luck. No hassle. No need to say, 'I'm Frances Drummond, widow. Would-be teacher. No virtues to speak of and every vice from A to Z . . . oh, and I'm always running away from difficult situations.' Tonight she'd told Martin to turn off the TV and he'd answered, 'No, I won't.' She'd hesitated a moment and then slipped from the room. Slipped, slid, slithered, sidled. She tucked her bag resolutely under her arm and lifted her chin. 'Three Rivers Social Club, here I come!'

She was standing inside the gloomy passage when a man entered. For no good reason she decided he was a Securicor man. He had the air of downtrodden seediness she had noticed about Securicor men . . . unless they were unloading at banks, in which case they walked like kings!

'Looking for the club?' She nodded and smiled, and he ushered her into a large room with a pool table at one end and a dais at the other. A woman standing at the dais met Fran's eye and weaved towards her. 'New member? That's nice.' She wore a bulging Chanel-type suit, a ton of bracelets and a tiny diamanté fob-watch that could only be read with a microscope. She was so like Sybil Fawlty that Fran looked round for Basil. Any moment he would appear with his funny loping stride and aim a blow at Manuel.

'Well, actually, I just saw the advert . . . I don't really have time to join anything . . .'

The woman was shrewd. 'I know,' she said. Famous words! 'I know. We'll find you a seat and you can see how we go on.'

The man who'd ushered her in appeared and placed a half-pint glass in front of her. 'Lager and lime,' he said. 'I guessed you'd be a lager and lime.' She threw profuse thanks after him and sipped. She had never had lager and lime before. Lager on its own she had tasted once and hated, but this was nice.

Sybil Fawlty brought everyone to order. 'Right-oh . . . let's get the business over and then we can enjoy ourselves.' Fran got comfortable against the wall and looked around. She was one of the youngest in the room, perhaps the youngest. Most of the men were forty-plus and the women thirty-five to fifty. They were having a furious discussion about the spring trip when a girl slipped into the room, glanced round, and made for Fran's table. 'Can I join you?' She was already easing into a chair.

The newcomer was in her twenties, thin and pretty with long dark hair cascading over a suedette coat. She leaned towards Fran. 'They could go on like this for hours. That's why I don't rush to get here.' She cast a quick look around. 'No new talent . . . except you.'

'Is that agreed then?' There was a murmur of approval and then a scraping of chairs as the organizer declared the business meeting over.

'What happens now?' Fran said, alarmed at the flurry of activity.

The girl raised her brows. 'You don't know about Funsville?' There was a tinkling of piano keys and Fran turned to the dais where a woman was seated at the piano and a man was assembling a drum kit. 'I'm Linda,' the girl said, 'and that's Tommy and Madge up there. They play for ballroom, and after

9.30 it's records so everyone gets a chance to do their thing. But I'm off for a quick one, I only look in here in case they're enrolling Tom Conti. D'you want to come?'

Fran nodded. 'I might as well.' She was gathering up her bag when Linda groaned.

'Too late ... she's coming to get your perticks! I'll be in the snug, if you manage to get away.'

Sybil Fawlty bustled up and cast a jaundiced eye in the direction of the door. 'Linda gone, has she? I was hoping to get some subs tonight ...' She turned back to Fran and gestured to a seat. 'Let's just get one or two particulars and then you can enjoy yourself.' Particulars! *My name is Mary Smith. No fixed abode.* But she was British and middle-class and C of E into the bargain, and therefore could not lie on official forms. And all forms were official; their very black and whiteness made them so.

'You're a widow ... what a shame ... and only thirty-two. You don't have to tell me, my dear. I know, I know.' It was finished, down to her interests and her date of birth, and she parted with fifty pence. 'Now get up and dance. They're a friendly lot here.'

Linda hailed her as she passed an open door. 'You got away then ... I got you a lager.' The golden glass was bitter and strange without the lime, and if it had not been for giving offence she would've pushed it away. She fished out her cigarettes and they both lit up.

'I suppose you're like me ... always going to pack in?' Linda's fingers were thin and brown.

Fran nodded. 'I can't afford them ... well, I keep on affording them, but I shouldn't. It's burning money, isn't it?'

'I'm divorced,' Linda said and waited for Fran.

'I'm a widow. My husband died in the summer.'

Linda nodded. 'That's tough ... if you got on. Any kids?'

This was safe ground. 'One, a boy. He's just turned ten. What about you?'

'Three ... two boys and a girl. I must've been mad. But I used to feel really great when I was pregnant. That's about the one thing I can't blame El Soddo for . . . although I couldn't've done it without him.'

Fran tried to unscrabble the sentence. 'El Soddo?'

Linda grinned. 'El Soddo . . . Buggerlugs . . . The Impossible Bulk . . . my Ex.'

She looked perfectly happy about it, so Fran felt free to laugh. 'Was he that bad?'

Linda stubbed out her cigarette. 'How long've you got? It'll take weeks.'

Before Fran could reply a man came up to Linda. 'What're you drinking? And your friend?'

Linda perked up. 'A snowball, please, Jimmy.' She turned to Fran.

'Not for me, thanks. I'm fine.'

The snowball was a glassful of candy floss, and the man placed it carefully in front of Linda. 'Coming in?'

Linda nodded. 'As soon as we've had a chat. I wouldn't miss me bit of dance.' When he'd gone Linda picked up the snowball and sipped. 'That's nice.' A thin line of froth ornamented her upper lip and she licked it in. 'Do you fancy a dance?'

'I'm afraid I can't . . . I just popped in . . .' She was marshalling more excuses when Linda interrupted.

'You don't have to convince me. It's as dead as a dodo to-night . . . no talent. I was going to say, what about going round to my place? We could have a drink, and I'll fill you in on this lot.'

Fran was taken aback. 'What about your friend?'

Linda was belting her coat. 'Jimmy? He's not my type. Bo—ring! That's why I want to get out . . . before he comes back.'

Linda was impressed with the Mini. 'That's what I need, wheels. I took some lessons once . . . I'll start again when the ship comes in.' At her request they stopped at an off-licence. 'I've got nothing in, but I can get a bottle of draught sherry here.' She refused to let Fran pay, but accepted 75 pence. 'We'll go halfies. It's only £1.50 if you bring your own bottle.' She emerged with a bottle labelled Green Ginger Wine. 'She loaned me this 'cos I'm her most regular customer.'

They pulled up in the middle of a row of small terraced houses. 'It's flats,' Linda said as she opened the door. The stairs were steep and dark and covered by the thinnest of carpets. They pounded to the top and into a dimly lit room where a telly blared in one corner and four children were camped about the settee.

'This is Debbie,' Linda said, pointing to a small child in a brushed nylon nightie, 'and Carl and Damian ... and this is Sharon, who babysits.' Sharon was slightly older than the others, but not much. Linda pressed a coin into her hand and pushed her out of the door. 'Tarra, Sharon. Thanks a lot.' She turned back. 'She lives downstairs, so it's handy. What I'll do when she starts courting I do not know.'

She lifted up the little girl. 'Say night-night to the lady.'

They were nice children. Fran smiled encouragingly at the little girl, and held out her hand to the oldest. 'I've got a son at home. He's called Martin. You must be a help to your mam, a big boy like you.' Suddenly she was back in a Durham street and filled with insensate rage. What a bloody silly remark! She gave Debbie a kiss and Linda shepherded them out of the room.

Left to herself, Fran looked around. The moquette three-piece was shiny and the same paper-thin carpet covered the floor, but the place was clean. A solemn-faced oriental stared out above the electric fire. If Harold could see all three bars burning it might make him appreciate her, Frances's, thrift. She was smiling slightly as Linda came back into the room and curled up on the settee. She couldn't be more than twenty-one ... twenty-two, at the most.

In the event she was twenty-seven, had been married for seven years and divorced for two. 'Carl's seven ... yes, we just made it ... Debbie's three, and Damian's four.' She poured sherry and pushed a glass over the flowered coffee table. Fran sipped. It was thick and sweet and at least a thousand calories a glass. And yet Linda was reed-thin, hip, knee and shoulder-bones sticking out like a harness.

She was steeling herself for a second sip when they heard the call. 'Mam! Mam!' Linda unwound her legs like a new-born foal. 'Just a minute while I shut them up.' She disappeared on to the landing and Fran could hear a hectic conversation. At least Martin was good about bedtime. Smugness was momentary: TV was coming between him and his wits, and she hadn't a clue how to cope. Her midriff felt huge under the band of her new skirt and she burped. She had never realized lager was so gassy.

Linda settled back. 'I've dared them to shout any more. They think they've got the lend of me.' Her words were fierce but the tone was indulgent, and Fran felt a surge of fellow-feeling. Kids were hell. Hell to be with, and hell to be without.

Linda returned to the subject of the club. 'Don't be put off ... you get nights like tonight, totally talentless ... just the no-hopers ... and then one night you go and there's a real canny bloke there. I've never found one who was interested once he found I had three kids. We've had a few weddings, though, and two couples just shacked up. Once bitten, twice shy.'

'Would you get married again?'

Linda extended a thin leg and examined it carefully. 'I suppose so, if he wanted it ... but I'm easy. I want a feller, that's all. I suppose it's different for you. You had a good marriage and you can hang on to that. But after a divorce you think ... he was a villain, but how much of it was my fault? If I'd been different, better ... would he've been better?'

Fran got out her cigarettes. 'It's funny but I always thought it would be easier after divorce. You know ... you just got angry and walked away, and that was that.'

Linda sniffed and drew her hand across her nose. 'Bloody sherry. Makes you bloody morbid. I know what you mean ... it should be like that, it just isn't.'

There was sympathy between them that not even a further cry of 'Mam' could destroy. This time Linda was away for longer and her voice was harsh. Afterwards they finished the sherry and then had coffee in Oxo mugs.

'I don't get out much,' Linda said as they drank. 'Just to the Singles, and once a fortnight we all go to El Bitcho's for the Saturday afternoon ... El Bitcho being El Soddo's sod of a mother. Apart from the kids, it's money. You can't afford to go out unless you let your rent go, or the electric. And I never let the telly go ... I'd be hairless without me TV.'

Fran thought of her £1,139, and felt a small warm glow. 'Do you work?' she asked. Linda shook her head.

'If I did I'd just lose it on me SS. I get for me and the kids, and they collect maintenance from him. When they can find him and when he's in work. I tried home work once, carding buttons ... but they only paid a pound a thousand and then Damian got one up his nose and we were all down the Infirmary. So I packed it in. It drives me up the wall being here all the time. Can you get out?'

Fran nodded. 'I've got a good babysitter ... well, she's a friend really. But I work, I'm doing teacher training.'

Linda whistled. 'I wouldn't mind that. Nice hours and everything. Did you have O levels?'

Fran felt a desire to comfort. 'Yes ... but you can get them at night schools.'

Linda laughed. 'I never even got CSEs. "You're wasting yourself, Linda," they said, and I thought, "Silly old bags, who wants CSEs?"'

Fran reached for her bag. 'Look, I'll have to go ... can you scribble your address down? Perhaps you could come to tea one day. And I take Martin to the Welfare swimming pool ... we could take all the kids, they'd like that.'

Feeling her way down the dark stairs, she vowed to do something. It was bad enough being cooped in at night but at least she got out during the day. Linda's life was a wasteland. As she drove, she thought about the whole evening. El Weirdo! She would have to go again, though, or think of a good excuse. They had her name. That was the only reason she would go back; she didn't want a feller. She would never get married again ... except for desperation. Like yesterday when the sink blocked. She had poured in kettles of boiling water till the level in the sink rose dangerously high and had to be baled out. Halfway through Brian Malone had appeared with a wrench, and heaved and banged beneath. And then ... shades of Frank Spencer ... the waste pipe had come away in his hand, covering everything with tea-leaf glue and slime.

She had laughed about it to ease Brian's discomfiture, but really it had been the ultimate straw. Sinks never blocked when you had husbands; mice made detours to avoid your property; men like Edward and Dennis treated you with respectful indifference; and everything was easy! If she cried after all that lager and sherry, the tears would be absolute alcohol. She gripped the wheel and launched into song. '*I'm getting married in the morning*' . . . very Freudian. Of course she could never re-marry. It was so much more than a second ceremony; it was comparison and precedence and terrible things like heaven. Did 'many mansions' include a granny-flat for a second husband?

All the same, she would have to be careful to manage. If she went on spending she might wind up like Linda, living in a threadbare home with carpets like best brown paper. She felt quite righteous about Linda buying draught sherry, until she remembered how she bought booze with the groceries. Same difference. One day soon she might be waiting for them to cut off the electricity. She started to make promises, like a naughty child hoping to evade punishment. '*I'll be good. I'll be thrifty. I'll never look at a drink again.*' She kept it up until the lights of Belgate appeared and beckoned, and folded her safely into the warm.

15

Monday, 21 November 1983

While they waited for the bus she checked and rechecked her bag. Notebook, two pens, four books in case she had to read to them, packet of paper hankies for runny noses, and paracetamol in case she developed a headache. 'You won't need half of that . . .' Edward had said. 'All we do is observe. They won't let us within arm's length of actually doing anything.'

They trooped out to the waiting bus, fifteen students well leavened with tutors. Fran sat next to Gwen and sucked gratefully on a boiled sweet until they reached the school. 'This isn't ours,' Gwen said soothingly as Fran grabbed for her bag. 'Broad Street's the second one.'

Broad Street Juniors was tall and red-brick and had the old, familiar smell of school. 'We're class Four,' the education tutor said, and shepherded them down a corridor.

The teacher was young ... incredibly young ... and had a voice like a talking weighing machine. 'Say good morning, class.' The class obliged. 'Class, get chairs.' The class moved as one. 'No, not up here, Gordon. At the back.' Fran walked down the aisle and subsided gratefully on to a pinewood chair. The tutor conferred with the teacher in low tones and then took a back seat. The morning had begun.

The first thing that struck Fran was the teacher's control. It was arts and crafts, and enough split peas to have fed the five thousand. They might have picked them up in handfuls and hurled them against the walls. Instead they fell to, brows raised, tongues protruding, short fingers weaving magic to one degree or another. At least their mothers would love the results. She pinned all Martin's efforts on the kitchen wall.

She would never be able to teach. She looked at Gwen, hoping to see signs of equal depression, but Gwen's face was rapt. A small girl applied a final piece of vermicelli and sat back satisfied. Fran would have liked to lean forward and admire, but she dared not. Perhaps you weren't supposed to hob-nob. The little girls worked speedily; the boys were slower and one or two fidgeted with boredom. Girls were more confident than boys at this age. She hadn't needed the tutor to tell her that: she saw them every day in the Belgate streets, bossing the lads, laying down the law, tottering around in their mother's high heels. Desperate to grow up and reach the promised land of womanhood. Someone should tell them.

She wriggled to get a glimpse of their shoes. She would have to get Martin new shoes. His brogues were only slightly scuffed, but ever since the sociology lecturer had said shoes were indicative of home standards she'd been scared. It wasn't just sociology ... psychology classes were minefields. Deprivation! Parental lack! She was glad when a bell clanged and it was time to file out.

Members of staff were polite, handing out cups and making a conscious effort at conversation. 'What made you take up teacher training?' a spectacled man asked, in tones that implied there were better things to do. The biscuit in her mouth turned to ash. What *had* made her take up teaching? She had to say something.

She was too old to lift her shoulders and answer with one of Martin's shrugs. 'I like children,' she said at last. 'You'll soon be cured of that,' he said and dipped his biscuit in his tea.

It was a relief when another bell clanged and the staff room emptied. They struggled along the swarming corridors and resumed their seats. 'Get out your jotters. We're going to do maths.' Fran found new maths incomprehensible, the squeak of chalk a signal from outer space. But hands kept shooting up with answers. Ten years old, and minds like Einstein! *They* wouldn't get their chequebook counterfoils wrong! She'd lain awake most of the night worrying about money . . . and sooner or later she'd have to tell Bethel about the will. You couldn't just make someone a guardian without getting their consent. If she died, there would be money from the house. Bethel would say, 'We'll manage' . . . but it wasn't that simple. She ought to get insured, but how would she pay premiums on top of the mortgage? Even binary numbers were less agonizing than that question, and she switched her attention back to the class.

At lunch-time they boarded the bus for the journey back to college. The students were deep in thought, the tutors looked smug. 'They think we've been cut down to size,' Fran thought wryly. Gwen popped in a sweet and sucked reflectively. 'They were a good set of kids. How did you feel?'

It had been all right really, Fran thought. 'Well, it passed in a flash,' she said.

They chose a corner table in the refectory and loaded the spare chair with their coats and bags. 'You won't keep him away that easily,' Gwen said drily and then, as Edward appeared, 'Oh God, why am I always right?'

He looked as perky as a worm-filled robin. 'Of course it was A-stream material . . . not your actual hard cases . . . but I was itching to get on with it. All this preliminary skirmishing gets me down.'

Gwen scraped up the last of her shepherd's pie. 'I could do with a little more skirmishing, thank you. There must be a trick or two to learn . . . but then Fran and I are mere women, we need all the help we can get.'

'You haven't forgotten tonight?' Gwen said as they crossed the quad. As if she could!

'No fear, I'm looking forward to it.' She stood aside to let Gwen precede her and disentangled her handbag when it got caught on the door.

'I must empty the flaming thing,' Gwen said ruefully. 'I found one pound fourteen the last time I did it. Talking about tonight, I still feel guilty about not asking Edward ... but he'd simply take it as encouragement to start chasing you again, and I'm not having that.'

Gwen was polishing the lenses of her spectacles. Everyone needed glasses eventually ... around the forty mark. She would be forty in eight years' time. After that it was down the slope to sans-everything. Everyone was growing old – here, in this room, cells were dying, sloughing off. Every time you washed you flushed a bit of yourself away. Dead cells in the sink ... down the plughole to the sea. Dead cells in the green sea. Fish food. So when you bought a pound of cod, you were buying back yourself. She pressed the point of her Biro and got down to work.

At four she went into town to get Martin some shoes. The shop windows were turning over to Christmas, display artists running up backcloths of red and white and gold. Christmas colours, and it was still autumn. At the weekend she would take boy and dog into the open air and run. The park would have a spare beauty now, bare earth and Chinese patterns of twigs. She tucked the black lace-ups under her arm and put the receipt in the back of her purse in case they had to be changed.

She was staring into a window full of furs when her arm was seized and a wave of Madame Rochas engulfed her. 'Fran, what are you doing here? I thought you'd be beavering away in your temple of learning ... oh no, God, it's quarter to five! Look, would you like a cup of tea? I'm parched.' Fran allowed Min to sweep her into Dunn's and up to the restaurant.

'I've trailed round all day looking for some pewter courts ... shall we have Danish pastries? You wouldn't think that was beyond their powers, would you, plain grey court shoes? And tea for two, please. Now, tell me all your news!'

The bangles tinkled as Min proceeded to give Frances her news. 'I'm sick of Dennis's parents . . . well, her really. We had them round to a meal last night – did you enjoy the party, by the way? . . . and she was off everything. Listing the bloody calories! If it hadn't been for pa-in-law, I'd have smashed the bloody food over her head.'

Fran smiled with what she hoped was a look of sympathy. 'Is she scared of middle-aged spread?'

Min snorted. 'It's not middle-aged spread with her, it's committee woman's arse. She's obsessed with do-gooding. My God, if I was the humble poor and I saw her bearing down on me, I'd expire! You know what it is, of course . . . guilty conscience. Now that she and pa-in-law don't know what to do with their money, they're riddled with guilt. Riddled! Typical nouveau riche.' At school Min had worn her sister's cast-offs and her shoes were always split at the back. Perhaps being nouveau riche by marriage didn't count.

Min finished her in-laws along with the pastry, and poured another cup of tea. 'What d'you think about Eve and this baby? Honestly, she's so taken up with it, it's a hoot. You know why, don't you? It's religion . . . I mean, she's not Catholic or anything but I think she thinks it isn't nice unless it's for procreation.'

Fran felt an uneasy need to defend Eve. 'I think she just likes a family . . . and they haven't got a boy.'

Min blew a cloud of smoke into the air. 'Well, catch me having another. I've done my bit. I mean, you've got to go on with it, but God bless the pill.' She filled the teapot with hot water and held it up.

'Yes please,' Fran said, and pushed forward her cup. Perhaps that was what was wrong with Dennis . . . he was tired of being regarded as a chore.

As they went down in the lift she tried to think charitably of Min. She was always good for a laugh, you had to admit that. Committee woman's arse! She kept in her laughter until they'd made their goodbyes, and then let it out in the High Street.

They had tea in front of the TV. Martin ate absently, eyes glued to Sooty and Sweep.

'Don't you think you're a bit old for this?' she asked

'There's nothing else on,' he replied. She wondered if she should point out that conversation was on, reading was on, cheering up your widowed mother was on . . . but decided against it.

She was glad when Bethel arrived and she could go upstairs to get changed. Nee-wan followed her hopefully. 'Not tonight,' she said ruefully. 'Tomorrow, I promise.' She leaned over the banister. 'Martin . . . switch off that TV and let the dog out.' Nothing happened. '*Martin, do you hear me?*'

She heard Bethel march along the hall. 'Did you hear your mam?' There was an answering murmur and then Bethel again. 'Never mind "wait on". He needs a wee, not a "wait on".' And then the sounds of boy and dog going out of the door.

She thought about the papers on the mantelpiece as she drove north – bills and brown officials in equal proportions. There should be a dictionary of leaflet jargon to help you unravel the forms. They all mentioned her 'entitlement' but not the entitlement to comprehend. She would have to come to grips with them soon. Since meeting Linda she had given more thought to the future. Still, no one starved to death in Britain. *Vive le* Welfare State.

Gwen's house was small and modern and warm. Books on shelves and well-thumbed magazines on a stool. There were five or six others there and Lewis, Gwen's husband, introduced them all. He was tall and slightly bald and wore a cravat in his open neck. 'Doesn't it make you sick?' Gwen said, patting his trim midriff. 'Eats like a horse and looks like a greyhound.'

The atmosphere was congenial and Fran began to relax. 'You're at the Poly with Gwen, aren't you?' The man's wrists projected too far from his cuffs and it made her feel protective.

'Yes, I'm a fellow sufferer. Do you teach?'

He shook his head. 'I'm a librarian.' There was a ripple of laughter.

'He keeps all the best books in the back,' Lewis said.

'I won't have any books to keep anywhere shortly if Maggie Thatcher has her way.'

There was more laughter as Lewis plonked down on a stool in

the centre of the room. 'There you are, Eric, there's your soapbox.'

A girl in a white crêpe blouse leaned towards Fran. 'They shouldn't encourage him. He thinks he's the insufferable Donald Soper . . . I know, 'cos I'm married to him.'

Fran heard herself say, 'What do you think about public spending?' There was a muted roar as answers came, and she leaned back. It was going to be all right. They were going to have a lovely argument and no one was going to say, 'I know'. She had a funny feeling that they didn't know and wouldn't care if they did. She reached behind her to move the cushion, and then opened her mouth to put her point of view.

16

Thursday, 24 November 1983

She could hear Bethel in the kitchen, a comforting medley of sounds that meant order. She let the last sliver of guilt melt and lit a cigarette. This was the first time she had skipped lectures, but everyone else did it. And they were open about it! If anyone asked her about it tomorrow, she'd say she'd been sick.

She could hear Bethel telling Nee-wan what a useless article he was, in tones so tender that they made him roll over and squirm with pleasure. It was nice to encounter love, any love, all love. Man to animal, man to man, nation to nation. She wondered if that was a philosophical thought? Gwen kept trying to interpret philosophy to her, but the lectures were so woolly you could stitch on buttons and wear them for cardigans. Still, college was working out better than she'd imagined and her first teaching practice had been positively nice. 'I told you you'd cope,' Gwen had said afterwards. Nice Gwen. Comforting, comforting Gwen.

Tomorrow she would tell her about Steve. 'You'll never guess who phoned . . . Steve Carter . . . the man who bought my car.' She had picked up the phone, expecting it to be Harold with the latest bulletin on the Greenway flats, and a voice had said, 'Mrs

Drummond? Steve Carter here.' She felt an overwhelming delight that his name was Stephen. A nice solicitor's kind of name.

Now she looked at the clock. Half-past two, time to give Nee-wan a run. As soon as she reached for her walking shoes the dog began to perform, racing along the hall, bounding into the air, paws bunched beneath him. 'I'm taking the dog for a walk,' she called to Bethel.

'Aye, I heard him going light. I'll have the kettle on when you get back.'

As Fran walked towards the door she felt tears pricking her eyes. 'You won't need that funny woman of yours when you move,' Eve had said last night, 'so that'll be a saving.'

The park gate was rusty and howled in protest when she pushed it open. She searched for stones and sent Nee-wan scudding left and right. There was a garden at Greenway, that was something. What she must decide was when to tell Martin. It would be weeks before they moved; the house was still to sell, and there was packing to be done. Time for him to come to terms – or time for him to eat out his heart?

In the end it had been easy to say yes. It made sense. The house was too big for two; too big to heat, too big to clean, and when it came to outside painting or repairs she'd be lost. She'd made one last attempt when they took her to look over Greenway. 'I thought, if I stayed, I could let one or two of the rooms . . ?'

Eve and Min had moved agitated hands. 'You mean *lodgers*?' Yes, lodgers. People. Humans. Someone to have a crack with, as Bethel would say.

Harold had quelled the protests and spoken in reasonable tones. 'You'd have endless trouble, Fran. It sounds tempting, I know, but talk to people who've tried it. I could tell you tales . . ! They bring in their friends, and before you know you've got a hippie commune on your hands. They get in and you can't get them out . . . or get rent out of them. You end up with whacking bills, and no income.'

As he dried up, Min took over. 'Just look at this flat, Fran. Ducted heating, everything streamlined, easy to clean . . . there's even a refuse disposal unit.'

Fran had looked round the minuscule rooms. She'd need a disposal unit for everything that wouldn't fit in. 'What about the dog?' she'd said defensively.

'Ah well . . .' Harold said, in his Baptist lay-preacher voice, 'it's a question of priorities.'

Eve was strategically placed to see Fran's face, and leaped to mend the dyke. 'No one's suggesting you can't keep the dog . . . it's quite a small dog. Heaps of people keep dogs in flats.'

Min had looked daggers at Dennis who'd failed to contribute. He lifted his chin. 'You don't have to do anything you don't want to do, Fran. We think you'd be better off here: it's a pukka area, and the schools would be better for Martin. But when it comes down to it, it's your decision.' Poor Dennis . . . trying to back her up, and as much use as a two-legged stool.

She spoke slowly. 'I suppose it makes sense to be nearer college . . .'

Min had swooped in for the kill. 'There you are! I said you'd see reason in the end.'

She ran out of stones, and had to make pretend motions with her arms. Nee-wan didn't care: the chase was the thing. She looked around. The trees were bare, the earth barren, roses and shrubs cut back for spring. When she was little her mother had explained: 'The seeds are there, in the ground, waiting. And if it gets too cold, God sends the snow to wrap them up.'

If her mother had been alive, everything would've been different. 'Now don't worry . . . Mammy's here.' Perhaps she should say that to Martin? Except that it wouldn't work. The delicate brows would stiffen, the mouth slacken and droop. He was happy in Belgate, you could tell. The others might go on about colliery schools, but she wasn't so sure. Every night in the local paper there were stories about former pupils making good. She whistled up the dog and turned for home. She could see the roof of her house from the park with all its funny chimneys. It was an ugly house really, but full of character. Looking back as she left Greenway, she'd had difficulty picking out which flat would be hers. She would have to give it the personal touch, that was all. A carriage lamp at the front door, and a candlewick mat on the netty lid!

She started to laugh, but it was a crying kind of laughter. '*We don't need you now, Bethel. We're moving away.*' There was no way she could say that, and no nicer way to put it. She shut the gate with such force that it forgot to whinge, and clanged shut.

She tried to make Nee-wan come to heel at the kerb. He was anxious to please but hadn't the least idea what she was on about. She was saying 'Stay!' in martial tones when the small blue car drew up beside her. 'Hallo, Walter.'

His face was creased in what he obviously hoped was an evil grin. 'That's the dog, then. She said it was a bonny-funny-queer'un, and she wasn't far wrong.'

Fran laughed. 'He's lovely, and you know it.'

Walter shook his head. 'Nowt of sort . . . he's a bloody nuisance, like all dogs. I hope you've got a licence for it?' *Licence!* She was getting ready to worry, when she remembered you got six months' grace for a puppy.

'Listen, why don't you come in for a cup of tea? Mrs Bethel's making it now, and she'll be pleased to see you.' He shook his head and she had to restrain a smile. He was a small boy waiting to be coaxed. 'Oh, come on . . . just to please me.' There was curly grey hair growing in front of his ears and his eyebrows jutted like prows.

'Well, it'll only have to be for a minute. I've got far ower much on to waste time on you.'

She reached the front door as he drew up. He slid back the side of the car and started to drag out a folded wheelchair. Fran put out a hand, but he barked, 'Get off! Get yersel' in and tell her to brew up. And keep that mongrel from under my wheels!'

'What's up now?' Bethel asked, as Fran wrenched open the biscuit tin.

'Your friend Walter . . . he's on his way in.'

Bethel raised her brows. 'Is that what you're getten' yourself worked up about? Where is he, then?'

Fran nodded towards the door. 'He wanted to come in by himself.'

Bethel sniffed. 'Is that what he told you? Any minute now he'll be shouting you left him stranded.'

It was thirty seconds before the anguished shout of 'Howay'

booled down the hall. He was in his chair on the path, hands gripping the wheels, indignation in every line. 'Howay, howay! You invite people to a house with forty-two steps, and then bugger off and leave them!' Fran was laughing so much she could hardly manoeuvre the chair, and had to give way to Bethel.

'Don't laugh at him. Don't give him the satisfaction. Get your elbow in there before you damage the door ... and try and behave yourself in someone else's house.' She pushed him through to the kitchen, scolding and grumbling as she went.

'I know how to go on, Sally Bethel. Anyway, she's nowt but a townee.' He took control when they reached the kitchen, positioning himself where he could command the room. 'Where's the tea then? She said you had it masted. I wouldn't've come if I had to wait.'

Bethel proceeded to make the tea as slowly as she could, measuring, shaking, warming the pot. He took no offence, in fact there seemed to be a gleam of satisfaction in his eye.

The upper part of his body was broad and muscular, the sleeves of his tweed jacket protected with leather, and his collar and tie immaculate. His lower limbs were covered with a tartan rug and a leather strap bound them. She tried not to let her gaze dwell on him, but once, when she caught his eye, he looked at her directly as though to say – 'Go on, get it over.'

There was a faint sweet smell about him and she guessed he must use some sort of urinal. If your back was broken, it didn't end at your legs. She shifted the idea around her mind and decided it was unimportant. He was exciting, vital. The more she saw of him, the more she liked him. If this were a story he would marry Bethel and that would be lovely. But it wouldn't happen in real life. Too many pros and cons.

He criticized the tea and then pushed forward his cup for a refill. While Bethel watered the pot he turned to Fran. 'She says you're going to be a teacher? Well, they take all sorts nowadays.' She smiled her thanks and sat waiting for more. She ought to go away and work, but this was too good to miss.

'Aye, the country's gone to the dogs.'

Bethel filled his cup. 'It's not like you to talk a bit sense.'

He bridled. 'Oh, you haven't got me in the Tory party yet,

Sally. Not by a long chalk. But that's not to say I can't see what's what. Take the NCB – too many chiefs and not enough Indians. Twelve collar-and-tie men for every silly bugger down below. We fought tooth and nail for a five-day week, and now half of them's Sat-Suns.'

Fran looked to Bethel for explanation but it was Walter who spoke. 'Sat-Suns? How long have you been in Belgate, and you've never heard of Sat-Suns? They lie abed through the week and then go down at weekends for double time.'

Fran leaned her elbows on the table. 'There must be somebody down through the week?'

He leered satisfaction. 'Oh, there is. Them as knows no better. Them as believes you work for your pay. But there's not many of their sort left. We're swamped with shirkers now . . . and not just up here, you can't beat your average southerner for skiving. This country's doomed. The sooner we get the Ruskies in the better. That'll make them sit up.'

Bethel was moved to intervene. 'I hope you're taking no notice of him, mind? I've given up expecting sense from him.'

He smacked his lips on the last swallow of tea and wiped his mouth with a white hanky. 'That's because you're a Tory and don't know sense when you hear it.'

Bethel gave a groan of disgust. 'I haven't said whether I'm a Tory or not . . . and if I was, it's no business of yours. Not that I can't see points in favour. I mind when Lady Londonderry or one of the girls came here every week God sent, in their long white gloves . . . *and* knew who you were when they spoke to you.'

Fran sat forgotten now that battle had commenced in earnest. 'Don't mention Londonderry to me . . . it's him and his Irish blacklegs we've got to thank for all the micks we've got here.'

Bethel turned to Fran and scowled. 'That's what happens when you talk to him . . . he drags up the past.'

Before Fran could open her mouth Walter was in. 'And when did the last pair of long white gloves put in an appearance?' He was half out of his chair in anticipation.

'I can remember them clear enough,' Bethel said.

He sat back, the trap sprung. 'Exactly! Because you're an old woman, Sally. Senile, that's your trouble.'

They could say anything to one another, these two, and make it sound like a love song.

'Walter . . .' Bethel's tones were considered, 'I'm not keeping up this conversation. Trying to talk sense to you's like tapdancing in treacle.' Fran smiled, but thinking about it as they manhandled the chair over the step she realized that half the trouble with the North-east stemmed from its long memory. Some cast their vote for remembered pain, and some for remembered glory, and very few at all for the needs of the day.

'I like Walter,' she said as Bethel struggled into her coat and hat.

'Aye, he's all right,' Bethel said. She sounded like a fond parent.

'I didn't realize you were so far apart politically,' Fran said.

Bethel looked at her in amazement. 'I agree with every word he says. I just won't give him the satisfaction.'

Fran's mouth opened in astonishment, then shut. She might have known.

When Bethel had gone she tried not to think about the evening ahead. It would have to be an anti-climax. She had built him up in her imagination, and tonight she would find his chest wheezed, or he picked his teeth. It was sure to be a let-down, and in a way she hoped it was. She was in the mood for getting rid of loose ends.

She was spooning beans on to buttered toast when Martin came in.

'Is it beans?' He looked far from enthusiastic and she couldn't resist a moan.

'You like beans. You're always asking for them!' She followed him along the passage with the tray and met him coming out of the living room. 'Where's the dog?' he said.

She had a sudden vivid picture of Nee-wan, tongue lolling, watching them push Walter out to the car. They had scampered back inside, stung by the November weather, and had never checked whether or not he was safe.

'Has Bethel got him?' There was a tearful note in Martin's

voice and she felt a surge of resentment. He was going to cry, and if he cried she couldn't.

She went into the hall and shouted the dog's name. There was no answering patter of feet, no whisking tail. She reached for her coat. 'I'll go out and look for him . . . he won't have gone far.'

Martin was shrugging into his anorak. 'I'll come as well.' They went into the half-dark and turned towards the allotments. The street lamps had a fuzzy aura like pink angora: that meant fog.

'Dogs always come home when they're hungry,' she said cheerfully.

'How do you know he knows how to get home?' The tone was aggressive, but she knew he was dying to be convinced.

'It's his wees, that's why they do them . . . marking the spot. He'll be able to smell his way right back to his own door.' She had made it up, but it sounded sensible. They turned on to the rutted path and began to call out. She watched every dark patch, hoping to see a black and white shape erupt. He was always so pleased to see them, that was the best thing about him.

They gave up after an hour. The fog had come down and the streets were emptying. If he was gone for good she would go out and get another one straight away, the same day. Before they had a chance to stop her. They would like that, Harold and Co. '*It's for the best, Fran. It's Fate. You weren't meant to have a dog.*' She would spit in their eyes and kick and swear at them, the worst words she could think of. She started to cry and couldn't be bothered to hide it. Everything went, everything!

'Come on, Mam. You know what we ought to do?' She shook her head. 'We ought to dial 999.'

She searched for the police station number; she wouldn't dare dial 999, not even for murder or rape. 'It'll be down on the beach,' the voice said at the other end. 'They all wind up down there. It's like *A Hundred and One Dalmatians*. Wait till it's run itself into the ground, and it'll be back. We get dozens of calls like this and they all turn up.'

Martin came back with Gary Malone, and she was relieved. She'd been half afraid he'd suggest going down to the beach. It might be high tide and she wasn't too sure of the cliffs – if there were a fall she might wind up losing Martin, too. But if he were

gone there would be nothing left to lose ... which equalled
safety.

She went upstairs and began to get ready. Her eyes in the
mirror were rabbit's eyes, pink-rimmed. '*I'm late for a very
important date.*' She put the plug in the sink. They wouldn't get
the dog back because that would be nice, a story-book ending,
and they weren't that lucky. Daft little dogs got caught on roads
and tossed aside to die, limp bundles of dirty fur. She would take
a towel and gather him gently into it for burial. No furnaces or
tips.

When she heard the knock on the back door she turned off
the tap and fell on her knees beside the bath. 'Please God, let it
be the dog. Let it, let it, let it be the dog. Just this. I'll never ask
for anything again.'

Martin stood at the foot of the stairs, Nee-wan in his arms
looking dirty and sheepish and thoroughly ashamed. 'Where was
he?' she said, and heard Brian Malone's voice from the kitchen.

'He was on the blast, Mrs Drummond. I thought he might be
there.' His hands were in his pockets, his shoulders hunched
with pleasure. She knew the blast, the place where they tipped
the pit waste and let it tumble untidily into the sea.

When Brian had gone she tried to remember if she'd thanked
him enough. Tomorrow she would take his hand and say, 'I love
you, Brian Malone.' Except that you seldom carried out good
intentions. Reason intervened, and caution, and inhibition ...
and in the end you did little or nothing. Well, she must make
sure she did.

She could only see a car's length ahead as she drove into
Sunderland. She kept one eye on the kerb and the other on the
white line, and let her thoughts range free. She would have to
say something to Bethel soon because the *For Sale* board would
be going up and she mustn't find out that way. '*It's money, you
see,*' she would say. And if the other woman's lips trembled.
'*We'll be here for Christmas ... you won't get rid of us before then.*'
Christmas. Christmas.

The fog lifted for a few yards and then settled down again.
She would try to find joy in Christmas, not just for Martin's sake
but her own. Without Christmas there would have been no

Easter, and without Easter there was no hope. Her foot came off the clutch in surprise. That was a profoundly religious thought, and she didn't even believe. She must have read it somewhere . . . except that she never read that kind of book.

Steve was waiting in the car park and she sighed with relief that he was not driving the Rover. 'You're prompt,' he said. She might have known he wouldn't bring the Rover. She knew him better than that.

'It's pretty foggy,' she said. She didn't ask where they were going. Wherever they went would be nice. Nice. She would tell him about the dog, and that was nice too. She settled in her seat as Sunderland slipped away and they took the Chester-le-Street road.

17

Saturday, November 26 1983

Linda sat opposite her at the kitchen table, both of them basking in the virtuous feeling of a job well done. The afternoon at the Welfare pool had been a riotous success. Linda's children had never seen a pool before, let alone swum in one, and Martin gloried in his superior ability. Linda plodged around at the shallow end, holding Debbie in her thin arms and dipping her feet in the water from time to time. She looked no more than a child herself, in spite of the jutting nipples and yard-long legs. Beside her Fran felt positively hefty.

She encouraged the little boys to splash about and restrained Martin's showing off when it threatened to get out of hand. The chlorine made her eyes sting and she felt strangely exposed in her one-piece suit, but she could see the children were having a wonderful time and that made it worth while. In the end they had to be dragged, shrieking, from the water and only shut up at the promise of orange drinks and an introduction to Nee-wan.

'I should get them a puppy,' Linda said as they towelled the children dry. 'I've always fancied one of the Old English Sheeps

. . . like you see in the Dulux ads. I might see about it at Christmas.' Fran was just about to point out the foolishness of keeping a dog at all, let alone a giant, when she remembered Eve and Min and kept her mouth shut.

When they got home, to mountains of beans and sausages and chips and euphoria over the dog, Fran felt good . . . and there was still the promise of tonight. 'I'll take you home on my way to college,' she said when the children were seated in front of the TV. She had refused Linda's offer to help with the washing-up and they were relishing a few moments' peace in the littered kitchen.

'Come across any new talent?' Linda's face was hopeful, but Fran was cautious.

'Not really . . . well, I'm just between home and college . . .' She was still amazed at her own capacity to lie when it was necessary for self-protection. Tonight she was meeting Steve again, but for reasons she could not quite analyse she was unwilling to admit it to Linda. 'Haven't you been to the club lately? That's where you'll find new talent.'

Linda's nose wrinkled in distaste. 'It's getting really draggy, I think I'll pack it in. Anyway, I'd need a mortgage to catch up on me subs. I'm going to watch out for another one . . . more on the lines of a disco. They have them, some places.'

They nattered about men or the lack of them, El Soddo's misdeeds and David's virtues. Once or twice she was tempted to come clean about tonight, but she resisted the impulse. She liked Linda . . . they were chalk and cheese, but oddly compatible. In a way Linda's deprivation was balm to her own wounds, but that wasn't the only reason she'd kept in touch. There was something about Linda's personality that was strangely uplifting. Each time they met Fran felt more resilient, surer that things would work out eventually. But she still needed to keep her secrets.

When she went upstairs to get ready she took an unopened bottle of Coty L'Aimant . . . Aunt Em's Christmas gift . . . from her drawer, and gave it to Linda when she came down. She still had her Youth Dew, enough to last for ages if she used it sparingly – and Linda could do with a little cherishing. Her eyes grew wide at the gift. 'Eeh no . . . I couldn't. Are you sure? Oh

God, I'll have to go back to Funsville now. This'll rattle Jimmy's marbles . . .' And then the thin arms were round Fran's neck. 'Ta, Fran . . . you're a mate.' Her body was fragile and crunchy like Martin's. And yet Linda had given birth to three sturdy children, and was holding her own in a harsh world.

She dropped them at their door with promises to be in touch soon. 'I'll have to rush now, I'm due at college at eight. But I'll definitely be in touch . . . Martin will make sure I am.' Debbie's little face glowed at the mention of 'the big boy's' name. Boy-conscious at three years old! God, let her have better luck than her mother.

As she negotiated the town centre she thought back to her first date with Steve. They had spent three hours together but you could telescope memories, erase the unimportant bits so that you got the nub. She loved that word. Nub. Sweet kernel. Essence. You strove and strove to reach it, and seldom did.

The pub had been long and rambling and the menu short and sensible. Steve hadn't commented on how little she ate and when she said no to the sweet-trolley he didn't seem to care. As they ate he had made her laugh about car sales. 'I can sell them all right, it's getting them to drive away that's difficult . . .' He'd asked after Harold and was sympathetic when she told him about the bubble bath and the thermostat. 'All the same he means well. He's determined to make sure you come out on the right side.'

When they parted she'd felt good. It had been a nice night. No niggling doubts or tremors, no randy fantasies! It had just felt right. Tonight they were meeting outside a town-centre pub. The Saracen was a bit of a dive, but no one she knew would be seen there. She felt her spirits rise at the prospect.

They settled in a booth, padded plastic behind, melamine table before. She drank lager and lime with extra lime. It was light and fresh, and she was coming to like it. She thought back to the days after David had died, the jumble of whisky and rum and whatever came to hand. If she tried to drink like that now, she would sink to the floor and be carried out on a shutter.

Steve asked if she had made up her mind about moving, and somehow the conversation turned from houses to politics. 'You sound like a socialist,' she said inquiringly.

He grinned. 'And me a bloated capitalist flogging cars? I like the idea of socialism ... the brotherhood of man, the strong supporting the weak, from each according, and that sort of thing. But I draw the line at your socialist politician. He keeps his HP sauce on the kitchen table and his Châteauneuf du Pape in the back room. The Tories may be swine, but they're open about it.'

Fran laughed. 'You can't stop there ... let's have a hatchet job on the Liberals and the SDP.'

He rose to his feet. 'I'll need another drink before I tackle that lot. They're an unknown quantity.'

It was nine o'clock. An hour and a half to go. 'I could stay here all night,' she said. 'It's just nice ... not crowded but nice.' At school the English teacher had crossed out 'nice' each time she used it, and had written 'Meaningless' in the margin. Which just showed that English teachers didn't know everything.

'How long have you been on your own, Steve?'

He thought for a moment. 'Two years. Seems longer.'

She knew what he meant. 'I know. I've got Martin, but in a way that makes it worse. When I get home tonight and Bethel goes ... she's off like a flash to see to her fire ... I want to talk. I want to say, "Guess who I saw tonight?" or "What do you think about this?" And I want to run upstairs and wake Martin, and I know I can't.'

He blew smoke into the air. 'I knew a fellow once who used to ring the speaking clock, just to hear another voice ... and he was kidding himself because it's a recording.'

She wanted to say, 'Was it you?' but didn't dare.

'Anyway,' he said, 'what are we doing about a meal?'

She wasn't hungry but perhaps he hadn't eaten all day. 'What do you want to do?'

He lifted his shoulders. 'I'm easy.'

She felt she ought to persist. 'What did you have for lunch?'

He smiled. 'Liquid refreshment.'

She tutted. 'I wish I lived nearer. I'd cook you a meal and make you eat it.'

There was a moment of silence. 'We could go back to my place. That's near, and I could make you a Carter special.'

She knew he wouldn't repeat the invitation. Return of service was up to her. She downed the last of the lager. 'Come on then ... let's see what the Carter cuisine is made of. I mustn't be late home though, or Bethel will worry.'

She felt light-headed as they threaded towards the door. And it wasn't the drink. Something important was happening, and she wasn't sure she was up to it. She followed his tail-lights through town, watching him make meticulous signals in case he lost her. She wondered briefly what his flat would be like, and then curiosity gave way to more important matters. If they were alone together they would probably make love. It stood to reason. She had never had sex with anyone but David. With someone else it might be awful. Or full of unimagined delights. Whichever it was, she mustn't cry. If she could handle the whole thing with dignity it would be all right whether it was all right or not.

She saw him signal right and swerve to a halt in front of a tall terraced house, and tried not to meet his eyes as they mounted the steps. Perhaps this was an everyday occurrence for him, but she thought not. He had his own front door opening off the hall. 'It's a bit cramped,' he said, 'but it's self-contained.'

In contrast to the entrance his living room was spacious and the antique furniture exuded chill. He hung up her coat and hurried to switch on the fire. There was a pair of slippers beside the fire, scuffed at the toe, with worn linings. She wanted to pick them up and hold them to the heat before slipping them on to his feet. 'What about a drink?' he said.

She couldn't look directly at him. She could only walk up close, averting her face like a child. His arms came round her. 'Do you want to make love to me?' She had never spoken so directly in her life, and he was equally sparing of words. 'Yes.' His neck was smooth and firm and smelled of soap. She moved against it blindly. 'Well?'

It would be impossible to uncouple now, to move away and face him. She wanted to move sideways, like a child dragging its mother with it ... 'You do it, Mammy.' Or she could say, 'I'm sorry, I made a mistake,' and reach for her coat.

'Could you show me where the bedroom is?'

He followed her, holding her elbow gently to guide her. 'The furniture in here is mine. Everything else came with the lease but I furnished this myself.

She seized on it with relief. 'It's lovely.' There was an open paperback on the bedside table and she was relieved to see it was a thriller – if it had been even faintly pornographic she would have turned and run.

'The bathroom's next door,' he said and left her alone.

In the dressing table mirror she looked white and gaunt, her eyes too black, her lipstick non-existent. There was a sharp rap and in the mirror she saw the door move. '*Not yet, please God, not yet.*' His face was flushed with embarrassment. 'Look, just one thing. I've got the blanket on a time-switch. It always comes on at nine. I just didn't want you to think . . . to think I expected . . . well, anything.' When he disappeared she put a hand on the nylon counterpane. It was faintly warm. He would come home each night, cold and tired and more than a little drunk, and climb into the warm and empty bed. Poor Steve.

She went into the bathroom and locked the door behind her. The painted walls were blistered but the towels were clean and his toilet articles neatly ranged above the bath. She had to think. She didn't want to go back in there and climb into the warm bed. Perhaps sinning should be done between cold sheets? She felt a sudden compulsion to pray and started to kneel down. You had to kneel down or it didn't count. She stopped halfway and straightened up. If prayers were going to work, they would work hanging from a chandelier. 'Please God, help me sort it out.'

She heard Steve cross the hall and go into the bedroom. He would be unbuttoning his shirt, dropping garments one by one, climbing into bed. If she was going to stop him it had to be now. He might get nasty – after all, she had forced the pace.

Perhaps she should let it happen. She liked him. If she walked in there he would put his arms around her. Comfort her. 'There now, everything's all right.' Suddenly she thought about contraception. She had been infertile with David, but would that be enough? The fear was paralysing and helped to make up her mind.

When she went into the room he was sitting on the side of the bed, his tie loosened, a glass in each hand. 'I brought you a drink,' he said. She fumbled for words that would not hurt but it was Steve who spoke. 'Come on, don't look so tragic. I was none too sure myself.'

'Don't you mind?' Her voice was shaking.

'Yes, I mind . . . but not enough to go over the cliff. I'd mind a lot less if I drank this whisky.' They sat side by side on the bed and he reached for her hand. 'There'll be other times. You won't run off and never see me again, will you?'

Her voice was fervent. 'No, I definitely won't do that.'

He saw her out to the car. 'Sure you'll be all right? I could run you home and you could pick this up tomorrow?'

She shook her head. She needed the run along the coast road. Time to think, time to put on a sensible face for Bethel. 'I'm fine, Steve. Honestly. Will you ring me?'

He stepped back on to the kerb. 'That's a silly question. You know I will.'

The sky was bare of stars as she drove back to Belgate but the moon was up. It was a clear night and her mind was clear to match. Unless you actually experienced something you never knew what it was like. She had expected divorced people to be angry or bitter, but in fact they were sad. And everyone expected widows to be noble, and nobility was the last thing she felt. She looked at her watch and tried to decipher the hands. It must be late because she was tired out. She would have a cigarette when she got home and then go straight to bed. No drink, no pill. If she couldn't sleep she would just lie there until she heard the first feet in the street. Four o'clock. Tub-loading. Or was it fore shift? She must ask Bethel tomorrow.

In bed she closed her eyes and tried to compose herself for sleep, but the image of the pit intruded. The wheel against the moonlit sky, the colliery buildings a frieze. And below men were sweating and straining in the pursuit of coal, oblivious of the stars. What had Walter told her the last time they spoke? 'All I thought about was getten the shift ower . . . getten back to the cage.' He'd been thirteen when he went down the pit, employed to lift the leather trap each time a pony and tub came through.

'I mind on, that first shift . . . I had a lamp and it gave a canny glow. "It's not so bad, this," I thought. "Just sitting here in the warm and pulling the string for the lads." And then this bloody big putter stumbled out of the dark! "Howay, son," he says, "I'll have to have your lamp. Mine's gone out, and I'm on piece – I need a light to make me money up." He legged it back to the face with me lamp, and I sat in the dark, scared witless.'

For once he had been speaking without mockery. 'It wasn't just the dark – I could stand that. But when you got your pit ears you could hear the layers creaking above you. I kept thinking, "That's it . . . this time there'll be a fall."' He had twitched the tartan rug that covered his knees then, and Fran knew he was remembering the fall that had taken his legs. 'And then there was the everlasting bloody squeaking. Talk about mice! There was thousands of them, they came down in the ponies' feed, and bred. You can smell things in the pit – if a lad eats an orange half a mile away, you get the whiff – and you could smell those mice. I mind once we caught one with a lump of stone and you could see the lops leaping off it the minute it died.'

Fran had shivered at the thought and Walter returned to form. 'You're a proper townee . . . nee guts. You should've been there when the blacklocks used to go for me bait, so bloody shiny you could see your face in them.'

Fran turned on her side and punched the pillow for sleep, but Walter lingered. 'I always remember the summers. You'd lie in the fields baking yersel' till the skin peeled. With me it was always me arms went first. And then you'd cadge a lift in-bye along of the putters, riding the limbers behind the pony. If he'd just been physicked, and if you didn't watch it, he'd lift his tail and it'd scrape your burned arms like a wire brush . . . by God, it knacked.'

Fran had winced in sympathy and Walter poured scorn. 'There you go, pulling a face. Life's not all sugar and spice, miss . . . you should know that by now. It lifted its tail and scraped you raw, and if you didn't get out of its way it shit on you.'

In the darkness Fran grinned. Walter was a devil, really – loving to shock. But he was a jewel too, a nugget, and she was glad he inhabited her world.

18

Saturday, 3 December 1983

The temperature outside the bedclothes was a thousand below zero. She put her arms inside the blankets and stroked them to feel the gooseflesh. The boiler must have gone out. She gave a groan and turned on her side. Assume the foetal position, curl up until Bethel appears and puts it on again.

'Come on, Frances.' It was Saturday morning so Bethel wouldn't come, unless on a social call. Anyway, she could cope with the boiler now ... and watching the needle rise on the thermostat was the nearest thing to orgasm she knew. She gave a chuckle and snuggled down again. Five more minutes, then *action!* If she leaped out of bed and dragged on some clothes before she lost her body heat, she might prevent frostbite setting in.

The sky was grey and threatening, and clouds seemed to be scudding past the window with alarming speed. If it was windy she would put on a headscarf. Her mother had hated headscarves but the Queen did it. God save the Queen. So ... a headscarf, and her sheepskin, and trousers. Battle clothes ... which was silly because it wasn't going to be an ordeal. *'They're canny kids,'* he'd said, *'you'll like them.'* And it had been a compliment. He only had one day a week with them, and to ask her along meant a lot.

It was ages since she'd spent a Saturday in Sunderland. Sunderland! The move, the terrible, terrible move. She would have to tip the removal men and she never got it right. Gave too little and squirmed with shame, or gave too much and cursed herself for a sucker. Men were so good at tipping. 'Please God teach me how to tip.' She would learn in time. You couldn't go on getting things wrong for ever. When she was grey-haired and a deputy head she would tip correctly. She giggled again. She'd got a 'Quite Good' for her English last week, but that was no cause for megalomania.

Her eye fell on the bedroom cupboard. She'd been shoving

things in there ever since they moved in, and now you had to hold back the junk with one hand and force the door shut with the other. She'd have to make a start soon – if she didn't Eve and Min would come, and that had to be prevented at all costs. Eve would raise her eyebrows at Fran's domestic arrangements, and Min would decree everything 'cheapex' and throw it out. And she would wear her rubber gloves! She wore them at the least hint of grot. Perhaps she wore them for making love, which she seemed to think grottier than almost anything else. Poor Dennis, unless he was a rubber fetishist he'd find it very off-putting. Fran plumped up her pillows and tried to think constructively.

Bethel would help. 'We're going to move, I'm afraid. Not from choice. It's force-push.' She'd had to say it straight out; you couldn't beat about the bush with Bethel. 'But we'll come back every week, and you can come to us. Stay, even.' She'd be able to stay if it wasn't for her ruddy fire!

'I suppose it makes sense, the travelling and everything.' Bethel's acceptance had been more hurtful than a show of force.

Fran had appealed to Steve for advice but he'd refused to be drawn. 'You have to work it out for yourself. The one thing I know is you can't run away from things.' They'd gone on to talk of his own affairs: a marriage cracking at the seams, holding together for the sake of one child, producing another in an attempt to paper over the rifts. 'That's why Julie's so much younger than Ian.' There'd been pain in his face and Fran had been reminded of Linda, wiping her emotional nose and blaming the sherry. She must get in touch with her soon. Action today, tomorrow at the latest. And a note to the Singles Club to say she was busy at college but would be back soon. And an embargo on Martin's TV. And a rein on expenses . . . if she lay any longer the list of jobs would need a lavatory roll. Better freeze to death than die of anxiety. She leaped out of bed.

When she got downstairs she could hear the television set . . . Martin giving Mike Reid the best of attention. She felt resentful, but it was mean to deny him TV on a Saturday. Nee-wan was weaving about her feet, and she considered the possibility of taking him into Sunderland. He could stay in the car during

lunch and then, if they went for a walk, he'd come into his own.
It might be a good idea.

She gave Martin some Ready Brek, revived the boiler, and
was on to her second cup of coffee when Bethel came in. Since
news of the move her face had been grim, her nose pinched as
though in disappointment. Today, though, she had the light of
hot gossip in her eyes! Fran spooned coffee into a cup and stirred
as Bethel unfastened the neck of her coat and divested herself of
her folded scarf.

'Aye, well . . . I've got a nice piece of news!' Her tone implied
the worst. 'Mind you, you'll trot out every excuse: "It's only
nature . . . it's all the fault of his upbringing." It isn't his
upbringing he's done it with . . . well, that's not what *I* call it.'
Someone had conceived! Fran spooned in sugar and waited.

'Mind, I don't blame the lad. You'd have to be cast-iron to
grow up straight in that family. I've seen better floating on broth!'
The Malones! Fran went cold.

'You don't mean Brian?'

Mrs Bethel's unbound breast quivered in a paroxysm of
satisfaction. 'Oh, but I do. Your blue-eyed boy's got a girl into
trouble. Mind, I don't blame the lad . . . or the girl either.
Carruthers's lass, poor little bit of a thing, wouldn't know B from
a bull's foot. They're only bairns and they've only done what
many another's done before them. No . . . it's *her* I blame, the
mother. Swanking off about it, mind. In the shop! "Our Brian's
lass's got a bairn on the way, so I'm doing out the back bedroom."
She thinks that bloody house's elastic! Come one, come all. I
told the rent man, "I can feel that house next door expanding," I
told him, "I might as well move out now before they come
through the wall!"'

Fran threw back her head and laughed, but there was a tinge
of regret to her mirth. Brian had been her property in a way –
her protector. Now he belonged to someone else. She took the
proffered cigarette. 'They're getting married, then?' Indeed they
were, church wedding, white dress, bridesmaids and a honeymoon in Southport.

'They'd've done better to look for a flat, if you ask me – not moved in along of seven bairns. Still, pigs'll fly before that lot see sense.'

In the end they took Nee-wan with them. Fran saw the hopeful gleam in his eye, and that clinched the matter. After one mad scramble to get on to Martin's knee he contented himself with the back seat, and sat alert. Perhaps they were beginning to train him. She felt almost optimistic as they covered the miles into town. Even Martin looked reasonably cheerful.

When she'd told him about the move he'd been bewildered. 'What about school? How will I get home?'

She'd tried to keep her voice level. 'There'll be a new school near the flat, and that'll be your school.' His lips had set angrily and then trembled. Useless to tell him what Eve had said about catchment areas and the importance of going to school with your equals. Today, however, he looked reasonably OK so she could worry about something else.

She'd have preferred to go to Newcastle but it had seemed a cheek to suggest it, as though she were ashamed of being seen with Steve's family. You never knew who you'd see in Sunderland, that was the trouble. Yesterday she'd stopped to look at earrings in Weinberg's and seen Lilian Sparks through the glass. She was trying on a ring . . . a thin gold band . . . holding it up for her Malaysian's reaction. He was nodding and smiling, and Lilian's face was almost girlish. Almost beautiful. 'She is becoming what he believes her to be,' Fran thought, and moved on.

She was glad of the dog when they met Steve and his children. It bounded from one to another, administering tongue-licks, dashing madly round in the joy of someone new. 'This is Ian,' Steve said, 'and this is Julie. And this must be Martin.' Martin's face registered no emotion except pride of ownership in the dog. 'He's reserving judgement,' Fran thought.

Ian was thin and tall, almost at the lank and spotty stage. She fell into step beside him when they'd put the dog back in the car. Mustn't seem to be monopolizing their father. The little girl was small and dark, dressed in a red hooded coat with Fair Isle knee socks and mitts. She was obviously a daddy's girl from the way she hung on to his hand. Steve turned towards Fran. 'Where are we going then?'

Fran felt a flush of disappointment. He was less sure of himself than usual. 'Wherever you like.' She patted the ball back.

'I want to go to Santa Claus,' Julie said, and settled the matter.

Santa was red and wrinkled with a beery nose and a patently false beard. The queue inched forward and he lifted each child on to his knee, casting apprehensive glances at the head of the toy department to see if he was doing it right. Once, in a paper, she'd read of a Santa, well into pensionable age, who'd been dismissed for groping the fairies in the enchanted grotto. She wished this Santa had been a raver instead of a scared old man trying to make a crust.

Some of the children backed off when their turn came and had to be forced on to the red velvet knee. Julie grew uneasy and whispered in her father's down-bent ear. 'She's changed her mind,' Steve said apologetically.

'Don't force her,' Fran said and put out a hand. The little girl shrank back. 'She'd rather face Santa Claus than me,' Fran thought, and wondered why it hurt.

They ate lunch in Dunn's, and food broke the ice. Martin and Ian chose a mixed grill and Ian hooked Martin's finger to say 'snap'. 'He's nice,' Fran thought. Steve made a fuss of divesting Julie of coat and gloves, settling her in her chair, steering her through the menu. She disliked everything, but settled for shepherd's pie. 'I'll only eat the potato, Daddy.' He'd have agreed if she'd suggested boiled serviettes. 'I really dislike her,' Fran thought, and pressed her knees together in an act of contrition.

She tried to remember what Steve was like usually, how strong he seemed. Obviously Julie was his Achilles heel, as her mother had been before her. Except that all single parents were suckers. Martin was inching his way to total control in the Drummond household, so who was she to judge? When lunch was over she wanted to pay her share, but Steve refused to catch her eye and she let it go.

They went into the toy department, where Fran could see Steve was torn between loyalty to his daughter and duty to his guest. 'I'll just pop along and look at the fashions. Shall we meet back here?'

They were waiting for her when she came back and they filed on to the escalator. Julie put both hands on the rail and Steve turned to take Fran's arm. It was nice having someone to cherish you. She wished they could go on for ever, floating down, touching discreetly ... and then it was time to leap for terra firma, and the little girl in front not getting out of the way. 'Are you all right?' She held Julie by the arms and looked into the mutinous little face. If only she were old enough for truth. '*You see me as a threat, darling, but I'm as frightened as you. Shall we declare a truce?*' But Julie was locked in a seven-year-old world that only admitted daddies and mammies, and all the blandishments in the world were so much crap. Like Martin – except that his world had no dad, and his mam was only allowed in by arrangement.

When they had collected Nee-wan they made for the park. 'Julie likes the ducks,' Steve said. Fran doubted the presence of ducks on a day like this, but kept a diplomatic silence. She was glad of the headscarf and her sheepskin jacket. She'd have liked to pull up Martin's hood and zip his anorak but she didn't dare. On winter days her mother used to warm her coat for her at the fire before she put it on. Nice. Nice. Still, Martin was behaving well today, better not spoil it.

She knew the park well. Her father used to bring her here on summer days and buy her a Walls from the kiosk. The lake was bounded on one side by a stone balustrade complete with stone lions. She watched Steve lift Julie on to their stone backs, just as her father had done. She could still feel their cold flanks against her bare legs. But her childhood lions had seemed huge and fierce; now they were pathetic, eyeless and worn. Someone had daubed their faces with red paint and it fell from their open mouths like gouts of blood. And the lake was murky, its edges choked with litter, and not a duck was to be seen.

They moved on, trying to escape the wind. She could hear the note of pride in Steve's voice as he talked to Ian of his O levels, see the tilt of his head that hoped she was listening. What funny mortals parents were. She had a wicked desire to pin their ears back with Martin's *Treasure Island*, but managed to force it down.

They were on the top of the park now, the town laid out before

them, tower blocks and steeples, dockside cranes and houses . . .
homes. Thousands and thousands of homes. Too many people
for a town. Sunderland should be a city with a Lord Mayor and
some clout. The children were in their element, wheeling and
swerving to avoid a dog mad with delight at escaping its lead.
Fran shivered inside her sheepskin, and felt the bones of her
face ache at the onslaught of the wind.

'We can't stay here much longer,' Steve said. 'You must be
freezing. I never know what to do on Saturdays. Mostly we just
stay at my place and watch TV.'

Fran tried to look sympathetic. 'It must be difficult. I never
really realized before. I think I thought divorce was quick and
clean, that you didn't bleed because you were full of anger . . . a
kind of cauterization.'

Steve rested his forearms on the railing and looked out at the
town. 'I don't feel angry . . . except when she plays me up. Like
Saturdays, for instance. She knows it's my busiest day at the
showrooms, but she insists I make it my access day. I've a good
set of lads but some deals need my say-so. Sundays we can't sell,
of course. Display, yes – but sell, no. So I could have them on
Sundays and lose no business, but that won't do for Jean. Too
simple.' He didn't sound bitter, he sounded flat.

Fran put her hand on his arm and squeezed. 'They'll be grown
up one day, and then they'll make their own arrangements.'

It was weird, really, the two of them up here with their
children. Two halves that did not make one whole. You wouldn't
have found this situation some years ago. She couldn't remember
a single divorce when she was a child. Not one. On the other
hand she couldn't remember a death either, and there must've
been some. Beyond the houses she could see Tunstall Hill, the
highest point in Sunderland. She had walked there with her
father, holding his hand. She felt a sudden pain in her chest, so
fierce that she put up her hands expecting to find a wound. Why
did you have to grow up? Move on? Why did it hurt so much to
know you'd left it behind for ever?

They rounded up the children and turned for home. 'Will you
come back for some tea?' Steve said.

Fran shook her head. 'If you don't mind I'd like to get out of

town before the football crowds turn out. But I did enjoy meeting
your children. They're nice.'

He smiled. 'Your own lad's not so bad.'

'Perhaps you could all come to tea some Saturday . . . or better
still, lunch?'

He thrust his hands further into the pockets of his coat. David
used to do that when something gave him pleasure. 'I'd like that.'

They parted at the car and he helped her bundle in boy and
dog. 'Goodbye, Ian.' As he smiled farewell she wondered if he
had done this before with other women of his father's. It might
be a regular occurrence, but she thought not.

When they got home she hurried through tea. She was in the
mood to work and if she once sat down to relax it would be fatal.
'Did you enjoy today?' she said as they ate.

'It was all right.' All right was a bloody silly expression. No
one knew what it meant. She wanted to take him by the shoulders
and shake him. Translate! Translate! *Parlez double vite!* Instead
she went upstairs and opened the cupboard. She would throw
out the lot, be ruthless. She settled on the floor.

The things you kept! Rubbish. Junk. A notebook of her father's
with odd jottings in it – she couldn't throw that out. And Martin's
first arts and crafts, a bloated snowman shedding tinsel. The
next thing out of the cupboard was for the chop, God's honour.
It was a Pitman's shorthand manual and she put it aside with an
easy mind. What if it had been something vital? Could she have
consigned it to the bin? You shouldn't make vows.

She drew out some battered Christmas decorations and put
them with the shorthand book. They were making streamers at
Broad Street School, fumbling lop-sided things that breathed
the spirit of Christmas. 'It's not worth your putting up decorations,' Eve had said, but she could go to hell. Except that she was
already booked in at the maternity hospital. She fished a small
suede-covered book out of the box: *A Shropshire Lad* by A. E.
Housman, her mother's favourite poet. She opened it up. '*To
Mary with gratitude and fond remembrance from your ever-loving
friend Janet Winter. 1 September 1936.*' People had dared to be
sloppy in those days. If you gave another girl a book of poetry
now they'd put you up for Gay Lib. She sat for a while wondering

if her mother had known what lesbian meant. She couldn't really believe she had ... on the other hand, with your own mother, you couldn't be sure. She turned the pages. '*Loveliest of trees, the cherry now ...*' That one had been in her school anthology. But the best one was further on. She found it on page 60.

> *Into my heart an air that kills*
> *From yon far country blows,*
> *What are those blue remembered hills,*
> *What spires, what farms are those?*
>
> *That is the land of lost content,*
> *I see it shining plain,*
> *The happy highways where I went*
> *And cannot come again.*

She had always loved that poem ... because it was short and easily remembered. But her love had been unthinking.

She had thought of '*an air that kills*' as a keen wind, freezing the blood. But she had felt that air today on top of the park. Nostalgia. A longing for the past that could overwhelm you. And '*yon far country*' was childhood and youth, and everyone had their '*blue remembered hills*'. She had stood with her father on Tunstall Hill and counted thirteen spires and two mill chimneys. And every day had been sunny, and what wasn't sunny her dad could fix. She put down her head and wept until the tears reached the folds of her neck, and it was time to go in search of comfort.

19

Tuesday, 6 December 1983

As she followed them down the stairs she braced herself for their parting words. 'What d'you think?' the man said to his wife, avoiding Fran's eye. All the men passed the buck, left the women to do the dirty work. This one was clever, though, and passed it smartly back. 'It's up to you ... it's a nice enough house.' His face began to assume a hunted expression and Fran wondered if she should throw open the front door and say, 'Come back when you've made up your mind.' He fidgeted with his car keys. 'Could we have another look at the front room?'

They were the sixteenth viewers. The first night the house was advertised the phone never stopped and people trooped in and out with permits to view. 'Ah, that's nice . . . lovely window . . . I love your paper . . .' And then, as if they'd admitted too much, they would pick on something and say, 'Oh dear . . .'

With some it was the bath. 'It's never full-size, is it?' It was a lovely bath, her favourite place, and their comments stung. Others fingered the stain under the tap as though they expected the enamel to come off on their fingers. Several of them said, 'We're really after a bungalow.' One day, when she was rich, she would put up a *For Sale* board and then slam the door in the face of prospective purchasers.

'Houses never sell at Christmas,' Harold had said on the phone last night. Why the hell hadn't he told her that before, and postponed the whole thing until after the New Year? Afraid she would chicken out, probably. The man's face was growing more hunted by the minute but the woman was getting into her stride. 'It's awful moving, isn't it? I see your husband's keeping well out of it. I suppose he's like this one, doesn't want to move.' She was fishing. Come to the surface, Fran, and take the fly.

'I'm a widow. I'm going back to my home town.'

The woman said, 'Oh, I'm sorry,' and let it drop. She'd been hoping for a juicier skeleton. Bereavement was boring.

Fran took pity on the man. 'Why don't you go away and talk it over? It's a big thing, a move.' She shut the door as they scuttled gleefully down the path. 'Please God let the next one be more serious. I can't stand much more.' It was the ultimate breach of privacy, strangers in your home, poking into your cupboards and running their fingers over your bath. Before she bathed again she would scrub it from end to end with Vim. She let Nee-wan out of the scullery and went into the living-room.

'Come on, Martin. You know we agreed on an early night.' Last night he had demanded an extra hour to see the end of a cops and robbers. 'All right,' she'd said, 'but you'll have to go up early tomorrow.' Now he was unwilling to keep his word. 'Come along. Martin. You know what you promised!' She hoped there was a note of steel in her voice. The iron had certainly entered into her soul.

Martin changed his position on the chair and said, 'Wait on.'

'I'm going to give you five to get out of this room ! One . . . two . . . three . . .' He went, with every bit of dignity he could muster, leaving her weak with relief. What would she have done if he'd defied her? She went through to the kitchen and checked Bethel's supper. Leek and potato pie by special request. It had turned out well, she must be getting back her pastry hand.

She heard the lavatory flush and the tap running in the bathroom. She gave him the count of ten to get into bed and then went up to his room. She couldn't bear to leave the house on bad terms, but she knew what must be done.

'I'm not going to argue now, Martin, but tomorrow we're going to talk about this. *I* decide when you watch TV and *I* decide when you come to bed. Christmas is coming and there'll be lots of excitement, and you won't want to be tired and run down, will you?' He was looking at the ceiling, giving a good imitation of a dead body. If she lifted the covers there would be a tag on his toe. She smoothed them down instead and ruffled his hair. 'I love you, Martin, but you must understand there are limits.' She turned away and began to fold his clothes. He would never forgive her for thwarting him and she would never forgive herself for sounding so pompous.

She heard him wriggling on to his side and resisted the impulse to turn, shifting a little until she could see him in the mirror. He was lying on his side, eyes shut, and the expression on his face was pure relief. Confused, she stood there, pulling his sweater into shape. When she looked up again there was no mistake. He was pleased with the way things had gone!

She wanted to shower him with kisses but it wouldn't do. She crossed to the door. 'Goodnight. Sleep well.' She was on the landing when his reply came. 'Goodnight, Mam.' If she'd lived through a more pleasurable moment it didn't come immediately to mind.

*

As she drove into Sunderland she thought over what she'd said to Martin about Christmas: '*There'll be lots of excitement.*' Well, he would have a good time. His ticket to the Welfare party was on the mantelpiece, gift of Brian Malone, and Gary had painted the event in glowing terms. 'Me dad's marrer comes round with a sack, letten on he's Santy, and everybody gets something. Everybody.'

How would she cope with Christmas? Already the morning post was an ordeal, although she could tell the cards had been carefully chosen. No unrestrained hilarity, no drunken mice in drooping nightcaps. Religious pictures mostly, with 'Seasons Greetings' in place of 'Happy Christmas'. But Christmas was Christmas, however you played it down. Gwen had said 'Come to us'; Eve was taking their coming for granted; but she wasn't sure. Anyway, after the party she wouldn't be able to afford Christmas, so it would be turkey with Eve and Harold or a tin of Kennomeat between three!

She still couldn't understand how it had happened. She had met Eve and Min for coffee, and conversation had followed the usual lines. Min was having one of her periodic clear-outs . . . everything in the house vanishing to be replaced by the contents of Fellowes' main window. Eve was having a new bathroom suite installed and was afraid for her paintwork when the bath went up the stairs. 'When we get this lot over we'll have to have a do,' Min had said, and Fran had answered on impulse: 'It's my turn next.'

Eve had looked uncertain. 'Well, if you're feeling up to it it might do you good. We'll come, won't we, Min? . . . and the rest of the girls'll be over the moon.'

Fran had wanted to punch Eve, reach out over the Danish pastries and bash her face. 'I don't want them there . . . Valerie and Co. Besides which, we'll have to have men . . . I owe a lot of hospitality.' She saw them both suspend breathing and it made her reckless. 'I know I never get asked to mixed things now, but it doesn't mean I can't give a mixed party myself, does it? Anyway, a party's nothing without men.'

She might have been swinging defiantly on a childhood gate saying, '*I will if I want!*' Fool, fool, fool! Men meant beer, and beer was a mystery. She couldn't ask Steve for help, it would be presumptuous. She would just have to manage by herself. Once she got her last day at Broad Street over she'd get down to it.

She was enjoying Broad Street. Streamers up, and pictures of 'What I want for Christmas' on the wall. Eleven portable tellies and seven radio cassettes, to name but a few small items. Kids had big ideas nowadays. Lots of things were slipping into place, though. On Sunday they had gone to the cemetery, carrying a holly wreath. Martin had walked beside her, sucked-in cheeks betraying tension. 'You'll be pleased, Mrs Drummond,' the stonemason had said. 'It's a pity they don't allow kerbs these days . . . they gave a nice finish . . . but you'll be pleased with the stone.'

It was white and solid and the letters stood out clearly. 'DAVID ALEXANDER DRUMMOND, *a beloved husband and father.*' She turned to Martin. 'Do you like it?' she said, and let out her breath when he nodded. 'You put the wreath on . . . Daddy would've liked that.'

He handled it carefully to avoid the prickles and struggled to get it placed. His feet strayed on to the grave and she was about to pull him back when she remembered how David would have liked his son's foot to fall above him. 'Dad's initials spelled "Dad",' Martin said, looking at the stone.

'I know. I used to tease him about it when you were a baby.'

As they walked away they saw a boy and a girl, arms locked, oblivious of the stones. 'There's Brian and his girlfriend,' Martin said. She wondered if he knew about the baby but dared not inquire. They were obviously getting a bit of peace from the Malone household. Fancy having to take refuge in a cemetery!

Now, as she drove into Sunderland, Fran thought about Brian Malone. He would make a good husband and father. And lover. And that was important.

Steve was waiting for her in the car park. 'How did your sales technique bear up?' he asked when they were sitting down and she told him about the prospective buyers.

She wrinkled her nose. 'I was OK. They couldn't make up their minds.'

He nodded reassuringly. 'Don't worry. It'll sell. Everything sells, given time.'

They sat in silence for a while, sipping their drinks, each aware of what the other was thinking, each waiting for the other to make a move. 'What do you want to do tonight?' Steve said at last.

Her shoulders were half-lifted in a shrug when she remembered how irritating that could be. 'We could go to your place?' And then they were out in the street and it was all right.

He went into the kitchen to make drinks and left her to go to the bathroom. Locked in, she tried to pass water. Useless. She made an effort to relax . . . there was no need to hurry. When at last she felt her bladder empty she almost cried with relief. She washed her hands at the basin, regarding herself in the mirror above. She looked awful. The skin under her eyes was papery and wrinkled, and the muscles of her face were taut. What did he see in her?

She ran her lipstick over her lips and then wiped it away. It would be dreadful if she left lipstick on his pillows. She knew they would wind up in bed, had known it since they sat in the pub. She felt curiously detached about it, as though it were happening to someone else. It would be all right. He would take care of her. The men in her life had always taken care of her, ever since she was daddy's little girl. But the face in the mirror was too haggard to be the face of a child. Life was catching up on her. She took her Youth Dew from her handbag and sprayed it behind her ears. You had to keep up your morale somehow.

In the end it was surprisingly easy to get into bed. They sat either side of the electric fire and then he came across to sit beside her. Their lips met once or twice, gentle dry kisses that were as nice as she had expected them to be. And then she let him lift her to her feet and guide her towards the bedroom. They undressed back to back and slid between the cold sheets. 'No blanket tonight,' she thought . . . and then, 'He was expecting this.' It was too late for outrage and she didn't feel any. She had been expecting it, too. She put out a tentative foot and realized he was trembling.

'Are you warm enough?' he said, sliding an arm under her head.

'Yes, yes . . . I'm fine.' Her voice was shaky and she hurried on. 'I'll warm up in a minute.' There was an innuendo in her words if he looked for it, and if he found it she would die.

She was still holding her breath when he spoke. 'I'm sorry, Fran. I can't.'

He sounded defeated and she wanted to comfort him, but what could she do? Impossible for her to coax him. That was something nice women couldn't do: men didn't like it. She didn't know much, but she knew that! It was only prostitutes who could take the lead. All the same, someone must do or say something, for the silence was becoming unbearable. 'It doesn't matter,' she said at last, trying to sound cheerful. 'Let's just talk.' She knew it wasn't enough. She wanted to help him over his embarrassment but she didn't know how. She didn't even know how they were going to get out of bed and retrieve their clothes without losing what little remained of their dignity.

She reached for his hand. 'Tell me about your day.'

20

Saturday, 10 December 1983

One minute it looked enough, the next she was not sure. 'Who's coming? The Russian army?' Bethel said as they laid it out. When Fran thought of what it had cost, she felt sick but still determined. It was a sort of farewell gesture and damn the expense.

A streamer drooped forlornly and she repositioned the pin. They'd put up the decorations last night in an effort to mitigate Martin's misery about the coming move to Sunderland. He didn't argue or sulk, but there was a touch of the tumbrils in his expression and it hurt. She would bring him back to Belgate once a week. At least once a week. She covered the food with clean tea towels and went through to check the fire.

It burned huge and bright. An abandoned fire. The coal had arrived two days before, delivered by a furtive little man from a lorry. 'Drummond?' he'd asked as he staggered past, a leather sack on his back.

'Wait . . . there must be some mistake! I haven't ordered coal.'

He had let the sack empty in a gleaming rush. 'It's from Sally Bethel. Five bags off her allocation. She says it's for Christmas and it's all you're getten.' Fran stood back and let him get on with it, gratitude and pain lying in equal proportions on her chest. Five bags! Enough to do them until they left. 'That's it then, missus . . . and mind, not a word. I could get the sack for this.' Fran remembered that coal allocated to miners or their widows could not be given or sold elsewhere.

'You shouldn't have done it,' she had said lamely.

'I'd rather face the NCB than Sally,' he said, and quit the yard.

Now Fran kneeled down and rattled a poker between the bars. There was a hiss as gas flared and a lump bubbled with tar. Strange stuff, coal. If it had been less plentiful they might have kept it in museums or worn it like gems. Maybe they would one day, when the pits ran dry.

She was on her way back to the kitchen when the doorbell rang. It couldn't be Brian, he would come in the back way. She opened the door and saw the florist's van. 'Drummond?' She hadn't had flowers in cellophane for a long time . . . not since the sympathy cards shot through with faith. She carried them through to the kitchen and untangled the card. *'See you tonight, Steve.'*

You had to crush the stalks of chrysanthemums. She found a hammer and began to bash them. There would be petals later, wet petals turning brown, putting on corruption. But the world was full of flowers, and you couldn't take a thing against them because of memories.

It was nice of Steve to send flowers, but he was a nice man. Guilt stirred. They had met twice since their failed love-making but now they were careful not to be alone. In the fug of the Saracen they laughed and chatted, but Fran thought she could detect an air of defeat about him – and no wonder. What had he said that night as they lay side by side? '*You haven't missed much. According to Jean, I'm a lousy lover.*' How could a woman say that to a man . . . even if it were true? And in Steve's cases he doubted that it was. If he ever got around to it he would be kind . . . and passionate enough. She put the vase on the hall table and stood back to admire.

Steve was suffering from rejection, that was the trouble, but there was nothing she could do about it. She couldn't handle things like that, they were beyond her. She put out a hand and flicked a flower into place. If only life could be arranged so easily.

Brian Malone came into the kitchen as she got back, carrying a crate. 'What are you doing about beer?' he had asked when she invited him, and she'd fallen on his neck with relief. Now he went back and forth to the yard, bringing in crates. 'And that's the stout for the Black Velvets,' he said finally. He grinned at her blank face. 'Never heard of Black Velvets? It's Sally Bethel's drink – Guinness and cider. And here's your change. I got the off-licence wife to write it all down. Shout if there's owt else, and me and Treesa'll see you later.'

She made Martin eat in the kitchen, and there was no demur. 'What time is Gary coming?' she asked.

'Half-past six. Can we watch *Family Fortunes*?'

She made a rapid calculation. 'Yes, but then it's straight upstairs after you've said hello to the guests. And no running round!'

He eyed the covered trays. 'What about supper?'

She couldn't resist a grin. 'I'll bring something up . . . git lumps of meat.' His answering grin was the best he'd given for ages.

She sent him out to walk the dog while she washed up. Mustn't have a cluttered draining board. There'd be chaos tonight when things really got going. She felt a moment's panic, and then remembered Gwen. Gwen would lend her Lewis if things got out of hand.

She was getting out clean tea towels when Bethel appeared, resplendent in peacock-blue Crimplene and the ceremonial brassière. She looked around the kitchen. 'This is a good house for a do. Roomy. Beats me why you want to leave it.'

There was no point in saying it all again. 'Don't let's think about it tonight . . . think about Walter. This might be the night he proposes.'

If Bethel had been bra-less she might have bridled. As it was she had to make do with a scowl. 'Let's have no more of that,' she said and took the tea towel from Fran's hand.

Upstairs Fran ran water into the basin and looked at her face through the steam. Older and thinner but still here, and that was something. She leaned her forehead against the glass and wondered if she dared risk it. Why not! When she closed her eyes David was there . . . just like last night. Smiling as though he'd just come into the room. It had happened suddenly, just before she fell asleep, his face coming unbidden into her mind. She had been afraid to try again in case of failure, but now she had done it and it worked.

Gary Malone was in the kitchen when she went down. He had been polished, taken up like a window apple and burnished until he shone. 'You do look smart,' she said and he nodded agreement.

She whisked Martin upstairs to change his shirt and socks. He submitted but she could tell his thoughts were elsewhere. 'Will Gary be able to sleep at ours when we move?' he said at last.

'Of course. We'll pick him up on Fridays sometimes and he can stay the whole weekend.' So he had accepted that the move was inevitable! She would bring him back as often as possible. Except that you never kept faith with former haunts. You meant to, but you never did.

After that there was little time for thought. Greeting new arrivals, taking their coats, asking their preference, filling their glasses . . . how full did you fill? It had been hard work when there were two of them. Now she was alone.

Steve arrived, and she thanked him for the flowers. 'Flowers! How lovely. We should have thought of that,' Min said as she entered.

They had brought a bottle each, tissue-wrapped. 'We thought it should be BYOB,' Harold said, and carried them through to the kitchen. He started at the sight of Steve and then covered his embarrassment. 'Nice to see you, old chap. Business going well?'

Nee-wan became frenzied as the house filled up, and had to be shut in the scullery. His look of reproach as she shut the door was a masterpiece.

Fran felt better when Gwen arrived, as though the cavalry had còme. 'Need a hand?' Lewis began to move about filling glasses.

'You needn't've bothered with Guinness,' Bethel said gruffly but Fran could see she was pleased. God bless Brian Malone!

'Have you seen our friend?' Gwen whispered. Edward was sitting on the arm of a chair, legs elegantly crossed to show the socks that matched his tie, one arm along the back of Linda's chair. Reed-thin and waif-like, Linda sat gazing up at him. 'I hope she's a good listener,' Gwen said with feeling. 'Who's the guy in the window?' she added. 'He looks nice.'

Fran measured her words. 'He is nice. He's the guy I got the Mini from . . . you know.'

She thought she had handled it with nonchalance but Gwen's reply deflated her. 'Oh, he's *that* one!'

Fran crossed the room to talk to Brian and Treesa. The girl was very young but already her breasts were swelling and it gave her an odd maturity. Fran was about to speak when there was a racket at the door. 'I knew he'd make a show of himself,' Bethel said with satisfaction. 'Comes in late, and expects everyone to fall flat.'

There was a rush of helping hands but Walter thrust them aside. 'Howay then, what about a drink?' Someone passed him a pint glass and he raised it. 'Here's to the lady host. She's only a townee but she's a canny lass for all that.' He looked round the room for contradiction and then across at Bethel. 'All right, Sally?' She rose and crossed to sit beside him, doing her best to show she was bestowing a favour.

'Do I scent romance?' Steve said in Fran's ear, and she nodded. 'I think so.'

At nine she shooed the boys up to bed. 'Get ready and I'll bring you some supper.' Brian carried up the second tray for her. The children were sitting up in bed bristling with anticipation. They fell on the food, throwing her mangled thanks, and the last word was left to Brian. 'Watch yersel, our young 'un. Nee carry on.'

Downstairs she lifted the covers from the food. Once again she felt doubtful, but Gwen calmed her fears. 'Not even I'll be able to get through this lot.' Lewis began to fill glasses. She saw Steve move to help and sank back in relief.

Conversation blossomed over coffee. 'You haven't started packing?' Min said, glancing round.

Fran passed her a cup. 'I have . . . where you can't see it. I started on the glory-holes first. It's amazing the junk you hang on to . . . still, it's got to be done. Harold says I'll be killed in the rush of buyers when Christmas is over. I hope he's right.'

Min nodded reassuringly. 'I'm sure he is . . . and don't forget I'll help.' Suddenly her eyes lit up. 'Has Eve told you the latest about Lilian? Spring wedding at Monkwearmouth . . . all the trimmings . . . well, as many as you're allowed the second time around. And you know that surgeon, the one you met at our place, double-barrelled name and everything . . . well, he's taking Margot Davison out. You know, Manky Margot we called her at school because she had greasy hair and wanted to be a social worker?' Fran wondered if she should tell about the phone call, but it wasn't worth it. Instead she went round with the after-dinner mints.

Harold and Steve were deep in conversation in the window seat with Dennis lounging nearby. 'Could I have another drink?' He mouthed the words across the room and nodded towards the kitchen. If this was an excuse to get her alone, she'd be furious. She was about to mouth 'Help yourself', when he gave another jerk of his head and raised his brows. Scenting a mystery, she followed him into the kitchen and he closed the door like a conspirator.

'I got a shock when I saw old Teddy. How do you know him?'

Fran filled his glass. 'Edward, you mean? Edward Pattison?'

Dennis nodded. 'Yes, Teddy Pattison. They used to live beside us when Mam and Dad had the semi . . . when we were all at Bede.' Fran could remember the Fellowes' semi, although she was sure they'd rather forget it.

'What about him?'

Dennis took a drink. 'I'm surprised you don't remember. It was in all the papers. His father died when he was . . . oh, twenty or so. I was just a kid then. Teddy was in the drawing-office at one of the yards and his younger brother had just left Bede – head boy, A levels, the lot. Got a scholarship to Cambridge. Brilliant future. The mother was always besotted with him . . . Geoffrey, I think his name was. Well, he got this illness, some sort of bone disease, and died . . . just like that.' Fran could tell there was more to come.

'They got the funeral over, and Teddy was running around after her . . . he always was a bit of an old woman . . . and then she killed herself. Left a note saying she'd nothing left to live for now she'd lost her son.' He made a face. 'You see?'

Fran saw, all right. Poor Edward. No wonder he had to keep reminding you he existed.

'Come on, givvus a kiss,' Dennis said as they moved towards the door.

'Get off out of it,' Fran said and held the door wide. He went cheerfully. He'd undoubtedly end up a DOM, but he had his good points.

When they got back to the living room Harold was holding forth. 'It's the image we project . . . cloth caps and strikes. And all this whingeing about the past . . .'

Fran looked at Walter. If he decided to take issue, it would be light the blue touch-paper and retire. As if Gwen had read her thoughts she intervened. 'Don't take it too seriously. Andy Capp's a joke, they know that down south.'

Min rattled her bangles. 'He may be a joke down there, darling, but he's not so funny up here. Women are downtrodden, positively downtrodden . . .'

From the depths of the settee Bethel's bra heaved and emerged. 'Don't talk so daft.' The light of Black Velvet was in her eye. 'It's a throwback, this downtrodden business . . . from the old days when a man got his face ground in the muck at work. He crawled home, and his woman, having a bit of sense, made on he was lord and master. That put the stiffening back in him. But she wasn't downtrodden – she was fly!'

There was a buzz of reaction and then Walter was leaning forward. 'You admit a man got ground in the muck then, Sally . . . and you still vote Tory?'

Fran couldn't help smiling. They were off! 'Hold on, Walter. I never said I voted Tory, but if I did it's no business of yours. When I vote I use me head. If Labour put a brush up, you'd vote for it.'

Walter bristled. 'And what about your Tory brushes? They put London fellers up here that's never put coal on a fire, let alone hewed any.'

They glared at one another, horns locked, and Brian Malone held out an olive branch. 'Howay, you two . . . you know you're on the same side.'

Bethel turned on him. 'I don't need help from foreigners, thank you. I can stand me own ground.' Foreigners! The last Irish strike-breaker had come to Belgate sixty years ago, but Bethel had a long memory. 'They've killed the Labour Party, this new bunch. Scargill? He'll not rest till he's smashed the lot.'

For once Walter was in agreement. 'Aye, you're right there, Sally. They had a good 'un in Gormley, he pushed them to the top but this one . . . he's far ower busy combing his pageboy.'

There was a tinkle of laughter, and then Brian chipped in. 'Arthur's all right, Walter. You're taking him too seriously. We let him do the shouting but we do the deciding. That's what a ballot's for.'

'If you believe that you're as daft as a brush,' Bethel said tartly, and Walter nodded.

It was Lewis who saved the day. 'I propose we found a Brush-Haters Party.' There was a relieved titter and then Min was turning up the record player for dancing.

'You didn't tell me you lived in a battle zone,' Steve said as they moved on to the floor. 'Are they often like that?'

Fran grinned. 'Only all the time.'

It was nice to dance with a man again. She looked to see if Eve was disapproving but she was deep in conversation with Gwen. God bless Gwen, she was a one-woman lubrication system. When the music ended Fran made her rounds, topping up glasses, offering cigarettes. Duty done, she went upstairs to check on the sleeping children. The trays were picked clean. '*Git lumps of meat, and as much as you liked,*' – and this time no one had needed to die.

Min and Eve were waiting in the hall. 'There you are, Eve, I said she'd only gone to the loo. All the same, Fran, it'll be nice when we get you away from the pit and these narrow streets . . . and that fire-eating dragon in there. I wouldn't like to cross her! Did you hear what she said to me? "Don't talk so daft" . . . I nearly died.'

There was a moment, Fran thought, when you knew a party was all right. When you could stop fanning it and let it race away. 'Viva l'España' was throbbing from the stereo, and the other dancers moved back to leave the floor to Min and Brian Malone. Min stamped and strutted, whirling an imaginary cape for his charge. Every movement showed off her figure. It was funny, but she did that all the time – wiggled her bum and heaven help anyone who believed her. She was purely a promises lady.

Treesa was watching the dance, smiling slightly, hands folded in her lap. Not a trace of jealousy, because she knew her man. Eve sat next to her, hands resting on her swollen belly. Fran thought of the coming baby and found it didn't hurt any more. She would've liked to reach out and touch, send a welcome to the life in the womb. But you couldn't do things like that. People would think you were mad.

She danced with Steve again. 'Feel better now it's going well? I knew you were worried, but don't fret . . . no one else noticed. It's just that I know you quite well.'

She was still thinking over what Steve had said when Harold buttonholed her. He had cast off his jacket and looked vulnerable in his shirt sleeves. Perhaps he woke rumpled in the morning as David had done, and that was why Eve loved him. 'I want to tell you, Fran, that you've given a splendid party . . . very fine effort. It was a big thing for us all, you know . . . losing David.' He was going to unburden himself, and if he did, it might be too much for both of them. 'It made us think . . . Eve and I have been closer just realizing it might have been us.'

He was looking uncertain now, and Fran squeezed his arm to comfort him. 'I know, Harold, I know.'

The drift home began around midnight. 'It was *good*,' Gwen said. 'And don't forget about Christmas if you change your mind.' Lewis kissed Fran's cheek. 'We mean that.'

Fran was turning back to the living room when Edward appeared, using his important voice. 'I'll see Linda gets home.' Linda came downstairs with her fun fur and he handed her into it. 'We've had a marvellous time, haven't we, Linda?'

Linda was lit up, the little face as perky as a Yorkshire terrier's.

'I haven't forgotten about the swimming,' Fran said. 'I'll be in touch.'

Before Linda could speak, Edward did it for her. 'That'll be nice, won't it?'

Walter departed in a blaze of glory, tooting his horn in a derisory fanfare. 'It hasn't been a bad night,' he said, which Fran took to be a fairly florid compliment.

'He's been in his element,' Bethel said as they watched him depart.

'What about you?' Fran asked.

The craggy face drooped. 'I cannat get over you going.'

Fran shook her head despairingly and Bethel nodded. 'I know, I know . . . it's the money. By, I wish I could get the pools up.'

Fran was determined not to cry. 'I'll come back every week.'

It seemed that Bethel had shrunk. Normally they stood eye to eye, but tonight she seemed smaller. The hair on the top of her head was thin and the scalp showed pinkly through. 'She's getting old,' Fran thought and was filled with love. They stood together until Steve appeared with Bethel's coat. The fur hat was planted on the grey hair, the silk square folded about her neck and held with her chin as she slipped into her coat. 'Leave this lot to me to clear up. I'll be here first thing.' They went over the step arm in arm.

'I'll ring you tomorrow,' Steve said and then, looking at the frosted ground, 'I hope Walter gets home in that car.'

Bethel's head cocked. 'Walter? He could drive that car in the Monte Carlo rally.'

'We must go,' Harold said when she got back to the living room. 'I'll be over next week to take some of your fragile stuff . . . let's get cracking in plenty of time.'

Fran crossed to the sideboard and took out the matineé jacket. 'Here you are, Eve. Worked with my own fair hand.'

Min was ready to go. 'Absolutely lovely party, Fran. Haven't enjoyed myself so much in ages. They're really quite human when you get to know them . . . and I've told Lewis and Gwen they must come over to us soon.' Dennis had grown weary and was settling himself in a chair. 'Dennis, for goodness' sake, go and get the car started!'

Fran found Brian and Treesa in the kitchen, he stacking crates, she rinsing glasses. 'Would you like another drink?' Fran asked. Brian balanced the last crate. 'Thanks very much, Mrs Drummond, but Treesa's still with her mam, you know, and she watches the time. I'll be over tomorrow to get rid of the empties. Mind, we've had a good night – a canny drink and a dance and a bit talk . . .'

Fran grinned. 'We nearly had a fight on our hands when they got on about Scargill.'

Brian shook his head. 'They're wrong about Arthur. I didn't vote for him, mind . . . I never vote, one vote here or there makes nee difference . . . but our Terry's a big union man, and he's for Scargill out and out. He'd bloody die for him.'

Fran knew Terry Malone, a crew-cut boy in a denim jacket who hardly looked old enough for union politics. 'Do you think there'll be a strike?' she asked as Treesa shrugged into her coat. 'I know Belgate's threatened with closure.'

Brian was confident. 'Nee chance, Mrs Drummond. Not with all that coal stockpiled. You'd be crazy to strike with that lot lying about – and they'd never close Belgate, a good little pit like that. Nee chance.'

Treesa was looking meaningfully at him. 'Oh, and by the way, we'd like you to come to the wedding. January the fourth, St Mary Magdalene's. And your Martin, of course.' She wanted to ask if there would be git lumps of meat, but managed to refrain. It would be a lovely wedding, and Gary would exploit it to the full.

Alone in the house Fran moved from room to room, emptying ashtrays, throwing litter into a cardboard box. Edward would be pulling up at Linda's door now and telling her what they would do tomorrow. 'I hope I haven't done something awful,' she thought. He would take down the El Cordobes and put Sanderson paper on the walls, but the bills would be paid and Linda wouldn't have to worry any more. He was already doing her talking for her, soon he would be doing her thinking, too. Except that Linda was tougher than she looked, and Edward, now that Fran knew his history, was easier to understand. What he had seen in her was her wounds; he'd needed her pain to assuage his own. Perhaps he and Linda would be good for one another.

She went to the back door and pointed a stern finger at Nee-wan. 'Go out and perform. Immediately!' When he came back she shooed him into his basket and checked his water. He was watching as she put up a hand to the light switch. 'I love you, dog,' she said and plunged him into darkness.

Martin lay on his side, Gary lay on his back. She could see traces of Brian in him, but there was a more determined set to the chin. They said there was no future for children in the North-east, no opportunity but the dole queue. Gary would survive, though ... and Martin, probably. She turned off the lamp and felt her way out to the landing.

As she washed she decided the night had gone well. Later on she might wince over her mistakes. 'No *dry* Martini?' Min had said, as though Fran had confessed to having no navel. But she'd seemed perfectly happy on sweet ... in fact you'd have thought she'd been wound up. Fran laughed into the towel. Poor Min! Suddenly and desperately she wanted David. He had always loved to make her laugh. Now she could make jokes of her own, and she wanted to tell him. Today she'd put a new fuse in the rollers and nothing had blown. She wiped the steam-mirror and regarded her face. Funny face, creeping towards corruption but not yet showing it.

She was wide awake now, unbelievably awake considering how she'd crawled up the stairs. She sat on the edge of the bed and lit a cigarette. Tonight she had cared for people, made them happy. It was the best feeling there was and, wife or widow, no one could take it away because it was part of the female condition.

She put out the light and drew back the curtains. Outside the sky was high and clear. 'Bethlehem weather', her mother used to call it because it came at Christmas. This would be her last Christmas in Belgate but she would always remember it. It was part of her land of lost content, and she would ache for it if she chose.

21

Saturday, 17 December 1983

It was Bethel who'd brought the news but this time there was no lip-smacking satisfaction. 'Malone's lad's dead. Gone in the pit.'

Fran's voice was cheerfully disbelieving. 'Not Brian ... you don't mean Brian.' And then the unbearable singing in her ears that she had wanted never to hear again.

He was dead, crushed between tubs. 'Went out like a light they say ... never suffered.' And this time there was a degree of satisfaction. Fran had sat down at the kitchen table, clutching her cup. They would drape the banner on Gala day and march with solemn slowness, and she would never see him again. She raised her hand and spread the fingers wide. 'It isn't *fair*,' she had said and struck the table with all her force.

Now they sat in St Mary Magdalene's, the Catholic service enfolding them, beautiful but beyond understanding. 'I want to go,' Martin had said and Fran had said 'No' until she saw his longing to be part of it. He sat between her and Bethel, hymn book resting on small scarred knees, drinking it in. 'Is this what happened to Daddy?' he whispered and there was satisfaction in his face when she said yes.

Suddenly she sensed movement in the aisle and Min was slipping into the pew, bobbing her head to the altar. 'Eve told me,' she whispered. 'He was so young ... the other night ... I can't get over the waste.'

She means it, Fran thought. She's really sorry he died. She put out a hand and touched Min's arm. 'I'm glad you're here.'

The church was dressed for Christmas ... a baby in a crib. No comforting Joseph for Treesa's baby. Not now. She had gone to the Malones when Bethel brought the news. 'There's not a mark on him,' Mrs Malone had said fondly as they looked down.

Beneath the shroud the chest would be fragmented, the pelvis torn and twisted, but his mother was choosing to ignore what could not be borne, and Fran understood. She remembered a wet patch on a white shirt. '*Bloody hell*,' he'd said. '*Bloody hell*.' She'd put out a hand and touched the cold cheek. 'I liked him so much.' In the living room Treesa sat, hands folded on the little mound of her belly. She's only eighteen, Fran thought, and felt ashamed in the face of such resolve. Only Gary showed signs of tears, the others were buoyed up by faith.

Now, as the Requiem Mass continued, she strained to see the front pew, red-headed father and brothers, women's heads uniform in black chiffon. The priest's voice rose and fell, but Fran kept thinking about the Miner's Memorial. '*Remember before God the Durham Miners who have given their lives in the pits of this county.*' Please God, remember Brian Malone. '*He breaketh open a shaft . . .*' She struggled to remember the rest but it eluded her. It was something about being forgotten, but she would never forget him. Kindness entered into your blood and was passed on through your genes. So Brian would live on, not only in his own child but in her child and her children's children. She wondered if this was a philosophical thought and decided it was. Gwen would have been proud of her.

They stood by as the funeral party climbed into cars and ebbed away. Mrs Malone was weeping and Terry Malone, strangely different now that he was the eldest son, supported Treesa. 'I'd better get back,' Min said, suddenly embarrassed at being there. They walked with her to the car. 'We'll meet again, Mrs Bethel,' Min said. 'Fran won't lose touch.' Bethel gave a condescending nod and Fran felt a warmth in her chest. They were both her friends, and they got on!

Ahead, Martin walked alone, sometimes scuffing his toes on the pavement. When she'd told him about Brian she'd expected tears . . . at least a quiver of the lips. When she'd told him of David's death his face had dissolved into little pieces, like suds popping on water. But this time he had looked at her for a moment and then turned on his heel. 'I'm going to see Gary.' She was about to call him back when she remembered children were balm, and let him go.

Bethel was ready to pronounce on the service. 'It was all right. They put plenty of feeling in, I'll give you that. All the same you can't beat a good Sally Army hymn. 'I want "Fight the Good Fight" when I go. Mind on about that.'

Fran walked the dog when Martin went back to school. Alone in the park, where wood pigeons flitted ghost-like through winter trees she thought about Brian Malone. When it came down to it, the getting of coal was man against nature and the NUM and the NCB were merely bystanders. Brian had never talked about the pit but Walter Raeburn had . . . the frightened child left alone with a small circle of lamplight for comfort, losing even that when a marrer needed it more. As she left the park she wondered about Brian. Had he been afraid in the pit, the whitewashed antiseptic pit of the eighties that was still the nearest thing to hell on earth?

When she got home she baked three sponge cakes to put in the freezer. The surfaces cooled and dimpled in just the right way. She hadn't lost the knack. She bagged them and tagged them neatly '*Sponge. 17 December 1983*' . . . the day they buried Brian Malone.

Gary came home with Martin, a subdued little boy who had no glorious tales of funeral teas. 'Would you like to stay tonight?' Fran said, but he shook his head. 'I best get back to me mam.'

When Martin was in bed Steve rang to ask how the day had gone. 'I'd have been there if I could. It doesn't make sense. He had everything to live for.'

When Fran put down the phone she cried for Brian who'd had everything to live for, and for Steve who had nothing to live for except Saturdays.

She was still weeping when Bethel came. 'I've banked up me fire, so there's nothing spoiling. Get yersel' out.' It was an order. Fran drove into Sunderland on the coast road, past the pit. The wheel was turning against the night sky and beneath her men were working in their pit togs and white helmets. '*They are forgotten of the foot that passes by . . .*' That was the bit she hadn't been able to remember.

Treesa would never forget Brian. She had his child to remind her. Suddenly, like computer terminals clicking, her own feelings for Martin came clear. It wasn't that she didn't love him, it was that she loved him too much. And she had tried not to love him, even to hate him sometimes, so that the fear of losing him would not overwhelm her.

As she turned into Steve's street she waited for panic to engulf her. He might have someone there ... another woman. He might be out. He might not want company. He might shut the door in her face. Well, if he didn't want her she could always go home, and if he was out she could sit on his step and wait.

He was wearing the shabby slippers and his tie was loose at his neck. 'I'm glad you came,' he said and drew her over the step. They sat by the electric fire, drinking whisky and water, marking time for what they both knew must come. When she climbed into his bed she felt calm.

She lay for a while, sensing the fear in him, then she raised herself and straddled him, putting her lips to his body, missing no inch of skin, lingering on ridges and burying her face in hollows. Her arms ached and she felt exposed, but her mind was clear. She went on loving him until she felt his body rise to meet her own, until his breath came out in a sigh, and he was quiet.

'Are you happy now?' she said, the question that never needs an answer but always needs to be asked.

Driving home, she realized that there was no need to compose her face for Bethel, no need to fear discovery. Only one opinion mattered – her own opinion of herself.

'All right?' Bethel asked when she came in, and then, seeing her face, 'Aye, well, I'll be off. The bairn's never stirred but that little bugger ...' Nee-wan was quivering with energy. Happy dogs who never knew about death.

She stood in the garden while he snuffled among stones. What would he make of Greenway? And what about Martin, lying peacefully when she looked in on him? She'd been proud of him today. She always would be proud of him. One day, quite soon, he'd ask about God, about life after death. She'd seen the questions forming in the church. She would just have to be honest and say she didn't know, and that would be enough for now. More and more she was coming to believe that man was too illogical to be anything other than Divine, but her thoughts were still amorphous.

When she was ready for bed she drew back the curtains on the dark garden and the orange sodium lights beyond. The *For Sale* board stood out like a sore thumb. Sooner or later it would lure in someone, and the house would sell. Then it would be goodbye Belgate. '*That is the land of lost content, I see it shining plain, The happy highways where I went and cannot come again.*' It would be nice if life could be like poetry, having form and rhyme, but life was lumpy and jagged, and often unbelievably cruel. There was one thing about it, though: sometimes, just sometimes, you could make it any damned shape you liked.

The ground was frozen and the chill struck through her mules. Nee-wan stood, head cocked to one side as though admiring her nerve. There would be hell to pay tomorrow – Harold and the estate agent, to name but fourteen. She grasped the post and tugged. As she pulled she realized she had never loved David more. She didn't need him to cosset and protect her, she could do those things for herself. But she loved him with all her heart. Except that she also loved Steve. How much and in what way she wasn't sure, and she would have to think about that tomorrow. Even when you were strong there were some things you had to postpone.

She felt the earth quiver, and then the *For Sale* board was in her hands and she was lowering it to the ground. Around her she fancied Belgate sighed, chiding her gently for being so slow to catch on. 'Still, better late than never, pet. We knew you'd come round in the end.'

Part II

A Year of Winter

1

Wednesday, 22 February 1984

In summer the car park would be a sea of cars, red, blue and yellow, disgorging families eager to enjoy the beach. Today it was empty, except for a man wheeling a bicycle in through the gate. Fran looked towards the sea. There was a tiny blob on the horizon, a cargo ship or a rig drilling for coal. She felt a glow of pleasure. It was nice to stand here, warm in her sheepskin coat, and look at the grey North Sea.

Behind her, in the trees, Nee-wan was dashing about, winter twigs cracking beneath his paws. She bent to pick up a branch and threw it in an arc. He went past in a flash of black and white, and returned with the branch in his mouth. It was his new trick and he was proud of it.

The pit stood above the cliff, its wheel and headstock almost dwarfed by a mountain of stockpiled coal. Each day the papers were full of an impending strike, but everyone knew you couldn't strike with so much coal already on the ground. She had come late to the life of a pit village, but even she knew that.

There was an impatient bark at her feet. 'Another stick?' She bent to fondle the dog's ears but it jerked away its head. 'Slavedriver!' She threw another brittle twig and moved forward out of the trees.

As she drew near she recognized the cyclist. It was Fenwick, a miner who lived a few doors away from her. There was a wicker basket strapped on the back of his bicycle and he was studying his watch. She slowed, knowing he was engaged in serious business and must not be interrupted. Pigeon flights were carefully timed, recorded, and checked, and Fenwick's birds were prizewinners. She had taken Martin to see them once, not long after they moved to Belgate. David had arranged it over a drink in the club. *'It's all right, Fran. Your precious son'll come to no harm. Birds don't bite.'* Martin had been eight then. They had taken him by the hand into the aviary and heard a soft coo of protest at their intrusion.

Now, as she watched, Fenwick lifted the lid of the left-hand basket and a bird flashed up. Close to, it would be grey and white and iridescent blue, beady of eye and red-legged. At a distance it was a black speck hurtling skywards. Another followed. She imagined the other birds waiting for release, light filtering in through the wickerwork. Did they dream of freedom or wait, docile, for whatever came? Impossible to be sure. But she knew that a finger planted at the base of their neck would encounter endless feathers – down, down and never a hint of spine. Fenwick raised the right-hand lid and they were free!

All four birds reached their zenith and hung there, marking time. They started to circle, small sweeps at first and then wider, as though searching. From that height they would see the tower blocks of Sunderland to the north, the spires of Durham to the west, Middlesbrough a smoky blur in the south. Were those their markers, or was it some indefinable scent that pointed them home? Whatever it was, they found it, taking wing to the south, Indian-file. A moment and they were gone.

'Were they the bedsocks birds?' she asked when she came up to Fenwick.

He grinned at the remembered joke. When they had visited his aviary there had been a pair of birds with feathered feet. 'They look as though they're wearing bedsocks,' Fran had said in amazement and they'd all laughed. She felt tears prick her eyes at the memory but Fenwick was shaking his head. 'They're not mine, Mrs Drummond. I'm letting them go for another fancier. They're on their way to Stockton now. Time trials.' He cleared his throat. 'I haven't seen you since . . . well, not to talk to. I was sorry about your man. He was a canny bloke.'

Fran nodded and smiled, and saw his relief that she was not going to cry. 'Yes. He was nice.'

They fell into step towards the gate, he pushing the now empty bike, she fumbling to put on Nee-wan's lead. 'We used to have a crack at the club,' Fenwick said. 'You know, just a quiet pint. He liked to hear about the pit.' His grey jersey was shapeless but clean, and the hands clasping the bike handles were huge and weathered, flecked with the blue marks of the collier. 'I would've come round when it happened, but you never know what to do for the best. I came to the church. Anyway, like I said . . . how's the lad doing?' This was safer ground.

'Martin's fine. He's ten now. He misses his father but he's accepted it. At least, I think he has.'

Fenwick's mouth drooped. 'Aye.' They walked on in silence for a moment. 'I don't remember my dad. He went in the war. Burma jungle. They say I saw him, but I don't remember.' Fran made a rapid calculation. If he was a baby in the war he must be middle forties now. 'Then me mam went in 1962, and me sister married. I've been on me own since then.' He chuckled. 'I've never wed . . . but I've had plenty birds . . . feathered variety.' Fran was about to say that there was time for the right woman to come along, but refrained. He seemed perfectly happy as he was.

'Are you having a rest day?' she asked.

He shook his head. 'I'm tub-loading. Came up at six. I'll get me dinner and then have a bit kip before I go in tonight.' Before them the pit loomed.

'Is there going to be a strike?'

He shook his head. 'I doubt it. The lads'll not go for a strike. They can't afford to lose money – too many commitments. There'll be a ballot and I'll vote to take action, but they'll not get a majority.' He sounded regretful.

'You would strike then?' Fran asked.

'If I had to. They'll finish off this coalfield if we don't watch out. If we give the executive a mandate to take action, it gives them more clout in negotiations. But there must be a ballot: that's an NUM rule.'

He sounded so determined that she looked at him inquiringly. 'There's some as wants short-cuts. Hot-heads. But NUM history's based on the ballot, you can't get round that. Any road, if this overtime ban lasts much longer there'll be no need to strike – they're not keeping up with maintenance and safety work. There's a few pits round here'll be shut down before long. It's gone on for months, you know.'

They had reached the gate and he watched her try to subdue the dog before they came out on to the road. 'By, it's a handful, that one. What's it called?'

It was Fran's turn to chuckle. 'Nee-wan.' He waited, scenting a joke. 'When we got it I asked what kind it was and someone said, "Nee-wan knaas." So we christened it that.'

He shook his head at her folly. 'Nee wonder it's daft.' His grey flannel trousers were wound round his calves and fastened at the ankles with clips. He swung a leg over the saddle and felt for the pedal. 'I'll be off then. Send the lad round any time he's a mind to see the birds.'

She was almost home when she saw Treesa ahead of her. She was obviously pregnant now, the lines of her figure blurred, and when she turned at Fran's greeting her face was puffy. 'Hallo, Mrs Drummond. I thought you'd be at college.'

Fran fell into step beside her. 'It's half-term.' It was difficult to know what to say to Treesa. She liked her so much, but conversation was a minefield. In a few months Treesa would give birth to the child of her dead lover: was that a matter for congratulation or commiseration?

'It's cold, isn't it?' Treesa's shoes were pink patent leather scuffed at the toe and oddly down at heel, as though they ached. 'Can you still manage the standing in the shop? I know they'd be sorry to lose you.'

The girl's thin fair hair had blown across her eyes and she tidied it behind her ears before replying, 'I've got a chair out the back. The boss is canny about things like that. If he's not watching the ovens he pops out and serves. So I can manage a bit longer.'

They parted on a corner where ice glinted on drain covers and the edges of the kerb. 'Come round to tea when you have a day off,' Fran said. If Brian Malone had lived she would have gone to their wedding, bought a gift, drunk their health: instead he had died in the pit, and Treesa had been left alone. 'Don't forget. We'd be so pleased to see you.'

"I saw Treesa today,' she told Martin when he came home to lunch. 'She's coming to tea one day.' Before then she would have to explain about the baby. He had idolized Brian Malone, which meant he had a right to know. But not yet. This afternoon she had to write an essay on the educationally subnormal child. Sufficient unto the day!

'It isn't fair, you being off when I'm not,' he said when it was time to go back to school. 'College should be just the same as school.'

Fran pulled a face. 'Jealousy gets you nowhere.' She wanted to reach out and hug him until the breath left his body, but it wouldn't do. Since his father's death he had been wary of too much emotion. It was enough that he liked her. More than enough! She pulled up his socks and helped him into his anorak. There were times when he seemed not to mind dependency, and she treasured them. She watched from the back door until he was lost to sight, then scuttled back into the warm. This was the moment when she would have liked a cigarette, but now she had given them up. Besides, there was work to be done.

She laid out pens, paper, reference books and dictionary. Outside the window the back-yard wall blotted out the sky. She always worked here because there was nothing to distract. And she was so easily distracted! She selected a piece of paper and picked up a pen. If Bethel arrived and found her shirking there would be trouble. She uncapped her pen and began.

When she had filled a page she flexed her wrist, rotated her neck, and allowed herself a moment's escape. Tonight she was meeting Steve in the Saracen. For a drink, no more; she mustn't go back to his flat. Not tonight. She was happy in his bed but afterwards the guilt was all-consuming. A night out that did not end in love-making would be a demonstration that she was in control.

She was dying to know if making love with Steve was adultery but there was no one she could ask. They were both free, but did that make it right? She had looked up 'adultery' in the dictionary and it hadn't helped: '*Sexual unfaithfulness of husband or wife.*' But was she a wife? She was a widow, but was she still a wife? Or Steve a husband? His wife had rejected him, had left him impotent in the wake of that rejection. So did that make it right?

Bethel arrived as she was writing the last paragraph. 'Nice to see you doing a bit work for a change.' She was unpinning her hat and placing it upside-down on the dresser. Her wool gloves went inside, followed by her nylon scarf, carefully folded.

'Get the kettle on,' Fran said.

They settled either side of the table, papers tidied away. 'By, it's cold,' Bethel said, eyeing the boiler. 'Let it go out again?'

Fran shook her head. 'I can work it now. It's simple.'

Bethel cackled. 'That's about your level, then.' They drank their tea, each enjoying the other's presence.

'Any gossip?' Fran said at last.

'Nothing much. Mind, I've never been across the doors till I came here.' She looked round the kitchen. 'If you get out of me way I'll bottom this place before tea-time. It's a mass of dog hairs.' Nee-wan pricked up his ears. 'Yes, you. You have a good right to cock a lug. You're more mess than you're worth.' Her voice was the voice of the doting grandma and the dog's eyes narrowed in ecstasy.

'I saw Treesa today,' Fran said. 'I couldn't help feeling sorry for her.'

Bethel sniffed. 'You make your bed in this life . . .' The grey hair was scraped back from a weathered brow, but the pale blue eyes were kind.

'She's only a child,' Fran said.

Bethel pounced. 'Exactly! Only a child, but she's been playing with grown-up toys, hasn't she? Not that I blame her – or him, come to that. He knew no better, and he's dead and gone. No, it's the upbringing he had. You can't grow up straight in a madhouse.'

'Be fair,' Fran pleaded. 'I know they're a big family and a bit untidy, but they do no harm.'

Bethel's eyes rolled. 'No harm? I hope you don't live to rue those words, miss. Letting your Martin run the streets with their Gary, in and out of that house. You don't know what he might pick up. As for that oldest lad, he's a communist – no more, no less! He's down on his knees praying for a strike. Begging for it.'

'He is a bit militant,' Fran said, 'but he's still a nice boy. Very willing.' Last week Terry Malone had located the stopcock for her and prevented a flood. She would not have him maligned. 'Anyway, there's not going to be a strike. Fenwick says so.' She knew she sounded smug but she couldn't help it. Usually it was Bethel who had the gen; today it was her turn. 'I met him today, setting off some pigeons. He says there can't be a strike without a ballot, and a ballot will say no.'

Bethel shook her head. 'I heard he's been making his mouth go. He wants to watch out. They don't like anyone that thwarts them. You should get Walter on about the militants . . .'

Fran seized on a change of subject. 'How is Walter? Set the date yet?'

Bethel bridled, drawing her folded arms to her ample breasts. 'No, nor yet likely to, Miss Impudence.' Her eyes twinkled. 'We're just good friends. And now get out of my way. The bairn'll be in next, and nothing done.'

Later they all sat down to tea together in front of the television. Martin had perfected the art of finding his mouth without taking his eyes off the screen. Fran worried about it but couldn't bear the thought of making him eat in the silent kitchen. When David was alive, meal-times had been fun. Now they needed a spoonful of media to help them down.

'What rubbish is this then?' Bethel asked.

Martin grinned. 'It's a quiz, Bethel. It's good.'

Bethel emptied her mouth. 'Good for nothing. And less of the Bethel if you don't mind. Show a bit of respect.'

Martin raised his hand in mock salute. 'Yes, sir!'

Bethel glanced at Fran. 'Remember what I said about who he was mixing with? He's picking up cheek.'

The local news programme began with pictures of jostling miners, demonstrating at the visit of MacGregor, the new National Coal Board supremo. The portly American came into view, incongruous in a donkey jacket. Fran saw a face loom up in the crowd, a man in a cap enjoying the mêlée. His hand came up, seemed to clutch the elderly man, and then MacGregor was sprawling backwards, the camera was swinging. 'Did you see that?' Bethel was outraged. 'He knocked him down. The young thug!'

Fran was watching the inert body on the screen, sprawled over a fence. 'I don't think he meant to knock him down. It happened so quickly.'

Bethel stood up. 'Where's me hat? If I listen to your excuses much longer, I'll be no more good. If you lunge at someone like that it doesn't matter what you meant, it's what you've done that counts. Well, if they've killed him I hope they hang. I've got no room for Yanks, but that was disgusting.'

When she had made her exit, Martin grinned. 'I love it when she gets mad.' He searched for words. 'When she does, her thingies shake.'

Fran looked at him. 'You mean her boobs?' He was blushing now and she laughed. 'Yes, they do. You're quite right.' On the day of David's funeral when Bethel's breasts had escaped above and below and made interesting little bulges beneath her dress, Fran had wanted to share the joke with David. But they had shut him away.

The phone rang. 'It's me . . . Min. Did you see that on the box just now? Those rampaging miners? We told you not to stay there. You can't say we didn't warn you!' She assured Min that Belgate was in no immediate danger of insurrection and then tried to get away. The clock was ticking round and she wanted to look her best. 'I rang Eve this afternoon,' Min said. 'She feels vile, and there's still three weeks to go. Still, this might have taught her a lesson. It's easy enough to conceive, but that's not even half of it.'

When Min had put down the phone, Fran sat still. *'It's easy enough to conceive.'* Tell that to the strained faces in the infertility clinics. *'Don't give up, Mrs Drummond,'* the consultant had told her a year ago, *'we've still a few tricks up our sleeve.'* And David was dead, and it was too late.

Steve was waiting in the car park at the Saracen, uncoiling from the seat of his car at the sight of her Mini. The street lamps sparkled on his dark hair and threw his eyes into shadow. He looked thin and intense and strange, and she felt a frisson of excitement. 'Hallo,' he said and leaned to kiss her cheek.

He smelled different, an exotic but definitely male odour. She sniffed appreciatively. 'That's nice.'

He had taken her keys from her and was locking the door of the Mini. 'Do you think so? It's some stuff Jean sent for me at Christmas – we keep up a front for the kids. It's a touch of the casbahs, isn't it. Still, might as well use it.'

The pain burned in the centre of her chest as they walked towards the pub door. It was there while he found them a corner seat, and remained while he stood at the bar for their drinks. Jean, Jean, always Jean. For the hundredth time she wished she could see her rival in the flesh. For the hundredth time she reminded herself that Jean was not a rival but Steve's divorced wife, part of the past. But the pain remained.

'There you are,' he said, putting her sherry in front of her. 'Now, tell me about your day.'

It was what she usually said to him, and they both smiled. 'Nothing much,' she said. 'I took the dog out this morning.' He listened while she told him about the pigeons. 'You could see they were getting their bearings, and then off they went. It was marvellous. He's a nice man, Fenwick.'

They talked of the strike. 'I hope it doesn't come off,' Steve said. 'I get a lot of trade from the mining community.'

She had never thought of the knock-on effect of a strike. It would not just cripple Belgate and the other mining communities – the ripples would widen. 'Well, if it's any consolation he's sure it won't happen.'

Steve was looking at her quizzically. 'Penny for them?' she said.

He leaned towards her. 'I was thinking we could be back at the flat now, just the two of us.'

She looked at the clock. 'There wouldn't be time.'

He smiled. 'That's not the point.' She enjoyed it when they had this sort of conversation, and at the same time she was horrified by it. It was funny to be out in the world again after years of marriage, to be sitting in a pub with a man and carrying on a flirtation.

'What is the point?'

He leaned closer. 'You know.'

She shook her head. 'I don't.'

He smiled again. 'Then I'll spell it out. Do you want me?'

She dropped her eyes. 'You know I do.'

He leaned back. 'That's all right then. That's all I need to know.'

They talked of everything and nothing then. She asked

questions and gave answers, but all she could think of was the intimacy of his questions. How stupid to worry about Jean's gift of aftershave when he was here beside her in the flesh. She felt euphoric on the way home. There was nothing like being virtuous for cheering you up. They had wanted each other, but they had stood firm. 'Next time,' she'd whispered when he kissed her goodbye. He had nodded and hugged her close, then handed her into the car.

She was still filled with elation when she changed gear and turned into her own back street, parking in the right place to turn once she had the garage doors open.

She had just climbed out and was fumbling for her keys when she heard the noise of feet. Her heart lurched and then steadied. Muggers didn't hunt in packs, and besides she had nothing worth mugging for. The next moment they were passing her, young men in dark clothes. One brushed past so close that she smelled the male odours of sweat and tobacco. 'Sorry, mate . . . I mean missus.' Her smile began and then froze, for his eyes had gleamed at her from slots in a mask. It couldn't be – except that it was. As they passed beneath a street lamp she saw that they were wearing ski-masks. Their heads looked like malevolent pumpkins. They had smelled and sounded normal, but they had not been nice. She knew that by the pricking of her thumbs.

She mustn't mention them to Martin. It was not that he would be afraid – no, his eyes would widen with curiosity. '*Who were they, Mam? Where were they going? Why did they have masks on? I bet they didn't. You always get things wrong.*' But this time she had not been mistaken. Here, in Belgate, in 1984, a gang of men had run by her, much as the rum-runners must have run from the customs men two centuries before. An old poem was coming and going in her mind . . . '*Watch the wall, my darling, while the gentlemen go by.*' As she went up to bed she decided they had probably been joggers, wrapped up against the cold. Half your body heat was lost through the head, she had read that somewhere. She relegated the joggers to the safer recesses of her mind while she said her prayers; and only remembered them when she drew back the curtains for a last look at the stars and

saw the blue light of a Panda car winking as it raced past the end
of the street.

2

Thursday, 15 March 1984

It was still dark in the bedroom but Fran could hear the clamour
from the pit-head. The shift must be changing, tub-loading over,
back shift going down. The Durham coalfield had been officially
on strike for three days, but still the Belgate men were going
doggedly to work. Yesterday there had been Yorkshire pickets
waiting. A car had been overturned and stones thrown. A few
Belgate men had turned back but the majority had gone through
with Fenwick as their leader. Thinking of Fenwick she turned
on her side, trying not to remember. It was useless. She would
never be able to forget! Even now, three weeks later, the memory
made her cringe.

Bethel had brought the news. 'It's Fenwick's pigeons. Gone,
every one of them. Necks wrung, feathers all over the place. He's
just sitting there holding the cock bird. It's dead as a dodo, but
he won't admit it.'

Fran had gone round to offer condolences. 'It was too late
when I saw them, Mr Fenwick. Even if I'd dialled 999, it was all
over by then.' The birds were laid out in rows in front of the
cree, limp bundles that had once flown free, heads dangling from
the wrung necks. It was windy, and the fine breast feathers
stirred. Impossible to believe they would never again soar and
circle and head for home.

Fenwick had not moved or spoken, and it frightened her. She
had wanted to provoke him to some emotion, even grief. 'I'm so
sorry. I know how much you loved them. People are saying it's
because you were demanding a ballot before you would come
out on strike – but I can't believe anyone would do such a thing.
Not for such a trivial reason.'

As she waited for a reply he stood up and began to gather up the birds. Methodically, showing neither reverence nor contempt. He was packing them into a box that bore a garish label: 'Canary Island Tomatoes'.

Fran felt her face twitch. She felt out of her depth. 'Well, I must go now. I just wanted to say I was sorry.' Mustn't mention replacements. That was the ultimate insult to the bereft.

As she reached the yard door he spoke. 'Thanks for coming round.' His voice was flat. When she was through the yard gate and into the back street she had heard him clear his throat. While his birds had lived he had cradled them in his hands, preening the breast feathers with a forefinger. 'Aye, bonny lad. Aye there, cocker.' When they were dead he had had nothing to say. But he still went to work. She had seen him only yesterday when he had passed her window.

Remembering his pinched expression she decided to abandon sleep and lifted herself on her pillows. It was resolution time! In half an hour she would leap up, let out the dog, stoke the boiler, cook Martin a nutritious breakfast, wave him off to school, and sit straight down to her essay. Until then her time was her own. She felt goosebumps rising on her bare arms and snuggled down again. Ten to one the boiler had gone out and would need resuscitation. Bloody clinker. Bloody, bloody clinker! The one sure thing was that she mustn't let coke or clinker or anything else interfere with her essay. She still felt guilty about skipping lectures. If she didn't make good use of the time she would be consumed with guilt and end up as clinker herself, consigned to some Hadean scrap-heap.

She flung back the bedclothes and dived for her dressing gown. A car sped by in the street, gathering speed. That was what they did each morning now, tried to dash through before anyone could stop them. Sooner or later there would be an accident. She lifted the curtain and looked out. The street lamps were still on, lending a ghostly glow, and a kind of freezing fog hung in the air. Her bare feet were cold and she was about to hunt her slippers when the man came into view. He walked hands in pockets, hunched like a Lowry figure, all browns and blacks and misery. A cap was set forward on his head, his bait box tucked under his arm.

As he came near, the noise from the pit-head grew louder. She saw the man hesitate. His hand came up and drew his collar about his throat. Fran clutched her own neck in sympathy. The man was frightened! He walked on a step or two, and then turned back. She watched him out of sight before she let the curtain fall.

The strike couldn't last. What had the *Echo* said on the first day? '*Coal mountains at pit-head and power station, summer almost here . . . the miners are cutting off their nose to spite their face.*' There was more traffic in the street, tub-loaders going home, gunning their engines to escape. Once they had gone there would be peace again until the first shift came up at noon. It had taken her a long time to work out the shifts and learn their names. Sleepless after David's death she had begun to listen for the first footfall in the street: 4 a.m., first shift. Now that she was coming to terms with life again she was grateful to those tramping miners, and she grieved for them in the grip of a strike that some of them didn't want and some of them craved.

She carried her radio through to the bathroom and listened to the news as she washed and dressed. Every colliery in the North-east was idle, according to the newscaster. So the men of Belgate didn't count! They would continue to work until they got the ballot that was their right – but if the media ignored the fact of their working, what hope was there? What point in their making a stand? She cleaned her teeth to the details of violent picketing in Nottingham which had left a Yorkshire picket dead on the ground.

'Aunt Eve might have her baby today,' she told Martin over breakfast. She made a determined effort to sit down to meals with him now.

'She wants a boy, doesn't she?' Martin asked. Fran nodded and he gave a smirk. 'That's sensible.'

Fran rolled her eyes. 'I don't know about that . . . girls have their good points.' She felt love for him well up and hurried to school her face. At ten you were embarrassed by shows of emotion. It was enough that they had shared a joke.

When he had gone she took another look at the boiler. The coke she had put on first thing was still silvery and unconsumed, the glow behind it even fainter. 'Burn, damn you. Or at least keep going till Bethel comes.' Bethel would fettle the boiler, bring up-to-date news of the strike, and restore the house to harmony. If she ever became a fully fledged teacher she would split her salary with Bethel. Except that Bethel would push it away and tell her not to be so daft.

She gathered her notebooks and sat down to begin her essay. '*The Value of Audio-visual Aids in the Teaching Situation.*' She underlined the title and then filled in the holes in the letters. She added a firm full stop, and then turned it into a flower. She would have to write the whole thing out again anyway. She began to embellish the title with leaves and flowers on a trellis until the importance of audio-visual aids was lost to view. She was seeing Steve tonight and would wear her flowered velvet skirt.

Everyone knew she was seeing Steve but no one could be sure how far they went. She could see the question in their eyes when they reassured her. '*I* don't blame you, Fran.' The emphasis on the 'I' implied that everyone else thought you a whore. 'David wouldn't have wanted you to shut yourself away.' That was what they said out loud. '*But you needn't have gone this far,*' their eyes said, and flicked nervously away.

'*I am too sensitive.*' She wrote it on the pad and circled it with a balloon emerging from the mouth of a skirted matchstick man. So that was how the day was going to go: doodling and dawdling and no essay to hand in tomorrow. She got a fresh sheet of foolscap and began again. The trouble was, she wasn't cut out for adultery. Or for dissembling. She might have kept quiet about Steve but she couldn't stand the strain, so she had told them at a girls' night. 'There's this man ... it's not a grand passion. It's really quite platonic ... but he's lonely and so am I, so we go out.' She didn't add, 'so there' but it hung in the air. They had all looked back calmly as though it was nothing out of the ordinary, but the relief when she went to the loo had been almost tangible.

By eleven Fran had filled three foolscap pages and was running out of steam. She put on the kettle and watched the clock for Bethel's arrival. Dear Bethel, who smelled of soap and nutmeg and told you not to be daft if you got too sloppy. Fran would never have survived David's death without Bethel. She wrote '*I love you, Bethel*' on the Shopping Memo, and wiped it out before she mashed the tea.

'You smelled it,' she said accusingly as Bethel came through the door.

'Never mind the cackle . . . get it poured,' Bethel said. The gleam in her eyes foretold news. 'By, there's been trouble there this morning!' 'There' always meant the Malone household. 'Bawling and shouting, thumping tables . . . you can hear them at it through the wall, hammer and tongs. And her . . . I've always said she was daft, but she stands there, wringing her hands, saying . . . "Come on, now, Dad; come on, our Terry." She wants to clash their heads together, never mind "Now, Dad."'

Fran poured tea as a way of evading reply. She hated it when Bethel criticized the Malones, and this was a particularly vexed question. The Malones, father and son, were miners but there the resemblance ended: Terry was for Scargill and the strike, his father for the NUM rule book and the ballot. 'I'll come out when I've had my say,' he'd told Fran last week, and that was what most of the Belgate men said. That was why they continued to work. But how much longer could they hold out?

As if Bethel had read her thoughts, she spoke. 'They'll be out by the week`nd, it stands to reason. Maniacs like Terry Malone putting themselves about, and worse coming from Yorkshire. They'll come out, they've got no more sense. And then they'll feel the pinch.' Her face shadowed as she remembered other strikes. 'We pulled together in the old days. We always managed. Well, we had nothing to start with so there was nowt to lose. But this lot, with their videos and their dishwashers . . . mark my words, they'll be crying their eyes out in a fortnight.'

Bethel had another piece of news. 'Treesa's given up her job, and not before time. Standing in a shop with a bump like that. I don't know what we're coming to.'

Fran drained her cup before she answered. 'She didn't have much choice, did she? How else would she have managed? – And don't say they get everything given nowadays because they don't . . . you get something from the state, but it's never enough.' As Bethel sniffed her disagreement Fran thought of her own widow's pension – if she hadn't started teacher training, they'd have starved. 'Anyway, I expect it makes sense for her to give up now. The baby's due in June, isn't it?'

They fell into a discussion of giving birth. 'She's always a bit pasty, that friend of yours,' Bethel said in tones of foreboding. 'She has a chance to have a hard time.'

It was true, Fran thought, Eve was pale – but how much did that mean? The phone rang in the hall and she scampered to answer it.

'It's only me.' Min's voice was apologetic, as though she had known Fran was waiting for news. 'I've just rung Harold. He's tearing his hair. She hasn't had a single pang yet . . . nothing. She'll have to have an induction. They stick a drip in your arm, and out it pops.'

Fran sat down to her essay when Min rang off, but it wouldn't come. Damn Min. Damn thoughts that lay comatose for months and then were resurrected to torment you. They had wanted another baby, had tried so hard . . . '*I love you, Fran . . . I love you . . .*' In her mind David's arms, David's body turned into Steve's. Steve alive, sweating with effort, loving her. '*Oh God, Fran, I do love you.*' She felt her face flush. Guilt, that was what it all boiled down to in the end! She had felt guilty after David's death, ashamed of breathing, eating, laughing . . . especially laughing. And now, less than a year after his death, she had a lover and a life of her own, and didn't turn up for lectures into the bargain.

She went back to her essay, ignoring distant rumblings from the pit as the shifts changed. 'First shift's out,' Bethel said when she brought in lunch, 'and that lot's still hanging about for the back shift to come up. They want to fetch the pollis in.'

'That's all we need,' Fran thought. Aloud she said, 'I expect it'll be over soon.' If it went on she would have to take sides. Eve and Min were always on about the miners – '*Salt of the earth? I know what I'd do with them . . .*' Well, if it came to the push she was on Belgate's side. One day, if she lived to be ninety, there might be an issue on which she could be 100 per cent sure of where she stood. Until then, she would have to make do with Hobson's choice.

*

Min rang up again at two. 'I'll go up there and drag it out shortly,' she said with feeling. 'Why can't they give her something and get it over with? My God, they talk about advances in medicine and we're all sitting waiting like aborigines squatting under a bush.'

Fran laughed. 'Maybe we should organize a fertility dance.'

Min's reply was tart. 'Harold did the fertility dance nine months ago . . . that's why we're all suffering now.'

As Fran put down the phone she wondered once more about Min. '*Harold did it.*' Not Eve and Harold together, making love, making a baby. Just Harold. In Min's eyes the woman was used by the man.

'I'm going through to Sunderland,' she told Bethel. 'I'll take the dog out before I go, and finish my essay tonight. Min says Eve's in the dumps so we're going to cheer her up.'

Bethel's leer was a masterpiece. 'By, they're soft, those friends of yours. The least little thing upsets them and you've got to go and hold their hands. What a pity!'

Fran was still laughing when she emerged from the back gate with Nee-wan on his lead.

She had passed the allotments when Terry Malone joined her. The red hair curled around a naturally rebellious face, but he smiled at the sight of her. 'Who's taking who for a walk?' She tried unsuccessfully to bring Nee-wan to heel. 'He doesn't improve, does he?'

They fell into step. 'So you've come out on strike?' She knew the answer but she was curious to hear his views.

'Aye, I've been out from day one. We'll have the rest out before long . . . once they see sense. It's do or die now, Mrs Drummond. We can lie down and let the buggers walk over us – excuse the language – or we can stand by Arthur and fight.' The speech had obviously been made before but was no less sincere for repetition.

Fran chose her words carefully. 'Are you sure a strike's the right way?'

His eyes were fervid. 'It's the only way. The *only* way. We won't be pushed around, not any more. Maggie Thatcher's met her match this time. She's wiped out British Steel, she won't cripple us. Not a single pit goes, and that's our last word.'

Fran wondered if he knew about the world recession or the sad faces on the streets of Sunderland where one man in four was out of work. Could miners demand a safer world than other workers? Half of her said yes; the other half rebelled. Life should be fair. Except that fair shares of misery was not fair at all, and if a pit died the village died with it – or so they said.

They had reached the parting of the ways. 'Well, I hope it's over soon for everybody's sake. And I hope there's not going to be any more beastliness.'

She was thinking of Fenwick but his reply chilled her. 'I don't want trouble, Mrs Drummond, but this is war.'

Fran shook her head. 'You're wrong, Terry. It's an industrial dispute. You won't solve it with your fists. Look at Fenwick . . . he was all *for* a strike till they killed his pigeons. Now he'll keep on working till he drops.'

His face winced at the mention of Fenwick. 'That was wrong. Senseless. Not that it was definitely our lads – it could've been cranks or someone with a grudge. But if it was to bring him into line . . . well, it was wrong, but you must understand how they feel.'

As she walked away, Fran felt a sense of despair. Left to himself, Terry Malone would not harm a fly. Now he was at least halfway to condoning something that was vicious and wrong.

Harold was waiting in the drive, dressed as usual in neat pinstripes. Fran had left her Mini at Min's and accepted a lift in her new fuchsia-pink Capri. 'It's good of you both to come round,' Harold said, almost wringing his hands. 'She can't seem to find a resting place and I haven't liked to leave her, but there are a few things at the office . . .'

Min was pushing him towards his Audi. 'Stop being a wally, Harold. It's too late to agonize now. The damage is done.'

He cast a pleading glance at Fran. 'Off you go,' she said. 'You'll be all the better for a break, and we'll take care of Eve. Twenty-four hours from now it'll all be over. It's worth all the aggro.'

'You're far too soft,' Min said as they watched him drive away. 'He's had his pleasure, now poor Eve has to pay the price. You shouldn't pamper him.'

They were both shocked at the sight of Eve. Her face, usually pink and rounded, was pale, with blue shadows beneath the eyes. There was a line of moisture along her upper lip and her forehead gleamed beneath lank hair. But it was her body that had changed most in the last few days. 'Yes, it has dropped,' she said, following their eyes to her belly. Her arms and legs looked sticklike, and when she tried to get up she resembled a struggling beetle that has fallen on its back.

'For God's sake sit still,' Min said. 'What is it you want? If it's anything except a pee, I'll do it for you.'

Eve subsided. 'I was going to make some tea.'

Fran went off to the kitchen to see to tea and Min opened her handbag. 'What you need is an uplift. Come to Aunty Min.'

As she waited for the kettle to boil, Fran thought about the two women in the adjoining room. At school, by mutual consent Eve had been leader because she knew how to keep in with the staff. Min had been thin and shabby and never had money for extras. She had married Dennis for his money, and now even her bra and pants were designer models. She was still thin but she had the gait of a mannequin and a haircut that turned heads wherever she went.

Eve . . . Eve was still Eve. Miss Goody Two-Shoes who never got order marks and had name tabs in all her clothes. She had wanted this baby desperately, a son to add to her two daughters. She had planned it down to the last detail. But even the best-laid plans could go awry. There had always been something of the saint about Eve, a Maid of Orleans quality that would burn at the stake for an ideal . . . or a son. 'Please, God, let her be all right.' As Fran scalded the tea she prayed, 'Let things stay as they are, God. No more missing pieces. I want peace!'

When she got back to the living room, Min was showing off her handiwork. 'There now, that looks better, doesn't it?' She had looped up Eve's hair at the sides and taken up the back in a French pleat. Now she produced a small onyx case containing cosmetics. 'A little shadow. Green, I think. It's more you. And a

little blusher there . . . and there. And some lipstick. There you
are, that's more like it.' The lipstick looked incongruous on Eve's
strained face and her hair had already begun to straggle. As if
she sensed her efforts were less than adequate, Min produced a
slim gold container and sprayed Eve lavishly from head to toe.
'Madame Rochas, you can't beat it. I try other things but they
never measure up. Here . . .' She pressed the phial into Eve's
hands. 'Keep it. It'll do wonders for your morale and I've gallons
more at home.'

Normally Eve would have refused such a gift. Today she was
too weary. She took the cup of tea Fran offered and raised it to
her lips. Her fingers had the spotless but unclean look of an
invalid's, and Fran felt a sudden terror. Surely it *was* going to be
all right? They never lost mothers or babies now. Not in 1984.

'I hope he's pleased with himself,' Min said again, as Harold,
newly returned, waved them goodbye. 'And I hope he's going to
get a snip before he does any more damage.'

Fran couldn't let the injustice pass. 'Oh Min, you know this
baby was Eve's idea. I don't think Harold even wanted it, much
less forced it on her.'

Min lifted her hands and banged them down on the wheel. 'I
know, I know. But it doesn't make any difference, Fran. I wish
you wouldn't be so bloody reasonable!'

She refused Min's offer of a drink, and made for home. Poor
Eve . . . it *was* the woman who paid in the end, although she
wouldn't admit it to Min. As the pit came into view she thought
of the women of Belgate who would be crucified if the strike
lasted any length of time. Last week a group of them had given
Scargill a noisy reception when he came to Sunderland. They
were demanding their husbands' right to a ballot, but he had
dashed from his black Rover without speaking to them. And yet
they were as involved as their men.

She had five minutes to spare before she needed to get ready
to meet Steve. 'I've made the tea,' Bethel said. 'Get something
eaten. You look peaky. I'm coming back when I've seen to me
fire, but if you ask me you want to get your feet up. All this
rushing about . . . it wouldn't do for me.'

Fran pecked at Bethel's cheek. 'You're an angel, but if I have a cup of tea I'll be fine.'

She opened the evening paper – details of the death on the picket line that had featured in the morning news, and further trouble in Nottinghamshire. The Durham mechanics had rejected the strike call and union activists were making threats. 'I've told you,' Bethel said. 'They'll not be content till they've drawn blood.'

Fran put the paper aside. Belgate had seemed the safest place on earth, a bolt-hole to hide in after David died. Now it was getting ready to erupt.

Harold's phone call put paid to her premonitions, substituting real fears for imaginary ones. 'Her waters have broken . . . just after you left. They're taking her in now, she's in a bad way. Eve's mother's coming round to see to the children but if you're not busy . . . well, I might be at the hospital a long time . . .'

His unspoken plea could not be denied. 'I'm on my way,' she said and put down the phone.

She explained to Bethel and dialled Steve's number. 'Of course you must go . . . I hope everything goes well . . . I'll miss you . . .' She shrugged into her coat as she ran for the car. If anything happened to Eve it would be more than she could bear. 'We've been friends since school,' she said to Bethel by way of explanation.

'I know, I know. Get yersel' off and stop slavering on.'

Harold was waiting outside the labour room, wearing the look of a convicted felon. 'We shouldn't have done it, Fran. I've been thinking that all along, but Eve had her heart set on a boy.'

It was time for stern measures. 'Stop whingeing, Harold. In an hour or two they'll both be fine. Eve knows what she's doing.' She was amazed at the confident sound of her own voice. It was strange to be in command – strange, but not unpleasant. She went in search of coffee for Harold and made half-hourly inquiries as to Eve's progress.

'She's fine, Harold. Getting regular pains. And there's no sign of foetal distress.' He was still wearing his office suit but he had light-coloured loafers on his feet and it made her want to laugh.

She had never seen Harold improperly dressed before ... in all the years. At school he had worn the uniform correct to the last button. Dennis had been the one who broke the rules with six-foot Dr Who scarves and olive-green chukka boots. And David ... David had always had style – or else she had been so in love that she had endowed him with some special grace.

'Do you think she's all right ... it's been ages.' Harold was leaning forward, his eyes fixed on her face. There was a blueness along his upper lip and around his jowl.

'I'm sure she is but I'll go and ask.'

The nurse was suddenly noncommittal. 'We'll let you know.' After reassuring Harold, Fran offered up a silent prayer: '*Take care of Eve. It isn't much to ask.*' When the doctor emerged and decreed a Caesarian section, she gave up praying. It never worked anyway. Eve would live or die according to the script ... or the director's whim. She and Harold were merely the audience and had no say in the plot.

She rang Min from the call-box in the corridor. 'I couldn't bear it if anything happened to her, Fran. I know she's a pain sometimes, but she's always there when you need her. If she gets through this I'll never talk about her again ... not behind her back, anyway.'

Fran smiled into the telephone. Oh, the power of good intentions. 'She'll be all right, Min. Now stop being silly and get on with Dennis's meal.'

At 10.45 Eve was delivered of a son. Seven pounds four ounces and apparently perfect. 'You're sure it's a boy?' Harold asked, incredulous.

'Fairly sure,' the midwife said tartly. 'I've delivered a hundred and three, so I hope I know by now.'

They were allowed to peer at the baby through a window. 'He's wonderful,' Harold said, his breath frosting the glass. The baby's eyes were closed but his face was troubled, as though he was angry at being brought into such a world. 'He'll still be at school in the year 2000,' Harold said suddenly and then, apologetically ... 'Sorry, I must be rambling.'

Eve was only half returned to consciousness. 'I'll wait here,' Fran said. 'They only allow the husband on the first day.'

A trace of Harold's self-importance returned. 'It's different in here,' he said. 'It's private.'

So Fran followed in his wake, and saw him lay his lips to his wife's flaccid fingers. 'Thank you, darling, for being a clever girl.' If she had given David another child he would have been grateful too. Fran wondered how much more pain she would be called upon to bear.

'I'm so happy for you, Eve,' she said. Eve still bulked huge in the bed, although a frilly nightie had been pulled over her head and down to meet the bedclothes in honour of the visiting husband. A line of white flesh showed, but all traces of gore had been tidied away. When David had come to her after Martin's birth he had put his lips to her cheek and whispered, 'Hallo mother.'

She left them alone and went to give Min the good news. 'Thank God. I've bitten my left little finger down to the quick. It's a good job I'm due for a manicure tomorrow. Still . . . as long as it turned out all right.' She made the contribution of her little fingernail sound as important as Eve's incision and stitches.

'Min,' Fran said, and her voice was fervent, 'don't ever change.' She put up a finger and wiped a tear from her eyes.

'What do you mean?' Min said.

'Exactly what I say,' Fran answered and put down the phone.

'There now. It's over,' she said as she bundled Harold into his car. She couldn't accuse him of insensitivity in asking her to be in on the birth. He meant to be kind, to make her feel wanted. He couldn't see inside her mind, her jealous seething mind that begrudged Eve the new life lying neatly in the blue-tagged crib.

'I couldn't have coped without you,' he said and held her wrist to his cheek.

'I wouldn't have missed it for the world,' Fran lied cheerfully, and waved him on his way.

She pulled into the car park on the cliff when she got back to Belgate. The pit was tranquil, the wheel still. Only lights in cabins and walkways betrayed men working. In a few hours there would be all hell let loose, but for a little while there was peace. She laid her head against the side window. A baby. A life for a life. David gone, the baby safely arrived. 'I *am* glad,' she told

herself. 'And if I'm not, I must try to be.' She turned on the
engine and let out the clutch. She would have to finish her essay
before she went to bed, disentangle the audio-visual aids from
the flowered trellis. That was real life. Small and pedestrian and
safe.

3

Wednesday, 21 March 1984

'Well, they've done it!'

The smell of new bread was filling the kitchen but Bethel was
flushed more with the light of gossip than the exertion of baking.
So it had happened: after ten days of conflict the die was cast
and Belgate was on strike!

Fran dropped her books on to the table and sank into a chair.
'When did they decide?'

Bethel was filling the kettle, words spilling faster than the
flowing tap. 'The union men came down from Durham this
morning . . . "Come out or else," they said, and the daft buggers
just downed tools and walked out.'

'Even Mr Malone?'

Bethel's satisfaction rose in the air like steam. 'Oh yes . . .
"Our Gerry won't come out," she says this morning. "Not
without a national ballot," . . . an' the next minute he's slinging
his pit boots in the back passage and off down the club. She'll
feel it now! Debt? They're up to their eyes . . . three wage
packets coming in and it's tick this, tick that. Her back garden'll
be that full of clubmen next week, they'll think she's growing
them.'

Fran smiled to acknowledge the joke but her thoughts were
elsewhere. Tomorrow there would be no angry clamour from the
pit-head but no reassuring footfalls either. She had listened for
those feet in the days after David's death. Now, for a while at
least, they would be silent. Still, it was probably for the best. The
pickets' mood had been getting uglier every day – the *Echo*

headlines had told the story: '*Blue Army Keeps Peace at Pits*' – and the streets seemed full of Panda cars and sinister blue vans.

'Has Fenwick come out too?'

Bethel nodded. 'Him as well. They've cut their throats, throwing the rule-book out of the window. They'll pay for that.'

Fran had long since given up trying to understand the ballot argument ... national ballot, pit-head ballot, area ballot ... Belgate's air was thick with jargon. She would have to ask someone to explain it to her.

Bethel was still in full spate when Martin arrived. School had been OK, playtime had been OK, but *Grange Hill* was on the telly and could he have some Ritz crackers with marge not butter? While she filled his order, he told her about Gary Malone. 'He's off sick. Something he ate. Their Anne brought a note and she says the priest's been round again about them not going to the Catholic school. He won't have to leave before we go to the comp., will he?'

Fran tried to make a noncommittal answer. 'I don't know. I wouldn't worry about it until it happens.' It was not enough.

'What do they want a different school *for*?'

Fran could feel Bethel drawing breath to do her Ian Paisley impression. 'I don't know but take these biscuits and we'll go round and see Gary later on. You can take him some comics.'

He was examining the biscuits as though inspecting them for weevils and she struggled not to show irritation. 'Hurry up, darling.'

'Wrap up!' muttered Martin.

'How dare you?' said Fran, and saw him flush.

'Well, Gary says it.'

Bethel drew in her breath. 'The impident little monkey. Still you can't blame a bairn ... it's what he learns at home. Religion? They don't know the meaning of the word. That's what's the matter with them ...'

Fran knew what was coming next and she wasn't in the mood. 'Take your biscuits and off you go,' she said. 'And don't get marge on the chairs.'

When Martin had gone, Fran turned. 'Don't start about religious segregation, Bethel, because I haven't got any answers.

Besides which, it's the Malones' business, not ours. So drink your tea.'

Bethel obeyed, but managed to turn defeat into victory. 'Aye, they've got bigger troubles than schools. Four young bairns there, all impressionable, and a girl having a baby out of wedlock that their brother fathered. What'll their Gary make of that?'

'I expect he'll understand. After all, he's ten. They know everything at that age, nowadays.' Suddenly Fran was filled with fear. If Gary knew about free love, so did Martin. They shared every thought. She would have to tackle him about it in case he got the wrong ideas. But what were the right ideas? Was she qualified to enlighten him, she who never knew her own mind from one moment to another?

'Mind, I'm sorry for that Treesa,' Bethel said. 'She's not getting on with her mam and dad. They're upset about her not being wed. Still, they had every intention if it hadn't been for tragedy. And the lad would've stood by her, I'll give him that. He was the only one of that family with any gumption.'

Fran hid her smile. Alive, Brian had been a Malone with all the dreadful implications of that name. Dead, he was beatified.

'If she has to get out, I hope she gets a place of her own . . .' Bethel's eyes rolled upwards. 'If she goes in with that lot . . . Hell'll freeze over before Winnie Malone sees sense . . . She's having wall lights put in now!'

Obviously Fran was supposed to react to this ominous news. 'Wall lights?'

'That's what I said. Wall lights in her front room, and half the time there's nee bulbs in the upstairs. I can hear them groping around through the wall trying to find the bed.' Fran could not hold in her laughter. The picture of Bethel, ear to the wall, listening to the Malones' nocturnal ramblings was irresistible. 'All right, miss . . . you have a good laugh, but if this strike keeps up she'll know what's what. You can't eat wall lights.'

Once again Fran was torn by divided loyalties. She loved Bethel and hated to cross her, but the Malones were special too. In their funny, haphazard way they had comforted her in the worst moments after David's death. Gary had come and gone, cheering Martin, chivvying him, making her laugh. And Brian . . . ! She reminded herself that dead people must not be elevated to the sainthood. Not straight away, anyway. But the Malone ménage produced happy, well-rounded human beings – in spite of wall lights and importunate clubmen and disapproving neighbours! She decided to speak out but when she looked up, Bethel's eyebrows were jutting ominously. 'I expect they'll manage,' she said sheepishly, and afterwards felt ashamed.

Belgate's decision to join the strike was front-page news in the evening paper. The union leaders were relieved: '*By voting to strike Belgate is paving the way for the county's miners to speak with one voice for a national ballot.*' The Durham officials were notifying National Executive Headquarters in Sheffield that the Durham men wanted a national ballot as soon as possible. Fran felt a surge of optimism: a national ballot would settle things, one way or another.

Her good cheer was short-lived. A small paragraph revealed that the DHSS were setting up temporary offices to deal with the rush of claims. So somebody somewhere thought it was going to last! An uneasy vision of soup kitchens and hungry children lasted all through tea and put her off her poached egg.

They took Nee-wan for a walk after they'd eaten. Martin ran hither and thither, whooping with delight, an ecstatic dog at his heels. Ice glinted from the rutted track. Winter was unwilling to give up its grip – that should help the strike! Once more she wondered about her own allegiance. They were striking over job losses ... but no one would be losing a job. It would all be done painlessly by voluntary redundancy or moving to other, more productive pits. Lots of men would give their eye-teeth for a chance like that. But if the pit went, if the men were bussed away, what would happen to the village? Would it wither bit by bit until all that was left was a husk?

'Boo!' Martin leaped out at her from behind a fence and she chased him, laughing, all the way home.

She paused at the Malones' gate while Martin knocked, and asked after Gary. Mrs Malone appeared in the lighted doorway and beckoned. 'Come out of the cold, pet. It'd freeze the brass balls off a monkey.' Inside the single living room a huge fire

burned, an abandoned fire leaping up the chimney. Mr Malone
was toasting his socked feet in the hearth and Gary lay on the
settee under a quilt. He fell on the comics with cries of joy, and
Mrs Malone pressed Fran to a chair. 'I've just brewed up . . . it's
nee trouble.'

Mr Malone was renewing acquaintance with the dog. 'He's
twice the size.' Mrs Malone gazed at them fondly. 'Our Brian
loved that dog. He was that pleased when it went to you. If it
hadn't been for the cat, it could've stopped here.'

On the windowsill the battered tom closed its eyes in disgust
and Fran smiled. 'I wouldn't be without it now.'

Mrs Malone sighed. 'I wonder what our Brian would've made
of all this trouble. There's his brother upstairs in a freezing
bedroom 'cos he won't share a fire with his own father. And if
he does come down, it's a slanging match.'

Mr Malone spoke. 'That's enough now, Mother. Mrs Drummond hasn't come here to be entertained to our troubles.
Besides, it's a storm in a teacup. They'll see sense soon.'

Fran could hear Bethel's voice in the hall as she and Martin let
themselves back into the kitchen, and then a tinkle as the phone
was replaced. Bethel was rubbing her ear as though contact with
the hated instrument had somehow defiled her. 'It was that
friend of yours. That Minnie.' Bethel insisted on calling Min
after Mickey Mouse's partner.

'She'd kill you if she heard that,' Fran said, grinning.

A trace of a smile crossed the older woman's face. 'Well, she
shouldn't call herself after a furniture polish, should she? Any
road, she says she'll see you at the hospital. There'll only be you
and her there. The husband's laid out, apparently. Less than a
week of coping on his own, and he's exhausted. What a shame!'

Poor Harold! Fran knew she should stick up for him but she
didn't have time. Instead she scampered upstairs to get washed.

Min was already there when she arrived at Eve's private room.
It was heady with flowers and festooned with cards, all of them
depicting babies with large heads and bright blue eyes. The real
baby was remarkably like its paper images, but the eyes were
shut. 'He's gorgeous,' Fran said, and wished she could have

thought of something original. Unless her memory was failing, that was what she'd said last time.

'You're looking better.' This time her words were sincere. Eve was sitting up now, hair tidied, a trace of lipstick and a powdered nose.

'Min's telling me about Vivienne ... she thinks she's pregnant.'

Fran's spirits lurched. Another baby to be glad about; it would probably be more than she could bear.

'It's your fault, Eve.' Min was peeling herself a grape with perfect scarlet fingernails. 'It's like a disease ... it spreads. One person goes down with it and the rest become broody. Well, it won't strike me!' She reached for another grape. 'I'm never going to be caught in that trap again. I want some fun. There's no earthly reason now why a woman should serve a nine-month sentence for a little bit of fun. No reason at all.'

Fran couldn't put a finger on it but she felt there was some significance in Min's words that was not immediately apparent. She looked across at the bed, but Eve seemed oblivious of any hidden meaning.

'Is the strike over yet, Fran? You're hot from the scene of the crime ... have they seen sense?'

If she made a joke of it the conversation would fizzle out and she wouldn't have to take a stand. For a moment she wavered, but the sardonic tilt of Min's eyebrows tipped the scales. 'No, it's not over, Eve. And not likely to be. They've got a grievance ... well, they feel they've got a grievance ... and they're standing firm. The Belgate men joined the strike today. They want a ballot but they're still solid behind the union.' She was going over the top with her defence: the Belgate men were not solid for the strike, they were split in two. But she was not about to tell that to Eve and Min, not when they were being so smug.

Min removed a pip from her mouth and wiped the corners just in case. 'They can strike till they're blue, as far as I'm concerned. We have gas central heating and the cooker's electric. Coal's a fossil fuel anyway. It's time it was done away with. Then you could come back here and be sensible. You could have been in Greenway now, nicely settled in with ducted heating. Instead you're stuck out there with that ghastly boiler, surrounded by left-wing loonies. Well, don't come to me for sympathy.'

Eve detected a note of acrimony and moved to deflect it. 'Would anyone like a cup of tea? They're awfully good here . . . you can have anything you like, within reason.'

While they waited for tea to be brought Fran looked around at the room. Laura Ashley curtains and the crib trimmed to match. A television on a swivel stand, and cotton rugs to take away the hardness of the rubber floors. Treesa's baby would lie on a paper sheet in an NHS ward, and Treesa would be sent home after seven days.

She was deflected from the unfairness of life by Eve's voice. 'Did you hear what I said, Fran? We're calling the baby David Ian. It'll be Ian for everyday use but the David will be there just the same.'

David, David, help me David. I don't want them to use your name, to give it to this small, strange alien. Aloud she said, 'That's lovely, Eve. David would have liked that.'

Afterwards, driving to Steve's, she tried to gauge her feelings. They were doing it to please her, to honour their friend, to keep his memory alive. One day they would tell the baby the origins of his name, praise David . . . that was nice. So why did she feel such anger? Soon she must sit in the library all day and read Freud – and when she had come to a decent understanding of the workings of her mind, she would throw herself under the first passing bus!

The laughter was still on her lips when she reached the flat. 'You look happy,' Steve said and bent to kiss her mouth. She was entitled to this, she reminded herself as she kissed him back. She was an animal, no more – with animal needs and animal desires. As long as she remembered that there was no need to feel ashamed.

He had set the table in style, down to a candle in a brandy snifter. Watching him as he dished up the meal, she could see that his face had filled out, there were fewer lines around the eyes, the shoulders were less slumped. She had done that for him. Made him a man again. But what had he done for her?

'Penny for them?' He was looking at her, brows raised.

'Nothing important.' She reached out and covered his hand. She still had the power to bring him down, that was certain, and it must never happen.

They carried their coffee to the fire and switched on the nine o'clock news. Domestic coal stocks were already running down but the power stations were safe. Pressure was building up for a miners' national ballot, but Scargill was standing firm. 'I hate that man,' Fran said and was surprised at her own vehemence.

'It all depends on the triple alliance,' Steve said when they switched off. 'If Scargill reactivates the steel and railway workers, he's got a chance. Without it . . . well, spring's on the way, the power stations are stocked to the gunwales – Maggie's seen to that. I think he's in for a hiding. He hasn't even got his own men behind him. North Wales has rejected a strike two to one, Lancashire's split down the middle, the Midlands is three to one against, the Notts men are drifting back, and Derbyshire won't be far behind them . . . No, he's had it.'

She still felt self-conscious with his arms around her. Even after he turned on the lamp and doused the centre light, she felt uncomfortable. To ease things she turned in towards him and buried her face in his neck, knowing as she did so that it was the wrong thing to do. They moved to the bedroom slowly, unwilling to disentangle, tied together more by embarrassment than ecstasy. 'I love you, Fran.' She felt a tenderness for him, an awareness of his vulnerability that made up for lack of passion. He needed her. She moved with him, tailoring her movements to his, trying hard to meet his every requirement. 'I love you, Fran.'

She laid her lips to his forehead, moist now with fulfilment. 'I know, I know.'

While he slept she thought about those magic words, 'I know.' The formula for all situations: 'I know how you feel.' Except that no one ever did. You were alone from the moment of birth, alone in all the things that mattered. When she and David had been together she had believed they were one. She had loved David, really loved him. Now, though, she realized that their love had not been infinite, it had had parameters that had been hidden until his death. Now she loved Steve, even cherished him, but that love too had limitations. Perhaps desire shifted as you moved towards it, so that you never really achieved complete fulfilment. Perhaps that was the secret of the universe, that the goalposts were ambulant. She chuckled silently and smoothed the hair from Steve's forehead. In the darkness the alarm glowed green: 10.30. In fifteen minutes it would be time to take the Belgate road, but meanwhile she would enjoy the comfort of another body breathing close, and try to tell herself that all was well.

4

Saturday, 31 March 1984

'I'm taking the dog out.'

Martin was glued to *Dr Who*. 'I'll come if you want.'

She declined his reluctant offer and let herself out of the back door. Nee-wan strained at his lead and tugged her towards the allotments. 'Not there,' she said, struggling to restrain him. 'Not when I'm on my own.' It was a dark night, no trace of moon or stars. The orange street lamps glowed through a fine mist of rain. Her hair would frizz, but it didn't matter. There would be time for a bath before she went to Min's and she could use her heated rollers in the steam.

Another 'ghastly girls' night'. Every five minutes, or so it seemed, Min said, 'It's time we had a do.' Sometimes Fran enjoyed them but tonight would be awful. They would all get on about the strike and look at her accusingly, as though she were coal incarnate. 'I live in Belgate, I don't own it,' she'd told Min last week. 'Don't blame *me* for the strike.' But she had thrown in her lot with the miners the day she elected to stay in Belgate. For ever more, Eve and Min would hold her responsible for the price of coal.

And the price was escalating, it said so in the *Echo*. Up 86p a bag in Sunderland, and stocks fast running out. It wasn't just money either: the getting of coal had always exacted a toll in blood, and even with the pits idle that toll continued. A striker had already died on a picket line in Nottingham. According to the papers there was a breakaway group within the union, and NUM leaders in Durham were under police protection after anonymous threats. The radio said Durham was solid behind the strike, but it wasn't true – Durham was struggling in torment and the strike was not a month old. There were mutterings of protest but everyone was watching their tongues. 'It's hateful,' she said out loud to a passing lamp post, and almost jumped out of her skin when a man loomed out of the mist.

He was trundling a wheelbarrow piled high with wood. To her horror she saw it was saplings, slender young trees chopped off at the base and shorn of branches. He looked at her as they drew level. 'I'm not going without a fire.' His tone was defiant.

She smiled noncommittally. 'I expect it'll be over soon.'

His reply was thrown over his shoulder. 'Nee chance! The bugger'll drag on for months.'

Fran stood watching the white-lettered NCB on his donkey jacket until it faded and was lost to view. He was stocking up for a siege! Horror-stricken, she whistled up the dog and turned for home.

She had nearly reached the back gate when she met Treesa on her way to the shop. 'I'll walk along with you.' Treesa was moving awkwardly; breasts had merged with belly, coat buttons now strained, her face looked swollen and tired. 'Not much longer now,' Fran said hopefully.

'Eight weeks . . . well, eight an' a bit.' The voice was almost tearful and Fran looked at her with concern.

'You're not scared, are you? We go on about it being awful . . . well, we have to, don't we? . . . but it's not so bad.'

Treesa shook her head. In the lamplight, gleams of mist showed in her hair. 'No . . . I'll be glad to get it over.'

Fran felt panic. Perhaps it was grief, plain, unadulterated grief for a dead lover. And if it was, and if Treesa expressed it, how would she, Fran, cope? 'Selfish, selfish bitch!' she told herself. 'Always thinking of yourself.' They walked in silence for a second and then she took the bull by the unacceptable horns.

'I expect you miss Brian terribly?'

She couldn't look at Treesa but she could feel the quivering lip, the filling eyes. Except that when she turned the eyes were dry, the lips composed. 'I miss him, Mrs Drummond. I expect it'll be worse when the bairn comes – knowing he'll never see it grow up.'

There was only one reply: 'I know.' Somewhere back in time, Neolithic man must have grunted those same all-embracing words.

But Treesa was continuing. 'It's being at me mam's. It's not working out. I'm still sharing with our Dawn and our Mary. There'll be no room for a cot or anything. Me mam's already creating about the nappies and things I'm laying by. I'll have to move out . . . I've got me name down with the council but you can wait months.'

'You couldn't go to the Malones, just for the time being? No, of course, they're crowded too.' But willing. What had Mrs Malone said when she first heard of the pregnancy? *'I'm doing out the back room . . . our Brian's girl's got a bairn on the way.'* It had been a cause for rejoicing then, with Brian alive and earning. Now it was a problem that must be accommodated. 'I hope you find something soon, Treesa. I'll ask Mrs Bethel . . . she has her ear to the ground.' The shop doorway was open, spilling light. She followed Treesa inside, unwilling to abandon her just yet.

The shop was run by a husband and wife, together with one or two part-time assistants. Usually it was a hive of activity but tonight the atmosphere was subdued, the faces on both sides of the counter gloomy. Fran recognized the woman being served – she had a daughter in Martin's class, and they had chatted at sports meetings and open days. Botcherby. Angela Botcherby's mother. A bit of a gossip, but nice.

Tonight, though, she kept her head averted, her shoulders hunched. Her hand clutched and unclutched her big leather purse and the knuckles showed white. She was buying sparsely . . . two pounds of potatoes, a sliced loaf, two ounces of chopped pork. She eyed some ageing tomatoes, then turned back. Her voice dropped. 'I think that's all . . . can you mark them down?'

The shopkeeper was already reaching for his ledger, the 'tick book' about which Bethel was so scathing. He began to write, then looked up. 'You can have those tomatoes half price, if you want them. They're not selling., Everyone's in the same boat, pet. I've cancelled the usual order till this lot's settled.'

As Mrs Botcherby eyed the tomatoes again he raised his brows to Fran. 'It's a right carry-on, isn't it, Mrs Drummond? I don't know how they expect us to manage.' His customer's face was scarlet. He leaned forward and patted her hand. 'I don't mean you, pet. You're like the rest of us – puppets. Do this, do that . . . Arthur's running round in his Daimler organizing the troops, Maggie's on her high horse, and I'm sitting here watching a good little business go down the drain.'

Mrs Botcherby shrugged, obviously lost for words. Her yellow hair had black roots, the first time Fran had noticed them, and the pores on her cheeks were obvious, stained with rouge. She was packing her purchases into a string bag with fingers that trembled slightly and were brown with nicotine. 'Let me help you,' Fran said, and held open the mouth of the bag.

Even when Treesa had made her purchases and they were out in the street Fran was remembering Mrs Botcherby. It was all very well for Mrs Thatcher to talk about standing firm. There was room to do that in Downing Street. It was not so easy in the corner shops of the Durham coalfield. 'It's terrible, isn't it?' Treesa said suddenly. 'That's half the trouble in our house. Me mam doesn't know where to turn and it's making her ratty.'

Fran touched Treesa's arm and bit back the sympathetic 'I know' that had rushed to her lips. 'It can't last for ever, Treesa. And I won't forget about somewhere for you . . . I'll ask Mrs Bethel tonight. I know the muddle over Brian's compensation is awful but they'll sort it out eventually – and then you can get a proper home.'

As she walked away she thought about her own house. Seven rooms for two people: space to swing a tiger let alone a cat. And Treesa's baby would share one room with three. '*You* could do something about it,' her conscience said tartly . . . 'but you won't. You never do.'

The phone was ringing when she came into the kitchen. 'Fran?' She recognized the voice. It was Edward, fellow student who had dropped out of the teaching course after Christmas.

'Hallo, Edward. Nice to hear from you.' Her voice was cautious. She assured him that she and Martin were well and waited to hear what he had to say. If he asked her out again she would plead pressure of work, or tell him Steve had a prior claim.

'I'm ringing with some news . . . good news. Perhaps you can guess?' Fran's mind was suddenly running on six cylinders. Linda! Edward and Linda! She had introduced them at her party, and they had seemed to click. Over-protective Edward and poor little Linda with money troubles and legs like matchsticks. Poor little Linda whom she, Fran, had vowed to befriend and had recently forgotten. And now Edward was going to marry Linda and Fran's guilty conscience could be laid to rest. 'Oh Edward, I'm so *glad*!' She had never meant anything more.

When she got to college on Monday she would tell Gwen. Her eyes would widen in amazement: '*Edward*? Getting married?' Fran realized she was wriggling with pleasure at the thought of Monday. It was lovely to hear a bit of news when it was good news; even lovelier to impart it.

Lying in the bath, she thought about Edward and Linda. Edward would revel in his new-found responsibility. But would they love? She sank lower in the water and pondered love. She had loved David totally, or so she had thought. But Steve had shown her other dimensions – not better dimensions, just different ones. She had adored David, set him on a pedestal; towards Steve she felt protective, even maternal. But for neither of them had she felt passion – she had only just realized that. Perhaps it didn't exist except in Harold Robbins . . . or, sanitized, in Barbara Cartland. She was definitely a Cartland character, knees pressed together, buttoned to the neck. Except for Steve. And adultery! She rested her head on the rim of the bath and thought about Steve, trying very hard not to think about adultery. It was no good. Seizing the loofah, she began to scrub her legs as if by exfoliation she could banish the last lingering trace of sin.

She wore her new shirt for the girls' night – jade polyester crêpe de Chine, and simply cut. She had put on weight in the last few months so her shoulder-blades no longer jutted, but the face in the mirror was still gaunt. Probably always would be, now. She was thirty-three years old, two years off the point of no return, and it was beginning to show. All the same, she felt good as she walked into Min's hall and deposited her bag on the monk's bench. 'You look marvellous, Fran ... fabulous ... now come and see who's here.'

The usual faces turned to smile a welcome. Sally, Valerie, Dot ... no Eve, because she was still recuperating. 'I miss Eve,' Fran thought. Her heart sank as they resumed their chatter and the hum of totally feminine conversation engulfed her. She never got asked to mixed dos now. She was a widow, an oddity, a terrible reminder that marriage might not be for ever, so there were no intimate dinner parties, no groups to play badminton or go dancing ... just ghastly girls' nights, where lepers could be accommodated without too much pain.

Her moral indignation at society's treatment of widows fizzled out as she recalled that in ten years of happy marriage she had not once invited a single woman to her home other than for morning coffee. If she married Steve and was readmitted to the magic circle, she would make sure she changed her ways.

She looked around at the other girls. A bunch of exotic flowers in their boutique clothes, walking adverts for Estée Lauder, who was spreading through the British departmental store like wildfire. She had nothing in common with them now. They spent their days filing their nails and operating their microwaves, waiting for husbands with incipient beer-guts to come home from the office. Only with Eve and Min did she feel a rapport, and that was based more on nostalgia than compatibility. They had been too close as girls to be sundered now.

Min was leading her to a sofa. 'Look who's here ... you remember Margot? I ran into her in town and insisted she come tonight.'

Of course Fran remembered Margot. Manky Margot of the greasy hair and spectacles and the regulation school uniform down to the last durable item. Always top in RK and the last one to get a bra. 'Of course I remember you, Margot. You haven't changed a bit.'

As she sipped her wine she hid a smile. Min had more faces than a town-hall clock. She had never been able to stand Margot, especially since she became a social worker, and presumably had invited her tonight so that she could be suitably stunned by Min's lifestyle.

'Min tells me you live in Belgate?' Margot's eyes were strangely opaque. Contact lenses.

'Yes. We moved there for David's work, and after he died I decided to stay.'

Margot nodded. 'I heard about David. I was so sorry. He was nice.'

Fran wanted to feel grateful to Margot but she couldn't. Her condolences had a professional touch to them, like a key sliding into a well-oiled lock. 'You must feel very involved with the strike,' Margot was continuing, a note of envy in her voice. 'Have you made contact with the women's support groups?'

Fran shook her head. 'I don't think we have one. As a matter of fact . . .'

She never got a chance to tell Margot that no one in Belgate was keen on the strike, for Margot was launched, riding on waves of enthusiasm. 'It's so marvellous to see them making a stand beside their men. I'm doing my bit of course . . . I can put you in touch with their fund-raisers if you haven't got the address. Someone has to call a halt to this government. Not that it'll be easy. They've made very sure of the police; they're up to all those tricks. It's economic nonsense to close pits. When we wake up to the dangers of nuclear power we'll need coal. There's no such thing as an uneconomic pit . . . investment, that's all it takes . . .'

'She doesn't know what she's talking about,' Fran thought, letting the tirade wash over her. Pits got old and tired, ceased to be fertile and bring forth. But Belgate's was safe, hardly middle-aged even. Sunk in 1928 – that was no time at all.

'They've established a workers' collective at Barfield . . . we've promised total support . . . total. They must stand firm!'

'*No matter what the cost*!' Fran was thinking about the corner shop, strain on both sides of the counter and two ounces of chopped pork to give protein. 'I must see if Min needs a hand,' she said, rising to her feet. Yesterday she had seen *Scab* painted

white on a gable end – like a wartime newsreel: *Juden*. Only a
word, scrawled large. Only a word, but deadlier than a knife
thrust.

They were talking about sex in the kitchen, uninhibited
because Eve was not there to disapprove. Fran busied herself
with the cups and saucers, and smiled noncommittally from time
to time. In an hour or two she could escape to the car, drive back
to Belgate, sit for five minutes in the car park and watch the
moon on the water, the lights at the pit-head. Pretend there was
no strike, no ripple on the surface. *'Please God, let it be over soon.'*
If it went on, she would have to take sides, form opinions, stand
up for her beliefs. Panic stirred ... and then Min was bearing
down on her, exuding Madame Rochas and self-satisfaction in
equal proportions. 'What did you think of her, Fran? That hair!
She had it landscaped by Incapability Brown. And the brooch is
a gallstone, I swear it!'

5

Monday, 2 April 1984

'It'll never work.' Gwen licked in the last morsel of chocolate
pudding and shook a regretful head. 'Edward'll organize the poor
girl until she can't take any more, and then she'll put prussic acid
in his muesli and be up for manslaughter.'

Fran grinned. 'We could give evidence. "She was driven to it,
m'lud ..."' She was about to expand her performance when
shame overtook her. 'No, Gwen, we're being mean. There's a lot
about Edward to admire. He'll never let her down ... and he'll
do his best for the kids ... and anyway, Linda's nobody's fool.'

Gwen's eyes lit up. 'Perhaps she'll organize him. Turn the
tables. Oh, I'd like to be around to see that.'

Once more Fran's conscience smote her. Edward had shown
nothing but kindness to her ... and to Martin too. 'He wasn't
really bossy, Gwen. He was trying to be protective.'

Gwen's eyes rolled in pain. 'Fran, you can't have forgotten!

He was the bitter end. We used to sit in this refectory and will him to sit at another table. And it never worked. If he hadn't left when he did, I'd have been in jail now for GBH.' Her face softened. 'Still, he did have his good points. I used to borrow his notes sometimes if I missed things, and all the lecturers used to pick on him so we got off scot-free. But better Linda than me. Actually, it's quite brave of him to take on someone else's kids. Lots of men wouldn't.'

Fran bit down on her cracker, trying not to show she minded, but Gwen was too quick. 'Come on, why the hurt face? Anyone would be willing to take on Martin, he's a pet. Besides, he's almost grown-up. He'll be off and away before you know it.'

Usually Gwen was tact personified but today she seemed to be losing her touch. 'I don't want him to be off and away. I know it'll happen, but that doesn't mean I want it to.'

Gwen burped gently and tugged at her waistband. 'God, I've got to stop eating. I'm frightened to get on the scales. Lewis . . . all ten stone of him . . . keeps saying it's my nature to be plump. If I ever leave him, I'll cite that as unreasonable behaviour. Anyway, enough of me.' She patted her midriff. 'More than enough of me.' She raised her coffee cup. 'Here's to good old Edward – may he live happily ever after. And may Linda be given the strength to endure it!'

They talked about the respective strengths of Edward and Linda until it was time to gather up their books and head for the next lecture. 'You put me off, telling me the news about Edward,' Gwen said as they settled in their seats; 'I meant to ask about the war zone. Are they fighting in the streets yet? Lewis says there's a steady drift back in the Midlands . . . p'raps it'll be over soon?'

As she half-listened to a dissertation on the teaching methods of Montessori, Fran thought about the strike. Belgate seemed quiet now that all the men had come out. There was only a token picket and apart from the odd rumble about Fenwick everyone seemed to be bearing up. But there was strain beneath the surface. Yesterday she had waited in the bank as man after man queued to cancel his standing orders. Cars and mortgages and finance-company loans were all suspended, pending a return to work. As each one had finished his business and turned away she had seen bewilderment in his eyes, and anger, and the beginnings of fear.

There was a group of miners outside the pit as she drove home, huddled in the gateway, woollen-hatted and mufflered against the cold, but still shivering. A tattered banner proclaimed *Coal not dole* and someone had sprayed *Maggie out* on the left-hand gatepost. It was a relief to leave them behind and drive into the back street. Here, at least, normality reigned.

'I'm dying for a cuppa,' she said as she entered the kitchen.

'It's already masting.' Bethel's tone was smug. She loved being one step ahead. 'Get that down you,' she said as she pushed forward the cup. Her tone implied that this was the good news, the bad news was to come. 'You're out of coke. As good as, anyway.'

Fran sighed. 'How many days left?'

Bethel grimaced. 'Two . . . three if you damp it well down. And there's none to be got – folk cannat get a fire, never mind central heating. There'll be power cuts an' all, if the deputies come out.'

Fran groaned. NACODS, the deputies' union, was meeting on Friday. If they decided to come out, the strike would be 100 per cent effective. Not even safety work could take place without a deputy present. 'Don't fret yersel',' Bethel said, drawing on her cigarette. 'They're only holding a meeting, an' that'll be hot air.'

'Do you think they'll come out?' Fran asked.

'Nee chance. They'll sit on the fence till their bums grow corns. Oh, they'll huff and puff, but they'll not give up their pay . . . not that lot. Too many airs and graces to keep up.'

'I suppose you can't blame them,' Fran said. 'It's easy for us to talk, but it can't be easy for any of them to decide . . . one way or another.'

Bethel's snort spoke volumes. 'It wouldn't take me long. They had a rule book . . . if they'd stuck to that, they could've decided the way they've always done: by the ballot box. Still, they'll learn the hard way. Some of them's seen the light already. Fenwick's going back on Monday if they haven't fixed up for a ballot.'

Fran shook her head. 'I suppose he's desperate. He won't

qualify for social security, will he . . . not having any dependants?
But he can hardly go back by himself. They won't let him.'

'He says they won't stop him . . . he's always been a peaceable
lad but his dander's up now. You don't persuade a man like
Fenwick with rough stuff.' As Martin came through the door,
demanding instant heat and food, Fran remembered the day she
had seen Fenwick on the cliffs, a pigeon basket strapped to his
pillion, a smile on his face because he was out in the open air to
fly his beloved birds. And now he was girding his loins for a fight
with his marrers. Truly the world had gone mad!

When he had changed his shoes and raided the biscuits,
Martin went off to watch TV, Nee-wan devotedly at his heel.
'More tea? I've watered the pot.'

Bethel pushed forward her cup. 'I shouldn't but I will. Have
you seen Treesa lately? By, she has a poor look. The sooner her
time comes the better . . . though how she'll bring a bairn up in
that house I'll never know. She's holding water, you can see it in
her face. I never like that in a lass. Aye, it's easy enough makkin'
bairns but carrying them's different.'

The *Echo* plopped through the letter box. 'More good news,'
the old woman said with sarcasm. 'You want to stop that paper
before it cheers you up!'

As she collected the paper, Fran looked in on Martin. 'What
do you want for tea?'

'Anything. Except sausage and beans.' Last week sausages and
beans were the only things he would eat, and she had laid in a
store.

'Oh God, the joys of motherhood,' she said and reached for
the eggs.

There was a sudden toot from outside the door. 'That's
Walter.' Bethel made no move.

'Let him in,' Fran said.

Bethel folded her arms across her chest. 'I'm sitting tight.'

A few moments later there was a shout from the door. 'Howay,
let me in. You pay a visit, you ask for a bit help, and you get
ignored.'

Bethel was arming the wheelchair over the step. 'If I'd come when you called, Walter, you'd have buzzed off round the block leaving me on the pavement like a tin of milk.'

His howl was anguished. 'Me? Now I know you're senile, Sally. I've never done a thing like that in my life.'

She had lifted off his cap and was tugging at his muffler. 'You want to think on what you're saying, Walter. God's listening.'

Fran cracked more eggs into the bowl. Having Bethel and Walter here was the best thing she knew. 'Will you stay to tea?'

The bushy eyebrows shot towards the hairline. 'If it's not begrudged. If you'll keep this geriatric hooligan off me back. If I get a cup of tea that's not stewed.'

Bethel passed him a cup and he drained it. 'It's a bit past it, but it'll do.'

A heavy sigh issued from Bethel. 'One of these days you'll say something's all right and I'll drop dead of shock.'

Walter's grin was wicked. 'That's why I grumble, Sally. I want to keep you healthy.'

'I love them,' Fran thought as she tipped up the pot. 'I love having them here arguing, fighting, scoring points.' When they were here they filled the house, made it a home again.

Bethel moved to set the table and Walter accepted a second cup. 'Hear the news?' His tone was sombre. 'There's a Wheatley Hill lad tossed hisself in front of a train. They reckon he got punched at the club last night cos' he wanted to work. The poor bit lad was saving up to get wed, and she was the ambitious type. Well, he's out of it now, poor bugger.'

Fran turned the first omelette on to a plate and put it in the warming oven. 'How long is it going to last, Walter?'

He shook his head. 'As long as it takes, bonny lass.'

Bethel bridled. 'Listen to that. "As long as it takes" – never mind the worry and the pain of it, never mind the suicides, as long as you score points. No wonder the young 'uns is daft, if you can't get sense from an old man.'

Fran intervened. 'I wish you'd explain something to me, Walter. The rule book says there must be a ballot before there can be a strike. There *hasn't* been a ballot but the men *are* on strike. How can that be?'

Walter's finger plucked at the tartan rug that covered his knees. 'Aye, well, there you are . . .'

Before he could continue, Bethel chortled. 'Hit you on a sore point, has she, Walter? You're as upset about the ballot as anyone, but you try to put a good face on it. Why don't you tell the truth?'

He glared at her for a moment, then his jaw came up and he turned to Fran. 'It's like this . . . listen and take it in 'cos I'm not saying it again. The NUM's a federation. Each area's separate but they come together in a federation. So you can have a national ballot . . . countrywide. Or an area ballot, in your individual coalfield . . . or a lodge ballot. That's at the pit-head.' He looked round, daring them to question.

'Go on then,' Bethel said. 'Finish off.'

He held up his hands, strong from manoeuvring the wheels of his chair. 'Well, that's it . . . they had lodge ballots . . .'

Bethel let out a howl of triumph. 'And they voted not to strike. Come on, say it!'

Walter hit the wheels of his chair, causing it to buck. 'Shut up, you silly old woman. I'm coming to that. They voted not to strike, but then they changed their minds.'

Fran could stay silent no longer. 'Because they were lied to, Walter. The union men promised to press for a ballot if they came out. But then they didn't . . . they voted *against* a ballot. They broke their word!'

Walter adjusted his rug. 'It wasn't exactly like that . . . they had a delegate conference . . . oh, I'm not going on with this! Am I getting fed or not? Just say.'

Fran served up the omelettes, chattering brightly to cover his confusion. She knew what he was so shy of saying. The delegate conference had over-ruled the wishes of the miners. The men had not been given their traditional right to decide, and no amount of huffing and puffing could disguise it. Even Bethel seemed to sense that she had drawn blood. Honour satisfied, she was prepared to talk amicably, her subject Martin's wish to eat in front of the TV.

'Aye, times is different now. It's another world. We had time in the old days. Leisure? This lot don't know the meaning of the word. We had days out in the hayfield, your bait in a tea towel. Down the beach round a driftwood fire ... They're like yo-yos now – if they move too far from the telly the elastic snaps them back.'

Fran nodded. 'I know what you mean. And yet there never seems to be enough time.' The absence of time in a world of mod-cons had long puzzled her.

Bethel nodded. 'Two days a week we washed – round the poss tub all Monday, starching and ironing Tuesdays. No drip dry, no permanent pleats, no steam irons. Just Robin Starch and a good flat-iron. Now all they do's press buttons, and they're still running to catch up.'

Walter laid his knife and fork on his empty plate and wiped his mouth with a spotless hanky. 'Aye, you're right, Sally. It's nowt like the old days. No means test, no workhouse, no diphtheria, no standpipes on the corner, no night-soil men to empty the privies. The march of progress has a lot to answer for.'

Bethel turned to Fran. 'Ignore him, he's addled. The trouble today is, no one waits for anything any more. It's all live in advance. You can get everything on tick, so they're up to their necks in debt. It's the new disease round here, credit. And more money lenders than garden gates. They get loans at sixty per cent, and hand their family allowance books over.'

Fran was horrified. 'That's illegal!'

Bethel smirked. 'There you go ... it can't be true because it's illegal. It's a fact, miss. They live on the never-never and the very first week their man doesn't make bonus, the whole world falls to bits.'

As she washed up later, Fran thought of Bethel's words. It was true. If you lived on weekly pay your world did fall apart in the first week of deprivation. Mrs Botcherby was proof of that. If you were salaried, you were cushioned for a little while. Nothing had really changed in the weeks after David's death, except for Harold's constant reminders that she must cut her spending.

The rates bill, tucked out of sight behind the clock, sprang into her mind's eye. If she paid it in full, even with the rebate, she would have nothing left. Well, almost nothing. The upkeep of the house was beyond her: Harold had said it from the outset, and he was right. Bloody Harold! It was a relief when the phone rang and interrupted her thoughts.

'How was your day?' Steve sounded weary.

'OK. How was yours?'

His day had been quiet. No actual sales, two prospective customers. 'Though I doubt if they'll clinch. No money, that's the trouble. No one has cash for the deposit. Did you see the paper yesterday? Sunderland's in line for EEC help as a poverty-stricken region – there's something to be proud of.'

Fran was taken aback at the bitterness of his tone. 'I'm telling you, Fran, Tyne and Wear's near the bottom of the European prosperity table, so if we bow and scrape nicely we'll be thrown a few pennies. Not that I care, as long as some of the loot comes my way.'

She tried to cheer him. 'I'll miss you tonight.' They had agreed not to meet that evening, but if he asked her, she would go.

'Well, mustn't keep you,' he said. 'I expect you've got piles of work.'

She put down the phone and sat on the bottom stair, hugging her knees. Did she love Steve? Or he her? Did she know him? Or he her? They conversed, they coupled, but did they comprehend? At last, weary of speculation, she rose to her feet and returned to the washing-up.

6

Saturday, 7 April 1984

Martin's interest in shopping flagged after five minutes. If David had been alive he would have taken him to the park to see the crocuses, or even the football match. Sunderland were locked in yet another relegation struggle; father and son could have gone along to give support. Briefly she wondered if she should go herself and make an effort, but it didn't take a moment to decide against the idea. She would be terrified in a football crowd. The first shout of 'Howay the lads' and her knees would go! She would just have to file football away for the moment and hope for a miracle. That was what Sunderland football club were always hoping for, so it was quite appropriate.

'Do you remember Linda?' she asked as they sat in Dunn's, having pastries and fizzy drinks.

'Carl and Damian's mam?'

Fran nodded. 'And Debbie . . . you remember Debbie?'

He wrinkled his nose. 'She's a girl.'

Fran pulled a face in return. 'That's not a crime . . . not any more. Anyway, she's getting married – Linda, I mean. To Edward. You remember Edward?' This time Martin just grinned and Fran felt herself blush. So he had been aware of her feelings towards Edward.

'He was OK,' Martin said condescendingly. 'I expect they'll get on.'

While she told him about the cheeseboard she had bought as an engagement present, Fran pondered that last remark. What would he have said if she had suggested she and Steve might marry – '*I expect we'll get on*'? Or would the bottom lip have jutted, the brows come down? He was growing up and she could not be sure of his reactions.

By mutual agreement they called on Linda. The stairs were still steep and dark, the carpet paper-thin, but Linda was strikingly different. Her face had filled out, the long hair was ear-length now and curled about her face. 'Fran! Come on in, we were only talking about you last night. And Martin . . . wait till Debbie sees you. She'll go berserk.'

Fran looked apprehensively at Martin but he looked quite chuffed and certainly able to take adoring toddlers in his stride.

When the children had grouped round the toys, she settled with Linda on the settee, both of them clutching mugs of coffee – bone china instead of pottery with 'Oxo' on them, so Edward was already making his presence felt. 'I'm so happy for you, Linda. And Edward. It'll be nice for him to have a family again.'

Linda grimaced. 'There's no "again" about it. He never had a family, as far as I can make out.' So Linda knew about Edward's unhappiness. It was funny, but Fran had never thought he would tell Linda about his mother's death. As if Linda had read her thoughts, she spoke. 'He didn't tell me, you know. Not a word. It was his cousin. She's really nice . . . a bit posh, but you can't hold that against people.' She grinned and patted Fran's arm. 'You're a bit posh, but you're OK. Any road, she told me his mam always idolized his brother, had no room for Edward. Then his brother got ill and died, and she killed herself – as though Edward didn't matter. I'm not much of a mother, Fran, but I wouldn't do that to a dog, let alone one of the bairns. Did you know about it?'

Fran nodded. 'Someone told me. Yes, it was awful; but she must have been sick. It's not as though Edward wasn't a good son – according to this friend of mine, he idolized his mother. And he's a good friend. I never meant to let so much time slip by before I saw you both again. We were expecting Edward back at college after Christmas . . .'

Linda nodded. 'He was coming back . . . I mean he was keen on teaching . . . but this job came up that was too good to miss. Not his old trade: he's in insurance now. So he took it.'

It was Fran's turn to nod. 'I'm sure it was for the best.' Edward had been a fish out of water on the teaching course, but this was not the time to say so. Anyone who criticized Edward, however slightly, would probably be hung, drawn and quartered by his wife-to-be.

'We heard about that young lad,' Linda said. 'The one who was dancing at your party. It was such a shame . . . dying like that in the pit. How's his girlfriend? Has she had the baby?' They talked about Brian Malone's death and Treesa's baby, and agreed that Treesa had a hard row to hoe. 'Being a single parent is hell on earth,' Linda said. 'No other word for it. Hell on earth.'

Fran's voice was rueful. 'Well, you won't have to endure it much longer.' If she had had patience with Edward she might be making wedding arrangements herself now, preparing to load half the burden of single parenthood on to a willing shoulder. Except that you couldn't marry where you didn't love. It never worked. Did Linda know that? Or was she scheduled to find out the hard way?

Fran looked round the room. The moquette three-piece suite was still shiny, but there were new velvet scatter-cushions on it and a thick pile rug at the hearth. Edward must have bought them to give comfort to the bare room. She looked at Linda. Still thin with yard-long legs, but the tension had gone from her face, her bones no longer jutted like prows. 'She's happy,' Fran thought, and was faintly mortified by the discovery.

'Have a tab?' Linda said, proffering a packet of Benson and Hedges.

'I've given up,' Fran said, 'too expensive.'

Linda nodded. 'I know. I'm trying. It worries Edward ... not the money, but I'm a bit chesty. I've told him I'll pack them in when I get the wedding over. Wedding! Even the word makes me mouth go dry.' She looked at Fran. 'What are you smiling about?'

Fran shook her head. 'Nothing. I've just noticed your bullfight poster's gone.' What had she said to Gwen last year when she had introduced Edward to Linda and seen them click? '*I bet he takes down the El Cordobes*.'

'See you in church,' Linda trilled as the Mini drew away. The children clutched Martin until the last minute and had to be forcibly detached. 'I think they like you,' Fran said, and received a smug 'I know they do' in return.

Nee-wan was ecstatic when they let themselves into the house. 'Steady on,' Fran said, trying to keep her tights away from his raking claws. 'We've only been to Sunderland, not Australia.' They put him on the lead and set off through the dusk, pulled behind a dog mad for freedom. 'I think he likes living with us,' Martin said.

Fran puffed. 'As long as we're doing what he wants. I know some boys like that!'

Martin ignored the jibe. They had reached the safety zone, the dog could be let off the lead, and boy and dog ran, whooping, into the blackness.

After a moment Fran's eyes adjusted to the dark, and familiar shapes appeared. Light was reflected from puddles and glinting cold frames, even the occasional greenhouse. The fences around the allotments were cobbled together from whatever had come to hand, railway sleepers and old doors, corrugated iron and chicken wire. As she passed one plot she heard the soft cluck of hens disturbed by Nee-wan's presence. There was something about a new-laid egg, brown and dirty and feather-strewn – something safe. Except for cholesterol. Bugger the experts – sooner or later they'd destroy the enjoyment of everything!

They had turned for home and were nearly back to the street lamps when they saw Terry Malone in the distance, hands in pockets, shoulders hunched. Since the strike he seemed to be always walking the streets. To get out of the house and away from his father, presumably.

'It's a cold night, Terry.'

His face in the lamplight was pinched. 'Aye, Mrs Drummond, I think winter's set to stay. Someone wants to tell the bugger it's springtime.' He fell in beside her. 'Have you heard about Treesa?'

Fran's heart lurched. 'There's nothing wrong, is there?'

He shrugged. 'She's in hospital. They talked a lot of stuff about tension – blood pressure and all that . . .'

Fran comprehended. 'Hypertension, was that it?'

'Aye, that's it. Any road, she has to stop in bed. Her mam wasn't keen, so me mam said she could lie up at our place, but there's no rest there . . . not with a houseful of bairns. So the hospital took her in. It's all for the best, I suppose. Her mam's a bundle of nerves, what with the strike an' all.'

'It'll be a good job when it's over.' Fran's tone was tentative, for Terry was nothing if not militant; but his reply was cheerful.

'It won't be long now, Mrs Drummond, not with the deputies balloting. Once they're out, that's it.' He seemed to have no doubt that the deputies would vote for a strike; no sense of the irony of men denied a ballot of their own being so dependent on the ballot of others.

'Give my love to Treesa,' she said when they parted. 'I'll go in and see her myself before long.'

She would go in. Sunderland was a long way off if you didn't have a car and she could easily pop in one evening before she met Steve.

She collected the *Echo* from the doormat and glanced quickly through it. She was meeting Steve at 8.15 and time was running out.

NUPE was calling nurses into the picket lines and there was the usual controversy in the letters column. According to one writer, striking miners had only struck so they could carry bags of logs to coalless OAPs. Another letter blamed the whole thing on a 'vociferous minority'. But it was the account of the Kent men's march on the Nottinghamshire coalfield that took Fran's attention. The march had begun at Dover four days before, and would reach Nottinghamshire on Friday. The former general secretary of the Kent NUM explained, '*We are marching into the Midland coalfield to defend jobs. We removed Heath in 1974. Now is the time to remove Thatcher.*' Was he defending jobs or pursuing a political aim? Or were they one and the same? Not that it really mattered about the aims: Belgate and other villages like it were being crucified, and nothing could justify that.

Steve was waiting for her in the Saracen. He shook his head when she told him about Treesa. 'Poor kid. She needs a man and a settled home, that'd do more for her blood pressure than a stay in hospital. It makes you wonder . . .'

Something in his tone made her look at him sharply. 'You think she was wrong to keep this baby?'

The shaking of his head was vehement. 'I never said that. But it's not straightforward, is it? Kids were meant to come into a happy home with two parents. Sometimes it can't be helped – take you and me – but if you have a choice . . .'

Fran felt chilled, too chilled to point out that Treesa's pregnancy had been advanced when Brian had died, or that she had loved him and probably wanted to bear his child. Too chilled to say that babies were lovely and well worth any amount of suffering, and that she would change places with Treesa right now. She had done nothing about contraception, and infertility was fickle protection.

What if she were pregnant? Would Steve marry her or give her another little speech about abortion?

The thought niggled all the way back to the flat and lay between them in the bed. It was only banished when another more uncomfortable thought came to oust it. 'That was good, Fran.' He lay on his face, his arm heavy across her belly. 'Good for you too?' She squeezed his arm in reply. 'I wish you didn't have to go home. It spoils things.'

She spoke indulgently. 'I have to go home . . . I live there.'

Suddenly he was sitting up, reaching for her. 'That's what I mean. You should live here, you and Martin.'

She kept her tone light but her mind was hitting the fan. 'Are you proposing to make an honest woman of me?' How would she tell Martin? Face other people? Face David on the Day of Judgement? Would he be good to David's child? He loved his own children to distraction, but would Martin equal them? Questions. Always questions.

He whispered, 'I suppose I am,' against her ear, and she turned it into a joke.

'I never accept proposals on Saturday. Ask me again on May thirty-second.'

He seemed happy enough to end the conversation there, and suddenly she was peeved. What sort of proposal fizzled out when treated with frivolity? And what sort of woman froze with fear at such a proposal and then took offence when it was not pursued?

The questions stayed with her. 'Frances Mary Drummond, you don't improve,' she said as she swung the car towards Belgate and saw the moon's path on the water as clear as the road ahead.

7

Wednesday, 2 May 1984

She could see the figure through the swishing wipers, head down, inadequately clad against the driving rain. She would have to pick it up, him or her. Thoughts of knives driven into drivers' sides intruded, but you couldn't leave a dog out on the open road on a day like this. As she slowed and drew level, she saw it was a woman. 'Mrs Botcherby . . . what are you doing out here in this weather? Get in!'

The woman stood for a moment, apparently uncertain. Rain streamed down her face, her yellow hair was moulded to her head on either side of the black untouched roots. 'Get in!' Fran's voice was uncertain now, the situation beyond her. Mrs Botcherby put a hand to the door, then bent into the seat.

It was better with the door closed and the noise of the rain diminished. 'Are you going home?' Dignity was beginning to reassert itself; Mrs Botcherby had taken the sodden scarf from her neck and was wiping her face.

'Yes. Stafford Street. The end of the street'll do.' There was no gratitude, no explanation of her presence on the road between Belgate and Sunderland, inadequately clad, without handbag or head covering. Her bare legs steamed in the warm air from the heater and she stroked them with fingernails bitten to the quick. It was no time for polite questions and Fran kept her mouth shut.

She drove right up to the Botcherby's door, halfway down a sloping terrace. She knew it was the Botcherby's home because Angela was on the doorstep, soaked cotton dress protruding from a sodden anorak. She peered at the approaching car and then scampered back into the house, reappearing behind her father. He too was rain-soaked, a muffler crossed over his chest, his face drawn. 'Where've you been, lass? We've been frantic.' His eyes flicked to Fran and he smiled. 'Thanks for bringing her back. The lads are out looking; I had to come back to see to Angela.' The nine-year-old, suddenly mature, had taken her

mother's hand and was leading her into the house. Relief broke
on the man's face. 'I thought . . . well, never mind what I thought.
She's back. Where was she?'

'Out on the Sunderland road. Did she miss the bus?' Damn
you, Frances; still trying to keep the lid on things! Mr Botcherby's
face closed as quickly as it had opened. He had been glad to see
Fran, now he wanted rid of her. 'Aye, well, thanks very much.'
He peered into her face. 'It is Mrs Drummond, isn't it? We know
your lad, he's in our Angela's class. Well, thanks for bringing her
home, I'd best be getting in . . .' He paused, feeling something
else was needed. 'It's this strike, you see – she takes things very
serious, always has. Money's short, things have to go . . . we're
all in the same boat, I tell her, but she takes no notice. Any road,
we'll have the doctor in. He'll give her something to tide her
over . . .'

Long after she had driven away Fran could see Mrs Botcherby's face in her mind's eye, blank, almost vacant, except for the
agitated eyes. The sight of that face had been almost as upsetting
as the sight of Angela, old before her time, leading her mother
into the house.

She called in at the corner shop on her way home, running from
the car, her handbag held over her head to protect her hair. The
bell jangled a welcome but the shopkeeper's face was sombre.
'Nobody's got any money, Mrs Drummond.' He was scooping
potatoes into the scales. 'Every time that bell jangles, it's someone
wanting tick – or else it's a support group wanting handouts. I'd
like to say "Get lost", but I'd only lose me windows. So I shell
out. I just hope I can keep going till they see sense.'

Fran looked around the shelves for something else she needed –
anything to promote a little cash trade.

'Don't get me wrong, Mrs Drummond, I think they've got a
case. Coal not dole. It'd be different if there was jobs for them
to go to . . . but there's nothing but the pits round here, is there?
Not a blessed thing.' She bought two pounds of sugar and a
quarter of PG Tips. You could never have too much tea and
sugar.

'Never mind, love,' he said as she left the shop. 'It'll be over soon, and I'll be killed in the rush.'

'You know I'm going out tonight?' she said as they ate tea.

Martin nodded, eyes fixed on the screen. 'To an engagement party, I know . . . you've told me twice.'

The invitation had come out of the blue: '*We've decided to have a small gathering, a few close friends . . .*' Edward was trying to be nonchalant but she'd sensed the underlying excitement. 'Don't let him down, Linda, Please, please don't let him down,' she thought. She had bought them a cheeseboard as an engagement gift, flower-strewn melamine with a gilt ribbon through the handle. It lay, gift wrapped, on the hall table, along with the card of congratulations. It was nice to be celebrating something.

She wanted to visit Treesa tonight, so there was only time for a quick skim through the evening paper as she dried the tea dishes. Howls of protest from the NCB about the American coal order, the first from the US in ten years. If Durham coal stocks remained strike-bound, the order would be lost. 'Fed-up Striker' wrote that the silent majority was suffering, and he wished it had the guts of the Notts miners; 'Fair Play' said Labour had closed pits but hadn't paid a pensioner to do it. Well, he had a point there! 'Back to Work' gave statistics: from 1960 to February 1984, ninety-five pits had closed in County Durham, fifty-five of them under Labour, forty under the Conservatives. With friends like those who needed enemies, he asked, and ended with a plea to buy British. £2 saved on a shirt meant the dole queue for someone. Fran looked guiltily at the tea towel she was holding, nervous of seeing a 'Made in Taiwan' label. You could never be sure nowadays, not even when there was a Union Jack on the packet.

She turned the page. Durham's member on the National Executive was appealing to miners not to ring the Coal Board's redundancy hot-line: '*You are giving the NCB propaganda to undermine morale.*' The suds were settling on the washing-up water and Fran's spirits were sinking too. If everybody left the pits, what price Belgate? Some villages in Durham already had 21 per cent unemployed. If the pits went, that figure would soar. Suddenly another item caught her eye – the Northern director of ACAS was warning against too much optimism on the jobs front!

Treesa's was the only unvisited bed in the ward, hers the only locker without a bouquet of spring flowers. She lay, eyes closed as though to shut out the attentive fathers and doting parents. 'Hello, Treesa.' Fran laid magazines and fruit on the jacquard counterpane.

'Mrs Drummond! I'm glad you came in.'

Fran drew a chair closer to the bed and sat down. 'How are you feeling?'

Beneath the counterpane there was a baby, boy or girl, arched in the foetal curve. Fran felt a sense of longing so intense that she had to shake her head to get rid of it. 'No, it's all right, Treesa. I'm OK. A bit of a dizzy spell, that's all. Now tell me about yourself.'

Lying there in the metal bed, Treesa looked even younger than her years. And clean. Amazing how people in hospital always looked so clean. 'So if you could take it, Mrs Drummond . . . just until I get back home?' Treesa was worried about the layette, the things she had put by for the baby. 'There's that many bairns you see . . . and me mam doesn't have much control. They'll have everything out and on their dolls if I'm not careful, and it's not as if I've got much . . .'

Fran left, promising to collect the layette the next day. 'You're sure your mam won't mind?'

'Why, no, Mrs Drummond . . . she'll be pleased to see the back of it.'

Fran was out in the hospital car park before she realized they had never talked about Brian. He had fathered Treesa's baby, provided the vital spark . . . now he was shut out of their conversation for no greater crime than that of dying. 'Brian Malone,' she said out loud to the driving mirror, as though by speaking out she could redress the wrong.

The engagement party was being held at Linda's, and Fran rather admired Edward for that. His own house in Queen's Crescent was a spacious three-bedroom semi. The old Edward would have jibbed at inviting his friends to Linda's threadbare flat. Or would he? Had she credited him with a snobbishness he did not possess, as she had credited him with so many other small defects? She was still trying to decide as she mounted the narrow stairs and held out her gift to her waiting hosts.

It was a lovely party. Edward's friends and relations seemed genuinely pleased at his new-found happiness, and Linda's were relieved that at last she was out of the wood. 'She's done all right for herself this time,' one portly uncle confided. 'He was a bad 'un, that first husband of hers. Good for nowt but makkin' bairns. This one's a gentleman, you can tell from his shoes.'

It all came down to shoes in the end, Fran thought as she drove home – just as the sociology tutor said. And you were still being judged when you were turned forty and gone grey at the temples. All the same, it had been a happy evening. They had toasted the engaged couple and Edward had clutched Linda by the waist in a proprietory gesture and received a smacking kiss for his pains. 'I'm dead scared about the ceremony,' Linda had confided in the kitchen as they made a hasty second batch of sandwiches. 'I want to do it properly.' Fran had promised to procure a book on wedding etiquette and act as a consultant on protocol. 'You know about these things,' Linda had said trustingly. 'I knew you were classy as soon as I laid eyes on you.' They had laughed then about the Three Rivers Social Club and the Sybil Fawlty figure who ran it. ' "I just need some perticks," ' Linda mimicked, and stuck out her flat chest to emulate Sybil's pouter-pigeon boobs.

Fran was driving along the coast now, the beach silver in the moonlight, the tide a white ribbon at its edge. She would have liked to stop the car and run barefoot along the sand to watch the sea-coalers filling their sacks at the tide line, but she was scared of the deserted beach at night and the sea-coalers were gone, banished by the strike. Her eyes flicked to the dashboard clock: 11.30. In normal times tub-loading would just have begun, the night-shift men would be ascending in the cage. She put thoughts of the strike firmly out of her mind. It only made her miserable, and she needed to keep cheerful for what must be done before she went to bed.

'*It's not as though I have that much.*' Those words of Treesa's had haunted her all evening. Brian Malone's baby was coming into the world in style if she, Frances Drummond, had anything to do with it. When Bethel had handed over the reins and gone home, she went into her bedroom and kneeled down by the ottoman. Inside were those baby clothes of Martin's she had saved for a second baby, and the items she had bought from time to time while she prayed for another child. She fingered the voile and Viyella, the broderie anglaise and terry towelling that had made up the fabric of her hopes. When she had repacked them in a case for Treesa, she put her head against the ottoman's padded lid and cried.

8

Tuesday, 5 June 1984

'And it's there in the window. It is, it really is,' Martin said as though he expected her not to believe him.

'What does it say?' She was peeling potatoes for lunch but she dried her hands and sat down at the kitchen table. As he quoted she realized the notice was imprinted on Martin's mind. '*To whom it may concern. If the strike is not settled by Monday 18 June I will be going in*. That's all ... and it's signed *W. Fenwick*. Someone's already smashed the window, and he's taped it up with sticking plaster. And Gary says if he scabs they'll expel him from the union, and that means he'll be finished.'

The child's eyes were gleaming with excitement and Fran felt a sudden distaste. 'Well, I think it's awful, darling – a man having his window broken just because he wants to go to work.' She was suddenly aware she was making a political statement. It was wrong to indoctrinate your children, an abuse of parental power. 'It's not that I'm against the strike ... well, not altogether ... but if they've got the right to strike, then he's got the right not to strike. Hasn't he?'

Martin shrugged and she began to dither. 'Well, they shouldn't throw things at his window ... no matter what he's done ... and it isn't as if he's done anything yet. He's only saying he will if they don't sort things out . . .'

She might have been mistaken, but there was a faint smirk on Martin's face that might have been contempt. 'I wouldn't scab,' he said, 'not if I was a miner. I'd occupy the pit until they promised to leave it open for good.'

Fran looked at him. He was enjoying the excitement, the anger, the increased activity. It was only child-like, but it filled her with unease. And there was no escaping it. Bethel's latest bulletins filled the kitchen, TV and radio were obsessed with the picket line, the local paper read like a supplement of *Coal News*. North-east miners had already lost millions of pounds in wages, but their leaders were asserting that they could not afford to lose the strike . . . 'the only way out is victory'. Once more the Falklands! No wonder Martin was confused.

Sooner or later she would have to talk to him about it, but first she would have to work out where she herself stood. There was right on both sides but eventually someone would have to give way. If it was the miners, there would be no holding Maggie Thatcher, and if the government was broken, anarchy would reign. Once more the Devil and the deep blue sea.

'Can I go down the beach?' Martin said, suddenly erupting back into the kitchen. 'It's a lovely day. And can I have some sarnies and an apple and some pop, and Gary says not to wear good shoes in case we have to plodge.' It was summer half-term and she ought to take him out somewhere, but the thought of five minutes' peace on her own was glorious. She gave him a bagful of sandwiches and a can of Coke, and warned him against drowning. 'I am getting better,' she thought as she waved him away. 'I am learning to let him go.'

She was thinking of afternoon tea when Bethel arrived. 'His lordship's on his way in. He says you'll be glad to see him, even if I'm not.' As usual when she spoke of Walter her face was poker-like but she turned to fill the kettle before she removed her hat. The next moment there was the ritual shout from the open door.

'Howay! Howay! Two of you in there gobbing on, and me

stranded.' Fran left Bethel to manhandle the wheelchair, and got out cups and saucers.

'Aye, well . . .' he said, when he was settled. His shirt collar was as crisp as ever, and once more Fran wondered if Bethel did his laundry. He spread his hands on the tartan rug that was strapped about his legs and regarded them solemnly, turning them palm upwards for a closer look. A heavy sigh followed and Fran could not repress a grin at the thought of what would come next. 'You'd think,' he said solemnly, 'that a woman of Sally Bethel's age would be above lying to a poor feller that's bound to a chair. But no, she's not. "Come in, Walter," she says, nice as ninepence. "The tea's all brewed. Biscuits ready, home-made." Gets you in with a nice little tarradiddle, and the bloody kettle's not even on. And I bet it's packet biscuits. Pap!' Bethel went stolidly about the tea-making as though she had not heard but Fran was willing to wheedle.

'What would you say to chocolate bourbons?'

He sniffed. 'They'll do. But it's tea I want. Now! I'm clammin'.'

Though he had lost the use of his legs he was still every inch a man. 'If he'd been nearer my age I'd have given you a run for your money,' Fran had told Bethel once.

'You can have him,' Bethel had sniffed with a nonchalance that convinced no one.

Now, as they sipped their tea, she told them of Fenwick's notice.

'There'll be trouble,' Walter said. 'Still, he's made his row and he's hoeing it.'

Bethel's snort was a masterpiece. 'They'd better not cross my path. He has his rights . . . a lad that's lived here all his life. Half of this lot causing trouble's incomers.'

Walter put down his cup. 'There's the Tory talking.' But he spoke automatically, as though he half-agreed.

'I'm no Tory, Walter, but I'll tell you what . . . this carry-on has a chance to make me Tory. They're acting themselves like animals, some of them. I class myself better than that. Billy Fenwick would have stuck out if they'd left well alone, but no – it's do what we say, or else! So he's going to show them. And he'll not be the last. What else can single lads do? They've got no social to depend on – it's work or starve.'

'You do not scab, Sally. That's the miner's Bible, that. You do not cross a picket line. You might have doubts, you might not like the cause, but you *never* scab. You have your say in the meeting, then you accept the democratic decision.'

Bethel leaned forward. 'You don't fool me, Walter, not for a moment. You keep on spouting, but you don't like what's going on any more than I do, do you?'

His brows bristled. 'I don't like scabs.'

'Answer the question, Walter. You don't like what's going on any more than I do.'

He put his hands on the chair wheels and moved a little backwards. For once he was seeking words, and Fran was amazed.

'Well, no, I don't . . . But that doesn't affect the issue, Sally. We can't all be ruled by slop. Oh, poor Fenwick, let's all have a sob for Fenwick – that's not the main issue. You've got a woman in Downing Street that hates the working class. You've got a Yank in the Coal Board that hates the human race. I've got no room for Scargill – he's a bloody fool, or else a bloody agitator – and your average miner doesn't like him either. But they hate Maggie! And they despise MacGregor, for all his power! They'll not stick out for love of Arthur Scargill, they'll stick out to show her she can't beat the miners. They'll eat grass to prove that. If I had legs, I'd be out there with them, and don't you believe anything else.'

Long after they had gone and the tea things were washed and put to dry, Fran was remembering Walter's words, or rather the feeling behind them. The strike was escalating now, for all the papers might say about deadlock. Feelings were sharpening on both sides, you could sense it in the air. She got out her knitting and tried to concentrate on the matinée coat she was knitting for Treesa's baby – white with a touch of lemon.

She had collected the layette as Treesa had asked her: three polythene carriers and a soap-powder box containing a potty and some plastic bath toys. She added her own store of baby clothes, and then looked through for omissions. Hence the matinée coat.

There was a visitor by Treesa's bed when she reached the ward later that day: Terry Malone, scrubbed till he shone, blue denim neatly pressed and red hair slicked down. He leaped to his feet when he saw Fran. 'Sit here, Mrs Drummond. It's good of you to come.'

Fran felt *de trop*, but to turn and go would cause further embarrassment. 'I wish I'd known you were coming,' she said. 'I could've given you a lift.' Treesa looked rested now, her hair brushed and looped up with slides. Only the swollen belly beneath the bedclothes betrayed maturity. 'Not long now,' Terry said, nodding at the bump and blushing furiously, when Fran caught his eye.

Treesa smiled. 'It can't come too soon for me.'

Terry was fumbling with his jacket pocket. 'I brought you these . . . I forgot.'

Her eyes widened. 'Peppermint creams! Lovely!'

As they ripped off the cellophane, Fran watched them. Two kids, still with the round faces of childhood. No trace of militancy in Terry tonight, but the scarred hands were surprisingly large and strong. He must be nineteen or twenty. She accepted a peppermint cream and wondered how to get away. 'I expect your mother's dying to see the baby. It'll be her first grandchild, won't it?'

For the first time, Treesa's brow clouded. 'I suppose she is. She doesn't say much.' Terry's shoulders hunched under the blue denim and he rubbed his chin on his T-shirt. 'You did get the baby things, didn't you?' Treesa asked.

Fran nodded. 'Yes, they're safe. And I've added a few things I'd been saving . . . if you want them.'

She saw Treesa smile and then suddenly redden, realizing what lay behind the gift. There was silence for a moment and then Terry cleared his throat. 'How're doing for coal, Mrs Drummond? If you've got nowt left I can get you a bag from the mineral line. It's wick with duff, that place. I'm digging it out for me mam, so you only need to say.'

Suddenly he was Brian . . . *'It's nee trouble, Mrs Drummond,'* was what Brian used to say when she was down and desperate, and missing David.

'I'm fine at the moment, Terry. But I'll remember if I get stuck.' No point in telling him she needed high-grade coke to fuel the boiler. Why kick a gift-horse in the teeth?

She left them, leaning towards each other across the jacquard cover, and as she walked away she wondered how they felt about one another. Was it loyalty to a dead brother's child that had brought Terry here? Or gratitude that made Treesa's face light at the sight of him? If it was love . . . or anything like love . . . it was a fairy tale, and those were thin on the ground in 1984.

Thinking about them disquieted her. That, or the thought of the coming baby. She sat behind the wheel, a hand against her chest, wondering if the burning sensation beneath her ribs was angst or indigestion. She felt flat and over-excited at one and the same time, unwilling to move and yet unable to stay still. In the end she switched on the engine and turned towards the town centre. She had not arranged to see Steve, had even vowed to stay away from him tonight, but nothing less would still her agitation.

'Fancy a curry?' Fran said when Steve answered the door. 'Chicken Bhuna, double pulao, poppadums and a bindi bhaji?' She decanted them on to the table, refusing to think about what they had cost, and took off her jacket.

She told him about Fenwick as they ate. 'It sounds pretty terrible,' he said.

'It is. How much longer can it go on – before something dreadful happens?'

Steve shook his head. 'It won't finish this month. Or next. Scargill's hanging on for the end of the summer, isn't he? That's when power cuts would bite. If he can keep going till October, he's cracked it.'

She pushed away her plate. 'You can't be serious? October! That's four months away.' If it went on until winter, there would be no trees left, no fences. Fenwick would have vanished beneath the onslaught and would never fly pigeons again.

Long after, when they lay together in Steve's bed, it was

Fenwick's face she saw imprinted on her closed lids, the new,
austere Fenwick, who had not a friend in the world. Soon he
would leave his neat council house with its looped lace curtains
and run a gauntlet of hate to the pit. Before the strike began,
miners' wives had heckled Scargill when he visited Sunderland.
Now those same women, or at least some of them, were
supporting him. When a safety worker had been killed in the pit
recently they had withdrawn the official picket, but one woman
had declared it a fitting end for a scab. She would have told
Steve about that too – but his mouth was sealing hers, cutting off
breath, banishing unpleasant thoughts to some far-off box-room
of the mind where they could stay until morning.

9

Sunday, 17 June 1984

She moved the car forward and got out to close the garage doors
behind them.

'Hurry up, darling.' Martin was struggling with dog and lead,
and shrugging into his anorak at the same time. Fran resisted the
impulse to interfere; he hated it when she made a fuss. She was
trying to look nonchalant when Bethel came round the corner,
indignation in every line. Fran dispensed with formal greetings.
'What's happened?'

'What's happened? You might well ask.' Suddenly she cast an
uneasy glance in Martin's direction and dropped her voice. It
was too late. He was pretending to fiddle with the lead but his
ears were cocked like Mr Spock's. 'Animals . . . that's what they
are. Not fit to live in a decent society.' Fran struggled to hold her
tongue, knowing the penalties of interruption. 'Someone's nailed
a dead pigeon to Fenwick's door.'

Fran shuddered. 'Who did it?'

Bethel's brows flew skywards. 'They've done it. *Them!* By,
you're slow! He said he was going back tomorrow, didn't he, so

they showed him. There's spray paint everywhere. *"Learn the scab,"* it says on the door. *"Stop out or else."'*

Martin's face was grim, lower lip trembling and tears not far away. As Fran bundled him into the car, Bethel spoke. 'They've spoiled their bloody selves. He's no blackleg, he was only talking. But he'll go in now, all right, and God help anyone that gets in his way.'

The dog had got caught in its lead and was yelping discomfort. 'You're never taking it through the town?' Bethel reached for the squirming body. 'Give 'im here. I'll walk him down the allotments, but he better behave himself. You can't take a dog to a christening.'

Fran smiled her thanks and slid behind the wheel. Nee-wan would be better off with Bethel. She looked at Martin, who was still struggling with the news of the pigeon's death. He was too soft-hearted, that was the trouble. And wanton destruction was hard to take at any age.

They were passing the pit when Martin spoke, the question she had been dreading. 'Whose side are you on, Mam?' The pit was deserted and still, except for the police van in the entrance, a bored copper slumped behind the wheel.

'I don't know, Martin. But they shouldn't have hurt Mr Fenwick's pigeons.' That, at least, was clear.

'Who did it?'

She moved up a gear and shook her head. 'I don't know.' Mustn't tell him about the ski-masked men. 'Someone who was angry, I suppose.'

His tone was impatient. 'I know that. But I mean who would do it . . . no one we know?' It was a plea for reassurance.

'No, Martin, no one we know would behave like that.'

She hoped he was convinced by the lie. They knew everyone in Belgate – well almost everyone – so chances were they knew the pigeon-killers. Perhaps the one who had brushed by her was a neighbour, a fresh-faced boy who whistled his way to the pit and had 'Dire Straits' embroidered on his denim jacket. She was glad when they left Belgate behind and the pit could be forgotten for a little while.

They had almost reached the town centre when she remembered David. It was strange – for long periods now she didn't think about his death or the happiness that had preceded it. And yet she loved him more than ever. The trouble was that living reasserted itself, whether you liked it or not. Once she had been whole, single of purpose. Now there was one Fran who loved David, one who almost loved Steve, and one who increasingly loved no one and yearned to find something . . . but what? She indicated a left turn towards Eve's and resolved to stop philosophizing. She had no talent for it and it never got you anywhere, anyway. That was why she got such low marks for philosophy: it was like trying to hold water in a sieve.

As soon as she entered Eve's living room she knew something was wrong. 'I'll tell you later,' Eve said. 'Does this dress look all right? I've had to let it out at the waist.'

Harold was holding the baby like a wand of office. 'Here you are, godmother. Over to you. Are we all ready? It's twenty past.'

Fiona and Elaine were dressed in Laura Ashley prints with wide pink sashes. They watched critically as she gathered their baby brother into her arms. 'This baby's going to be ruined,' Fran said, wiping a bubble from the fat pink mouth.

'He's gained four ounces,' Fiona said. 'That's an awful lot.'

She looked at Fran, defying contradiction. Fran pulled a face to indicate that she was suitably impressed and shifted the baby to her other arm. Elaine looked dubious above the pie-crust collar. Life was always difficult for a second child. Fran put out a hand and touched her cheek. 'He's lucky to have sisters like you.'

They trooped out to the waiting cars, Fran given precedence as godmother. The baby slept in her arms, gorged on milk. 'He should be OK till we get back,' Eve said anxiously. She smelled of milk, and suddenly Fran was reminded of childhood holidays, up in the hayloft, cows lowing in their stalls, a nest of kittens under the eaves suckling from an alert mother cat.

And then they were in church and she was straining to catch every word so that she could fulfil her role. Behind her Min was tanned and elegant in white crunchy knitted cotton, and strangely enigmatic. Perhaps she was put out at not being chosen godmother – if so, they would certainly hear of it. And what had Eve meant when she said, 'Tell you later'? The baby stirred in her arms and she rocked it gently. It was strange to be standing there before the blue and red stained glass, holding a baby that was not your own, making vows that were seldom if ever kept. 'I baptize thee David Ian.' She looked at the sleeping face, puckered as though with all the cares of the world, and made her own promises. She would love this baby, take an interest, never ever allow herself to envy Eve's possession of him. She would be good! Thoughts of all the other times she had vowed to be good rose up in her mind and were sternly put down. Church was a place for new beginnings.

She walked out into the sunlight and handed the baby to Eve so that the polaroids could have their fill. Fiona and Elaine jostled to get on either side of their mother and the new baby. 'He'll be a little prince,' Fran thought, 'adored by all his women.' Harold was doing his David Bailey act, coming on with the camera from every angle.

'Doesn't it make you sick,' Min murmured in her ear.

Fran kept on watching the display. 'I don't know, Min. It's a special day . . . nice to have mementos.' When Martin had been christened, David had made a ciné film and screened it *ad nauseam*. She turned to look for Martin. He was standing a little way off with Min's Althea, Peter and James. They all had a faintly deprived expression, as though Fiona and Elaine were getting an unfair share of the limelight. Min had followed her eyes. 'Jealousy gets you nowhere,' she called out, and when Althea, the eldest, scowled – 'Your face'll stick like that one of these days.'

Dennis moved protectively towards his children. 'Race you back to the car,' he said, ruffling Peter's hair and hugging the toddler, James, against him. He reached out and tweaked Martin's tie into place. 'That's better,' he said, and Martin smiled.

The fatherly gesture touched Fran. 'You're lucky to have Dennis,' she said, but Min had already turned away and if she heard she gave no sign. The cameras stopped clicking and people began to drift towards the cars. It was over and it hadn't hurt at all. Well, hardly at all.

Back at the house she handed out sherry, then wine, refilled buffet tables, acted the perfect godmother and best friend. Eve's thanks were fervent. 'I couldn't have managed without you, Fran.'

As they waited in the kitchen for coffee to brew, their eyes met across the hissing percolators. 'What are we going to do about Min?' Eve said suddenly. 'No good pretending it's going to go away. I've tried that. She actually wanted me to ask him here today. Here! With Dennis!'

'What do you mean?' Fran asked.

Eve put down the cream jug. 'You mean you don't know?'

Fran shook her head. 'I haven't a clue.'

Eve crossed to the door and closed it. 'We'll have to be quiet. Dennis is just outside the door.' She pursed her lips. 'You remember Hindson-Evans, the surgeon from the Infirmary? You met him at Min's.'

Fran nodded. She had loathed Richard Hindson-Evans on sight, so it had been no trouble to refuse his invitation to dinner.

'Well, Min's having an affair with him. I wouldn't believe it at first . . . when Sally told me I went down her neck. But it's true. And she wanted him here today! I thought you knew – Sally was simply broadcasting it! But of course you live in Siberia. I said no when she asked me to invite him here – she tried to look wounded and astonished, but I was quite firm. Harold nearly had a fit. He can't understand why Dennis doesn't twig. She'll get no encouragement from me. And if I *had* asked him . . . well, Harold's foaming, I can tell you; I wouldn't put it past him to take Hindson-Evans by the lapels. Not that I blame *him* . . . well, it's man's way, isn't it? They take what they're offered.'

So that was how Eve's mind worked. All men were natural marauders and not to be held responsible. It was up to women to be chaste. That was probably why she never took her eyes off Harold, in case he gave way to primeval impulses. The thought of Harold beating his pinstriped chest was so lovely that Fran smiled.

'It's no laughing matter, Fran. She'll never get away with it. And asking me to lie for her! I'm shocked. She's always been headstrong but this . . . I hardly dared tell Harold. He says we should say something to Dennis, but I keep hoping she'll come to her senses.'

Fran held up a hand. 'Whoa. What has she asked you to lie about?'

Eve took a deep breath. 'She wants to go to a conference with him. A drug company's paying. Two nights at the London Hilton. She's cock-a-hoop about it. "Back me up to Dennis," she says. "I'll say I'm going to visit an old schoolfriend, and you back me up."'

'She hadn't any friends at school, except us,' Fran said, 'and we're here.'

Eve nodded. 'Exactly what I told her. He'll be on to it straight away.'

Harold came into the kitchen then, and Eve made a great show of making coffee. They carried the pots out to the waiting guests, trying hard not to look at Min, draped elegantly across a ladder-backed chair.

'Coffee, Min?'

Min put out a languid hand. 'I'd rather have a drink, Fran. Has Harold locked up the rest of the booze?'

Fran had emptied her tray. 'I think there's some Asti in the kitchen.'

Min unwound from the chair. 'Lead on, Macduff.'

They filled two glasses and consigned the empty bottle to the waste-bin. 'Here's to crime,' Min said and clinked glasses. Fran's cheeks felt hot. Was she supposed to know? Min's eyes were twinkling. 'Come on then, give me a rocket. Everyone else has. I'll rue the day and all that sort of thing.'

Fran shrugged. 'It's not up to me to criticize, Min. But I hope you know what you're doing.'

Min was examining her perfect oval nails. 'It's just a bit of fun. Richard's here at a loose end and Dennis is out several nights a week. I meet Richard now and then for a laugh, that's all.'

Fran wanted to ask about the London Hilton but didn't dare. 'Cheer up,' Min said, draining her glass. 'You've gone all goody-goody like Eve. I can't stand two of you doing a Saint Joan. I thought you'd understand.'

Fran was saved from having to reply by the advent of Valerie.

Her eyes flicked from face to face, but she feigned nonchalance. 'We need another pot of coffee ... and Harold's aunty wants tea.'

As she filled the kettle, Fran wondered how long it would be before Dennis found out. Already half a dozen people were in the know, and a secret was something known by one person.

Harold buttonholed her when she appeared with the tea and grilled her about money. 'I hope you've had second thoughts about the house, Fran? Get it on the market and move back here. You'd be far better off. I'm not saying anything against Belgate, but it's no place to bring up David's son – especially at the moment. He's ready to change schools and God knows what their idea of secondary education is. And if you were nearer, I could keep an eye on your finances. No use having a friend who's an accountant if you don't make use of him.'

Fran tried to look as though she was paying attention, but she could hear the children whooping and hollering around the garden. Harold was proud of his flowerbeds: if Martin trampled the carefully planted annuals she would simply die! Her own garden had grown rampant with summer, straying over paths and straggling on walls. The garden had been David's province; now it was up to her.

'You will do that, won't you, Fran?' Harold was waiting for an answer and she gave him a fervent assurance. Anything for peace.

10

Friday, 29 June 1984

There was no one about as she passed the pit. Morning was the time for pickets, but the police van still lurked in the gateway, its occupants trying to look unobtrusive and thereby looking ridiculous. She felt hot and sticky, in need of a bath and a long drink and a seat in front of the telly to watch Wimbledon. When David was alive he had always made a fuss of her in Wimbledon fortnight, doing the chores so she didn't miss the good bits, and once bringing her strawberries on a tray.

It was over a year since David had died. Impossible to believe that. On the day itself, she had gone alone to the cemetery and brushed dirt from the stone with her fingertips. '*David Alexander Drummond, a beloved husband and father.*' There would be no strawberries on a tray for Wimbledon, and no watching either. She had a million things to do before she went to visit Treesa, and all of them urgent.

'Sit down. I've got the kettle on. The bairn's had his tea.' The light of a good tale was in Bethel's eyes and it was not long before it spilled out. 'You know the Botcherbys? Halfway down Stafford Street? Poor-looking little thing, dyes her hair? She was a Connor before she wed, and they were a funny family. Any road, she's taken this strike badly. A maniac for the house she was, HP here, HP there. There's any amount like her, but they're not taking it so seriously.'

'What's happened to her?' She couldn't wait any longer for Bethel to spill the beans.

'Overdosed!' Bethel's tone was triumphant, which meant Mrs Botcherby had survived. Bethel never gloated over real tragedy. 'Took a bottle of sleeping pills and brought them back up. Sick all over the place. Botcherby fetched the woman over the road – she used to work in the fever hospital. She says it was in the bedclothes, on the carpet, all up the wall.'

By night-time, Fran thought wryly, it would be dripping from the chandelier. 'But she's all right.'

Mrs Botcherby of the bitten nails and the untouched roots was indeed all right, and probably all the better for a 'good clear-out' according to Bethel.

'I'm going to visit Treesa tonight,' Fran said, glad to broach a more cheerful subject.

Bethel lit a No. 6 and blew smoke. 'And that's another tragedy . . . a bairn coming into the world to nowt. She'll get no help off her own family and even less off that sackless lot.'

Fran felt prickings of indignation. 'I suppose you mean the Malones. I think they'll be very supportive. Mrs Malone loves babies, and it will be her first grandchild.'

Bethel's sniff would have done credit to a water buffalo. 'Yes, God help it. Of all the nutty varmints to have for a grandma, *she* takes the biscuit. Any road, I don't hold with all this free love, having bairns to fulfil yersel'. I'd've liked a bairn after Tommy went . . .' her words slowed as she thought of the young husband killed in the pit before his time, '. . . but I wasn't that selfish. You hear them on telly now – "Ooh, I must have a baby . . . I'm shopping around for a man to spark it off . . . I can rear it on me own." Go out and buy a doll if you feel like that, that's what I say. Don't bring a live bairn into the world to have no dad.' Their eyes met and she saw the dawning resentment in Fran's eyes. 'I'm not talking about people like you. You've been landed with a situation you had no hand in. I'm talking about women who say, "I want". Someone should tell them "I want" never gets.'

'Treesa's not like that,' Fran said defensively. 'She meant to get married . . . the wedding was fixed.'

Bethel's retort was sharp. 'Then she should've have kept her hand on her ha'penny till she left the church. Now look where she is . . . flat on her back in a hospital, and no place for her or the bairn when she comes out. There'll be compensation when they work it out but God knows when that'll be . . . or who'll get it. In the meantime, her mother'll take her in all right but she'll pay for it! You can be sure about that.'

As she drank her tea, Fran wondered what Bethel would say if she, Frances, were to become pregnant. Not that she would ever dare to confess it. She would rather face the Spanish Inquisition! She filed the worry of contraception away for later and asked for news of the strike.

The Malones, father and son, were still at loggerheads and Fenwick's windows had gone for the umpteenth time, although he was still only talking about going back to work. 'A lump of concrete *that* wide went clean through the quilt. His sister told me herself. Not that she's sticking up for him; she says he's caused more trouble than enough for her and her man . . . by, she's bitter. She says he's always been awkward.'

'He was happy enough when he had his pigeons,' Fran said. 'All he wanted was to be left alone to go to work. I don't think that's asking much. He talked about breaking the strike, but he probably never would have done it if they hadn't killed his pigeons.' Remembering that night, the padding footsteps in the dark, she shivered. 'What kind of men ... young men ... can kill defenceless birds?'

They were deep in argument over the effects of a) TV violence and b) the demise of corporal punishment, when there was a call from the back door. 'Hallo?' It was Manky Margot.

'What on earth is she doing here?' Fran thought, and then, 'I must stop calling her Manky. We're grown women now.'

In spite of the heat, Margot was wearing a shapeless knitted sweater in an indeterminate sludge colour, her only ornaments two badges, one for CND the other *Coal not Dole*. 'I couldn't pass your door without calling,' she said, flashing Bethel a wide smile that said, '*We're all sisters, aren't we, and class doesn't matter at all.*' The trouble was that to think class didn't matter implied that you recognized its existence, which seemed to make non-sense of the whole thing.

'Come in and sit down,' Fran said, suddenly remembering her manners. 'Would you like some tea?'

Bethel was preparing to go but she reached for the kettle.

'No, ta ... I'm awash with tea. We've made gallons of it for the boys. I've been lending a hand at the support centre. You knew we had the welfare hall? It's marvellous to see them come in and get a square meal. We've all got to help, haven't we? I know it's a fight for pits and jobs but it's the class thing, too – that's why they must stick out to the bitter end. We must all give till it hurts; that's why I'm through here every spare moment – pitching in.'

There was a dry cough from the doorway. 'I'll just be going.' The set of Bethel's jaw told it all: she had had enough.

Margot was on to the subject of women now. 'There'll have to be positive discrimination in the end. We've tried to change sexist attitudes with subtlety but it hasn't worked, so it'll have to be direct attack. We've formed a collective in Sunderland ... you must come along one night ... and we're making strides; but there'll never be equal participation without positive discrimination.'

Wicked thoughts were rising up in Fran's mind. Positive
discrimination was what Hitler had practised in favour of Aryan
blondes, and Paisley in favour of Ulster Protestants. Positive
discrimination was all right if you were doing it, and all wrong if
it was the other fellow. She looked at the clock. Ten to seven:
not enough time to enter into an argument, and she was not
going to be ashamed of her relief. 'I'm awfully sorry, Margot, but
I have to dash. I'm visiting a friend in hospital . . .'

Margot went, in a rush of promises to call again. 'I'll be
standing in whenever I can – I've told them at the office that I'm
taking all my lieu days. They understand.' Her tone implied that
any good liberal would, and, to her subsequent shame, Fran
nodded to indicate agreement. Anything to get Margot over the
step.

She had picked some flowers from the garden, and started
looking for a sheet of wrapping paper. She had found the
aquilegia among the knee-high grass. David had planted it two
summers ago and called her out to see the first blossoms. She
must find a way to cope with the grass and let the flowers
breathe. It was the least she could do. And she mustn't be
tempted to call on Steve again when she was in Sunderland. She
was becoming a nymphomaniac . . . or she would, if she wasn't
careful.

She gave up looking for the wrapping paper. Newsprint would
have to do. She was rolling the flowers in an old *Echo* when some
figures caught her eye. She looked at the date: 17 March, when
the figures of the regional ballots had been coming in. South
Derbyshire had been 83 per cent against, Northumberland 52
per cent for, but North Wales, Lancashire and the Midlands
were all two or three to one against. There had been a gradual
drift back in the Nottinghamshire coalfield and a call for a
national ballot everywhere. With that degree of opposition, how
had the strike ever got off the ground let alone lasted for four
months?

As she drove towards Sunderland she realized how little she had
done since she got home. She might as well have watched
Wimbledon, for all she had accomplished. Next weekend she

would let everything go and watch the finals. They wouldn't be able to go shopping anyway, for the money in the bank was dwindling rapidly: £998 at the last count. Less than four figures, and Martin would need kitting out completely for the winter. The thought depressed her so much she began to sing. '*When I'm faced with a day that's grey and cloudy, I stick out my chin and grin and say – tomorrow, tomorrow, I love you, tomorrow . . .*' When David died she had driven the roads screaming her agony, seeing startled faces as she flashed by. Now the same startled expressions greeted her vocal cords. She shut her mouth firmly on the last '*tomorrow*' and concentrated on the road.

Treesa's bed was empty when she reached the ward, but the young nurse was full of information. 'She's in the labour room. Her waters broke at three o'clock. Any time now, I should think. Her mother's waiting in the corridor. She'll probably be glad of some company.'

Treesa's mother was small and thin, a complete contrast to her daughter. 'Yes, we're not alike; she takes after her dad. They all do.' She looked as though the paternal resemblance gave her no pleasure. 'I don't know how it's going to work out, I'm sure. Thoughtless, that's what she's been. I've told her that. "It's all very well to be grown-up," I've told her. "You have to act grown-up. We've got no accommodation for a baby." Besides, I thought I'd put all that behind me – broken nights, and the clothes horse round the fire all the time – not that we have a fire at the moment, but that's another story. She'll have to buckle to and find somewhere. I've told her that. As soon as she's on her feet. I've told her that. And she'll have to chase up the compen. money. If the Malones get their hands on it, she won't see a penny for her or the baby. I've told her that.'

How awful to be told so many things when you were about to give birth, Fran thought. Poor Treesa. Poor little baby.

She looked at the wall and wondered why she was sitting in on a birth for the second time in weeks, she who had not been able to give birth at will. It wasn't fair. But life was never fair. It worked out how much you could bear and pushed you to the brink.

'It's a boy!' The baby was firmly wrapped in cellular cotton, a

face like a pink walnut the only thing on show. The staff nurse
held it in one arm and guided the foot of the trolley that bore
Treesa with her free hand. The porter at the other end was
whistling 'Memories', but he wasn't a patch on Elaine Paige.

'Are you all right, Treesa?' Her mother's tone implied that she
better had be.

'A bit sore, but that's all. Have you seen him?' Mrs Carruthers
nodded grimly, unwilling to acknowledge that an illegitimate
grandchild was anything else but a drawback. 'Yes. He's very
nice.'

Fran leaned to squeeze Treesa's arm above the plastic name
tag. 'He's beautiful.' There was a streak of dried, bloody mucus
on her arm and a terrible odour of antiseptic.

When Treesa was safely in the ward and the baby whisked to
the nursery, they sat either side of the bed. 'How many stitches
did you have? They won't send you home too soon, will they? I'm
counting on a day or two to get put straight.'

Treesa's eyes were half-closed and there was a terrible
resignation about her mouth. 'I don't know, Mam . . . I don't
know how many stitches I had . . . I don't know how they go on.'

Birth shouldn't be like this, it should be joyful! Fran made one
or two efforts to deflect Mrs Carruthers, but she was indefatig-
able. 'You'll have to go round the councillors, Treesa. Tell them
you've lived here all your life and you must have a place. Say we
can't keep you.' No wonder Treesa had loved Brian Malone: like
all the Malones he took life a day at a time, trimming his sails to
whichever wind was blowing.

When the bell signalled the end of visiting time, they left the
ward together. 'I wish I could give you a lift, Mrs Carruthers, but
I'm not going back to Belgate yet.'

She waited till the other woman was out of sight before she
ran back to the ward. 'I won't be a moment,' she told the startled
staff nurse. 'It's something urgent I forgot.'

Treesa's eyes were closed and sweat gleamed in the blurred
sockets. 'Treesa, I know you're dying to go to sleep . . . it's just
that I've been thinking. We have so much room, Martin and I,
plenty of room for you and a baby . . . if you'd like to come?'

Treesa was nothing if not honest. 'Oh, Mrs Drummond . . .
I've been praying you'd say that!'

As she drove towards Eve's, Fran felt mingled delight and
terror. To have a baby in the house again . . . would that be
unalloyed pleasure? Or exquisite pain? Treesa had promised to
pay her way, so it wouldn't rock the financial boat and the
company would be nice. And nice or not, she wouldn't have sent
a hyena back to Mrs Carruthers' tender mercies. All the same –
lodgers! When she'd suggested them after David's death, Harold
had thrown up his hands in horror. However would she break
the news to him?

She reached the corner that led to Steve's flat and turned
resolutely in the opposite direction. Mustn't importune. The
trouble was, she was not cut out to be on her own; she was meant
to be half of a whole. She thought of him in bed, muscled
forearms lying on top of the duvet, his hair rumpled on his brow.
Gwen had said he was a bit like Richard Gere and it was true. If
he proposed properly she would properly say yes. Except that
people would disapprove, and she couldn't bear that. On the
other hand, if she turned him down, could she live without him?
Anyway, she didn't have to decide just now. Steve was preoccu-
pied of late – bowed down with worry about his business
probably. The strike was beginning to affect everyone. She
shivered, remembering what Steve had said about it lasting till
October or November. The sky was high and clear, the moon a
kindly face. She banished thoughts of General Winter from her
mind and opened her mouth to sing.

11

Saturday, 7 July 1984

'Well, I only hope you won't come to regret it.' Bethel's tone
implied that Fran undoubtedly would, but she still bustled
around the spare bedroom, making everything spick and span.

'It looks nice, doesn't it?' Fran said placatingly.

'All right,' Bethel said. 'At least there's plenty of room.'

Fran had always loved the spare bedroom, with its white walls and blue and white curtains. Perhaps, subconsciously, she had made it a nursery for David's baby that was never to be. Anyway, it was perfect for Treesa and Brian Christopher. Bethel had snorted when she heard the chosen names: '*He'll need St Christopher to find his way around that lot.*' Nevertheless, she had worked hard to get ready for the homecoming. Fran said, 'I love you, Bethel.'

The older woman sighed. 'There you go again. Slop, slop, slop. That's why you get nowt done. Too much jaw.'

While Bethel peeled potatoes for lunch, Fran popped to the corner shop. For once she was not the only customer. Two women stood at the end of the counter holding on to a large cardboard box. The shopkeeper was packing it with goods – a plastic bag of potatoes, sugar, two packets of dried peas, a bottle of tomato sauce. So somebody at least had money. Behind Fran the doorbell jangled and someone entered the shop. One of the two women looked up and nudged her neighbour. The other woman turned her head, gold earrings swinging at the movement, and regarded the newcomer. Fran was dying to turn round, but it would look too obvious – and something was certainly up. The shopkeeper's professional smile turned into a fixed grin that suggested terror more than bonhomie. He looked appealingly at the women. 'Shall I just serve Mrs Mather?' He turned to the newcomer. 'Is it much, Mrs Mather?'

As she advanced to the counter, fumbling with her purse, the two women at the end of the counter began to converse. 'By, I could do with something nice for me tea. A nice bit of roast pig . . . I mean pork . . .'

Her stooge was quick to respond. 'It's the only way I do like pig . . . I mean pork. Roasted. That's what you do with pigs. Fry them.'

Fran couldn't resist a peep at the shopkeeper and his customer. She had pointed to a punnet of tomatoes and he was putting them on to the scales, fumbling in his haste to get her served and out of his shop before there was trouble. As Fran watched she saw that the woman's mouth was set to cover a tremble, and her hands clasped and unclasped her purse, just as Mrs Botcherby's had done. But this was no striker's wife, not if she could afford tomatoes.

She paid for her purchases and turned, but the sight of the tomatoes had enraged the other woman. 'It's all right for some isn't it?' They were talking to one another but their remarks were for broadcasting. 'Them as don't mind breeding pigs. Pigs can afford tomatoes. Snouts in the bloody trough. Still, we'll be the ones that's laughing before long. Fenwick got the message; he's seen sense. The pigs'll have to take the consequences, won't they?'

The bell jangled, the door closed. The shopkeeper turned back to the box and threw in two or three cans of food. 'There now, is that OK?'

The gold-earringed woman pulled a doubting face. 'We're short of washing-up liquid. All them dishes. Still, if you can't manage . . .' He reached for a small Fairy Liquid, hesitated, and then chose the largest size.

They hefted the box between them and made for the door. Fran held it open for them and received a nod for her pains. The door closed and the bell ceased to jangle.

'By God, that's shortened my life.' The shopkeeper was wiping his brow, and Fran looked at him inquiringly. 'They're from the support group . . . well, they *are* the support group, the rest's just followers. In here every week for a load like that, and I'm not taking twopence ha'penny.' He gestured to the shelves. 'This shop's getting galloping alopecia, bald spots everywhere, but I can't afford to restock. Try telling the wholesale you'll pay them when the strikes over. They'd laugh in your face! And I'm not the only one – we had a meeting last week, retailers from all over the coalfield. It's the same story everywhere. You've got your regular customers, good payers when they had the money . . . you can't see them go without, can you? I've got women never ticked on in their lives. They come in here and you can see the pain of it on their faces. Humiliation. And then there's the other lot. If I want customers after the strike, I've got to keep them sweet now . . . so I filled their box. Nobody's balloted *me* about the strike; it's pay your dues or else. There'll be wholesale bankruptcies before this lot's over.'

Fran nodded sympathy – she hadn't liked the look of the two women. On the other hand she would murder to feed Martin, so how could she blame them for what they were doing? 'Who was the other customer? The one who bought the tomatoes?'

He shook his head. 'I'm sorry for her. She's a widow. One son. Her man was a miner, got dust, took his redundancy, and snuffed it. But the son's a copper. Bright young lad, used to do a paper round for me . . . did it for years. Never missed a day, rain or shine. He was a police cadet and then he joined the Northumbria Constabulary.'

'So he doesn't work round here?' Fran said.

'No, but he visits. And they know who and what he is. Talk about Northern Ireland – they'd put a bullet in his back as soon as look at you.'

He put his hands on the counter and leaned forward, his face sombre. 'Mrs Drummond, I don't have political opinions. Half the time I don't bother to vote. It makes no difference who's in power; we suffer. I don't see how you can keep uneconomical pits open, and I don't see how you can shut them and toss whole communities on the scrap heap. But I do know someone's to blame for this lot . . . neighbour against neighbour, father against son, miner against miner, lads that have grown up in a community afraid to come back to see their mothers. Someone somewhere's to blame for that . . . And I hope they think shame of themselves.'

It was a relief to get back home, even though she was immediately called to arbitrate in another row. 'He says the baby's more his than ours.' Martin was bristling with pride of ownership, and Gary was looking to Fran for justice.

'He doesn't belong to anybody . . . he's himself,' Fran said, weakly, and then caught Gary's reproachful eye. 'Well . . .' If she went into Gary's position as uncle she might get into deep water, but there was no escape. 'Well . . . Gary is Christopher's uncle, because Christopher's daddy was his brother. So in a way it *is* more his.' Gary was looking decidedly mollified, even smug. 'But Christopher will be living here for a while, so you'll be sort of a big brother.' Pride stirred in her as Martin assumed a modest expression and did not gloat. It was incredibly easy to talk to children really: they never raised irrelevant issues like illegitimacy, they were more concerned with possession.

'I'm turning this oven off now,' Bethel roared from the kitchen. 'If you can't be bothered to eat it, I might as well not've cooked it.' They sat round the table, munching cheerfully, four sets of legs underneath to jostle. If she married Steve they would move away, leave behind this funny house with its even funnier kitchen. And then the ambulance was drawing up at the door with Treesa and the baby, and it was time to think of someone other than herself.

'Aye, he's a bonny bairn all right. I see his dad in him.' Bethel was being unusually magnanimous in admitting the Malone strain. Now she looked up at Treesa. 'You look peaky. You want to get yersel' built up. Calf's-foot jelly, that's what you want, not this chemical muck they give you nowadays.' She extolled the virtues of Scott's Emulsion and stout, whilst she donned her hat and coat and left in a blaze of injunctions to the children. 'You'll have that baby a bundle of nerves if you don't stop your carry-on. And help your mam and Treesa.' Her parting shot was directed at Gary. 'You've got no home to go to, I suppose . . . or not what most people would call a one.'

When the children had drunk their fill of the baby and zoomed out of the house, Fran sat down opposite Treesa. 'How do you feel? I remember when I brought Martin home, I felt so weak! How'm I going to manage, I thought. But I did.'

They drank tea and discussed the pros and cons of living together. 'This is nice,' Fran thought. 'Like having a sister.' When the baby cried she picked him up and soothed him, moving him instinctively to her shoulder where he hiccuped wind and tiny gobbets of undigested milk.

'He's marked your dress,' Treesa said apologetically.

'It doesn't matter,' Fran said. Nothing mattered except the unfocused blue eyes that fixed on her face as though it held the secret of the universe.

She was about to ask when Treesa's mother would be calling when the phone shrilled in the hall. It was Linda. 'I'm just ringing to say your invite's on the way. Eddy's made it out for Fran and partner, so bring a feller.' Fran didn't know which was

the bigger shock, the double invitation or the idea of Edward as
Eddy. It conjured up a whole new persona. Eddys made saucy
jokes, got holes in their socks, made love on the hearthrug or in
the bath. Where had immaculate, precise Edward gone? 'Did
you hear what I said? He'll be very welcome.'

Fran demurred. 'It's very kind, Linda, but I'm sure you've
more than enough as it is. Besides, he has his children on
Saturdays . . .'

Linda was not at all fazed. 'Bring them . . . they'll be company
for my lot and your Martin. He's included of course . . . our
Debbie's made sure of that.' Her tone changed, becoming less
certain. 'Did you manage to get that book?'

It was time for a whopping lie. 'No. It's out of print. But I've
got all the gen from one of the women on the course, so I'll pop
over next week and fill you in.'

She *had* been able to get a book on wedding etiquette, a silver-
backed volume packed with advertisements. She had looked for
the section on second marriage and found it towards the end. It
advised soft pedalling on everything the second time around.
'Discreet dress' obviously meant sackcloth and ashes; 'no ostentation at the reception' meant send out an apology with the
invitation; and the final straw was a recommendation to dispense
with bridesmaids and music. She had sent it spinning into the
wastepaper basket. One marriage in three was second time
around now, but no one seemed to have realized. There was no
way she was going to cast Linda down when she was so happy.
'Gwen says you should do what you did the first time,' she said,
'but I'll give you the details later.'

She was about to put down the receiver when Linda cleared
her throat. 'By the way, Fran, I've been meaning to say this . . .
ta for the introduction. I'm going to make him happy, you can be
sure of that.'

When she got back to the living room she found Mrs Malone
had arrived and was cooing over the baby. 'He's like his dad,'
she said, pushing at one tiny fist with her forefinger. A tear
gathered in the corner of her eye and ran down the fat cheek.
'He didn't have much hair, our Brian. But what a good bairn.'

Behind her Terry grinned. 'Not like me, you mean. I bet I was a right little sod.'

His mother looked at him indulgently. 'Still are,' she said. She turned towards Fran. 'It's a relief she's here, Mrs Drummond. We're not that well placed, but I wouldn't have seen her beaten. It'll be different when they get the compen. sorted out. It's the bairn's by right, no doubt about that. His and Treesa's. It's only a pity they want it proving.'

Fran nodded. The legal wheels were grinding slowly. No one knew what to do about a baby born to a miner long dead in the pit. 'Not that she needs to worry,' Mrs Malone said. 'If they reckon it's ours, we'll pass it straight on. No fear about that.'

Treesa was raising her arms, proffering the sleeping baby to Terry. 'I can't hold bairns,' he said awkwardly, but he took it just the same. 'There's a good lad,' he said to the sleeping head. 'You lie quiet for your Uncle Tel.'

Fran tiptoed away and made tea, carrying it in on a tray. 'You shouldn't've bothered,' Mrs Malone said, but Fran could see she was pleased.

'You didn't hear the news,' Treesa said. 'Terry's just been telling us – Fenwick's taking the union to court.'

Fran handed out tea. 'Can he do that?'

Terry looked suddenly more mature, launched on to his favourite subject. 'Oh yes, Mrs Drummond, an individual member can take legal action. He won't win because he's got no case, but he's entitled to try. What the lodge wants to know is who's behind him. He didn't think that up on his own, and he won't be paying for it.'

'He could be getting legal aid,' Fran ventured.

Terry shook his head. 'I hope not . . . seeing as none of our lads are allowed it.' His expression was bitter.

'I thought everyone got it, unless they were rich?' Fran remarked.

'It's like a lot of things, Mrs Drummond. They look all right till you come to rely on them.'

'Like being insured for everything except what got on fire?' Fran said, and he nodded.

'It's a pity he's done this. It'll only make things worse, prolong

the dispute, cause more bitterness . . . Still, like I said, he's got
the right.'

Mrs Malone had been silent; now she sighed. 'I doubt things
can get worse. I never thought I'd see a bairn of mine not
speaking to his own father.' She looked at Fran. 'I'm not saying
anything I haven't said already. There's no excuse for two grown
men being at loggerheads under one roof.' She leaned forward
and tickled the baby's cheek. 'I mind on when you were like this,
our Terry, and your dad carried you everywhere. Our Brian was
always my bairn, and you were your dad's. And now this.'

Fran looked at the young face, as resolute as the north face of
the Eiger. 'He knows my views.'

Mrs Malone turned back to Frances. 'See what I mean?'

Long after they'd gone the unhappiness hung in the room.
'It'll get over, Treesa,' Fran said. 'When they get back to work,
the bitterness'll go.'

Treesa shifted the baby to her other arm. 'I'm not so sure,
Mrs Drummond. They feel it deep, both of them. Both sure
they're right.'

'Who do you think is in the right?' Fran asked, but Treesa
shook her head.

'It's too deep for me. I only wish Brian'd been here. They
wouldn't have fallen out if he'd been between them.'

Steve rang at half past nine. 'Is she settled in? And you'll be
drooling over the baby, I suppose . . . We went to the park, then
I fried chips for tea. It's far too hot for chips, but they won't
touch salad. Julie didn't eat anything as usual, but Ian made up
for it. He's shooting up.' There was always pride in his voice
when Steve spoke of his children. 'Anyway,' he said at last,
'what's the news of your wayward friend?'

Fran laughed. 'You mean Min? Nothing new. She's still
planning her illicit weekend and Eve's having kittens about it.
The one good thing about it is it's stopped her having those
ghastly girls' nights. She's too taken up with her boyfriend.'

'What about *your* boyfriend? When does he get to see you?'

She smiled into the mouthpiece. 'Boyfriend? I haven't got a
boyfriend.'

His voice dropped. 'You have, you know. And he misses you. It's no cop, me here and you ten miles away.'

She tut-tutted. 'You're exaggerating, it's only eight miles.'

'Eight inches would be too much right now. I love you, Frances. I want you. I need you.'

She went into the kitchen and spread out the books she needed for her essay on 'The Learning Situation'. She tried to concentrate on Piaget, but her mind wandered. For some reason she kept thinking about Min. Nowadays she looked like the cat who was getting the cream – which was funny, really, because she had always moaned about sex: '*You have to go on with it, it's the price you pay for marriage. But that doesn't mean you have to like it.*' Now, if Sally were to be believed, she was at it like knives. Perhaps she was attracted to his being a doctor? Or forbidden fruit, the ultimate aphrodisiac? In any event, she wasn't suffering pangs of guilt. Not visibly. 'Not like me,' Fran said aloud and for good measure wrote it on her nice clean page.

Why couldn't she be permissive? Not promiscuous, just reasonably carefree? Instead hell and VD were ever-present threats. Her mother's teaching had been specific: if you were wicked, you went to rot and bits dropped off ... but Min was visibly blooming, waxing on her sin. Life was one long enigma. She, who did like sex, tried to keep out of one man's bed; and Min, who did not, had taken not one man into her bed but two. The thought of Hindson-Evans getting into bed in his custom-tailored suits made Fran laugh out loud. Perhaps he did it in his white coat with a stethoscope round his neck? Perhaps Min was a surgical-mask fetishist? Or had to be given a general anaesthetic? Coitus nitrous oxide!

'You want to stop being hysterical and get some work done,' Bethel said disapprovingly from the kitchen doorway. 'I'm on me way back from the bingo and I bought you some cod and chips. I nearly had the holiday flyer, but I needed one number. Still, I had a canny little win on me last card, so get them down you. And there's some for that Treesa. She needs a feed.'

When Bethel had gone and Treesa's cod had been carried upstairs, Fran took her own plate through to the living room. The telly was switched off and she left it silent. She was tired of pictures of picket-line violence interspersed with American cops and robbers. She picked up the evening paper for her daily shot of the letters page. Dame Flora Robson was dead . . . one more pillar of childhood gone. Arthur Scargill was saying, '*We are going to win*,' and the Bishop of Durham was quoted: '*I am going to do a Brer Rabbit now . . . lie low and say nothing*.' Fran smiled to herself. The Bishop had the over-excited look of someone new to the limelight who, having found it, doesn't intend to be out of it for a minute. She munched her batter. The letters page was as productive as ever. '1984 *is coming true*.' '*Comrade Scargill will close more pits than MacGregor ever intended to*.' Another writer mocked Scargill's constant promise of victory: '*It's like Sunderland football team being two goals down and the manager saying "Keep it up lads, we're winning."*'

She was putting the *Echo* away when she saw the picture of a railway line where men were excavating for coal. '*NE Mineral Lines a Danger. Two men already killed in Scotland and Yorkshire in vain attempts to get fuel*.' She must show it to Terry Malone and tell him not to dig out the mineral line any more. If anything happened to him it would surely break his mother's heart.

She carried cocoa upstairs and knocked on Treesa's door. 'I thought you'd like a drink?' They sat on the bed to sup their cocoa. Treesa's nightdress was wet at the nipples and clung to her. She had the body of a woman but the face and hands were those of a child. 'Is this all right for you?' Fran said, gesturing round. 'Tell me if there's anything you'd like changed.'

'It's lovely, Mrs Drummond. It's so peaceful. I'll try not to be a nuisance . . . well, we'll both try.' The baby slept soundly in Martin's crib.

'It's nice to have a baby in the house again. If David hadn't died, we'd have liked more children.'

Treesa nodded. 'You do, when you love someone, don't you? It's only natural.'

'We can talk,' Fran thought. 'We can talk about them without it hurting. As though they were both here.'

Treesa licked cocoa from her upper lip. 'I'm glad I've had the bairn. I know it's not right, not being wed and everything . . . but at least I've got something out of it. It's not as though Brian didn't count.'

When they had paid homage at the crib and said their goodnights, Fran walked across the landing to Martin's room. He lay asleep on his back, his copy of *Bert Vegg's Nasty Book* open in an outstretched hand. She took it from him and laid it on his desk. There was a faint down on his upper lip and perhaps the hint of an Adam's apple in the childish throat. She put out a hand to the lamp. 'Thank you, David,' she said, and plunged the room into darkness.

12

Saturday, 11 August 1984

There was a spattering of letters on the mat as Fran came down the stairs: bills and circulars and a DHSS envelope for Treesa. She carried them through the kitchen and submitted to Neewan's onslaught of welcome. 'All right, all right. You'd think I'd been to Nova Scotia, not just upstairs in bed.' That was the best thing about dogs, they were eternally pleased to see you. The sun was shining through the kitchen window, and when she let the dog out into the garden a cabbage white was spiralling above the buddleia. At least Linda was getting a lovely day.

She carried tea and toast upstairs for Treesa. She was curled in the chair by the window, the sated baby asleep against her breast. His cheeks were puffed with satisfaction and milk dripped from the pouting mouth. 'He's lovely, isn't he?' Treesa said and transferred him to Fran's arms. As she put him down and tucked him in, Fran was proud of herself. She had come to terms with the baby problem. They were for other people, not for her, but she could still love them if she chose.

'I think that's your Giro,' she said. It was indeed the magic slip but the figure was still wrong.

'I'll have to go down again,' Treesa said. 'They never listen, that's the trouble.' While they drank their tea they talked about the DHSS. 'It takes at least three visits to get things straight. They never have time to get it right. Everyone else behind you is coughing and groaning, and the bairns are crying. You look at them through the grille and you see their eyes go funny. And then they say, "You'll get something in the post", and you know it won't happen and they know you know, but they still say, "Next please".'

Fran reassured her that there would be compensation money sooner or later, and gave silent thanks for her own teacher-training course. She had made the trip to the DHSS office at the beginning of her widowhood, and the mingled odours of sweat and despair were in her nostrils still.

'You'll need a good wash and your things are laid out on my bed.' Martin had never been to a wedding before and excitement was exuding from every pore. She hoped he wouldn't be disappointed. He had looked forward to it for so long, but in life you got what you wanted and then waited for elation to strike, and it didn't.

Bethel arrived in time to do the washing up. 'No, go and get yersel' ready. It's not often you get a day out. I'll fettle this lot.' She looked at Nee-wan. 'And not a cheep out of you, mind. Or else.' The dog rolled on his back, paws languid. No matter the words, the tone told him he was loved.

'Fenwick's going in on Monday.' With a start Fran realized she had not thought of the strike this morning. How could you forget something so momentous, even for a wedding?

'Do you think he'll really do it this time?'

Bethel's nod was emphatic. 'Oh yes, there'll be no turning back this time.' Fenwick had been signalling his intention of going back for weeks. 'He's sat down there in the library day after day, head buried in law books, scribbling things down. He's never been the same since those pigeons. I reckon he's gone funny.'

And now he was going back to work, and there would be trouble. Fran reminded herself that this was Linda's wedding day. Time enough to worry about Monday morning when the wedding was over.

Bethel was standing up to the elbows in suds. 'I expect we'll have her round on Monday, wringing her hands and spouting rubbish. That friend of yours, I mean. That Margot! Solidarity? The only solid thing about her's her backside.'

Fran felt bound to put the other side. 'She means well . . .' She got no further.

'Means well!' Reddened arms were withdrawn from the sink, suds flying. ' "Means well" is the cause of the trouble. Thatcher "means well", I daresay. Scargill "means well". If they'd all stop "meaning well" and let the miners get on with it, all this trouble'd stop. Besides . . .' The parting shot was half meant for Fran. '. . . she's only a townee. She doesn't know what she's talking about. Pits are for pitmen. And their women. She should keep herself to herself.' She dropped into a wicked imitation of Margot's accent. 'They must see it through to the bitter end. I've done my bit to see they're not starved out. Mrs Thatcher will never break the miners.' She reverted to her own voice. 'Mrs Thatcher won't break them but the do-gooders just might manage it.'

It was nice to be dressing for a gala occasion. Fran was wearing a suit she had bought just before David died and seldom worn, navy linen with red and white blouse and lapels. She spent a lot of time on her make-up, keeping one eye always on the clock. She had promised Linda that she would be there in time to give her a final inspection, and nothing must interfere with that. It was funny to think of Edward marrying Linda. She had invited them to her Christmas party to salve a guilty conscience, nothing more. And now they were getting married. For every action in life there was a consequence. Sometimes you knew nothing about it, but it was there just the same.

When she went through to the bedroom in search of her red earrings, the stack of files and textbooks on her dressing table was a reproach. She had taken to working in the bedroom lately, away from Martin and the TV. She would have to get down to some work next week. There were still weeks and weeks of summer holidays left, but she had a daunting list of essays to complete, and Martin to kit out for his new school. She regarded herself in the mirror. She looked nice, but would she ever make a teacher? She consoled herself by listing some of the idiots she knew who had risen to senior posts in the teaching profession, and then went down to check on Martin.

He looked suitably clean, his hair plastered to his head and his tie knotted loose on the clean shirt. He protested when she made to tighten the knot. 'Nobody wears their tie like that now, Mam. Except the fascist junta, and they want throttling.'

Fran looked at him. 'Is that the police you're talking about?'

He put up a hand in the Nazi salute and the other forefinger under his nose. '*Jawohl*,' he said.

Fran licked her lips. 'Do you know what it means?'

He grinned. 'No, but I know it's rude. They're like the Argies . . . bang, bang.'

Fran sought for words. How could she explain the difference between the Falklands battlefield and the Durham coalfield when a British MP had stood at a miners' rally and demanded victory for extra-parliamentary action? Still, she mustn't over-react. He was only a child, after all.

'Yes. Well, we'd better get on. It'd be awful if we were late.'

Bethel waved them off, restraining a frantic dog. 'You don't look bad, quite classy. Behave yourselves.' And then, in an aside to Fran, 'If that feller of yours is there, it has a chance to be a double wedding.' It would have been nice if Steve could've been there, but she understood about his access day. She had told him of the invitation. 'Linda says bring them along, but I don't think you can. I'm not sure I should be taking Martin. Edward's paying for it all and Linda seems to have asked the world and his wife.'

He had shaken a rueful head, and today he would wander the park or the seafront, trying to wrap a week's worth of fatherhood into two or three hours, while she stood alone at Linda's wedding, trying to appear as though it was from choice.

They were almost at Linda's house when the traffic slowed. 'I bet there's been an accident,' Martin said, leaning out of the window for a better view. A flashing blue light could be seen in the distance and the faint beating of a drum. It was five minutes before the marchers came abreast of them, with familiar banners – *Coal not Dole* and *The Right to Work* – an effigy of Mrs Thatcher hanging from a pole and another that might be MacGregor or any other elderly gent. Margot was in the third rank, arm in arm with a girl in dungarees pushing a pushchair and a middle-aged man who looked like a union official. From time to time he tried to disentangle his arm from Margot's but she held cheerfully on.

Fran turned away, fearful of being seen, and caught Martin's eye. 'Do you see what I see?'

He nodded, grinning. 'It's that Margot.'

The traffic was beginning to move and Fran let out the clutch. 'We used to call her Manky when we were at school.'

His grin widened. 'What does it mean?'

Fran shook her head. 'I don't know . . . but something awful.' The spectacle had put them both in a good mood. Even when she put out a hand and squeezed his knee he didn't seem to mind.

She had expected pandemonium at Linda's flat. Instead there was ordered calm. The children were resplendent in new clothes, faces shining, wearing an aura of importance. Debbie was clutching a silver horseshoe in a cellophane packet and the two boys had boxes of confetti. Fran fumbled in her bag and produced her own box for Martin. When the white-coated driver arrived and spirited all four children away, Fran had time to take stock of Linda. 'You look lovely,' she said. It was true. Linda's angularity had softened to slenderness, her bust looked fuller, her cheeks rounder. The cream dress with its neat collar looked exactly right for a second-time bride, the bunch of silk roses that formed her hat set off the long dark hair.

'Are you sure?' For a second the old Linda looked out, uncertain and afraid.

'I'm sure,' Fran said firmly and then, suddenly feeling responsible. 'Are *you* sure you're doing the right thing? There's still time.'

Linda smiled, suddenly at ease. 'Oh yes, I'm sure. You think he's funny, I suppose – I know everyone thinks that. I've seen the looks. He does fuss around and he likes everything just so. But he's thoughtful, Fran. He makes me feel I'm important . . . even the kids, they know they count. I only hope I don't let him down, that's all.' She put up a forefinger and wiped her nose. 'My God, I'm getting bloody maudlin again and I've never had a drop.' She crossed to the wall unit and took down two glasses. A bottle of sherry was produced from the cupboard. 'I'm trying to give this up but I need one now. Bloody hell, you don't get married every day. I'm trying to give up swearing too, for Eddy's sake.' She sipped. 'Ooh, lovely!'

Fran held out her glass and they clinked. 'To marriage. May it be a happy one.'

They clinked again. 'I'll bleeding well make sure it is,' Linda said and drained her glass.

'Dearly beloved, we are gathered here . . .' She had turned and smiled at David then, and he had reached for her hand and squeezed it. Someone had let out a sob behind and she had known it was her mother. Now she sat in the unfamiliar church and listened to the service. Linda and Edward were being married in the Reform Church, which permitted the marriage of divorced people at the minister's discretion. She looked down at Martin but he was rapt. He was always rapt in church. Perhaps he would wind up a vicar. She was picturing her mother's celestial delight if such a thing came to pass when someone moved into the pew beside her. 'I made it,' Steve whispered, and bowed his head in prayer.

She felt a sudden exultation, a clutching at her chest that could hardly be borne. He was here, he cared! She was glad when the organ pealed out 'Love Divine' and she had to concentrate on her hymn-book.

She had accompanied Linda in the bridal car, leaving the Mini at the flat. Now she climbed into Steve's car for the journey to the reception. Martin had made himself part of the official bridal party and would ride with Linda's children. 'They looked happy, didn't they?' Steve said as they drove out of the churchyard. They had looked happy, both of them. Linda had looked cherished and Edward had kept a protective eye on the children as photographs were taken.

'He'll love being a father,' Fran said.

Steve laughed. 'I give him two weeks. It's not as easy as it looks.'

Suddenly Fran realized he was thinking of his own children; picturing them, if Jean remarried, walking down the aisle behind a new father-figure. She wanted to say something reassuring but as usual she couldn't find the words.

Linda had banished her family from the house before she left for the church but they were prominent at the reception – aunties and uncles and cousins by the dozen, all in the mood for a knees-up. Hilarity accompanied the speeches and the nudge-nudge, wink-wink telegrams, and grew to a peak when Edward rose to make his speech. Fran looked at him apprehensively. Poor stuffy old Edward . . . how would he take all this?

Edward, a lock of hair falling on to his forehead, looked at least ten years younger. He was, he said, the luckiest man imaginable. Not only did he have the loveliest wife in Britain, he had the three best children in the world. Linda allowed him a fair measure of hyperbole and then gave a gentle tug to his sleeve. 'That's enough, dear.'

Edward looked round as if to say, 'See how gloriously hen-pecked I am already?' and sat down.

'I thought you told me he was bossy?' Steve whispered, and all Fran could do was shrug.

The couple were seen off in a snowstorm of confetti and silver horseshoes. Edward kissed all the children and promised untold treasures upon their return, and the car clanked off in a flurry of Ostermilk tins tied to the rear bumper. Linda's cousin was looking after the children. 'She says I can go too, Mam. Four's no more trouble than three. Besides . . .' Martin tried to sound nonchalant . . . 'she says I'm a good influence on them. She wants me to come.'

Fran sought out the cousin and checked. 'Of course he can come. They'll all have to bunk in, I've told them that. But he's a proper little gentleman, isn't he? That polite! He's been here before, that one.'

So it was arranged. 'It feels funny to be free,' Fran thought as they left the hotel. Nothing to go home for except Nee-wan, and Bethel was seeing to him.

'Where shall we go?' Steve said. 'Do you fancy a big night out?' He had managed to persuade Jean to let him take the children tomorrow, so he too was free.

'I'd like a cup of tea,' Fran said, 'and I'd like to take off these shoes. There's something about weddings that goes to my feet.'

They talked of the strike as they drove to Linda's to pick up the Mini. 'So he's really going to do it this time?' Steve said when she told him about Fenwick. 'If one or two of them make a start it'll open the floodgates. But they won't get in without a fight. The mobile pickets are hit-men, nothing less.'

Fran shivered. 'Don't let's talk about it. I don't want anything to spoil today.'

It was cool in Steve's flat, cool and dark after the heat of the day. They stood in the centre of the room, mouths together, fingers fumbling with buttons and zips. 'I love you, Fran.'

She wanted to say, 'I love you, Steve,' but some tiny mechanism held her back – until he was moving with her and through her, taking away her consciousness so that the dead man's handle fell away and she could cry, 'I love you,' and feel no shame.

Beside her Steve stirred. 'What are you thinking about?'

She put out a hand and laid it on his belly. The flesh did not quiver as it would have done before they made love. Now he was at peace. 'I was thinking about them. Do you think they'll be happy?'

Steve considered for a moment. 'They've got as much chance as anyone else. More, probably.'

She turned on her side, sliding her hand further so that her arm was around his waist. 'Do you ever think about Jean? You know what I mean?'

Again he paused before answering. 'Sometimes. We were married a long time you know. You remember.'

It was not the answer she wanted. It was emphatically not the answer she wanted. Of course he would remember a wife of fifteen years' standing. Reason told her that, but instinct could not bear it. She wanted to get out of bed, pull on her clothes and rush from the house. Instead she laid her lips against his chest and moved her hand to fondle his cheek.

He groaned. 'Not again. I don't believe it. This woman is insatiable. Help!'

She giggled and started to tickle him, seeking the places where she knew he could not bear it. 'This is good,' she told herself. What did the experts say? '*A good laugh in bed is worth a thousand orgasms.*' They had loved and now they were laughing. It was all right.

But long after they were still she thought about that shadowy figure, the woman who had given him his children, and knew that she was right to be afraid.

13

Saturday, 1 September 1984

Even after she was back in the house the horror of the scene clung to her. She had come out of the shop and heard a clamour. At first the distant sound had not been frightening – a compound of excitement and laughter, children's voices, a barking dog ... And then one word rose above the rest: 'Scab. Scab. Bloody scab!' She had stood, stupid, in the street, arms full of purchases, and wondered what was going on.

And then Fenwick had rounded the corner; Fenwick who now went doggedly to work each morning and returned in the afternoon from his permanent, lonely back shift. Around him women and children swirled, taunting, mocking, spitting hate. Teenage boys, faces alight, lunged forward to aim a blow, or mouth an insult. But it was Fenwick's face that held Fran's eye. The lines of good humour were gone, the double chin was now a slack pouch, the eyes stone-hard and fixed ahead. He walked on steadily, not heeding the blows, the hard words. He walked as though the crowd around him did not exist, not even when their spittle flew through the air and landed, glistening, on his clothes. Some of the women in the crowd Fran knew from the school gates or the corner shop, but they were strangers now, fierce creatures exulting as though around the guillotine, wielding their pushchairs like scythes. Fran moved back against the shop window as they came nearer. 'Scab, scab ... fucking scab!' Children used the oath freely, recognizing it as a word that would

not bring rebuke – not now, while Belgate was at war. Fran
recoiled at the sound. No matter what the cause, it could never
be right to teach children to spew out hate.

And then, as Fenwick drew level and she saw the tic at the
side of his mouth, she was filled with a sudden and insensate
rage. Who had a right to block anyone else's path? She moved
forward, determined to fall in beside him, demonstrate solidarity.
A woman's face loomed up, grinning: 'Get the scabby bastard!'
Her eyes flicked over Fran's face and then back to it, sensing a
stranger, someone out of step. Gold rings hung from her huge
lobes, the holes of their insertion pulled down by the weight. It
was the woman Fran had seen in the corner shop. Her eyes
locked with Fran's and challenged: '*With us or against us?*' they
said, without room for compromise.

Fran dropped her eyes and turned, clutching her shopping
before her like an excuse.

The cock-crow sounded in her ears a thousand times before
she reached her own door and was safe inside.

The house seemed cold, or else what she had just seen had
chilled her. She went through to the kitchen and checked the
boiler. They were burning the dust from the coke house now.
She put a poker through the bars, but there was no answering
glow. She shivered and shut the boiler door. She could pile on
cardigans when winter came, and anyway she was at college all
day and Martin at school. But what about Treesa? If the
unthinkable happened and the strike went on till Christmas, what
would become of the baby? As she straightened up she resolved
to keep Treesa and the baby warm somehow, even if she had to
chop up the furniture. What else could she do? The whole area
was picked clean of anything that would burn, even fences and
park benches. Besides, she would never have the nerve to steal
wood. But she would keep Treesa warm, one way or another!
She looked at the calendar: 1 September. *Surely* this misery
couldn't last till Christmas?

She put Nee-wan on the lead after lunch and went prospecting
for fuel. She had hoped Martin would come with her but he was
off on some jaunt with Gary. 'You find the wood or the coal or

whatever, and we'll come and carry it later on.' He was turning into a thorough little procrastinator! Gary was more helpful: 'I could get you a bag of duff. Our Terry's digging tons out of the railway. Me mam says she can do without anything except a fire, so he gets it nearly every day.'

Fran felt bound to point out the dangers. 'The banks could cave in, Gary. I've seen warnings in the papers. It's happened in other places, and people have been buried alive.'

Gary's smile was pitying. 'Our Terry's a face-worker, he knows all about getting coal.'

Looking at his face, full of pride, Fran knew it was useless to argue. 'Well, I expect he has plenty to do, keeping your fire on. Don't worry about us, we'll manage.'

Martin was less tactful. 'Does your dad dig coal off the line?'

For perhaps the first time, Fran saw Gary Malone nonplussed. His eyes dropped. 'No. Me dad doesn't go down the line.' Then the old spirit reasserted itself. 'But he could if he wanted!'

So the conflict between Terry and his father was getting to Gary. As Fran got the car out she wondered for the thousandth time if Scargill and Thatcher had any idea of the havoc they were causing in ordinary people's lives.

People had changed in the last few months. They looked older, more determined – or perhaps her view of them had altered. She was certainly reacting to the coal strike. It was still summer, the air was warm, but she was possessed with the need for fuel like the rest of Belgate. She could heat water with the immersion heater but it would not do. She wanted a fire, a living flame, a symbol that life in the coalfield still went on. That was why men tramped the woods for sticks or flitted through the darkness with buzz-saws. It was a sign that they were not yet defeated.

As she drove towards the blast, she thought about the first time she had gone there. David had told her of the beach beneath the colliery where they tumbled waste into the sea, but nothing had prepared her for the sight. Now, as she crossed the mineral-line tracks, the landscape changed, as though someone were dropping grey filters one by one before her eyes. She drove between banks of rubble, a compound of earth and shale, with everywhere twisted wire and cable, and once the remnants of some ancient tree. The sea came into sight, and then the beach; but this was no Hawaii. A fine grey silt sloped to the sea, rising like smoke at every footfall, turning to slurry when the tide lapped at its edge.

On her first visit she had stood there horror-stricken, and known this was the landscape of the future, when man had blown himself out of existence. There were no birds, no blades of grass; no fish could swim through that sludgy sea. She had picked up a rounded stone from her feet and it had fallen to pieces in her hand.

Above them the pit had stood castle-like against the sky, the gantries of the tippers like Triffids, silent and watchful. She had shivered and turned to David. 'This is a place of desolation.'

Now she parked the car and walked forward, hoping to pick through the waste for enough to keep the boiler going for another day. Others were there before her. A man in a pork-pie hat went by, pushing a bike. A half-filled sack lay across its saddle. 'There's nowt left, pet. It's picked clean.' The beach came into view and she saw them, heads bent, scrabbling for nuggets in the blackened sand. As she watched, a woman straightened up, empty-handed, and shook her head in a gesture of despair. Fran turned away and went back to the car.

She parked above the allotments and let Nee-wan out of the car. He bounded ahead, stopping now and then for some extra special smell. Everywhere she looked there were signs of de-forestation. The newly cut stumps shone white through the greenery, raw evidence of the search for fuel. And always the saplings. No one had time to take the old, dead trees that could be spared; they took easier prey, trunks no bigger than a man's wrist, logs that would flare up for a moment and then subside to grey ash. God damn Arthur Scargill, Fran thought. Thirty years from now his mark would still be left on the British coalfields.

She was turning for home when Nee-wan went into a frenzy of barking. The man was almost up to her before she recognized him. 'Hallo, Mr Botcherby. It seems we had the same idea.'

He had a bundle of twigs under his arm, small pieces that had been missed by earlier gleaners. His shoulders were hunched under the navy donkey jacket, and he needed a shave. 'Aye, it's a sad carry-on when a collier's reduced to this.' He had stopped to speak but he avoided her eye.

'How's your wife?' Suddenly she was afraid of intruding and hastened to give him a get-out. 'And Angela? I haven't seen her lately.'

He shifted his wood to a more comfortable position. 'The bairn's all right. The missus . . . she's bearing up.' He sought to change the subject. 'You'll have run out of coal by now, I suppose?'

Fran was relieved. 'Yes, well, almost . . . it's coke I use. I had the offer of some duff from the mineral line but I didn't think it would burn in my boiler.'

A trace of a smile crossed his face. 'I was all for going down the line till I got a look. It's Piccadilly Circus down there. There's that many backsides sticking out of them embankments, it looks like a Butlin's Bonny Bottoms contest.'

Fran laughed. 'Is it safe?'

He was getting ready to move on. 'Safe enough for them as knows what they're doing. Besides, safe or not, what else can they do? We're all living dangerously now, Mrs Drummond, and God knows what the end'll be.'

Long after he had passed from sight and she and Nee-wan were back in the car, she was trying to work out what he'd meant.

Treesa was in the kitchen when she got back and the kettle was on the boil. 'Tea! Lovely!' Fran subsided into a chair and opened the evening paper. There were the usual letters for and against the strike, and one from 'Industrial Democrat' who said the ordinary miner could truthfully say, 'I am the union', and, if he wanted to go to work, cross picket lines with a clear conscience. Mrs Thatcher was saying miners who returned to work would end the strike, which Fran felt would surely prolong it by another week or two. Every time the leaders of either side opened their mouths, it was a setback.

But it was the 'Quote for Today' that caught her eye and made her look across at Treesa, curled in a chair with a mug of tea clasped in both hands, her eyes fixed on nothing in particular. It came from the Director of the Population Institute: 'A girl who has an illegitimate child at sixteen suddenly has 90 per cent of her life's script written for her. Her life chances are few.' Treesa was not sixteen, but she was little more, and for the next sixteen years at least her role as a mother would overrule all others. If Brian had lived it might have been different. Then again, it might not. Could you find undying love at eighteen or nineteen? Or would you wake up at thirty and find yourself married to a stranger?

She looked up to find Treesa's eyes on her. For a moment she was disconcerted, feeling Treesa must have known what she was thinking. But Treesa had something else on her mind. 'I've been thinking . . . now that the bairn's settled down and I've got a bit more time, I think I'd like to give the women a hand.' She looked at Fran apprehensively. 'Would you mind?'

'Of course not.' Fran's answer was swift. 'I know some of them go on a bit, and Margot's a pain, but I agree with what they're doing. Especially for the single men – I don't know how they're surviving.'

Treesa nodded. 'Brian would've been in there helping, wouldn't he? That's why I want to do my bit.'

It was true. Whether or not he had agreed with the strike, Brian would have pitched in, loyal, cheerful . . . to the bitter end.

'I know he would,' Fran said, 'and I think you should help. It'll get you out a bit, too. You haven't had many laughs lately, have you? And I'd love to babysit when I'm here.' She was about to suggest Bethel as an extra babysitter when there was an urgent knock at the door.

'Let me in, Fran! Hurry up!' Min was shouting through the letterbox in her haste to gain admission. 'Oh God, Fran, I'm in such terrible trouble,' she was babbling all the time Fran was pushing her into the front room and closing the door for privacy.

'Shut up a minute, Min. I can't take it in if you talk like that.'

For the first time in years she saw signs of the old down-at-heel Min of their schooldays. Her nose was red with crying and mascara streaked down her cheeks. Her blouse clashed with her jacket and the sleek black hair was spiked with anguish. 'It's Dennis. He's gone berserk. Like a maniac! I've tried to explain but he won't listen ... you'll have to go and see him ... he's always had a soft spot for you, Fran. Tell him it was all a joke. I'd never have let it get out of hand, you know that!'

Fran took a deep breath. 'Min, sit down and pull yourself together. I suppose Dennis has found out about Hindson-thingummy. Well, it serves you right. Eve did warn you. I expect it'll all blow over ... ?'

She was about to suggest a nice cup of tea when Min began to jump up and down. 'Oh for God's sake listen, Fran ... blow over? *Blow over?* He's packed my bags! I'm out in the street. He's got it all worked out ... maintenance, access to the kids ... he's going to sell my Capri ... it isn't that I mind *that*, so don't say it is. I know you all think all I care about is money, and I admit it's important ... but I actually like Dennis. I like living with him. But he won't listen, he's shown me the door, Fran. I'm telling you ...'

Fran left Treesa to make tea for Min, and got out the car. What *was* she going to say to Dennis? She could hardly accept Min's picture of him as a raging bull, but she still wasn't sure how to handle it. '*Now look here, Dennis ... ?*' Or, '*Before you speak ... I know you've got every right to be angry ... ?*'

In the end it was Dennis who began the conversation. 'Come on in, Fran. I wasn't sure whether it would be you or Eve. Of the two, I'm glad it's you.'

He led the way across the parquet-tiled hall to the kitchen. A bottle of Blue Nun and two glasses stood on the table. He poured wine for them both, sat down, and swung his crossed feet on to the table. 'Come on then, get it over. The kids are at Mum's, so you can feel free. And I know what you're going to say, it's all been a misunderstanding, she's really a good little girl, and can she come back?'

Fran took a good swig of wine. 'Something like that.'

He held his glass to the light and squinted at it. 'Well, between you and me, the short answer is "yes".'

Fran felt a sudden desire to laugh. Surely it wasn't going to be this easy! She fumbled for the right words. 'I really think she's sorry, Dennis ... and after all, it didn't get that far. I mean ...'

She was on dangerous ground here. 'Well, you know Min, it's more talk than anything else.'

He was grinning. 'Yes. She's big on promises but not so hot on performance.'

Fran felt herself blush. When all this blew over, she would murder Min for putting her in this situation. 'Shall I tell her to come home then?'

He looked at his watch. 'Not yet. We'll give her another hour, just to let it sink in.'

Fran looked at him for a moment and then took the bull by the horns. 'Dennis, I think you're enjoying this.'

He lifted the bottle and topped up their glasses.

'With a bit of luck, Fran, I am going to have the best year of my life out of this lot. When she comes back, I'll tell her she's on probation. I've told her I've seen a solicitor – I didn't tell her it was for a drink at the squash club. If she gives me a touch of the geishas, it'll stay on the file. Otherwise . . .' he tilted further back in his chair and smiled, 'it's out into the cold, cold snow.'

Fran began to laugh, wiping tears of merriment from her eyes. 'How long have you known?' she said at last.

'From the beginning . . . but there's always a psychological moment to intervene. You learn that in business.'

Fran reflected that Dennis had more nous than anyone had given him credit for. No wonder his family had made so much money out of their furniture business. They had the business instinct! As she left the kitchen, Dennis gave her an affectionate pat. 'Don't let her off the hook, Fran. It's for her own good.' So she would tell Min she could go back home on sufferance, and in all probability Min would be grateful to her for acting as go-between. It was a bit of a cheat but it was all in a good cause.

Fran sent Min on her way with a final word of warning. 'Don't forget it's hanging by a thread, Min. I talked him round, but it wasn't easy. You'll have to tread carefully for a long while.'

When Min had gone, she sat down on the bottom of the stairs and hugged her knees. She felt devious and wicked. It was lovely to lie and not feel really sinful. She was wondering how much of the evening's events she should relay to Eve when the letterbox rattled. 'Fran?' Min stood on the step, still dishevelled but resolute. 'Look Fran . . . I don't think we need to tell Eve about this. You know what she's like. She'll be looking at me as though I was in the condemned cell for the next ten years, and as for Harold – he'd just gloat.' She pulled the collar of her jacket into place and touched up her hair. 'Dennis may have been a swine tonight, but I'd rather be married to him than a stuffed shirt. Actually . . . well . . .' A fatuous smile was spreading over her face. 'Well, Dennis has his points.'

When Fran subsided on to the stairs again it was to wonder whether Min really liked the new dominant Dennis, or whether she was simply convincing herself that she did.

She could see the light under Treesa's door and was about to knock when she heard Martin call out. He was sitting up in bed, eyes bright. 'What happened?'

She played for time. 'What do you mean?'

He gave her a knowing look. 'About Aunty Min getting thrown out. Are they getting divorced?' He had overheard some of Min's conversation and put two and two together.

'You mustn't say a word to anyone,' Fran said, and gave him an edited version. He seemed to appreciate being made a confidant.

'Sit down a minute,' he said, patting the bed. She felt as honoured as if she had been asked to share the throne. 'Do you think the strike'll last long?'

'I don't know. It's difficult to judge. They're still talking, so I suppose that's something.'

He was looking down at the duvet. 'I don't know which side I'm on.'

So that was it! 'I don't know either. I try to make up my mind, but then something happens to change it.'

He nodded. 'It's awful now.' She waited. 'We used to play Police and Pickets, and it was all right at first. But now it's not much fun.' There was an even longer pause. 'People cry sometimes.'

Fran nodded. 'I know. What does Gary think about it?'

Martin shook his head. 'He's the worst. He gets mad with everybody because his dad and Terry don't like each other any more. And he likes them both.'

When she had put out the light and was safely on the landing she let out her breath in a gust of anger. Whatever they were currently discussing in their political seaside hotels, it wouldn't be the agony of one small boy torn between loyalty to father and brother. And yet what could be more important?

14

Wednesday, 24 October 1984

The trees on the campus had shed most of their leaves by now and shivered in the east wind. Fran pushed open the refectory doors to allow Gwen to pass, and the mingled odours of coffee and overheated fat enfolded them. The red-topped tables were mostly unoccupied, condiments still neatly grouped around vases of plastic roses.

'It's quiet for a Wednesday.' Gwen put her books down to bag a table and reached for a tray.

Fran followed suit. 'No one's got any money.' That morning she had totted up the stubs of her cheque book and total depression had ensued. Christmas was looming larger with each passing day and funds were dwindling in direct proportion.

Gwen looked around at her fellow students. 'Well, they haven't spent it on their backs. I know we were too subdued in my day but, God . . . ! Take any two items; if they clash, wear them!' It was true. The students looked bizarre, boys and girls alike. But cheerful!

Fran looked up to find Gwen's eyes twinkling. 'I'm showing my age, aren't I? And I'm jealous. Look at those waistlines.' She sat down, looked at her sausage roll, lifted it, and bit firmly. 'After today, no more.' She emptied her mouth and licked her lips. 'Heard anything of the newly-weds?'

Fran shook her head. 'I must get over there soon. They've moved into Edward's house; Linda loves it. And him! She was on the phone at the weekend. She says she goes from room to room, counting.'

Gwen shook her head. 'I have to take your word for it . . . that she loves him, I mean. Loving Edward! The mind boggles. When you think what we endured with him prosing on all the time. He knew better than us, he knew better than the lecturers . . . he knew the lot!'

Fran nodded. 'Yes, he was a bit of a pain, but I think he was frightened. Uninvolved and frightened! He was out of his depth on the course, and then he went back to an empty house. He had to be pompous to keep his nerve. He's quite different now, he's always laughing. If you saw him with Linda's kids you wouldn't recognize him.'

It was true. Edward looked ten years younger, fatter, more muscular. 'In fact,' Fran reflected wryly, 'I half wish I'd nabbed him myself.' But Linda had done for Edward what Fran had been unable to do. Had she, Fran, done better by Steve?

'You're doing it again!' Fran looked up as Gwen spoke to find the other woman's eyes bright with affection.

'What?'

Gwen smiled. 'You know! Going moony. Thinking about that boyfriend of yours. You ought to set the date.'

Long after the conversation had turned to the coming teaching practice, Fran felt an uncomfortable flushing of her face and neck. It came whenever she thought of remarriage. She couldn't stand in a church and make the same vows. It would be a mockery.

'I'd like to get Broad Street again,' she told Gwen, remembering that her first teaching practice at Broad Street Juniors had been the pleasantest of experiences.

'I shouldn't think you will,' Gwen said. 'They like to shuffle us round. We might get too happy if they didn't.' They grinned in mutual antipathy to their college authorities and began to gather their books.

'How is Martin's new school going down?' asked Gwen, struggling with her holdall.

'He loves it. Having Gary there makes all the difference.'

Gwen nodded. 'At least comprehensives have that benefit . . . friends aren't split up and sent hither and thither. I've seen it cause misery, separating sheep from goats, leaving kids without their pals at a crucial time. Still, I'm glad all's well with your offspring. He's a good lad.'

Fran flushed again, this time with maternal pride. 'He's all right,' she said.

'How are things in Belgate?' Gwen asked as they left the refectory. 'I keep forgetting you live in the battle zone.'

As they walked back to the lecture room, Fran tried to explain what Belgate was like now. 'You think before you speak all the time. You stand next to someone you've known for ages and the subject of the strike comes up and you think . . . Dare I speak? Are they for or against? It's awful. You want to say what you think, but you don't want trouble.'

As they passed through the lecture room doorway Gwen pulled a face. 'That's how these things happen in the first place. The majority are afraid to speak out.'

All through the psychology lecture Gwen's words were uppermost in Fran's mind. Perhaps you should speak out, and to hell with the consequences. But if you did you'd be in constant hot water. And the issue of the strike was more complicated than most: even Walter was confused. He and Bethel had always argued over politics but it had been light-hearted, almost a game. Now their disagreement had a cutting edge. Yesterday he had lashed out at Bethel over the Christmas appeal that Wearside miners had launched. She had looked at him stony-faced. 'They should think shame on themselves. They've always had good wages, and now they're cadging. What about them as has no jobs? Who's begging for *their* bairns? There's some been out of work in Sunderland two or three years.'

Walter had bristled. 'There you go! They can't do right in your eyes, can they? They're in a war, you silly old git. Front-line troops. That's why we should see to their bairns . . . because they're fighting our battle.'

'I'm not going to take offence, Walter. You've always been proud of the NUM, but you're seeing it dragged in the dust and it's turning you nasty. Well, I'm not going to crack back – although I could – because I'm sorry for you.'

He had glared at her for a moment and then booled his chair

towards the door. He was lost for words and Fran did not enjoy the spectacle.

Fran was halfway between Sunderland and Belgate when an ominous thudding began. At first she thought it was the engine, but then the wheel began to buck in her hands and she realized she had a flat tyre. She was on an unlit section of the road and her heart sank. She knew the theory of changing a tyre, but would she have the strength? David had always grunted with effort when he loosened the nuts. And what about the spare? She hadn't checked the spare since she got the car. It rolled to rest at the side of the road and she switched off the engine. The lights of Belgate winked through a mist of rain. She could lock up the car and walk, but the road lay between open fields. Anything could be in there . . . anything! A car might come by and stop, but ten to one it would be driven by a psychopath. With her luck, that could be practically guaranteed!

She had opened the boot and located the jack when the car nosed in behind her. The sight of its blue flashing lamp was at first balm, and then full of terror as she tried to remember if all her documents were in order. 'Having trouble?' Inside the police car the dashboard crackled with tango messages as the driver stated their location. 'Looks like a lady driver in trouble. Yeah!'

His answering laugh to the dashboard's obvious quip brought out the femininist in Fran. 'It's only a puncture. I can manage.'

A young PC uncoiled from the passenger seat and put on his hat. 'Let's have a look . . .'

As he changed the wheel with minimum fuss, she recognized him. It was the young policeman whose mother lived in the wide back street, the woman she had seen in the shop that day being taunted by the strikers' wives. 'You come from Belgate, don't you?'

He nodded without taking his eyes from his work. 'That's right.'

Fran sought for a topic of conversation. 'Do you lodge in Sunderland?'

He shook his head. 'Share a flat.' There was a pause. 'Just as

well, at the moment. I'm not too popular in Belgate right now.'
His tone was bitter.

'But you don't do picket duty there?' Fran said.

He was swinging the spare wheel into place. 'No, I went down
to the Midlands through the summer. It was quiet up here once
they got all the pits out. There was plenty of trouble on the
open-cast sites with them being privately owned ... the men not
in the NUM ... but our lads could cope; so we were sent to
Notts and Derbyshire to help out. But since some miners have
started going back up here, it's been all hands to the wheel.
None of our lads can be spared – in fact we've got men from
other forces coming in to help us. I don't do duty in Belgate ...
that's the county force, and I'm Northumbria Constabulary. But
you get your local hot-heads picketing away from home and word
gets back.' He started to tighten the nuts. 'It's not too nice for
the old lady, but I just shrug it off. According to them, I'll be
able to retire on me overtime pay, so I suppose that's a
consolation.' His tone belied his words.

His partner had left the car and come to inspect progress.
'They say we gloat about the pay; that they've got nowt and we're
coining it in.' Suddenly Fran remembered Walter's tale of fat
pay packets waved in the faces of hungry pickets. 'But we don't
need to rub it in. They're not daft, they know the score. What
are we supposed to do – offer to do picket-line duty for free? I
know what they'd say about that.' His tone was flat. 'Besides, you
get sick. There's no time off. You're out there doing twelve on,
twelve off, and you're covering for the men on picket-line duty.
Either way, it's work, work and more work. As for days off ...
I've forgotten what they are.'

'You sound fed up,' Fran said as the wheel was lowered to
meet the ground. 'I don't know how to thank you. I was scared
stiff till you came along.'

They stood as she climbed into her car. 'No need for thanks,
pet. It's nice to be popular for a change!'

As she drove back to Belgate, Fran thought about the two
policemen, both in their twenties, both local lads, but outcasts
now. If anyone believed the 'fascist junta' was enjoying the strike,
they were wrong.

*

The door was open when she got home, streaming light into the yard. Terry Malone appeared in the doorway, carrying a bucket full of rubble. His hands and forearms were black with soot. 'It's done, Mrs Drummond. Opened up and a good fire going.' She had forgotten about the fireplace! When the coke had run out, she had switched on electric fires to keep everyone warm. It was no good worrying about bills with a baby in the house. But still they had shivered. 'Open up the fireplace,' Terry had urged on one of his visits to Treesa and the baby. 'Open it up, it's only filled in with hardboard, and I'll keep a fire going. Nee worry about that.' She had jittered about years of disuse and the capped chimney, but he had waved her objections away. All the same, she had never thought he would actually do it.

Indoors, a fire was burning brightly, duff coal piled on broken pieces of the timber that had framed the fire throat. The hardboard sheet which they had supported stood against the wall. 'I took it down carefully,' Terry said. 'We can put it back when things are back to normal. And I shinned up the roof and took off the cap. That can go back, an' all!'

Bethel was in the kitchen, Treesa's baby propped on one hip, teapot in the other hand. 'Sit down and get that door shut. This bairn's nithered with all the comings and goings.' She gave Terry a malevolent look. 'I hope he'll be around when the trouble starts. You can't open up a fire just like that. You'll get smoke pouring out of everywhere, bricks coming down, God knows what. The mess here today . . .' Her eyes rolled upwards.

Terry gave a grin and sat down at the table. 'H'away, Sally, give the workers a cup of tea and stop slavering on.' Bethel snorted, but she poured his tea just the same.

'Is Treesa at the church hall?' Now that Treesa helped the support group, Bethel had come into her own. Not only a house to fuss over, but a baby too. It was nice, Fran thought. Nice to see them all getting on together. One good thing out of all the bad. Once it would have been impossible for Bethel and Terry Malone to sit down together and talk. Now they were doing it. Whatever the rights and wrongs of the strike, whatever your position, it was drawing communities together . . . except that it was also separating families.

It was warm in the kitchen, heat flowing from the open oven. She had told Bethel to warm whichever room the baby was in, and the oven was the obvious answer. The immersion heater was ticking away upstairs, heating the water for the nappies. When she went to jail for debt, she would have the comforting feel of duty done.

They were on to their second cups when Treesa came in. She turned towards the baby but did not hold out her arms. She looked tired and the fair hair was lank. 'It's taking too much out of her,' Fran thought. 'It's too soon after the baby.' She pulled out a chair and Treesa sank into it.

Terry did not speak but there was satisfaction on his face as he looked at her. 'I'm not tired,' she said, taking the proffered cup of tea. 'Just a bit weary. I've peeled that many taties this week I'm ready to drop.' Her hands looked red and sore, with brown patches down the side of the left index finger. 'It's been a thin week, so we've been making stovies.'

Fran had never encountered stovies till she came to Belgate – layers of sliced potato and onion cooked with butter or marge and topped with cheese, if you were in the money. 'Is that all they get?' she said. She was always haunted by thoughts of protein. Miss your protein for a day and your legs gave way. She knew it was crazy, but she couldn't help it. And miners, used to four good meals, were now reduced to stovies.

Treesa had revived with the cup of tea. She held out her arms for the baby. 'Who's been a good lad, then?' He lay in her arms looking up into her face. She smiled at Bethel. 'I don't think he wants his mammy, he's happy with you.'

Bethel struggled to keep a poker face and lost the battle. 'He's a good bairn, I'll say that for him. It's nee trouble to me to keep an eye on him. Not that I agree with what you're doing, mind; don't think that. Dragging everybody back to the soup kitchens. It's a disgrace. They want to get back to work.'

Terry drained his mug and put it down on the table. 'Come on, Sally. It's the right to work we're striking for. We could take redundancy, sit back or get bussed to another pit. Then they close Belgate. What happens to your young lads then, the ones coming out of school? Where's their jobs? I'll tell you . . . down the drain, because we sold them out. I'm not facing them year after year to tell them why there's nowt but the dole queue.'

He's right, Fran thought. They *are* fighting for more than their own jobs.

Bethel did not agree. 'Hold hard, there. You've got it all down nice and pat; Scargill's got you well trained. But stop and think a minute. Take your bad pit . . . it costs you £90 a ton to bring coal up. You sell it for £30. Who foots the difference? The government? They've got nowt, only what they take off the people. So they take extra to keep your pit open. And the ones they've taken it off – what about them? What about their jobs? It's all very well to say, "Make sure I'm all right, Jack." But what about the other feller? Look at the middle of Sunderland – it's getting to be a ghost town, with shops closing that can't afford to stop open for the rates and taxes. So they close, and a few dozen shop-girls get tossed on the street. Never mind, as long as the pits stop open! You'll face them, will you, and say "Hard lines"?'

Terry was shaking his head. 'That's half the trouble, you know. Everybody's an economist, they've all got a recipe. "Do it this way and it'll come up roses." Arthur's got the only answer: operate the pits for people not profit.'

Fran was trying to put her finger on the weakness she knew was somewhere in his argument when Bethel spoke, not in her usual sharp tones but a more measured way. 'You may well be right, Terry Malone. I am an old woman, and ten to one I see things too simple. But I know how to spot a bad 'un and I had Arthur Scargill spotted long afore he was elected to anything. He wants to play God and move a few mountains, and as long as you silly buggers let him get away with it we'll all have to suffer.' Suddenly the old fire flickered. 'He's set son against father. Don't tell me that's right.'

Fran felt her cheek flush. That was hitting below the belt. She saw Terry's Adam's apple bob, but when he spoke his voice was equable. 'I'll say this for you, Sally, you've got a wicked tongue on you sometimes.'

Bethel grinned. 'I can stick up for meself. Don't go forgetting it.'

Treesa launched into a hasty discourse about the support

group, designed to pour oil on troubled waters. Fran drank her tea and gave thanks that the argument had gone no further. There was one thing about life in Belgate: it got down to the nitty-gritty. None of the dissembling of life in Sunderland – and no generation gap either. Terry was a third of Bethel's age, and yet they had been able to argue without any sense of strain.

Suddenly she realized Treesa was talking to her. 'Sorry, Treesa, I was miles away.'

Treesa smiled. 'It was nothing. I just said that friend of yours was there again today, the one with the CND badge. Nobody can stand her. I mean, it's good of her to come and everything, but . . . well, she doesn't do much.'

'You want to tell her,' Fran said and Treesa grinned.

'Someone did. "Let's have less solidarity and a few more taties peeled." That's what they told her. Well, Ella Bishop did. She dares say anything.'

Fran looked inquiring. 'Do I know her?'

Treesa nodded. 'You're sure to. She's a big wife, dark hair, wears big gold hoop earrings. She's got her man and her two sons on strike. She works like a slave; she can lift the sacks about like feathers. And she's a wonder at getting stuff off the shops.'

Fran nodded. 'I know she is. I've seen her at it.'

Before Treesa could reply there was a loud crack, and then a clatter as Nee-wan shot out from the living room and ran behind the dresser.

'God's mercy, what was that?' Bethel said. Nee-wan was pressed against the wall, eyes wide, his body racked by shivering.

They moved as one to the living room door. 'Jeez,' Terry said.

A fire still burned in the grate but they could see it only dimly through the pall of smoke that hung in the air. As Fran watched, huge particles of dust began to settle on everything. 'I warned you,' Bethel said with grim satisfaction. 'You can't say I didn't warn you.'

While they cleared up, they had a heated discussion as to the cause of the explosion. Bethel blamed the unused chimney, Terry some impurity in the slack coal. 'It could've been a detonator,' Treesa said, but Terry laughed at the idea.

'We wouldn't be sitting here if it'd been a detonator, Treesa pet. We'd be sitting on clouds playing harps.'

Bethel did most of the clearing up, wielding the Hoover like a badge of office. Fran retired to the kitchen and put on the kettle again, and Treesa followed, the sleeping baby in her arms. 'It's amazing the way they'll sleep through things, isn't it?' Fran said. 'Even wars. As long as they're safe in their mothers' arms, nothing else matters.'

Treesa nodded. 'I know. It's the mothers that suffer. I feel sorry for the women in the support group, the ones that's got kids. They have to keep refusing them things . . . daft little things you'd take for granted, like an ice cream or a penny bubbly. The kids don't understand. One woman cried today. She said, "My bairns look at me as though I begrudged them." I felt really sorry for her. And she's not the worst.'

Bethel had come back into the kitchen and was listening as Treesa continued.

'They were on about Mary Botcherby today. You know, she lives in Stafford Street? They say she's in a bad way. He's beside himself, but what can he do? He's always been a big union man.'

Bethel was shaking her head. 'I've been expecting this. She may be the first, she won't be the last. It's tick; they've got that much tick, no one could keep it up. Mind, I'll say one thing for Mary Botcherby – she never ticked on her grub. Some of them buy the week's groceries with a Provvy, and then they're paying for it for the next twenty weeks. But she had more sense than that. It was always cash on the nail for her week's shopping.'

Fran was remembering the scene in the corner shop not long after the strike had begun, when Mrs Botcherby had asked for credit for a few items of groceries. So that was why she had been so upset that night; the bastion of her financial affairs had been breached.

'I had a flat tyre on the way home,' Fran said as they drank more tea. 'I was trying to change it myself when a Panda car stopped. It was that boy whose mother lives in the wide back – he did it for me.'

Bethel cast a jaundiced look in Terry's direction. 'Aye, he's always been a good lad.'

Terry smiled. 'I'm not arguing, Sally. He is a good lad. He was one of our Brian's mates in school, and I've never heard a wrong word said about him. I know they've given his mam some stick, and I've told them it's wrong. But you can't blame them for having it in for the pollis, not after what's gone on on the pickets. They join arms to hold you back and it looks as nice as ninepence; and then, when there's nee cameras around and you're up close, they lift their knee.' He grunted. 'Just like that. And you're knackered for a week. They know all those little tricks.'

Fran could not believe that the entire police force was bent on disabling the striking miners, but there was no mistaking the sincerity in Terry's voice. Whether or not it had happened, he believed that it had.

When they had all gone she carried the evening paper through to the living room and sat by the spitting fire. There was a terrible smell of soot but it was nice to see a flame. The front page carried pictures of the deterioration of Durham coal-faces. '*Recovery will take months.*' NACODS, the deputies' union, was poised to do a deal and avoid a strike; and 3,000 pickets had faced six rebel miners in Yorkshire and failed to turn them away.

The day before yesterday an angry crowd had besieged the police station in the next village to Belgate, howling allegations of police intimidation: but what about the intimidating effect of mass pickets? There had been road blocks at Easington when the strike first broke and hundreds of men had pitted themselves against one returning miner. What were the police supposed to do? Cut off his brush and throw it to the waiting hounds? The word 'scab' had once meant the healing of a wound: now it was a missile to be hurled between former friends, with the police caught in the middle. Even in Belgate she could sense the tension when a police uniform appeared. The Sunderland MP had accused the police of a massive abuse of power and an erosion of civil liberties. But whose liberties?

There were the usual newspaper columns about men in court for stealing coal – but how could anyone expect them to sit and shiver in the shadow of stockpiled coal that seemed to mock their misery? Several times she had seen men scurrying by with coal, and once a cruising Panda had driven past and ignored the culprit. She minded them stealing coal a lot less than she minded the carnage in the woodland. Every time she saw them scavenging for wood she meant to protest, but their cold pinched faces stilled her tongue.

She put down the paper and turned on the telly. As she'd feared, the image of Arthur Scargill appeared. He was countering questions about men going back to work with his usual defence: 'There are more men out now than at the beginning of the strike.' As with most of his statements, it was based on truth but a distortion of that truth. The Belgate men and others like them had come out two weeks late on the promise of a ballot, so the numbers on strike had risen. But they had not come out because of fervour for the cause, as Scargill was suggesting; they had come out in the belief that by doing so they would get a ballot, and would then be able to vote for the strike to end.

It was a relief to climb into the car and drive away from Belgate. 'I will not think about the strike,' she said aloud as she passed the pit. The taste of soot was still on her tongue, in spite of cleaning her teeth, and enough was enough. They were eating Chinese tonight and she meant to enjoy it.

They chose a corner table and relaxed in each other's company. 'This is nice,' she said over coffee. 'Just sitting, not having to talk.'

Steve smiled. 'You're easily pleased.'

She put out a hand and touched his arm. 'I like being with you.'

Even in the shaded light of the restaurant she could see there was something sad about him tonight, an air of harassment. 'How's business?' she said. 'I know it can't be easy at the moment.'

He shrugged. 'Business never is easy. Beats me why there's always another mug ready to strike out on his own. But it's not that – it's Jean.'

Fran's heart sank. Steve's first wife was not her favourite topic of conversation.

'She knows about us. I suppose Julie let it out – Ian wouldn't say anything. He gets the brunt of it if she gets her temper up. Anyway, she's determined to play me up over the kids. She thinks they should spend every second Saturday with her, and they have to visit her mother on Sundays. She's trying to make it so difficult that I'll pack access in, but she'll have a long wait.'

Fran was puzzled. 'Why should she mind about us? She didn't . . .'

The words died on her lips. They were not flattering, but Steve finished them for her. 'She didn't want me? Of course she didn't. Not while no one else did. But now you've come on the scene, it's different.'

They made an effort to change the conversation. 'What about Min?' he said. 'Is she still toeing the line?'

She regaled him with tales of Min's new role as Dennis's personal and private geisha. Steve laughed. 'It won't last. It's against her nature.'

Fran was not so sure. She looked at Dennis with new respect nowadays. He had handled his crisis very well indeed. She had always thought him weak, but she had been wrong. When the occasion demanded, he could be strong enough. Stronger than Harold – if Eve had taken a lover, Harold would have gone to pieces.

The thought of Eve taking a lover was so hilarious that she laughed out aloud. 'Come on, share the joke,' Steve said, and she had to explain.

But in spite of the joke he still had a hangdog look about him. She gathered up her jacket and bag. 'Let's go,' she said. She would take him home and comfort him in the only way she knew how.

15

Thursday, 15 November 1984

The classroom walls were covered with the trappings of Christmas, red-nosed reindeers and bloated Santas, three Marys and Josephs, and a dozen babies spilling out of straw-filled cribs. Even the hamster's cage was topped with artificial holly and the ceiling lights cascaded tinsel. Fran looked down at the child's jotter once more. The heading 'Preparing for Christmas', neatly written and underlined with more gusto than precision. A holly leaf was carefully crayoned in one corner with the statutory three berries underneath, but it was the words that held Fran's attention. '*We are not preparing for Christmas. There will be no Christmas till someone gets that slimy bastard Scargill off my dad's back.*'

She looked at the sea of down-bent heads. They were reading *Charlie and the Chocolate Factory* and every face was rapt. She turned back to the essay: '*My dad has been on strike for thirty-two weeks. We go to my gran's on Sundays for a feed, and my mam has given the dog to some people. He was a good dog but she says he had to go. I want a BMX and Tracy wants a Sindy doll and some clothes, but my dad says when he goes back to work. I don't mind much but he does. He doesn't go out any more and my mam has stopped dying her hair. She says she feels old. Last Christmas was good. This one will be all right but we are not preparing much.*' She put '7/10' in the bottom right-hand corner and closed the jotter. If only she could write with so much power! If only she could show that essay to Scargill and Thatcher.

She wanted to tell Gwen about it in the staff room, but Gwen was surrounded, and had tears of mirth in her eyes. 'So the kid was halfway out of the door when he turned back. "Here, miss, are you a student?" I said yes, and he thought a bit, and then he said, "I said you weren't. You look too old." I pushed him into the corner and I said, "I looked all right when I came in here this morning, but you lot would get anybody down."'

The bell signalled the end of coffee break before Fran got

Gwen to herself and by then it was too late, but the thought of that bleak appraisal of life in a striker's home stayed with Fran throughout the next lesson and up to the bell.

It was two weeks since the NCB had offered a bumper pay packet to those who returned to work; £658, and no tax to pay. But still the Belgate men stayed firm. It was crazy really. They had voted against the strike in the first place, had been brought out by an untruth, and still they refused to cross a picket line. Not even for £600. Terry had tried to explain it to her. 'They voted to stay in – a lodge ballot. So it was all right to go on working. Well, I didn't think it was, but that's by the way. Then they came out . . . once they'd agreed to come *out* they couldn't go back and cross a picket line. That would be blacklegging. You won't get a Durham miner blacklegging. They won't be bribed, not if they were offered £6,000.'

She had tried to express her puzzlement. 'But they were lied to, Terry.'

For the first time he had looked uncomfortable. 'It's not as simple as that, Mrs Drummond. They weren't exactly promised.'

She had referred to all the letters in the local paper from men who felt that they had been betrayed, and he had taken refuge in incomprehension. 'Don't ask me, Mrs Drummond. I don't know what they're on about. I only know they came out under Rule 41, all straight and above board. And any road, even if Arthur has made mistakes, who else have we got to stick up for us? Tell me that. He said, "Come out," and I did!'

And he would stay out, she had no doubt about that. No matter what the privation, he would stand firm. There was the uncomfortable glow of a zealot in his eyes, and she both admired and feared it. He would stand firm while Belgate bled, while trees and fences went up in smoke, and men scrabbled in the earth of the mineral line for the makings of a fire. This morning she had seen a battle bus for the first time: a single-decker, every window covered with metal grilles. Behind the armoured windscreen the driver sat tense, his face obscured by a rapist's hood for fear of reprisals. There had been three men in the bus, that was all – fewer than the number of police accompanying them.

She had felt a frisson of fear as she drove past. It was 1984, after all, and Winston Smith nearer than she had thought possible.

When she got home Treesa was already pouring tea. 'Eeh, Mrs Drummond, you're in for a laugh when you go in the room.'

A fire smouldered in the grate, duff was piled on to old wood. Nee-wan sat behind the settee, shivering uncontrollably, eyes wild. From time to time he peered cautiously round the edge of the furniture to check on this strange new addition to the home. A stick caught fire and cracked in a shower of sparks, causing the dog to twitch convulsively. 'He'll be a nervous wreck by the time things get back to normal,' Fran said, and sat at the kitchen table to drink her tea. The *Echo* headlines were stark. The leader of the back-to-work revolt at Wearmouth had had the windows of his home shot out. In spite of this discouragement, 139 more men in the North-east had gone in. The trickle back would continue, and with it all the misery of a divided coalfield. Every night there were lists of men in court for picket offences or stealing coal. Every family in the mining villages was becoming involved. Fran herself, although she had no direct connection with the pit, could think of nothing but the strike. But more and more her chief emotion was disbelief. How could a strike which the majority did not want drag on for nine months? She put aside the *Echo* and went upstairs to get ready.

She ran a wickedly hot bath. Now that the boiler was out of use she was using the immersion heater, which lurked in the airing cupboard, a voracious beast, gobbling up ohms or watts or whatever they called them. When the bill came in she would rue every moment spent in getting clean, but for now she was going to enjoy it. As she lay in the scented foam she thought about Steve. If they were married, he might be standing at the basin, shaving, making jibes. He might cross to the edge of the bath and flick the suds or scrub the unreachable places between her shoulder blades. If they were married, he might pull her dripping from the water and make love to her there and then on the curly carpet. 'I wish I were seeing Steve tonight.' Saying it aloud seemed to exorcize her longing, and she got on with preparing for an evening at Min's.

The one sure thing about tonight was that Margot would not be there! Since she had espoused the miners' cause, Margot had been put back on Min's list of no-longer-desirables. It had been strange to watch Min over the three weeks since she had arrived, tear-stained and distraught, on Fran's doorstep. She was as well-groomed as ever. She still made quips about Dennis, but once when she called him 'hopeless' her eyes had met Fran's and suddenly been filled with confusion. It made Fran feel powerful, being the only one who knew about the showdown. She was still curious about Dennis: there seemed to be a new set to his jaw, although he was as affable and apparently *laissez-faire* as ever. Did she just imagine the change, or had there always been a hint of steel beneath the sugar coating? Just as Harold was marshmallow underneath, for all his blustering?

The suds were beginning to settle now. She hated that moment. In the bath you were safe, isolated from your troubles; once you stood up and lifted a foot over the rim you were back on the treadmill. She settled down in the water, determined to postpone reality for one more moment.

It was difficult to know who had come out on top in the Min/ Dennis situation. Dennis had appeared to dominate; on the other hand Min had got clean away with things. She had even kept her Capri. Fran realized she was grinning like an idiot and shut her mouth. The all-important Capri! It was true about cars being phallic symbols. Min enjoyed driving around in her fuchsia-pink penis, and would give up anything to keep it. So who were the weaker sex? Who finally won out?

On Saturday Fran had gone with Treesa to the support group. It was partly curiosity that took her there, partly a desire to help. Food was dwindling as shopkeepers felt the pinch. The local Co-op had set up a box by the door and people were tipping in one or two groceries as they left with their shopping, but it was never enough. Treesa's tales of families whose only meal of the day was at the church hall, and particularly of the plight of the single lads who had no income other than their picketing fees, had touched Fran's conscience. She had seen a boy going by with his meagre gift of food and felt her eyes fill. So on Saturday morning she had cleared out her tins cupboard and accompanied

Treesa to the church hall. Remembering the gold-earrings woman she had been scared, but the faces that turned to her were welcoming. 'Come and look at this, girls!' someone shouted. 'Corn in Egypt.' They had oohed and aahed over tins of soup and packets of suet. 'Let's get stuck in then, lasses,' a thin elderly woman said, and began to peel carrots.

Fran's intention had been to dump her gifts and run, but somehow she found herself dutifully chopping turnips. 'It's Irish stew,' her neighbour said, wiping away a tear. 'I don't know whether this bugger's grief or onions,' she went on, smiling at Fran. 'I'll be glad when I'm cooking for four again instead of feeding the five thousand.'

Fran nodded. 'It must be a strain.' She had a sudden feeling of sisterhood with the woman. It was not as she had imagined; these women were ordinary wives and mothers, neither bold nor militant. Certainly not menacing as Gold Earrings had been. Perhaps the bold ones were sent out to forage; the gentler ones stayed home to stir the pots. As if the other woman had read her thoughts, she grinned. 'It's awful, isn't it . . . having to scrounge? It's not what we've been used to, but when it's a question of feeding your bairns you don't split hairs. I daren't go round cadging, so I'm on permanent onions. It's not as though I agreed with the strike, but we're all in it together now, aren't we? Whether we like it or not.' There was a pause, then she continued. 'I know who you are . . . and your little boy. I was sorry when you lost your man. He was no age. And it's good of you to help out.'

They looked at one another for a moment and then went back to the vegetables. Emotion was misting Fran's eyes, and she took out her hanky and blew her nose. 'It's the onions,' the other woman said. 'The bloody things get everywhere.'

When the stew was bubbling away in the huge open pans they sat round the table together, elbows on the board, discussing life in general and the strike in particular. 'It'll last into next year.' The speaker was relighting a cigarette stub no longer than her thumbnail.

'My God, Jenny, if you can't say something cheerful, say nowt.' The smoker blew a defiant ring. 'I'm telling you! My man's never liked going down the hole. He's in his element now. He's got an old settee outside the pit gate, and he sits there declaring solidarity. If it's left to him, they'll be out till he's sixty-five.' There was a roar of laughter. 'All the same, we've got to stick it out. If Maggie Thatcher beats the NUM she's got the working classes by the short and curlies.'

There was a murmur of agreement. 'I've told my man I'll cut his balls off if he goes back.' The speaker was young and plump and determined. ' "I'll suffer," I've told him. "I'll give the bairns and do without meself." But if he scabs he'll come back to find the door shut.' The mood around the table was changing. Some chins were thrust out, other heads down-bent. The sound of the door clashing broke the spell.

'Treasure trove!' Manky Margot advanced, her arms full of goodies. 'Take these, they're defrosting.' She recognized Fran. 'Oh good, you've come at last.' She leaned towards her. 'I've emptied Jean Goodison's freezer. "It's no good pontificating," I told her, "you have to be active." So she gave the lot.'

Relieved of her burdens, she put up her hands and tucked her lank hair behind her ears. Her sweater was brown. '*The colour of faeces,*' Fran thought and blushed at the very idea. Her CND badge was still in place but *Coal not Dole* had been replaced by *I'm Supporting The Miners*. She turned towards the women, rolling up her sleeves. 'Right then, lead me to it.' As she walked towards the sink, the onion peeler lifted the frozen leg of lamb she was holding and brandished it at Margot's back. 'I'd like to,' she mouthed at Fran; and Fran, to her shame, had nodded agreement. Margot was a pain.

Since that first visit ten days ago, Fran had been back once, to deliver a sack of potatoes paid for by Gwen. 'Tell them I think they're mad but I like their guts,' Gwen had said when she handed over money.

'I wouldn't dare,' Fran had answered.

Gwen nodded. 'Then say they came from St Jude. He's the patron saint of lost causes, isn't he?'

The bath water was stone cold now and Fran heaved herself to her feet. If Min or any of her cohorts rubbished the support groups tonight, she would defend them. After all, what else were girls' nights but middle-class support groups? Except that sister-hood only lasted until you went to the loo and it was your turn to be done over.

In the event, no one was really interested in the strike. There was a little gloating when Fran appeared, but it was soon over. 'There's a hundred and thirty-nine gone back today, Fran. Good old Maggie, she's going to win.' Fran smiled noncommittally and they returned to their previous topic of conversation, the inquest on Diana Dors's husband. Half of them thought it romantic that he had died rather than live alone; the other half were sceptical. 'He'd lost his meal ticket, hadn't he? So he lost his bottle. Heaps of people lose their partners, but they go on living.' They looked to Fran for confirmation. She had wanted to die after David's death, but life had reasserted its hold.

'Can't we talk about something cheerful?' Eve said, always pulling the irons out of the fire.

They ate from the usual groaning board, making the usual vows to diet tomorrow. Eve carried her plate to where Fran was sitting and perched on the arm of the chair. 'Everything all right?' Fran knew what Eve was after: she wanted information about Min's affair, but was too proud to ask.

'Fine,' she said ingenuously. 'How's the baby?'

But Eve was not to be deterred. 'He's blooming . . . but that's not what I'm worried about.' Her voice dropped. 'What's Min up to? One minute she was flaunting that Hindson-Evans man, and then suddenly everything went dead. I can't get a word out of her. She just plays dumb when I hint and puts on a saintly expression.'

Fran made a show of wiping crumbs from her mouth while she worked out what to say. 'I'm sure it's over, Eve. In fact, I'm certain.' Eve was torn between desire to believe what Fran was saying and a fear that Fran was more in Min's confidence than she was herself. 'She didn't tell me,' Fran said hastily. 'I heard it from someone who works at the Royal. Hindson-Evans has a new girlfriend. A staff nurse in the theatre. Apparently it's quite serious this time.'

Satisfaction flitted across Eve's face, to be replaced with solicitude. 'Poor Min . . . still, it was only to be expected.'

As Eve moved away, Fran glanced up to find Min's anxious eyes on her. 'OK,' she mouthed, and had to repress a smile at the look of relief on her friend's face.

They ate and drank, then used up some of the surplus calories by dancing to a Wham LP. 'It was marvellous, Min,' Fran said as she made her escape.

'Drive carefully,' Min called as she climbed into the Mini. 'It worries me, the thought of you going back to that place. God knows what they'll get up to next.'

As though to belie Min's words, Belgate lay tranquil and silver in the moonlight without a sign of discord. Fran would have liked to pause in the car park and drink in the sight of sea and sky, but it was after eleven and she knew Treesa could not sleep in an empty house. Remembering how scared she had been in the days after David's death, Fran always tried to be home before midnight.

Treesa was not alone when she entered the kitchen. Terry sat by the cold boiler, huddled in his donkey jacket, an Adidas grip at his feet. 'He's left home,' Treesa said, looking at Fran round-eyed. 'His dad's going in in the morning, and they've had a row.'

Fran looked at the boy's face, pinched now with misery. 'I can't stop with a scab, Mrs Drummond. He's betrayed the union!'

Fran's heart sank at the boy's words. The strike was starting to crumble, but Terry refused to face it. In spite of the brave sentiments at the support group and Scargill's cockiness on TV, the dyke had been breached – only a few men as yet, but the return would snowball.

She unbuttoned her coat, fumbling for the right words. 'He doesn't see it that way, Terry. He thinks it was the union who betrayed him. Can't you at least try to understand his feelings?'

The reply was swift. 'Scabs don't have feelings!'

Inside Fran something snapped. She was tired of trying to see both sides. 'For God's sake, it's your father you're talking about, not a total stranger. *He* has a right to work if he wants to, just as *you* have a right to strike.'

Terry got to his feet and reached for the grip. 'I won't argue, Mrs Drummond. You're entitled to your point of view.'

Treesa's eyes were beseeching. 'He's got nowhere fixed up, Mrs Drummond.'

Outside a fine rain was falling and the wind was from the east. 'You can stay here tonight, Terry. I can't let you freeze. But I won't be drawn into a family quarrel. Your parents are my friends. You'll have to make other arrangements.' She saw his chin come up and hurried on. 'And don't give me any rubbish about pride. It's pride and arrogance that's responsible for all the trouble in this village. If you won't stay for your own sake, stay for Treesa's. She's got enough on her plate without worrying about you.'

Before she got into bed she pulled back the curtain and looked at the rain-soaked pavements. Where was it all going to end? Margot's badge had proclaimed *I'm Supporting The Miners* – but which miners? Those who had been forced into a strike against their will and who were trickling back day by day? Or the diehards like Terry, who would rather lie down in the gutter than share with a scab? Even when that scab was the man who had given him life.

16

Saturday, 1 December 1984

The sweaters were soft and luxurious and hideously expensive. She hesitated between beige and loden green, and decided the latter was more sensible for a man on his own. There were tiny Christmas trees at each end of the counter, and the till was covered in tinsel. While she waited to pay she thought about last Christmas, her first without David. She had wandered from shop to shop, rudderless, uncertain what to buy for Martin, turning her eyes from the sight of couples rapt with the magic of

Christmas. Now, a year on, she was buying a lambswool sweater
for Steve.

A wave of longing for David washed over her. They had filled
Martin's stocking together on Christmas Eve, one holding open
the pillowcase, one putting in the parcels, laughing and whispering, standing at the foot of the bed to gloat over the child they
had made together. She was roused from an ache of nostalgia by
the salesgirl's 'Can I help you?' She put down the green sweater
and turned away. 'Thank you, I haven't quite made up my mind.'
Impossible to buy gifts for one man while you were remembering
another!

She went up to the restaurant and bought herself a cup of
coffee. There was still money about in Sunderland, in spite of
the strike. The Wearmouth pit was huge, but its workers were
only a small part of Sunderland's population. In Belgate the
strike had killed Christmas. Streets that in times past had bristled
with lighted trees in uncurtained windows were dark now,
curtained to keep out the cold. But the cold got in just the same.
That was the overwhelming impression now, as though winter
had got into everyone's bones.

People who had never gone without a fire in their lives still sat
by empty grates, as though by concentration they could restore a
flame. 'I haven't been warm this year,' an old woman had told
her yesterday in the street, and she had seen that the misshapen
knuckles were blue. She sipped her coffee and tried to remember
the summer. They must have been warm then. The summer had
been grim but quiet, before the strike got its second wind.
Scargill had promised that General Winter would defeat Mrs
Thatcher, but it was his own troops who were succumbing and
still he was marching on towards Moscow, oblivious of casualties.
The faces of the strikers and their wives were desperate, but not
as desperate as the faces of the tallymen who moved from house
to house in search of payments they knew would not be
forthcoming. The economy of Belgate was based on tick. Now
the pendulum had slowed to a standstill.

She looked at her watch. Still half an hour before she was
meeting Steve. A woman cleaning tables loomed into sight, and
Fran raised the empty cup to her lips. She never dared to occupy

restaurant tables unless she could be seen to be there by right. She wondered if Steve was in the store already, guiding Julie around the toy department, and wondered once again what would happen at Christmas. He hadn't mentioned it yet, and she didn't like to ask. The attendant began to clear the next table, throwing half-eaten food into a plastic container and stacking plates. Across the world in Ethiopia people were dying of hunger, and here the means of their salvation was shovelled into swill. Fran gathered up her bags and rose to her feet. If she sat here any longer she would get the blues, and she wanted to be in a good mood when she met Ian and Julie.

She bought the sweater and some new lights for the tree, and quelled her rising panic over money. There was only one way to cope with Christmas: get what you needed and worry about it later. If you once paused to cost it out, you would wind up carving an Oxo cube. In each department the clocks ticked remorselessly towards four o'clock. She thought of Laurence Olivier urging 'Once more unto the breach', and made her way to the rendezvous. Last year Julie had been a small dark-haired girl in a Red Riding Hood coat and Fair Isle knee socks. Today she wore cord jeans and a fur-trimmed jacket, but the small, closed face was the same. Last year she had ignored Frances. Today she muttered a sulky 'Hello' and tugged at her father's arm. Each time they had met in the last twelve months, Fran had made an effort. It couldn't be easy to leave your mother behind and meet your father's girlfriend. But there was something faintly insolent in the child's attitude that made forbearance hard. The boy was different.

'No Martin?' he said. There were small pustules on his brow and a faint moustache along his upper lip.

Fran smiled. 'He's gone off with Gary Malone to look for firewood. They're going to make a fortune in one afternoon.' He had always been kind to Martin and she was grateful. 'How are the A-levels?' He fell into step beside her and she nodded sympathetically as he recounted his troubles.

They paused in the rainwear department. 'What about Santa Claus?' Steve asked hopefully.

Julie's nostrils flared. 'No way!' Last year she had been a child afraid of the bearded figure; today she was a woman, contemptuous of the very idea. It was too swift a transition. She turned to her father and administered the *coup de grâce*. 'It's a proper con, Mam says. They only give you rubbish.'

As they sat in the restaurant, Fran toyed with haddock and chips and thought about the future. If she and Steve were married, Julie would be her step-daughter. Access days would be statutory, even access weekends. The fish turned to wormwood in her mouth, and she chewed frantically. Suddenly she caught Ian's eyes. He was looking at her sympathetically, as though he knew what she was thinking. If she married his father, there would be Ian too, so it wouldn't be too bad.

She was about to ask his plans for Christmas when she realized what a minefield that would be. Would he expect to spend it with his father, or accept that his father's place was now with her? At seventeen could you relinquish your father to another home, another family's Christmas? She was glad when the meal was over and they made their way from the store. 'See you tonight,' Steve murmured, eyes bright with fear that she might expect a kiss in front of Julie. She curbed an unreasoning impulse to clasp him around the neck, and made her dutiful goodbyes.

She called at Bethel's, on the way home, to hide the gifts she had bought for Martin. 'I like him to be surprised,' she told Walter, who was drinking tea by Bethel's one-bar fire.

'Well, he won't find out from me,' Bethel said, shutting the cupboard door on the gifts to emphasize her point. 'But I doubt you'll keep quiet.'

Fran opened her mouth to protest but Bethel had moved on to higher things.

'The money's pouring in for that taxi-man's bairns.' She pushed a mug of tea towards Fran. 'Pit folks sending in out of shame, I shouldn't wonder.'

Fran looked at Walter but he was uncharacteristically silent. The day before, a man driving miners to work had been killed when a concrete block crashed through the window of his taxi. 'They've come down to murder,' Bethel said, remorseless. 'The miner used to carry his head high but now . . .' She caught Fran's apprehensive glance at Walter. 'Oh, he'll say nowt. Ask him about Libya . . . watch him squirm!'

Walter's mug thudded to the table and the wheels of his chair spun for the door. Fran could bear no more. 'Walter, please . . . she's only teasing. I know she shouldn't, but don't fall out!'

He turned at the door. 'I don't have to stay here and listen to rubbish, and neither do you. Hadaway to your own home and see to your bairn. You'll get nothing out of that one. She's far ower bitter.'

Bethel's reply was triumphant. 'I've stung you this time, Walter, haven't I? Your precious NUM's gone cap in hand to Gadaffy . . . that's what you cannat stomach.'

To Fran's horror she saw Walter's lip tremble. 'No, I can't stomach taking cash from them as shot down a nice young girl, Sally Bethel. But think shame of yourself for rubbing my nose in it. It's bad enough to hear union men saying, "We'll take cash from anyone." It's bad enough to see the union I had pride in prostitute itself for money, but to have a friend ram it down me throat . . . that's too much.'

When he was gone Fran felt her face going stiff. She was angry with Bethel and she would have to say so, but she didn't know how. It was Bethel who broke the silence in uncharacteristically meek tones. 'Aye, I suppose I went a bit far.' Fran tried to look reproachful, and Bethel bristled. 'But was it or wasn't it the truth? They're messing in the gutter now, and we might as well all admit it. Canny lads like Fenwick being tormented night and day . . . no, it's time to stop excusing it. This is not a pit strike; the bugger's political, and that's wrong! We'll shift Thatcher through the ballot box. No other way!'

As Fran parked the car in the back street she resolved not to think about the strike any more that night. She wouldn't read the *Echo*, not even if she got withdrawal symptoms. She was contemplating a hot bath and a blow-wave when Martin met her in the kitchen doorway, eyes bright. 'Mrs Malone's here.'

Fran motioned him to precede her. 'All right then, let me get in. It's cold out here.' Their eyes met and he grinned. 'Yes,' Fran said drily. 'And it's cold in here. I hope you took Mrs Malone in to the fire.'

The big, red-haired woman was sitting by the fire, her grandchild on her knee. 'By, he's lovely, isn't he? The image of his dad.' Treesa was sitting proudly on the other side of the fire, enjoying praise of her son.

'Have you had some tea?' Fran asked.

Treesa nodded. 'It's not been made long. I could top it up. Would you like a cup?'

Fran was about to refuse, having had about as much tea as she could drink, when she saw Mrs Malone's face. There was a plea in the blue eyes. 'OK,' she said. 'Yes, I'd like a cup.'

As soon as Treesa had carried away the teapot, Mrs Malone moved forward. 'I don't want her to hear, Mrs Drummond. She's that thick with our Terry, she's sure to tell him and then he'll turn awkward. I want you to speak to him, Mrs Drummond. He'll listen to you. It's killing his father. Killing him. He lost one son to the pit, now he's losing another. I'm not sure this isn't worse, seeing a lad you've brought up walk past you in the street.'

The baby on her lap stirred, disturbed by the vehemence of her tone. 'There now, pet, hush a minute for your nana. It's breaking my man, I'll tell you that for nothing. He's stood up to a lot in his time, but this'll finish him. Him a scab, him as stood by the union right and wrong for years! I've seen him cry . . . and I'll never forgive Scargill for that. You know why he went back – because they tricked him out. Betrayal, that's what he calls it. I don't know the ins and outs, I cook and clean, I'm not political . . . I don't blame Scargill any more than Thatcher. But they're trying to murder this coalfield between them, I do know that.'

There were sounds of Treesa's return from the kitchen and she drew back. 'Mind on what I said . . . don't let him know it was me that asked – but do what you can.'

There was no time for a bath after Mrs Malone's departure, so Fran picked up the evening paper after all. Scargill was in the high court fighting over NUM assets. Nothing new there! She turned to the letters page for her daily fix. As usual the letters all had pseudonyms, derived from the same fear that caused men to appear on local TV with their backs to the camera. Shades of Big Brother! One writer wanted the NCB to invoke the law. Another, signing herself 'Fed-up Miner's Wife', wanted to know where cash donated to miners' families was going, because she wasn't getting any of it. 'Plain Common Sense' wanted Maggie Thatcher to '*Climb down and help this country*', and 'Worried Mother' vowed that if the council helped the miners at Christmas she would never vote Labour again. '*My husband has been out of work for four years, and we have had nothing.*'

As she folded the paper Fran reflected that the strike was turning the out-of-work against the miners, and that was a pity. A recent article had asked sympathy for the pregnant wife of a striking miner, but at least she had a wage to look forward to at the end of the strike. For the out-of-work there was nothing.

She met Steve in the Saracen. He was making jokes, fussing over her drink, but she could feel the unease in him. It reminded her of dates with Edward a year ago – an attentive escort who was nevertheless on hot bricks. It was not a pleasant feeling.

She sensed his relief when she mentioned the strike. 'How's your support group going, or have you chickened out?' She told him about her last flying visit. 'I took some potatoes, and they were pleased. But that big woman was there . . . the one with the hoop earrings . . . she scares me. It's as though she's ready to explode all the time.'

He smiled. 'Who says women are the weaker sex?'

'You don't think it'll end before Christmas?' Fran knew the answer even as she asked the question.

'No chance. They're making their preparations for a striking Christmas – toys from France, turkeys from Germany. All your showbiz do-gooders rallying round to help the miners and none of them with a blind idea of what the miners really think . . . the real miners. The ones that go down the hole instead of attending union meetings.'

'Things'll have to be different when all this is over,' Fran said. 'The rank and file'll have to have more say. And I think they will. They've learned their lesson.'

Steve shook a doubtful head. 'They'll forget the pain. They'll start to earn again, and they'll forget.'

'I think you're wrong,' Fran said. 'It's gone too deep. Families split, marriages cracking . . . they'll remember, all right.'

They were on to the coffee now and suddenly tension was there again. 'Look, Fran, there's something I must get straight . . .'

He was not going to be with her at Christmas. Jean had invited him to stay over the holiday to be with the children. 'I've said yes . . . you know how much it'll mean to Julie. Besides, Jean would only take it out of Ian if I said no. But I'll make it up to you at New Year. You know who I want to be with, don't you?'

Fran hung on desperately to her dignity. It would be all right as long as she didn't cry. 'Of course you must go. I wouldn't want to be separated from Martin at Christmas. I understand.'

Driving home she felt anger wash over her. Damn Jean! Damn Julie! Damn Steve, for that matter! What about *her* Christmas? And Martin, with no man around? How bloody dare he drop her at Christmas and run back to his wife? His ex-wife, for whom he seldom had a good word? She knew she was being unfair, but she couldn't help it. She understood the anger: it was the emotion you substituted for other deeper emotions that could not be borne. A return to the primitive, a beating of the chest at the absolute bloodiness of life. It wasn't as though she was madly in love with Steve. As Belgate came into view she tried to analyse her feelings for him, but it was difficult to know where love began and fear of a vacuum ended.

She moved into a lower gear and into her own back street. She had brought the car to a standstill when she saw the masked figure, all dark except for the white patch that contained his eyes. And then another and another, coming over a back-yard wall further down the street.

When at last she plucked up courage to get out of the car, the back street was empty. Useless to tell herself that she had imagined them – they had been real and sinister.

When she got in she would dial 999. But even as she thought it, she knew she would not.

17

Christmas Eve 1984

'Will it do?' Treesa's face was anxious. The dress, which had fitted her before the baby, now bulged at every seam, riding up over her stomach.

Before Fran could speak Bethel sniffed. 'You want some sugar on your ankles!'

Treesa's face was blank. 'Sugar on me ankles?'

Bethel smiled as the well-sprung trap closed. 'To see if you can 'tice that skirt down a bit!'

Fran laughed nervously but Treesa's eyes filled. 'I knew it was too short! Well, that's it, I just can't go.'

It took five minutes to calm Treesa down. 'Honestly, Bethel,' Fran said when Treesa had gone back upstairs. 'Honestly ... she hasn't been across the doors for a year. Now Terry's persuaded her to spend one night at the club – it took him weeks, and he can ill afford it – and you've done your level best to ruin everything. You're getting worse.'

Bethel looked back, unrepentant, cheeks rosy beneath the grey hair. 'If she's that easy put off, she's better stopping at home.' She saw Fran's lips forming an angry retort and hurried on. 'Any road I didn't come round here to argy-bargy over Treesa Carruthers. I came for two reasons. One – are you going out with that feller of yours tonight? I need to know if I'm wanted, I can't drop everything. And second, what time do you want Walter round here tomorrow? I'll be coming early to do the veg, but we don't want him here criticizing.' She paused for breath, and then delivered a final thrust. 'And to go back to Treesa for a moment, I wouldn't be encouraging anything between her and that lad if I was you. He's not like their Brian – *he* did have a bit about him ... the only one of that family that wasn't barmy. This one's a proper little communist. He's left of Mao Tse-Tung, if you ask me.'

Fran stood up. 'I'm not going to rise to the bait, Bethel, not on Christmas Eve. You know how I feel about the Malones. I'm going to put the kettle on and we'll have a nice cup of tea.' She ignored Bethel's allegations that she would be waterlogged from tea-drinking if she came round here much more, and brewed the tea. She didn't refer to not going out with Steve later on, and with surprising tact Bethel did not repeat her question. Instead she brought up the matter of Christmas toys.

'They've all been gloating over what they were going to get from the miners in France. Toys? You'd think it was double-decker buses they were expecting, not Dinky cars. Any road, there's only a few stocking-fillers come, by all accounts. I met one lass this morning, crying. Her man's COSA – good enough to strike with the NUM but not good enough to get the toys. They're for NUM only. Not that she's missing much – Ellis's wife went for her four bairns, and came home with two plastic skittles for the little 'un. She was nearly hairless when I saw her. Serves you right for counting your chickens, I told her.'

Fran groaned. 'Honestly Bethel, talk about a Job's comforter.'

Bethel's eyes flashed. 'I've got no comfort for this sackless lot. They want to get back to work before there's no work left to go back to. There's faces collapsing right, left and centre. I've told Walter – Scargill'll close more pits than MacGregor could. Mind, I've got no room for that American bugger; he's less use than a one-legged man in an arse-kicking contest, if you'll excuse the language. But this business of begging here and scrounging there ... they're out in Durham market place with tins, bold as brass. My man won't be turning in his grave, he'll be spinning. Money from that mad Arab ... all right to pal up with murderers, but they'll cross the street if they see Fenwick doing his bit shopping. And there's Botcherby trying to put a good face on it while his wife goes round the bend and his poor little bairn gets old afore her time. If that's pride, if that's loyalty, I think he's giving it to the wrong ones.

'And that's not all! You've got daft wives with bairns in pushchairs marching on the Electricity Board protesting at being cut off for non-payment. It's not fair, they say. And while they're protesting, their men's dancing round the power stations trying to get us *all* cut off, old-age pensioners and everybody. "Make your mind up," I told one. "Do you want to freeze, or don't you?" Old people there, never done any harm to anybody – they've cut off their concessionary coal, or if they get it it's full of stone. They're sitting shivering over one-bar fires, and the strikers are even trying to stop those. "It's not Mrs Thatcher you're punishing," I've told them. "It's your own kith and kin." But they don't listen.'

Fran tried to point out that Mrs Thatcher had cut £1 off heating allowances and slashed regional aid, but Bethel was deaf to reason. 'There's Alfreton pit collapsing for want of safety work. You know why? One girl went in to type and the safety men downed tools: "We're not playing if she's playing!" Talk about bairns? I told Walter, and he says the lass should've known better . . . the lass should! He's getting worse!'

She was still on her soap-box when Fran escaped to the shop for some last-minute purchases. Normally at this time the shop was crowded both sides of the counter. Last Christmas Eve she had stood in rank to wait her turn. Now the shopkeeper coped alone and the only other customer was Mrs Malone. Fran's heart sank. She had tried to persuade Terry to go back home but had come up against a stone wall. '*I cannat, Mrs Drummond. It's not that I wouldn't . . . but how can I ask the lads not to scab if I sit down at the table with a scab meself?*' When Fran had relayed a version of his answer to his mother, she had put down her head on her kitchen table and cried. Tonight she gave Fran a wan smile. 'Eeh, it's not like Christmas Eve, is it? There's nobody in the streets. You'd think it was the middle of the night.'

The shopkeeper joined in. 'It's the daft little things you miss – that's what they tell me. The nuts and tangerines and the big fire, getting your hair done, even wrapping paper. There was a woman in here last week cried over the wrapping paper. "I've got nowt to wrap up," she said, "but I still hanker for a nice bit of paper and string."'

As Fran had walked home she was remembering the Sunderland vicar who had warned that miners' marriages were on the brink of disaster. That had been weeks ago. This Christmas would make them or break them, but none would escape its effect.

She made the stuffings when she got home: sausagemeat for

the neck, and sage and onion for the inside. The trifle base was already in the fridge, the roast potatoes par-boiled and coated with butter to preserve them. She deserved a rest! She carried the *Echo* through to the spluttering fire and curled up in a chair to get out of the draught.

According to the paper, an uneasy peace had settled on the coalfield since the pits closed last Friday, and there would be no picketing of safety men over Christmas. MacGregor had gone to the States for a family Christmas there, and the thought of his departure cheered Fran enormously until she read that Arthur Scargill would be having a working holiday. 'Oh dear,' she thought, and went back to the kitchen.

Martin was at the fridge, filling two glasses with milk. Gary sat at the kitchen table. 'You look miserable,' Fran said.

His usual cheerful face was glum. 'I'm all right.'

Martin closed the fridge door with his elbow and carried the two glasses to the table. 'No, you're not.' Gary's brows came down in warning but Martin was not to be deterred. 'He wants their Terry home for Christmas, but he's stopping at his lodgings.' Gary's eyes were on the glass of milk but he did not drink. 'Go on,' Martin said, 'tell her. She knows already. You can't keep a secret from someone who knows already.'

Suddenly Gary was out of the chair and round the table. 'Shurrup,' he said, between clenched teeth. His fist caught Martin in the chest and sent the milk flying. Gary looked at Fran, eyes half-afraid, half-wild. 'I don't care,' he said, and then again, 'I don't care!'

When the kitchen door slammed behind him, Fran fetched the dishcloth and mopped up the milk. Martin rinsed the glasses in the sink and stacked them on the drainer. She wondered if she should speak, but wasn't sure what to say, and it was a relief when the phone jangled in the hall and called her away.

'I'm off now,' Steve said. 'Girded up for the ordeal.' She knew what he was trying to do – assure her that it was the children he was going to see and not Jean.

'It won't be so bad,' she said, wishing her voice carried more conviction.

'Thanks for the parcel,' he said. 'It feels nice. Don't open yours till tomorrow.' There was a pause and then, 'I love you, Fran. You know that.'

She made tea and carried a cup to Treesa. 'Don't panic,' she said. 'Just drink your tea and then we'll fix things up. I've got heaps of things, and I'm bigger than you.'

Treesa slurped her tea and sniffed. 'Nobody's bigger than me. I feel like a house end.'

Fran nodded towards the crib. 'He was worth it, wasn't he?' The baby slept serenely, unaware of tensions within and without the house that was his home.

Treesa smiled. 'Yes. Well worth it.' She blew her nose on a tissue. 'I'm sorry to be going on like this, but it's been a bad couple of weeks.'

Fran nodded. 'I know.' Last week had been the anniversary of Brian's death in the pit. Treesa had carried the baby to Mass and returned dry-eyed and composed, making Fran ashamed of her own reddened eyes. Now she sat down on the edge of the bed. 'Things will get better, you'll see. They'll sort out your compensation soon; the strike will end eventually . . . it has to. And then things can get back to normal.'

Treesa nodded and was about to smile when a thought struck her. 'You won't want us out of here, will you? When the money comes? Not straight away? That's why I've never grumbled about it taking so long to prove about Christopher being Brian's bairn, and having a right to claim, and everything. Because I was happy stopping here.'

Fran reached out and covered Treesa's hand with her own. 'You and Christopher belong here. For as long as you want to stay.'

One day, if things went right, Treesa would have a home of her own and a man to love her, but this was not the time to mention it. As if on cue the baby stirred and woke, and they could crowd round his crib to admire. Sometimes, Fran thought as she went downstairs, sometimes it seemed children were the only worthwhile thing in life. The only thing that didn't cause you pain. Then she remembered the Malones, and the pain caused there by son to parents. So there was no escape after all, no area of life which guaranteed you peace.

It was hard to imagine Terry as a militant when he knocked at the door and entered the kitchen. His hair had been trimmed of its wildness and he wore a collar and tie. She couldn't resist a comment. 'You look smart.'

The rosy cheeks grew rosier. 'I thought I'd make an effort, seeing as it's Christmas. One of the women at the support group, she used to be in a big hairdresser's. She's doing cuts. She does a canny job, doesn't she . . . 50p for a married man and 25p for lads.' He grinned. 'Another good reason for not getting wed.' He looked down at his clothes. 'I got the shirt and jacket from the nearly-new last Wednesday, and the tie's me mate's. His wife said put it on.' Suddenly there was a silence between them. Mention of his new lodgings was a reminder of the home he had left, and of Fran's efforts at persuasion on his mother's behalf.

As she licked her lips to try again, he spoke hurriedly, as if to stem embarrassment for them both. 'Is Treesa ready? We'll have to get down the club or we'll not get seats.'

Fran was not so easily put off. 'Are you going to call on your parents over the holidays? You can say it's none of my business and you'd be right. But the strike's over now, surely you can see that? Why prolong the bitterness? I feel so sorry for your mother, losing Brian and now you. And think of your father . . .'

He cut across her words. 'He didn't think of me did he, before he betrayed the union? I've taken some stick because of him. I'll never forgive him. Hard? I know it's been hard – hard for everyone. But we've stuck it out. We will stick it out, Mrs Drummond, don't get any wrong ideas. The rats can scuttle back, but the men'll stop out till Doomsday if they have to. Look at Billy Botcherby – *there's* a bloke to be sorry for, if you like. A wife bad with her nerves, and everything. But he doesn't crack! He's on the rack, that man, but he doesn't scab! My dad's always had good money; he could've stuck it out . . . so I'll never forgive him, Christmas or no Christmas.'

Fran felt bound to defend Mr Malone. 'He hasn't gone back for the hardship, Terry, or the money. He's gone back because of what he sees as an injustice. He wasn't given a say; they've even denied the men meetings. There are others who feel the same, Fenwick for one. It's an NUM rule that you ballot on a strike, isn't it?'

His nod was contemptuous. 'Yes, let's have the old chestnut trotted out again. As for Fenwick, he's made his bed. I didn't agree with his pigeons being brought into it, but that wasn't the union, that was hot-heads. There's been attacks on union men's homes, don't forget that! It's not just violence by our side. Everything that's been done in this strike's been strictly according to the constitution. Arthur's a good union man, he plays it straight. Everything he's done's had the backing of the executive. And them as go against the decision of the executive are scabs.'

Fran's spirit failed in the face of such intransigence. Terry was marching to his own drum, and nothing and nobody would change him. He had scrabbled for duff to earn the money for tonight's outing – pointless to spoil it with an argument, especially one that could not be won ... 'I'll go up and see if Treesa's ready,' she said, and left the room.

She found Treesa sitting on the edge of the bed, one hand on the crib where her baby slept. She was dressed in her slip, covered by a wool cardigan. 'I cannat go, Mrs Drummond. I cannat get into me dress ... an' anyway, even if I could, I can't face it. Everyone'll be thinking about Brian. I know it, I can see it on their faces. They don't understand about Terry and me ...' Suddenly she looked up. 'You know there's no funny business, don't you?'

Fran offered up a swift prayer for guidance and sat down on the bed. 'Yes, I know exactly how things are between you and Terry, Treesa. I know how you felt about Brian. But I also know Terry's made sacrifices for tonight. You know he's had nothing but the money he's got for picketing, and that's hardly enough to keep body and soul together. He got the money for tonight by selling duff from the mineral line. He did it so you could have a good time, to take your mind off your troubles. If you don't go, all that'll be for nothing.'

Treesa made no reply but she ceased to rock the crib and folded her arms across her chest. 'Sometimes,' Fran said slowly, 'sometimes women have to do things they don't want to do. Not because they're weaker than men, but because they're stronger.'

Suddenly she was back in Steve's flat a year ago, hiding in his
bathroom because she was afraid, emerging at last because he
had such need of her. 'I'm not asking you to enjoy tonight,
Treesa . . . although I think you might . . . I'm asking you to go
for Terry's sake – and Brian's. Do what you can to heal the
break with the Malones. Maybe not tonight, but when you can.'

Treesa sighed and nodded. 'I know.'

As Fran scurried in search of suitable dresses for Treesa, she
vowed to afford herself a shield one day and use '*I know*' as her
motto.

Twenty minutes later she stood in the doorway watching them
leave, giggling a little to cover the awkwardness but with at least
a touch of anticipation. Treesa looked good in the jade blouse,
the black wraparound skirt and her black mohair cardigan. When
Fran shut the door she felt the first stirrings of Christmas.

Eve rang at seven to make sure she hadn't changed her mind
about staying in Belgate for Christmas. Min rang at seven-thirty
to point out what she was missing. 'I'd have thought you'd be
glad to get Martin out of that hell-hole. God knows what they're
plotting as a holiday diversion – blowing up the railway line or
rifling the Co-op store. We're having goose . . . turkey's so
plebby now. I've really excelled myself, and it's not too late to say
yes.'

She assured Min her answer was still no, and put down the
phone. She lit the tree and put out the centre light before Martin
brought in his cocoa. They sat either side of the fire, strangely
content, discussing the exact moment they would give Gary
Malone his gift. She had first suggested delivering it to his
mother for inclusion in his stocking and then had thought better
of it: Belgate stockings would be thin this year, or even non-
existent. She had gone to town on Gary's gift at Martin's
insistence. Better avoid comparison with what his parents would
manage. Mr Malone was back at work but they were still deeply
in debt. So the boxing gloves and punchbag were wrapped in all
their knobbly glory and hidden in the front room. 'When he
comes round tomorrow,' Martin said, wriggling with pleasure at
the very idea, 'when he comes round, we'll push him in there
and . . . wow . . . I can see his face!'

After he had gone to bed, uncomplaining in his haste to bring on the morning, Fran was suddenly lonely. She went in to check on the sleeping baby and pulled aside the curtain to look on the frosted street. It was quiet and strangely peaceful, as though the holiday had brought about a hiatus in the strike. A truce, so that you almost expected to hear 'Silent Night' and see opposing troops come out from their trenches to fraternize. If only she could have moved Terry Malone. The thought of his relentless young face drove her down to the kitchen in search of coffee and a tot of the Drambuie Gwen had given her and which she had been saving for New Year.

She made up the fire, sorting carefully through the dust for pieces that were not slate. Slate cracked when heated and ricocheted round the room, reducing Nee-wan to a jelly. 'Good dog,' she said when he settled behind her chair. He was the only companion she had, so better make the most of him.

Her textbooks looked at her reproachfully from across the room, but she was not in the mood for work tonight. Not on Christmas Eve. A group was on the TV, two boys, two girls, as bland and wholesome as corn cobs wrapped in tinsel. '*Love, love, love,*' they sang, and were followed by a comedian who spewed out hate. Most jokes were barbed, if you thought about it. Other people's discomfiture was funny: 'It didn't happen to me, goody-goody gum-drop.' So you could afford to laugh. Steve had been funny tonight – distant and strained. 'I love you,' he had said before he rang off. He always said that, but tonight it had been ... a shibboleth. And where on earth had she got that word from? She reached for the dictionary. '*Shibboleth, a party catch-word.*' Appropriate or inappropriate? She couldn't decide.

She was suddenly horribly depressed, worse even than last year. In Belgate they were thronging the clubs for one good night out. In Sunderland, Eve would be putting the final touches to her feast, filling stockings, standing with Harold to gloat over the new baby. She poured herself another Drambuie and kicked off her shoes. A new and uncomfortable thought was pricking at the back of her mind and must not be allowed to emerge.

A quarter of the way down the Drambuie she accepted defeat and brought the unbearable into view. In Sunderland now Steve would be sitting with Jean, Julie asleep in the bedroom above. Ian off somewhere with his friends. Perhaps he had cooked a meal, put a candle in a glass. Perhaps Jean would turn to him just like she, Fran, did and he would draw her to her feet and up the stairs to bed. She had a sudden mad impulse to ring Jean's house and put the cat among the pigeons, even going as far as looking up the number. And all the while a voice in her head reminded her of her doubts. Did she love Steve? Would she marry him if he asked her? Or was Nature simply abhorring a vacuum and so causing her to suffer like this?

In the end she put away the phone book and went upstairs to wash her face. Christmas, Christmas, you longed for it from afar and when it arrived it was often more than you could bear.

The baby was still asleep, a fist to his chin. As she watched, his brow wrinkled and then cleared and his mouth moved in a quick smile. It was only wind but it cheered her enormously. There was something about babies that was balm. In all the arguments over Warnock, no one could deny that. She wanted to pick him up and hold him but she knew she must not. She contented herself with a touch to his cheek. 'Happy Christmas, Christopher,' she said and tiptoed to the door.

When she was ready for bed she collected Martin's gifts from behind the chair where Bethel had hidden them earlier and carried them upstairs, listening through the crack of the door to make sure he was asleep. She was halfway across the room when he spoke. 'You can put the light on, Mam. I'm not asleep.'

She put down the parcels and put on the light. He was propped on one arm and he patted the bed. 'Sit down for a minute. I promise not to look.' He grinned. 'That is, if there's anything to look at.'

She pursed her lips. 'Oh, there's the odd thing. Nothing much.'

There was silence for a moment, and then he spoke. 'I remember you and Dad doing it. I used to pretend to be asleep, but I never was. You used to giggle and whisper, and then he'd give you a kiss.'

She felt tears fill her eyes, but made no move to brush them away. 'Yes, Dad always enjoyed Christmas Eve.'

He changed his elbows. 'I've been thinking about things.'

She waited. 'Tomorrow, could we send something to Ethiopia? A cheque, because the post office's shut.'

She nodded. 'That's a good idea.'

He looked relieved. 'I'll pay my half.'

She nodded again. He looked away and she wondered what was coming next. 'I'm sick of the strike,' he said. 'At first . . .' Now he was looking sheepish. 'At first I thought it was fun. You know, exciting. Always someone fighting, and things. But now it isn't funny any more. Gary fights with everyone all the time, and sometimes . . . well, it's just not nice any more.'

She smoothed the sheet and settled him down. 'It can't last much longer, darling. One way or another it has to be over soon.'

In her own bedroom she prayed for Belgate, wondering as she asked favours if the God who had allowed the strike to start had the power or the inclination to bring it to an end.

18

Tuesday, 8 January 1985

Down below her, the tiny figures moved with precision, enacting a familiar ritual. She had watched it often during the holidays, and she knew the pattern. In the clifftop car park, a few hundred yards from the pit, the battle-buses were waiting, with metal-meshed windows and masked drivers. Clustered nearby was a gaggle of blue police vans, their occupants outside, jumping and clapping to escape the cold. Sometimes they kicked a ball around, scoring between imaginary goalposts and cheering superior moves. Then the convoy would drive into view, blue flashing lights on the vans, strained faces behind the wheels of the ordinary buses that were considered safe as long as they were away from the pit. In summer the car park lay between fields yellow with wheat, dappled cows in green pastures, a sea striped blue and sunlit. Now the landscape was barren, striking in sympathy.

The normal buses disgorged working miners, tiny men in parkas and woolly hats, bait boxes under their arms, looking neither right nor left till they reached the safety of the armoured buses. A quarter of a mile away, three or four hundred men were waiting at the pit gates to chant and jeer and jostle and bang impotently on the battle-bus sides. At first Fran had held her breath, expecting a raid by pickets on the car park, but none came. The battle-buses would leave the car park unmolested, drive a few hundred yards, and enter the pit in a hail of stones and abuse. The empty shuttle buses would drive out of the car park and vanish; the police would laugh and joke and climb into their blue vans, leaving the car park again deserted, with only the distant ugly clamour to prove an exchange had ever taken place.

Some men had refused the shelter of the buses, preferring to walk in, heads erect, eyes fixed on nothing in particular as though oblivious of the shouts of 'scab', the blows, the spittle that flew through the air to land on shoulders and chests and wincing, unprotected cheeks. Fran could never decide whether they were extra-brave or merely foolhardy. Most of the men rode safe in the armoured buses, and moved obediently through the exchange in the car park like marionettes.

Today was routine. From the shelter of the trees Fran watched, wondering how much it was all costing, wondering how grown men could participate in such a charade. The whole coalfield was moving obediently through some ghastly minuet, no one quite sure whose music they were dancing to, but dancing all the same. Striking miners chanted at the pit gates, working miners embarked and disembarked. Police glided here and there, forming and re-forming with expertise. These were the police who had collected for the strikers' children at Christmas. Now, in a glad New Year, they were facing those same strikers on the battlefield and would mount a baton charge if they had to. If everybody stood up and said, 'Enough,' it would be over – but no one did. Only MacGregor and Scargill spoke, and theirs was a barren language. Yesterday she had seen Angela Botcherby in the corner shop, spending the family purse with the gravity of a pensioner.

When the car park was empty, Fran retraced her steps into the wood. Next week she would be back at college, and walks with Nee-wan a luxury, so she meant to spin out today. To right and left, raw stumps gleamed white amid blackened outer trunks. Even the bridge across the beck was gone now, chopped down in the night and spirited away like the park benches. The union was distributing logs to pensioners and no one could begrudge them, for old people felt the cold more keenly. She felt warm inside her 'sheep' and full of resolutions. She liked new years, they reminded her of brand-new exercise books. She walked on, enjoying the crackle of winter twigs beneath her feet, the sparkle of spiders' webs in crevices hoary with frost. She must persuade Martin to come out with her sometimes. He was missing so much beauty. She was ready to whistle up Nee-wan and turn for home when she came across the clearing. It had been a natural space in the wood, a circle of grass. Now it was scorched and blackened, with here and there pieces of broken glass.

She stood, stupid, thinking of Martians and extra-terrestrial fireballs, until a more mundane but equally horrifying explanation dawned. Someone had been throwing petrol bombs! She felt a sudden desire to laugh. This was Belgate; this was an English wood. This was an idiot making a mushroom cloud out of a molehill. Except that before Christmas a bus full of working miners had been attacked with petrol bombs on its way to the pit.

Nee-wan was digging furiously in the ash. Fearful of cut paws, she snatched him up and carried him to safety.

Lunching with Martin, she struggled not to tell of her discovery. He was too young for such a disclosure; he was sensible and steady, but even sensible children experimented sometimes. Better not put ideas into his mind. 'Bethel and Walter are coming to tea,' she said.

He grinned. 'That'll put you in a good mood, then; I'll be all right for a loan.'

She smiled, a little taken aback at his perception. 'How do you know it puts me in a good mood?'

He tapped the side of his nose to suggest wisdom. Suddenly his eyes gleamed. 'Do you want to hear a song?'

The tune was 'What shall we do with the drunken sailor?' The words were new:

> *'What shall we do with Maggie Thatcher?*
> *What shall we do with Maggie Thatcher?*
> *What shall we do with Maggie Thatcher, early in the morning?*
> *Burn, burn, burn the bastard,*
> *Burn, burn, burn the bastard,*
> *Burn, burn, burn the bastard, early in the morning.'*

She let him finish and gave him a lecture on democracy, but she knew her words were falling on deaf ears.

She was washing up when Terry arrived. 'Where d'you want it?' The paper sack was filled to the brim with duff and exuding dust from every seam. She made a place for it behind the pantry door and thanked him. As usual he refused payment. 'Not from you, Mrs Drummond. Besides, it's for Treesa and the bairn as well.'

Fran closed her purse. 'Well, it's very kind of you. And I hope you're being careful, Terry. That bank's completely overhung now. It must be dangerous. The *Echo*'s on about it nearly every night. There's been people killed in other parts of the country.'

He shook his head in derision. 'They weren't miners, Mrs Drummond. That's the difference. Don't you fret yoursel', I know what I'm doing. And I never go in without me marrer there. There's nee danger if you're careful.'

Fran gave way. 'Well, if you're sure ...' They were so confident, the Malones – so certain and optimistic. Was it their Catholic faith or their Irish blood? She could never be sure.

She sat down to do an hour's work on her holiday tasks. She was reading Piaget but the words just wouldn't penetrate her brain. Eventually she put her books aside and started preparations for tea.

'I hope you don't get him on about the strike,' Bethel said when she arrived. She had put on her Crimplene dress in honour of the tea party, but scorned underpinnings so that her bosom heaved right and left in glorious abandon.

Fran nodded. 'I know. Everybody's sick of it.' She had wanted to confide in them about the petrol bombs, but perhaps it was best to keep quiet. They might advise her to dial 999 and she wasn't sure how she would react to that. Anyway, the police had ways of knowing things, so it wasn't really up to her to be a nark. She was pondering the concepts of honour and informing, when Walter arrived, abusing the steps and Bethel in the usual equal proportions. 'It's the last time I'm coming here. Of all the God-forsaken ways to get into a house. He was a step-fanatic, the feller that built this. It wants bulldozing.'

Fran felt herself relax as she always did in Walter's presence. He was such fun!

As they settled down, complaining about the fire, she mentioned her visit to the blast. 'I've been meaning to tell you for ages. It was like walking on the moon. Bare and desolate, nothing growing. I felt frightened.'

Walter positively glowed. 'Frightened? Frightened! That's a townee for you: nee guts. You should've seen the blast before the war. People lived in the caves down there . . . they'd have frightened you, all right! Loppy Dick with his staring eyes and his woman, Blast Martha . . . and Sandshoe Sammy. Characters, that's what they were.'

Fran knew better than to interrupt. She merely widened her eyes.

'They turfed them out about 1937, but they kept on going back. They liked living like that, free to come and go. They didn't want council houses . . . or they didn't want rent books, more like. The military went in while the war was on, blew the place up. Aye, they'll not be content till we're all homogenized. He was crawling with lops, old Dick, a bit of sacking round his shoulders, hair like a raggedy mat. I mind on he used to stand and rub his back against the corner walls, just to stop the itch. He came from a good family, you know. Richard Thomas was his name. Proper gentleman . . . but filthy.'

Fran was intrigued. 'How did he live?'

'Door to door. Bit of tea here, bit of sugar there, sixpence here or a box of matches. He managed. Then there was Ganny Airship. She lived alongside the Bottleworks, long skirts, always saying she was going away in a flying ship. By, she was a character. They won't stand for that nowadays. We've all got to fit the mould.'

The thought of Walter fitting a mould was so hilarious that Bethel and Fran burst into laughter. 'Aye, laugh away, hinnies. But you mark my words.'

Bethel leaned over and dropped her voice. 'I told you to get Walter on about the blast.' There was a note of pride in her voice.

'I must give you back your copy of *Peter Lee*,' Fran said. Walter had loaned her Lord Lawson's biography of the miners' leader at Christmas, and she had read it twice. 'I liked it. He was everything you said he was. And there was one bit . . . someone had underlined it . . .'

Walter closed his eyes and began to recite. '*Not only men but nations must realize that the human family is thus so linked together that we must work together in a co-operative spirit if civilization is to endure.*'

Fran nodded. 'You know it by heart.'

Walter sighed. 'Aye, he was a great man, all right. God only knows what he'd make of this lot.'

Bethel groaned. 'Don't start. Think of your blood pressure.'

But it was too late. Walter was into his stride. 'They've only got themselves to blame. If they'd stuck by the rule book there'd've been none of this. They've buggered the union. A hundred years of striving thrown away on one man's bloody vanity. It makes you weep.'

Fran daren't look at Bethel who would be gloating over Walter's apparent change of heart, but she couldn't resist a question. 'Why don't they go back then? They didn't want the strike; they only came out because they were promised a ballot. So when that promise was broken, why didn't they go back, together, in a block?'

Walter spread his hands over the tartan rug that covered his knees. 'It's not that simple, bonny lass. They had a lodge meeting and they voted to stay in. So they could cross the picket lines at the start because they'd made a joint decision. Then they met again, and they swallowed a lot of pap and voted to come out. Once they were out they couldn't go back in because it would mean crossing a picket line. And that would be scabbing, and scabbing is something a miner does not do. Do you understand?'

Fran shook her head. 'No, not really. Why don't they have another meeting and vote to go back in?'

He smiled. 'Because the union never lets the dog see the rabbit. And if they did get a meeting, it'd be a show of hands and you'd have the militants down the front counting . . . but really marking down anyone who crossed them. It'd take a brave man to stand up to that lot.' He leaned towards Fran. 'I'm talking about your boyfriend, young Malone. Butter wouldn't melt when he's in here, but you see him out there making his mouth go. That's a different story!'

Bethel set down her cup with a clatter. 'I'm glad someone else is telling her. Gullible, that's her trouble. But mark my words, there'll be bloodshed here before we're finished. Look at Botcherby's lass . . . she'll never be right again.'

Fran nodded. 'Has she always had trouble with her nerves?'

Bethel's snort of contempt was instant. 'Nerves? It's not nerves that ails her, it's stark bloody fear of the club woman.'

Fran knew about clubs, the slip of paper that entitled you to buy goods in the stores of Sunderland and for which you paid week after week. Bethel was continuing. 'She's not the only one – they're battening on each other now. Them as has money's saying, "Take a ten pound club out and I'll give you five for it." They're that mad to get a bit cash, they do it. The five pounds is gone in a flash, and they have ten to pay back – more with the interest. There's some of them so far in now they'll be lucky to be left with what they stand up in.'

Walter had fallen to musing, anger gone. 'We dreamed about nationalization, you know. Before the war there was a miners' MP tried to put a bill through. We thought it'd be a piece of cake once we were the masters . . . but the first fifteen years after nationalization were my worst in the pit and no mistake. We put up with it because we believed in the dream. We thought if we got rid of the slag-heaps we'd have a green and pleasant land. But we've got coal they can't sell, piled higher than the slag-heaps ever were. Now you've got too many chiefs, and what Indians there is is barmy. When a pit's done, it's done – it doesn't have to be exhausted. I mind on when there was coal there, tons upon tons of it, laughing at you from behind a fault . . . and you had to let it go. Now they've had near enough a year of neglect. If I was still a pitman I'd be witless with fright to go down again and sort those faces out. There'll be more than a few too dangerous to work. It'd never have happened in Attlee's time. He'd've sorted it.'

Fran nodded. 'What about Kinnock?' Walter's face lit up with delight. 'Our Neil? He needs a cure for fence-sitter's arse, that one. Never send a boy to do a man's job. Not that he's not a sight better than Thatcher. She'd curdle milk.' He sighed. 'Aye, it's a sad day for the miners.' His fingers touched the rug over his knees, as he began to hum and then sing:

'The flour barrel is empty now, their true and trusted friend,
Which makes the miners wish today the strike was at an end.
The pulley wheels have ceased to move which went so swift around,
The horses and the ponies too are brought from underground.'

He looked up as he ceased to sing. 'That was written in the Durham lock-out in 1892 but it's still true today.'

Treesa came into the kitchen, the baby in her arms. 'Aye, it's not a bad little bairn,' Walter said when Christopher was presented for inspection. 'Let's hope it takes after its mother's side when it's grown.'

Fran saw Treesa's brow cloud and rushed to repair fences. 'He's like his daddy, and we love him for it.'

Walter's grin was evil. 'His dad was all right, it's his uncle that's causing all the trouble.'

Fran looked apprehensively at Treesa, but the young girl stayed calm. 'You can witter on as much as you like, Walter, but you won't change my opinion of Terry. I don't agree with everything he says or does, but he's all right. And it's not just miners causing trouble – there's a few policemen got something to answer for, not that they'll ever have to.'

The best thing about Walter, Fran reflected, was that you never knew which way he was going to jump. 'Aye, you're right there,' he said, as meek as a lamb.

*

While she washed up she thought about the evening ahead. She wanted to enjoy tonight, make Steve enjoy it too. If he wanted her to go back to the flat, she would go. She pictured him in her mind's eye, smiling, drawing her towards him, his lips tracing mouth, throat, breast, belly ... they had not made love since before the New Year. Which meant they had not made love this year. Which was a long time. At New Year they had both been tired and more than a little drunk, and since then he had been worried about business. 'It's only money,' she had teased, and had seen his irritation. It was more than money to a man; it was prestige and virility and being able to look your neighbour in the eye in the pub.

They met in the Saracen, Steve rising from the fog of smoke to wave a welcome. 'It's packed tonight,' she said, squeezing in beside him. They were sharing a table with three young men, heads together, faces turned away from strangers. While Steve was getting her a drink she realized they were miners and for the strike. They sipped their halves of Exhibition carefully, spinning them out, and she strained her ears to catch their conversation. 'I don't hold with that, Jimmy. Not the position he's in.' One was advocating some sort of mayhem, another disagreeing. The third stared into space, obviously weighing the matter.

'Look at it like this, Jimmy,' the second one said. 'He's a one-parent family through no fault of his own. So he gets social for the kids but they keep fifteen quid off, which leaves nowt. Well, as good as nowt. Now in my book the union's got two choices: tell him to stop out and pay for his bairns, or let him go through. You can't say stop out and let your bairns starve. Them kids has no mother.'

The first man shook his head. 'You let one through, they'll all be at it. It's hard, of course it's hard, but this is a bloody war we're fighting!'

The third one finished cogitating and put down his empty glass. 'I'd go in if it was my bairns,' he said and wiped the last wisp of froth from his lip.

As Steve slipped into the seat beside her, the three rose to their feet. 'It's a bad do when you've got to make do with a half,' one of them said, laughing.

The third man slapped him on the shoulder as they moved away. 'You should thank Arthur for getting rid of your beer-belly for you.'

His friend laughed and hitched up his slackened jeans. 'It's a good job I can thank the bugger for something.'

When they had gone Steve grinned. 'Bloody but unbowed?'

Fran nodded and moved closer. 'Tell me what's been happening to you. I'm sick of the strike.'

There was only one thing she wanted to do, go home with him and climb into his bed, but first she must play out the charade of drinking and talking like civilized people. She put out a finger and traced the tendons of his hands. She liked his hands, lean and brown with the wrist-bone somehow vulnerable where it protruded from his slightly fraying cuff. 'Let's get out of here,' she said when desire overcame discretion. 'It's ages since we had time to ourselves.'

The wind was bitter and whipped her hair into her eyes. She reached for his hand and urged him to run for the car. Some lines of poetry came into her mind, remnants of a long-dead literature class . . . '*to bundle time away that the night come.*' She would have liked to share the poem with him but two things stopped her. He was always embarrassed if she launched into a literary discussion, saying, 'that's too deep for me' – and she still did not feel safe enough with him to admit she wanted him to take her to bed.

Instead she stayed silent as the car threaded the Sunderland streets and drew up outside his flat. 'Do you want a drink?' he said, switching on lights and struggling out of his coat. If she waited, the moment would be past. They would drink and talk, and the clock would move round too fast. She let her coat drop to the floor and reached for him.

As she moved against him she felt his body respond, and a flicker of triumph ran through her. 'I love you,' she said against his ear, half-whispering, half licking his so-desirable flesh.

'Oh Fran,' he said and then again, 'Oh Fran.'

They moved into the bedroom, she stumbling out of shoes, he trying to hold them both upright. Some innate modesty made them turn away to undress and then they were between the cold sheets and reaching and turning.

She knew almost at once that he could not make love to her. He was going through the motions but she had a distinct sense that his mind was elsewhere and that elsewhere was not a pleasant place. 'What's the matter?' she said at last, sliding her arms around him to show him that all was well. If they could lie there for a moment, if he could relax, everything would come right. But he was pulling away from her, sliding from beneath the clothes to sit on the edge of the bed, head in hands. 'If you can't it doesn't matter. You know it doesn't matter . . .'

He cut through her words. 'It's not that . . . well, it's not just that. I've been trying to tell you for weeks now. I'm going back to Jean.'

As she drove through the bleak winter night, her tears were tears of indignation not tears of loss. He had known for weeks and had not spoken. He had allowed her to attempt a ridiculous, humiliating seduction, and still he had not spoken. The thought of being naked in the bed with him made her feel unclean – because there had been three of them in bed; Jean had been lying between them, watching them behave like fools.

She tried to rationalize her feelings. She had always known he was weak; that had been half the attraction, his need of her. So why did it matter so much that he had proved what she had known in her heart all along? Perhaps only women were brave? Perhaps she should not be crying after all.

19

Saturday, 2 February 1985

She felt a sense of release as she breasted the bank and saw the Palace Green laid out before her, shimmering still with frost at ten in the morning. She had tried in the last few weeks to keep busy, and look happy, but Bethel was hard to fool. 'So it's off then, the big romance?' It was a statement rather than a question and only required a shrug in reply. 'Aye, well, there's better fish in the sea than ever came out of it.' And then, when that failed to elicit an instant, glowing response, 'For God's sake get yersel' off this weekend; buy something you can't afford and cheer up. I'll mind the bairn. There's that many long faces round here nowadays, it gets a body down.'

Obediently Fran had arranged a trip to Durham, done her grocery shopping in advance and left the day free for sybaritic pursuits. She had with her the magnificent sum of £2 mad money. Except that there was nothing she wanted to buy, nothing she wanted to do. As she neared the door of the cathedral she prayed as she had done for the last few nights, *'Please God, give me a quiet mind.'* It wasn't much to ask, just freedom from the thoughts that had racketed round her head since that night with Steve ... shame, indignation, a sense of loss. And if she was truthful, a feeling of relief. He had dumped her – that was the harsh truth! And in dumping her he had relieved her of the necessity of making any sort of commitment. She was back in mid-stream, treading water and well away from rocks or rapids. Except that she wanted to be loved; she even indulged in fantasies where figures of authority, uniformed and in command, made love to her with unofficial fervour.

She slipped into a pew and fixed her eyes on the rose window, hoping to exorcise her randy thoughts; but the image of her phantom lover remained in her mind. She closed her eyes and buried her face in her hands, seeking to fill her head with prayers. It was useless. She stood up and moved into the aisle. A year ago, in the aftermath of David's death, she had come here with Martin and prayed for God to ease her path. Instead he had piled difficulties her way. True, she had overcome them but the going had been tough. Now she was tired of struggling.

She found herself in front of the Miners' Memorial, a masterpiece of carving, with tiny, distorted miners guarded by fat cupids garlanded with vines. *'Remember before God the Durham Miners who have given their lives in the pits of this county.'* If the strike came to an end with an honourable settlement, she might cheer up. There was no fun in Belgate now, a war-torn town in a ravaged countryside. Yesterday she had seen a dog, ribs sticking through its skin, scavenging dustbins as they stood in the back street for collection. And Scargill and MacGregor, urbane and smiling, continued to preside over a civil war that was cracking communities throughout the country.

She put 50p in the collecting box before she left, to pay for lack of reverence in her thoughts. She had hoped to find peace in the cathedral and found only stone.

She was halfway down Silver Street when she heard the shout – 'Hold on, Stirling Moss!' The last time she was here she had met Steve in the Market Square and her knees had threatened to give way at the sight of him. This time it was Min with Dennis in tow, loaded with dress bags. 'Where are you off to in such a hurry? I saw you from the boutique window, and we raced out but you were gone. Anyway, we've found you now! Where's Martin?' Min's eyes were bright with curiosity, and not about Martin. 'Is he here . . . Robert Redford?'

It was time for a statement. 'Martin's at home and I don't see Steve any more. He's gone back to his wife.'

Min's eyes flashed 'I told you so' in Dennis's direction, but he was rearranging his parcels to free an arm.

'We're going for a drink,' he said when he'd succeeded. 'You look as though you need cheering up, Fran, and I've got a mouth like a birdcage.'

They settled in the Market Tavern, hemmed in by market traders come in to escape the chill. Fran smiled at Dennis. 'Long time no see.' As the words left her mouth, she regretted them. The last time she had seen him, apart from fleeting glimpses, they had been discussing his wife's adultery. How unkind of her to remind him! She raised guilty eyes and found him smiling.

'Cheer up, Fran. What can I get you?'

When he had shouldered his way to the bar, Min moved closer. 'Are you upset? About the car man, I mean? He wasn't your type, Fran. He was nice . . . sexy, even, if you like them thin and intense. But he'd never have been another David.'

Fran licked her lips. Min, Min, insensitive bloody Min. 'I didn't want another David . . . you won't replace someone just like that. Steve was – is – a good friend. It was never more than friendship.'

Min made a face to show tolerant disbelief. 'Don't take my head off, I only asked! You know I care about you. If you knew how many times Dennis says he wishes you were out of Belgate . . . he thinks the whole place will erupt before long. Someone at Ladies' Circle was saying they're all being sent for training with the IRA . . .'

Fran threw back her head and laughed. 'Sometimes, Min, you are so *ridiculous* . . .'

The nice thing about Min was that she took insults on the chin. Her face drooped, and then brightened. 'Well, as long as I've made you laugh . . .'

Dennis walked back with her to the car park to deposit the parcels and return for more. 'Take care, Franny,' he said as she was about to climb into the Mini. On an impulse she straightened up and kissed his cheek. 'And you,' she said warmly. 'Don't change, Dennis. I like you as you are.'

She drove out of the car park and took the Belgate road before she let the tears come. She didn't know why she was crying, but she knew it was right that she should. When the tears ceased, she pulled into a lay-by and dried her eyes. She felt cleaned out, rested. As she put the car into gear again, she thought that perhaps God did exist after all. She had gone to the cathedral to beg for a quiet mind and, in the most roundabout of ways, she had found it. Remembering the mad money still unspent, she went into the fish and chip shop before she reached home and bought cod and chips for everyone.

They had finished eating and were sitting companionably, elbows on table, when the kitchen door opened. 'It's only me!' Margot was wearing a Friends of the Earth sweatshirt under her duffle, which provoked Fran to think uncharitably of Nature in general and the Earth in particular. Margot was a walking mass of allegiances, nothing more. Pull out the front of her jumper and there would be a junction box with wires and a voice box that went on whirring 'Demonstrate!' long after the robot that housed it had shuddered to a halt.

By way of penitence for her thoughts, she gave Margot her chair and watered the pot. 'Lovely,' Margot said, clasping the mug around its middle in what she probably hoped was true working-class fashion, '*Stop nit-picking*,' Fran told herself sternly, and pulled up another chair.

Margot was wearing her 'I've-done-my-little-bit-for-the-miners' look. Something was coming. 'We're having a women's rally next month. And a vigil. The whole department's giving support, and there'll be token attendances from all over the region. Some of the women from the support group may come, but I've told them it's optional. The whole point is to show that *non-mining* women are in this struggle with them, shoulder to shoulder. We're planning a token ... something quite massive for each month: the rally and the vigil for March, and a Day of Hunger for April ...'

She never got around to May. Bethel had risen to her feet and appeared to be steaming at the nostrils. 'A day of hunger for April? Well, now, that's nice. There's been hunger around here for twelve months in case you've missed it. And how many bellies will you fill with your token-this and token-that? I'll tell you – none! You lot'll watch this strike drag on week after week because it suits your purpose. I'd even go so far as to say you're wetting yoursel' in case someone solves it. Get away to hell out of it, before I forget I'm a lady and bash the life out of you.'

Fran accompanied a flushed Margot to her car. 'I'm not going to take umbrage, Fran. Poor thing, it's her age. I'd have a word with the doctor, if I were you. I can give you the address of the Alzheimer's Society ...' Seeing Fran's blank expression, she explained. 'Alzheimer's ... it's just the trade name for senile dementia ... the silent epidemic?' She looked at Fran expectantly.

'I don't know about epidemics, Margot, but I do know Bethel isn't senile. OK, she may have been a bit outspoken ... rude, even ... but there's nothing the matter with her brain.'

Margot unlocked the door of her car and turned with a tolerant smile. 'Well, let's hope you're right ... but give me a ring if you need advice.'

For 'if' read 'when', Fran thought, and loathed herself for waving goodbye to the retreating Volkswagen.

To banish the last lingering trace of Margot's visit Fran whistled up the dog and went for a walk. The days were drawing out now, but still the daylight would not last for much longer. She made for the allotments because they were within easy reach and because their very haphazardness was a comfort. Old sinks and galvanized buckets and blunted spades were thrown aside there, and within days had become part of the landscape, their edges gentled by grass, their colours muted by wind and rain. There was a new addition since her last visit, a hand-printed notice pinned to a gate: 'THIS PLOT BELONGS TO A STRIKING MINER.' There had been bitter tales of winter produce that vanished in the night, and this was the result. She peered over the fence to see if the notice had been obeyed, but the earth was barren, whatever had grown there gone.

She came out at the other end of the path and walked down the alley that led to the main street. The wooden fence that bounded the path had almost disappeared; only the concrete plinths remained, the rusted hoops that had held the posts dangling empty. When the brick wall began it was daubed with graffiti: '*Kill the Pigs*' and '*Scabs are Shits*' and everywhere the plaintive '*Coal not Dole*'. Even the war memorial had not escaped. When she reached it she saw that beneath the dates 1914–18 and 1939–45 someone had added '*1984–5 The People's War*' in white spray paint.

She put Nee-wan back on the lead for fear of traffic and turned into Stafford Street. The problem was, who were the people? As far as she could see Britain was turning into a mass of pressure groups, all of them maintaining that they spoke for 'the people'. But she doubted very much if any of these self-appointed spokespersons had much in common with the British people. She was searching her mind for something she had read once about the voice of England that 'has not spoken yet', when Nee-wan whined and pulled on his lead. She turned and saw Terry Malone behind her. He bent to fondle the dog and then fell into step beside her.

'Have you seen Treesa today?' she asked.

He shook his head. 'No, I was just coming round now.'

Fran grinned. 'You're lucky you weren't in an hour ago!' She told him about Bethel's treatment of Margot, expecting him to laugh, but his face clouded.

'That's half the trouble with the strike, Mrs Drummond – outsiders sticking their fingers in. I don't mean you, you belong here; but the likes of her . . . what's *she* doing coming over here every day? She's just a laughing-stock to the men. They call her Tokyo Rose because she's always spouting propaganda. OK, she's only a joke. But you get all sorts on the pickets. They wouldn't know a pit from a pot-hole, but they're in there, causing trouble – and then we get the blame for it. It's the same with the pollis, they come from everywhere but here. If we'd been left, just local lads on the pickets, local bobbies on the police lines, you wouldn't've had half the trouble. Not half of it. And . . .'

Fran was never to hear what else he had to say. She was still glowing from his description of her as 'belonging' to Belgate when she saw his words freeze on his lips and his eyes widen. She followed his gaze and saw the cause of his consternation. Mrs Botcherby had emerged from her front door, head erect, arms at sides. She was naked except for her fur-trimmed slippers that slopped absurdly on the ends of her spindle legs. Fran stood looking at her, thinking of Norman Mailer and something he had written about naked men and women moving forward into gas chambers. '*Here a titty and there a twat* . . .' Mrs Botcherby's tiny breasts sagged pathetically, there were silver stretch-marks on her abdomen and her pubic hair was black, tinged with grey. Long after Terry had shrouded her in his parka and was shepherding her back into the house, an image of her nakedness remained in Fran's mind. In a frozen chicken factory the live chickens were hung from wires and rotated so that someone could slit their throats. They had tied Mrs Botcherby and hung her on the wires, but no one had had the courage to administer the *coup de grâce*.

Monday, 4 February 1985

It was a relief when light began to filter through the curtains.
She had slept fitfully, never more than twenty minutes at a time,
waking always in a fever of anxiety over a dream. In one she had
been terribly conscious of having sweaty feet; people had moved
away from her and she had been ashamed. In another she had
tried to crawl through a gap between two stones. On the other
side was freedom and pure air, but the gap narrowed as she
struggled through, so that she woke scrabbling at the duvet to
escape.

She looked at the clock. Ten to seven. If the rumour was true,
Terry Malone would be nearing the pit gates now. She couldn't
believe it, but Bethel vowed it was fact and Gary, when tactfully
probed, had not denied it. She snuggled down to escape the chill
and pondered her dreams. What had caused them? In her waking
moments she had thought almost continuously of Terry Malone
and sometimes of shortage of money. She had wondered briefly
if Steve was curled round Jean in sleep or if they were occupying
distant edges of the mattress, but she had put such thoughts
resolutely aside. Whatever she was going to lose sleep over, it
wouldn't be a man.

At five to seven she jumped out of bed and snatched for her
dressing gown. Outside the world was ice-bound. Two birds
hunched morosely on the frozen telephone wires and there were
frost patterns inside the window panes. She wondered if Treesa
had taken the baby into her bed and hoped she had. He was
seven months now, too big to smother but too small to resist
hypothermia. Downstairs she put on the oven to warm the
kitchen and began Martin's breakfast. 'Have you heard anything?'
he asked as he came into the kitchen.

She shook her head. 'Not yet.' The radio was spilling news,
but there would be no figures for a return to work for another
hour or more. And then they would not mention Terry Malone.
They would not know of his existence.

She couldn't believe Terry would go back, not even after the trauma of Saturday. They had bundled Mrs Botcherby into the house and Terry had sprinted for the phone box. Fran had stayed until Botcherby arrived, carrying a sliced loaf and a bottle of sterilized milk. He had listened in silence, then mounted the stairs to check on his wife. Angela sat on the settee while all this went on, methodically buttoning and unbuttoning her cardigan, not saying a word and – more significantly – asking no questions.

When Botcherby came downstairs, Fran had sensed he wanted her to go but was too polite to say so. 'It's the pressure,' he said as he saw her to the door. 'Pressure, pressure, always more pressure. She couldn't stand not being able to pay her way.' Now Mrs Botcherby was in hospital and Belgate seethed with rumours, the chief one being that Botcherby was returning to work and so was Terry Malone. Could one incident change a deep-held conviction? She had seen pain on Terry's face on Saturday, and pity – but no sign of wavering.

Martin was snap-crackle-popping with gusto, the milk leaving a white moustache on his lip. In some Belgate homes this morning there would be no breakfast. And yet, for the most part, they stood firm. They had not wanted the strike, they had fought against it; but now, after eleven months of deprivation, they still stood firm. It was an enigma, but a marvellous one. They had stuck together and survived with only a handful of casualties. But if Terry went back today, she had a feeling the dyke would break.

Martin was finished now, scraping his chair back from the table. 'I might know before you,' he said. 'I might find out off Gary.'

'From Gary,' Fran corrected.

He nodded irritably. 'I know, I know. But if he goes back, will it be right?'

Fran shook her head. 'I've told you, I don't know. If a man has a right to strike, he surely has a right to work. The trouble is they all think they're right, the strikers *and* the workers. They're both convinced.'

'So they do things like fighting, because it's in a good cause?'

Fran nodded. 'They think it's in a good cause ... but that doesn't make everything they do right ...' Her voice trailed away. How could you explain civil disobedience to a eleven-year-old? Even when that eleven-year-old was determined to have an answer?

'Well, what would make you do things like that?'

Suddenly it was easy! 'I'd only fight if they tried to stop me voting. That's the most important thing. If you can vote, you can change things. And don't you forget that!'

She felt quite light-headed with wisdom until she remembered that nowadays there was hardly anybody worth voting for.

She got Nee-wan on his lead and sent Martin to school. The streets seemed oddly empty, the houses eyeless and closed. 'It feels like wartime,' she thought. Any moment resistance fighters would spring out from a back street and tanks rumble round the Half Moon corner. And then a film crew would materialize and shout 'Cut!' It was all unreal. It was too early for shoppers, but the single woman she passed, hurrying to the corner shop in carpet slippers, was raking in her purse as she went. She looked up as Fran drew level. 'It's a bugger, isn't it?' she said.

Fran was opening the back door when the man hailed her. He was wheeling an ancient bicycle with a sack strapped to the saddle. 'Want some coal, lady? Proper coal, no rubbish?' He looked cheerful inside the shabby parka. *Coal not Dole* was pinned to his chest. She wondered where he had got 'proper' coal, and the question showed in her face. 'Fell off a lorry,' he said. 'And you can't turn down a chance like that nowadays, can you?' So it was stolen . . . from the pit-heap probably.

'No thank you,' Fran said politely. 'I wouldn't dare.'

He grinned. 'Who's to know, missus? The evidence goes up in smoke.'

She shook her head. 'No, sorry. I'm too scared.'

He shrugged and began to walk away. Her conscience pricked. What if he was on strike and needed the money? 'Never mind,' she called out, 'the strike'll be over soon.'

His face, when he turned, showed consternation. 'I hope not, missus. I'm working up a canny little business here.'

She had to wait until ten o'clock to hear what had happened. She sat down to work on her essay but the radio kept diverting her. At nine o'clock they predicted a record return in the North-east – well over eight hundred 'new faces'. But of the most important face of all there was, predictably, no mention. When Bethel arrived she insisted on putting on the kettle and removing her hat, coat and scarf before she was willing to talk. 'Come on,' Fran urged. 'Just tell me . . . did he go in?'

Bethel took out her cigarettes and lit up. 'He did and he didn't.' She was being deliberately perverse but urging would have a reverse effect. Fran sat back and waited.

'I got it off Mary Whiteside, who went down with her man to make sure he got in all right. She says they were shouting and bawling, and them at the back were throwing rocks . . . only half the time they were hitting their own men, not the pollis. The buses went in, and then half the pickets ran round the back because some men were getting in over the fence behind the washery. And then Botcherby comes round the corner with Malone's lad beside him, and Mary says it all went quiet. Botcherby's face was a study, she thinks he was drugged; and Terry Malone had a funny little smile on his face. Then someone at the back shouted 'Scab!' and they surged forward, and then Ella Bishop . . . you know, the big wife with the gold hoops? . . . she got on Botcherby's other side and fended them off.' Bethel paused and drew on her cigarette. Something good was coming! 'And then . . . they got up to the gate, and Botcherby went through, and young Malone turned round and walked back. Without a word. Not a look to right or left. Mary says they might've known he wasn't going in because he had nee bait and nee towel, but nobody twigged.'

'So he just went along to make sure Botcherby got in safely?'

Bethel nodded. 'I think he was mad not to go in hisself but . . . well . . .' She gave a leer that might have been a grin. 'I'll say nowt more, or you'll be going on and on about all the Malones being angels. Funny angels, that's all I can say.'

Before they could further discuss the Malone family, Treesa appeared in the doorway, the baby in her arms. 'It's all right,' Fran said. 'Botcherby went in all right, but Terry didn't.'

Treesa sighed. 'Thank God for that. I couldn't stand any more trouble at the moment. I don't think the bairn's very well. He's been whingey all night, and I've just got him off.'

Bethel and Fran moved nearer. 'Poor bairn,' Bethel said soothingly. 'Well, he looks peaceful enough now.'

Fran touched his brow. 'He's rather warm.' The baby's face quivered with a spasm of wind, and all three women smiled. 'It makes you wonder how anyone could hurt them, doesn't it?' Fran said.

Treesa shook her head. 'They were talking at the group yesterday about a lass in the wide back street. She's got two bairns under five and she fell again, so she's had an abortion.' Her face was full of Catholic conscience. 'I know it's bad times, but there was no need for that.'

Bethel's face sharpened. 'Don't go criticizing other people, miss. Unless you're a fly on the wall, you don't know all the ins and outs.'

Fran saw Treesa's chin come up and hurried to smooth things over. 'Come and have a cup of tea.'

Treesa shook her head. 'I've got to get down there and get the dinners on. I came to see if you'd watch the bairn down here, seeing he's off colour.'

Fran looked at the blank sheets of essay paper. The relevance of Montessori to the present-day teaching situation could wait another day. 'Better than that,' she said. 'You stay with the baby and I'll go in your place.'

She walked to the church hall, glad of the time to pluck up her courage. It was always a bit of an ordeal to walk into the support group. She was still an outsider among women who had grown up together and were bound together now by a fierce belief in what they were doing. In some ways they seemed more fervent than their men. '*I've told my man he can go back in*,' one had said last time, '*but I'll have the door locks changed when he gets back.*' If it was true that northern men had dominated northern women in the past, the wheel had certainly turned full circle.

As she reached the end of the street she heard a rhythmic thudding. In a front garden stood a beautiful Victorian sideboard, intact down to the original brass drawer-fittings. A man and a woman were laying into it from either side, raising their axes

shoulder high in their haste to shatter the ancient wood. Fran
wanted to protest, but it was too late. The axes had gouged
through layers of age and veneer, and the raw wood was exposed.
As she drew level the woman looked up. 'It's a nice state
of affairs when you're chopping up your home to keep warm.
Still . . .' She gestured at the man, '. . . he's in his element 'cos
it came from my side an' he's never liked it.' The man grinned
and redoubled his efforts as Fran moved on.

In the event the support group was less of a strain than she
had feared. Today the women were mostly silent, chopping and
stirring with a tense dedication. 'Aye, lasses, let's give them a
good meal,' the gold-earrings woman said. 'Cheer their little
cotton socks.'

The woman next to Fran sighed. 'Poor Ella. She won't admit
it's over bar the shouting.' It was the woman she had peeled
onions with, the first time she came.

Fran turned off the tap and pulled the plug. 'Do you think it's
over?'

The woman leaned closer so as not to be overheard. 'I bloody
well hope so.'

Their work done, they carried mugs of tea to a quiet corner.
Looking at her closely, Fran saw that she was no more than
thirty, her brown hair covered by a cotton scarf, her eyes ringed
with black pencil. 'I thought they were right to come out; I still
think so. But they've had it now. The sooner they go back, the
better. Mind, there'll be scores to settle – I won't forget some
people. And the pollis! I've brought my bairns up to respect
them, but never again.'

Fran looked at her inquiringly. 'What changed your mind?'

The woman's face darkened. 'They've enjoyed this. Not just
bashing the men – that was fair enough, to give as good as they
got. But the way they've treated the women on the pickets is
disgraceful. If they could give you a dig they did. That's what's
bitten into my man – seeing me pushed around.'

Fran had never been on a picket but she had seen the jostling,
swaying masses on TV. Who could decide who had injured
whom in such a mêlée? And after all, if there had been no pickets
there would have been no policemen. She was wondering

whether or not to defend the police when the woman groaned. 'Oh my God, where's the fall-out shelter?'

Fran turned and saw Margot in the doorway, swathed in what looked suspiciously like a horse-blanket and handing out goodies right and left. 'She gets right up my nose,' the woman said. 'She doesn't care about us, she just wants to be able to say she's on the side of the workers. It makes you sick. You know what the men call her?'

Fran nodded. 'Tokyo Rose.' She shrank down in her seat and prayed Margot would not notice her and claim kinship.

She managed to avoid Margot as the diners thronged through the doors and took their seats. Then it was all systems go as plates were filled, delivered, cleared, retrieved, scraped, stacked and washed. 'By God, that was good,' a man said, giving a vigorous belch.

'You know what it was, marrer?' his neighbour said. 'Kit-e-Kat stew.'

The man belched again. 'I was that hungered, it could've been pussy-cat stew. It all goes down.'

Fran smiled but she looked at the children, eating wordlessly, eyes raised above spoons to look around. What must they make of this?

As the room cleared, Margot bore down on her. 'Hello, Fran. Doing your bit, I see.'

They left together, Margot insisting on giving her a lift. 'I'd ask you in, Margot, but I simply must work on my essay. I only left it to help out Treesa.'

They were passing the bridge near the Co-op when they saw the man running up from the mineral line. His hands waved in the air and his mouth hung open in an anguished O. 'There's something wrong,' Margot said and slammed on her brakes.

Fran was first out of the car. 'He's down ... there's a ton of earth on top of him ... I've tried ... hopeless ...' He went off at a shambling run to get help. There was a low stone parapet to the bridge and Fran leaned over. The overhung bank had fallen, that much was plain. But all that could be seen of the trapped man was a pair of jeans and track shoes, both holed in the centre of the sole.

'It's no good, Fran,' Margot was behind her, her voice sombre, but Fran was already climbing the parapet, her feet feeling for the bank below.

She started to dig, clutching at clods of damp earth, feeling the sharp edges of rock and shale but sensing no pain. Her nails were breaking but she clawed away, weeping as more earth tumbled down for every piece she removed. And then someone was shouldering her aside. 'Howay pet, this is men's work.' He was heaving, digging, making way.

She looked up and saw two policemen scrambling down the bank. One shot his watch from his cuff. 'How long?' he said to her and when she did not answer . . . 'How long has he been under, missus? Pull yourself together!'

Fran drew breath. 'A minute. Perhaps a little longer.' His eyes dropped to his watch and he began to count. His mate had joined the digging, pausing only to snatch off his helmet and hurl it aside. It was not until they had scraped enough away to pull on the legs that Fran saw the blue parka and the striped T-shirt beneath, and knew it was Terry Malone.

The policeman's voice intoned, 'One minute forty . . . forty-five . . . fifty . . . fifty-five . . . two minutes . . .' But Fran was back in her own kitchen more than a year ago. What had Brian Malone said then? *'Our Terry would die for Arthur Scargill.'* His face was the colour of storm clouds, the lips blue. The miner who had begun the digging moved back, defeated, but the policeman put his fingers into the dead mouth and pulled forward the tongue. 'Never mind counting, Ted . . . it's past that.' As his mate moved forward he drew breath and bent to the open mouth, sealing the nose with his fingers. 'Ready?'

The other placed his hands, wrists inward, on the striped and lifeless chest. 'Ready.'

As they blew and pressed alternately, Fran glanced up at the bridge. Margot stood there, a crowd around her, arms folded across her chest. Fran looked back at the body and the two figures bearing down on it. Someone would have to tell them to stop. It wasn't seemly. She would have to tell them it was too late. Why was it always her? The two policemen were Terry's age; in another place, another time, they might have been his friends.

'Geronimo!' one of them said suddenly and grinned like a child.

The ambulance arrived while the breathing was still shallow and reedy. 'He'll do,' the ambulance men said, and fastened an oxygen mask over Terry's mouth.

Suddenly Fran's legs gave way. She was always amazed when old wives' tales proved true: you did wring your hands at moments of stress, and your legs did fold at the knees when you had had enough. The policemen were looking sheepish now that the crisis was over, fastening buttons and donning their official positions with their helmets. 'We'll need a statement, miss,' one said and hauled her up the bank.

Margot was back to normal. 'Here's my card, officer. My home number's on the back. I saw it all. You did your best, but of course there'll be brain damage . . . deprivation of oxygen . . . I saw you counting. Still, jolly well done.' Suddenly her eyes flickered, checking the crowd, and Fran knew what she was thinking – *mustn't be seen to fraternize with the instruments of repression.*

As Margot reached for her arm, Fran leaned towards her. 'Fuck off, Margot,' she said, and felt an unholy satisfaction as the words went home.

She drove the Malones to the hospital and sat with them in the corridor. 'He was always a daring lad,' his mother said to no one in particular. 'He could never take a telling.' She still wore her pinny beneath her coat, and there were traces of flour around her fingernails.

It was getting dark outside and lamps sprang to life in the street. The doors swung open and the sister appeared. Her high-heeled shoes looked incongruous with the navy uniform, but her eyes were kind. 'Relax,' she said. 'He's young and strong . . . and lucky, according to our Registrar. You can go in for five minutes – two of you. Visit tonight and bring his gear.'

Mrs Malone stood up. 'Come on, Dad.'

Mr Malone sat still. 'Better not, Mother. We don't want to
upset him. You go in on your own.'

He's frightened, Fran thought. After all that's gone on today,
he's still afraid of being rebuffed.

She left him, weeping, in the corridor and went to tell Treesa
all was well. Except that all was far from well when a father was
crying for a son who might not want to see him, after all.

21

Saturday, 16 February 1985

Fran felt virtuous as she put a match to the fire. Eight-fifteen on
a Saturday morning, and she was out of bed. She pulled her coat
around her and watched the flames licking uninterestedly at the
duff coal. 'Burn, damn you, burn!' Outside the world was in the
grip of winter. Blizzards last week and two dogs drowned in an
ice-covered pond the day before yesterday. General Winter had
come, as Scargill had prophesied, but he was firing on his own
lines. Everyone in Belgate was cold, which made their misery
that much harder to bear. The flame flickered, and in desperation
she covered the fire opening with a sheet of newspaper to act as
a blazer. She kneeled to hold it in place and looked at the
headlines. There had been a demonstration in the Commons
over the bill on experimentation on embryos, and terrible violence
at the Sunderland match the night before. She searched for
something cheerful. The Bishop of Durham had opened his
mouth again: that was always good for a laugh. And a lodge
official wanted working miners banned from the streets of
Easington. 'How bloody dare he!' she thought, and then had to
snatch her hands away as the paper caught fire.

She carried tea up to Treesa and urged her to stay in bed till
the house warmed up. 'I'll still be here at Christmas then,'
Treesa said and struggled on to one elbow to drink her tea. Her
nightdress was topped with a sweatshirt and cardigan, and beside
her the baby was swaddled in blankets.

Fran bent to look at him. 'Wait till spring, little one. We'll have sunshine then.'

Treesa sighed. 'Sometimes I wonder if the sun'll ever shine again. It's been like a year of winter.'

Downstairs Fran put out cereal for Martin and let Nee-wan in from the garden. 'Sit down and be quiet,' she told him. 'I've got work to do.' She laid out her pens and pencils to write up her teaching practice: it had to be handed in on Monday and nothing must interfere. Her fingers were icy and she flexed them to warm them up. Cold as she was, she was faring better than most people in Belgate. She had never been used to fires roaring up the chimney winter and summer. 'There's grates in this village never gone cold till now,' Bethel had said the other day, and the perished faces on the streets of Belgate gave substance to her words.

At half-past nine the phone rang. 'It's only me,' Min said. There was an odd note in her voice that might have been glee. 'I won't keep you a second.' Fran's heart sank – that meant it would take at least until lunchtime. 'But I wanted you to be the first to know . . . I'm pregnant! It was all the fault of Christmas.'

'You mean Santa Claus did it?' Fran asked, playing for time. Babies, babies, always babies. It wasn't fair.

'No, it wasn't St Nicholas,' Min was saying, 'it was St Dennis.'

Fran grinned. 'How's he taking it?'

There was a giggle from the other end of the line. 'As though it was the first ever. He's eating out of my hand.' Min's tone was triumphant.

'Is that why you did it?' Fran asked.

'How could you think such a thing!' Min said. 'It was an act of God . . . I just pushed his hand a bit.' They rang off after Fran had agreed to come over for a drink after tea. 'Just you and me, Fran. Dennis is at a Round Table do and we don't want Eve. I've never had a chance to thank you for what you did, so tonight it'll be Moët et Chandon and we can really let our hair down. We can't talk freely if Eve's there . . . she's still dying to know what happened, and you know how she agonizes over our feet of clay.'

Fran had just put down the phone when Bethel arrived. 'Get the tea on!' she said, walking through the living room. Nee-wan

had emerged from behind the chair to greet her, but shot back
as the fire erupted and a piece of stone ricocheted around the
room. 'Aye, mind, that Terry's got a lot to answer for,' Bethel
said. 'I warned you about letting him smash that fireplace.'

Fran retrieved the stone and put it in the hearth. 'We'd have
frozen without it, Bethel – especially Treesa and the baby. And
don't forget he nearly lost his life for that fire.'

Bethel shook her head. 'He'd've been nee loss. It's his sort
caused all the trouble.'

Fran went in search of the teapot. 'I'm not going to rise to the
bait, Bethel. I've got work to do.'

She took the dog for a walk after lunch, avoiding the woodland
and sticking to the streets. She could no longer bear the sight of
butchered trees, and if there had been more petrol-bomb
throwing she didn't want to know about it. She had pondered
many times whether or not she should have dialled 999. The
trouble was, you could never be sure you were not reporting your
neighbour. Since the accident Terry Malone had been subdued
but he was still militant ... not the type to throw bombs, but
then which of the Belgate lads looked like would-be arsonists?
Some of them must be.

As she turned for home she thought of last Saturday at this
time. She had gone into Sunderland in search of shoes for
Martin, and in the high street had come face to face with Steve
and his wife, Julie between them. The little girl had nudged her
mother and whispered, and Steve's eyes had met Fran's in silent
apology. Jean had been short and dark and older than Fran had
imagined. She had waited for her heart to lurch at the sight of
them together, and there had been nothing. Only a kind of pity.

She was crossing the top of Stafford Street when she saw the
young policeman who had changed her tyre. He was in mufti
and carried a holdall. Fran smiled. 'Been to see your mother?'

He gestured with the holdall. 'Been to board up her window.
Some brave he-man put it in last night.'

They walked on, Fran seeking desperately for the right words.
'I wouldn't mind if they hit at me,' he said. 'OK, our lads haven't
been perfect. They haven't been half as bad as they've been

painted, but we've got our black sheep. Still, there's no excuse for taking it out on an old woman.' Fran smiled wryly. His mother looked all of fifty . . . so that was old age.

'Are you still doing picket-line duty?' she asked.

He shook his head. 'Not at the moment. I was up at an open-cast the week before last – we were there in force, and so were they. The lorries came. They pushed, we held firm. I could hear the vehicles thudding past behind me, and then I saw this bloke's face . . . he was pushing forward and I could see it in his eyes: "That bastard's going to have me under the next lot of wheels," I thought. I tried to hold, but he was coming forward all the time. I felt the bonnet brush against me and I thought . . . "I'm going to die." That was all. Not about me mam or me girlfriend or anything. Just . . . "I'm going to die." And then the line broke and I thumped him. So I was sent home and suspended – no more gravy-train for a naughty boy. I've never been so pleased in me life.

'It makes you sick!' he went on. 'I watch the telly night after night, and we get a rollicking from the commentators. They don't say "police brutality", but they might as well. What do they expect us to do – stand bare-headed and let them pelt us? You should see some of the weapons they've used . . . not just half-bricks, worse than that . . . things they've spent time crafting, just so as they can do more damage. Over seventy of our lads injured. What came first, the riot or the riot shields? Then they say we've brought the army in. What a load of rubbish! I wish we had brought them in, let *them* take some of the stick. I was at an open-cast site not long since . . . out in the wilds . . . they dismantled a dry-stone wall and skimmed the rocks at us along the ground. You had police falling like ninepins. But that doesn't make the papers . . . oh no, it's all MPs on about police brutality and civil liberties.'

Fran stayed silent, unable to halt the flow of his frustration.

'Whose liberties? That's what I want to know. They say we're oppressing the miners: which miners? There's more miners back at work than on the pickets, far more. So who are we supposed to stick up for: them going in, or them standing outside the gates? Someone should tell us, because we can't win. There was this little lass the other day . . . just knee-high. The lads gave her a bag of apples but I said, "You want to watch what you're doing. If she eats that lot and gets a bellyache, we'll be in more trouble!"'

He was into his stride now, not expecting answers. 'Why would I have it in for the miners? Me own dad was a miner; he died coughing up dust. Now I have to stand and take gobs of spittle off lads that's scarce seen the inside of the shaft. I'm not bitter – I'm sad!'

Fran tried desperately to divert him. 'Tell me something . . . I've watched the battle-bus exchange on the car park near the pit. A few hundred yards away at the pit gates there are hundreds of pickets yelling for blood. But none of them come to the car park. When the buses get to the pit they'll try to wreck them, but they don't try to stop the exchange. It amazes me.'

For the first time his face lightened and his voice took on a note of pride. 'We saw to that. We explained to their leaders that rendezvous points weren't NCB land. They're public places, not the scene of an industrial dispute. So if they tried anything on public land, we'd have them. Our bosses have tried to cut out aggro where they could. Talk about the National Reporting Centre as much as you like, policing this area's a job for local forces and I think they've done a bloody good job.' Once more anger entered his voice. 'We're there to see that people can go about their lawful business unmolested. That's what we did! That's what I thought I joined the force for . . . protecting people. Now I'm told I'm a puppet. Well, nobody's pulling my strings except the chief, and he's only doing his job. But who's pulling their strings, who issues the orders to them . . . and finances them? Try asking that for a change, and you might get some surprises.'

They parted on the corner and she entered her own back street. Halfway down a group of lads stood grouped round a back door. She recognized one of them as the lad who lived there, a young miner. His mates were leaning against the wall and one had defied the frost and sat down on the edge of the kerb. Nee-wan rushed to greet them. 'Fed up?' Fran said. There was a chorus of assent. 'It'll soon be over,' she said.

One of them laughed. 'Seems like I've heard that before.'

Fran nodded. 'I know, it does seem to go on and on. But it can't last much longer. Were you for the strike?'

They shrugged defensively, reminding her of Martin when she asked him unanswerable questions. At last the boy in the gutter spoke. 'Put it like this, missus. There's five per cent at this end mad for Arthur ...' His left hand shot sideways. 'And there's five per cent at that end Maggie's men.' His right hand shot in the other direction. 'As long as they get their redundancy, they wouldn't care if the pit caved in. The rest of us are here in the middle, bleeding bloody bewildered.' There was another chorus of agreement.

'It's over but we can't go back,' a second boy added. 'You'd be marked for life if you went back now. It's really bitter.'

When Fran got into the house she put on the kettle and brewed tea. Seven mugs and a packet of biscuits, milk and sugar on a tray. She carried it into the street. 'Here's something to cheer you up. I'd invite you inside but it's no warmer in there.' She presided over the pot while they dished out the biscuits.

'Thanks missus, there's nothing like a cuppa.' The boy on the kerb lifted his mug. 'Here's to a settlement.' There were murmurs of disbelief. 'Sometimes I feel we'll never get back. No one thinks of us single lads with nowt coming in. They say it's all young 'uns on the picket, but we've got nee choice. That's the only money we can get, picketing fees.'

Fran filled the last mug. 'Don't you want to picket?'

There were shakings of heads. 'There's a few goes for it ... hot-heads. They're always looking for a punch-up, or running round in balaclavas causing trouble. But your average lad, he just wants a bit peace ... a few bevvies on a Friday night ...'

There was a roar of laughter. 'And a nice bit of snogging on a Saturday, eh, Clogger?'

The boy blushed. 'Nee chance of takking a lass out nowadays.' He tried to change the subject. 'Any road, you've got to picket if you want your parcels. Look at Pearson's lad, he won't picket – he never liked trouble, not even at school – and he can't get for his bairn.'

Fran knew Paul Pearson. She had seen him about the streets

during the strike, his baby in his arms. 'You mean they've refused him help because he won't picket?'

The boy nodded. 'If you don't picket, they mark you down, then when you turn up they say there's nowt left. You can't argue. No one knows what the union men's got or not got. They're walking round with the funds in suitcases, dishing out here and there. If your face doesn't fit, you get nowt.'

Another boy spoke up. 'It was the same at Christmas with the toys. If your grandad was lodge chairman it was a bloody bonanza. If not it was, "Sorry pet. Santa's all cleared out."'

Fran could not contain herself. 'But why do you stand it?'

They shrugged 'Nee option. They're running the union, that's it. Anyway . . .' The speaker looked a little ashamed as though they had all been guilty of betrayal. 'Anyway, we've got nee room for that other lot, Thatcher and MacGregor. It's not so much supporting the union, it's standing up to the others. They'll not best the miner, not in the long run.'

There were murmurs of agreement. 'Miners have long memories. We won't forget Thatcher . . . and we won't forget the pollis either. We'll never forget them!'

Back in the kitchen, washing the tea things, Fran thought over their words. Someone was going to have to heal the breach between miners and police, but it would need a Solomon. The sad thing was that individually the policeman and the miner were perfectly compatible; but in the mass, given rocks on one side and riot shields on the other, they were enemies. And there had been wrongs on both sides. Put people under pressure and cracks would appear – in Northern Ireland, or Belgate or anywhere else.

When she had wrung out the dishcloth and hung up the teatowel she went to the corner shop. It was strange to be looking at baby foods again. They had changed since Martin's babyhood, become more exotic. She selected a dozen tins of Junior dinners and asked for a brown paper bag. 'A few things for the baby,' she told Paul Pearson when he opened his door. 'To tide you over till you're back to work.' As she walked away she decided it would be nice to see Min tonight, to giggle and be daft for a little

while. Living close to the nitty-gritty was becoming almost too
much to bear.

Min did not disappoint. 'Come in. I've banished the kids to their
beds so we've got the place to ourselves.' She was dressed in a
georgette cat-suit with a gold lamé belt and sandals to match.
'Might as well dress up while I can – it'll be smocks and
elasticated trousers soon enough. All the same, maternity wear's
much more imaginative now, isn't it? Not that I'm going to
overdo it. I'd like to get something lasting out of all this. Ma-in-
law is simply over the moon, so I hinted I'd like a memento. And
I've told Dennis I'd like a white gold choker. I've seen them in
London. A kind of mesh so you can breathe, but quite savage-
looking all the same. You know, the slave-girl effect. He hasn't
said no, so I'm quite hopeful. If only your lot would get back to
work! Dennis says business is in the doldrums because of the
strike – they're not even replacing the company cars this year,
that's how bad it is.'

Fran loosened her jacket in the overheated room and wondered if she should try to convey the cold and desolation of
Belgate. But this was another country. Instead she held out her
glass for a refill. 'Tell me what Eve said when you told her.'

She felt mellow when she left Min's in spite of refusing too
many refills. They had eaten Tandoori drumsticks and profiter-
oles, and reminisced about schooldays. 'Do you remember when
David and Dennis shinned up the flagpole and put up those
psychedelic bloomers?' Fran asked. 'And Harold pretended he
had to go home because he thought they'd be expelled?'

Min had left her seat and come to kneel at Fran's chair. 'I love
it when you talk about David like that, as though you were glad
he was once alive. I couldn't do it because I'm a weak bitch and
if something hurt I'd have to run away. But I want you to know I
admire you for doing it.'

Fran hugged Min for a moment and let her go. 'You're not as
black as you paint yourself . . . just a little bit grey round the
edges.'

*

As she drove out of Sunderland she thought of the old days, and the six of them together thinking nothing would change, except to get better. They had been short-sighted but it was the only way to live. She was smiling at the remembrance of David when she saw the glow. At first she thought it was the pit, but then the wheel came clear against the skyline and she saw the fire was over to the west. A moment of panic came and went. Someone would have phoned her if the house had burned down.

She drove past the pit and, turning towards the house, saw the running figures before she heard the noise: the clanging of a fire engine, the roar of voices, the crackling of flames that shot skywards. Ahead was an eddying, swaying mass of people, police and protesters locked in combat. The car slowed to a crawl as a police constable loomed up and slapped the bonnet to halt her. She wound down the window and a smell of burning filled the car. 'You can't get through here, miss. Someone's fired the pub. Best go back and take the high road.'

Fran shook her head 'I live here . . . a few yards on. I must get through.'

'Go back, miss. The road's closed.' Suddenly he lurched over the bonnet as something hit him in the back. He turned towards the crowd, Fran forgotten, and lunged forward. She realized she was pressing the accelerator, gunning the engine, and eased her foot. They had fired the Golden Hind, a pub that had closed last year. Of all the crazy things! Suddenly the crowd surged towards her, struggling and fighting. She wound up the window as the car began to rock. If she had dialled 999 when she'd found the fire-bomb site, none of this might have happened. But in her heart she knew she could no more have stemmed all this than stilled the North Sea.

Suddenly she realized someone was banging on the near-side window. A man, face anguished, was mouthing, 'Let me in!' through the glass. She saw the cameras round his neck and reached for the handle, but the door was held shut by the struggling bodies, both sides raining blows indiscriminately on anything that came within reach. She saw the photographer lift his hands to cover his head and then blood was running between his fingers. She pushed at the door and when it opened began to pull at the straps of his camera till he was in the passenger seat and the door was closed. 'You can't go forward, go back!' He was blinking through the windscreen as blood ran down into his eyes.

'I must go on . . . my little boy's through there and this is the only road.'

She let out the clutch, praying as she did so that no one would fall under her wheels. She felt detached, quite ruthless and single-minded. She was going home! A man's face loomed through the windscreen, distorted with rage and mouthing like a fish. She trod on the brake.

'It's no use . . . for God's sake . . . you'll get us both killed.' The photographer was struggling to rid himself of the tangle of cameras so he could take over the wheel.

'I have to get through,' she said, wishing with all her heart she had not let him into her car.

'Go back. Go back!' He was trying to put the gear into reverse, treading on her foot as it guarded the clutch pedal. There was a banging on the roof and the car began to rock. 'Christ!' the man said and turned to open his door.

Fran clutched at the wheel. They were all around her now. The car was no longer a haven, it was a trap. She glanced in the rear-view mirror. The road behind was clear except for a single cavorting figure. He would have to take his chance. She threw the engine into reverse and pressed down the accelerator. The photographer pulled his door shut and the figure behind leaped away. A second later they were clear of the crowd and booling down the centre of the road. She changed into neutral and steered for the kerb.

'Are you all right?' In the light from the street lamps she could see he was quite old and his face ashen beneath the blood. He looked back at the dancing figures, silhouetted against the flames. 'That wasn't protest,' he said. 'That was a bloody riot.'

'I've got to go, I'm afraid. I'll get through on foot,' she said, searching in her bag for a tissue to stem his bleeding. She wanted him out of her car.

'I've got a van back there somewhere,' he said. 'I expect I can find it. Ta.' He took the tissue and wiped his face. The tissue turned red under his fingers. 'Bloody hell, I didn't think it was that bad! It doesn't hurt much.' She was leaning past him to open the door, ready to bundle him out if she had to. 'Hold on . . . you don't want to leave the car here. They'll wreck it.'

She was torn between desire to reach Martin and fear for her precious Mini. If she lost it, there would never be another. She switched on the engine and reversed into a side road. 'That's it . . . right down. Away from the lights.' She made her goodbyes and locked the car, trying desperately to remember the web of streets that lay between her and home. She could come upon the house from behind, through the allotments, but that would take time. Who knew where the rioters would go if the fire spread or police reinforcements appeared? She must be with Martin and Treesa and the baby if there was going to be trouble.

With a pang she realized she had never thought of Treesa and the baby until now, only of Martin, her own flesh and blood. She slipped the strap of her bag over her head so her arms were free and began to run. A blue police van passed the head of the side road, then another and another. With so many police about, it would be safe to go straight home.

She had worn her patent court shoes to Min's. Now she cursed them as the spindle heels wobbled beneath her. She tried running on the balls of her feet but the pavement jarred. Nothing for it but to run barefoot. She tucked one shoe in each pocket and set off again. She felt the feet of her tights hole, and ladders flickered up her legs. One shoe fell from her pocket but she did not falter. They had cost her fifteen pounds in the Dolcis sale, but what did that matter now?

As she drew near she could hear the crowd, distinguish faces. There was a sudden roar and a flame shot skywards, showering sparks. Helmeted police were trying to restore order, but it was useless. The shouting took shape: they were singing the song that Martin had sung that day in the kitchen. '*Burn, burn, burn the bastard. Burn, burn, burn the bastard. Burn, burn, burn the bastard, early in the morning.*' She could smell fire and the pavement was awash. You never thought of water in a fire, but it was there, swilling over her feet and running into the gutter.

People were dashing past her, young boys, faces alight with a strange excitement. 'Howay the lads!' They looked like football hooligans but it wasn't a game. A girl passed and caught Fran's eye. 'This'll learn the sods!' An elbow dug into her ribs, too hard to have been accidental. They're enjoying this, she thought.

There were firemen ahead, yellow legs gleaming. If she went on they would grab her, make her turn back. As she looked for a turn-off she saw terrified faces peering from windows. A door opened and a policeman shepherded out a family. 'Hurry along . . . fast as you can.' A little girl was crying and he scooped her into his arms. The man of the house carried a Jack Russell terrier, its eyes rolling with terror. The mother was holding a baby. 'My God,' she said bitterly, to no one in particular. 'My God . . . is this Britain?'

Suddenly the wall of the pub collapsed in an ongoing roar. It was still a hundred yards away but Fran felt the impact as the old bricks crumbled and fell and went on falling. She saw a car in the middle of the road, turned on its roof like a dead beetle. Flames appeared, the petrol tank exploded and the car was engulfed. The flash caught her face, but it seemed not to matter. Perhaps that would happen to the Mini.

There was a crack as a window blew out somewhere, and unbelievably people were laughing and dancing with glee! Something flew past her ear and she heard her hair sizzle. Her ears throbbed with noise and her eyelids burned. This was what hell would be, an escalating agony.

A voice boomed through a loud hailer and suddenly the crowd surged back, taking her with it. She struggled forward, beating them with her fists until she remembered the other shoe. When it was free of her pocket she held it by the toe and used the heel as a weapon.

Her nose started to run and she licked it into her mouth. Someone trod on her bare foot and smoke filled her lungs as she screamed in pain. The strap of her bag caught on someone's arm and she lashed out. 'Let go, damn you. Let go!'

'Steady on, lass. Steady on.' It was Fenwick, tall and gaunt in a shabby parka, but recognizably a friend.

Her arms fell to her sides and she dropped the shoe. 'Take

me home, Mr Fenwick,' she said, and felt his arms go round her
like a shield.

22

Sunday, 3 March 1985

'It's over, Terry. You might as well face it.'

Terry shifted the baby to his other shoulder. 'There now, pet,
stop crying. You'll make yersel' bad.'

Treesa shook her head in despair and looked at Fran. 'You
tell him.' The baby whimpered again and Treesa held out her
arms. 'Let me have him.'

Fran stood up. 'I think we'll all have a nice cup of tea.' The
strike was over! Well over 50 per cent of the men were back, and
the Durham NUM had backed the call for a return to work
without a negotiated settlement. But still Terry stood firm. 'Are
you well enough to go back?' she asked as she poured his tea. He
was pale and his face was thinner, but they might be more the
marks of maturity than of his ordeal on the embankment.

'I'll be well enough when the time comes,' he said and dipped
his biscuit in his tea.

Fran felt a sudden pity for him. 'It's not exactly a defeat,
Terry. You've all been brave.'

The biscuit threatened to crumble and he helped it into his
mouth. 'We'd've won if we hadn't been let down. Trade union
solidarity? Don't make me laugh. They've produced more steel
through this strike than they do when times is normal.' A picture
of Bill Sirs, the steelworkers' leader, came into Fran's mind: a
face tortured by the need to keep his own men in work. She
wanted to point out that the miners had asked the impossible
and that they had continued to mine coal when the steelworkers
were on the rack . . . but it didn't seem the time. Instead she
said, 'You can't decide men's lives for them without giving them
a chance to have a say, Terry. There should have been a ballot.'

He said nothing, simply shook his head as if in pity for her ignorance.

Terry left as Bethel arrived with the latest news. 'They say there'll be a march back on Tuesday. Behind the banner. But most of them are going in tomorrow to get a full week in. They're going round as though they've won the pools 'cos they'll get a pay packet next week. They've forgotten they'll have the butcher and the baker and the candlestick-maker down on them like vultures. They've hung back while there was nowt to get, but you wait till Friday . . . it'll be a massacree!'

Fran went for a walk after lunch. Walter was coming to tea and Bethel was pretending to be unconcerned but in reality cooking up a storm. 'I won't be long,' Fran said and turned up her collar against the cold.

They had boarded up the windows of the Golden Hind and nailed planks across the doors. What brickwork remained was blackened around every orifice, where tongues of fire had licked the outside walls. It had served its purpose, that last wanton act. As though all the pent-up animosity of a twelvemonth had been consumed in one sacrificial flame, Belgate had been quiet since then, almost subdued. She walked up into the woods, devoid today of woodcutters. The trouble was, she was no surer now than she had been when it started. Hearts had been broken, the landscape scarred, and for what? It was noble to suffer for a principle, but had the principle been preserved? Had it been there in the first place? And more important, would Belgate recover? The coal industry was changing: whether or not they liked it they would have to face the fact. Nothing stood still for ever, however much you wanted it to. That was what frightened her most, that neither side seemed to have learned from the last twelve months. Instead, they seemed more confirmed in their entrenched attitudes and the words of the TV pundits still had the consistency of candyfloss.

The wider view was frightening and she narrowed her thoughts. How would Belgate be affected? The sea-coalers would return in the moonlight to take coal from the blast. The pit would continue to disgorge, but what of the heart of Belgate? She remembered Fenwick as he had half-led, half-carried her through the rubble of the riot and delivered her to her door that night. She had tried to thank him, to offer some hope for the future, but he had brushed it all aside. 'What's the use?' he had said and there was a note of finality in his voice. She had passed his house the next morning when she went to retrieve the Mini, but his windows were curtained and eyeless behind the boarded panes.

And what of Fran when the peace came? Treesa's affairs would be settled, she would have money for a home of her own. Without the baby the house would be empty once more.

She turned when she reached the top of the rise and looked back at the sea. It was flat and grey, no whitecaps to break the dark expanse. There were big ships on the horizon, leaving the Tyne or heading for the Tees, and two coasters waiting for the tide to turn so they could enter the port of Seaham. When she was a child her father had taught her to be proud of Sunderland, of being a Wearsider, but the mighty shipyards of the Wear were almost silenced. She felt afraid for the North-east, doubtful of Martin's future. And yet their history stretched back to Bede and before. Surely they would survive?

Walter was already ensconced by the fire when she got home and his mood was sombre. 'There'll be worse trouble before long. They're all drawing breath and saying, "Whoopee!" – but watch out. The NUM's crippled, and the whole trade union movement weakened. When Scargill took over from Gormley he said he wanted to unite the union . . . and he's smashed it to smithereens. She must be rubbing her hands in Downing Street.'

Fran tried to console him. 'Well, at least it's the end of Scargill.'

Walter's snort held more sorrow than anger. 'You're wrong there, bonny lass. By next week he'll have convinced them he masterminded this lot. All part of the Grand Design. He's better at pulling rabbits out of hats than Paul Daniels.'

Bethel had come in from the kitchen, for once without the light of triumph in her face at Walter's admissions. 'You're mebbe right, but if they can't see what's in front of their noses they deserve no better. It'd never've happened if Gormley'd still been there. This one thinks he's the Messiah, never mind a union leader.'

Walter was shaking his head. 'The only mission he's got, Sally, is lust for power. He wants to see if he can make everyone dance to his tune and, by God, half the time he can. They've got a Star Chamber now to castrate anyone who disagrees with him. If you'd asked me twelve months since whether that could happen, I'd've told you "Never". But I've seen a lot of things in this strike I wouldn't've credited. There's been more fiddling in the NUM than in the Royal Philharmonic. And not just the officials.' He leaned forward in his chair, eyes twinkling. 'If you don't laugh at this you get your money back . . .'

Fran felt a constriction at her throat. At least he hadn't lost his sense of humour.

'There's an open-cast site in Durham . . . doesn't matter where . . . and there was never a shortage of pickets. "Put me out there," they were all saying, "I'll shut the bugger down." Turns out they were picking up a fee from the union to close the place, and a fee from the owner to keep it open. They stood there shouting "Scab" and shaking their fists while the lorries went in and out like yo-yos. Beat *that*!'

Fran shook her head. 'I don't believe it . . . the picketing at the open-cast sites was savage!'

Walter sat back. 'Please yersel'. But I'd believe anything now.'

'Is there a cup of tea going?' Treesa looked tired as she came into the room and Fran made room for her at the fire.

'Sit here and I'll top up the pot. Is Christopher asleep?'

Treesa nodded. 'Yes, he's dropped off. He's cried that much! Still, he's asleep now; I think he's worn himself out.'

When the tea was watered, Fran handed Treesa her cup and topped up Bethel's. It was growing dark outside, and she moved to shut the curtains. 'It'll be nice to have a proper fire again.' She went into the kitchen and drew the curtains, and then went up to the landing window. The moon was already up, a sliver in the west, and the sky was clear. Spring would be coming soon.

She drew the curtains in Martin's room, then her own, and tiptoed into the room Treesa shared with the baby. She knew before she crossed the room that something was wrong, was afraid before she touched the baby's brow and felt the dry heat. Its breath seemed to be drawn up from troubled lungs, an agonized sound that seemed to grow worse even as she listened.

She knew she must go down, tell Treesa something was wrong, but she felt disinclined to do so. They would all look at her, expect her to take charge, and she was not up to it. She was tired of struggling with life, tired of being pushed to the limits. Except that limits, like everything else in life, were endlessly accommodating. She picked the baby from the cot and wrapped it securely before she carried it downstairs.

She saw the faces turn to her, at first surprised and then perturbed. Terry was standing in the kitchen doorway, mouth already open. 'There isn't time to argue,' she said firmly. 'We have to take Christopher to hospital. Will somebody get my coat?'

As she drove through the darkening streets, lights were springing up in the houses. Treesa sat beside her, crying quietly as the troubled breathing came and went. 'I think it's diphtheria,' Fran had said to Bethel. 'Except that no one gets that nowadays. But that's what I think it is.'

Now she drove as fast as she could on to the Sunderland road, watching the signs flick past. Eight miles, seven, six. When David was dying they had lifted him into an ambulance and sent it jangling through the crowded streets. An ambulance man had held a mask to his face, and she had held his hand and asked him not to leave her. She had looked from the windows and seen the rush-hour traffic and known they would not get through. But the cars and buses had parted in obedience to the siren and David had died in an iron bed in a side ward five hours later.

This time she gave thanks for the empty Sunday roads, willing the baby not to give up. Diphtheria formed a web in the throat and closed the airway; they had to cut a hole in the windpipe and divert air to the lungs. People had done it with penknives before now, and the sufferers had lived. But Peter Lee had banished diphtheria from the streets of Durham when he gave them pure piped water. So why was it happening now? She heard Terry in the back seat, clearing his throat. 'Not much further now,' he said and she knew he was afraid.

They took the baby away through swing doors. 'Sit here,' the nurse said. 'I'll come back as soon as I can.' When she came back her face was expressionless. 'He's going up to Ward 5. There's no need to panic. Doctor just wants another opinion. You can stay, Mum and Dad. Your friend might as well go.'

Fran was glad to escape. Terry had not disclaimed parenthood, he was holding Treesa's arm and doing his best to console her. He was the proper person to stay. 'I'll come back if you need me,' she told Treesa. 'Maybe they'll let him go later on. Just ring me and I'll come.' They both knew it was nonsense but they nodded agreement.

It was Martin who comforted her. 'It's a strong little baby, Mam. Remember what it did to the Poody dog. It won't die.' She cried then, and clutched him, and he did not draw away. 'It's all right,' he said, and she nodded. Babies who could pull the legs off Poody dogs could surely defeat diphtheria.

In the end it was not diphtheria after all. 'It's quinsy,' Terry said when the call-box pips stopped. 'It's only quinsy, and he should be all right. They've got him on antibiotics, massive doses. If he responds . . . and they say nine out of ten do . . . he'll be all right. If not, they can do an operation . . .'

'A tracheotomy?' Fran asked.

'Yes, that's it. They do that while they find out the proper treatment. But the main thing is, he's going to be all right. The doctor says it was the right thing to bring him straight in. It's made all the difference . . .'

'Thank God,' Bethel said when Fran went round and told her. 'I don't hold with praying for favours, but I've asked for a few tonight.'

Fran nodded. 'I should have prayed but I was too muddled up. Anyway, Treesa's staying till the baby settles and then they're coming home in a taxi. I offered to go for them but Terry said no.'

Bethel looked agitated. 'Will he have any money?'

Fran nodded. 'I gave him something before I left. I said we could sort it out later.'

The older woman settled back in her chair. 'Quinsy. I haven't heard of quinsy for years. They used to wrap your throat in flannel but it still closed up. Many a one died of it, couldn't even open their mouths.'

Fran patted her arm. 'It's different now. They've got antibiotics, and all sorts of things. You'll have your precious baby back before you know where you are.'

As she went back to her own house she passed people scurrying here and there. She had forgotten the strike was over! There was a new air of activity, even at that time of night. In the darkness a woman was collecting washing from a line. 'I've just been airing his pit clays. They've been in-bye for a year, and they hum.'

When she'd switched on the immersion heater she looked in on Martin. 'Try and go to sleep, darling. We know everything's going to be all right, and it might be ages before Treesa comes back. I'm going to have a nice bath and go to bed myself.'

He shuffled down under the covers but his eyes remained alert. 'Will the strike be over tomorrow?'

Fran nodded. 'All over bar the shouting. Some people . . . the very strict union members . . . will stay out till Scargill says to go in, but most of the men will go back tomorrow.' She sensed he had something to add. 'Will Terry go back home now?'

Fran sat down on the edge of the bed. 'Do you want him to?'

He nodded. 'Yeah. Not just for Gary. I think it's better if families stick together.'

She wanted to reassure him but it wouldn't do. He trusted her to tell the truth. 'I don't know what'll happen. I'm fairly sure they'll get friends again, but once you've been away from home it's hard to go back. Anyway, when you get to Terry's age you'll want to leave home.'

His tone was confident. 'I won't. I won't ever get married.'

She felt the first frosts of panic as she stood up. If she got things right he would go: that was the irony of motherhood. If you did it properly you lost your stake.

She shook her head to rid herself of fatigue. It wasn't just today – it had been a hell of a year, and now it was catching up with her. Two years, really – a chapter that had begun with David's death. She would always date things from then. AD . . .

the year of David. There would not be a year of Steve. She would remember him only as an interlude.

But she would remember the strike, as a time of deprivation and anger and comradeship and tragedy. If there had been good leaders on both sides, it might have been different. Instead MacGregor had been the urbane godfather figure, always saying he had nothing to give. And Scargill ... he had played his followers like a master puppeteer, but he had paid a price. Tonight, on television, the signs of strain had shown on him. A strike was like an atom bomb: you could drop it on your enemy, but you couldn't escape the fall-out.

When she was ready for bed she collected Walter's book on Peter Lee, turning once more to the marked page. '*Not only men but nations must realize that the human family is thus so linked together that we must work together in a co-operative spirit if civilization is to endure.*' If only she could spray those words on the walls of Belgate. If only Peter Lee were here today to draw the miners together once more. He had been ruthless in the pursuit of social justice but he had been a militant who preached conciliation, and she liked that. He had banished open drains from his county and with them the toll of infant deaths. No wonder they had named a town after him. Where was his like today?

It was two o'clock before the taxi drew up outside but she was still awake. She looked from the window and saw them facing one another, a foot apart. As though she had willed it, they moved forward and melded and clung. She let the curtain fall back into place and climbed into bed.

She was still awake when the first footfall sounded in the street. It was a trudging step, and those that followed were no more jaunty. She wondered if the lone footstep was Fenwick's, but dared not look. It would not be Terry Malone, that was sure. He would march in at the union signal, not a moment before. But he would go back. Yesterday she had asked him a question she had never dared ask before: why he clung to a pit that had robbed him of his brother. 'Is it because there's no other work, Terry?'

He had not answered for a moment, and she wondered if she

had gone too far. Then he looked up and smiled. 'It's just my place, isn't it? It's in the blood. Going down the hole, that's what Malones do. We're good at it. Pit ears, pit eyes . . . we can read that bitch like a book.' There was affection in his voice and a kind of reverence.

'He's looking forward to going back,' Fran thought and was amazed.

But he would not go back today. A few streets away he would be lying, listening as she was listening to the halting return. Down below someone struck up a tuneless whistle. It was 'Colonel Bogey', but no one joined in. Fran felt her lips purse in sympathy as the lone whistle died away. There was silence for a moment, and she held her breath until there was an anguished stage whisper beneath her window. 'Howay, lads!' A voice picked up the 'Colonel Bogey' theme but the words were his own:

> *MacGregor has only got one ball,*
> *The other is in the Albert Hall.*
> *Scargill, dear Arthur Scargill,*
> *Drives us all right up the wall.*

One by one voices joined in, the tempo quickened. Fran lay, smiling, as the feet picked up rhythm, the drift back became a march. The Belgate men were going in! She turned on her side as the heart of Belgate steadied and returned to its old, familiar beat.

Part III

Blue Remembered Hills

1

Friday, 28 June 1985

The pub at lunchtime was usually cold and always seedy. Dust showed in the folds of the leatherette seats, and the floor was scarred by a hundred stubbed-out cigarettes. Today, though, end-of-term euphoria lent it a cosy air. 'Move along,' Gwen said, squeezing behind a table. 'Thank God that's over.'

Fran nodded. 'The last two weeks have dragged. I'm not going to think about work for a month. Then I'll get down to some real graft.'

It was end of term. Their second year of teacher training was over, the third and critical year still twelve weeks away. Time to unwind.

'One lager, one lager and lime. The snowball's for Jenny . . . God knows how she can drink that muck . . . and that's Gordon's Exhibition.' Tony Lund emptied his tray and returned to the bar.

'He fancies you,' Gwen said, licking froth from her upper lip.

'Hush!' Fran tried to sound nonchalant. 'The others'll be here in a moment. We don't want them hearing nonsense!'

Gwen was not to be deterred. 'He fancies you – hence the drinks all round. I'm not averse to a free half, but watch your step. He's a bit too fly, that one.'

Tony was waiting for his change, dark hair unruly above an open-necked shirt, as befitted a sociology tutor. His navy jacket was shiny in places but his shoes were custom-made and must have been expensive. Fran suspected he was a bit of a fraud – anti-establishment on the outside and an élitist where it didn't show. He was affable with all the students but lately she had found his attention to her disconcerting. He seemed always to be secretly amused by her, putting her completely off lectures and making her respectable end-of-term mark in his subject a blatant fraud.

Now he sat opposite trying to catch her eye, grinning when he succeeded. She snatched away her gaze. 'Damn men,' she thought. Still, it was nice to be fancied, why deny it? And why worry about it, when there were other and more frightening things with which to contend? Tomorrow she had promised to take Martin to Seaham Harbour to try out his new fishing tackle. Not only the sea to fear, but a complex mass of rod and line!

'Cheer up!' Gwen said suddenly. 'This is out of school drinkies we're having, not a wake!'

Fran smiled and raised her glass. 'Here's to crime,' she said recklessly, the first words that came into her mind.

'I'll drink to that.' Tony grinned and clinked glasses and Fran felt a blush begin. Of all the ridiculous things to say! Trust him to twist it . . . there was no mistaking what he meant.

The conversation turned to holidays and she sat back to contemplate her fellow students. No chance of a holiday for her this year, so she had nothing to contribute. Not that she had a hankering for foreign parts; just to be at home for three whole months would be bliss.

Gwen was going to Greece with Lewis, her husband, and her face was alight at the thought of sunshine and food. 'I'm going to lose half a stone before I go, then I can just enjoy without any mad guilt feelings.'

Fran smiled. Gwen's attempts to diet were notorious for their failure to produce results. She would go to Greece at thirteen stone and come back five pounds heavier, but she was the most reassuring person Fran knew and could be forgiven any amount of wishful thinking.

Jenny and Gordon were young and earnest and in love. They were going to do France the hard way, on foot with half a ton of equipment on their backs. Fran closed her eyes as they talked, remembering long French roads lined with poplars. She and David had spent two weeks of honeymoon in France, weeks filled with laughter and love-making that no longer needed to be illicit.

She opened her eyes to find Tony watching her. 'I'm tired,' she said defensively. He seemed always to be teasing. Even when he said nothing, the challenge was there. David had been dead for two years and still she felt on edge with men.

She had never really felt comfortable with Steve unless they were close together, limbs entwined, cheek to cheek, so that it was impossible for eyes to meet and transmit disconcerting messages. Now it was happening again.

'Can I give you a lift?' The others were rising to go and Tony was between her and the door.

'Thanks, but I've got the car.' Not for the first time she blessed the Mini. Once inside it, she was safe.

They all came out into the sunlight, suddenly anxious to get away. It was always like that at the end of term. You thought you would miss your fellow students, even promised to keep in touch, and then suddenly you were free and wanted to forget them.

'Take care.' Gwen's cheek was soft and powdery, reminding Fran of her mother's cheek which had always smelled of 4711 cologne.

'And you! Enjoy Greece and don't forget to come back.' The inane exchanges continued until Gwen turned the corner and Jenny and Gordon were striding purposefully in the other direction.

'Well, if I can't give you a lift let me see you to your car.' There was no escape and, worst of all, he was grinning at her discomfiture.

Fran felt a sudden anger. 'Haven't you a home to go to?'

Her heart sank at the sound of her own voice. She didn't sound distant and superior, as she had intended. She sounded as though she were checking up on him, and that would imply interest. He was shepherding her over the zebra crossing towards the car park and his reply was detached. 'Two actually . . . the flat here and a house in York.' They were on the pavement but he still held her arm loosely, above the elbow. 'But there's no little woman waiting, just cold empty rooms.' So he *had* thought she was probing! 'You're supposed to say "Aaah" when I say that,' he said mildly, and she found herself grinning.

'I'm not in the least sorry for you.' The door of the Mini was open, safety just inches away. She could afford to be generous. 'But I hope you have a good holiday.'

He was winding down the window and closing the door. 'I'm here for at least a week, tying up ends. We might have a meal one night?'

Nothing to do but nod and smile. She eased into reverse and

the car was under way. 'Bye!' She was out on the road, steering with one hand and winding up the window with the other before she realized that she was quite glad about the invitation. It would probably never come to anything but it might be nice if it did.

She was wandering through C & A, looking at racks of bright holiday clothes, when she saw Min. She was six months pregnant now but still glamorous, black hair a shining cap, limbs tanned from two weeks in Tenerife. She was riffling through maternity dresses, rattling hangers disdainfully along the rail as each one failed to please.

'Min, what are you doing here?'

Min turned from the dresses and clutched Fran's arm. 'Slumming, darling. Dennis is on one of his economy drives and says no more maternity wear. "Let something out," he said at lunchtime. Men? Give me alligators! Anyway, I'm glad you're here. I was dying for tea and cream cakes but it's so naff to sit by oneself. There's nowhere to put your eyes.'

Useless to say she didn't feel like cream cakes at two in the afternoon. Min was normally determined; pregnant, she was unstoppable. Fran watched her across the table as she ordered. 'And some of those choux buns with cream. Lemon with the tea and we'd like a toasted teacake to start.' Her throat and face were the colour of caramel above the beautifully cut white silk shift.

'How much did that cost?' Fran asked.

'A lot!' For a moment Min looked guilty. 'But it's not every day you have a baby, is it? And it's such a drag. I need something to cheer me up.

'I'm quite pleased about it really,' she said as she poured the tea. 'You know I am, so don't look so disapproving. But you get fed up with feeling like a tank and being trapped in the house all the time.'

Fran could not conceal her smile. 'You're just back from Tenerife!'

Min was unrepentant. 'I know, but that was a wash-out ... apart from the sunshine, which was bliss. But it's no fun on your own, not when you've got a bump. I said to Dennis, "You don't need to worry about me being good. I couldn't give it away looking like this."'

The teacake had arrived and Min fell on it with gusto. 'Thank God I don't put on weight. You sure you don't want some? Good! Now stop looking like Mary Whitehouse and tell me your news. I hope you've done something wicked. If I can't do it myself, hearing about it's the next best thing.'

For a moment Fran was tempted to remind Min that less than a year ago she had been grovelling to Dennis for forgiveness, and forswearing even unchaste thoughts; but it would be a waste of time. There was no hope of Min's changing now. Not that Fran would want her to change.

'I'm sorry to disappoint you, darling, but there's more shenanigans in the Vatican than in my life at the moment. Although I *have* just been propositioned by my sociology tutor ... at least I think I have. But I doubt it'll come to anything.'

Min's eyes were suddenly wise. 'You mean you hope it won't come to anything. You can't mourn David for ever, you know. He wouldn't want you to. You're thirty-four years old, Fran. Someday you'll find someone. Not the same as David, but just as good. Anyway, that's what we all hope.'

Fran felt her eyes prick. 'Thanks but no thanks, Min. I've got enough on my plate bringing up Martin and attempting the course. If I can just qualify and get a decent school to teach at, I'll ask for nothing more.' She could have pointed out that she had already tried replacing David: her affair with Steve had been traumatic and Min knew it. Instead she changed the subject. 'How's Dennis?'

Min was on to the choux buns. 'Vile. All he talks about is business and that ghastly strike. He says it's worse since they went back to work. Nobody's buying furniture. All their branches are flat; even the Sunderland shop's struggling. They've got rid of ever so many staff and that makes Dennis feel guilty. No one likes putting people on the dole, not even me. Especially when there's no other work available. But that's business. If you can't stand the heat, and everything. And Harold doesn't help, going on about all the liquidations he's handling. Accountants are vultures, nothing more. They get fat on other people's downfall.

If we hadn't been friends with Eve and Harold since school, I'd cut them dead. Eve's so smug. She'd like to see Dennis go broke.'

Loyalty to Eve made Fran demur. 'I'm sure you're wrong, Min. Eve can be a bit of a pain sometimes but she's very loyal.'

'She may be loyal, Fran, but she's sanctimonious. She says I should humour Dennis. She doesn't have to live with him. It's a good job I'm preggers because I doubt if he's got the energy for sex. Still, the baby'll take his mind off his troubles when it arrives, and things'll pick up for Christmas. They always do.'

She rattled on through another choux bun while Fran marvelled at her certainty. The baby would be born safely and the business would pick up: no thought of stillbirth or liquidation. And yet businesses were folding left and right – every night the *Echo* told the dismal story. The strike had been over for three months but still the ripples were widening.

'What about Martin? You must bring him over in the holidays. The kids were asking about him last night.' Min let out a tiny burp. 'That's better.'

Fran smiled. 'Martin's fine. He's developed this sudden passion for sea-angling. We went to Seaham a couple of weeks ago and he saw some anglers on the pier. I thought it was just a phase, but he went on and on and then Bethel found this ancient rod which had belonged to her husband and he just went mad. So tomorrow I'm taking him to try it out, and I'm terrified.'

'Trust that old witch to cause trouble.'

'She's very fond of Martin, you know that, Min. The rod means a lot to her . . . it's jolly kind of her to give it to him.'

Min pulled a face. 'Sorry, I forgot I mustn't criticize Mother Teresa. I'll try not to do it again.'

She was paying the bill now, changing a five-pound note. 'No, Fran. It's my treat. Besides, if Dennis cuts my allowance much more it'll be you treating me next time.'

They parted at the entrance to the beauty salon. 'I've got a manicure at three. Don't forget about bringing Martin over. Anyway, I'll ring you. And don't think I've forgotten about the sociology tutor. I'll await developments.' She patted her belly. 'That's all I can do at the moment.'

As Fran drove back towards Belgate she thought about Dennis and Min. When they married they had moved into a custom-built, split-level luxury home and Min had a new car every year. Their children went to private schools and Min's perfume cost £42 a bottle.

But Fellowes' shops were situated in colliery areas, their customers mostly miners who bought on credit. They must have felt the draught. Impossible to believe they could go bust, but it was bound to be difficult for a while. There were still strained faces in Belgate, and if Bethel was to be believed things would not get better in the near future. A Russian paper had reported Scargill as claiming that the miners had scored 'a brilliant victory'. If it were true, they had paid a terrible price for it in broken and scarred relationships. Fran felt a sense of despair now whenever she thought about the strike. Bitterness seemed to have increased. Myths abounded, and increasingly people forgot that a ballot had been denied the men, even those who had fought vociferously to obtain one. It was all talk, now, of the government against the miners and not a hint that miner had been against miner, father against son.

The fading graffiti on the railway bridge caught her eye: '*Scabs are shits!*' And a new slogan, white and bright and startling: '*UDM is Scum*'. No one in Belgate had joined the breakaway union but in Sunderland there were quite a few members.

Fran changed gear for the roundabout and saw the chimneys of her own home ahead. The strike was over, no point in thinking about it now. What was real and imminent and frightening was the prospect of that bloody fishing rod. They would never get it put together, and if they did they would never catch anything. Since David's death she couldn't bear to see Martin disappointed. Still, as long as he didn't fall into the sea nothing else mattered. She glanced at her watch. Only half-past three, and no need to settle to her books tonight. Suddenly she felt like a kid out of school and it was a pleasant feeling.

2

Saturday, 29 June 1985

Now that she was on holiday a Saturday morning lie-in was no longer a luxury, so she was up by eight o'clock, drawing back her bedroom curtains on an unkempt garden. It was painful to see the flowers David had planted run to seed. Aquilegia and marigolds were lost in waist-high grass. Today, however, she was full of good intentions. Some time during the holiday she would transform the garden from a wilderness to a perfumed pleasure place.

She had always liked alliteration in English classes. Now she repeated the felicitous phrase aloud twice before she acknowledged its idiocy. She was as capable of creating a garden as she was of writing Italian opera. Still, at least she could tidy it up.

Not today, though. Today, unless the gods were kind and sent rain, she was taking Martin fishing. The sky was leaden, so she might have a lucky escape. She brushed her hair off her face and skewered it with hairpins. Later on there might be time for a bath but first she must riddle the boiler.

As she squatted gingerly among the ash, trying to break up clinker, she wondered once more if it might have been wiser after all to move back to Sunderland after David's death. There was no denying this house was too big. Its heating system burned money and gave back very little in return. She gave one last vicious twist of the poker and shut the door. There had been a small patch of red glowing faintly through the grey: with luck there would be hot water.

Martin had not made a sound yet. Perhaps he'd forgotten about the fishing trip? If he had, she would take him somewhere else. Somewhere they could do things together, things she could manage.

This was when she missed David most, in the upbringing of his son. No one to talk to about Martin's character, his good and bad points. If you discussed your offspring with outsiders you felt a traitor and they felt compelled to say the child was a saint, so constructive discussion was out. Only with the other parent could you talk freely.

There was a handful of circulars on the mat and one brightly coloured postcard. Jersey. '*Having a wonderful time. Weather good. Food good. See you soon. Edward, Linda and family.* PS: *Debbie sends kisses for Martin.*' 'Edward, Linda and family' – seeing it written down like that made her feel good. And jealous. And guilty. She must contact them soon.

She sat down at the kitchen table and riffled through the morning paper. Wimbledon was front-page news, McEnroe and Navratilova expected to retain the titles they'd won in 1984. Their winning would be predictable and therefore boring unless McEnroe threw a tantrum. But his tennis was bliss, so the next two weeks would at least be pleasurable.

She was reading her fortune ('Not a good day for excursions. Stay close to home') when Nee-wan sat up, ears pricked. The next moment there was a bang on the back gate. As she padded down the yard, dog at her heels, a fine drizzle touched her face.

Gary Malone stood in the back street, red hair beaded with rain. 'Is your Martin in?'

Fran ushered him into the yard, retrieved the dog who was keen to explore, and re-bolted the door. 'He's still in bed, Gary, but you can go up if you like.' She made a quick calculation and decided to be brave. 'We're going through to Seaham shortly, to try out his fishing rod. Want to come?'

For a moment interest gleamed in the blue Malone eyes but it was transient. 'No thanks.'

As he vanished upstairs Fran reflected on how much he had changed in the last eighteen months. His militant brother still passed his rule-book father in the street as though they were strangers but it was the little boy who had suffered most. He had to cope with divided loyalties.

He was coming down from the bedroom now, clutching a borrowed football under his arm. 'See you this saffa,' he called back upstairs.

Martin hung over the banister to reply. 'Yeah. Gerra game fixed termorrer and I'll play.'

Fran's smile was pained. Talking to his friends, her son was an elocutionist's nightmare.

When he came down his enunciation had returned to normal. 'Yuck! Mush!' he declared when she showed him Linda's postcard.

'It's a nice day,' he said firmly as he ate his muesli, daring her to contradict. 'Just right for fishing.' Outside the sky glowered, the yard gleamed wetly.

'It'll be awful on that pier,' Fran said doubtfully, wanting to put him off, no longer able to say a straight 'no', now that his twelfth birthday was in sight.

He grinned at her. 'I'm still going, mam. You get more fish when the sea's a bit rough. They bash their heads on the rocks and it knocks them silly. Then you just dangle the hook . . .' He made a cast with an imaginary line . . . 'and you've got fish and chips.'

She was consumed with love for him and proud of his persuasiveness until a new and terrible thought struck her. 'You're not expecting me to clean them, are you? Because I couldn't.'

In the end they agreed that any catch would be admired, measured and thrown back, and he went off to get ready. 'Wrap up!' she called after him and received the predictable short reply.

She was stacking the breakfast things when the yard door rattled. 'It's me, Bethel.'

'That tea's stewed,' she said, feeling the pot. 'Get the kettle on.'

As they drank their tea Bethel recounted the local gossip. The deeds and misdeeds of the neighbourhood were catalogued and graded, and local funerals listed. Bethel would be attending the Methodist church at 2 p.m to see off her second cousin. 'Never was strong . . . a chest like an old tin can.' After the funeral she was expecting company.

'Anyone special?' Fran inquired but Bethel's lined face remained impassive.

'Walter . . . I doubt you'd call him owt special.'

'Do you think he'll pop the question today?' Fran asked innocently.

Bethel sniffed. 'He can pop as much as he likes, the answer'll be the same.'

'Go on,' Fran urged. 'Admit you love him.'

Bethel stood up and reached for her hat. 'I can see I'll have to go. You're in one of them moods. Impudent! I'm old enough to be your mother, so show some respect.'

Fran wound her arms around Bethel's neck, against only token resistance. 'You know I love you, Bethel. I only want what's best for you. Let Walter make an honest woman of you. I'll be bridesmaid.'

'Let me out.' Bethel broke free and rammed her hat on to hair that was thinning with age. 'I can see how it's going to be. Twelve weeks of torture. That college of yours wants to get down to some work instead of letting the likes of you loose to torment decent old women.'

In spite of her outrage she stayed long enough to fettle the boiler and wipe down the draining board. 'I'll be in on Monday, and make sure you've simmered down by then. You're worse than the bairn.'

There was no sign of the sun as they drove out of Belgate but the drizzle had eased. Perhaps they would get on and off the pier without mishap. 'You mustn't go near the edge,' she warned for the umpteenth time.

'I know, Mam. You've already told me.' His tone was weary and she made a mental note not to be so over-protective. Kids survived, even kids who were unsupervised, sometimes unloved. That thought created a fresh terror: perhaps she loved Martin too much, so that he was almost singled out for disaster? She glanced at the landscape for diversion.

The last house flashed past and there was a brief interlude of fields before the outskirts of Seaham began. Seaham was a town boasting three working pits and a shopping centre. Last week she had taken Martin to see the harbour. Now she wished she hadn't, for he had gone on and on about the anglers ever since. Bethel had overheard and appeared next day with an ancient rod. Martin had gone into ecstasies, Bethel glowed with benevolence, and

Fran had found herself promising to mount an expedition for which she was totally unfitted.

A wooded dale led towards the sea. The road was lined with neat houses and green spaces where people were exercising their dogs. Nee-wan lay on the ledge behind the back seat, looking out at the other dogs and occasionally uttering a token growl.

'We can't take the dog on the pier,' Fran said. 'It isn't safe.' To her relief Martin didn't argue. He was too taken up with the rod. Its massive handle was bound tight with string that had turned yellow with the sweat of its owner's palm. Bethel's husband had died in the pit forty years before, aged twenty-nine. He must have come up from the darkness of the shaft and revelled in open air and sea.

'You're lucky to have that rod,' she told Martin. 'Take care of it.'

His eyes, when they met hers, were exasperated. 'I know, I know. It belonged to her husband. I'm not daft, you know, Mam.'

Fran's anxiety increased when they got to the pier. She tried to ignore the swirling water below the sheer drop, by concentrating on the assembly of the rod. 'It's easy,' Martin grimaced, trying to force one length into another.

'It screws,' Fran said. The brass ends were grooved but the pieces refused to join.

A seabird waddled forward to get a closer look. Fran was about to offer help when she saw the set of Martin's lips. It had become a matter of honour now, a challenge. 'Look,' she said, trying to sound reasonable, 'let's lay the pieces out in order and then try again.'

His fingers were stained with rust and suddenly looked immature, the hands of a child. He looked up and saw her sympathetic face. 'It's a bugger, isn't it?' he said.

'Don't swear,' Fran said automatically but they both knew more was at stake than words. They needed David. They needed a man to flick the pieces of rod into place and make everything simple.

She looked towards the end of the pier. Two men were hunched over their rods. Even if she dared walk out that far, they would hardly appreciate interruption. She was still staring seawards when the voice came from behind. 'Need a hand?' She let out her breath in a sigh of relief and turned.

Martin was already holding out the segments of the rod. The newcomer was dressed in a grey sweater and slacks, too well pressed for the pier, but the hands manipulating the rod were deft. He wasn't from around here, though. The accent was southern, even a little Cockney. His eyes flicked up and caught Fran's. 'I used to have one like this . . . well, something like this.' They grinned in mutual appreciation of the rod's venerable age.

'There now.' The last segment clicked into place and he handed the completed rod to Martin. 'Watch what you're doing.' He had laid a pipe and tobacco pouch down to handle the rod; now he picked them up.

'Watch him,' he said to Fran, in a lowered tone. 'The rod's a bit big . . . if he swings it too enthusiastically it could topple him.' A wedding ring gleamed on his left hand. 'I'd stay, but I have to get back.'

Fran nodded. 'I'll be careful. You've been very kind.' He wanted to be away now and she turned her back to set him free.

'It's not as easy as I thought,' Martin admitted after a half-dozen abortive casts.

To the north, over Sunderland, the sky was turquoise and streaky. Down below, the beach stretched into infinity: golden sand, free from rocks, but almost empty because of the weather. It was always cold here. If this beach were in the south or on the west coast, it would be renowned. But if it were anywhere else it would have lost its trademark – the faint patina of coal dust that lodged at the tide line, reminding her, as it always did, of the black edge of a mourning card.

She turned to the south. Below, in the small dock, brightly coloured fishing boats bobbed at anchor. Once this harbour had throbbed with life. They still sold fish here, fresh-caught and silver, but it was a hard trade and one made no easier by bureaucracy. Over in the main harbour a ship was moving through the gates. Sailors home from the sea. Behind, a pit bulked, mountains of coal and foothills of scrap iron: industry and dereliction. She felt love well up in her for this place, this bleak coastline that was her heritage.

'You're not scared, are you?' Martin was looking at her, wide-eyed.

'No.' She shook her head and blinked her eyes. Impossible to explain patriotism. She didn't even understand it herself. 'I was thinking about the lifeboat.'

He let the rod sag, interest aroused. 'Where is it?'

Fran shook her head. 'They don't have one any more, they share Sunderland's. They had one once, when I was your age. It went out on a rescue and then it went down and they were all drowned. We had a collection at school, and everyone was sad.'

Martin's face was sombre as he went back to his fishing. Perhaps mention of the lifeboat had put the sea into perspective. It could lap your feet at the tide's edge, or swallow you up like a flake of foam.

The drizzle had returned and the greening stones of the pier were slippery. Once or twice Fran took a grip of the middle of his jacket, only to have her hand shaken angrily away. 'It's raining,' she said, looking gratefully at the sky. 'We could come back next week.'

Martin lowered the rod, honour satisfied. 'OK. I'll be better at it by then.'

They couldn't dismantle the rod completely but managed to separate it into two halves. 'There's a pub on the seafront,' Fran said. 'We could get lunch there if you'd like?'

Martin was in a good mood, grateful that she had not ordered him off the pier. 'Can we afford it?' he said.

She felt a surge of goodwill towards him. 'Definitely. Providing you don't want champagne and caviar, you can have anything you like.'

He settled for fish and chips. 'Fish is better in batter.' He chewed for a moment. 'I was a bit worried about catching anything. I mean, they flap around. I've seen it on the telly.'

Fran nodded. 'I know. You're supposed to hit them on the head or something.'

He crunched his batter. 'We'll find out before next week.' They both knew there would be no second expedition but the myth had to be sustained for the time being.

They were on to dessert when the man from the pier came in.

The barmaid greeted him like an old friend. 'Eating in today?'
So he was a resident! Fran turned away, anxious lest he saw
them and was caused embarrassment.

'What do you want to do?' she asked. 'Go to the casino?'

Martin's eyes gleamed.

'OK, but I can only afford 50p, and we can't leave the dog
much longer.'

The money vanished into the fruit machine like snow from a
griddle. 'It's a mug's game,' Fran said, 'it never pays out.' And
was turned into a liar as the bandit gushed out silver for the
person who had taken Martin's place.

They drove into a wooded dene beside an ancient church and
set free the dog. Fran watched it run, wild with delight, turning
at intervals to make sure they were following. A dog was a
responsibility but worth every ounce of effort. 'I'm enjoying
myself,' Fran thought and hugged the idea to her until the damp
grass penetrated her flimsy summer shoes and brought her back
to reality.

They called at Treesa's on the way home. It was six weeks since
Treesa and her baby had left them for her new council house.
Every time Fran passed the spare bedroom she felt like pushing
it open to see the small head rear up from the pillow and smile a
welcome.

'Come in. I was hoping you'd come round.' Genuine pleasure
showed on Treesa's face – pleasure and pride. The tiny living
room was packed with new furniture and the shag-pile carpet
ran from wall to wall.

'It's lovely,' Fran said but each woman knew what was in the
other's mind. The money that had furnished the room had been
blood money, bought with a death in the pit. 'I'll pop up and get
the bairn,' Treesa said. 'He's ready to wake up and he'll be over
the moon to see you, Mrs Drummond.'

'It's Frances,' Fran said. 'I've told you before ... call me
Frances or Fran. We've been friends long enough for that.'

Treesa smiled. 'I'll try, Frances, but I'm that used with saying
Mrs Drummond, it just slips out.'

A new stereo gleamed in the corner, and a video under the

TV. You needed such things when you were alone, Fran thought, remembering how she had clung to music after David died, to records that would make her cry and let her emotions run free.

'There now, look who's here.' The baby was still sleepy but his eyes lit up at the sight of Martin.

'I've got him.' Martin was proud of his skills with the baby, and the two women relaxed.

'You must stay to tea,' Treesa said. 'I'll be glad of a bit of company. You don't feel like eating when it's just yourself.'

Fran nodded. 'I lived on cottage cheese after David died. Just cottage cheese off a spoon. I never set a table. Still, you've got to look after yourself. Don't your family come round ... or the Malones?'

Treesa twitched out a non-existent ruck in the new hearthrug. 'No. Mam comes sometimes, and the bairns call round. Me dad's been once, to see how I'd got the place. He liked it.' She was picking at an imaginary hangnail until she looked up defiantly. 'And Terry comes round ... just to see there's nothing needs doing. Well, he is the bairn's uncle.'

Fran wanted to reach across and soothe the jerky young hands, but it wouldn't do. 'He's a very kind young man. Just like Brian. You remember how kind Brian was with me when I was on my own? Well, you used to come with him sometimes, didn't you? After Brian died, Terry just took over. I don't know what I'd have done without him. Still don't know.'

She was getting better at fending for herself but there were times when a man's strength was indispensable. The day before yesterday Terry Malone had forced back the bent mudguard on Martin's bike and stopped it from scraping the tyre.

Treesa stood up. 'I'll pop the kettle on and then we can talk. I've got heaps to tell you.' There was an air of excitement about her under the unease, and Fran understood the emotional turmoil that engulfed Treesa. She had been seventeen when she became pregnant, eighteen when Brian had died. And now Terry was in love with her and that love was returned: Fran had seen signs of it before Treesa moved out, and had sensed how afraid of her feelings the girl had become.

When Treesa came back into the room she made a determined

effort to change the conversation. 'I'm taking the bairn to a playgroup twice a week. He likes the company.' In the corner the baby rocked back and forward, trying to force a plastic bucket into its mouth, eyes bright with laughter at Martin's antics with a jack-in-the-box. 'He's good with babies, your Martin. It's a pity . . .' Treesa's words died away as she realized their implication but Fran didn't mind. She had now come to terms with the fact that Martin was her only child and likely to remain so.

'We'd been trying for another baby for years,' she said, smiling to show she was not upset. 'In and out of clinics. They couldn't find any reason, it was just one of those things. If David had lived we'd have persevered. We might even have adopted eventually.'

Treesa was still embarrassed. 'Well, you still might . . . I mean . . .'

She was floundering and Fran came to her rescue. 'Tell me about your new neighbours. Are they nice?'

Treesa launched at once into an account of neighbours right, left, and opposite. Right and left were elderly people who kept themselves to themselves. It was opposite that interested Treesa. 'He was sacked after the strike. He was taken to court and fined, but he lost his job just the same. You can't say that's fair.'

Fran shook her head. 'No. If that's true it's not fair.' The plight of the sacked miners was a sore point in mining areas. Fran did not believe that men who had done bodily harm to others should get off scot-free, but she had heard too many stories like Treesa's to be happy about the situation. 'Can't he appeal?'

Treesa's laugh was scornful. 'Appeal? Who to? It's been left to the area directors and we all know whose pocket they're in.'

As Treesa went to scald the tea, Fran fought hard to restrain a smile. The sacked miners were no laughing matter; what was funny was the way Treesa's voice and attitudes were beginning to mirror Terry's.

Over the tea it emerged he was coming round that night. 'He wants to fix the tiles in the toilet,' Treesa said. 'There's nothing in it, I mean, I wouldn't. Even if he was interested . . . which he's not . . . well, you know I wouldn't get up to anything.'

She was still vowing chastity when she waved Fran and Martin off. 'Be happy,' Fran said as she left. 'Don't worry about anything else.'

The trouble with being cryptic was that it got you nowhere. Treesa would take no notice and go on worrying just the same.

'Are you stopping in tonight?' Martin asked as she got out to open the garage doors.

'Don't I usually?' she answered drily.

He shrugged. 'How do I know? Anyway, if you are, you can't watch mush on the telly. *Sports Special*'s on.'

Fran gave a theatrical groan. 'I'll go to bed then. Poor old Mum. Thirty-four years old and no rights.'

He was smiling, relieved that she had not given him an argument. Secretly, she was pleased. She didn't need telly. A nice long bath, with nothing to prepare for the morning. Bliss!

She was turning on the immersion heater when the telephone rang. 'Frances?'

Her heart leaped and then steadied to beat twice as fast as usual. 'Hallo. I didn't expect to hear from you.' It was true, she had not expected Tony Lund to ring, in spite of his words.

'I suggested a meal, didn't I? When are you free?'

They arranged to meet on Tuesday night and she put the phone down slowly, waiting to hear the click at the other end before she let go.

'Who was that?' Martin called as she crossed the hall.

'No one. Well, no one special.'

When she was safely in the bath, suds up to her chin, she thought about Lund. He wasn't special. Quite a typical lecturer except for the disturbing eyes. He had nice hands, good finger-nails, his hair touched his collar, and his breath quite often smelled of exotic food. Par for the sociology course. So why the agitation?

She had arranged to meet him in Sunderland. She still couldn't bear the thought of another man picking her up here, in David's house, but she was looking forward to the meeting. Some sixth sense told her that, like Byron, Tony would be mad, bad and dangerous to know, and she was in the mood for some excitement. She reached for the loofah and began to scrub.

3

Tuesday, 2 July 1985

She had looked forward to the ritual of dressing up but when it came it was an ordeal. Foundation caked as she applied it, mascara clogged and beaded, and had to be wiped away, leaving her chipmunk-eyed. She sat on the edge of the bath and drew breath. She was going out for a meal with a man, that was all. No big deal. David had been dead for two years. No one could expect her to live in purdah, no one except herself.

She put on her navy suit with the red and white blouse and lapels, then decided it was too formal and changed into a pink linen shift-dress. Now her red lipstick clashed and had to be replaced. She cursed gently as she tried to wipe it away. Somewhere in Sunderland Tony Lund was washing his face, perhaps changing his shirt – no more. Men had all the luck. Thoughts about the chore of daily shaving intruded but she put them resolutely aside. It was her turn to feel deprived and no one was going to stop her.

Bethel arrived as Fran was making Martin's supper. 'Leave that to me. You don't want your best dress mucked up.'

Fran sat down gratefully and watched Bethel bustle about. 'She's like a mother to me,' she thought, emotion pricking pepper-like at her nostrils.

The older woman was stooping to peer under the grill. 'It's not the same,' she said gloomily. 'Not that anything is nowadays, but toast has no taste. The bread's pap and you can't beat a fork to the fire.'

Suddenly Fran understood. Bethel was angling to keep open the living-room fireplace. Now the strike was over Fran was preparing to have it blocked off again, but if it stayed open Bethel could give her part of her concessionary coal – and she was determined the fireplace should remain.

'You never wanted me to open up that fireplace,' Fran said accusingly, but Bethel was not abashed.

'That was because you set a madman loose on it. If you'd gone about it sensibly I'd have been all in favour. Anyroad, stop raking old coals. It's open now and it's daft to shut it. You could keep a fire going for next to nothing, and burn all your rubbish besides. And you wouldn't get cardboard when you wanted toast.' She banged two pieces of toast on the bench to illustrate her point. 'It's a good job that lad of yours has a good set of teeth.'

Fran promised to reconsider the fireplace and made her goodbyes. 'I won't be late and I won't do anything you wouldn't do and I'll try to be a lady.' Bethel's snort of disbelief followed her through the hall.

Tony was already at the town-centre hotel, lager in front of him and the *Guardian* open at the leader page. While he collected her drink she glanced at the headlines. 'I *thought* you'd read this,' she said, indicating the paper as he slid into his seat.

'Compulsory,' he said, returning her grin. 'No good sociologist is complete without it.'

So far, so good, Fran thought. Away from the college environment he seemed more vulnerable, less of a threat. 'Tell me about yourself,' he said suddenly and set the alarm bells ringing once more.

'You know all about me.' She sounded defensive and the teasing gleam returned to his eye.

'Not the important bits. What makes you tick, Frances Drummond?' He was going to probe! Worse than that, he was going to analyse. He had probably invited her out as part of some terrible sociological research project and he was waiting for an answer.

'What makes me tick?' she said. 'Oh, the usual things. Home, children, getting through college ... surviving. Just general surviving.'

He was expecting more and it wasn't fair. David had always dictated topics of conversation he knew she could follow. She and Steve had shared misery and comforted one another. This man was offering no comfort.

'Why have you stayed in Sunderland?' she said, suddenly determined to carry the war into the enemy's camp.

He grinned in appreciation of the ploy. 'I wanted to see you.' And when she blushed – 'I like to see you go pink. You do it in group discussion, every time I ask you to take up a point.'

Fran was nettled. 'So that's why you always pick on me.'

There was crisp dark hair in the open neck of his shirt and along the backs of his hands. He reached out a forefinger and momentarily touched her wrist. 'You shouldn't complain. I'm bringing you out of your shell. And you still haven't told me about yourself.'

She was into the game now. 'I live in a shell. I'm a single parent of limited intelligence who had the temerity to think she could cope with a teaching course. Correction, the entirely misplaced temerity.'

He was laughing and it gave her confidence. 'I can't help getting myself into situations where men far cleverer than I ask me impertinent and unanswerable questions, to which I can give only the sketchiest of answers.'

'Men? So I'm one of a long line?' He had caught her.

'No, that's not what I mean . . .'

He had very good teeth and he knew it, allowing his tongue to touch against them when he smiled.

'So I'm the only man in your life?'

Careful, Frances. Don't say too much. 'The only clever man. So please don't torment me.' She was useless at conversational tilting. That was for the Germaine Greers of this world who were born with a thesaurus in one hand and a lance in the other.

He didn't take her arm when they came out into the evening air but his presence was all around her. He was sexy, she decided over her prawn and almond balls. Or rather, sexual. And sensual. Sometimes he laid one fingertip on her upturned wrist to emphasize a point, and afterwards she looked down, convinced she would find a burn mark.

His mood changed abruptly with the lychees. 'What made you go in for teaching?'

She chewed for a moment, trying to gain time. She could hardly tell him she had chosen teacher training because it seemed to postpone taking an actual job, or because she could just manage to live on the grant and, most importantly, the hours coincided with Martin's school times. Besides, it was no longer true. In the beginning she had felt no great calling, but things had changed. With each spell of teaching practice she felt more involved. Perhaps she might make a teacher after all.

'I always wanted to do it but David . . . my husband was called David . . . wanted to get married as soon as we could and it didn't seem worth training if I was never going to teach. So I worked in a bank, just marking time.'

'Your husband didn't believe in working women, then?'

She couldn't resist a smile. 'I don't think he ever thought of me as a working woman.' She felt suddenly disloyal. 'No, that's not quite true. I never saw *myself* as a career woman. I wanted to be David's wife. From the first, that was all I wanted; and then Martin came along and we were very happy until . . .'

He filled her glass and then his own and showed no sign of wanting further information. Fran was first grateful and then piqued. His interest didn't last for long.

'What about you?'

He was smiling again. 'What about me? You know it all. I'm an open book. I'm thirty-seven years old, I teach sociology and I read the *Guardian*. I have two homes, a rather poky flat in Sunderland for term-time and a house in Yorkshire for off-duty . . . not that there's much of that.'

Fran was not to be fobbed off. 'You've never married?'

His smile deepened. 'There's no Mrs Lund.'

Fran felt her cheeks burn. 'I wasn't meaning that.'

They talked of the course, then, of students and lecturers and the possibility of a job at the end of it all, but the uncomfortable flush still mantled Fran's cheeks. He must think her a complete square.

She had parked the car underneath a tree in a well-lit side street. He walked her back to it and waited while she fumbled for her keys. When the door opened she moved inside but he reached out a hand. 'Whoa. I don't bite.' He was holding her lightly and she could move away if she chose, but she was powerless to pull away and they both knew it.

He kissed her lightly on the forehead, then on each closed eye. His lips barely touched her but she found herself stirred out of all proportion. 'I'll ring you,' he said, suddenly distancing himself. She wanted more. She kept her eyes lowered, willing him to move back and uncomfortably aware that if she looked up, his eyes would be amused. She felt like a naughty child now, anxious to be away and yet incapable of moving.

He made it easy for her, opening the door wider and holding her elbow lightly to turn her car-wards. 'Sleep well.'

She was out on the Belgate road before she realized she had not said thank you. It was a fresh embarrassment to add to the rest. She couldn't handle him, that was sure, and yet he turned her on in a way that was new to her. He had made none of the usual moves and still she was hooked. She *wanted* him or, rather, the unknown quantity in him. Sex with David had been warm and comfortable. Sex with Steve had been an act of mercy, giving rather than receiving. Sex with Tony Lund would be – ? She thought about it for more than a mile without finding a single suitable adjective, but that there would be sex with him she had no doubt.

She felt distinctly sinful as she let herself into the house. 'Not a word out of either of them,' Bethel said. In his basket Nee-wan lifted an ear, then half-rolled on to his back in the hope of a tickled belly. 'Good night?' Bethel asked.

She knows, Fran thought, busying herself with the kettle. She knows I'm having randy thoughts. 'It was all right. He's just one of my lecturers.'

Bethel nodded. 'So you've been having a night class. By, it's nice to see someone dedicated to their work.'

They were both laughing now, sitting down at the table to share coffee and sympathy. 'Anyway, he's probably got someone else.' She was thinking over Tony Lund's words: *There's no Mrs Lund.* That meant he had no wife. It didn't mean he was unattached.

Bethel blew out smoke. 'If he is, drop him. If they'll play away once, they'll play away twice. All these lasses nowadays, snaffling other folks' husbands. Proud of it, some of them. Beats me why they can't see it. On the other hand, he might be a single feller. If he's been at college he might not have had a chance to meet a lass.'

Fran considered explaining the sexual mores of university life and decided against it. 'Well, we'll soon know for sure.' The possibility that he might be living with someone had obviously never entered Bethel's head and Fran was glad.

She put Nee-wan on his lead and set Bethel to her gate. The July sky was still tinged with pink and there was night-scented stock in someone's garden. Fires burned in the grates of Belgate in spite of summer and smoke rose into the air from several chimneys. 'Watch what you're doing, lass,' Bethel said as they parted. 'You're enough to drive a body up the wall but I wouldn't like to see you come to harm.'

'I'll be careful.' Fran felt good now, at peace with the world as the adrenaline subsided. He might ring tomorrow and if he did she would handle it better. He was attractive and he knew it, but that was not a crime. If all he wanted was sex, there were others in the class who would be happy to oblige and much better at it than she. 'Perhaps he's after my mind,' she said aloud. 'In which case he'd better bring a magnifying glass.' She was still chuckling when she was safe inside and bolting the door.

4

Saturday, 13 July 1985

She was out in the garden before 8 a.m., gathering up weeds by the handful and piling them neatly in a corner. It was the height of summer and couch grass tickled her bare legs and poked through the crevices of her sandals. Nee-wan had trotted after her at first. Now he had lost interest and lay, belly upwards, in the sun.

Ever since end of term she had felt guilty about the garden, which David had planted and she had let run to seed. Coming to grips with it was a tremendous relief – and enjoyable! She had not realized how satisfying it would be to rescue a clump of iris from encroaching weeds, trowel the hard-baked earth until it was black and moist, and leave the green spears standing proud.

She would garden a lot more now that she knew she could do it. That was her trouble: she shirked because she feared her own inadequacy and other people's competence. Having discovered a Titchmarsh-like talent, she would be at it all the time, hoeing, pruning, tying up with twine. She tried to straighten her back and found herself doing a Richard-the-Third hobble. Time for breakfast!

She poured water into the dog's bowl and he lapped noisily, droplets leaping from the bowl and spattering the floor. At last he looked up and turned expectantly towards the biscuit cupboard. 'Just one, then.' To think she had gone thirty-two years of her life without knowing the love of a dog! She had taken the puppy to comfort Martin and had found endless comfort for herself. She bent to fondle the silky head. He was a noble dog, despite his tangled genes.

She was still enjoying a flush of emotion when the phone rang. It was Min. 'You're OK, aren't you?' She was making rapid calculations about Min's dates. It couldn't be the baby, not yet!

'I can't talk, Fran ... not now. But I've got to see you!' Though Min was usually impassioned when she wanted something, this sounded different.

'I could come over about seven; I'm coming in to Sunderland then, in any case.'

'No, that's no good. You've got to come now! Dennis is out ... and I don't know how long for, but I've got to talk to someone.'

Fran's heart thudded towards her boots. 'Oh Min, ... it's not Hindson-Evans again?'

'Are you mad? I can hardly cope with one man at the moment – I can't see my feet ... No, this is serious, Fran. Too serious to talk about on the phone – you must come over. Now!' If Fran hadn't known that Min never cried she would have thought she detected tears.

'I've promised to take Martin to Seaham. He's not going to

fish, thank God, but he wants to watch. I'll come to you first. Martin can play with the kids . . .'

Min's tone was flat. 'They're not here.'

Now Fran was really alarmed. 'OK. Let's not go on about it. I'll be with you as soon as I can.'

Martin was mutinous when she suggested a change of plans. 'I don't want to go. You promised we'd go to Seaham.'

In the end Fran compromised. 'I'll drop you off there, but you're not to go near the water.' Martin's eyes rolled heavenwards. 'All right, I know you're eleven but that doesn't mean I don't want you to make twelve! Stay where it's safe and I'll get back as soon as I can.'

She was getting the car out when Terry Malone came into view. At a distance he looked remarkably like Brian, but as he drew close the tilt of his chin, the direct gaze, were his own. Brian had been as easy as an old shoe; Terry was made of sterner stuff. The strike had been over for months and still he had not gone home.

'Hallo, Terry. I was going to pop round to your mam's in the hope that I'd catch you.'

He was bending to fondle the dog. 'Good lad . . . all right now, no need to jump up. What can I do for you, Mrs Drummond?'

She wanted him to babysit. 'Bethel's got a chance of a holiday flyer, so she's Bingo bound tonight – though what she'll do with a package holiday abroad I do not know.'

Terry was more knowledgeable. 'They sell them. There's always someone wants it. You get half-price, mebbe a bit more if it's a fancy place.'

The mysteries of the holiday flyer had only recently been explained to Fran – every Bingo winner received a ticket entitling them to take part in a special game whose prize was a package holiday. 'Treesa goes to Bingo, doesn't she?' Fran asked. 'It'd be nice if she won a holiday. You could go with her and take the baby.'

She had made the remark innocently enough but he blushed to the roots of his hair. She was about to make some mollifying remark when she changed her mind and opted for defiance. 'I know you're fond of her, Terry. A blind man could see that. She hasn't said anything but I'm certain she feels the same. So why shouldn't you go on holiday together?'

He shook his red head. 'Don't ask me, Mrs Drummond. I'm not the one with the mucky mind. It's all the tongues round here, that's what's got Treesa scared.'

Aloud, Fran made light of public opinion. Privately, she conceded Treesa had a point. Belgate was like any other place, full of sympathy for a widow unless, and until, she decided to retire from the widowed state. It had taken them a while to concede to Treesa the status of widow. Having given her a grudged respectability, many would disapprove if she took up with another man, especially if that man was her dead lover's brother.

Terry was willing, even eager, to sit with Martin, and Fran finished getting the car out. Martin appeared before she could shout. 'Come on, let's get going.' His tone was imperious and he fastened himself into the passenger seat with aplomb.

'What are your orders, sir?' she said once she was behind the wheel.

'Drive on,' he said, waving a lordly hand, and shaking out his comic.

'Yes, sir,' she said and let out the clutch.

They had left Belgate behind and were driving between fields when she saw a familiar figure in the distance. It was Fenwick. She was used to seeing him alone now, wearing the aura of the outcast. Damn the strike.

She cheered herself up by remembering that she had two cans of lager at the back of the fridge. She would put them out for Terry tonight. He was still short of money, still repaying debts incurred during a year without work. What spare money he had went on Treesa's baby, so he would appreciate a drink.

'Wake up, Mam. You'll miss the turning.' She swung the wheel and left the A19. 'The sooner I'm old enough to drive the better,' Martin said smugly and returned to his comic.

She left him at the harbour, urging him to stay away from anything that might be in the least dangerous. He nodded reassuringly, spitting on his hand to reinforce his promise, but she was still anxious as she walked back to the car.

'I see he hasn't brought the rod today.' It was the man who had helped them on the pier.

'No. I think one day was enough.'

He was tapping out his pipe on a stone wall and he caught her looking at it. 'That's all I seem to do with this thing. Fill it up, have a dozen goes at lighting it, and then knock it out.' He shook his head ruefully. 'Cigarettes were so much easier.'

Fran felt the instant sympathy of the fellow nicotine addict. 'Have you just given up? Stick it out . . . I gave them up a while ago and it was hell at first. Now I'm glad I did.'

Suddenly she remembered Min and was guilt-stricken. 'I'll have to go. A friend of mine is in some sort of trouble . . .' She looked back towards the harbour, seaching for Martin, and he followed her eyes.

'Are you leaving him? Don't worry, I'll be hanging around for a while. I won't let him fall in.'

She was grateful and then suddenly afraid. A man wandering about? He looked respectable, but who said psychopaths had to dress in rags? As if he had read her mind he fished in his pocket. The wallet was shabby and bulging and opened to reveal a photograph of two children, boy and girl, a small picture of a woman superimposed. As she admired them, he fished in his wallet for a business card. 'There you are: my bona fides. I'll be down here for an hour or so, I've nothing else to do. So off you go!'

Fran felt suddenly ashamed of her doubts. 'I didn't need your card . . .' she said, and was fumbling for the right words when he cut her short.

'Don't apologize. It pays to be careful.'

As she let out the clutch and moved back on to the road, his face was in her mind. A nice face, even good-looking. But not her type. She could be on a desert island with him for ten years and feel not a flicker. The pier man faded and Tony Lund took his place. That was different. Last night he had fingered the nape of her neck and she had felt her vaginal muscles contract. It was crazy but it was true. Just like that – a reflex action but quite devastating.

She looked up and caught her own eyes in the rear-view

mirror. Guilty eyes. She tried to banish randy thoughts and fixed her mind on Min. What could it be? Surely Dennis had not strayed from the straight and narrow? Lots of men did when their wives were pregnant. On the other hand, Dennis's delight in the coming baby was genuine enough – she would bet on it. She was still conjecturing when Min's driveway loomed up, and the car ground to a halt in the gravel.

Min's eyes were huge in a white face. 'She's got no make-up on,' Fran thought, and knew that whatever was wrong must be very wrong indeed.

'We've gone bust,' Min said when they were sitting at the kitchen table. 'Finished. Kaput. Not a penny!'

Fran's first reaction was relief. So it was only money! Then she thought again: money was life-blood to Min. What did you say to someone when their life collapsed like a pack of cards?

'I'll make us a nice cup of tea,' she suggested.

'It can't have *all* gone,' she ventured later, when they were supping the tea.

'All,' Min replied flatly. 'Shops, houses, cars – they're all company property. Some nasty little man from the Official Receiver's office came round this morning and immobilized the cars. He says the Receiver will take everything. The kids will even have to leave their schools . . . my God, I could weep when I think of it.'

Fran tried to marshall her thoughts. 'I thought Fellowes was a limited company, and that meant they couldn't touch your possessions?'

Min's tone was bitter. 'That's what I thought. But Fellowes got into deep water during the strike – you know all their business was in mining areas. There was stock unsold, no one paying their HP . . . The business needed cash to keep going, so they put up our houses as security.'

'Your in-laws' too?' Fran asked.

Min nodded. 'I can't help feeling sorry for them – awful to build up a successful business and then see it pulled down by a bunch of shits.'

Fran couldn't let that pass. 'It wasn't as simple as that, Min.

The miners didn't strike on purpose. They thought they had a cause.'

For once Min was not disposed to argue. 'Oh, all right. What does it matter, anyway? Whoever's to blame, it's done.' She put a hand on her swollen belly. 'I've got to keep calm for the sake of the baby. If it wasn't for that, I'd get in my car and drive it into the nearest wall . . . just to stop them getting their thieving hands on it. I loved that car!'

Fran couldn't resist a smile. 'Oh, Min, trust you to think of your Capri.'

A ghost of a grin touched Min's face. 'I know. I'm upset about the whole thing, but the car really hurts. And the thought of Eve! She's going to *love* all this. Harold rang Dennis this morning to say he would help if he could. I should bloody well think so! He's been our accountant for the last ten years, he should've seen this coming. God knows what he's made out of us. Now we lose everything and he keeps the lot. It makes you sick!'

Fran listened while Min poured out her anger and fear for the future, but her mind kept straying to Martin and the North Sea, sucking greedily at the harbour walls. 'I'll have to go,' she said at last. 'But you know where I am. I'll do anything.' She hesitated, wanting to help and yet afraid of putting her foot in it. 'Remember, we've got heaps of room. If you and Dennis and the kids need a place – in between houses – Martin and I would be glad of the company.'

Min looked suddenly confused. 'I never thought of that. Where will we live?'

Suddenly Fran remembered her own fears after David's death. 'I'll tell you one thing,' she said firmly. 'However things turn out, it won't be nearly as bad as you think.'

In the hallway Min suddenly reached out. 'Oh, Franny, isn't it a bloody life?' She looked down at her bump. 'Still, we'll have to make the best of it! And Dennis, poor sod – I'll have to keep going for his sake.'

Fran smiled. 'You'll be all right, Min. It'd take more than liquidation to get you down.'

Martin was sitting on a wall when she got to Seaham, watching cranes swing backwards and forwards. The pier man was expounding about imports and exports. 'You're back,' he said, as Fran reached them. And then, seeing her face: 'Bad news?'

Fran shrugged. 'It could've been worse. All the same . . .'

Martin looked suddenly perturbed and she hastened to calm his fears. 'No one's hurt, so it's not really bad. But Aunty Min's had a shock. Uncle Dennis's business will have to close.' She looked towards the pier man to explain. 'They're friends of ours, close friends. And she's expecting a baby soon.'

He had taken out his tobacco pouch. Now he put it away. 'I think you could do with a drink,' he said and, looking at Martin, 'Coke for you – or lime and lemon?'

As they walked up the bank towards the pub on the seafront, she wondered how old he was. Late thirties? There was something careworn about him, a fatherly quality. And something else, less reassuring. They were almost at the door of the pub when she realized what it was: an air of defeat, as though he were coping with a terrible despair.

They chatted about Min and Dennis over the drinks. He didn't know their name or location, so it didn't seem disloyal to discuss them with a stranger. He was sympathetic and knowledgeable about the strike. 'We did quite well out of it,' he said. 'We brought in coal to some of the smaller harbours . . . but it was different for other people.'

Fran remembered his card, still in her pocket. He was something to do with shipping.

He walked them back to the car and she thanked him. 'It was a great help, knowing you were there,' she said and he smiled.

'It was no trouble. That's a nice lad you've got there.'

She was driving away before she realized he had said nothing about seeing them again. 'Ships that pass in the night,' she thought.

'His name's Jim. He used to go to sea,' Martin said, turning back from waving. 'He's been to every continent. He says he'll show me some photographs next time.'

Fran nodded. 'That's nice.' All the same, she would have to check. You couldn't be too careful; he'd said that himself.

The phone was ringing when she got home. 'I thought it might be you, Eve,' she said, trying not to sound acid.

'Of course, they'll lose everything,' Eve said. 'I know she's brought it on herself – I mean, the mad extravagance! – but you can't help feeling sorry. Still, Harold will help. I've told him to pull out all the stops.'

Alone in the hall, Fran winced. She remembered what it was like to be on the receiving end of help from Harold and Eve. Eve had expected her to live like a pauper and Harold had tut-tutted over the least extravagance. She was tempted to tell Eve to leave Min alone, but they had been friends since infants' school and it wasn't that simple.

'It may not be as bad as they think,' she said but Eve was not to be gainsaid.

'Harold says they'll lose everything, and are lucky to be in liquidation, rather than bankruptcy. *That* means they can take everything, down to your undies. They only need to leave you a bed and a chair. You can't even have an electricity bill when you're bankrupt.'

Fran tucked the telephone under her chin and began to push back her cuticles. In an hour or so she would be meeting Tony. They would go for a drink, perhaps a meal. Perhaps go back to his flat. She put up a hand and felt her hair. There would be time to wash it if Eve would just shut up.

Martin appeared from the kitchen and she began to signal. 'Who is it?' he mouthed, and she mouthed back, 'Aunty Eve!' and rolled her eyes to the door. He nodded and tiptoed away. The next moment the ring of the doorbell pierced the air. 'I'll have to go,' she told Eve, and then ran upstairs to get ready.

5

Monday, 12 August 1985

The smell of new-baked bread was like no other, Fran decided. 'Aye, they're not bad,' Bethel conceded when Fran showered praise on the plump rolls and crusty loaves that covered the kitchen table. Bethel had only lately agreed to bake in Fran's kitchen, declaring the electric oven a menace until she had mastered it.

Today Eve and Min were coming to tea. 'Min'll adore these,' Fran said, breaking off red-hot crust to reveal the steaming, doughy bread beneath.

'She'll be lucky to find any left,' Bethel said tartly. 'I'll be glad when you get back to that college of yours and let me have this kitchen again.'

Outside, the August sky was still blue but this morning Fran had seen a browning leaf. Autumn, autumn. Worse still, autumn term, the beginning of her final year. The thought was so frightening that she turned back to the bread.

When Min arrived she would ply her with hot rolls and butter. Actually, Min was being amazingly brave. Every night, or so it seemed, notices of Fellowes' liquidation appeared in the evening paper, alarming, official notices that made the whole thing seem to roll on remorselessly. In spite of all this, Min carried on, cheering Dennis, encouraging the dazed children, and preparing to give birth.

Eve was scathing each time she phoned. 'She won't stay. You wait till this baby's born. She'll be off! I mean, what will there be to stay for? You know Min, money mad! And the best Dennis can hope for is some sort of job in retail. Harold's always said you can't beat having a qualification. If Dennis had a few letters after his name, he'd be in a better position now.'

'What's the matter with you?' Bethel was glowering at her across the kitchen table. 'Your face is tripping you up.'

Fran nodded. 'I know. I was thinking about poor Min.' She was saved from Bethel's scorn by a knock at the yard door.

A man stood in the back lane, his bike loaded with bags of coal beside him. 'Need any coal, missus? It's proper coal, not duff.' That meant it was stolen, Fran thought.

'Thanks a lot but I've got plenty for the moment. I have it delivered.'

He nodded and turned away as though he had been expecting a refusal. If he had argued, pushed even a little, she could have closed the door but his resignation was harder to deal with. 'How much is it? Perhaps I could take a bag.'

The coal was £2 a bag: half-price. But what was a saving of £2 if you went to gaol?

'You know who that is?' Bethel was peering out at the man tipping the bag into the coal-house and her voice spoke volumes.

'No,' Fran said, raking through her purse for two pound coins.

Bethel bridled. 'He's a right villain! You've done it now, miss, throwing in with the likes of him.'

Fran forbore to answer until the back door was safely rebolted and she was back at the kitchen table. 'I haven't thrown in with anybody, Bethel. I've bought a bag of coal, probably stolen, definitely cheap. I've told him I have it delivered so it's unlikely I'll see him again, and there's no need for you to get uptight. However, I can see from your face that you're going to give me chapter and verse, so let's get it over with.'

'You should've told him to hadaway to hell, never mind getting it delivered. He's a real hard case, lives opposite Treesa. She wants to keep her doors locked. Lost his job for GBH – nearly maimed a man. And that's just what they can pin on him ... God knows what the truth of it is.'

So he was the sacked miner Treesa had mentioned. That explained his downcast air. The coal would have come from the stockpile at the pit. Stealing was rife and the police seemed to do little about it. 'It hasn't been fair,' Fran said defiantly. 'If they really did wrong, they should lose their jobs but the policy hasn't been fair. You can't say it has, Bethel! They've been taken back in one place and left sacked in another, for the same offence. That can't be right?'

Bethel took refuge in a mighty sniff which meant she knew she was on shaky ground. Fran decided not to push her advantage and poured herself a second cup of tea.

The man hadn't looked like a villain, he'd looked like a confused boy. Technically he was a thief, but he was taking what he felt to be his due ... the fruit of the Durham earth, hard, black, unyielding coal. He was a casualty of the strike, like Fenwick and Mrs Botcherby.

As if she had read Fran's mind, Bethel spoke. 'Botcherby's lass's home from the asylum.'

Fran was pleased. 'That's good. How is she now?' If she was

home her husband might lose his haggard air and her little girl
look like a child again, instead of a woman cut down.

'Not too bad, by all accounts. But you can't tell when they first
come out. It's what they're like when they're under pressure that
counts.'

The front door banged and Martin appeared in the doorway,
Gary Malone behind him. 'We want Penguins, or custard creams
if you've got none, and Coke, and Gary's shoelace's broke. Can
you put a knot in it?'

Fran hunted for a spare shoelace while Bethel told both boys
what she would like to put a knot in. 'Aunty Eve and Aunty Min
are coming to tea,' Fran said while they swilled biscuits and
orange, the nearest thing she had to Coke.

'I'm off then,' Martin said and made for the back door.

'His manners don't improve,' Bethel said, oozing satisfaction.
'I warned you about bad company. Give your Martin a week or
so, and he'll be worse than them he's learned it off.'

Fran smiled sweetly. 'That's why I love you, Bethel. You're
such a ray of sunshine.'

Bethel grinned. 'I do my best.'

Eve and Min arrived at four, Eve fussing around Min like a
mother hen. 'Watch that step. There you are, Fran, I brought
you a jar of my lemon curd. I know you like it.' And then in a
lower tone, 'I'm far too busy to take an afternoon off, but I
couldn't let her come on the bus, could I?'

Fran groaned inwardly. So that was how it was going to be.
They got the difficulties of dressing for so many functions with
the bread buns, and the impossibility of finding decent domestic
help with the Victoria sandwich. This was after Bethel had
clumped in wielding a steaming kettle and topped up the teapot
with a muttered aside about hollow legs.

Min's face was a mask of impassivity but Fran knew it must be
irking her. Eve had taken Min's place at the top of the heap and
was being none too subtle about it. Fran's thoughts wandered: if
David had lived she would have continued to see Ladies' Circle
as the hub of the universe. She might even have been elected to
office like Eve, and had a medallion on a ribbon to prove it.

At five to five the phone rang, and Eve jumped to her feet.

'It'll be for me. I left your number with the girl, I knew you wouldn't mind.' Eve's 'girl' was a wide-eyed Sunderland teen-ager, as near to an au pair as they could get.

'They pay her peanuts,' Min said as Eve rushed to answer. 'Sheer exploitation! It's enough to make you take out a Party card.'

The idea of Eve's reaction to Min's joining the Labour Party struck them simultaneously and they had to stifle their laughter in case it percolated through to the hall. 'We're being hysterical,' Fran thought and was suddenly sober.

'Seriously, though,' Min said at last, wiping her eyes. 'Let's talk while she's out there.'

Fran took another slice of cake and pushed the plate towards Min. 'She'll be there for hours.'

Min nodded and fell into a passable imitation of Eve's voice. 'I'm doing my best for Min . . . well, what are friends for? I drove all the way to Belgate in second gear in case I brought on premature labour and on the way home I'll help her to count her blessings.' Her merriment subsided. 'Not that that'll take long.'

'How are things?' Fran asked.

Min shifted her bulk into a more comfortable position. 'Fairly bloody. If only I could get out from behind this bump and get cracking!'

Fran was sympathetic. 'Not long now. Three weeks?'

'And two days . . . and then we might see some progress. Dennis does his best but he's still punch-drunk. His father kept him in the dark about the money side. You know Dennis ran the shops . . . he knew sales were down – God bless Scargill for that – but he didn't realize the cash position was so desperate.'

Fran was going to ask about the house but decided against it.

'Even when the house was put up to the bank, he didn't twig. His father had the deeds; he just said he needed a temporary guarantee, and Dennis signed. So did I, God help me. I'll read what I sign from now on. Not that it would have made any difference – if he'd said they needed the house to save the business, I'd have said "Go ahead."'

'So there's nothing left?' Fran said.

A ghost of a smile flitted across Min's face. 'Next to nothing but not actually nil.'

Fran was intrigued. Out in the hall Eve was beginning her goodbyes. Fran leaned closer. 'What d'you mean, Min? Hurry up, we've only got a minute.'

Min glanced at the closed door and then wriggled around to bring her face close to Fran's. 'Well, you know how they take everything from the business? I mean, everything! Well, Dennis had this box of ornaments . . . ghastly things, sort of cheap Capo di Monte imitations. Fellowes used them in window displays, but customers could buy them if they wanted to for thirty or forty quid. Anyway, the ornaments kept getting smashed in the warehouse, so he brought boxes of them home and stuck them in the garage. He was going to take them and give them to the liquidator! "Are you mad?" I said. So I've got them.'

Fran was puzzled. 'What will you do with them?' Min's home was stacked with *objets d'art*. Overstocked, by Fran's standards.

Min was looking at her with a jaundiced eye. 'Sometimes, Fran, I can't believe you did GCE! I'm going to flog them, of course. I'm going to flog everything I can get my hands on. We need a stake if we're going to get back in . . .'

She would have continued but there was a ping from the hall as Eve replaced the receiver, and both women sprang back into place. Min smiled angelically at Eve, but Fran could think only of what Min had told her. It was illegal, but was it immoral? Not that Min would care. Something had awakened in Min: a burning desire to protect her family.

They left at half-past five. 'Take care,' Fran said and gave Min a hug. It was difficult, the bulk of Min's swollen belly protruding and keeping them apart. Min's eyes rolled skywards. 'How long, oh Lord? How long?'

She was trying to squeeze into the seat, where Eve was holding out the safety belt with an impatient hand. 'Sorry to rush you,' she said, 'but I've so much on.' Fran's eyes locked with Min's for a second and saw fleeting pain there. Once Min would have said 'Shut up, Eve,' and Eve would have obeyed. Once Eve would not have dared tell Min to hurry. Once Min would have had her own gleaming pink Capri and not have been dependent

on Eve at all. As if Min had read her thoughts she smiled. 'How
are the mighty fallen,' she said quietly, and closed the door.

Fran was still waving to the departing car when Walter's three-
wheeled invalid car drew up at her side. 'Hello, Walter.'

He had wound down his window but made no move to get
out. 'Hello, yourself. Never mind the hellos. I've come for me
bread . . . if Sally Bethel's going to keep a promise for once.' His
tone implied this was unlikely but his eyes were twinkling. He
was dressed in his usual tweed jacket in spite of the summer's
day, his knees covered by a plaid rug bound with a leather strap.
'Well?' His eyebrows jutted. 'I know I'm a magnificent specimen
but you should've seen enough of me by now. Hadaway in and
get me a flat cake. Well done, mind. None of your pale imitations
of a good stotty.'

Bethel carried the flat cake out herself, wrapped in a clean tea
towel. 'Here it is, Walter, as promised.'

He unwrapped the bread and looked at it critically. It was
perfectly baked to a rich golden brown lightening to cream at the
edges, and still floury. 'Aye, it'll do. It's not what I'm used to, but
I'm in no position to argue.' It was exactly what they had expected
him to say.

'Bethel's sitting in for me tonight,' Fran said coaxingly. 'Why
don't you come to supper? She'd be glad of some company.'

Bethel's snort was pure outrage. 'Company – him? I'd sooner
be put in a cageful of monkeys.'

Walter's voice was silky, his remark addressed to Fran. 'She
plays hard to get but we all know she fancies me. Silly old moo.'
Fran was giggling.

Bethel was less impressed. She pushed the stotty cake close to
his chest and leaned in the window. 'You've got your stotty,
Walter. Take it home and let your meat stop your mouth. And
don't bother coming round tonight or you'll get a bucket of water
over you.'

He had put the car into gear and was moving off. 'Will you be
coming?' Fran called.

He was nearly at the corner when his reply came drifting back.
'I might . . . if I've got nothing better on.'

She left Bethel in the kitchen, preparing Martin's tea, and ran upstairs to get ready. If Walter came round it would be nice. She could relax with Tony without guilt about Bethel sitting alone in Belgate. She tried not to think about the other guilts that might strike her tonight. 'Nothing to be gained by crossing bridges, Frances,' she said aloud to the mirror.

Her face looked back, thin still and pale but more resolute than it used to be. The brown hair still curled but there were lines at the corners of her eyes and two distinct furrows between her brows. She would have to stop frowning.

She inspected her upper lip. Every magazine she picked up told you about the ageing upper lip which developed thousands of cracks into which your lipstick bled if you didn't watch out. Her upper lip bore even the most searching examination and she got down to basics, turning on the hot tap and fastening up her hair.

In the bath she thought about Tony Lund, acting out various scenarios in her mind. She was pleased about his interest in her, no two ways about it! When she thought of the beginning of term, the one bright spot in an otherwise gloomy picture was the prospect of telling Gwen ever so casually that she was in cahoots with a lecturer. Not just any lecturer, but the most personable of the lot. He would never marry her, he wasn't the marrying kind. All the same she ran through the acceptable wedding colours and settled for cream.

As she rubbed herself dry she pondered the divisions of the mind. With one bit you could think something quite barmy – like believing you would ever be married to a handsome sociology tutor – with another bit you knew you were fantasizing, even despised yourself for doing it; and yet the two parts could co-exist quite happily.

The thought sustained her through two goes at getting her make-up right, telling Martin to go to bed when Bethel told him, bearing Bethel's disapproval of her slit skirt, and driving eight miles to Sunderland. She felt quite serene as she walked into the cocktail bar and accepted Tony's smile of appreciation as though it were her due.

They went back to his flat for a meal, and as she teased him about his culinary abilities, her mind was in a ferment. She knew

what would happen. She was thirty-four years old, a married
woman, not a novice. They would eat and drink, and they would
make love. No big deal. She let out her breath in annoyance.
Martin was always using that stupid Americanism; now she was
doing it.

To take her mind off the evening ahead she looked around the
flat. It was not what she had expected. She had had two distinct
sets of expectations. In one daydream, he had been surrounded
by Victoriana. Not expensive bits, but good. One or two rare
prints, a worn but valuable Persian carpet, and shelf upon shelf
of books. In the other setting it had all been high-tech: plate
glass and chrome, original cartoons on the walls and a cord
carpet. The reality resembled neither.

It was shabby. Not nice shabby, like comfy old shoes that had
once been expensive, but cheap shabby. Hardboard sides and
wafer thin veneers, a shag-pile carpet and rampant tigers in
lacquered frames. 'Don't blame me for this,' he said, catching
her unawares, 'It's rented and, as I don't use it except to sleep
and work, I've refrained from imposing my personality.'

Fran doubted if you could impose much personality on shag
pile and jungle prints, but there were other things to worry about.
He had planted a dish in front of her. 'Crudités,' he said. The
dish was piled with strips of raw vegetable: carrot, cauliflower,
celery, marrow, and a couple of things she couldn't identify.
There was a bowl beside it, containing what looked like speckled
mayonnaise.

'Tuck in,' he said, gathering a handful of strips. His fingers
were lean and brown, and his nails immaculate but a trifle long.
He was dipping a strip of carrot into the bowl and munching.
His teeth were his best feature. She bit on a piece of dipped
marrow and found it delicious. She was going to enjoy this after
all!

They had chicken Kiev to follow . . . Marks and Sparks, from
a microwave she guessed . . . and then cheese and biscuits. He
served things, leaving her to eat what she chose. She liked that.

He was in the kitchen, collecting coffee, when the phone rang.
She waited for him to hurry through the door but the ringing
ceased and she heard him talking. There must be an extension

in the kitchen. She couldn't hear exactly what he was saying but it sounded like a casual conversation. He gave no explanation when he came back, simply put down the coffee and slid easily to the floor to pour.

There was a tape playing in the background, a piano trio making pleasant but unrecognizable music. 'Loussier,' he said, and Fran nodded sagely, although she hadn't the faintest idea what he meant. The coffee was strong and dark and good, the perfect finish to a meal. He patted the floor beside him. 'Come here.'

She said, 'Yes, lord and master,' but she went just the same.

He was touching her mouth, her neck, her breasts with the one gentle tracing finger. 'Funny Fran.' He was lifting her chin so that their eyes would meet but she struggled, unwilling to look at him. 'Are you scared?' His tone suggested that if she were scared it was for nothing, and yet his finger undid the buttons of her blouse and pulled it free of her skirt. 'I want to love you, Fran.'

She put her face into the hollow of his neck. 'I know.'

His hand was running gently up her spine, unfastening her bra. 'Can I? Is it all right?'

There was nothing to be afraid of, after all. He was letting her decide. She could call a halt and he would not be angry, nor contemptuous. Not even defeated, as Steve had been. 'Yes,' she said and began to get to her feet.

'Where are you going?' He was holding her arm, drawing her back.

'To the bedroom.'

He laughed gently, pulling her against him and rocking her gently to and fro. 'Oh Fran, what a baby you are. Haven't you done it anywhere else but in bed?'

He didn't expect an answer and she gave none. Instead she concentrated on the parchment shade of the ceiling light and the single burning bulb, trying not to mind about the indignity of shedding skirt and tights. He was holding her head in the hollow of his hand, murmuring encouragement, and she was suddenly grateful. She must pretend it was good. Perhaps it would be, if only she weren't so aware of the lights, the open kitchen door, the bentwood chair legs only inches from her eyes.

'It's all right isn't it, Fran darling?' She was forced to meet his gaze, not comprehending the question. His pupils were light blue, almost turquoise, flecked with green around hard, dark pupils. 'You are on the pill? We don't want you preggers in your final year.'

She nodded and nuzzled his neck again. No point in explaining she was as safe as the rock of Gibraltar inside her infertility. 'It's all right,' she said and gave herself up to pleasing him.

6

Wednesday, 4 September 1985

The stamp of Tony's personality was more evident in the bedroom. Black sheets with tiny coloured diamonds here and there to match the duvet; two pairs of slacks hung neatly on the wardrobe front; paperbacks and folders everywhere, as in the living room; a diverse and rather touching jumble on the ghastly, glass-topped dressing table. Perhaps, after all, he was an ordinary man. Fran closed her eyes and snuggled down. It was more than three weeks since the first time they had made love but she still felt the original excitement and the same post-coital inertia.

Tony was in the shower. He always showered after making love, emerging clean and pressed and totally asexual. Which was strange, because beforehand he was totally the opposite.

She was finding it difficult to define her relationship with Tony. He came and went between his homes, and when he was in Sunderland he wanted her in his bed. No, that was not strictly true. He wanted her. The bed was at her insistence, which caused him to call her 'a complete pleb'. He had smiled when he said it and seemed not to mind, but she was left with an aftertaste of guilt, as though she were hanging on to some outmoded convention. Everyone she knew made love in bed. Or did they? Most of the pillars on which life was based were assumptions.

You thought you knew what went on behind the closed doors of your friends, your colleagues, your bank manager, but in reality you never did.

The thought of her bank manager orgiastic on the hearthrug was so delicious that she laughed out loud, but cut it short in case Tony overheard and thought she was laughing at his performance. Which would have been unfair, because he was good at making love, leaving her at peace. She moved her legs in the bed and remembered him inside her.

She was roused from a pleasant re-run of the last hour by the shrilling of the bedside phone. In the kitchen there was a faint echoing peep-peep and in the living room too. When she found he had two extensions she had thought it the ultimate extravagance; now it seemed a good idea. She waited for him to pick the phone up but it rang on. He must still be in the shower. She looked at her watch: four-fifteen in the afternoon. It was OK for her to be there. She picked up the phone.

'*Tony, the kettle's on the blink. Bring the Russell Hobbs with you. Don't forget . . . and remember we're out to dinner.*' There was a pause and then, '*Tony?*'

Fran moistened her lips. 'I'm afraid he's not here at the moment.' She was prepared to stammer out some explanation of her own presence, but the caller seemed not to need one. '*Oh . . . all right. Tell him about the kettle. Boiling pans is bloody and I haven't time to shop for a new one. He'll have to do that at the weekend.*'

When Fran had replaced the receiver she lay still. At the sound of the woman's voice she had wanted to put down the phone but you couldn't do that. So he was married, after all! Such a domestic message could have come from no one else but a wife. Which made him a liar.

He came through the bedroom door just as she had pictured him: clean and shining and precise, all the languorous, teasing quality of his pre-coital performance gone.

'Someone rang,' she said, sitting up, hugging duvet and sheets to her breasts. 'They didn't give a name, but they want you to take the kettle with you. The other kettle's gone wrong.' He didn't answer, forcing her to add, 'It's terribly important. And you're to remember you're out to dinner.'

He was nodding, shovelling change and other paraphernalia from the dressing table into his trouser pockets. 'Are you getting up? Otherwise, I'll have to leave you here, I'm afraid.'

She tried to wriggle into her clothes under cover of the sheet. She knew it was crazy after such uninhibited love-making, but she couldn't help it. Her modesty was superfluous. When she looked in the mirror he was busy filling a leather grip, quite oblivious of her presence.

They went out to their cars together, his arms full of files and loose-leaf folders. 'Don't forget the kettle,' she said as she climbed into her car.

For a moment his old teasing manner returned. 'I won't forget, Miss Nags. Can't get it out of your mind, can you? It was just a friend. We share things. If she needs a kettle she shall have one. Now go home and forget it. You've got four more days of freedom, so enjoy them!'

She went up to the bathroom when she got home and stepped out of her clothes. At the beginning he had offered her the use of his shower, but when she had refused she could see he was relieved. He liked to keep his shower to himself, which was exactly the way she felt about her bathroom. It wasn't just that, though; it was that he wanted rid of her afterwards. She was trying not to mind, to get it into perspective, but it wasn't easy.

She lowered herself into the warm water. Four more days to relax, and then she must work hard. In less than a year she would be a fully fledged teacher – if she passed. He *wasn't* married: no wife would be so offhand about a strange woman answering her husband's phone. Outside she could hear Martin shouting. Shouting gleefully, which was all right. She sank lower into the water and gave herself up to luxury.

She was trying to pretend that the water was not cooling when she heard the phone ring. Still smarting from the effects of the call at Tony's flat, she decided to let it ring, but the impulse was short-lived: if it stopped ringing she would spend the rest of the day imagining the worst. Better get it over with. In the end she half leaped, half stumbled down the stairs, clad in towels.

It was Dennis. 'She's started, Fran. She wanted you to know.' He sounded less than jubilant.

'Has she gone in?' Fran was making rapid calculations.

'Not yet. We thought it'd be best to hang on . . .' Min's bed in an expensive nursing home had been cancelled when the money ran out. She was having the baby on the NHS and Dennis's sombre tones said it all.

'She'll be all right, Dennis. It's terribly efficient in the District General. That's where I had Martin.' She stopped then, anxious not to labour the point and worried that her towel would slip and leave her naked in the hall. She felt uneasy, just like she did in communal changing rooms: you were defenceless without the clothes and jewellery that were your identity. She cut Dennis short. 'Look, I'm coming over. Tell her to hang on.'

As she struggled into the first garments that came to hand, it seemed to her that her life revolved around other people giving birth. No one had asked her to go to Min, but it was obvious where her duty lay. 'Oh God,' she said aloud, 'I sound just like Eve.' Should she ring Eve? There would be hell to pay if she didn't, but worse if she did and Min didn't want it. She decided to be cautious.

It was Wednesday, Bethel's Bingo night. She would forgo it if Fran asked, but it wasn't fair. It would have to be Terry and if he failed, Martin would have to go to Treesa's. Except that she couldn't be sure how long she would be away. Some babies took hours. She would have to explain to Martin and then seek out Terry.

He was in when she called at his lodgings, coming to the door in his stockinged feet. His T-shirt was old and shabby but his arms were amazingly strong and muscled. She had noticed that about young miners . . . their faces were the faces of children, their hands were huge and powerful, almost out of place.

'Why aye, I'll watch him, Mrs Drummond. It's nee bother.' He nodded towards the living-room door behind him. 'They'll be glad of the place to themselves for a while.' He was lodging with a young miner and his wife, both as militant as Terry and glad to give him a home. All the same, it must be difficult at times.

'Martin was over the moon when I said you might come round. Can you stay if I don't get back in time? You never can tell with babies.' Terry assured her that she could stay away for a week, and watched as she went down the front path. 'Leave it all to me,' he called as she got into the car.

Driving towards Sunderland, she thought about Min and Dennis. At the moment they were both bearing up, Min better than Dennis. This baby would tip the scales one way or another, would be a millstone or a blessing, depending on their attitude.

The H of the hospital sign came into view and she shuddered. Till the end of her days that sign would remind her of David, strapped to the stretcher, lying grey and quiet as the ambulance skidded and swerved to get him there on time. '*He'll be all right now,*' the driver had said when they got there, but he had still died. She shook her head to banish morbid thoughts and took the turning for Min's. At least she lived near to the hospital; that would make it easier for everyone.

Dennis was in the hall when she got there, with Althea, Peter and James, all unnaturally solemn and clad in their outdoor clothes. 'Dad's coming for them,' Dennis explained. 'If they're round there, it leaves me free.' The three little faces were tense. Poor kids, Fran thought. They must have been aware of the business collapse. A *For Sale* board stood in the garden, and now they were being shipped to their grandparents.

'You'll have a new baby by tomorrow,' she said. 'Do you want a boy or a girl?'

The reply was unanimous. 'A boy!' 'We don't want another girl,' James said and gave Althea a look of scorn.

Usually Dennis was good with his children. Today he seemed not to care. 'Go in,' he urged Fran. 'I'll take the kids down to the gate. Dad should be here any moment.' She was moving away before she realized he didn't want her to meet his father. She had known Mr Fellowes all her life, had watched him grow from a one-windowed shop proprietor to the owner of a chain of stores. He had gloried in his increasing wealth and new-found status. Now it was gone, he was probably anxious to avoid prying eyes.

'Thank God you've come,' Min said. And then, suddenly anxious, 'You didn't ring Eve, did you?'

Fran shook her head. 'No, I'll ring her when it's over. How do you feel?'

Min's face gleamed with sweat as she pushed down with her arms and tried to shift her body into a more comfortable position. 'Bloody ... but I don't care. As long as I get it over with, that's all that matters. Do you want tea?'

'No, but I'll get you a cup.'

Min shook her head. 'I'll only want the loo if I drink and I can't face getting up. I feel as though I'm coming adrift.'

A spasm of pain crossed her face and she started to pant short breaths. 'I don't know if this stuff helps, but might as well try it.' Her breathing slowed and she relaxed. 'That's it for a while ... about twenty minutes, I think. When it gets to ten-minute intervals, we'll go.' She licked her lips. 'I'd love a gin.'

Fran was alarmed. 'You can't drink, Min. Not now. It's dangerous.'

Min threw back her head to laugh. 'It's bleeding impossible, darlin, 'cos we haven't got none. Just another of life's little luxuries gone down the plughole. Still, I've always got Eve to comfort me. She rang yesterday. "Don't worry about going NHS," she said. "It's not quite the same, but as long as you both survive it doesn't matter, does it?"'

Fran giggled. 'She didn't say that?'

Min's nod was emphatic. 'She did. The inference being that we'd be lucky if we did survive.'

Fran shook her head. 'She's wrong, Min. The treatment's the same, the standards are just as high. There are two differences: you don't get the etceteras like tea for visitors and Laura Ashley curtains; and they treat you with less respect.' She had never realized that until now, but it was true. Martin had been born in an NHS maternity ward. Most of her friends, apart from Treesa, had given birth in private wards. The only difference in attitude had been that the nurses in the public wards told you what to do, whereas in the private ward they asked. And yet you paid for medical treatment, no matter where you got it. By cheque or by taxes, you paid just the same.

Min was grimacing. 'I think it's another, Fran.'

Fran took her hand. 'Are you sure?' It was a labour pain all right. Min's knuckles showed white, and where she had gripped Fran's hand there were red marks.

'I'll ring for a taxi,' Dennis said, coming back into the room.

'Don't be stupid.' Fran was fumbling for her keys. 'Take the Mini.'

They half-carried, half-bundled Min into the car. 'Stay with him, Fran, when he comes back. I don't want him sitting around the hospital, feeling sorry for himself. See if you can get him to eat something. They'll ring when there's any action!'

Dennis was harder to persuade.

'I don't want you there, Dennis,' Min said. 'I absolutely, positively want to do this on my own. You won't help, you'll just divert everybody's attention from me. I want you to come back to Franny, and come in again when it's all over and there's a wizened little red thing with a big mouth for you to admire.'

She's trying to protect him, Fran thought. It isn't that she doesn't want him there, it's that she doesn't think it'll be good for him. 'Go and get on with it, kid,' she said, patting Min's arm. 'I'll see to everything here.'

Dennis was still dubious when he returned. 'I should've stayed.' Fran had tea ready on a tray, and they carried it through to the living room. 'Do you want the fire switched on?' he asked. She shook her head, remembering the days when Min's central heating, thermostatically controlled, had run round the clock. Now, like the almost empty fridge, it was in retirement.

'I don't expect it'll be long,' she said, handing him tea.

'They're going to ring when she goes into the delivery room. Then I'm going back.'

Fran raised her eyebrows. 'Does she want you to do that?'

He shook his head. 'No, but I'm going anyway.'

Fran smiled. 'Trust Min to be different. It's the fashion nowadays to have your husband in at the birth, but she has to do it her way.' Her tone was affectionate and he took it as it was intended.

'She's never run true to form ... not even now. I used to think all she cared about was the goodies – you know, clothes, jewellery ...' His voice faltered a little. 'That bloody awful pink car of hers. I thought she'd take it badly when everything went but no ... "We'll start again," she said. That's all.'

'And will you?'

He shook his head. 'No way, Fran. If we get this baby safely into the world, we'll sell the house so the bank stops moaning, find somewhere we can afford on a mortgage, and I'll get a job flogging something. We'll manage.' Fran would have changed the subject but he seemed anxious to go on.

'I should've seen it coming. I thought once the strike was over, things would pick up but I was wrong. It's been worse since the miners went back. They suddenly realized they had huge debts – debts they could never repay, in some cases. No one dunned them while the strike was on – you can't get blood out of a stone. But once it was over, everyone wanted their dues. The miners thought once the strike ended, everything would be roses. They were wrong.'

Fran knew what he meant. In Belgate the mood had changed completely since the strike. Even the perception of how the strike began was different. They did not see Scargill as the cause of their troubles now – that had changed on the day he was defeated and became the underdog.

'I wish I could offer you a drink, Fran, but the cupboard's bare.' Fran wondered if she dared suggest nipping out to an off-licence. She had the milk money in her purse, and cheering Dennis was a good cause. She was saved from decision by the phone.

'That's it, Fran. Can you drop me off?' Dennis was moving for the door as he replaced the receiver.

'I'll come in with you ... just till I know everything's OK.'

He made no move to drive and she got behind the wheel. Dennis's long legs looked incongruous shoved up against the dashboard. His own car had been a sleek Mercedes, and now he had no car at all.

'It's a girl,' the nurse said, when they arrived. 'You can look in the nursery window when they come out of delivery, and hubby can have a few words with Mum. Only a few words. We don't want the ward disturbed at this time of night.' It was nine o'clock and the TV was still blaring, but there was no mistaking that the nurse meant what she said.

Min came past them on a trolley. Dennis seemed overcome at the sight of her and it was left to Fran to say, 'Well done!'

Min smiled. 'I really wanted another girl. Two of each. Have you seen her?'

Fran shook her head. 'I'm going to have a look now, but I bet she's gorgeous. I'll wait for Dennis and run him home.'

Dennis had to wait while Min was returned to her bed behind drawn curtains. At last they were pulled back and the staff nurse gave an imperious nod. 'Off you go,' Fran said and turned towards the nursery. A midwife pointed out the right cot but Fran would have known it anyway. The baby was dark like Min, black hair, moist now but with a trace of curl, eyelashes fanned on cheeks. She's going to be a beauty, Fran thought, and was pleased.

It was a minute or two before she realized that it didn't hurt any more. She could look at babies and not feel anything except a surge of goodwill. The baby was not hers, never would be, but it had come safe into the world and that was cause for rejoicing.

She looked down the ward. Dennis was bending by the bed, kissing Min's cheek, and her hand was cradling his head. It was the first time she had seen Min show Dennis affection. So good could come out of bad, she thought – another old wives' tale proved true.

She turned away, a little ashamed of watching their intimacy and waited while Dennis looked at his daughter. 'She's lovely, isn't she?'

He nodded. 'A proper little Frances.'

She looked at him. 'What do you mean?'

He was smiling. 'She's going to be Frances Mary.'

'Oh Dennis . . . there's no need. It's such an old-fashioned name!'

He turned to wave to his wife. 'No use arguing, Franny, it's the boss's idea. You'll just have to put up with it.' Far down the ward, Min lay back on her pillows but her eyes were expectant.

'Tell her you're pleased,' Dennis said, and Fran mouthed her delight.

'We're going to be OK,' Dennis said suddenly as they drove home.

'I'm sure you are,' Fran said, and meant it. There was nothing like a baby for giving you a boost.

She felt tired but peaceful as she made for the Belgate road. The night sky was pink in the west, blue mother-of-pearl above her, and there was a bottle of white wine in the larder, a gift from Tony. As soon as she got home she was going to have a drink. She bloody well deserved it.

7

Sunday, 6 October 1985

Fran opened the car boot and reached inside. 'Take these, and keep them off your shirt.' Martin gave her a pitying look and held the tray of sausage rolls with one hand. 'I can take the vollies as well.' Fran gave him the tray of vol-au-vents as Min appeared in the doorway.

'Can I help?' Fran handed over the tin containing the cheese-cake and looked her up and down. 'You look smashing, Min.' Min had regained her figure, and her face, always attractive, was more interesting now that faint lines of worry punctuated her brow.

'It's an ancient suit,' Min said, 'but it's crêpe de Chine. You can't beat silk.' The suit was black and white, sashed with a broad red leather belt. Shoes and tights were black and Dallas-style earrings bright red. 'You've got style, Min,' Fran said.

Min was turning away. 'It's about all I have got at the moment, darling. But at least we've got some booze.' Fran gathered up the last of the food and slammed the Mini's boot.

The kitchen was awash with food but it was mostly home baking, not the extravagant cream- and sauce-smothered creations of

Min's former days. The booze stood on the freezer, an impressive array. 'Where did you get it?' Fran said in awe.

Min tried to look enigmatic. 'Balloon-seller with dog.' Fran was uncomprehending. 'Talk sense.'

Min shook her head. 'I am. That's how I did it. I sold one of the ghastly Capo di Monte fakes . . . "Balloon seller with dog". I went into the wine shop with "Girl with umbrella" under my arm, pretending I daren't leave it in the car in case it got nicked. I know the owner's wife – if someone else has something, she has to have one too. You know the type?'

'*Indeed I do*,' Fran thought but said nothing. This was a changed Min; no point in reminding her of the past. Min was continuing, 'I knew she'd be all eyes, so I said I'd been able to get it half-price, forty quid. Could I get her one? she said. I said probably not because they were supposed to be one-offs, and in the meantime could she take my booze order? Then I rang the next day and said she couldn't have one like mine because they were all unique, but she *could* have "Balloon seller with dog". Except that it was more expensive, so she probably couldn't afford it. Of course that clinched it! "Name your price," she said, so I said sixty pounds, which covered the bill.'

Fran was lost in admiration. 'You must be pleased with yourself.'

Min looked at her for a moment. 'Pleased? Yes, I suppose so. If only I can keep Dennis up. He's got to deal with all these ghastly official things like the winding-up process. Which really means grovelling to a bunch of supercilious accountants who have no real ability except that they can bear to make a living out of battening on other people's misfortunes.'

Fran knew she meant Harold. He was not the accountant charged with liquidating Fellowes Furniture Limited, but in Min's eyes he personified all liquidators. Perhaps it was time for a change of subject. 'Are you going to have enough food?'

They spent the next ten minutes setting out the buffet and fending off hungry children who all wanted Bethel's breadbuns. 'She's an old cow but she can bake bread,' Min said, looking at the high-piled basket. There had been a rapport between Min and Bethel since Min had come to Brian Malone's funeral but each of them would die before admitting it. '*Take her these,*' Bethel had said, '*and tell her she's lucky to get them. I'm past baking for all and sundry.*'

Eve arrived as they were finishing. 'Very nice,' she said, handing over her own contribution and eyeing the table. The words 'in the circumstances' were not said but hung in the air. When she turned to go back to the living room Min stuck out her tongue and jerked index and middle fingers upwards in a rude gesture.

'She means well,' Fran said, but her tone was uncertain.

Min put both hands on the kitchen table and leaned forward. 'Fran, we've all been kidding ourselves for years. I've had time to think during the last few months. Nobody's "friends for life". You say that at school and you mean it – but people change. Life changes them. And if you're honest you have to face facts. I've had to face the fact that for most of my life I've been an empty bitch. No, don't go po-faced and embarrassed. I was a shit to Dennis for most of our marriage, and I filled the kids' heads with a load of pseudo-upper-class rubbish. Well, the boys are too young to have taken it in but Althea has the makings of a right little pain if we don't watch out. I came from nothing and it didn't hurt me. We were as poor as church-mice. I've faced all this, and a few other things too, and I'll tell you this. I don't like Eve!'

Fran was groping for words. If she was honest, she didn't like Eve much now either. Half of her did, clinging to the memories of schooldays and shared confidences. The other half of her sometimes wanted to smack her old friend right between her neat blue eyes. On the other hand, she remembered the time after David's death, the terrible anger she had felt at everyone – particularly Min, if she was honest. Bereavement did that to you. Min had been bereaved, shorn of her lifestyle overnight. Perhaps her anger, too, was temporary. 'Well, we can't talk about it now,' she said at last. 'This is supposed to be a happy day.'

She carried the baby down from its cot, blue eyes startling between dark lashes. 'She may be your namesake but she's all Min, isn't she?' Dennis said, gazing fondly at his daughter.

'She's Min's image,' Fran agreed.

Dennis looked forlorn. His cheeks were hollowed and his hair, once so well cut, straggled over his collar. He was offering the baby his finger and the tiny fingers curled and gripped. He smiled, and would have gone on smiling had not Harold appeared in the hall.

'We'll take the proud parents. No offence, Fran, but a Mini's hardly the thing for a state occasion, is it? You can fit in Dennis's folks. Everyone else has wheels.'

Dennis disentangled his fingers from the baby. 'OK, Harold,' he said. 'Lead on . . . you seem to have everything organized.'

One day, Fran thought, as they made their way out to the cars, she would take a large pin and puncture Harold, so that all the self-importance oozed out of him.

The church was crowded, the christening a bit incomprehensible. It would no doubt be followed by the inevitable hand-shaking that seemed to be part of services now. It was all right, but it was no substitute for real brotherly love, which often seemed in short supply among church-goers.

The words of the christening ceremony flowed over her but she was thinking about her role as godmother. People took it so lightly, regarding it almost as a social cachet to have been asked. Eve had expressed relief at not being chosen. '*I'd have done it, of course, but I have so much on it wouldn't have been easy.*' Privately, Fran was sure she was choked.

'You're being bitchy again,' Fran told herself, and then offered swift mental apologies for thinking a dubious word in church. They filed back to their seats and sang 'The King of Love my Shepherd is' and then, as she had predicted, the people turned to each other and the hand-shaking began.

Outside, the baby was admired and pieces of silver pressed upon it. 'Everyone likes new babies,' James said. He sounded forlorn.

'Poor thing,' Fran thought, 'he's been the baby until now, and he feels pushed aside.'

But Dennis was scooping his younger son into his arms. 'I like new babies,' he said in a stage whisper, 'but I like four-year-olds better.'

Back at the house food and wine flowed. Everyone did their

best but no one could forget the *For Sale* board at the bottom of the drive or the grandparents, shadows of their former selves, sitting quietly in the corner. Mrs Fellowes had been a pack-leader in Inner Wheel, a golf-fanatic, a fierce worker for the more fashionable charities. Once Min had referred to her mother-in-law's middle-aged spread as 'committee woman's arse'. What would she do now? Remain a committee leader or seek a blessed obscurity?

Fran was clearing plates and stacking them in the dishwasher when Harold came into the kitchen. 'This is the last of the plates, I think. Where d'you want them?' She made room on the draining board and he took a tea towel. 'I'll dry some of these while we chat. I've been meaning to look you up for weeks. It's just that we have so much on, Eve and I. But you must come over soon.'

'How's business?' Fran asked, and immediately regretted it. Once launched on his favourite subject, Harold was unstoppable.

'Too good, Fran. There aren't enough hours in the day. Not that I have much to do with winding up ... we specialize, you know, and taxation's my forte. But the firm's burdened down with liquidations, and the workload spills over. Well, you know how it is.'

Fran nodded. 'I see it in the paper every night.'

Harold was shaking out his towel and folding it neatly over the rail. 'That friend of yours has had it. That motor salesman.'

Fran tried to look nonchalant. 'You mean Steve?'

Harold nodded. 'Yes, that's the guy. I told you we did his business. We tried to help, but it was useless. Stock he couldn't sell, a mountain of bad debt. The Inland Revenue applied for the order, but there'd've been others.'

'Has he lost everything?' Fran asked.

'Afraid so.' There was regret in Harold's voice. 'Not that there was much to lose, in the end. We'll be out of pocket, I should think. It isn't as though he had a house to sell – that went to the wife when they split, and she made sure that he had no claim on it when they were reconciled. She's quite a tough cookie, by all accounts.' Fran dried her hands. Though Steve had been her lover, she could barely remember his face.

Harold had turned to the miners' strike. 'That's what caused it, of course. All his trade was with the mining community – like Fellowes, but on a smaller scale. We haven't seen the last of the repercussions round here, Fran, I'll tell you that. I was in a warehouse this week piled to the roof with TV sets. Not old models, decent colour jobs. The miners packed them in during the strike, to save the rental and the colour licence. They made do with old black-and-white sets. Anyway, when the strike was over they wanted to begin hiring again . . . but they didn't want the sets they'd given back. Oh no! They wanted brand-new sets, never seen a plug. So this chap – my client – he's left with hundreds of nearly new sets that he can't hire at any price. He'll be lucky to give them away. I don't know about closing pits, but friend Scargill's closed down quite a few firms round here. I was talking to a credit bookmaker. All his business is done by phone, but half his clients gave up their phones during the strike, so he's lost out to the corner betting shop. I tell you, it's endless.'

As she drove past the *For Sale* board on Min's drive, Fran thought over what Harold had said. Poor Steve. Jean, his wife, had been hard enough to handle when he had money; she would be a poor companion in poverty. Except that you never could tell. She'd've said that about Min three months before, and look how that was turning out! As they made their goodbyes, Min had asked if she could borrow the car next weekend to join in a boot sale. 'Of course you can,' Fran had said. 'I'll help any way I can.'

It would be no great sacrifice. If Tony was staying in Sunderland for the weekend he would pick her up, and if he was away she would work, work, work.

'It was a good christening,' Martin said from the passenger seat. 'Can I go out when we get back?'

Fran looked at her watch. Six-fifteen. 'Well, for a bit, but there's school tomorrow, don't forget.'

He groaned. 'Wish I could.'

Ahead Belgate appeared, the sea foaming beneath. 'You like school, don't you?'

'It's OK. Bit boring. I like English, that's about all.' There was a pause and then . . . 'You won't teach at my school when you're done, will you?'

Fran giggled. 'You make me sound like a side of beef. No, I won't teach at your school when I'm done. Wouldn't you want me?'

His reply was fervent. 'No fear. You get bashed up in the bog if your ma's a teacher. I'll probably get it a bit, anyway, even if you're somewhere else.'

She wanted to chide his language but the thought of his being bullied was dreadful. 'They wouldn't really hurt you, would they?'

'They might try, but Gary sticks by me and I stick by him, so they lay off.' Solidarity, Fran thought. The secret of the universe.

8

Thursday, 14 November 1985

Outside, the November drizzle was so fine she had to cross to the window and look at the wet yard to decide whether or not it was raining. She had an old T-shirt under a blouse and cardigan, but still she was cold. Time to light the fire! She was still buying cut-price coal from the sacked miner, so she could afford a blaze.

As flames devoured paper and licked round sticks, she squatted by the fire. The coal was stolen property; she was an accessory before the fact because she knew he had pinched, was pinching and would pinch in the future. She was suddenly taken up by the word 'pinch'. It was a euphemism, an acceptable way of saying 'steal'. She was an honest woman and wouldn't steal or have any part in a theft, but 'pinching' was slightly different.

The sacked miner was called Dave, and increasingly she saw him as a Robin Hood figure. The NCB was rich, it had mountains of coal on the ground, not to mention stocks yet unmined. Dave stole from the rich to help the poor. He was out of work and therefore skint, and God knows she was poor. Thoughts of Christmas and present-giving slid into view and were shouldered aside. Don't think of Christmas, think of sacked miners. No greater balm for your own misery than to see the other fellow worse off.

Dave was thirty-two and had been a miner since his sixteenth birthday. He had four kids, twin girls of eight, a boy of five, and another just two years old. He had told her about the strike and the loss of his job, and Treesa had filled in the domestic details. He had been on a picket line in Yorkshire when he had seized a working miner by the lapels and butted him in the face, breaking his nose. There had been no satisfaction in his voice when he told her this; if there had been she would have been repelled. Instead she had listened, amazed by the violent details emerging from the mouth of this mild-mannered man.

'We'd had this clash with the police, you see. Me dander was up and then, there he was in front of me, bloody well grinning. Well, I thought he was grinning. Maybe he was just shit-scared like me. Anyroad, I butted him and there was blood coming out his nose and his mouth, and I just felt sick. It was like I'd taken it out of him for everything, no work, no money, our lass taking on so much. I knew I'd be clobbered in the court. I was fined a hundred pounds and got a twelve-month suspended sentence. The next week I got a letter from the pit – sacked on the grounds of misconduct. No appeal. Sacked just like that, after sixteen years.'

She had tried to cheer him up but there wasn't much she could say. He had little or no hope of a job, not in this area. There was no work for men even with clean records, so a conviction for GBH would be the bitter end.

'I thought there'd be an amnesty once it was over,' he had said last time. 'And then some of the men sacked for taking coal got took back and I thought, 'Maybe me next time.' Now I think I'll be pushing this bike around for ever. And I never even wanted a strike, I only came out to please the other lads.'

The fire was burning now, the coal consumed by flame. She put Dave and his troubles aside and sat down to her books. A buckshee day off always made her feel guilty. If she caught up on all her essays she wouldn't feel so bad.

She looked at the blank page and drew a female profile in the top right-hand corner. They said that if you doodled faces it meant you weren't satisfied with your own. Well, that was true. In seven months' time, if she worked, she could be a fully fledged teacher. Her name would be pinned on the wall – providing she'd passed the medical – and she'd be sent a scroll during the holidays. She put the blemished sheet aside for scrap and tried to begin.

She wanted a cigarette! It was months since she'd given up smoking but every time she sat down to work she wanted a smoke. She wrote a neat heading – 'Environmental Studies' – and then her name – 'Frances Drummond'. The trouble with ballpoints was they didn't need sharpening. If she'd been working in pencil she could have taken a knife and carved off satisfying bits of wood tipped with lead.

The clock showed nine twenty and suddenly she was galvanized into action. Tony was coming for a meal at seven-thirty, the first she had cooked for him. If she didn't get a move on it would have to be takeaway, which she couldn't afford. Fear oiled her pen, and once she was halfway down the page she knew it was going to be all right. She had finished 'Environmental Studies' and was on to the first of her psychology essays when the phone rang. It was Eve.

'They've sold it. Ninety thousand pounds, but Harold says it'll all go to the bank.' So Min's beloved house was gone. 'Heaven knows where they'll live now. Harold says they should apply for a council house. Can you imagine . . . after all that ostentation over the years? Min used to say their garage was bigger than a council house. Well, it goes to show . . .'

She had no sooner put down the phone than it rang again. It was Min. 'We've got a buyer!' Fran feigned surprise. 'They're coming here from the north. He's some sort of big wheel with that American factory at Peterlee. Oodles of money. Anyway, we got the asking price.'

'Where will you go?' Fran said tentatively. 'You know what I said about moving in here.'

Min sighed. 'It's lovely to know you're there in the background, and we're both grateful, but I hope it won't come to that. What you can do is lend me the car again.'

'Another boot sale?' If Min took the car every weekend, how

would she cope? On the other hand, how could she say no in such circumstances?

'No, it's not a sale this time. I've sorted out some of my clothes and there's this marvellous woman in Newcastle who sells second-hand models, only the best, mind, and gets you the most marvellous prices. Dennis has borrowed a pick-up from someone in Round Table . . . so he can get backwards and forwards and try to get work. Some people stick by you, isn't it funny? Anyway, I could ask him but I don't want him to see me flogging my clothes. He's down in the mouth as it is. I don't mind, I'm glad to be rid of most of them, and when I'm rich again I'll stock up with new things – but if you could lend me the Mini, he doesn't need to know. I'll pay the petrol. We got a lovely Giro today so I'm feeling flush.'

When Fran came off the phone she sat down. She was nonplussed, but she couldn't decide whether it was the idea of Min on Social Security that floored her, or what Min had said about getting rich again. In the end she decided that the most remarkable thing about the conversation had been the sensitivity Min had displayed towards Dennis's feelings. In the old days she would not have given a fig for them.

Martin came in at lunchtime and they shared their beefburgers and beans at the kitchen table. 'Before you ask,' he said, sitting down, 'school was OK.'

Fran was affronted. 'What do you mean, "before I ask"?'

He grinned. 'You always say, "How was school?" every time. As soon as I get in.'

'OK, cleverclogs. So you've got a predictable mother.' Round one to him, she thought, but at least he looked pleased.

'Are we going to Seaham this Saturday?' he asked. Most weekends now they went to Seaham. If she had given him a good day it made her feel less guilty about leaving him at night to see Tony.

'Do you want to?'

He shrugged. 'Don't mind.' This was something new.

'Have you gone off Seaham?'

His shake of the head was emphatic. 'No way. But Jim won't be there this weekend.'

She chewed carefully on her beefburger. Quite often they saw the pier man . . . she must remember his name was Jim . . . when they went to Seaham. He was good with Martin, but she hadn't realized how attached to him Martin was becoming. She would have to be careful. However kind he was to Martin, he had a family of his own in London. There would be a limit somewhere, and Martin was probably too young to realize that. She had seen a spasm of sympathy cross the man's face when she mentioned that David was dead, but sympathy only went so far.

'We might do some Christmas shopping,' she said. 'It's getting too late in the year for Seaham harbour, anyway.'

She would have gone on worrying about Martin's possible emotional entanglements if Bethel had not arrived with momentous news. The portents were there as she walked through the door. Usually she crossed to the sink and filled the kettle before shrugging out of her outdoor clothes. When she had *big* news she followed a precise ritual, unpinning her hat and sticking in the hatpins before laying it upside down on the dresser. Her silk scarf came off next, to be placed, carefully folded, inside the hat. After that came gloves, if the weather required them, and then her coat. After that she would fill the kettle. Then, and only then, would she give vent to the bombshell. And if you tried to hurry her, she became even slower, much more precise in her movements, to teach you a lesson.

Patience paid off. 'They're closing Belgate!'

Fran usually registered enough amazement to keep Bethel happy, but this time it was real. '*Belgate pit?*'

Bethel's scorn was boundless. 'No, Belgate Opera House. My God, no wonder bairns is getting dafter if you're a sample of what's let loose on teaching them. Belgate pit. P.I.T.'

Fran couldn't take it in. Belgate to close? It was unthinkable. They were on to their second cups, and steeped in gloom, when a car horn sounded outside. 'That's Walter,' Fran said. 'Shall I go out?'

'Just possess your soul in patience,' Bethel said, rising to refill the kettle. 'If you go rushing out, he'll feel he has to drive off so you won't take him for granted. I keep telling you that but you never listen.'

So they sat until Walter's outraged bellow permeated the kitchen. 'Howay, howay, give a feller a hand. I bet you're in there, Sally Bethel, stuffing tea while I bloody well struggle with these steps. I've said it before, and I'll say it again. The feller that built this house was a step-fanatic. *Sally?*'

The rising tone of his voice prompted action. Fran sprang to empty the teapot and Bethel armed the wheelchair into the kitchen.

'You've heard then?' he said, when a cup of fresh tea had been pressed on him.

'Heard what?' Bethel said.

'About the pit! About your friend Mrs Thatcher and her pal MacGregor. I told you they'd shut this village down, but you wouldn't have it.'

'I've heard,' Bethel said. A moment before she had been calling down curses on the government in general and their hatchet-man, MacGregor, in particular. Now, things were different. 'Well, it's Scargill we can thank for this. It was losing money before the strike, so it was hanging by a thread. Now he's finished it off.'

'You won't catch me with that one, Sally. You know how I feel about that shower. Belgate'd have a better chance if we had a united union. I'll never forgive him for what he's done to the NUM.'

'Do you think the pit'll close?' Fran asked.

The massive shoulders raised and then slumped. 'All I know, bonny lass, is that it'll stay open or close according to the powers that be. Little minions like you, me and the rest of Belgate'll have as much effect on the outcome as fluff.'

Fran was not in the mood for controversy but she couldn't resist the question. 'Well, was Scargill right about his hit-list of pits?'

The next moment the argument was away. Bethel and Walter enjoyed a verbal scrap and Fran adored seeing them at it. It was love-play: she had decided that a long time ago. Insults would emerge from either mouth and land on target, but the general effect was to bring the two even closer, where they would have driven any other couple apart.

In spite of the disturbing news it was a blissful afternoon. A good fire, toasted teacakes, two people she loved, and stimulating conversation. She didn't think about Tony and the evening ahead until Martin came home from school.

'Hallo, Walter,' he said. Nee-wan was leaping up to lick his face, and Walter scowled.

'Who trained that dog? If your mam does as good a job on her scholars as she's done on you and that dog, she'll be getting paid for nothing.'

Martin was grinning. 'I'm all right, aren't I, Bethel?'

Fran had to struggle not to chortle aloud. The little monkey! He had Bethel on toast now. She either must say he was a good boy or side with Walter, something she never did on principle.

She had underestimated Bethel, who took a third option and completely ignored the question. 'You've got company tonight, miss. It's time you got on with it, if you ask me.'

'I didn't half best her, didn't I?' Martin said when they were alone. And then the question she dreaded. 'What did she mean about company?' He didn't like Tony and he made it obvious. They had spent an agonizing afternoon at the Leisure Centre and only Tony's forbearance had stopped an explosion.

'Tony's coming to supper,' she said and adopted Bethel's strategy of ignoring his theatrical groan.

He went off to bed early because there was nothing on TV and he had two library books he wanted to read. They were both Goodies books. 'Very educational,' she said, secretly pleased at the innocuous nature of his reading. 'I'll bring you some supper up,' she promised and then, on impulse, sat down on his bed.

'I know you don't like Tony much, but he is my friend. I like him. You're growing up and one day you'll go away. I want you to go. Not because I don't love you, but because I do. I want you to make a life of your own and get married and be happy like Daddy and I were. So I have to make a life of my own, so that I'll be all right when I'm on my own. Do you understand?'

He was wearing his man-of-the-world expression. 'I don't know what you're going on about. It's no big deal.' She was halfway downstairs before she realized he had not made his usual statement about never getting married. So he was growing up after all.

She had prepared lasagne and bought an expensive bottle of wine. Whether or not it was good wine she had no idea, but the price had been mind-numbing. Bloody standards! That was the cause of half the trouble in the world. You couldn't ask anyone to a meal now unless you provided wine, whether or not you could afford it – which she certainly couldn't. Once you'd met that standard, there was the next hurdle: good wine versus bad wine. Hell, hell, bloody hell.

In the end she had worried for nothing. Tony arrived with a bottle of wine. Its label was not brilliantly patterned and it looked uniform and cheap, but she knew it was good. As Bethel would have said, she could feel it in her water. She put her own bottle in the larder and was about to put his in the fridge when he took it from her. 'Not red wine,' he said. 'It needs room temperature.' He took the sting from his words by stroking her hair behind her ears.

She felt the old familiar earthquake in her pelvic region but willed it to subside. She was not having sex here, in her own house, with David's child asleep in bed. Or not asleep, depending on how long she could avoid the subject.

The lasagne was OK except for the top bits, which had the consistency of steel sheeting. She kept those bits for herself and gave him the soft underbelly of the dish. That was a woman's lot, to eat up the undesirables.

It was the most domestic situation they had enjoyed. They often had meals at his place, very nice meals but eaten in an impromptu fashion. They had never sat either side of a table with white cloth and table mats and a cruet in the middle. 'Very nice,' he said, smiling at her. 'It's nice to be civilized occasionally.'

It was one of those remarks, inconsequential in themselves, which pack the punch of a nuclear warhead. '*This is not for me,*' he was saying; warning, even. It was funny because she hadn't invited him in order to demonstrate domesticity or draw him further into her net. With another man that might have been her intention, but not Tony. She had invited him here because for once she wanted to have the upper hand, and by golly she'd got it. He was running scared. She was so pleased that she allowed him to top up her glass so that there was hardly enough left for him – and she didn't even like red wine. 'Here's to crime,' she said, and this time laughed aloud at her own words.

9

Saturday, 14 December 1985

The air outside the bedclothes was as good as any calendar. Ten days to Christmas, and ten degrees below zero by the feel of it. She snuggled down for her Saturday lie-in. Before long Nee-wan would make his presence felt and she'd have to get up and let him out, but for now enjoy, enjoy!

Thinking of Nee-wan led to thoughts of Brian Malone. Soon it would be the second anniversary of his death in the pit, the pit that now was hanging between life and death. The NCB was waffling, and nothing was yet definite, but she had an uneasy feeling that Belgate was doomed. The pit would close. The younger miners, Terry Malone among them, would be bussed away to other pits and the older men would take their redundancy and haunt the street corners.

Fenwick came into her mind – gaunt Fenwick, the strike-breaker, who spoke to no one now. Before the strike he had been a cheerful man, devoted to his prize pigeons, but with their death the heart had seemed to go out of him. Fran doubted whether he would care if the pit lived or died.

Downstairs there was a thump and a scrabbling sound. Nee-wan was giving warning of an impending flood. 'I'm coming,' she said resignedly, and leaped out of bed.

The boiler was alight and the house warming up when the doorbell rang. Min stood on the step. 'I had to come through. I know it's daft to use petrol when I could have phoned, but I wanted you to be the first to see it – after Dennis – and I've got *piles* to tell you.'

'It' was a car, a battered Ford Fiesta sporting a Y registration.

'What d'you think?' Min asked, 'It's only done forty-five thousand, and they threw in two new tyres.' There was oil on her right cheek and lipstick on her teeth, but pride of ownership glowed from every pore.

'It's marvellous,' Fran said, averting her eyes from the bubbling paintwork of the wings.

'No,' Min said graciously, 'it's not marvellous, but it's mine. Well, mine and Dennis's. It's a start, Fran. We are back on the road. Now, where's the coffee. I can't stay but I must fill you in.'

'I can see you're pleased with it,' Fran said as she filled the kettle.

'Pleased?' Min said solemnly. 'Fran, I never knew what satisfaction was until now.'

Over coffee Min imparted the rest of her news. 'You're not going to believe this. I only half-believe it myself. You know we need somewhere to live? Well, the outlook was grim: two rooms above a butcher's shop, or a council house in an area no one else would touch. I said to Dennis, "We'll take anything . . . it doesn't matter because we won't be there long." But you know what men are like: he saw it as the end of the world. Anyway, he was seeing our solicitor about the sale of the house and everything, and he asked where we were going. Dennis said the street probably, or words to that effect, and then the solicitor came up with this marvellous offer.'

'What? Get to the point!' Fran could hardly contain herself.

'OK,' Min said, 'I'm getting to it. There's this family . . . he's a civil engineer and works abroad. The wife's a bit fed up and wants to join him. The kids are just at the right age to change schools for a while . . . anyway, they have this super home . . . it's even got a pool. It's in one of the best areas, quite near to Eve and Harold. These people daren't leave it empty for a year, so they want to rent, but they want someone they can trust because they're leaving absolutely everything behind. A Bendix and a double split-level gas and electric; two bathrooms . . . and all for a peppercorn rent!' She paused for a moment, her jubilation subsiding. 'We'll have to find the rates, of course, and it's oil-fired heating ... but I expect we'll manage.' She brightened again. 'At least it's a roof of our own, and a posh one!'

Fran felt as though she were going to cry. 'It's too good to be true, Min. But you deserve it. You've been so brave!'

Eve did not share her enthusiasm when she rang shortly after Min's departure. 'Of course, I'm pleased. I mean, no one wanted to see them on the street. But you can't help wondering how she managed it. If it had been Harold and I, we'd have wound up in a hostel. There's no justice. I knew Min would fall on her feet.'

Fran was dying to rub Eve's nose in the double hobs and the gold bathroom taps, but she refrained. Better to leave well alone. Besides, Eve had found a fly in the ointment. 'What will they do with all their stuff? If it's a fully furnished house, they'll have a problem.' In fact, Min was going to sell the entire contents of the house, and hoped to make a tidy sum. She had told Fran yesterday. *'They can't touch it, you see. They can take everything that belongs to the business; that's how I lost my car. But the goods and chattels are mine.'*

Eve was coming to an end. 'Well, I'll have to go. I've so much on. All I can say is, I wish them well. A house of that size and no income ... and she's just making light of it. She doesn't seem to care.'

This was too much. 'I think she's been jolly brave, Eve. In fact, I admire her.' When Fran put down the phone, she felt satisfied. She had spoken her mind. She could have added that the crash was probably the best thing that could've happened to Min, who had been bored, and now was discovering what life could be when it had a purpose other than party-giving and trips to Tenerife. All the same, the outlook for them was still far from rosy.

They set out for Seaham at two, well wrapped against the cold. 'We can't stay long,' she warned. 'We'll freeze if we do, and Treesa's expecting us for tea.'

Martin was belting himself into the passenger seat. 'I just want to see Jim. He's got a book about artics, and he said I could borrow it.'

She changed gear to gain time. 'Jim? And what on earth are artics?'

He heaved a sigh. 'Articulated lorries. You wouldn't understand.'

She understood only too well. 'Jim' seemed to be the most important thing in Martin's life now and it would have to stop, before he got hurt.

They had left the car and were walking down towards the harbour when they saw him. He was watching a ship easing through the harbour entrance but he turned at their approach. 'She's a timber ship – from Sweden.'

Martin nodded. 'She's not a light-ship,' he said solemnly.

Jim was smiling. 'That's right. She's down at the head.'

'They're shutting me out,' Fran thought. 'They're in their male world of technical jargon, and I'm not considered fit to take part.' As if he had read her thoughts Jim turned. 'Are you freezing?'

She nodded. 'Just about.'

He looked down at Martin. 'I think we ought to consider your Mum today. What about coming up to the hotel for a drink?' He looked at his watch and then at Fran. 'We've just got time . . . if it's all right with you.'

Fran nodded. 'If you let me pay. No, I won't come unless you do. You've been very kind.'

The pub was unbelievably warm and cosy after the cold outside. He ordered the drinks but accepted her five-pound note and handed over the change. 'I'll not be a moment,' he said and vanished through the residents' door. When he returned he was carrying a book and an oblong parcel in Christmas wrapping. 'There's the book I promised you, and a little something for Christmas. Not to be opened now.'

Martin was glowing. 'I got something for you.' The parcel was small and, at a guess, contained the tobacco which they had seen Jim use. He was looking from her to Martin and she shook her head.

'Don't look at me. I knew nothing about it.' It was true. The parcel was a complete surprise. So was the fact that her son was now capable of conducting his own affairs. She felt both proud and put out at the same time.

Martin went off to play the Quiz machine and Jim leaned closer. 'I think it's time for a few explanations. I can see you worry . . . no, I understand, honestly. I know what it's like to be a single parent: you do nothing else but worry. But I'm not some sort of pervert setting my cap for your lad. I have two kids of my own, as you know. They're with my mum in London. That's where I belong, as you may have guessed from the twang. I used to be in the Merchant Navy – navigating officer. Then my wife died . . . she had cancer . . . so I came ashore. If you're an engineer you can always pick up work, but a master's ticket fits you for nothing. My wife's brother had a shipping agency – that's how I met her. He offered me the north-east area, and I took it. It means I don't see much of the kids. I'm up here almost every week. I was used to being away from them when Dorothy was alive, but it's different now.'

'And Martin fills a gap?'

He nodded. 'He's a great kid.'

Fran smiled. 'I won't argue about that. He amazed me just now. He must think an awful lot of you.'

Jim looked across to where Martin was manipulating the machine. 'It's mutual, and I won't let him down. When he told me about his dad it seemed to click.'

'What was in the parcel?' she asked Martin as they drove back towards Belgate. It was getting dark now, dusk settling on the landscape like grey chiffon.

'St Bruno. It's the sort he likes.' There was uncertainty in his voice.

'Well done,' she said firmly and sensed him relax.

Treesa was waiting in the open doorway. 'I heard the car. Come on in, you must be frozen.' Treesa's living room was dressed for Christmas. A brand new silver tree stood ceiling high, laden with baubles. Every ornament and protrusion was garlanded with tinsel, and jovial Santa Clauses leered down from vantage points.

'I know it's a lot,' Treesa apologized, 'but I did it for the bairn.' She looked little more than a bairn herself and Fran could imagine how decorating the room had eased her boredom. Living alone with an eighteen-month-old baby would leave acres of silence.

While Treesa scalded the tea Fran thought about her own tree. She had put it up each year since David died, but it wasn't the same. Now she would have to bring it out once again. On the floor Martin was playing with the baby, building a tower with blocks and grinning at the baby's renewed delight when it tumbled. Fran put the tree out of her mind and enjoyed the spectacle.

They were gorging on hot sausage rolls and two kinds of quiche, with the Black Forest gateau to come, when Terry arrived. That he had not been expected was manifest from Treesa's agitation. 'What are you doing here?' she said.

Fran's heart sank. 'I'm pleased to see you, Terry,' she said to mitigate his embarrassment as his grin faded.

'I'll get a cup,' Treesa said and dived for the kitchen. Fran made room on the settee and beckoned Terry to sit down.

'What do you think of the bairn?' he said. Proud parenthood was in his voice.

'I think he's wonderful,' she said, 'and a proper Malone.'

Martin looked up. 'I expect he'll be just like Gary when he grows up.'

Terry's retort was fervent. 'I hope not. Our Gary's a cheeky little b . . . so and so!'

Tomorrow, Fran thought, or as soon as she could, she would sit down with Treesa and talk. About love and death and love after death and what right you had to make a new life when you were left behind. Except that she had never managed to work those things out for herself, so how would she convince someone else?

That evening she wore a red wool dress she had not worn for years. It had been David's favourite and she had not had the heart to wear it until now. Tonight she needed it for courage. Since the day Min had told her she didn't like Eve, Fran had been thinking hard. '*We've all been fooling ourselves,*' Min had said, '*but sooner or later you have to face facts.*' Fran put in her Dallas earrings and took a final look. Not bad.

At her suggestion she and Tony went to the Mohti Raj. She ordered Kashmiri chicken and managed to eat it all, although the sausage rolls were reluctant to give way. 'I wanted to talk and it's easier on neutral ground.'

He raised his brows. 'That sounds ominous.'

She smiled and shook her head. 'Not really.'

She had seen a fleeting anxiety in his eyes: perhaps he thought she was going to tell him she was pregnant! It was tempting to give it a whirl and send him home with a king-sized worry, but she decided against it. She was not a child, she was a grown woman.

'You've always said you weren't married, but there's someone, isn't there? I know you said you shared, but it's more than that.' Her question had turned into a statement and he didn't argue. 'Anyway, I've been thinking. I'm not the kind of woman who believes in threesomes.' Too late she remembered that meant three in a bed.

'Hardly that!' He was back to his mocking self now he knew she wasn't in the club, and it made her angry.

'Anyway, like I said, I've been thinking. We've had a fling, Tony: no big deal, as Martin would say. I'm not so naïve as to imagine I mean anything to you, or that not seeing me again will even ruffle your surface. It won't mean much to me either. I got a buzz out of going out with a lecturer. I should have known better at my age, but it's true. And you're good in bed, I don't need to tell you that. But I've realized that I prefer my men to be sincere. It may be frustrating at times but it's better than feeling like something that's just passed through a photocopier!'

Her fingers closed around a note inside her purse. Please God, let it be a fiver; she couldn't afford a tenner, and there was no way she could ask for change. 'That's my share of the meal. Thanks for everything. See you in class.'

He rose to his feet as she swept off, out of politeness not shock. She might have known she couldn't faze him, but she was glad she had done it all the same, and choosing the restaurant

had made sense. No need to be polite when you were neither
guest nor host.

As she drove home she felt free. She would be alone again at
Christmas, but that was no big deal. She looked for the Christmas
star and found it, just where she had expected it to be.

10

Tuesday, 24 December 1985

The kitchen had taken on a look of shell-shock. Dishes, tins,
opened packs of butter and marge, a pile of chestnut peel, a bowl
redolent of sage and onion. 'Well to be seen you were born a
lady,' Bethel said, eyeing the mess. 'The sooner you're out of my
way the better.' She started to clear up, putting lids back on jars
and sweeping flour from the table-top into her outstretched
palm.

'I'll tidy up in a minute,' Fran said placatingly. It was two
o'clock on Christmas Eve afternoon, still time, if she wished, to
hurry through to town for last-minute shopping. It was always a
temptation, to join the jostling crowd and be part of it all, but if
you did you found it an empty exercise. Far better to be at home.

'How many's coming?' Bethel asked.

Fran smiled. 'You know very well. You and Walter, me and
Martin.'

Bethel was running hot water into the washing-up bowl.
'That's who I thought was coming. When I saw the mess I
thought you'd invited the Russian army. Don't expect me to stuff
meself, mind. I don't know about Walter.'

She was taking the dirty dishes in precise order, clean things
first so as not to sully the water, then the slightly dirtier things. If
they were bad enough, they were first rinsed under the tap.
Gradually the kitchen was clearing. This was Bethel's gift, the
ability to restore order. 'I love you, Bethel,' Fran said, suddenly
overcome with gratitude and Christmas.

'Get off.' Bethel was fending off her hug with one hand and

washing up with the other. 'Put all that energy into something useful like making tea.'

They were seated at the kitchen table when Walter's horn sounded in the street. 'He smells tea,' Bethel said. 'If you brewed up under a blanket, he'd be there.' They went through the ritual of ignoring his presence until he was on the step, and then welcomed him in.

'Is it still on then, tomorrow?' He was dipping his biscuit into his tea and scooping the damp bits into his mouth.

'You know it is, Walter. You were properly asked and you said yes, so it's on.'

His eyes were twinkling. 'All right, Sally, all right. No need to take an old man's head off.' He sighed. 'Aye, it'll be a funny Christmas for some in Belgate. And a poor one next year if the pit's gone.'

'Do you think they'll really close it?' Fran asked. 'I thought it was a good pit.' Years ago, or so it seemed, Brian Malone had said, '*They'll never close Belgate, a canny little pit like that.*' Yesterday she had taken sponge cakes from the freezer to make the Christmas trifle base. Since she had started her teacher course there was never time to make things, but previously she had been precise. '*Sponge 17th December, 1983,*' it was labelled: the day they'd buried Brian Malone. 'I must go round to Treesa's later on,' she said, 'to take the baby's presents.'

The phone sounded in the hall; it was Eve, ringing to repeat her lukewarm invitation for Christmas. 'Oh well, as long as you're fixed up. We didn't like to think of you and Martin alone. Put the 8th in your diary; that's two weeks on Wednesday. The girls are coming and we'll have a super do.'

Another ghastly girls' night, Fran thought, as she put down the phone. They would all moan about the weight they'd put on over Christmas but it wouldn't stop them eating themselves silly. Vivienne would have news of someone's infidelity and at least one of them would be pregnant. Oh, well, it would have to be endured. If she cried off, Eve would summon a doctor. No one turned down a girls' night unless for birth or death.

*

They walked round to Treesa's as soon as Martin arrived, treading gingerly on the iced pavements. 'It's nearly dark,' Martin said, 'and it's only three o'clock.'

In almost every window a Christmas tree glittered, festooned with lights. There were no children on the streets but here and there a small face peered between curtains, watching for parents home from last-minute shopping. Martin had insisted on carrying all the gifts, and from time to time he took her elbow to help her along. She was about to say 'I'm not ancient', when she remembered how little chivalry there was nowadays. No need to kill it at birth.

'Do you like Christmas?' she asked.

His face gleamed in the light of a street lamp. 'Yeah, it's good. It's a bit miserable after, that's the only trouble. You've played with everything and read all the books and there's only school to look forward to. Ugh!'

She offered up a swift prayer that soon he would start to appreciate the joys of learning, and opened Treesa's gate. This was probably the last Christmas of Martin's childhood. Next year he would want clothes or a proper watch. And after that, aftershave and cigars; but it was silly to worry. Martin's childhood had really finished when David died. After that things could never be the same. She raised her hand and tapped on Treesa's door.

'Come in, Frances.' Treesa's face was alight at the prospect of company. Martin piled the gifts beneath the tree and then settled down to amuse the baby.

They had a sumptuous tea, baby included. 'Should he have fresh cream?' Fran queried.

'He loves it,' Treesa said, expertly scooping melba from the baby's chin to his mouth. The question of vitamins hovered on Fran's lip, but she bit it back. The legs and bare feet kicking beneath the tray of the high chair were rounded and sturdy. Treesa was doing all right without advice.

'What are you doing tomorrow?' Fran asked when Martin had carried the baby off to its 'lobster pot' and she and Treesa settled with a third cup of tea.

'We're going to Brian's mam for dinner and my mam for tea. It seemed the fairest way.'

Fran nodded. 'Keep everyone happy. What does your mother think of the baby? It's her first grandchild, isn't it?'

Treesa was slow to reply, and when she did it was not a direct answer to Fran's question. 'She's very set in her ways, me mam. Once she gets an idea, she doesn't let go. She never liked Brian. He was a Malone, that was enough for her. Anyroad, she doesn't like them seeing the bairn so much, specially Terry.' She was seeking for words and Fran came to her aid.

'Does she think he's round here too much?'

Treesa nodded. 'She says people'll talk. She says he's got his eye on the compen. money. I know she's wrong, but she keeps on about it.'

Fran was shocked. 'I think that's wicked, Treesa. Terry's the last person to care about money; he'd cut off his arm for a principle. And he idolizes that baby . . . and you.'

There was no answer.

'What about you?' Fran said gently. 'Sometimes I think you're fond of Terry, and other times you're quite short with him.'

'I do like him, Frances. Well, I could hardly help it, he's that kind. But . . . you were happy once, weren't you? You know how it leaves you. You can't just put it all behind you.'

'*You were happy once.*' The phrase was chilling. As she and Martin walked home, arm in arm under cover of darkness, Fran thought about the words. '*Happy once*' – as though it could never come again. And yet she *was* happy sometimes. Quite often, in fact, if you didn't count the times when she worried over money, or college, or things like that.

She couldn't resist broaching the subject with Bethel when she got home. 'How long have you been on your own, Bethel?'

The old woman blew a smoke ring. 'Forty years. No, forty-one.'

Fran poured the tea that always lubricated conversation between them. 'You've never thought about re-marrying? I know I pull your leg about Walter but, in a way, I'm serious. You're so fond of one another, it would make sense.'

Bethel blew more smoke. 'Not now, at my age. I'd lay down

my life for Walter, God forbid he should hear me say that. I'd do
any mortal thing for him except marry him. Not that he's asked,
mind. He's got more sense.'

She gave Fran a sharp look. 'You're not leading up to
something, are you, miss? Come straight out with it if you are.
No need to go all round the houses with me.'

Fran smiled. 'If I'm ever contemplating remarriage, Bethel,
you'll be the first to know. No, it's not me, but I sometimes
wonder about Treesa. Terry's very fond of her but something
holds her back.'

Bethel gave a snort. 'I should hope so. They want to call that
house where he lives Little Moscow. He's left of Mao Tse-tung.
I'm not saying I want to see the lass live alone, but there's a
happy medium and he's not it.'

Fran would have flown to Terry's defence if the phone had
not summoned her to the hall. 'I'll be on me way,' Bethel said as
Fran left the kitchen. 'I'll be round first thing to give you a hand.'

It was Min on the phone. 'You're sure you won't change your
mind? You're more than welcome. It's not our usual thrilling
repast, but there's plenty of it.' She assured Min that she was all
fixed up for Christmas, and referred to Eve's invitation for the
8th.

'Oh God. She hasn't asked me yet but I expect she will.
Unless I've been struck off the social register.' No chance of
that, Fran thought. Min would stay on Eve's list for one good
reason, so that she could see how Eve was occupying her former
place as queen of the heap.

'I thought you used to enjoy girls' nights?' Fran said, to cover
her thinking.

'I suppose I did. I mean, it was a chance to dress up and show
off and return hospitality. No one asks us out now ... well,
hardly anyone ... so I suppose I don't have to have do's any
more.'

There was an uncertain note in her voice, as though she
couldn't decide whether to be pleased or vexed. Fran sought for
a way of diverting her. 'D'you know what I used to call them last
year, when I felt bad? Another ghastly girls' night, I used to
think.'

Min's tone was almost incredulous. 'Even *mine?*'

Fran laughed. 'Sometimes even yours, Min.'

They said goodbye, promising to meet up on Boxing Day. As Fran went back into the empty kitchen faint sounds of canned laughter came from the living room and occasionally Martin's added chortle. She crossed the hall and pushed open the door. Martin was stretched out in one chair, Gary Malone in the other. Both of them had their shoes on the upholstery, but it was Christmas Eve after all.

'Want some supper?' she said, and then, 'Does your mum know you're here, Gary?'

Martin's reply was swift. 'His mother doesn't worry. She knows he's all right.' The inference was plain.

'Well, I'm sorry but I do worry. And so does Mrs Malone, whatever you may say, so if she doesn't know where Gary is, go round and tell her. Then I'll make you sausage and chips.'

Gary's legs were already swinging to the ground.

'With gravy?' Martin asked.

'Buckets of it,' she said, and let them scamper past.

When supper had been made and consumed and cleared away, she sent Gary on his way. 'Now we work,' she said. They sat either side of the kitchen table, wrapping, taping, writing tags. 'It's good, this,' Martin said. They were trying to make the paper meet round Bethel's boxed teapot set when the phone rang.

'Not again,' Fran groaned. It was ten o'clock. Who would call at that hour?

'I thought I'd just give you a ring, season's greetings and that sort of thing.' It was the pier man, sounding as though he were already regretting the call. 'It's Jim,' he said before she could reply. 'You know, from the harbour.'

She had collected her wits now. 'Of course, I recognized your voice. How is London?'

His reply was rueful. 'I wouldn't know. I've hardly had my nose outside the door since I got back. Well, you know how it is . . . a lot to do . . . and I can't ask my mother to see to everything.'

They swapped stories and sympathy for a while, and then she said, 'I expect you'd like to say Happy Christmas to Martin?'

'If it's no trouble. He's not in bed, is he?'

She laughed. 'I haven't suggested it. Besides, he's helping with the gift-wrapping. Wait till yours are that age.'

He groaned. 'I can't imagine them helping. Hindering, yes, that I can conceive. But helping . . .'

She was about to hand over the phone when she heard him clear his throat. 'I'll be back in the North-east the week after next, if things go according to plan. Anyway, I just thought, if you're free one night . . . you know I know you're tied . . . but if you could get a sitter . . .'

She had had stranger invitations but never more tentative ones. 'That would be lovely. Ring me when you're up here. Now I'll get Martin – and a very happy Christmas.'

While she piled up the wrapped gifts and put them ready for the tree she could hear Martin's excited chatter. 'That's long-distance,' she mouthed as she passed through the hall.

Martin pretended to ignore her but he wound up the conversation just the same. 'See you then, Jim. And I hope you have a good time.' She was reflecting on the propriety of his calling a man old enough to be his father by his Christian name when he came into the kitchen. 'I knew he'd ring,' he said. 'That's why I stopped up.'

Long after he had gone to bed she sat, staring through the gurgling television, reflecting on the ironies of life. If only she could be as enthusiastic about Jim as her son was, there were all the makings of a happy ending. Unfortunately, there was no X factor there, no weakening of the knees, no drying of the vocal chords. She wouldn't marry him in a million years. 'It's manners to wait till you're asked, miss,' she said aloud in a fair imitation of Bethel's tartest tones.

She poured herself a glass of Christmas booze and watched as the fire turned to ash and dropped, piece by piece, through the grate. Was she like that, a burned-out case? Perhaps she should feel something for Jim, some response. She was capable of love; why not with him? Inevitably, David came into her mind as she always saw him now, coming through the doorway smiling. She felt her own lips curl in sympathy but there were no tears. It was pleasant to think of David now, without pain, remembering only what was good.

But had she loved him? The thought was disloyal and she was tempted to put it aside, but it persisted. Had it been love or had she been swept along in the wake of other teenage pairings? Had she chosen David, or accepted his choosing her? She had never loved Steve; impossible now to believe she had shared his bed. He was someone remote, like a figure on a platform glimpsed from a moving train. She could remember Tony well enough, even without his presence at college to remind her. Why had she done it? Animal lust or a desire to be well in with authority? People fantasized about figures of authority, policemen, teachers, even Water Board men. She started to laugh out loud. The booze was making its mark: time for bed.

Upstairs she drew back the curtains and looked out on Belgate. Frost gleamed on the eaves of the houses and tinselled the gardens. Last Christmas Belgate had been torn apart by the strike, this Christmas it was under sentence of death. Last Christmas she had been alone, this Christmas she was still alone, and she would probably be alone next Christmas, too.

Perhaps she would never be loved again. At least it would do away with the hassle of second relationships that was plaguing Treesa now. And you could live without a man; that much she had learned in the years since David's death. Once she'd believed you needed a man for almost everything. Now she could do most things for herself.

Suddenly, she felt chilled and twitching the curtains back into place made her feel no warmer. '*Into my heart an air that kills . . .*' It was ages since she had read any poetry. She went back downstairs for her shabby volume of Housman and read until the distant church clock told her that Christmas Day was come.

22

Wednesday, 8 January 1986

She drove through the trough of darkness between Belgate and Sunderland but tonight that darkness was relieved by banks of snow on either side of a road whose surface sparkled like marcasite.

She felt the car skid slightly and eased her foot from the accelerator. Mustn't speed! Mustn't slow and change down, though. If you did that you could be left slithering in the road, your wheels unable to get a purchase on the ice. With roads like this she would have a good excuse for leaving Eve's at a reasonable hour, and she gave thanks for frost and small mercies.

If she was going to leave early she'd have to get there on time. Perhaps arranging to see Jim beforehand had been a mistake? You could hardly throw back your drink in one gulp and say thanks very much and ta-ta. He had been so good to Martin that she had felt under an obligation, which was why she had agreed to meet him. '*I'm going to a friend's house. It's been arranged since before Christmas. But we could have a drink beforehand, if you'd like?*' She had sensed a certain relief in him, as though a brief first meeting was not altogether undesirable, and had been faintly piqued.

The first lights of Sunderland loomed up, and after that she was too busy halting at junctions to worry about anything else. He was waiting in the foyer of the hotel. 'Hello,' she said and was struck once more by his aura of despair.

They carried their drinks to a corner table. 'What time do you want to be away?' he said. 'I don't want to spoil your night.'

She was suddenly filled with a desire to comfort him. 'Don't worry about it. I've got heaps and heaps of time,' and to prove it she took off her coat and scarf.

'Tell me how you wound up in the Merchant Navy and you a London boy.'

He was smiling. 'I'd never seen the sea till I was twelve. Then we went to Southampton for a family wedding, and I saw the big ships in the harbour. "That's for me," I thought, and after that there was plenty in London to fuel the flame. Stand on a London bridge at night and hear the hooting of the sirens down the river – that can get up a wanderlust on its own.'

'You sound as though you miss the sea?'

He raised his brows. 'Sometimes. Yes, I do miss it. Ireland like a jewel; going up the Rhine at Christmas with a lighted tree on your mast; coming into port just before dawn and seeing a city waken ... But it's a young man's life. I'd have come ashore anyway, sooner or later, but when Dorothy died, that changed everything. I couldn't let the kids grow up without either of us. They were pretty cut up, and I wanted to be around. I had this idea I could start up in marine paints. I had a few contacts, in the Southampton area, but you can't chance things when you're on your own. You must know that. So I settled for what I could get. Dorothy's brother had this shipping agency. They were twins, and very close. He more or less took it for granted I'd come in with him.'

Fran smiled. 'I know what you mean. I chose teacher training when David died because it seemed so safe. I'd never even thought about teaching before. But it seemed a good idea: the hours were the same as Martin's, and so were the holidays. I'm lucky, really, because now I'm actually doing it I quite enjoy it. How do you feel about your job?'

He shrugged. 'It pays the bills. I'm not mad about the paperwork, but I can cope. It's better than being out of work.'

This time her nod was fervent. Yesterday Min had told her about Dennis's fortnightly visits to sign on. *'There's a little bitch there who ticks him off if he's early and makes him wait till the end if he's a minute late. As though he were a little boy – a man who ran a company.'* There had been tears in Min's eyes, tears of rage and humiliation.

'Yes,' she said aloud. 'Anything's better than being out of work. Unemployment's nineteen per cent in Belgate, and it's changed everything. Miners used to scheme to keep their sons out of the pit. Now they're mad keen to get them in because there's nothing else.'

'Tell me about the pit,' he said, leaning forward. His amazement at finding she was a newcomer to Belgate was only equalled by his interest in her tales of mining life. 'I'll have to meet this Walter,' he said as they got up to leave. And Walter gave the excuse for an easy leave-taking.

'You must come to supper with him. And Bethel. Martin would love it if you did. Give me a ring.' A moment later she was in the car and away, congratulating herself that, for a while at least, while he had talked about the sea, he had looked no more than his age.

Eve was flushed when she opened the door, but it was the glow of triumph, not exertion. Through the open kitchen door Fran could see 'the girl' toiling at the sink, rinsing glasses. She looked all of fifteen. Any day soon Eve would have her decked out in cap and frilly apron like *Upstairs Downstairs*.

'Everyone's here.'

Fran was tempted to say, 'Even Diana and Charles?' but the sarcasm would have been wasted on Eve, who for years had fretted in Min's shadow.

'Come and meet the poor relation,' Min murmured in her ear. And then, flopping her skirts, 'Unclean! Unclean!'

Fran looked around uneasily. 'She'll hear you, Min.'

Min's eyes widened. 'I don't care. She makes me feel like a leper, so I'm acting the part.'

Now that Min could no longer afford to have her black hair cut every second week it hung in wings on either side of her head, and the longer length suited her. But it was her face that had changed most. It was thinner and the eyes were a little shadowed, but the mouth had softened and the old, bored pout was gone. 'You look a million dollars, Min,' Fran said.

They walked together into the room and the flow of gossip engulfed them. 'She said it was a model ... model Marks and Sparks, more like. I don't know why she does it.' 'Well, Geoff says he's had Tenerife ... never again.' 'Roger says protein balsam's the answer ... he won't perm it till it's in condition anyway. You know what he's like when he puts his foot down. So he took the ends off and I had it lamp dried.'

One or two acknowledged Fran and gave Min a beaming

smile. 'All right?' they asked brightly, and she replied, 'Fine! Marvellous!' in equally bright tones. 'Let's get another drink and get out of here,' she whispered at last.

Eve was circulating madly between the living rooms and the hall, with frequent trips to the kitchen to check on 'the girl'. She won't miss us for ages,' Min said as they climbed to the landing. 'We're not VIPs any more.'

They settled on the top stair and were about to chat when an upstairs door creaked and there was a subdued giggle.

'Who's that?' Min said, peering through the banisters.

'Me,' came the answer.

'Me who?' There was silence, then, 'Is that Aunty Min?'

Min started to climb the remaining stairs. 'No, it's the Big Bad Wolf and she's coming to eat you up!'

There was another giggle, a scampering of feet, and the sound of bodies hurtling on to beds.

'Shut up and give us peace, and I'll smuggle you some eats up when I go down again,' Min said, and shut the bedroom door.

'Eve won't approve of you feeding them,' Fran said.

'All the more reason for doing it, then,' was the reply.

'Hey, I've got something to tell you.' Min settled her back against the wall and sipped her drink. 'Remember Margot? Manky Margot we went to school with, who went all left wing and peculiar?'

Fran remembered Margot. 'She's hard to forget,' she said. Last year, during the strike, Margot had haunted Belgate, expressing solidarity with the miners and getting on Fran's nerves. She could still blush at the memory of Margot's astonished face when she'd finally told her to scram.

'She's shacked up with an anarchist,' Min said. 'According to Vivienne, he plants bombs and poisons Mars bars.' Given Vivienne's propensity for exaggeration and Min's own tendency to hyperbole, this probably meant he was an active member of the SDP, but Fran expressed suitable surprise.

'How's life?' she said, when Margot had been laid to rest.

'So so,' Min said. 'I mean, it's not as bad as I feared and it's not as good as I hoped. Does that make sense?'

It made eminent sense. 'That's how I felt,' Fran said. 'After

David died, when I had to start again, I was really frightened. But I always managed. Except that I always seemed to be up against it at the same time, so I know what you mean. Have you decided yet what you're going to do?'

Min shrugged. 'Not really. It's a relief to be getting the house, but that's just half of it. We've got to get an income but there's no work to be had. We'll have to start something of our own; it's the only way. We toss ideas around, but Dennis is just shit-scared, if you'll forgive the forthright language. I never realized what it meant to a man to lose his livelihood. It's far more than a job, it's his whole purpose.'

Yesterday Dave had said much the same as he tipped coal into Fran's bunker. 'There's nee point in life since I got sacked. Nee bloody point at all.' She was about to tell Min of the plight of the sacked miners when she realized that Min's sympathies were all with MacGregor and Thatcher.

'Something will turn up,' she said, trying not to sound complacent. 'When you least expect it, something will click.'

Min drained her glass. 'I hope it does. I've flogged those bloody ornaments to everyone short of the Lord Lieutenant. They've made the difference between living and existing. When they're gone, we've had it.'

They went down to supper and filled a plate for the kids. 'Poor little buggers,' Min said as they sneaked upstairs. 'Fancy facing adolescence with Eve and Harold for support.'

Downstairs again they tucked in to an array of meats and salads, asparagus rolled in brown bread, continental sausage and tiny kebabs on cocktail sticks. 'You know what's paying for this lot, don't you?' Min said, wrinkling her nose. 'All the poor shits who've gone into liquidation. The more of us down the drain, the fatter accountants get! Bugger them!'

Memories were stirring for Fran. In her own trauma after David's death, she had discovered the relief of using oaths. Admittedly she had done it under her breath, whereas Min said them aloud, but it was the same syndrome: the relief of anger and grief. Under the bold exterior and the constant quips, Min was afraid. 'Tell me about my namesake,' Fran said, steering her on to happier topics.

After supper they collapsed into chairs or sat on the floor, elegant legs tucked under expensive skirts. 'Oh God,' Vivienne said. 'I'll have to stop eating so much. I'm like a house-end.'

Pam was unrepentant. 'Well, I don't care. It was absolutely sumptuous, Eve and I'm not ashamed to say I pigged myself.'

They talked about losing weight, about the break-up of Lilian Sparks's romance with her Chinese/Malaysian/Polynesian, about the Princess of Wales and how Mrs Thatcher was saving or ruining the country, with the weight of the argument in favour of the former. 'You can't keep on supporting lame ducks,' one girl said. She had huge pearls in her ears and obviously believed she resembled Joan Collins. 'If a firm can't make it, it ought to go to the wall.'

There was a sudden uneasy silence as one or two eyes flicked to Min and back again. This is history repeating itself, Fran thought. Two years ago she had been the spectre at the feast, causing everyone to watch their tongues. Now it was Min's turn.

The penny had dropped for Joan Collins. 'Well,' she said desperately, trying to extricate herself, 'they can always start again. I mean, there's heaps of incentives, government help and everything. And there should be . . . I mean, I'm all in favour.'

Min was sitting with her back to the stone fireplace wall, her face bland. Eve was perched on the arm of a chair and looked as though she was about to give birth. 'Goodness, this conversation's getting serious,' she said at last. Any moment she'll rise to her feet and do her head-girl act, Fran thought. '*Parents, staff and fellow pupils, I am here tonight to demand we change the subject . . .*'

'It's OK, Eve,' Min said suddenly. 'It doesn't upset me. We went bust – so what? Actually, it was the best thing that could've happened. Dennis's always been the office boy as far as his parents were concerned. Now we're branching out on our own, and I'm going in with him. I can't say much at the moment, but watch this space!'

A relieved hum of congratulation and encouragement engulfed her. Min was not going to let the side down after all, and wasn't that splendid! Only Fran was puzzled. A moment before Min had been talking about the vague hope of something turning up; now she was hinting at something of Tiny Rowland proportions.

'What was all that about?' she whispered, as they collected their coats.

'Don't ask me,' Min said, a note of desperation in her voice. 'But I wasn't going to sit there and say nothing, was I? I'll just have to think of something.' The next moment someone called out that the Mini was blocking them in, and Fran had to rush down the drive.

All the way home to Belgate she thought about Min. Something had better turn up before the last of the fake Capo di Montes was gone, or Min's plight would indeed be desperate. Losing your home was one thing, losing face was another. She was sure Min could cope with the first. She was not so sure about the second.

12

Friday, 7 February 1986

She was applying eye-liner when the phone rang. 'Can you get that, Martin?' She had managed to finish the left eye and was stretching the lid of the right to match up when his face appeared in the bathroom door. 'It was Aunty Min. She says it's nothing special if you're going out. She'll ring another time.'

He was halfway back down the stairs when Fran called out, 'How did she know I was going out?'

He kept on descending. 'I told her. I said was it important 'cos you were busy, and she said "no". It's all right, I'd have got you if she'd said yes.'

'I wish you'd asked me first,' she said, glaring as fiercely as she could with one made-up eye. 'I don't mind you answering the phone, but I'd like to take my own calls.'

Martin had tired of the subject. 'Drop dead,' he said, *sotto voce*. She felt her lips twitch but pulled herself together before she spoke. 'What did you say?'

His reply was conciliatory. 'Nothing. I was just mumbling.'

She went back to the mirror to apply the rest of her make-up.

Martin was becoming quite single-minded lately. Jim's phone calls took precedence over everything; her going out with Jim was of paramount importance. He would kill to ensure their meeting, let alone get rid of Min. Sooner or later she would have to sit down and tell him the facts of life. Jim was nice, very nice, in fact. But if Martin had any rosy ideas of romance he would have to think again.

Last week she had invited Jim to supper with Bethel and Walter, and the evening had been a great success. 'He's all right,' Bethel had said, which was praise indeed. Tonight he was taking her out for a meal as a way of saying thank you. It was no big deal. She grimaced into the mirror: she really must stop using that stupid phrase. She would be saying it to her class at Broad Street if she wasn't careful.

While she slipped into the navy suit she thought about her teaching practice. The best one so far! She knew what she was doing now and it was a good feeling. This morning a small boy had taken her hand as she walked across the yard, and the touch of the small fingers in hers had been suddenly thrilling. 'He likes me,' she'd thought, and had had to restrain herself from grinning like a fool.

When she was ready she dialled Min's number. 'Hi . . . sorry I was upstairs when you rang. Is everything OK?'

There was a moment's silence and then, 'Which do you want first, the good news or the bad news?'

Fran felt behind her for the second stair and lowered herself to a sitting position. 'The bad news.' Always get the worst over first.

'I've finally flipped my lid, Fran. Gone bonkers, berserk, etc., etc. The good news is I'm going into business. In a small way, no big overheads and that sort of thing.'

Fran drew breath. 'Is that all? I thought something was wrong.'

Outrage came down the line. 'Is that *all?* I like that. Here I am chancing my arm, and all my best friend can say is "Is that all?" '

Fran smiled. 'No, I didn't mean that. I'm impressed. Very impressed, but I wish you'd tell me what you're on about.' The clock was moving forward remorselessly, and while Jim might not be the love of her life she didn't want to keep him waiting.

'Well, you know those ghastly Capo di Monte fakes I pinched from under the liquidator's nose? I sold the last of them last week at the boot sale, and I was just getting ready to clear up and come home when the woman who'd bought it came back and said did I have another because her friend was going mad for one. I said no, that was the last – and then I started to think. "Can you go back to the warehouse?" I said to Dennis, and he hummed and ha-ed a bit, but he said he could if we had cash because all the firm's accounts were closed and no one would give him credit any more. So I took the woman's name, and I raked up every spare cent. It was Giro week, and I'd just got a cheque from that woman in Newcastle for all the clobber she sold for me. So we went to the warehouse. Fran, I kid you not, it was Aladdin's cave. Pure kitsch. I wouldn't have given it house room. Anyway, we got another piece . . . it was the Pied Piper . . . but there were heaps of them, a lot cheaper. Dennis used to buy top of the market for the windows, but some of those things were only a couple of quid. So I sold the woman the piece she wanted and she . . . Oh God, this story's getting longer and longer. Fran, the fact is, I've taken a stall with Gamma Fairs . . . you know, they run the antiques fairs, but bric-a-brac's included. I start this weekend. I'll have to wrap up because the woman who runs it says you can freeze, but the main thing is, I'm in business. What d'you think about that?'

The idea of Min as a fairground barker was mind-boggling.

'What did Aunty Min want?' Martin said when she came off the phone. He was developing a nose for anything out of the ordinary and knew something was up.

'She's starting a business,' Fran said. 'A market stall.'

Martin's eyes widened. 'Selling what?' The news that Min would be flogging china dampened his enthusiasm. 'Can I have cod and chips for supper?' he said and brightened visibly when she fished in her bag for the money. There was cod in the freezer and frozen chips, but nothing home-made equalled the magic of that vinegar-soaked, newspaper-wrapped bundle. Not in Martin's eyes, anyway. So for once they would have to be afforded.

She was halfway through the door when the phone rang again, and she could never walk away from a beckoning phone. When she saw people do it in TV plays she always knew it was a poor script. Real people were compelled to come back and pick the damned thing up!

'Fran? I've just had Min on the phone . . . she says you already know and you approve. Surely, you can't be in favour of this crazy scheme? I've only had time to mention it to Harold, but he thinks they've gone mad. As if they're not in enough trouble already . . . Fran, are you there?'

She could put the phone down and pretend they'd been cut off, but Eve would only ring back and hassle Bethel. 'Yes, I'm here, Eve. Actually, I think it's quite a good idea. Better than just sitting around.'

The chill in Eve's voice was almost tangible. 'Oh, well . . . I suppose everyone's entitled to an opinion – ' Before Eve rang Fran had been nursing grave doubts about Min's latest enterprise, but she was not about to admit it to Eve.

As she drove into Sunderland Fran was uncomfortably aware that she would have to re-assess her friendships before too long. But not tonight. Tonight she was eating out with Jim and she meant to enjoy it.

A faint doubt stirred: was she leading him on? He liked her; more than liked. She liked him, too, but not in the same way. Perhaps she was presuming too much; perhaps he saw her not as a woman but as a mother figure? He was certainly fond of Martin. The chess set he had given him for Christmas was Martin's most prized possession and hadn't been cheap. As the lights of the town appeared ahead she tried to still her faint unease. It was only a meal, after all, not a nuptial mass.

They dined in a newly opened Chinese restaurant and she was amazed at the confident way he negotiated the menu and dealt with the waiter, until she remembered he had been at sea for fifteen years. He was wearing a dark grey suit and a patterned silk tie, and it made a difference. He caught her looking him over and gave an embarrassed half-laugh. 'Thought I might as well dress up.'

She knew enough about his job to know that suits were not *de rigueur*. He must have brought it from London in the hope of taking her out. A tiny bowl of fragrant soup was in front of her and he was waiting for her to start. 'Um, lovely,' she said, and gave herself up to eating.

In the end it was easy. They talked about food around the world, and then the difficulties of feeding families. 'I never cooked after David died. Well, not properly cooked. I'd fry something for Martin or do him something from the freezer but I lived on cottage cheese.'

Jim had been more ambitious. "I tried to carry on. Dorothy was a good cook, so I tried pastry, all that sort of thing.' He grinned. 'It was pretty disastrous. I could roll the stuff out all right, but when I put it over the pie-dish it would tear, and if I gathered it up again it'd have bits of pie filling in, so in the end it looked like a mosaic . . . and tasted worse.'

The thought of him struggling with a rolling pin was not unpleasant. 'I like him,' Fran thought. 'No violins, no knee tremors, it's just nice.'

'Was your wife ill for long?'

Dorothy had died of cancer after a four-month illness. 'I know it's selfish,' Fran said, trying to find the right words. 'I'm only thinking of myself, because it was better for David that he died so quickly, but I sometimes wish he'd been ill for a while so that I could have prepared. As it is, one minute he was there, the next he was gone. I kept feeling unreal, as though if I gave a really good shake of my head it would all dissolve and we'd be happy again.'

An enigmatic Chinese appeared for their plates. 'Coffee?' Jim said, and then when the waiter had gone, 'It doesn't work like that. You don't prepare. I knew practically from the beginning. Just by little things at first . . . sensing that they were sounding me out, seeing how much I could take. And then they said the surgeon wanted to see me. He sat there, just a little chap, very ordinary. He sat there toying with the notes and he said, "Three months." I argued. I remember I wanted to punch him because he was talking life and death and he didn't seem involved. I suppose dispassionate's the word. Anyway, I said no, it can't be like that, there are things you can do! But I think I knew, really. She was standing in the ward in her dressing gown when I came out of the sister's office. I looked along and saw her and she was laughing and I thought I'd never seen her look so well.'

He looked down at his plate. 'I'm sorry, Frances. I don't know why I did that. I've never talked about it, not to anyone. And then I ask you out for a meal and spoil it all. I can only say I'm sorry.'

She tried to coax him to continue but he was adamant. Instead they talked about recent films and what he liked on telly. 'I'm in my room most of the time. I pick small homely hotels, like the Harbour View . . . places where you're made welcome. And I like a pint. But you can't spend all your time drinking, so I watch TV and ring the kids. They like that. Kevin's quite good with the phone now. He's four. And Barbara's like a little old woman. "This is the Seymour residence," she says. It always creases me, the self-possessed little voice. Just like . . .'

He stopped then, before he mentioned Dorothy again. Fran would have put out her hand and covered his as it lay on the table but it would have been presumptuous. He had rather nice hands; she hadn't noticed that before but it was true.

She started to tell him about college then, deliberately choosing safe waters. 'When I look back I can't believe I did it. I must've been on automatic pilot because I have no recollection of applying and I only dimly remember the interview.' David had been dead for four weeks when she went for the interview and she had wandered, zombie-like, around a dress shop before she went in, but she decided to keep this to herself. 'The bonus is that I really enjoy it.'

He was smiling. 'Are you good at it?'

She rolled her eyes. 'That remains to be seen.'

He laughed when she told him about teaching practice, and expressed a wish to meet Gwen one day, and then the inscrutable Chinese was presenting the bill and they were out in the cold night air.

'I'll pick you up next time,' he said, taking her elbow to cross the road. 'It's silly to bring two cars.' A little frisson of unease came and went. He was taking 'next time' for granted, and although she would be happy to see him again she wanted to be the one holding the reins.

'I've enjoyed tonight.' She opened the car door and threw her bag across into the passenger seat.

'So have I.' The street lamp shone on his hair and threw his face into shadow, so that she could not make out his expression. He was thirty-nine years old; she had worked that out by simple addition. Thirty when he married, married for seven years and widowed for two. Or was it widowered? Whatever the name, the pain was the same.

'Goodnight, Frances.' In another moment he would incline his head and kiss her, and, even if she was quick to turn away her mouth, it would still imply a degree of intimacy. She put out her hand. 'Thanks for a lovely meal. I enjoyed it.' The next moment she was safe in the driving seat. He shut the door and, more forthcoming now that danger was past, she wound down the window. 'See you soon, Jim.'

He nodded and was about to stand clear when he changed his mind. 'I hope I didn't upset you, talking like that about Dorothy. I don't know what came over me. I'm not usually a blabbermouth.'

She leaned close to the open window and smiled up at him. 'I took it as a compliment. So don't be sorry.'

As she was driving away she looked in the rear-view mirror. He was standing there, hands in the pockets of the grey tweed coat, watching the retreating car. She would have to be careful not to hurt him. He was much too nice for that. And that was not the only complication: unless she was much mistaken Martin would be lurking on the landing, all agog to know how things had gone. 'Oh Frances,' she said aloud, as the street lamps fell away and darkness engulfed her, 'oh Frances, what have you got yourself into now?'

13

Friday, 28 February 1986

'For God's sake, Fran, don't look so guilty. We're two grown women, not little kids.'

Fran was unconvinced. 'We're still playing hooky.'

Gwen shook her head. 'It's not hooky when students do it: it's exercising judgement. If you don't think a lecturer's worth listening to, do something else instead.'

Fran quickened her pace. 'Well, I'll still be glad when we're out of here. I keep expecting to hear Ogilvie behind me, saying, "And where do you think you're going, Mrs Drummond?"'

'Don't look now, but that's him over there.'

Fran shot a guilty glance right and left for the principal before she realized Gwen was fooling.

'Honestly, Fran, it's a good job you didn't opt for a life of crime. One sniff of the policeman's armpit, and you'd've coughed the lot. I can honestly say I don't have a single qualm about taking this afternoon off. I've worked damned hard, my notes are up to date and I shall spend the next four hours wallowing in idleness. Besides, I'm tired of friend Lund and his teaching methods. He's so laid back . . . or so he wants you to believe. He's a real phoney.'

The car park was in sight and Fran was relieved. She had never told Gwen she was seeing Tony Lund, much less sleeping with him, but she felt bound to defend him. 'He's no worse than the others. I think he just wants us to feel his equals . . . I mean, not student and master.'

Gwen snorted. 'He needn't worry. I feel absolutely his equal, if not his superior. And I know you had a little fling with him, Fran. If I hadn't known before, I would now. Your neck's doing a litmus.'

It was useless to say 'I don't know what you mean.' Gwen was far too shrewd. 'It was nothing, really, just a couple of dates.' She could have added 'and a clutch of orgasms and a phone call from his lover' but left well alone. 'How did you know?'

They had reached Gwen's car and she was scrabbling wildly inside her massive handbag. 'I'll clear this damn thing out tonight, God help me, I will. How did I know? You were seen. Jenny saw you, or Geoff, or somebody. And then of course we recognized signs: he'd throw questions your way and flirt with you when you answered. Then there was your term exam mark. If I'd had lingering doubts, that did away with them.' She reached out and pulled Fran's arm. 'Cheer up. It wasn't illegal. It might've been immoral. I hope it was, a little bit, but there's no need to look like the scarlet woman.'

'I wish I'd told you, Gwen. I don't know why I didn't. It was fairly awful, really. He has a woman – they're not married . . .'

To her surprise Gwen was nodding. 'I thought you knew. Everyone else does. They've been together for years. She's quite famous, older than him, and they have a child. A boy, I think. She's on the box sometimes. Very arty, long dresses and brooches like foundry off-cuts. Deirdre Paul, her name is.'

As she drove towards Belgate Fran tried to build a mental picture of the woman in Tony Lund's life, but it was useless. What kind of woman could hold him for years and years? And, more intriguing, what kind of woman would wish to do so? When she looked at him now she was amazed she had ever fancied him. It had been a schoolgirl crush; but she was no wide-eyed schoolgirl, she was a mature student who should have known better. It was embarrassing to be taught by him now, remembering what had gone before, which meant that she could not concentrate. She tried to avoid his eye in class discussion but on the odd occasion that she did contribute he would listen gravely and then pass immediately to the next speaker as though her contribution was not worth comment. It was the perfect put-down, a favourite device of Robin Day, and at first it had stung. Now she didn't care, and that said a lot about Tony Lund. His impact, in bed or lecturing, was only transient. So why did Deirdre Paul put up with him?

The enigma of Tony Lund's love-life quickly palled. There were more important things to worry about. Today the review board would pronounce on the future of Belgate. Fran had only the dimmest idea of what happened when a pit closed. The colliery yard would be empty and barred, miners' buses would thread the streets carrying Belgate men away; but what would happen to the heart of Belgate? With a shiver she realized she was already assuming that the pit would be condemned. That was the kind of feeble acceptance that had landed the North in its present mess. Belgate would survive, and so would the pit! She put down her foot and watched the needle climb to eighty just to emphasize her point.

It was half-past one when she got home, time for her to take Nee-wan out before it got dark. Walks with the dog were great treats and she was in the mood for goodies of some sort. She kept him on the lead until they were on the old stagecoach road that ran above and behind Belgate. He was always overjoyed to be off the lead, running backwards and forwards in a frenzy of delight. 'Go on, daft dog. I'll be tripping over you in a moment.'

The path was scarred by tractor wheels, and here and there the imprint of a horse's hoofs. On either side the fields were black and rich, with tiny pockets of snow in sheltered corners. Ice had formed in the tractor furrows, and cracked at the impact of her booted feet. Ahead, the trees of the copse were winter black, but up close she would see buds pressing against the bark, ready to burst forth at the coming of spring.

Then fields would be filled with fragile green shoots that would turn into sturdy corn almost before her eyes, and the hedgerows, brittle and grey now that the hips were gone, would blossom with old man's beard and willow herb and beautiful, starry dog-daisies. Her eye was caught by a single leaf turned red and clinging to its stem in spite of winter winds. The sight cheered her out of all proportion, as though she had found a jewel.

She reached the top of the track and turned to look down on Belgate. Far off, the A19 stretched like a toy track with tiny Matchbox cars and buses speeding north and south. Below the road, the roofs of Belgate ran down to meet the coastline. There was the inevitable ship on the horizon, the familiar dark band where sky met sea. Somewhere to the west lay Durham city with its cathedral tower. South was the smoke of Middlesbrough, a sleeping giant waiting for jobs that never seemed to come. She bent down and touched the cold earth. Durham earth. Rich earth, that would bring forth good crops in the fullness of time. Rich earth covering even richer seams of coal.

Her eyes were pricking with tears, sentimental tears. It was a good job no one could see her. On her left winter sun glinted off window glass but the nearest house must be half a mile away, or more. Besides, who cared? Suddenly she remembered the time after David's death when she had been afraid to walk in the park and cry because someone was sure to be watching her. And now she dared weep at will and shout out loud and even take a precious half-day off.

A yard away, the dog watched her, hoping for a stick or a stone. Instead she threw up her arms and opened her mouth. 'Race you to the bottom,' she yelled, and began to run.

She had sobered up by the time she reached home. Bethel was sure to be there and would take a dim view of truancy for truancy's sake. She would have to invent a plausible reason for being home on a college afternoon.

She was spared interrogation for Bethel had news to impart. 'The NCB's decided.' Fran looked suitably impressed but kept her mouth shut. 'They've set a target: five thousand tons a day, or else!'

Fran let out a slow whistle. 'Can it be done?'

Bethel shrugged. 'It'll have to be, won't it? That pit's losing best part of a million pounds every few weeks. How long can that go on?'

'Yes, but five thousand tons. It sounds huge.' She thought for a moment and then decided to cheer up. 'Still, I expect it'll be all right. They'll never shut Belgate. It's a good little pit.'

Bethel was warming the pot, swilling it round and round against her bosom. 'By, you're green. You get older but you don't improve. "A good little pit?" It's losing millions, but it's a good little pit? Keep it open, God. We don't know where the wages is coming from but keep it open just the same.'

Fran was stung. 'What about the social consequences if it closes? There's no work in Belgate. They're paying off at David's old factory, and small firms don't take apprentices any more. Where are people going to work, Bethel?'

Bethel sighed deeply. 'That's not the point, is it? I never said put the lot on the dole. What I'm saying is that keeping a clapped-out pit open never solved anything.'

They were on to tea by now, elbows on table, Bethel's packet of No. 6 between them. 'I'd love a cigarette,' Fran thought and turned away her eyes. 'Well, what does solve it? I mean, whose responsibility is it? It's the government, they're responsible.'

Bethel shook her head. 'See what I mean: green as grass. The government's puppets, no more no less. Someone else has his hand up their jackets' . . . she gestured with her hand right and left . . . 'Yes sir, no sir, three bags full, sir.'

A delicious idea was forming in Fran's mind, a mental picture of someone trying to get his hand up Margaret Thatcher's frock. 'What about the Prime Minister? You don't think she's a puppet, do you?'

Bethel considered. 'No. She's a woman so she's not so easily led. And she's sincere, I'll give her that. She means what she says and she stands up for what she believes in.'

Fran was about to fall off her chair at this political conversion when the punchline came.

'The only trouble is, she gets everything wrong bar the date. We're saddled with one job-lot, and the alternative is worse, and you clap-trap on about it being logical. Get that dog some water and leave the thinking to folks that have the equipment for it.'

Fran was trying to decide whether or not Bethel was an anarchist when Walter's horn sounded. They sat still until they heard him fretting and fuming on the steps. 'Oh God, if ever a feller had a bunch of duds for friends . . . wouldn't even help a cripple up a lighthouse . . . hell and damnation. I'll best these bloody steps . . .'

'I ought to go,' Fran said, feeling guilty.

Bethel shook her head. 'Let the bairn play. It's the breath of life to him to complain. Don't spoil his pleasure.'

When Walter was safely in, he looked around. 'Well, I can see I'm going to be offered neither bite nor sup in this house, so I'd best get back on the road.' He spun his chair and then, as both women sprang into action, swung back and settled himself.

Terry arrived as they were drinking the tea. 'I've brought you some logs, Mrs Drummond. I thought you could use them.' He looked around. 'Sally. Walter. I haven't seen you for a bit. How are you?'

'I'm all right.' Walter's eyebrows were bristling. 'Except for worrying over what you lot'll do next.'

Terry grinned. 'What've I done now, Walter? I'm always glad to hear the latest episode.' He turned to Fran. 'It's nice when you can keep up with your own activities. I mean, I always seem to be the last to know.'

Bethel was scalding fresh tea at the sink but her eyes were on the two men.

'I hear you're talking strike again?'

Terry pursed his lips and considered. 'If you mean the lodge committee, Walter, we have discussed it. It's a legitimate working-class weapon. And there's never been a greater need for struggle – not even a die-hard like you can deny that.'

Walter fingered the arms of his chair. 'Aye, lad, you've got a bonny tongue on you. You dress it all up nice and you sound like butter wouldn't melt, but you're a bloody little agitator all the same. My union split down the middle, it'll never recover ... there's a dozen homes I could mention that'll never be the same again. The last strike was a bloody disaster, and you're talking strike again. God forgive you.'

Terry was shaking his head. 'The NUM's not split down the middle, Walter, not anything like it. There's a tiny fraction, a *tiny* fraction, split away and formed the UDM. They have no standing, legal or moral. We'll snuff them out and nee trouble. We'll see victimized men back to work, every man jack of them. And we'll keep this pit open. The strike wasn't a disaster, it was a breakthrough. We're politically aware now, Walter. We can't be pushed around any more. We've realized our power.'

Long after they had gone and she was preparing for her evening out, Fran was remembering Terry's words. So there was going to be more trouble.

She sat on the edge of the bath to put in her Carmens. A few hours ago she had been happy, perhaps as happy as she had been in a long time. Now it was spoiled. Damn Terry! And yet she liked him, with his cheerful, freckled face and willingness to do a good turn. And when he wasn't spouting Trotskyist rubbish, he could be good company. She was suddenly seized with curiosity about the word Trotskyist. She had been quick to use it but she hadn't a clue what it stood for. All she knew about Trotsky was that he'd been done in with an ice pick. She offered up a brief prayer for Treesa to marry Terry and make an honest man of him, and vowed to look up Trotsky the next time she was in the college library.

She was meeting Jim at his Seaham hotel that night. They hadn't seen one another for nearly two weeks, so she was looking forward to it. 'Come here for a meal,' he'd said. 'I've brought those photographs I told you about.'

Martin had been all bright-eyed and bushy-tailed at the thought of her seeing Jim. 'I hope he stays the whole weekend. I've missed him.' She had wondered if he might suggest coming with her but he seemed happy enough for her to go on her own. He was too young to be a matchmaker, really, but he was showing all the signs.

As Jim and Fran drank a fruity white wine in the bar, she felt her spirits rise. To hell with Terry and pit closures and the impossibility of her ever passing philosophy. Next birthday she'd be thirty-five: half her lifespan over. If she didn't start enjoying life soon it'd be too late. 'I'd love a rum baba,' she said when Jim asked about dessert. 'I'm full to the brim but I'm in the mood for going over the top.'

Afterwards, she would ponder her choice of words but as she uttered them she deliberately refrained from analysis. She had been on a seesaw of emotions all day. Now she was just glad to be here with Jim. He was nice – that much underrated adjective.

When Jim suggested going up to get the photographs she shook her head. 'I'll come up with you. We'll go out and come in again by the side door if that makes you feel better. No one will see.'

When they reached his room she could see he was both elated

and uneasy. He rushed to tidy a clutter of socks and underpants
and scooped his spare shoes under the bed.

'Sit down. There's only one chair but I'll squat down beside
you in a minute!' He passed her the album. 'I've got a bottle of
scotch here, if you'd like some?'

They had scotch and water in tooth-glasses, and turned the
pages of the album. His children were lovely, a pert little girl and
a camera-shy little boy who felt obliged to make faces at the lens.
'Your wife was very pretty.' A look of proprietorial pride touched
his face and Fran felt an irrational hurt. She skipped through the
last few pages and handed back the album.

Jim got to his feet and went to sit on the bed, looking first at
his glass and then at his hands. After a moment he switched on
the bedside radio and began to twiddle the tuner.

'This is crazy,' Fran thought. She put down her glass and
stood up. 'Do you want to make love to me?' she said. She had
asked that same question of Steve a long time ago. Asked it aloud
and been unable to believe her own ears. Now she waited calmly
until Jim was forced to meet her eye.

'Yes,' he answered. She put out a hand and felt his arm quiver
at her touch.

'It's all right,' she said, drawing him to her. 'It'll be all right.'
She held his head to her breast and soothed him, thinking all the
while of the girl she had once been who had always been afraid,
and wondering from whence her present boldness sprang.

At last they drew apart, both calm. He got to his feet to put
out the light, and she was glad. As her eyes grew accustomed to
the dark she crossed to the window and drew back the curtains.
A few hundred yards away a flat sea gleamed silver, only a faint
booming betraying the force beneath it. 'Beautiful, isn't it?' Jim
said, coming up behind her.

She turned into his arms and knew it was going to be all right.
Funny, funny life, teasing and deceiving you so that you mistook
sand for sugar and sugar for sand. He held her for a moment
then turned her slightly so that once more she could see the sea.

'I spent half my life out there. It's strange to think of it now,
that once it was my mistress . . . and my comforter. There's a

verse of John Betjeman's . . .' He tilted his head, seeking the
words, and then bent to recite for her.

> *'Here where the cliffs alone prevail*
> *I stand exultant, neutral, free,*
> *And from the cushion of the gale*
> *Behold a huge consoling sea.'*

She would never have guessed he loved poetry but the revelation
was a welcome one. 'I like that,' she said. *A huge consoling sea.* I
always thought Betjeman wrote funny stuff – good, but light.'

His arms were like a shield around her. 'You'll have to read
him again,' he said and touched her lips with his so that the last
word was almost lost.

They undressed slowly, helping one another sometimes,
neither of them afraid that the moment would slip away. 'Are
you sure?' he said, when at last they stood naked together.

'This is comfortable,' Fran thought. Aloud she said, 'I'm sure.'

They took time, exploring, reassuring. 'Oh, my love,' Fran
said at last and drew his body into hers. He took her with him,
lifting her in arms that were surprisingly strong, cradling her
head in one hand, touching her face with the other.

One tiny portion of her mind acknowledged his experience,
resented it briefly, and ceased to care. All that mattered was that
he was in her and around her and there was no possibility of
failure.

14

Friday, 21 March 1986

'I've put in for Broad Street or High Barnes,' Gwen said. 'It'd
be nice if we got on the same staff.'

Fran gave a hollow laugh. 'I just hope we both pass, Gwen. I'll
worry about *where* I teach when I know they're going to let me
teach at all.'

It was still winter but the earth was cracking to show impatient bulbs. They had almost reached the car park when Gwen dropped her bombshell. 'I was told last night that you were courting. It's the first I knew of it, I said . . . but when I thought it over I decided you'd been broody for a bit so it was possibly true.'

Fran felt guilty. 'I was going to tell you. It's not courting, not by a long chalk, but there is someone.'

Gwen's eyes were round with curiosity. 'Where did you meet him?'

'I picked him up on the dockside,' Fran said, and chuckled at the idea. 'It's true,' she said when Gwen expressed disbelief, and filled in the details while they stood at the car.

'He sounds nice,' Gwen said doubtfully. 'But with men who move around you can never be sure.'

'Sure of what?' Fran asked.

Gwen looked uneasy. 'Well, I mean, he says he's a widower but you only have his word for it . . .'

Fran's smile was wry. If ever she had seen a man with the stamp of bereavement on him, it was Jim when she first met him. Now he looked better but there was still some way to go.

Bethel had the kettle on when she got home. 'I'm dying for a good cup of tea. The stuff we get at college is foul. I don't know how they can spoil tea but they seem to have the knack.'

Bethel pushed a mug towards her. 'Get that down you.' She sank into the opposite chair. 'I've bottomed your bedroom and tickled up the front room.' She looked around. 'We'll have to do this place when the weather picks up. It's getting like the black hole of Calcutta.' It was true; the once-white ceiling was yellow, and in one or two places the paper was coming away from the walls. 'It doesn't do to let a house slip,' Bethel said. 'Not if you're intending to stop in it.'

'*If you're intending to stop.*' Fran thought about those words as she cooked sausages for Martin's tea. Last night on the phone Jim had asked her a question: '*Could you ever imagine living anywhere else but the North?*'

'I suppose I could,' she'd said and changed the conversation, but really she couldn't imagine leaving her roots. Couldn't bear to leave Bethel. Couldn't leave this funny red house in this claustrophobic little Durham village, let alone move miles away. And that was what he had meant. He was saying, '*Have we a future, you and I?*' The trouble was that neither of them had the answer to the question.

Exploring John Betjeman's poetry, she had found a verse that summed it up. 'On leaving Wantage 1972', it had been called, and the last few lines had struck her as appropriate:

> *From this wide vale, where all our married lives*
> *We two have lived, we now are whirled away*
> *Momently clinging to the things we knew –*
> *Friends, footpaths, hedges, house and animals –*
> *Till, borne along like twigs and bits of straw,*
> *We sink below the sliding stream of time.*

She shivered, suddenly downcast. The poem was right about leaving your roots: once you did that you were nothing more than straw. It amazed her to realize that she had never felt for any man as she felt for Jim, not physically. She had never been more fulfilled or more a partner in the physical sense. If that was love, then she loved him. Remembering the early days when she had had difficulty in recalling his name let alone his presence, she could hardly believe her present feelings. To be in his arms was now everything, with none of the desire to please she had felt for David, no need to be the crutch she had been for Steve, and no sense of being used, which had neutralized all Tony's expertise. Just a feeling of total pleasure that was all the better for its mutuality. It was only when they drew apart that the doubts began. It was as though he donned his other hats with his clothes and became father, businessman, grieving widower. And she returned to being foolish Frances, who was never sure of anything.

Martin was in a good mood at the tea table. 'I'm free. No more prison. I don't hate school, so you needn't make a face; it's just I like having freedom. We're going down the blast one day and Gary's making a go-cart. He's not half good with his hands, you know. I keep telling him he could be an apprentice, but he won't.'

'What does he want to do?' Fran asked.

Martin shrugged. 'Nothing much. I expect he'll be a dolie. There won't be a pit by the time he leaves school.' His world-weary tones suggested there wouldn't be much of anything in a year or two.

'You don't know that,' Fran said. 'They might hit the target and the pit might be reprieved. Anyway, there'll be other work by the time you grow up.' She tried to sound confident but he was not deceived.

'Like what? Unless we get more Japs, there won't be anything.'

He had a point. The Nissan car plant at Washington and NSK ball bearing at Peterlee were giving jobs to Belgate men, but there was precious little else. 'Well, I still think there'll be other jobs before long,' she said.

'When we get rid of Thatcher?' he asked.

Fran grinned. 'I wish it were that simple.'

He had finished his sausage and chips and was on to cake. 'Anyway, I might not want a job here. I might go to sea.'

Fran's amazement was unfeigned. 'What put that in your head?' and then . . . 'I suppose it was Jim?'

'Not really,' Martin said. 'Well, not just him. I was already thinking I'd like to go round the world a lot . . . like a pilot or something. Jim just said the sea was OK if you got all the tickets and everything and got good ships.'

Fran chose her words carefully. 'But wouldn't you mind leaving here? Leaving Gary and your other friends, and all the places you know?'

'Well, I'd rather not leave them but you have to sometimes. And anyway I could go backwards and forwards now. By myself. So I'd still be friends with him. Anyway, he might go in the army. He says he might do that if he doesn't go on the dole.'

Fran thought over their conversation as she washed up the tea things. A year ago, or little more, he had almost cried at the thought of having to change schools. Now he could contemplate a move with equanimity.

She was sorting the work she had brought home when Treesa arrived. 'Are you busy? Shall I go?' She looked miserable and Fran shoved her books aside.

'I should think not. I don't see half enough of you. Where's Christopher?'

Christopher was being put to bed by his Uncle Terry. 'It was Terry's idea I came round. "Go and see Mrs Drummond," he said. "She'll cheer you up."'

Fran settled Treesa by the fire and carried in instant coffee. 'Now, tell me what's wrong? It's not the baby, is it?'

Treesa shook her head. 'No, it's not us. But I'm that upset, it might as well be.'

In the hall the phone rang. 'I'll just let it ring,' Fran said. 'If it's important they'll ring back.'

Treesa's eyes widened. 'It might be trouble.'

It was Min. 'I'm just ringing to report on the first month's business. We've made a profit, Fran. But only just – not enough to live on.' She was trying to be cheerful but despair was in her voice. 'I'm learning, that's the important thing. There were one or two lines I simply loved but we couldn't shift them. So now I look for things in the worst possible taste and they go like a bomb. Dennis says it's early days, and I suppose he's right.' Her voice softened. 'He's beginning to pick up, Fran. He actually took my head off this morning and I thought, "Thank God". I don't believe in tyrants but a man shouldn't be crushed, should he?'

Fran was dying to hear Treesa's story but Min couldn't be cut short. 'Well, I think you deserve to succeed, Min. You've been an absolute brick.'

'And you didn't think I had it in me?'

It was time for truth. 'No, Min. I knew you weren't completely empty and money-mad . . .'

Min interrupted. 'Which is what Eve thinks.'

Fran ignored this and carried on . . . 'but I didn't think you'd have the guts to start again so soon, especially when Frances is still a baby. It can't be easy.'

Min was regaining her confidence. 'I'm going to make it work, I promise you. The truth is, Fran, that I've been an under-achiever. That's why I was such a bitch; too much undischarged energy. Now I'm plugged in, you just watch me!'

Fran was smiling as she came back into the room. 'Good news?' Treesa asked.

'Yes,' Fran said, 'I suppose so. But it's not so much the good news, it's the way Min keeps up her end. I've never known anyone like her.' Treesa's brows were raised. 'It's Min. You know, that friend of mine with the very black hair. She came . . .'

Fran suddenly realized what she was saying and stopped, but Treesa finished for her. 'She came to Brian's funeral. Yes, I remember her.'

'Now, tell me what's wrong?' Fran picked up her coffee. It was no longer hot but it would do.

'You know Dave, who brings your coal? Well, they've pinched him.'

Fran felt a jolt of alarm. 'For stealing coal?'

Treesa shook her head. 'No, much worse than that. They say . . . well, he did do it. They say he broke into a deputy's house and took a video and some coins. He sold them in a shop in Sunderland and they traced them back. His wife's in a bad way – they were on the bottom, that's why he did it. Now she says he'll go up for a long time and she's beside herself.'

'Oh, Treesa, I'm so sorry. And he'd never been in trouble before, had he, until the strike?'

Treesa was nodding. 'That's right. It makes you feel as though it'll never stop, all the trouble. Terry and his dad speak, you know, but it's not the same. I feel for his mam, I really do. I was feeling sorry for myself this afternoon, and then I heard about Dave and Audrey, and me own troubles just seemed nothing.'

'What troubles have you got, Treesa? I know you're on your own, but you have Terry. If only you wouldn't be silly and think you're being disloyal to Brian. I've told you before, he'd want you to be happy.'

Treesa's eyes were brimming and she twisted the sides of her cardigan. 'It's not that easy. I look at him sometimes and I think, yes, I do love him and we could work things out. And then it comes to it and I can't.'

Fran drew a breath and plunged. 'You mean you can't bear the thought of making love with him?' Treesa's down-bent head bobbed. 'I know how you feel. Brian was the only man you went with, wasn't he?' Again there was a nod, but the chin had come a little way from her chest. 'Well, it was the same for me. David and I fell in love at school, and after that I just never looked at anyone else. But I've had to make a new life.' Treesa's head came up, wearing an expression of shocked disapproval. 'Yes,' Fran said firmly. 'There has been someone else.' No need to say more than one: there was a limit to how much soul-bearing people could expect.

'And it wasn't easy, Treesa, for all the reasons you know. But in my heart I know it's right to love again. Not to replace David; I wouldn't do that even if I could. Love isn't like that, something you give once and have to take away to give again. It's a growing thing and it expands for each new love you make. Each real love, anyway.' Treesa was still gazing at her, waiting to be convinced. 'Look, when you had Christopher you loved him, didn't you? And you didn't have to take love from Brian or your parents. You grew new love. You've already grown new love for Terry, whether or not you know it. I've known it for ages, since Christopher was ill. So why not let things be?'

Treesa was wiping her eyes. 'Well, put like that, I suppose it makes sense. But there's something else . . . it's not just me.'

'Does Terry feel it's disloyal to Brian?'

Treesa shook her head. 'I don't think so. It's the money, with Terry. I've got all that compen., and he's just a working miner, and he thinks it'd be sponging. I think he'd like me to lose it all overnight and then he'd be happy.'

Fran's patience was going. 'That's stupid. That really is stupid. Just let me catch him saying that and I'll tell him what's what. He's got so much stupid pride, has Terry – that's what caused the trouble with his dad. He'll have to curb it before he's much older.'

When at last she sent Treesa off, comforted, she thought how pat her arguments had been. Off with the old love and on with the new – except that the old love remained to haunt you, so that you could cry out one man's name in the arms of another, or murmur the other's name in sleep. And when there were two ghosts, one on each side, the difficulty was compounded.

She decided to work off her blues and went to collect the

washing. She was feeding Martin's jeans into the tub when she felt the packet. King-size tipped. One whole cigarette, one fag end. That was all she needed, a twelve-year-old heading for emphysema.

The phone rang and she went through to the hall.

'Fran?'

She recognized the voice and was consumed with guilt. 'Linda! I was just going to ring you . . .' If there was a special hell for liars she was as good as there, but Linda was bubbling on, too happy to take umbrage.

'. . . and it's due in October. You ought to see Eddy, he's like a dog with two tails. Not that it'll make any difference to Debbie and Carl and Damian. He's got them ruined.'

When Fran rang off with firm promises to visit soon, she struggled to take pleasure in the news. Someone was happy. Where once there had been misery all was sweetness and light, with a baby to set the seal. Sometimes there were happy endings, and if for Linda why not for Fran in time? Except that for every winner there was bound to be a loser. Or two. Or twenty.

She was still feeling despondent when the phone rang again. 'I've been thinking, Fran,' Jim said. 'I was going to try to get up to your end in the holidays and then I thought, why doesn't Fran come down here? You could meet the kids, and we could have a night out in London. How does that sound?'

She heard herself agree but her rush of joy soon subsided. London was a long way away and belonged to Dorothy. When was life going to be easy? When would problems have simple answers and not be so overhung with emotion that they defied solution? She put a hand behind her and lowered herself to the stairs. 'I'm glad you rang,' she said. 'It's been a lousy day.'

15

Thursday, 3 April 1986

She felt better once they were actually on the road. Before that she had felt an almost physical pain at parting from Martin. 'It'll be all right, Mam, honestly. I'll like sleeping at Treesa's. She's better than you about stopping up. And Bethel'll be there if I need anyone.'

She had decided not to take him on this first trip. It was a voyage into uncharted waters and he was better out of it. Now, though, she wavered. 'Let him come,' Jim had said, sensing her distress. It was Martin who'd vetoed the idea. 'Go on. I'm all right, Mam. You're only going for two days.' His eyes said more: '*Have fun, Mam. Like Jim. Sorry about the smoking.*' So she had climbed into the car for the journey to Twickenham, and waved and waved until the corner was turned and her son was out of sight.

'I'm soft,' she said, blowing her nose. 'It's crazy really.' He said nothing, simply smiled and kept his eyes on the road.

Peterlee came and the smoky blur of Middlesbrough appeared. 'I hope you know where we're going,' Jim said. He always used the A1, but she had suggested taking the A19 as far as Dishforth.

'I do and it's simpler. You'll see,' she said, regretting her cocksureness when they had to queue to get on to the A1 and lost all the time they had saved. But at least she had seen the hills, the blue remembered Cleveland Hills. 'We used to have picnics there,' she said, and knew he understood.

Tonight she would ring Martin on Treesa's newly installed telephone. Tomorrow she would ring him again, and the next day. The day after, she would catch the three o'clock from Kings Cross and come home. As if he read her thoughts, Jim spoke. 'You must bring Martin next time. He'd get on well with Barbara, and Kevin would appreciate some male support. Barbara bosses him, I'm afraid. Well, she tries to mother him; I suppose it's understandable.'

They turned off at Newark and drove into the town to eat in

an old, timbered pub. 'I used to use the M1 at the beginning, but it's so monotonous,' he said. 'I found myself falling asleep a few times and I thought, that's it.' She nodded and smiled, and he reached out and touched her hand. 'That's better. You looked a bit woebegone before.'

'I do feel better.' She had enjoyed her meal and was feeling distinctly relaxed.

'It's like that when you set out on a journey,' he said. 'I used to feel it on the ship. Ashore, you had a thousand worries; then you got aboard and you saw the ship leave the side, and suddenly there was nothing you could do about it until you were ashore again. So you stopped fretting.'

Fran smiled. 'The huge consoling sea,' she said and he nodded agreement.

She drove when they got back on to the A1. At first he demurred, then he accepted gratefully. 'I could do with a snooze.' A moment later he had tilted his seat and was asleep. She couldn't believe it. David had let her share drives but he had always stayed alert in case she missed turnings. She drove as far as the Peterborough junction and felt inordinately proud of the fifty-five miles on the clock. As she drove she watched his profile. He was handsome; why had she not seen it from the first? Or had he changed since they had been together, blossoming as women were said to blossom when they fell in love? Perhaps it was all in the eye of the beholder and she was seeing what she wished to see. It didn't matter. She stretched out a hand to his thigh and left it there as the miles fell away.

London appeared on a road sign. 'Almost there,' he said and she could tell he was glad to be coming home.

'Do you love London?'

'Yes, I love the old place all right. You can't help it. "Dull would he be of soul," and all that.'

'"On Westminster Bridge",' she said.

He was pleased she recognized it. '"*This city now doth like a garment wear the beauty of the morning; silent, bare, ships, towers, domes, theatres and temples lie open unto the fields, and to the sky . . . The river glideth at its own sweet will; Dear God! the very houses seem asleep; and all that mighty heart is lying still.*"' He recited simply and well.

'You know your poetry.'

He laughed. 'Some poetry. The bits I can understand. I used to read a lot at sea.'

'What about Housman?' Fran asked.

Jim shook his head. 'I don't think I've heard of him.'

She felt smug. 'You must have heard of *The Shropshire Lad*?'

He wrinkled his brow. 'I thought that was the name of a pub. Yes, I've heard of it but it sounds a bit . . . bucolic?'

She let her enthusiasm show. 'Oh, it's not, it's lovely. You get the feeling of him being young and loving life and appreciating the things you appreciate. I won't go on about it, I'll lend you a copy when we get back. Then you'll see.'

As the outskirts of London began, she reflected that he was the first man she had talked poetry with. Real poetry, that is. David had liked the poems of John Lennon, but she wasn't sure they counted. Jim had introduced her to Betjeman and for that she was grateful.

They skirted central London and she didn't see a single familiar landmark. 'Never mind,' Jim consoled her, 'we'll go sightseeing tomorrow. There are things I've been meaning to show the kids . . . if you live in London it's amazing what you miss. We'll go tomorrow. We could start with Hampton Court, that's practically on the doorstep.' He changed gear as the traffic thickened. 'You really must bring Martin next time. London's magic for kids, a living history lesson.'

There it was again, that acceptance of a shared future that filled her with delight and terror. He felt right; more than a lover . . . he felt like a husband. Suddenly her happiness evaporated. He wasn't like a husband, he was a husband. Dorothy's husband.

At once the remembrance of his loving her was shameful, so that she shut her eyes and squeezed her lids.

'OK?' His eyes were on her, anxious.

'Yes, fine. Just a little headache . . . it's gone now.'

Twickenham was a town in itself. 'Lots of shops,' she said. It was half-past four and shoppers were still about.

'You can get anything here,' he said proudly. 'And there's a silversmith's down towards the river. Not many of them left. We're slap bang on the Thames, you know; you'll see tomorrow.' He was trying to sell the place to her and they both knew it. And they both knew that relocation would not be the only problem. 'That's just the beginning,' Fran thought.

His house was old and roomy and pleasant. 'We bought it cheap,' he said, showing her round. 'It was in its original state . . . stone sink, moulded arches. I kept what I could, but the plumbing's new, it's been rewired, that sort of thing. It's worth a lot more now, and it'll be mine in 1993!'

She asked about the children. 'I think Mother was taking them out after school. Just for an hour.' She could see he was on edge. 'I didn't want it to look like a reception committee . . . they're all dying to meet you.' He went off to make tea and Fran sank into a chair.

The room was impressively tidy. There were toys in a corner, but all boxed and neatly piled. She rested her hands on the arms of the chair. They were slightly worn. Worn by whom? Jim's slippers were placed neatly on the opposite side of the hearth, his pipe-rack was nearby. That was his side, therefore this had been Dorothy's side. Remembering how she had hated alien hands on David's chair, she withdrew her own and folded them in her lap.

It was a woman's room – flowered carpet, flowered curtains, embroidered cushions and a photograph in a silver frame. Dorothy and the children, all squinting into the sun above holiday smiles. There was a box beside the photograph, hand-carved with initials in mother-of-pearl: 'D.K.' D for Dorothy and K presumably for her maiden name. Fran was at once consumed with curiosity to see inside, and suffused with guilt at her own emotions. This was someone else's house. She moved her legs uneasily, tucking them neatly together. It was a pity he had kept the children away; they might have broken the ice.

'Do you need the loo?' He guided her to the upstairs landing and left her. 'Bathroom's on the right. I'll be in the kitchen.'

The bathroom was squeaking with Vim and elbow grease, and there was an embroidered guest-towel on the rail. On the way downstairs she passed an open bedroom door. There was a double bed and a man's jacket in a cleaner's bag hung on the wardrobe. This must be Jim's room, the bed he had shared with Dorothy. She sped down the rest of the stairs, praying for the front door to open and admit the children – anything to take her mind off things. Except that they, too, were Dorothy's, so there was no escape.

They came in when the tea had been drunk, their grandmother fussing over them and trying to make Fran welcome at the same time. 'Take your coat off, Kevin, there's a big boy. I do hope Jim made you some tea? We hurried back ... not there, Barbara, hang it up.'

Barbara was tall for her age, thin and intense. A freckled nose, hair scraped back into bunches in a style Fran remembered from childhood. They'd have trouble with her hairline in future if it continued to be pulled back like that. She would have to speak to Jim ... except that it was really none of her business. Barbara had seated herself close to her grandmother and bent periodically to pull up one sock or the other.

'Have you been somewhere nice?' The child shook her head and then decided some reply was necessary. 'We went to the library. Kevin's just joined. I've belonged for ages.' Kevin was eyeing the tea tray and seemed disinclined to talk. He was more like his father, with a determined, if chubby, chin.

'This lady's a teacher, Kevin. Show her your books.'

Fran's heart sank. She was not sure that being introduced as a teacher was the best possible start. 'I'm not a proper teacher. Not yet.'

She looked round the room, trying to find a safe topic of conversation. 'I see you've got Mousetrap. My son likes playing that.'

Barbara spoke with all the assurance of a septuagenarian. 'We don't play that any more. It's a bit babyish.'

Kevin scowled. 'I don't think it's babyish, I think it's good. Anyway, it's mine.'

Jim had come back into the room and was beginning to look agitated. 'Who wants some tea? Proper tea.'

Barbara stood up. 'I'll make it, Daddy. Tell me what you

want.' She's demonstrating ownership, Fran thought and was struck by pity for the child. Second relationships were difficult for everyone, children most of all.

Jim's mother offered to take her upstairs. 'I've put you in my room. It overlooks the back garden, so you won't hear the traffic.' It was a typical spare room with a single bed and a narrow ash wardrobe.

'I haven't put you out by coming, have I? I could easily have used a hotel.'

The older woman sat down suddenly on the bed. 'To tell the truth, I'm looking forward to being in my own home for a few days. Jim's so good to me but I miss my own place . . . well, you do after you've had it for forty years, don't you? Not that I mind. They're lovely children. You won't have a bit of trouble with them, and Barbara's getting very handy. The boy . . . well, it's just high spirits . . . you've got a boy of your own.'

Fran was dying to say, 'Don't worry, I'm predisposed to like them,' but it wouldn't have done. It was all getting too intense.

'Yes, I have a son,' she said instead. 'He's not a bad lad but he can be a bit of a handful at times.'

Jim's mother looked relieved and then at her wristwatch. 'There's a bus at six if I hurry. I don't want to take Jim away. It breaks my heart sometimes when I get home . . . it smells so foisty. Of course, it's shut up all the time.'

The children were already at the kitchen table and Jim motioned her to a chair. 'Sit down, Fran. I'll just see mother away.' He was flushed, and there were splashes of what Fran hoped was water but feared was fat on his trousers. Barbara was putting a plate in front of her. 'You can have beans as well, if you want them.'

Fran looked down at steak and mushrooms and chips. 'My, my. Your dad's a good cook. No beans, thank you.'

Barbara resumed her seat. 'Grandma cooked them. We just put them in the microwave.' There was a slight emphasis on the 'we' and Fran felt a spasm of irritation. 'All right, darling,' she thought, 'we all know you're in charge.'

The boy was easier . . . or perhaps she was just used to boys. One of Fran's mushrooms slid from under her fork and she pretended to chase it round her plate. That made him laugh, so she did it again. 'Stop playing to the gallery, Frances,' she told herself, and was glad when Jim came back to preside.

'Shall I wash up?' she asked when the meal was over. 'You two have worked hard. Let me clear up.'

Barbara was already piling plates. Jim had been right about her trying to replace her mother. 'You've marked the cloth,' she said accusingly when she moved Kevin's plate. He put a finger into the remains of his beans and made another smear to match the first. The little girl's face flushed. 'You're childish,' she said with contempt.

He put his fingers into his mouth and pulled the corners. 'Bugger,' he said, his eyes sliding towards his father.

Jim's expression was agonized. 'Kevin! That's naughty. Apologize to Frances. She didn't come here to hear that sort of thing.'

Barbara's eyes were on her, watching for the next move. 'What sort of thing?' Fran said, pushing back her chair. 'If Kevin and I give you a hand, Barbara, we could all have a game of something after.'

After that things were easier. Kevin, having been let off the hook, was disposed to be angelic, and Barbara was not displeased at the way things had turned out. 'She can tell him off but no one else should,' Fran thought, and felt a faint warmth for the determined little figure at the sink.

They played Mousetrap for Kevin and Trivial Pursuit for Barbara. Fran's eyes signalled, 'Intelligent, isn't she?' and Jim tried not to look overjoyed. They watched Russ Abbott and laughed at Kevin's uninhibited laughter more than the show itself.

'He's a happy little boy,' Fran said, when the children went up to the bath. '*What about her?*' Jim's eyes asked, and she hurried on. 'And Barbara's lovely. She adores you and Kevin, doesn't she?'

They came down, clean in cotton pyjamas, for milk and biscuits. Kevin climbed into the settee beside Fran and allowed her to put an arm round him for a story. *James and the Giant Peach* was his choice and she read his three favourite bits. Barbara listened gravely, giving the page numbers of the pieces he liked. 'You read it usually, don't you?' Fran asked and the child nodded.

'But you can do it. I don't mind.'

The atmosphere had undergone a remarkable thaw since tea time. 'We're like a family,' Fran thought, as they discussed the next day's sightseeing, and looked up to see the same thought on Jim's face.

Where would Martin fit in? How would he take to a small boy in her lap, which was where Kevin had wound up? If she was honest, he hadn't wanted to sit on her knee in years, so chances were he wouldn't mind. She was just about to suggest a pick-a-back to bed when the doorbell rang.

'Who can that be?' There was foreboding in Jim's voice and a weary acceptance of intrusion.

'It's just us!' The woman's voice was arch. They came into the room, giving false starts at the sight of a stranger. 'Oh, good Lord,' the man said, 'I'd completely forgotten you had a guest.'

'This is Desmond, Dorothy's brother,' Jim said. He didn't need to add 'my boss'; Desmond's bearing said it for him. 'And Janet, his wife. This is Frances Drummond, a friend of mine. She's here for a few days.'

Desmond held out his hand. 'Jim did tell me. I'm afraid it slipped my mind.' If John Wayne had been there he'd have said, '*the hell it did*'. All Fran said was, 'Hello.'

Janet's hand was warm and damp. 'Do you have a family, Mrs Drummond?' She didn't wait for an answer. 'We simply love children. Desmond can't see enough of them. It's understandable; he and Dorothy were twins. Identical.'

Fran was aching to point out that identical twins of opposite sexes was a contradiction in terms, but decided against it. Jim was fussing around getting everyone seated, in spite of the new arrivals' vowing they hadn't come to stay.

'Oh God,' Fran thought, as Janet settled herself for what promised to be a long stay. 'I thought things were going too well.'

16

Saturday, 12 April 1986

She was out of the house by seven-thirty and at the market by eight a.m.

'Fran, you're a brick. Now, it's perfectly simple . . .' A moment later Min was gone, leaving Fran in charge.

She surveyed the stall: dainty ladies, pipe-playing urchins, bespectacled cobblers, all portrayed in china, and a crowd of pixies on spotted toadstools trailing electric flex. It would be awful if she sold nothing. People passing on their way to work did not spare a glance.

It had seemed quite simple last night when Min had telephoned. 'Fran? How was London?'

She had started to talk about London's parks and gardens being further on than the North's, but Min had cut her short. 'Stuff the shrubs and bulbs, Fran; get to the nitty-gritty. How did you get on with his kids?'

A man passed the stall, looking uncertainly at her. 'She away then, the usual one?'

Fran gave him what she hoped was an encouraging smile. 'Yes, she's got some business to attend to, but I'll help if I can.'

He leaned forward and lowered his voice. 'She was getting me something a bit special . . . to help with the wife.' He gave a wink and a nod of his head. Surely Min was not marketing sex-aids under the cover of a china stall?

The sex-aid turned out to be a porcelain poodle twelve inches high, with a jewel-studded collar and a wicked gleam to its eye. Fran found it, after a long search, tissue-wrapped in a box under the counter.

'I told her the wife was hard to please. "Leave it to me. What's her likes and dislikes?" she says, and I said she was mad on the dog. A poodle. Daft little beggar, has to have chicken breast . . . Any road, your friend says, "I can fix that," and by gum she has. I'll be well in when the wife sees this.' He parted with the £8.50

marked on the box, and went off satisfied. So that was Min's gimmick – giving each customer personal service.

Min could come back any time now that there was money in the till. Honour was satisfied. It was nine o'clock and the crowd of people going to work had dwindled. At Min's suggestion Fran had put on her sheepskin coat, but her legs and feet felt numb. She stood up to stamp them gently and tried to think of other things.

She had told Min that everything had gone well at the weekend, but that was only part of the truth. All the way home in the train she had wondered whether or not she loved Jim. They fitted together, each of them tongued and grooved by marriage so that they could slip into the roles of husband and wife at will. Except that there was that other husband and wife, ghostly and yet substantial, pushing up through the floorboards, widening the gaps.

She had refused to share Dorothy's bed. She would have said no anyway, because of the children, but the thought of sex in the bed they'd shared, with Dorothy's trinkets still on the dressing table, her clothes, for all Fran knew, still hanging in the closets . . . that was not to be contemplated.

They had made love once in the back of the car, giggling at behaving like seventeen-year-olds again. But the giggling had been uneasy. They were not seventeen and there was no escaping it. What was possible, even desirable, at seventeen was out of place at twice that age, when you were no longer green enough to bend, and valued your dignity.

A woman came up, inquiring about the pixie lamps, and although she bought nothing Fran was glad of the interruption. It was no good dwelling on things, especially emotional things. The practical problems were enough. Desmond and Janet had hovered over everything, present in spirit if not in body, and they had been there in body often enough.

'We wouldn't mind if Jim married again,' Janet had confided as they washed up together on Fran's last day. 'Well, a house needs a woman, doesn't it?' The word 'housekeeper' hung unspoken in the air.

'Of course, it can never be the same. You know that from your own experience, I'm sure. But companionship's valuable.'

Fran had wanted to hurl the plate she was drying against the wall and shout, 'Sod companionship. We fuck frequently,' but even saying the word in her mind was shame-making. She felt her cheeks flush at the remembrance of it, and decided to rearrange the stock.

She was putting a white-faced pierrot next to a street band on a flower-encrusted base, when she recognized the woman eyeing the display. 'Hello, I thought it was you.' She looked younger and prettier than the last time Fran had seen her in the support group kitchen, when she had been thin and strained, brown hair covered with a cotton scarf, eyes ringed with kohl in an otherwise white face. Now she was carefully made up, well-dressed, and her hair was ash blonde. She smiled, seeing Fran's eyes widen. 'Yes . . . I do look a bit different, thank God. I wouldn't want to go through that again.' She looked at the stall. 'I never knew you worked here. Somebody said you were a student.'

'I am,' Fran said. 'I'm just minding the stall for a friend.'

The woman leaned closer. 'What happened to that friend of yours? You know, Tokyo Rose?'

Fran smiled. 'You mean Margot. Well, last I heard she'd moved in with a terrorist.'

The woman's mouth opened and shut. 'You're having me on!'

Fran shook her head. 'That's what I was told.'

The woman looked at her watch. 'Do you get a dinner hour?'

Fran nodded. 'I hope so. I'll freeze to the spot if I don't. Shall we have a coffee or something? Then we can swop all the news.'

They arranged to meet in the Market Tavern at twelve-thirty. Surely Min would be back by then. Business was picking up; the pierrot went and a ghastly pot shell that might have contained a sea-monster. 'You put plants in them. Trailers. She suggested that, the woman what's on usually. I tried and it looks lovely, so I'm having another. I'd buy one of those lamps, but you never know with electrics.'

Min and Dennis came back at noon. 'Well done, Franny. You've been an angel. I see you didn't shift those bloody pixies. I swear they're sneering at me. Now take this and buy lunch. No,

I won't take no for an answer.' They had been for the final interview with the liquidator and relief showed on both their faces.

'I don't want anything, Min. It was fun.'

She had enjoyed selling. Perhaps there was more of the entrepreneur in her than she had thought. She went off with Min's fiver burning a guilty hole in her pocket, but there was no point in arguing when Min had made up her mind – Fran had known that since their schooldays.

The woman was waiting in a corner alcove. 'I got you half a lager,' she said. 'Is that all right?'

Fran carried the menu from the bar. 'Lovely,' she said. 'And lunch is on me. I got paid unexpectedly, so you can help me spend it.'

Over Cornish pasty and chips, they reminisced. 'Peeling onions and taties,' the woman said, 'that's what I remember. Hundreds and hundreds of taties and onions.'

Fran nodded sympathetically. 'I only came now and again, but I can remember how the onions made you cry. Still, it was worth it.'

The woman shrugged. 'Sometimes I wonder. We suffered, I mean, really suffered. I watched my bairns go without and if there's worse torture than that I'd like to see it. And where do we stand now? The pit has a chance to be shut by Christmas.'

Fran hastened to reassure. Terry had briefed her on the likely scenario, so she was well-informed. 'The Coal Board has set a target, which the men might make. If they do, the pit's saved. If they don't, the Area Director will announce closure. The union at area level will have counter proposals, and if the NCB doesn't accept them, it'll go to national appeal in London, and after that to the independent review body – that's a panel of six, and they're not all Coal Board men. So there's lots of ground to cover before the pit goes. And if it does, there'll be voluntary redundancy, and relocation money if you go to another pit. Fifteen hundred pounds if you've been a miner for ten years.'

The woman nodded. 'Yes. Very nice. My man'll get his fifteen hundred, and they'll bus him to Seaham or Murton. But what about my lads? I've got one fourteen, one eleven: where'll they go for work if there's no pit? You tell me, 'cos I don't know.'

Fran made no attempt to tell her anything. There was nothing she could say. It was unthinkable to keep open pits whose losses regularly ran into millions, and equally unthinkable to present future generations with no occupation but the dole.

'Did you hear about Davy Sawyer? Him as got sacked for GBH? He's up for thieving. I'm not excusing it, but he'd never've done it if he'd still had his job.'

Fran nodded. 'I was talking to him yesterday.' He had staggered through her yard door, a sack on his back to be tipped into the coal-house. *'This is the last you'll get. I reckon I'll be out of circulation for a bit* . . .' He had looked old and defeated, and she had been too tongue-tied to help.

'It's made me think,' the woman said. 'I blame Scargill, I still blame the sod. He's a proper First World War general, that one. Over the top, boys; lie down and die for the cause! But as long as the working man doesn't involve himself there'll be people like Scargill to pull his strings. And people like Maggie to stamp him into the ground. We're on the bottom rung and we have to fight the system. I want power, not for power's sake but for the sake of my class.'

Fran listened, but half her mind was scrabbling around for something read in last week's papers. Scargill had been talking to a Russian newspaper about his 'brilliant victory': 'In the course of twelve months thousands of young men and women were politicized to a degree that seemed incredible just two or three years ago.'

The woman was warming to her theme. 'The men don't like it, you know. The minute the strike was over they said, "That's it, canny lass – back to the kitchen sink." Well, bugger that. Ever since I got married I've conformed . . . but now! I don't say "Can I?" I just go ahead. The strike made me political, which I never was before. Women have got to stick together. Mind you, I'm not anti-men – I love the sods!'

*

It was still light when Fran got back to Belgate. April was a lovely month. She thought of the evening ahead, of driving to Sunderland with a red glow in the western sky, Jim waiting for her and looking pleased to see her. That was the best bit of all. She was making him happy, so she could be happy herself, without guilt. 'I am entitled to this happiness,' she thought and went, smiling, into the house.

'Oh mind, that's a change. Something's pleased her.' Bethel was pretending to be sarcastic but it wouldn't wash.

'Hallo, lovely lovely Bethel. I've missed you, but I sold dozens of ornaments and earned a bomb and now I'd like a cup of tea.'

Bethel held her at arm's length. 'You've been drinking?'

Fran opened her mouth and blew. 'Yes. Alcohol. I'm under the affluence of incohol.'

She felt like being daft. She still felt like that when the tea was drunk and she was running upstairs to get ready. She didn't know why she was so euphoric, but no point in questioning a gift horse. She couldn't explain her present mood any more than she could explain the black moods that came for no apparent reason. Or why she had thrown herself at Jim, even suggested having sex when she considered such boldness unseemly.

She took her jewellery box and sat cross-legged on the bed to sort through it. She switched on the bedside radio and started to hand-jive to the beaty music. 'I'm being childish,' she thought, but carried on just the same. Lines from a poem by W. B. Yeats came into her mind:

> . . . But lived as 'twere a king
> That packed his marriage-day
> With banneret and pennon,
> Trumpet and kettledrum
> And the outrageous cannon,
> To bundle time away,
> That the night come.

That was what she was doing . . . bundling time away that the night come. 'I really want to see him,' she thought and went in search of the volume of Housman she had promised him. It was fun to share poetry with someone close. A new experience.

When she found it she carried it back upstairs and sat in the window, the book unopened in her hand. Could they be happy? Were they entitled to happiness the second time around? Could they take two different halves and make a whole? Would Barbara let them? Memories of Steve's daughter Julie flooded back, the mutinous little face resenting her very presence. And Martin might be put out at no longer being an only child, in spite of liking Jim so much.

If they loved enough, surely anything was possible? Barbara and Kevin were Jim's flesh and, loving him, she must learn to love them too . . . if she could. Or at least show affection.

They would have to take things slowly, one small step at a time. More trips to London, taking Martin with her; then a whole week with them up here. The kids would love Nee-wan. After that, a holiday together, somewhere in the sun. The book remained unopened as she indulged in daydreams that might become plans if they were given half a chance.

17

Saturday, 10 May 1986

'I'm taking the dog for a walk.' There was no response, so she called again. 'Did you hear me?'

Feet thudded to floor from arm of chair and the living-room door opened. 'Yeah. OK. I'll take him out tomorrow.'

She clipped on the dog's lead. 'Don't perjure yourself, Martin. And don't forget Terry's coming round tonight. Bethel's at Bingo. So no carry-on.'

He went back to his television and she let herself out of the back door and made for the allotments. 'There now,' she said, unclipping the lead as soon as it was safe. The fences around the allotments always fascinated her – old doors, mostly, railway sleepers, corrugated iron sheets, even a metal advertising board bearing half a legend. Once upon a time hens had clucked, but there had been so much skulduggery lately that the hens had been taken away.

Between the cracks in the fence she could see colour. Belgate men loved flowers. They would come up from the pit and hover over roses or gladioli, carrying off prizes for chrysanthemums the size of tea plates. And all that the South knew of the green-fingered North was its capacity for growing leeks! She smiled at her own fervour. She was becoming more northern as she grew older, or at least less ashamed of it.

She turned to look for Nee-wan as the alley to the main street came into view; he would have to be back on the lead before they encountered traffic. The alley had boasted a wooden fence once upon a time, but it had vanished during the strike, gone to fuel miners' fires like everything else that would burn. It had been replaced with metal-link fencing, but it was not the same and she was glad when she reached the brick wall.

Most of the graffiti from the strike were indecipherable now, but she could make out *Scabs are Shits* and one or two *Coal not Dole*.

A faint spasm of pain gripped her abdomen and she put up a hand to ease the top of her skirt. The curse must be on its way. She tried to remember the date of her last period: had it been early April or the end of March? Once she had counted the days of the month, hoping against hope that this time she would have conceived David's child; now she accepted the barrenness and the curse was just a nuisance. If she married Jim the yearning might return, except that he might think three children between them was more than enough.

She turned into the park and made for the beck. It was running clear today, leaping over stones and gurgling at its edges. She paused on the stone bridge, holding a twig she had picked up on her way. Years ago, when Martin was small, they had played on the bridge, dropping sticks in one side and rushing to see them emerge on the other. Sometimes they sank and never reached daylight, sometimes they re-surfaced and were whirled away. 'Borne along like twigs' to slip below the sliding stream of time. As usual, when she thought far ahead, she felt afraid. There was no mistaking John Betjeman's meaning: he was talking of death. But she had never felt more alive. Never in her whole life.

She had the dog under control and was walking along Stafford Street when Walter's car pulled up alongside. 'I thought you'd had that dog put down?' Nee-wan stood on his hind legs and put his paws on the car door.

'He wants to give you a kiss, Walter,' Fran said, wondering, as she always did, why Walter's presence so lifted her spirits.

'Kiss? I'll kiss him. You want to get rid of him, he's ruined. You can blame Sally Bethel for that . . . slop, slop, slop. It's not the dog's fault, poor beast.'

'Are you going to Bingo tonight?' That would guarantee an explosion, for he considered 'housey' to be a modern curse.

But with Walter nothing was guaranteed. 'Well,' he said, preparing to wind up his window, 'I might go. If Sally's going, I might force meself. Get her in the back row . . . pop the question between the Silver Chest and the Jackpot. She'll be all roused up by then, so you never know. Get your bridesmaid's dress out!' He was laughing so hugely he could barely steer, but Fran could only think how nice it would be if they did get together, in wedlock or out.

She was ready too early, but the pale, calm face in the bathroom mirror betrayed none of the doubts and fears behind. She knew tonight would be significant; she had sensed it in his voice when Jim rang and suggested the meal. 'We can talk there,' he'd said, naming a small Indian restaurant they'd used before. He was probably going to suggest marriage and if he did . . .

She came downstairs quietly and let herself into the front room. She could hear the television set on the other side of the wall, murmuring voices and studio laughter overlaid with Martin's constant chuckling. Thank God he had a sense of humour.

She sat on a high-backed chair, knees neatly together, hands on lap. She had sat like that on the day of David's funeral, all of the others watching her disintegrate. She had thought it the end of the world, but in a sense it had been the beginning of learning to cope.

In the wake of the self-congratulation came the terror. Could she mother another woman's children, take the place of a dead but still-loved wife? Could she flourish in the alien South if he asked her to move? Most important of all, how would it affect Martin? And Bethel, what would Bethel say?

A new and niggling doubt surfaced: what about Jim's wedding ring? If he kept on wearing it, it would be a constant reminder. On the other hand, she could hardly suggest he take it off.

It was a relief when Terry arrived. 'I'm not late, am I?' He would have settled down beside Martin but she waved him into the kitchen. 'I want a word, Terry. I haven't much time so I'll get to the point. And don't waste time telling me it's not my business because it'll fall on deaf ears. Treesa is my business and so are you, whether or not you like it.'

He was holding up his hands. 'All right, all right. I'll surrender now. I know when I'm beat.'

The smile left his face as she began, to be replaced by the look of resolution he had worn throughout the strike. 'It's hopeless,' Fran thought but she ploughed on. 'Treesa's told me how you feel about her money, Terry, and I might have known you'd have some ridiculous notion like that. What the hell does it matter whose money it is? She knows you don't give a damn for money; so do I, and so does anyone else who knows you. So if you love Treesa, and I'm sure you do, you'll marry her as soon as possible and give her some happiness and security for a change.'

His expression said, '*Can I go now?*' but she had not finished.

'Brian gave his life for that money. He can't be replaced, but you can try to make sure that things turn out as he'd've wanted them. That's the least you can do. If you turn away from Treesa, you'll break her heart – and all over some bloody silly idea that the man should be the sole provider. You think you're such a man, Terry, a man of principle. But you're letting every little street-carrier gossip in Belgate run your life for you. You're running scared in case one of them says you've feathered your nest.'

She had one final shot. 'After David died I was scared if a man even knocked on my door. "What will they say?" I thought. "Mustn't upset them." And then I grew up. I do what I like now, not because I don't care but because I value my own opinion more than the say-so of Tom, Dick and Harry.'

She had run out of steam and they both knew it. She picked up her bag. 'I won't be too late. Martin knows what's for supper.'

She was almost out of the door when he spoke. 'Thanks for the telling off.' There was a rueful note in his voice that surprised her.

'Did it do any good, Terry, that's the point?'

He shrugged. 'We'll just have to wait and see.'

She felt excited as she drove into Sunderland. Perhaps she had had the desired effect? He and Treesa might be happy ever after, and tonight her own fate might be settled . . . if they could agree terms. Perhaps he would move North; you never knew.

Jim was standing at the bar and she thought once again how ordinary he was until he smiled. Then he was devastating. She sipped her sherry and wondered if the alcohol had gone straight to her brain. Still, he was special to Martin, that was for sure.

They talked of the children, of the fall in oil prices, the Royal engagement, and a dozen other news items. Jim was quieter than usual, which increased her conviction that tonight was not purely a social occasion. She slipped her hand into his arm as they walked to the restaurant. 'We fit,' she thought again. 'It feels right.'

She ordered her favourite Kashmiri chicken, and ate it with gusto. She said no to dessert but accepted coffee. 'Fran,' he said, putting his coffee spoon carefully back in place. 'Fran. There's something I must say now, before I lose my nerve.'

She knew it was not a proposal. He had taken the old suede-backed volume of *A Shropshire Lad* from his pocket and was pushing it across the table. 'I brought that back. I knew it was precious.'

She knew, then, what he was going to say. That he couldn't go on without wanting to marry her, that he couldn't face marrying again.

'It's all right,' she said. 'I understand perfectly.'

'They've had so much upset, you see. I couldn't put them through another upheaval. Not just yet. I've got to think of them first; you read such terrible things about traumas in childhood. And we couldn't just marry – that would only be half of it. I'd

have to leave Desmond or you'd never have a chance; he and
Janet would see to that. I've thought and thought. I want you,
Fran, but for your sake . . . and the kids, all three of them . . . I
know how it has to be.'

He would have walked her back to the car but her refusal was
firm. 'No thanks, Jim. If you don't mind . . .' She held out her
hand. 'Goodbye. It's been really nice. I mean that. And thanks
for all you've done for Martin.'

He was shaking his head. 'I'm sorry. Can I still keep in touch
. . . for the boy's sake?'

'Of course,' she said. 'I hope you will.'

She felt completely calm, almost as though it didn't matter.
What was important was to get back into the car, that comforting
haven on wheels, without losing dignity.

Driving back to Belgate she wondered what she would say to
Martin. He would hang over the banister: '*Had a good time,
Mam*?' She could hardly tell him the evening had been dire. She
decided to postpone her homecoming – if she left it long enough,
he might be asleep. And Terry was babysitting: he wouldn't mind
if she was late.

The car park loomed up and she swung the wheel, coming to
a halt facing the sea. She had come here often after David died,
to cry in secret, away from Martin's apprehensive eyes. She used
to sit locked in the car, chain-smoking and trying to get a grip on
her emotions. Tonight was different: she felt calm, almost
dispassionate. But she would still give anything for a cigarette!

To take her mind off nicotine she tried to marshall the facts.
She had driven in to Sunderland expecting a proposal. Instead
she had got the old heave-ho. Her lips curved in a grin. Perhaps
she had BO – he was the third man she'd lost. Except that you
couldn't count David, who had really loved her and would have
stayed with her for ever if it had been allowed.

Steve had ditched her, though; he had sat on the side of the
bed, head bowed, and said, 'I'm sorry, Fran. I'm going back to
Jean.' Wives always won in the end – even dead wives like
Dorothy. Her eyes pricked and she felt in her bag for a tissue.
Instead, her fingers encountered the suede cover of the Hous-
man. '*Into my heart an air that kills* . . .' She shut her mind

resolutely on the rest of the poem. Poetry made you maudlin if you didn't watch out. Even Betjeman.

She went back to facts. He had said it was for the children's sake, but he had given himself away. His actual words had been, 'God knows I love you, Fran, but I can't face starting again.' That was it: the crunch! Easier by far to cling to the wreckage of your first love than start, painstakingly, to build a new one. It was fear of the unknown. At first you were mad keen to fill the vacuum. You met someone and you thought, 'This is nice. This is lovely.' But that turned out to be just the beginning. It was afterwards that the doubts began.

He'd made excuses: 'Mother's brought them up so far. I couldn't take it out of her hands, just like that.' She had wondered if she should tell him of the old lady's longing to get back to her own home, but decided against it. How terrible it would be to blow away his excuse and see desperation in his eyes as he sought another.

She turned on the engine and put the car into reverse. It was for the best. He might not have agreed to come north, and she could never have survived beyond the Cleveland Hills; not without Bethel. She was relieved, really, at escaping all the decisions, the traumas, the divided loyalties that would have beset them if they'd gone ahead. Yes, she was relieved. If she kept that in the front of her mind perhaps the pain of never seeing him again would go away.

18

Thursday, 26 June 1986

'I'll be in touch.' The students kissed and hugged, making arrangements to meet to compare notes when they got their postings. Fran joined in, smiling, embracing, promising never to forget; but all she could think of was the train ride to Birmingham and what would come after it.

Gwen walked with her to the car park. 'Did you say goodbye

to Lund? That second-year was hanging around him . . . the one who looks like Angela Rippon. Jenny says she's moved into his flat!'

Fran doubted that Tony would allow anything so restricting, but kept a noncommittal face.

'You can't really believe we did it, can you?' Gwen said, changing the subject.

'No, I can't believe it. At the beginning . . . well, I don't know what I was playing at, but I never seriously thought I'd qualify.' Fran meant what she said.

They had reached the car and Gwen was fumbling for her keys. 'You were still in shock,' she said, 'poor little white-faced thing that you were. We all felt protective towards you . . . and look how you've come on!'

Fran's smile was hollow. Gwen was suggesting that all was well, and all was far from well. It was simply that she had become a better liar. 'Let's hope we both get Broad Street.'

In a moment Gwen would drive away. 'Yes, that would be nice. I'll ring you as soon as I hear.'

Gwen's Ford reversed and then swung for the gates, but Fran kept her smile in place – you never knew about rear-view mirrors. Only when she was safe in her own car could the tears be allowed to flow, and then not for long. Martin would notice red eyes. If he didn't, Bethel would.

She had not been able to believe it at first. When it occurred to her that she might be pregnant she had laughed out loud at the absurdity of the idea. Not now! Not after all the years of trying! Not when it was utterly unacceptable that it should be so!

In the end, after lying dry-eyed and broad awake for three nights, she had driven to Middlesbrough to buy a pregnancy-testing kit in a back-street chemist, and had watched the yellow disc form on the surface with increasing incredulity. After that had come days of indecision. One night she had let herself out of the house and walked the dog down to the beach. It was three o'clock in the morning, and a cruising Panda car passed her, circled, and returned to ask if all was well. She had chattered brightly about insomnia, and the driver had warned her of the dangers of deserted streets before driving away. At any other time she would have been frightened out of her wits. Then, compared to the enormity of what was happening inside her, danger failed to register.

But the walk on the moonlit beach helped to clear her thoughts. The tide was coming in and foam edged gently further and further up towards the tide line. The sea was calm but even so it looked remorseless. No longer the huge, consoling sea of which Jim had spoken. Almost defiantly, she picked up stones and threw them for a dog hardly able to believe his luck. One stone, flatter than the rest, skimmed across the surface, bouncing into the moon's track and out again. She could walk down that moonlit track, easily at first and then with difficulty as the water dragged at her clothes; but if she kept on walking and, once afloat, offered no resistance, it would soon be over.

And then Nee-wan had pawed at her leg for another stone, and she had looked down into the expectant face. He depended on her. So did Martin. She wanted this baby, but she must do what was best for Martin.

At eight o'clock that morning she had got the advert she had clipped from yesterday's paper and dialled the Birmingham number. Five minutes later it was all arranged. 'Termination' was never mentioned, let alone 'abortion'. She would be 'helped'. 'Try not to worry,' the voice said with professional smoothness. She didn't feel worried, she felt quite detached. She had got pad and ballpoint, and begun to make a list of what had to be done.

Now, four days later, all was prepared. She had been 'summoned to the bedside of her aged Aunt Em in Hastings' and Martin was to stay with Treesa while she was away. In two days she would be back and it would be over. Something to be put behind her.

She had never seriously considered telling Jim. That he might have a right to know counted as nothing when set against the thought of what it would do to him. If she was tempted to shout for help she summoned up the thought of his careworn face the first time they had met, and temptation passed. She had allowed him to think she was on the pill, and he had been ready to accept it, as men were always ready to be relieved of responsibility. No, that wasn't fair – she hadn't given him the chance to take responsibility. Anyway, it was immaterial, now.

It was a tragic irony that a baby desperately sought with David had been conceived in a relationship destined to splutter out almost as soon as it had started. She couldn't keep the baby, not in Belgate, not and get a teaching post and explain to Martin and tell Bethel. She was not made of the same stuff as Treesa.

Belgate came into sight and she tried to put it out of her mind. She was going on a trip, then she was going to get a job at Broad Street and never think of the past. But she would have to be careful. Bethel was as sharp as a tack and already a little suspicious. So she must concentrate on the job of packing for herself and for Martin's stay with Treesa, and not think about things that could never be.

Bethel was warming the pot as Fran came into the kitchen. 'Sit down. We'll have five minutes, and then I'll have to get on.' The 'I'll' was accented to suggest the unlikelihood of Fran's getting on with anything of consequence, but Fran was too weary to rise to the bait.

They sat in silence for a while, Bethel occasionally rubbing her temple. 'Got a headache?' Fran asked. 'There's paracetamol in the larder.'

Bethel shook her head. 'I never take rubbish. It's only flitting, anyway. It'll go.' She changed tack. 'You haven't seen that London feller lately!' It was an accusation, not a question. Did she guess?

'No. It was just a friendship. We didn't have much in common.' She was saved by Walter's horn sounding in the street. 'I'll get him,' she said, glad to escape.

Getting the wheelchair up the steps was always difficult. Today, as she felt the tug on her abdominal muscles, she hesitated: there was life there. Then she remembered the pointlessness of caution and tugged until Walter was safely in the kitchen.

'Aye ... where's the tea then? I'm not having a stewed pot.' She smiled, waiting for him to work the old familiar magic, but today the mood was wrong. 'Lost a pound, found a penny?' he said, thrusting forward his head. She smiled more widely but it was useless.

'You're getting more like Sally Bethel every day. Sweet as a battleship.'

Bethel intervened. 'For God's sake, Walter, shut your mouth. The lass's just finished with that college of hers. It's only natural she's a bit upset.' The blue eyes were kind but shrewd as they rested on Fran's face. *Did* she know? Mercifully Walter was on to the subject of the pit, so Fran could pretend to give him her attention.

'Heard the latest? Output per man shift's up to 3.27 tonnes. Maggie must be rubbing her hands. More money to give to her rich friends.'

Bethel struck with lightning ferocity. 'They'll be the same ones that loaned her the £200 million?'

Walter's eyes flicked to Fran. 'What's she on about? £200 million. The poor old woman's wandering.'

He was not to be let off the hook. 'You know what I mean, Walter. The £200 million they lost in the Durham pits in the last two years. Who coughed up that lot?'

Walter decided to change the conversation. 'Did I ever tell you about the poor little trapper lad I started down the pit with?' he asked innocently. 'They set him to pull on the trap every time the ponies came through. Only they never told him the deputy'd fixed a bloody big hook on the back of it for his coat. So the first pony comes through ... wham ... hits the trap, sends it flying. The lad never came up at the end of his shift, and when they looked they found him stuck clean through with the hook, swinging backwards and forwards with the trap.' His look of pathos was a masterpiece.

'You've missed your vocation, Walter,' Bethel said. 'You're a better liar than Ananias. If the facts don't fit, make them up – and if you can't stand the facts, make up a fairy tale. Very nice!'

On a normal day Fran would have been grinning by now, but it was not a normal day. Bethel passed a hand over her forehead and the smooth grey crown of her head, and Fran felt her own head ache in sympathy. She was about to suggest paracetamol again when the phone rang.

'It's me, Min. How was your last day?' Before Fran could tell her she was hurrying on. 'I'm ringing to tell you the good news. Remember that line in nursery lamps I couldn't shift? A pixie and a toadstool? They needed plugs and all the paraphernalia, and it put the punters off. So then Dennis got interested. He's decided to go in for electricals ... well, you know, he's good with his hands. He's going to take half the stall, just on a trial basis ... but it's a start, isn't it? And it's Dennis's thing, that's the best bit. He'll sell batteries, flex, adaptors – do on-the-spot repairs. I know he can make it work.'

Fran was genuinely pleased. 'It's lovely, Min. The best news I've heard today.' She leaned her head against the wall. It was the *only* good news she'd heard today. 'By the way, Min, I'm going to Hastings for a couple of days. Aunt Em's not well ...'

Min expressed sympathy and then talked of practicalities. 'What about Martin? Oh well, if he's going to Treesa he'll be all right. As long as she hasn't got that commie brother-in-law of hers around.' Walter appeared in the kitchen doorway and Fran bade Min a hasty goodbye.

'I'm off before that senile old rattletrap convinces me black's white.'

Fran was helping him negotiate the steps when Martin appeared. 'I hope tea's ready; I'm famished. Hi, Walter. Come to see Bethel?'

Walter reached the pavement. 'I've seen more than enough of her for one day, young sir. Put your shin-pads on if you're going in there. She's bowling bouncers this afternoon!'

Bethel was unexpectedly kind when they got back to the kitchen. 'You sit there, son, and I'll get your tea. And *you* get yersel' upstairs and pack so that you can have a bit time off tonight. You look washed out.'

Bethel must know: that was the only thing that would explain her sudden mildness. But she *couldn't* know! It was only seven weeks, and she had watched herself carefully to give nothing away!

She was still speculating as she took down the tartan grip and began to pack. She had not reached any conclusion when Martin's voice rang out below. 'Mam. Mam. Come quickly. I'm frightened.' He was standing in the hall, his upturned face contorted with fear until it resembled a gargoyle.

'What is it, Martin? What is it – tell me!' Her own voice was rising, screeching in anger. Why was he doing this to her? It wasn't fair!

'It's Bethel, Mam. I didn't do anything. She just turned round and made a funny noise . . .'

Fran was brushing past him and the rest of his words were lost on her. 'Oh God, please God, let it, let it, let it be all right.'

At first she thought the old woman was dead. Her body lay slumped to the floor like an empty suit of clothes. Then she noticed the twitching of the eyelids and kneeled to reach for the pulse. Was that Bethel's heart beating or her own? 'She's still alive, Martin. Now, please, do as I say.' While he ran for the phone she tried to arrange the twisted limbs and put a cushion to the head but there was no response.

While they waited for an ambulance Fran held the hand, flaccid now and cold. 'I need you, Bethel. I need you now.' As if in answer the face twitched again and the eyes opened a crack. 'Bethel? Bethel, I love you, Bethel!'

The old woman's breathing was audible, issuing harshly from lips that were tinged with blue.

'It's all right, Mam.' Martin had got over his fright and was trying to support her. 'It's going to be OK. When they come, they'll have oxygen and all sorts of things.' And then, uncertain once more, 'Is it her heart?'

'I don't know, Martin. I think it is.'

A trickle of saliva had issued from the side of Bethel's mouth and was coursing slowly down her chin. Fran felt a momentary revulsion and then a surge of concern. She wiped it away with her hanky and patted the cold cheek. 'Here's a blanket,' Martin said, and helped her cover Bethel, tucking the coverlet tenderly around her. The next moment the ambulance men were in the room and Fran and Martin were put to one side.

'I'm coming with her,' Fran said and climbed the iron steps.

It was a stroke, a cerebral haemorrhage. As Fran heard the words she was back in that other hospital, with David lying beyond the door. '*I'm sorry,*' the doctor had said, and David had died. This time, however, there was hope.

'We won't be able to tell you anything definite tonight. Let's just keep her alive until morning . . . if we can do that, she's in with a chance. Now, if you can give me some details . . . ?'

As Fran struggled to offer up the facts of Bethel's life, she realized how little she knew of the woman who was closer to her than any other adult human being. When the doctor had gone she made a vow. '*If you let Bethel live, God, I'll make it up to you.*' But even as she bargained, she knew it was useless. It didn't work like that. If Bethel was to die she would die, and all the bribery in the world wouldn't change it. If Bethel died, she herself would be alone. She walked down the echoing hospital corridor, deserted now at seven o'clock in the evening. Without Bethel, there would be no one. Nothing.

There were decisions to make. Tomorrow she was supposed to take the Birmingham train and enter the clinic. She could still go: her presence would neither help nor hinder Bethel's recovery. Even as she acknowledged the fact, she knew that she could not leave now. And if not now, not ever. She would never be strong enough again.

As the tears started, a figure appeared at the end of the corridor. 'All right, all right, I'm here now.' Terry Malone was infinitely comforting, his arms around her like a rock. 'Your Martin came for me, he knew you'd be here on your own. Treesa's with him, and I'm with you. For as long as you want. Is she . . . ?'

Fran was nodding and laughing, wiping eyes and nose in a luxury of relief. 'She's alive. She's got a chance. It's a stroke . . . but Bethel's strong. She is, isn't she?'

It was Terry's turn to laugh. 'By God, it'll be some stroke that carries off Sally Bethel. Some stroke! And now let's get you home.'

19

Fran sat in the church, Martin quivering with excitement beside her. Across the aisle the Malone family were together, silent and reflective except for Gary. He was wearing a grey suit, white shirt and red tie and was acutely conscious of his new elegance. From time to time he shot his cuffs and turned them left and right, just to check. In between he lifted a foot to inspect brand new lace-ups and red fluorescent socks.

The organ played quietly, and now and again a footfall could be heard on the tessellated floor. 'How much longer?' Martin whispered. Down at the front Terry stared stolidly ahead but the neck above the tight white collar was a deeper shade of pink than usual, and occasionally he tugged at the unaccustomed collar as though desperate for air.

Fran was tempted to tug at the waist of her own navy skirt. It had been difficult to get the zip up to the top and it would never have stayed there without a pin. Every time she moved, the waistband bit, reminding her of her pregnant state. Panic rose and was marshalled back into place. '*Live a day at a time,*' that's what Bethel had told her years ago, after David died. '*Live a day at a time. It's as much as you can manage.*'

Now Bethel was lying in a high, white, hospital bed with a honeycomb counterpane, her lips making unintelligible sounds, only the fierce blue eyes betraying the agonized intelligence behind. At least she was still alive, that was the important thing. Sooner or later she would improve and come home, and they would all support one another. They would manage.

Gary Malone slipped from his pew and crossed the aisle. 'I can't come in your car. I have to go in the special one.'

Martin looked slightly peeved. 'We never asked you.'

Gary was not put off. Today his status was too elevated to permit of taking offence. 'Well, I'm only telling you. I'll see you at the reception.'

Fran's lips twitched. Gary's Belgate accent was overlaid with a touch of BBC received speech, as befitted the ceremony. As he returned to his seat Martin moved closer to whisper, 'He's going on as if it was his wedding.'

'Jealousy gets you nowhere,' she whispered back. Martin's eyes met hers, hostile at first and then laughter dawning in them. She reached out and patted his knees, decently covered in new, long grey trousers.

The music changed, and Terry was turning to face his bride. He looked troubled until he caught Treesa's eye, and then he smiled suddenly and was the old irrepressible Terry once more.

Treesa, on her father's arm, was dressed in a powder-blue crêpe dress, draped at the hip and broad-shouldered in true Dallas-Dynasty style. The fair hair was looped back and caught with a blue feathered band, and she carried a white missal with a single orchid attached. The outfit was formal and sophisticated, but the face above it was still the face of a child, a little chubby but serene, as though none of the trials of the last few years had occurred. Fran turned back to the altar as the bridal procession drew abreast. *Please God, let them be happy.*

Suddenly she remembered Brian's delight at the thought of his marriage to Treesa. It should have taken place in this church; instead everyone had gathered here for Brian's funeral. 'Crushed between tubs.' She closed her eyes, and then opened them to glance at Christopher, safe in Mrs Malone's arms. He would not understand as his mother made her marriage vows; for a baby, there were no complications other than hunger and wind. A twelve-year-old was different. Martin's face was rapt as he listened to the service. How was she going to explain the baby? '*Live a day at a time.*' She reached for her hymn-book and joined in, tremulous at first and then hearing her own voice gain strength at the familiar words: 'O perfect Love, all human thought transcending . . .'

The bridal pair disappeared to sign the register, a gaggle of family behind, and the congregation twittered. Martin was buried in the Order of Service and Fran looked around. There was something about a Catholic church, a busy feeling that she did not get from churches of other denominations. The hymn lingered on in her head: 'O perfect Love'. Love of God. God's love. Perfect as man's love never could be. Lately she had thought a lot about love, as difficult to find and hold as it was to define. She was glad when the organ pealed and the bridal procession appeared.

For the first time Fran could see Mr Malone's face. She had wondered if he would come to the wedding, until Treesa had confirmed it. 'They still don't speak, well, not what you'd call speaking, but I put my foot down. I said, "Ask him or else." Terry said, "I'll ask but that's not to say he'll come," so I said, "Leave it to me if he says no. I'll see to it." '

And see to it she had. Mr Malone was there in a dark three-piece suit, Treesa's mother on his arm in navy polka dots. They didn't speak on their way down the aisle but Mrs Carruthers' expression spoke volumes, especially when Gary, the youngest Malone, began to thread his way through the procession until he was immediately behind bride and groom. His father made an effort to grab his jacket and restrain him but in vain. Mrs Carruthers sniffed and rolled her eyes at the bride's side of the congregation to indicate that this was typical Malone behaviour and hasn't our Treesa burned her boats?

The pews began to empty and fall in behind.

The reception was held in the upper room of the Half Moon – chicken portions and salad, bread buns and bowls of beetroot, fresh cream trifles topped with hundreds and thousands in waxed paper cups, and a paper napkin by every plate emblazoned with the names of bride and groom in silver lettering.

'Very nice,' Mrs Carruthers said when it was over and she joined Fran for a chat. 'Not what I'd've wished, but our Treesa's turned very headstrong. Of course, she does what she's told now: he's got the upper hand.'

Fran glanced across to where Terry, looking distinctly hen-pecked, was obeying Treesa's instructions and cutting the cake. 'Do you think so?' she said. 'I'd've said Treesa would wear the pants. Terry'll huff and puff, but Treesa'll win in the end.'

It was too much for Treesa's mother. 'I must get round. You have to make yourself pleasant, don't you?'

Fran was relaxing into her chair when she heard Martin's whisper. 'She'll have a job!'

For anyone else she'd have told him not to be cheeky. Mrs
Carruthers was different. 'You can say that again,' she said.

She had almost forgotten her own problems, but now heart-
burn rose up to remind her. Soon she would have to make a plan
– who to tell and how, where to go and when. She couldn't live
from day to day for ever. There was a banging from the top table
and she turned her head.

Terry's best man was calling for order and making the usual
corny jokes. Then Terry rose to his feet. 'I would like to thank
Treesa's mam and dad for giving me such a lovely lass for a
bride . . .' Treesa's eyes were fixed on his face and Fran got the
impression their expression was steely. Terry swallowed and
looked down at the paper he held in his fist. 'And my mam and
dad for everything they've done for me, bringing me up.' Fran's
eyes flicked to the Malones. She was beaming above her petrol-
blue Crimplene; he looked ready to cry. Treesa sat back, task
completed.

'Are they friends now?' Martin whispered and Fran nodded.

'They will be after this . . . or Treesa'll want to know why.'
Martin's eyes met hers in perfect understanding.

At Treesa's request, Fran went to help her change. 'I've done
it now,' Treesa said as Fran tugged her free of the powder-blue
dress.

'You're not sorry?'

Treesa shook her head. 'No, not now. It's all right. I don't
know why, but it is.'

Fran nodded. She knew the feeling.

'I used to think Terry was tough and Brian was the quiet one.
You know, not pushy. And then I got to know Terry and it's all
talk. He needs me more than Brian did . . . Brian could always
cope. Everyone liked him. Terry makes a noise but half the time
he's scared.'

'You mean he's vulnerable?'

Treesa nodded. 'Yes, that's it exactly. Anyway, he's got me
now. And Christopher. We'll see him all right.' She fastened the
last button of her pink blouse. 'I've packed everything Christopher needs. I'm glad it's you having him. Me mam offered, but
she'd only upcast it after, and Terry's mam's got her hands full.

I know he'll be all right with you. I said he could stop with his gran till bedtime. Is that OK?'

Fran nodded. 'That's fine. I want to pop over to see Bethel when we leave. I won't get in as often while I have Christopher, so I'll go today.'

Treesa was stepping into the skirt of her grey going-away suit. 'How is she?'

Fran shrugged. 'Just the same. I think she knows me but I'm not sure.' To her horror her voice had an ominous break in it. She was alone and pregnant and would never look as Treesa looked now, dressing for her bridegroom to carry her away.

'I know,' Treesa said, holding out arms to embrace her. 'I know what she means to you . . . but it's not hopeless. You'll see. They can do a lot now.'

Fran felt ashamed. 'I know. I'm sorry. I shouldn't do this, today of all days.'

Treesa's arms were comforting as Bethel's arms would have comforted once she got over her shock at the news. She felt the truth trembling on her lips: '*I'm pregnant Treesa. And abandoned. And bloody frightened.*' Instead she smiled and detached herself. 'I ought to be shot, behaving like this on your wedding day. I'm sure she'll pick up. Come on, let's not keep everyone waiting.'

Treesa was grinning. 'You know something, this is the first day I've known Terry that he hasn't mentioned politics!'

Fran laughed. 'Maybe he'll give it up now he's a married man.'

Treesa shook her head. 'Nee chance!'

They went off in a haze of confetti and a rattling of Ostermilk tins. 'Keep it up, Terry,' the best man roared to an accompaniment of ribald laughter.

'They're coarse, aren't they?' Mrs Carruthers said. 'And going to Scarborough. I ask you! At this time of year.'

Fran didn't reply. Her eyes were fixed on the bridal car, where Terry's hand had emerged from the side window and gripped his father's outstretched hand. The perfect ending. 'It's been a lovely wedding,' Fran said, and her tones were fervent. 'And I love Scarborough. At any time of year.'

Mrs Carruthers had missed the hand-shaking, and would not have perceived its significance if she had seen it, but she had a parting shot. 'I suppose it's what you're used to . . . we're so used to Spain that I can't see the point of holidays at home. But if it's all you can afford . . .'

There were pictures of Prince Andrew and Fergie in the shop windows as Fran drove through Sunderland. Less than a week to their wedding. There would be crowds in the streets and a world audience, but no more love than there had been today.

'I must be glad for them,' she said aloud. They would be away for three days, and when they returned she could confide in them. They would understand, but they couldn't help. No one could help. She must carry the baby alone, support it alone, care for Bethel, and make sure Martin was not the one to suffer.

He had offered to come to the hospital with her today but she had persuaded him to stay with Gary. 'Well, I'm coming next time. I want to tell Bethel to get a move on and get better.'

But Bethel was deaf to exhortations, and dead almost, except for the agitated eyes. Fran sat by her bed and began to talk. 'It was a lovely wedding. You'd've liked her dress. And Terry was so good. Like a lamb. Martin sends his love. And Walter. He's his usual self, full of beans.' In truth Walter was a shadow, seldom venturing out and devoid of his usual fire. He had been like that since Fran had broken the news, simply shaking his head and saying, 'Not Sally Bethel. Not Sally,' as though denial would alter fact.

'We all miss you, Bethel.' The hands laid on the turned-back sheet were unnaturally white and blue-veined, the nails in need of trimming. 'Oh Bethel, please get better.'

In the next bed a white-haired woman in a blue bed jacket was talking incessantly, although there was no one to hear. Across the aisle an old woman rocked back and forwards in an armchair, a doll in her arms, her skirt above her knees to reveal bare white thighs and lisle stockings held up by elastic garters.

Fran turned back to Bethel. 'I'm going to get you out of here, Bethel. Home with me . . . and Martin. You'll get better there.'

A tear had formed in the corner of the old woman's eye and Fran removed it with a fingertip. A nurse loomed up.

'All right, Sally? Not long till tea-time.' She gave Fran a quick professional smile. 'Doctor's very satisfied with her. And she's a good girl, aren't you, Sally?' She twitched the pillow into place, causing Bethel's hair to straggle across the pillow. 'We'll have to get this cut, won't we, when the hairdresser comes round.'

In the other beds the women had bobbed hair, caught at the sides with clips or little girl's slides in pink and blue. Fran heard her own voice, surprisingly firm. 'I don't think she'd like her hair cut. And I'm making arrangements to have her with me, so you really don't need to bother.'

The nurse smiled again, a lighthouse grin that came and went. 'Well, we don't need to worry about it now, do we?' Another flash, and she was gone.

'I'll be back, Bethel. I'll come soon.' The face against the pillow looked smaller, somehow diminished, the eyes set further back. The lips twitched and pouted, and Fran bent closer. 'Lass ...' and then again ... 'lass'. But it had been a word. That was something.

As she left the ward she passed a side-ward, from inside which came a high-pitched voice, almost mechanical in repetition. 'Is there anybody there? Is there anybody there?' Fran turned and looked back along the corridor but there was no sign of a nurse. 'Is there anybody there?' She put her head through the door but the figure in the bed took no notice. 'Is there anybody there?' Her eyes were fixed on the facing wall.

Fran was about to withdraw, accepting there was nothing to be done, but something in the face caught her attention. It couldn't be ... except that the chart at the end of the bed confirmed that it was. '*Hilda Fenbow. Age 79.*' Miss Fenbow! Physics and Chemistry Fenbow who had terrorized Fran during her first year at Bede and then, mercifully, retired. Fran had hated and feared the woman, loathed the harsh voice and the cutting remarks that could reduce the most confident pupil to a jelly.

'Is there anybody there?'

Fran moved to the bedside. 'Miss Fenbow?' The eyes remained on the wall but the hands flew to Fran's arm and took possession. 'I'm here, Miss Fenbow.'

The head turned and the voice dropped to a whisper. 'Can

you get my cardigan. I'm very cold. They won't get me my cardigan. The mohair one that Ivy made.'

The bobbed hair had escaped the slide and straggled the forehead. Fran stroked it back and secured it. Outside, the July sun was still high, the room like an oven. The mohair cardigan lay across the coverlet, and she picked it up and arranged it around the thin shoulders. 'I want the mohair cardigan.' She was plucking it away as she spoke.

Fran stroked her arm. 'Wear this for a moment, until I can find the mohair one. The one that Ivy made.' The hands ceased to pluck. 'I'll go and find it now.'

As she neared the door to the corridor the voice started again. 'Is there anybody there?'

20

Friday, 25 July 1986

The door was double glazed and revealed a panelled hall. 'Posh,' Fran thought and then . . . 'Eve *will* be choked!'

Dennis came to greet and draw her in. 'Give us a kiss, Franny. I haven't seen you for an age.'

She wanted to put her head on his chest and give way but it wouldn't do. Instead she rearranged her shawl, knotting it at her waist. She had decided to wear it in case of prying eyes. She was thicker around the waist now and the zip of her dress proclaimed it.

'Come into the kitchen for a drink and then we'll go in. You've had a tough time lately and we want you to enjoy tonight.' He picked up a bottle. 'White?'

She nodded. 'Lovely.'

He held out the glass. 'It's not the greatest vintage, but it's wet. It's taken me years to realize what a lot of mumbo-jumbo is talked about wine. There are three categories, Fran: nice, foul, and bearable. This is bearable coming nice. I got it at cost from a guy at the market. Wheels within wheels.'

Fran sipped. 'It's gorgeous. Where's Min?'

Dennis nodded towards the door. 'In the living room, showing off. She looks like the Cheshire cat, and Eve resembles Mary Queen of Scots being stoic on the block.'

Fran laughed. 'I can imagine.'

Dennis had perched on the table, one foot on a chair. 'We've been damned lucky, haven't we? I thought it was going to be all downhill. Instead, we've got this place for a year. Min's making a bob or two, keeping the wolf at the garden gate, and I'm getting a foot in on the electrical side. I still can't see us making a living from it, but it's better than nothing and you never know. We could be lucky.'

'You deserve some luck. You've both been brave.' Besides, something had to go right for someone, some time. It couldn't all be black.

'Min's been brave! I never knew she had it in her, Fran. Right from the word go. Not a word of reproach, not, "What are we going to do?" – just, "Let's get on with it."' He sipped his drink. 'It teaches you, a thing like this. What your partner's really like. Who your friends are. You'll see a few faces missing in there tonight.'

'You mean they haven't come?'

Dennis chuckled. 'I mean they weren't asked! People we've been friends with for years, off into the undergrowth at the first hint of trouble. They want back in now but I'll see them in hell first. There was a guy we'd done business with for years. We made him, if I'm honest. Dad gave him his start, then he set up on his own. We owed him two hundred quid. Two hundred quid! He was never off the phone. "You must've known," he said, as though we'd screwed him deliberately. And Harold was very careful until he saw how things were going.' There was hurt in Dennis's voice now, and Fran couldn't think of anything to say.

'Anyway.' Dennis was standing up and holding out his arms. 'You were a brick, Franny.' He hugged her. 'You should hear Min about it. And remember, if you ever need a friend . . . two friends . . . you know where to come.'

As Fran followed him through to the living room, she won-

dered if he knew how soon she would have to take him up on his
offer. And then she was caught up in the comedy of Min seeing
her day with Eve, and it was all too delicious for anything else to
matter.

'I'm going to let it drop now,' Min said as they made coffee.
'I've shown her the pool, both bathrooms, the original oil in the
study by the man who painted Princess Margaret, and I've pulled
out every unit in here like Felicity Kendal in that advert. Now
I'm going to rise above revenge, sweet as it is, and return to my
usual sunny self. Bring the tray, Fran, and don't forget to tell
them the cups are Wedgwood.'

The party was deep in discussion of the Royal wedding.
Fergie, by common consent, had looked stunning, the bride-
groom suitably reverent, and the Queen noticeably pleased.
'Relieved!' someone said. 'Fergie'll sort him out.'

Fran moved about with the tray. 'How's Martin?' someone
asked, and Fran glanced at the clock. He had been alone now
for two hours, without a minder for the first time in his life.
'Please mam, I'm twelve now. And there's the telephone if I need you.'
So she had given in, expecting to be worried to death. Instead
she had hardly given it a thought.

'He's fine,' she said firmly, and moved on.

Eve accepted a cup of coffee and lowered her voice. 'I need
this to take away the taste of that awful wine.' She sipped. 'You'd
never think they hadn't a bean, would you? Entertaining! Look at
Harold, his face is a study – he knows the true state of affairs. If
they have any money they should be putting it aside, not splashing
it on a party.'

Fran was tempted to let it go but overcame the temptation. 'I
think they were right to give a party for their friends, Eve.' She
put emphasis on the last word. 'And anyway, the food's home-
made. Min must have baked and baked. Of course, she's got that
fabulous kitchen, so I suppose it was easy. You and I have to
struggle with the basics.' As she moved on she reproached
herself for bitchery, but she still couldn't repress the feeling of a
job well done.

'I'm going in to see your Bethel soon,' Min said as they saw

Fran to her car. 'Ring me and let me know when and what ward and everything. And what she'd like taken in.'

Fran nodded. Useless to say there was nothing Bethel could appreciate. If she began on that she'd end up crying.

As she drove home she tried to think things out. It was 25 July; the baby was due in February. If she took Bethel out of hospital now, would she be able to cope later on in her pregnancy? Treesa would help, and Terry, but there were limits. And before she did anything, she must tell Martin about the baby. Before someone else did. Before, for all she knew, he noticed for himself. Then there was Walter – something would have to be done for Walter, and there was no one else but her.

The sky to the west was still tinged with pink, with clouds like mother-of-pearl. If Martin had not been alone she would have stayed in the car park for a while, but it was time she was home. She must be careful too, showing pride that he had coped but not so much pride that it looked as though she hadn't expected him to manage on his own.

She put the car away and let herself into the yard. Light filtered through the living-room curtains, and she bit her lip. He had promised to go to bed at ten. Perhaps he had, and had simply left the light on to welcome her? There was no frenzied dog in the kitchen when she let herself in, so he was in the living room too. She walked through the hall and pushed open the door. The television was on, but it was not Martin who rose to greet her. It was Jim. 'Hello,' he said.

She was casting around for an adequate reply when she heard Martin call from the landing. He was hanging over the banisters, bright-eyed. 'Jim's here!'

She tried to keep calm. 'Yes, I know. Now go to bed.' She waited until his bedroom door was shut before she went in to face Jim.

'I've come back, Fran.' She shook her head in puzzlement. He moved forward. 'I don't know if we can work things out. I only know I can't live without you. Not now.'

Nee-wan was looking from one to another, expecting action. 'Sit down, dog,' she said.

There was no temptation to tell him, and she mustn't let anything slip. 'I think I'd like a drink. Shall I get you one?' If he moved forward and touched her, she would tell him. She could feel it in her chest, tears that would break through as a wail if she let them come.

He turned back to his chair. 'Yes please. Whisky, if you've got it.'

As she poured the drinks, she felt flat – that was all. Flat, uninterested, and perhaps a little angry. In fact, very angry! Walk out, walk in again: that was what men did. It was women who had to stay, tied to the fruit of a relationship as securely as branch to tree.

'I've been thinking, Fran. I could come north, if that's what you want? There are jobs up here if you look.' He was leaning forward in an effort to convince her.

'What about Desmond?' There was a taunting quality in her voice that she didn't like but couldn't help. 'He'd never let you get away from him, or be based elsewhere but London. Be realistic.'

Jim was looking hurt, and there was a devil rising up in her, a she-devil who wanted revenge for all the weeks of pain.

He had come back to her, that was what mattered. Except that it didn't matter. She was tired and she wanted him out of her house. 'We can't talk now, Jim. It's late and Martin probably has his ear to the door. There are lots of things you don't know about. Bethel's in hospital and I have to take her in here as soon as she's well enough to leave. And besides . . .' She would have listed other reasons, inventing them if necessary, but he had set down his glass to interrupt.

'Martin told me. How is she?' He had met Bethel several times, and concern showed in his face.

'She's had a stroke, a bad one . . . but that's beside the point. What about the children? How would Kevin and Barbara survive a move up here? I won't uproot Martin, not now.'

She was building a wall, feeling safer with each added brick. Safer and more despairing with each dollop of mortar, each ring of the trowel. 'We can talk another time. If you want to.' Her tone suggested, '*If there's any point*', but she left it unsaid.

She searched his face for signs of relief. She was setting him free, making it easy, so he should be bloody grateful! Her fingers were hurting and she realized she was squeezing the stem of her glass almost to snapping point. For a moment, as she tried to relax her hands, she contemplated breaking the news. '*Oh, and by the way, I'm pregnant. Now you're sure to scuttle and run.*' Only she mustn't tell him.

'I never said it would be easy. Do you think I don't see all the problems? I don't think I've slept two consecutive hours since we split up. But if there's a will, Frances . . . if we want it enough, we can find a way round everything.'

He was not going to give way. There was an air of dogged determination about him that reminded her of Martin at his most persistent. She must get him out of the house. All she wanted was to undo the zip now biting into her flesh, take off the too-tight bra, put on her towelling robe, and curl up somewhere, in the dark.

'I can't see the point, but if you've made up your mind we can meet tomorrow.'

He was getting up to go and she hadn't told him. Clever Frances. Brave Frances. Broad-shouldered Frances, who needed no help from anyone. Or any help from no one.

When she had bolted the door behind him she sat on the bottom rung of the stairs and cried until the dog brought comfort, and a reminder that Martin was probably awake upstairs and must not see her like this.

21

Saturday, 26 July 1986

She had intended to miss the class reunion but now it would serve her purpose. She began to get ready at four o'clock, washing her hair and letting it dry free, until it frizzed around her face. They were all meeting in the town-centre hotel and then going on to a restaurant. 'Not that I'll eat much,' Gwen had said on the phone last week. 'I'm trying to lose a stone.'

For once Gwen's promises to diet failed to raise a smile. 'What time?' Fran had asked without interest, because there was no way she could face them, feeling as she did.

Now, though, it was different. After weeks of drifting, postponing thought of the future let alone planning, she had a purpose! It had come to her in the night while she thought over Jim's insistence that they should meet.

She *would* meet him, looking her best, even blooming. And then she would leave him, as he had left her. Best of all, she would leave him to go to a party, so that he was discarded like so much used wrapping paper. Never mind that she shrank from the pub, the happy faces of her fellow students secure in their new jobs. It would have to be endured. She wasn't a good enough liar simply to pretend to Jim that she was going.

She felt almost excited as she put on her make-up. Lilac eyeshadow to match the cotton summer dress that floated mercifully free of her waist, pale lipstick outlined with darker pencil, two coats of mascara, and a third dip to emphasize her brows. God bless Estée Lauder, she thought as she surveyed the finished effect. She looked tarty but delectable . . . or as delectable as she was ever likely to look. Pregnancy had rounded her cheekbones and brightened eyes that glowed now with the desire for revenge. Tit for tat. Damn Jim for having reduced her to this charade.

She sat on the edge of the bath, suddenly aghast at what she was doing. It didn't make sense. But even as reason struggled to reassert itself she stood up. If she started to think, she would wind up going meekly to meet him, confessing all, and ending up in Twickenham with Desmond and Janet to oversee her rehabilitation from the state of fallen woman. She took one last look in the mirror and went in search of her hoop earrings.

He was waiting in the foyer, rising unsmiling to greet her. 'Thanks for coming.' He followed her through to the cocktail bar, dark and cool after the sunlit streets, so that she shivered momentarily, regretting her bared arms.

They carried their drinks to an alcove, although the bar was almost empty. She felt nervous now but still determined. Driving

to Sunderland she had considered his right to know about the
baby, and decided her right to keep the truth to herself was
greater. He didn't deserve to know – as long as she remembered
that, all would be well. 'Cutting off your nose to spite your face',
that's what Bethel would have said; but it had gone too far to
stop now.

'You look nice.'

Here it was, the opportunity. 'Yes,' she said, 'I'm going on to
a party.' She saw the shot register in a tightening of his lips, but
he didn't comment.

'I suppose you think I've got a nerve,' he said at last. 'Waltzing
out, waltzing back. It wasn't quite that simple.' His expression
confirmed his words.

'No, Jim, I don't think it was simple for either of us. But I'm
not sure there's anything we can do about it, either.'

'I love you, Fran. I knew that before, but I thought it wasn't
enough to cope with all the aggro. Now I know it is.' He put his
hand over hers. 'I love you a lot. And Martin. And we can make
something of it, I know we can.'

If she told him now, what would his reaction be? Concern or
panic? She could bear neither.

'I'll leave Desmond's business . . . if I'm honest, I've never
been happy there . . . and the kids could settle up here. They're
young enough to adjust.'

She was listening but somehow not comprehending. It was as
though a safety mechanism had come into play, blotting out
feeling. Words that would have meant so much a while ago were
now just words. '*Sound and fury, signifying nothing.*' At times of
stress forgotten phrases always popped up into her mind, and
they were not always appropriate. He was actually speaking
quietly and his words signified a great deal. The faulty reception
was in her. She withdrew her hand.

'I'm not angry, Jim. I understand how you felt, I always did.
But the fact remains that we each have our separate lives. I don't
see how we can get over that.' She would have to listen to his
arguments, keep up her own end. And then go to the Saracen,
laughing, smiling . . . '*Yes, it's marvellous, isn't it? All of us getting
schools. Good old LEA.*' She would have to watch out for Gwen,

though. Gwen was shrewd. Afterwards she could retreat, hide away in the car, and let go.

Her eyes flicked to the clock: ten past seven. Early evening, and already she was exhausted. Too exhausted to be angry, but the anger was there, whispering away. Not at Jim or the child inside her, not at men in general, or society, or any other recognizable entity. It was fate which had placed so many hurdles in her path, and left her so ill-equipped to deal with them. It was seldom others who caused your troubles, more the luck of the draw.

'I must go, Jim.' She was reaching for her bag. 'I'm meeting Gwen and the others from college in the Saracen. We're having a celebration. We've all been given teaching posts. I qualified, you know. You've never asked.'

The rebuke went home. 'I'm sorry. Congratulations. You've done well.' He pushed back his chair. 'I'll come with you. They won't mind, will they?'

She panicked. If he came with her she could never keep it up. 'Sorry, but I'm meeting someone there. Tony Lund. You remember Tony, my sociology tutor? I told you about him.' She didn't need to add 'He was my lover'; Jim was remembering all too well. He was the only man she had ever been able to talk to properly. She had confessed her affair with Tony and he had smiled it away. Now he didn't smile.

'I'm sorry,' he said. 'I should have realized.'

He offered to walk her to the car but she left him in the foyer. 'We'll be in touch. Martin will always be pleased to hear from you.'

Relief carried her out into the summer evening and through three sets of traffic lights to the Saracen. After that she was engulfed in chat. 'I got Broad Street. What about you?' 'Pass those drinks, Steve ... don't just stand there.' 'Hi, Frances. How've you been?'

'I hoped we'd get on the same staff,' Gwen said, when the hubbub subsided. 'Still, one of us can move eventually.' She would have to tell Gwen soon, watch the plump face quiver with concern. Or disapproval. You could never gauge reactions, not even with your friends.

'How's Bethel?' Gwen said. 'And that lad of yours? Enjoying his hols?'

Fran relaxed: Bethel and Martin were safe ground. She was about to reply when she saw Tony Lund, surrounded by female students still anxious to bask in his smile.

'I forgot to tell you lover boy was here,' Gwen said, following her eyes. 'No show without Punch, I suppose.'

Fran managed to avoid Tony. It wasn't difficult, for his eyes flicked over her as though she were a fixture. At the height of their love-making he had always used the same words – 'Oh darling, darling, Fran.' So much for passion!

She was deep in conversation when Jenny, discussing how friendly would be friendly enough with your first class, when she saw Jim come in and take a seat at the bar. At first she thought it was just a terrible coincidence, and then she remembered she had mentioned the name of the pub.

So he'd come deliberately! Emotions chased around in her head. He cared, cared enough to gate-crash. He had a cheek, barging in on her affairs! Worst of all, he would find her out in a lie: '*I'm meeting Tony. You remember Tony Lund?*' You always paid for lies. Her mother had told her that years ago and it was true.

She felt tears prick her eyes at the thought of her mother – a lifetime away, when everything had been easy, when she had played by the rules and been safe. She realized that her hand had dropped to her belly, the age-old protective gesture of the pregnant woman. She looked around, certain everyone's eyes would be on her, knowing everything. But no one was watching her except Jim, and there was no dawning knowledge in his eyes, only a steely determination. In another minute he would walk towards her and it would all be out of her hands.

She wanted to go home but if she went now Jim would follow and it would all begin again. 'Excuse me,' she said to Jenny and moved purposefully to the group around Tony.

One by one the others dropped away, some of them knowing what had gone on before, others aware of the chemistry. 'Fran. Long time no see.' He was keeping it light but his eyes were wary.

She plunged in. 'Tony! I couldn't let you go without saying goodbye.'

His eyes were like sea-washed glass, but she fixed them with her own, batting her lashes in spite of the weary contempt on his face.

'*Please God, let it be over soon.*' When she was safe in the car she would wind up all the windows and curl up and not think. In the meantime, she must smile and flirt until the stranger sitting at the bar got the message. Impossible to believe she had shared his bed. He was a stranger now, a glowering man in a dark suit, moving his glass from hand to hand and never taking his eyes off her.

Desperation made her bold. She swayed towards Tony, putting up a hand to finger the lapel of his jacket. It was enough. It took only a moment for Jim to swing his legs from the stool and shoulder his way to the door, but it seemed much longer. She made no farewell to Tony, simply turned away. It was five minutes to eight. At eight o'clock she could go home.

She made her excuses to Gwen, pleading an upset tummy. 'I'll ring you tomorrow.' As she crossed the foyer she felt her troubles slipping away. It would be lovely to be home, to begin again. It was always all right if you could get home.

Outside, the light was going and the sky was pearly. She felt suddenly free, energetic enough to walk to Belgate if she had to . . . but the car was there, waiting to be collected. She didn't need to hide in it now. She had handled things. No point in thinking how different it could have been. She had done it all for the best, that was the important thing.

She was fitting her key into the lock when he spoke from behind. 'I knew you'd have to come back to the car. I banked on him having his car with him. I'm sorry, Fran, but I only have another day here. I can't afford to be over-scrupulous.'

He climbed into the car and sat down beside her. 'I won't keep you long, Fran, but you must hear me out. I'm sure he'll wait five minutes.'

For a few seconds she hesitated, wondering if she could maintain the charade. And then she felt herself starting to laugh, and then to cry, and only ceased to hiccup when he took her by the forearms and shook her.

'Fran? Fran, what is it? For God's sake pull yourself together . . . if he means that much I'll get out of the way.' It was too delicious an irony, that he was preparing to go when every single particle of her being was longing for him to stay.

'I don't want him,' she said calmly, as he made to get out of the car. 'I don't even like him. I did it to make you pay. It wasn't much fun for me,' she finished lamely, and saw his look of outrage give way to a twitch of the lips.

'Oh, Fran,' he said at last. 'We're a pair of silly buggers, aren't we?'

22

Sunday, 27 July 1986

Fran spent the next morning in a half-pleasant, half-painful doze. Thinking of her bizarre behaviour the evening before made her cringe but she could understand it. She should have realized what lay behind that irrational anger and desire to pay back Jim; she had experienced anger before, in the aftermath of David's death, a wild, unreasoning rage that was really an antidote to fear. Be mad, and you could avoid total collapse, you were fuelled by a burst of adrenaline that would carry you forward regardless. She had seen it briefly in Min after their downfall, but Min had turned it to good use and become an entrepreneur.

All the same, excuse it as she might, the thought of making up to Tony Lund and feeding that fat ego was almost unbearable. She had hurt Jim too and risked ruining their relationship beyond repair, which had been daft.

Not quite daft enough, though, to give away her secret. She knew herself too well for that. If she had told him about the baby she would ever after believe he had stayed with her out of pity or a bad conscience. She wanted so much to believe he loved her as she loved him, madly and without reason. So she had kept quiet for the time being.

At two o'clock she roused herself. The lunch plates were still in the sink but first she must rinse her eyes, sore after a sleepless night.

She was crossing the hall when the phone rang.

'Mrs Drummond? I'm sorry to tell you Mrs Bethel is rather poorly. If you're thinking of visiting, I'd make it soon.'

Her ears were singing, the terrible hell sounds that come with the unbearable; and then Martin was coming through the kitchen doorway and taking the phone. 'They've rung off, Mam. What's wrong?'

'It's Bethel, darling. She's worse. They want me to go now.' She was trying to think, but her thoughts were woolly, running here and there like sheep, defying efforts to round them up.

'We need to tell Walter,' he said . . . 'and Terry.' His mouth was trembling but his voice was firm, and she was grateful.

'Yes, that's a clever boy. Can you tell them if I go?'

He shook his head. 'I'm coming with you. We can call and tell them on the way.'

She didn't argue. He had earned his place. Instead she concentrated on her driving, changing gear scrupulously at corners and using her mirrors. It was at times like this you made mistakes.

Terry's face clouded at the news. Fran was still behind the wheel but she could see him in the doorway. 'He's going to take care of everything,' Martin said, sliding back into his seat. 'I gave him my key, and he'll see to the dog and check the plugs and everything.'

Fran felt her own lips tremble. 'Thank you. That was sensible.' She didn't gush. The moment your son became a man was too important for that.

She left him in the car when she went in to Walter. 'It's not good news. She's very ill. Some kind of chest infection. I think you should come, Walter.' She knew it was hopeless from the set of his body, the hands on the arms of the chair as though carved from stone.

'There's no point, lass. Besides, I'm far ower old for hospitals. Let's know how it goes.'

She wanted to comfort him, but there was absolutely nothing she could say.

'I'll go in first,' she told Martin when they reached the ward. 'And then I'll come for you.'

The sister was bustling and impersonal. 'We've moved her to a side-ward. You can stay as long as you like.' There were tiny gold stars in her ears above the uniform collar and energy seemed to surround her like an aura. 'I wouldn't bring the child in, if I were you. I'm not saying no, but I don't advise it. She's his grandmother, is she?'

She was not expecting an answer but Fran gave one. 'Yes,' she said, 'she's his grandma.'

Bethel looked tiny against the pillow, a tiny, fretful doll of a woman who was almost a stranger. Outside the sun was shining and a painter was covering a window frame with white paint. To and fro his arm went, to and fro.

'Bethel?' She bent to the bed, hoping for an answer, but none came. She closed her eyes, trying to summon up the real Bethel. *'I went into service down London when I left school. I reckoned I might as well be paid for running after folks as do it for nothing.'* She had been the eldest of four, but three brothers had died in their youth, two in the war, one in the pit . . . the same pit that had robbed her of her husband. *'I worked in one house in Chelsea . . . she says, "I can't have a maid called Sally. You'll have to be Jane!" They were shouting "Jane" all round the house and I never budged. I let on I was daft and they gave in.'*

Fran realized she was smiling. If the sister looked in she would think her mad. But Bethel had been so funny. The past tense slipped from her and did not seem out of place. The figure in the bed was too still, too gentle: that had never been Bethel's way. When the strike was on she had taken on Margot, left-wing Margot of the feminist views. *'How many bellies will you fill with your token-this and token-that? You'll watch this strike drag on week after week because it suits your purpose. Get to hell out of it, before I forget I'm a lady and bash the life out of you.'* She had stood at the sink, arms akimbo, ready to take on the world.

'Oh Bethel, Bethel. I need you, Bethel.' She was crying now, wallowing in self pity . . . and then Martin was beside her, his arms round her shoulders.

'Come on, Mam. She wouldn't want you to cry.'

They sat on, watching over the figure in the bed until the restless eyelids ceased to twitch and the breathing slowed to a faint intake at intervals that drew further and further apart. 'I think you should go and find the sister now,' Fran said. 'She ought to check.'

There was one last thing to do before he came back. She took the hand from the coverlet and held it between her own. 'Thank you for everything, my darling. And thank you for saving my baby.' There was a small sigh from the bed. A faint coincidence, that was all.

'I think it's over,' Fran said when the sister came in.

'It's all right to cry,' she told Martin, when they were safe in the car. He was bearing up but now and again a gulp came and caught him unaware. She remembered that from childhood, when you had been naughty and punished and cried with remorse until you were comforted. 'Stop crying,' her mother would say, and she would try to obey but the gulp would overcome her.

She found she was taking the road to the hill – Tunstall Hill, high above Sunderland. 'My father used to bring me here,' she said when they had left the car and walked to the summit. 'We used to look out over the town and count the church spires. I think there were thirteen or fourteen . . . but it might have been more.' In the distance the cranes still marked the dockside. 'He used to say this was the greatest shipbuilding town in the world.'

'And was it?' Martin asked.

Fran smiled. 'I don't know, but it was a bit of a cheat, anyway, because he never told me about the shipbuilding cities. But he made me proud of the town. I'm still proud of it.'

There was a rocky outcrop in front of them and they sat down side by side. 'More than of Belgate?' The 64,000-dollar question!

'I love them both. That's the nice thing about love – it's not something you give and have to take back to give again. The more you want to give, the more you have. It's the fastest-growing commodity in the world.' And sometimes the quickest to wither, but this was not the time to tell him that.

'How old were you when your father died?' He was trying to sound casual but she knew he was thinking of David and of Bethel.

'I was quite old, twenty-four. But it hurt a lot. And right now it's hurting that Bethel has died. But we haven't lost her. It's hard to explain, but people you love become part of you. It's as though you absorb some of them . . . do you know what I mean?'

He considered for a moment. 'They teach you things, is that it? And then when you think, they're part of the thinking.'

She nodded. Bethel had taught her to stand on her own feet, to think and cope for herself . . . and so much else beside.

'I expect it'll hurt for a long time,' he said and she could hear the child in the boy's voice.

'I expect it will,' she answered and stood up to go home.

Jim's car was parked outside the house, and he was sitting at the kitchen table with Terry. 'Is she gone?' Terry said and shook his head when she confirmed it. 'I can't imagine Belgate without Sally. She was a character.'

Jim was taking her coat and pouring her a cup of tea. She smiled her thanks, and knew as she did so that she was glad he was there.

23

Thursday, 31 July 1986

She was ready long before time, checking and rechecking the funeral tea, laid out as Bethel would have wished it. Min stood beside her for a final inspection. 'I'm not going to say she'd be pleased with it because you know what she was like. I reckon she'd have said, "It'll do."'

It was so exactly what Bethel would have said that they both laughed. 'Cheer up, Franny,' Min said, squeezing Fran's arm. 'I know how you feel. I'm a bit choked myself, and I hardly knew her.'

'You're like her,' Fran said, suddenly seeing what she should have seen before. 'You're determined and wilful and you like to stir things up, but when you decide to stick to someone you'll do it through thick and thin. That's what she was like.'

Min looked abashed. 'I'd like to think you were right, Fran. Personally, I don't think I measure up to her bootstraps, but if it makes you happy to think so, go ahead.'

'There's something I've got to tell you, Min, but it's hush-hush for a while. I'm going to have a baby.'

Min's face was incredulous. 'Fran? I thought you *couldn't* . . . is it what you want?'

Fran nodded. 'Yes. I'm not saying I'd have chosen right now, but I want it very much.'

Min was sinking into a chair. 'Dennis said there was something. I should have realized . . . but I never notice anyone else, I'm so bloody taken up with me.'

Fran shook her head. 'You're too hard on yourself.'

Min was getting her wind back. 'What's going to happen? Are you . . . ?'

Fran finished for her. 'Getting married? I think so. I haven't told Jim yet. He wants us to marry anyway, but it's complicated.'

Min's eyes had widened. 'You mean you might have it on your own?'

'If that seemed to be for the best for everyone, especially Martin. So please, Min, don't tell anyone just yet.' Min was swearing secrecy when Jim came to tell them it was time to go.

Once more she was climbing into a limousine – just as she had done three years ago, when David died. Behind her the cars lined up for Bethel's friends. She had predicted a good turn-out, but it exceeded her expectations. Martin sat beside her, with Jim and Terry on the facing seats. Last time Eve and Harold had accompanied her, but Eve was otherwise engaged today and Harold had summed it up quite succinctly: '*Don't get too upset. I know she worked for you, Fran, but you can't grieve over everyone. She'd had a good run for her money.*' Still Min and Dennis were there, in the next car, and Walter was bringing up the rear. That was all that counted.

The Salvation Army Church was small and bright, the officer respectful, and buoyed up by hope. They sang 'Fight the Good Fight' as Bethel had requested long ago, and then Martin was standing at the lectern, earnest and self-important.

Fran had found the volume of John Bunyan in Bethel's sideboard. Her husband's name was on the fly-leaf and a dedication from some long-gone Sunday-School teacher. The book had opened at a marked page, and the words there came to life as Martin's young voice echoed round the hall.

'I am going to my fathers, and though with great difficulty I am got hither, yet now I do not repent me of all the trouble I have been at to arrive where I am. My sword, I give to him that shall succeed me in my pilgrimage and my courage and skill, to him that can get it. My marks and scars I carry with me, to be a witness for me, that I have fought His battles who now will be my rewarder!

'When the day that he must go hence was come many accompanied him to the river side, into which, as he went, he said, "Death, where is thy sting?" And as he went down deeper, he said, "Grave where is thy victory?" So he passed over, and the trumpets sounded for him on the other side!'

As he sat down beside her she murmured 'Well done!' but he stared straight ahead and she saw that he was struggling not to cry. They rose to sing the final hymn and Fran closed her eyes, remembering Bethel as she had been, fur hat set firmly on iron-grey hair, determined face beneath.

'Oh, Bethel, I don't think I can manage without you.' And then the voice in her head, the voice that would never leave her ... '*Let's have no more of that, miss.*' She looked down at the hymn-book and blinked until the letters swam into place and she could open her mouth to sing.

*

There were willing hands to help with the food – Min and Dennis, Terry and Treesa, and Jim, catching her eye from time to time to reassure himself she was OK.

'Walter didn't come, then,' Terry said, when everyone had plate and cup and they could relax. Around them the elders of Belgate reminisced. One or two wiped a surreptitious tear, but for the most part they laughed, remembering their youth and their friend.

'No, he wouldn't come. I tried to persuade him. He drove away as soon as the service was over.'

Terry nodded. 'He's taking it hard, Mrs Drummond. I've known him all my life and never seen him bested, but this has got him down.'

Treesa had joined them. 'I always thought they'd get wed in the end.' She looked at Fran for confirmation. 'I know they went on at each other, but underneath it was love.' There was a tremor in her voice and Terry put his arm round her.

'Of course it was, pet. It's a pity they left it too late, that's all.'

When everyone had gone Fran went about replacing the furniture, picking damp petals from the floor, just as she had done after David's funeral. It had been a joint decision to have Bethel buried from their house. 'I know she loved her own house,' Martin had said, deciding, 'but she loved us more.'

So Bethel had lain in the front room amid banks of flowers, and now the carpet was imprinted by the trestles and the debris of a funeral was there to be tidied away. But this time Jim was there to help her, and Martin too. Today she had noticed how thin his face had become – or perhaps it was his jaw showing through, the first angularity of youth.

When it was done, the three of them sat around the kitchen table and drank tea. Memories of Bethel, arms dusted with flour, face flushed from the oven's heat, opening her Players No. 6 and offering them, crowded in, but Fran put them aside. Bethel had always had a sense of priorities.

There was a soft plop from the hall and Martin went to collect the *Echo*. Last night he had read out the announcement: '*Bethel, Sarah Mary (née Heads) beloved wife of the late John Thomas and dearly loved friend of Frances and Martin Drummond . . .*'

Tonight there was better news. '*Belgate colliery reprieved. Best productivity performance in the Durham coalfield secures the future for Belgate miners*.' 'Bethel would've been pleased,' Martin said and then read a more stark announcement, prefacing it with his own headline: 'Our coalman's gone to gaol.' Dave, the sacked miner who had brought them their coal since the strike, had been sentenced to three months for burglary of a deputy's home. The strike had been over for eighteen months but still it was claiming victims.

When Martin had finished the *Echo* he stood up. 'The dog needs taking out.' And then, fondling its head, 'Poor thing. You don't know what's going on, do you?'

As boy and dog went out, Jim smiled at her. 'He's trying hard, isn't he?'

Fran nodded. 'It seems just like yesterday he was too lazy to do anything. "Walk the dog," I'd say, and he'd say, "Wait on." And Bethel would come through from the kitchen. "Never mind 'wait on'. It's wees that dog wants, not 'wait on'."'

She was fumbling for words when the phone rang. 'Hallo, it's Barbara.' Fran was about to say, 'I'll get Daddy for you' when the voice went on: 'Daddy says you're coming down soon?' and then a stern aside – 'In a minute. I said in a minute . . . get off! It's not your turn yet.'

Fran smiled. She would have liked more time to get to know Jim's children, but it would be all right. They were very normal kids.

She left him in the hall when he took over the phone, and waited in the kitchen. At last she heard the tinkle of the receiver going down and knew it had come, the moment she couldn't postpone any further, the absolute ultimate crunch.

'There's something I must tell you, Jim. I'm going to have a baby. It was my decision to keep it and I'm not asking for help, so don't feel you have to "do the decent thing". The decent thing in this situation is to be honest with each other.'

Mingled emotions were chasing across his face. 'Well,' she said at last, 'tell me how you feel?'

He grimaced. 'Absolute honesty?'

She inclined her head. 'Absolute.'

'Well then ... I feel ... wonderful ... and flabbergasted ...
and bloody scared, Fran. But I expect we'll manage.' As though
he had sensed his own inadequacy, he spoke again. 'I'm *glad*
about it, Fran. But not because I need another child. I'm glad
because it's a seal on our love, something we made together.
And, oh, I do love you, Frances Drummond.'

She leaned against him, trying to quell her mounting panic.
Commitment meant the prospect of pain and loss. But it meant
so much more. They would be together for ever now – for as
long as 'for ever' was allowed to be. She closed her eyes but
opened them in shock as he suddenly pulled away.

'Why didn't you tell me?' There was anger in his voice as he
measured the time she had kept silent.

'I don't know. I just didn't want to influence things. Whatever
happened, I wanted it to be for the right reasons.'

He nodded. 'I know what you mean, but you were wrong. I
should've known from the beginning. Anyway, I hope you're
satisfied now. I didn't come back to you for any other reason
than love.' He grinned and reached for her hand. 'And if I'm
honest, a little bit of lust. That figured in it, too.'

His kiss had little of lust in it – it was more a search for
reassurance. 'Is it what you want, Fran? That's all that matters.'

She lifted her free hand to touch his cheek. 'Of course it's
what I want. Surely you realize that?'

24

Monday, 15 September 1986

Bethel's house was already taking on the odour of disuse, and
everything Fran touched was chill. She decided to keep on her
coat and make a start on the bureau. She had looked there after
Bethel's death to see if there were instructions for the funeral,
and had found the will. She and Walter were executors and
could take their pick of Bethel's worldly goods. Martin got £848
in the Co-op Bank. Anything else went to the Sally Army.

Walter wanted nothing. 'I can't be bothered over what I've got already, without taking on more.' Since Bethel's death the fire had gone out of him, and with it the will to live. Apart from the day of the funeral, Fran had not seen his car on the Belgate streets and Treesa brought alarming tales of how little he was eating, which she'd culled from neighbours and shops.

Fran smiled, thinking of Treesa. In a few years' time she would be another Bethel, strong and upright, bossing Terry, probably wearing a fur hat and a silk scarf folded inside her coat. A proper News of the World! Perhaps she would even bake bread, although Fran doubted it. Treesa was a child of the sliced-loaf generation. Remembering Bethel's bread, Fran shivered. This kitchen used to steam gently in the glow from an abandoned fire, piled high with concessionary coal to heat the oven. There would be no more floury flat cakes, no crusty biscuit-coloured loaves to fall from their tins at the rap of an expert hand. But the memory was there, locked in her head, to be brought out reverently whenever she could bear it. Suddenly she heard Bethel's reproaching voice. '*You're sitting there as though you had corn growing!*' Obediently she lowered the lid of the bureau and settled to her task.

All she had to do was go through and remove the personal things. After that Terry had promised to see to it that everything was disposed of as the Sally Army wished. He was a good friend; so was Dennis. He and Min were to oversee the shipment of Fran's furniture to Twickenham and the subsequent sale of the house.

It had been easy for Jim and Fran to work things out once the principle of being together was agreed. She had suggested living together as an experiment and felt weak with relief when he gave a flat refusal. 'We're getting married, Fran ... and the quicker the better.' She was showing now, not to any great extent, but there was less and less point in concealment.

She had told Gwen when they met to talk about the future. 'Is it what you want?' Gwen had asked; it was the same question Min had posed, but this time Fran was more sure of the answer. 'Well, good for you,' Gwen said when Fran told her that it was.

Eve had been frosty. Her lips had mouthed uneasy platitudes

but her eyes had said, '*How could you, Fran? And you a grieving widow.*' For a second Fran had contemplated explanation, but there was no way Eve would have understood the intricacies of second relationships and, anyway, Fran was not sure she cared enough about Eve to enlighten her.

Jim understood: that was the important thing. 'I understand about David because I still love Dorothy. I always will. But I love you, Fran. Not instead of or in spite of . . . I just love you.' She had shivered a little, thinking of Dorothy, for ever thirty, never growing old, or arguing, or falling from grace. She it was who would age and rage and disintegrate with time. But she had smiled and touched his cheek. Sufficient unto the day.

'It'll be a relief to have someone to look after Barbara,' he'd said. 'Kevin and I can manage, but I used to wake up in the night and think, "What do you do with a girl? How do you explain womanhood, when it comes?"'

Fran had smiled, remembering her own fears. 'I used to have nightmares about Martin and shaving. I decided when the time came I'd just go into Boots and buy him the gear and hope it had instructions. But, really, we worry for nothing. Martin is growing . . . has grown up . . . with very little help from me.'

It was Martin's new-found maturity that had given her the courage to face a move. That, and the fact that Bethel was no longer there to lean on. 'It makes sense for us to come south,' she said when Jim demurred. 'You've got contacts down there – you said so . . . you wanted to go into marine paints? We'll talk about that in a minute. And your kids won't understand being uprooted. Not straight away. I want to talk to Martin first, but if he agrees, we'll come to London. You never know, I might come to like it in time.'

They were lying in his hotel bed, their gentle love-making over. 'I'm not suddenly made of glass because I'm pregnant,' she'd told him, but he was unconvinced.

'About work,' she said. 'You said once you'd have liked to go it alone, but it was too risky. Well, I'm here now to share that risk. I'm a trained teacher, remember. I can earn a salary once the baby's here. There'll be money to come from my house and you could re-mortgage yours. We could sell up and move to

Southampton if it made sense. But you must have a chance to strike out on your own!' She didn't add 'for all our sakes' but she knew he understood. She hoped in vain for instant agreement, but it would come with time. At least he'd agreed to consider it.

The confidence of her own thinking nowadays amazed her. Three years ago she had been a jelly, forced to recite her name and particulars to still the panic within. Now she could plot like a Machiavelli and face the world, warts and all. But she still shirked telling Martin about the baby, and she would have to tell him soon. He had been a brick about leaving Belgate, and deserved better from her. She got on with clearing out Bethel's bureau.

There were the usual bills and documents. A birth certificate for Sarah Mary Heads, born to Susannah and Thomas Henry at 12 Clanny Street, Belgate, on 17 June 1917, and another for John Thomas Bethel, folded with the certificate of his death from a ruptured spleen and multiple fractures, as the result of an industrial accident, on 18 October 1945. Fran put the documents carefully aside. They were the fabric of Bethel's life and must be preserved.

The bundle of letters were yellowing and flaked at the edges and were all dated 1937: Bethel's letters written from service to the man who was to be her husband, and his letters to her. Fran read through the formal phrases, stilted at first and then warming as their acquaintance deepened. '*I felt sad, love, when I saw you off at the station and then I thought of how soon we will be together, never to be parted again, and I felt quite cheered up. I have got a poker for you, made in the pit, a stout bit of iron and our first possession.*' Fran smiled, thinking how well he had known his love and her obsession with a well-stoked fire.

Bethel's letters were full of detail about the houses she worked in and her employers' peccadillos. '*Today we hung the winter curtains but they don't suit "madam" and will have to come down tomorrow. She says they clash with the new paper and he, poor fish, says yes dear, three bags full as usual. I'm thankful I'm marrying a man and not a soft article that isn't master in his own home.*'

She put the letters aside to be reread at leisure. She did not feel she was prying. It was as though Bethel had intended her to find them.

There was a baby's rattle in the next section, a mother-of-pearl handle topped with a silver bell, and all wrapped in tissue paper. It was not new, and had teeth-marks on the handle to prove it, so where had it come from? That too was put aside, and she took out a blue envelope that had once held a calendar. Inside was a yellowing cutting dated 1953. At first Fran thought it was a souvenir of the coronation, but the picture of Queen Elizabeth was incomplete and when she turned it over she saw that it was an account of an accident in the pit: '*Conveyor belt tragedy at Belgate.*' A miner called Sidney Jefferson had been killed and another, Walter Raeburn, was seriously ill in Sunderland's Accident Hospital.

Fran sifted through the rest of the envelope. Christmas and birthday cards from Walter, terse messages and restrained pictures, all signed with a flourish. There was an account of his chairmanship of the local disabled drivers' club and two letters written by him to the local paper, which had been carefully clipped and preserved by Bethel.

'She did love him,' Fran thought. 'She kept every little thing connected with him. *And* she loved her husband.' So Bethel, too, had loved twice. But she had never quite had the courage to confess that second love, and now Walter was left with nothing.

'I'll get it right, Bethel. This time I'll get it right for both of us.' She put the envelope in her handbag and went on with her task, but her mind wandered. First love, second love, mother love, all fruit of the same tree, all sweet. And so different to any other emotion. She had clung to Steve, desperate for companionship, and she had lusted for Tony Lund. But she had loved David, truly loved him, and now she loved Jim. Last night she had taken his head to her breast and known, as she did so, that her love for him was strong enough to deal with whatever might come.

Martin came in, Nee-wan on the lead quivering to be free. 'I want to talk to you, darling. Yes, now. It's important.'

He settled on a chair and coaxed the dog to a sitting position. He was looking at her, waiting, but his eyes were wary. She felt the rush of love that always overcame her when she looked at her child. But children needed more than love, they needed fair play.

'Sometimes it's easy to think parents always get things right. We encourage you to think that when you're little, so that you'll feel safe. Now you're growing up, you know that I don't always get things right.' He was smiling, trying not to look triumphant at her admission. She was seeking for words but the temptation to fob him off and delay the truth was overwhelming. She had felt like that about his father's death, knowing the secret could not be kept but hoping that if she waited it would go away.

'When people love one another they sleep together.' They were not the right words, he wouldn't understand. 'They make love ... because they love one another.' '*Make love*': another euphemism. She had always intended to tell him the facts of life but she had left it too late. The facts had preceded the telling.

His lips had come together now, the smile gone, and there was a flush on his upper cheeks. 'I know about sex,' he said suddenly. 'Everyone knows at school.' Of course he would know: she had known herself at going on twelve years old, in another and more innocent age.

It was easy to tell him, then, to discuss guilt and shame and love and the expectation of happiness. 'So I can't undo what's done, but I can try to make it better by making a happy life for all of us. If you'll help me.'

He had had enough of emotion. 'I will. Now, can I go?' He submitted to her embrace with good grace but she sensed his embarrassment and confusion. A baby like Christopher, alive and waiting to play, was one thing. A baby, mysterious within the womb, was quite another.

'I love you, Martin.'

He was frowning, uncertain of what to do next. She wanted to reach out for him but she knew it would be a mistake. Suddenly he grinned.

'It's right what Bethel used to say about you. Slop, slop, slop!'

As he quit the room she knew it was going to be all right.

When her work was done and the house left tidy for Terry and Treesa she let herself out and closed the door for the last time.

The lace curtains with their bottom frills were already jaded, missing their monthly soak to bring them up white. Next week the keys would be handed in, and a new tenant would polish and dust Bethel's domain. A Belgate girl with Belgate ways; another link in the chain.

She drove to Walter's house, taking the tape recorder from the seat, the volume of Bunyan from the glove compartment, and adding the envelope of his cards and cuttings. He was sitting in front of the fire and for the first time she saw him without his tweed jacket. He was tieless, shirt neck open and cuffs flapping at the wrists. There was a stubble on his chin and a smell of urine in the air. 'He's given up,' she thought and was afraid.

'I've been to Sally's. I know you didn't want anything but there's something I think you should have. This was her *Pilgrim's Progress*: it's yours now. And these were mementos of you she kept through the years. She loved you, Walter: for all the sparring and the ding-dong battles, you were the apple of her eye. And I don't know what she'd make of you today.'

She had hoped for some retaliation, a burst of anger as the barb went home, but there was nothing. He fingered the book and the envelope for a moment and then laid them on the side table.

'You're off the day after tomorrow, then?'

She nodded. 'Yes, Martin and I are driving down together. We'll sort things out there, and our furniture will follow later. Some friends of mine are seeing to it for me . . . and Terry's going to see to Bethel's house.'

'That young communist.' Once the words would have been flung like a lance, now they were simply a comment. Fran decided to ignore them.

'I'll be coming back often, Walter. Martin has friends here and so do I. So we won't lose touch. In the meantime, I want you to have this.' She held out the tape recorder. 'There's a tape in it, I made it last night. It just says a few things I want you to know. When you've heard it, you can record a message and send it back to me. It's better than letters.'

The massive head rolled slowly from side to side as if in amazement at her foolishness. 'I'm far ower old for that sort of thing. Tapes, buttons . . . why not get a space machine and I'll fly down?' She remembered Bethel's injunction: '*Don't give way to him. He likes everyone to dance to his tune.*'

'Well, it's there, Walter. Whether or not you use it's up to you. I'd like to keep in touch and so would Martin, but we can't make you.'

As she drove away she wondered if he was right: perhaps an old dog couldn't learn new tricks, not even push-button ones. She drove into her back street and got out to open the garage door. From a door further up a figure emerged, wheeling a bicycle: it was Fenwick. There was a basket on the back of his bicycle, and as he drew level she saw activity behind the wickerwork. 'New birds?' she said. For a year or more he had walked the streets of Belgate like a zombie, an outcast with no purpose in life other than work and sleep. Today he looked more relaxed. 'Aye, Mrs Drummond. I don't know if they're any good. We'll have to wait and see.'

As she let herself into the house she felt comforted. Fenwick was flying pigeons again. Birds to soar and circle, symbols of hope. And then again the memory of Bethel, floured arms akimbo, bringing her back to earth. '*Pigeons is nothing but shit-machines, miss. And don't you forget it.*'

25

Wednesday, 17 September 1986

They gathered for the last time in the kitchen: Dennis and Min, Gary Malone, Terry and Treesa, Christopher on unsteady legs, and Frances Mary in her carrycot. Fran had held them both in her arms from birth. Soon she would have two more children to care for and a baby of her own. After all the years of hoping, a child had crept up on her unawares and her son had grown to be a comfort. He was grinning at her now. 'Cheer up, Mam. Everything's under control.'

Gary Malone was fidgeting and Martin heaved a sigh. 'Come

on then, Gary. Let's get loaded.' Gary flew to the stairs and Terry tut-tutted.

'He's a right little vulture, that one. I don't know where he gets it. As soon as your Martin said there was some gear he could have, he was like a cat on hot bricks.'

Treesa smiled indulgently. 'He's only a bairn.' She turned to Fran. 'What time will you get to London?'

'About seven o'clock. I want to miss the rush-hour traffic. It should be over by then.'

Dennis's mouth had opened. 'Six hours to get to London! I thought you were going by car!'

Min gave him a playful rap. 'All right, Stirling Moss. Some of us quite like living. We're not all speed merchants.' Last night she had confided her chief ambition to Fran. *'I mean to get him some decent wheels again, Fran. It'll take a long time but I'll do it.'*

'There now.' Treesa put the tray on the table and began to pour. 'You can't beat a good cup of tea. And don't you worry about Walter, Fran. Me and Terry'll see to him.'

Terry grinned. 'I'll snap him out of it. A few digs about Scargill, that'll get his dander up.' It was true. Perhaps a good argument was what Walter needed.

'Arthur's a red rag to more than one around here,' Treesa said. 'I was talking to Ella Bishop's man the other day. You know the wife with the gold earrings, the one that was big in the strike? When the support group closed down she joined the Party. At it day and night, keen as mustard. I was saying to her man she'd gone very political, and he shakes his head and says, "I'll never forgive Scargill. He's ruined our lass."'

There was general laughter, and then Min returned to the subject. 'Terry's right, Fran. You're not to worry about a thing. He'll sort out Walter, and Dennis and I will see to things here. And then we'll all come down for the wedding, no matter where we get the cash. I'm planning a really snazzy outfit.' She thought for a moment. 'Of course, I won't go too far, I'll dress down. It's your day, after all.' She said it in generous tones and looked puzzled as Fran and Dennis burst into laughter.

'What about Eve and Harold?' Dennis said when the mirth had subsided.

'They won't be able to get away,' Fran said. 'Well, they have got a lot on. Isn't it a shame!' This time everyone laughed.

The next moment the door from the hall rocked back on its hinges and a flushed Gary Malone came through almost concealed behind a pile of books, comics, boxed games and half-completed models. He gave not a glance to the group around the table, merely steered for the back door. 'I'll come straight back for the rest,' he called as he exited.

'See what I mean?' Terry said. 'Mention something for nothing to that one and his motor starts.' Fran smiled, remembering Gary years ago, describing his grandmother's funeral. '*We had meat . . . not just gravy . . . git lumps of meat. And cream cakes. You could eat as much as you liked and the priest gave us all tenpence. I've still got one nana left.*'

The next moment he crashed back into the kitchen and through it without pause. 'He's a man in a hurry,' Dennis said. 'They're the ones who make the world go round.'

When Gary had tottered out under the second and final load, Martin said, 'I'm going to say tarra to Walter. I won't be long.'

Fran had made her own goodbyes to Walter earlier, once more exhorting him to keep in touch and receiving little response. 'We have to leave at one o'clock,' she said to Martin. 'Don't hold me up.'

Min and Treesa were clearing the fridge of perishable food and washing the tea cups while the men amused the children, so Fran mounted the stairs for a final check. She was sure to have forgotten something.

She had meant to check wardrobes and drawers, but she found herself drawn to the window. Three years ago she had looked out on the snow-covered garden and made her decision to stay. Now she was leaving but Belgate always would be her 'land of lost content'.

'We'll come back often, won't we?' Martin had asked last night and she had promised that they would. She would keep her word. Walter must not be abandoned, and there were Gwen and Linda and Edward. She had paid them a flying visit last night and vowed to come back for the christening. 'We'll be thinking of you on your big day, won't we, Eddy? We'd come down if it wasn't so soon.' Linda had looked at her swollen belly then smiled up at Edward.

'Take care of yourself, Frances,' he had said then. 'You'll always be special to us.'

Down below in the kitchen she could hear laughter, and her eyes filled with tears. Her friends! She had thought of them the night before as she walked on the beach with Martin and the dog. In the distance the sea-coalers toiled on the moonlit tide line. Beside her, Martin had walked, hands in pockets in case she was mushy enough to reach for one. Nee-wan, amazed at this night-time ramble, had run back and forth like a dog possessed.

'Do you know what I'm thinking about?' he said suddenly.

She shook her head. 'I don't know, darling. Is it about London? We'll be all right there, you know.'

He bent for a stone and sent it skimming across the surface of the sea. 'No, it's OK about London. Gary says he'll come down on the coach once we're settled in, and you said we'll come back. And Jim's OK.' There was a chuckle. 'He's the best boyfriend you've had. Since Dad.'

She felt her cheeks flush. 'I haven't had that many . . . you make me sound like Henry the Eighth.' If she wasn't careful he would start listing them! 'What *are* you thinking about?' she said hastily.

'I was thinking about the pit. Being here, under the sea. Men we know working down there with the North Sea above them. Gary's going to be a miner if he can get an apprenticeship, and he says he can. He says his dad and Terry can fix anything at the pit. Anyway, I was thinking I might be a mining engineer. Or an architect. Except that I'd quite like to work the market like Aunty Min.'

She was tempted to ask if he fancied brain surgery or fire-fighting but decided against it. At least he was thinking about the future.

'It's hard to believe the strike's been over for a year, and a half,' she said. 'Except that it still rumbles on.' Yesterday she had seen '*UDM is sods*' on a wall, fresh painted. And another slogan blaming the NUM for all the miners' troubles, as though to answer the first.

'They'll get over it eventually,' Martin said easily and bent for another stone.

Fran was still remembering that moonlit walk on the beach when Min tapped on the bedroom door. 'Fran?' She pushed the door to behind her and stood, arms at sides. 'Fran, there's no easy way to ask this but someone has to. You're not marrying Jim because it's the respectable thing to do, are you? Because if you are, you mustn't! Dennis and I are behind you every inch of the way, and you know you could cope. Don't say it's cheek to ask, because I'm not a bit ashamed. What's the good of having a brass neck if you don't stick it out occasionally?'

Fran went to Min, arms outstretched, and they clung. 'Thanks for saying that, Min. You sounded just like Dad. He offered me a final get-out before we left for church, and when I said I was sure I wanted to marry David he said, "Thank God. Your mother would've killed me if you'd called it off."'

'It's a lifetime ago, isn't it?' Min said, suddenly awestruck.

'Ten lifetimes,' Fran said, 'but I'm sure this is right, Min. Very sure. I love Jim.'

Min smiled. 'We've grown up, kid, you and I. A bit late, but we've done it all the same.'

They went out to the cars at one o'clock. 'I told Martin we were leaving at one,' Fran said, beginning to fret.

Fenwick was coming towards them, for once without his bike. 'You're off, then.'

Fran held out her hand. 'Goodbye, Mr Fenwick. But we'll see you again before long.'

He nodded and released her hand. 'Goodbye, Mrs Drummond. Watch out for that lad of yours.'

His eyes flicked to Terry – militant Terry, who had been known to spit at the sight of scabs. Fran held her breath until Terry inclined his head.

'Aye, aye, Billy lad.'

Fenwick merely bobbed his head in return, but Fran could see he was pleased.

'Oh, Terry Malone, you're a jewel,' she said when Fenwick was out of earshot.

'By,' Treesa said, putting her hand through the crook of her husband's arm, 'you're in my good books now, and no mistake.'

Terry was embarrassed and had to make a joke of it. 'Listen that,' he said to Dennis. 'The way they're going on you'd think I was a right sod usually . . . excuse the language.'

Martin came running up, panting. 'I'm not late, am I?' Neewan was shooed into the back seat. The babies were held up to be kissed, and Martin was hugged in turn. 'I'll see you, Gary,' he yelled – and they were away.

'Don't cry, Mam,' he said as she tried, through her tears, to negotiate the corner. 'They're still your friends. Besides, wait till you hear about Walter! He was trying to use the recorder and the air was blue. You know what he's like when he gets stuck. So I showed him, and he says he might send a tape. Which means he will, only he can never just say so.'

They were leaving Belgate behind and the rounded tops of the Cleveland Hills appeared in the distance. Once beyond the hills the North-east would be lost to view. 'It's a long way, isn't it?' Martin said suddenly, echoing her thoughts.

The comic he had begun to read was lying on his knee, and for the first time since London had been talked about he looked a little woebegone.

'Two hundred and sixty-five miles,' she said, sticking to facts. 'But it's only three hours by train.' He was silent. 'You'll like London . . . lots to see, heaps of history.' Perhaps they would learn to love the South in time, both of them.

They were approaching the junction with the A1. Soon she must turn west and then south. Instead she turned east and began to climb into the hills. The blue, remembered hills of Housman's poem. 'Why are you going to the Cleves?' Martin asked but she didn't reply.

She drove to Look-out Point, where they had picnicked so often with David, where she had driven in anguish after his death. 'Is this a kind of goodbye to Dad?' Martin said.

'No. We'll never say goodbye to Dad or Bethel. Or anyone we love. There's no need.'

Martin was grinning now. 'Dad fried sausages up here once, didn't he? And he set the pan on fire and said, "Hell's bloody teeth," and you said, "Shush, David, Martin's listening."'

Fran shook her head. 'You always have had *big* ears.'

She turned back to look out on a grey landscape, touched here and there with colour as the leaves turned with autumn and the fields, raped of their crops, blackened at the approach of winter. Ancient Northumbria, a kingdom by the sea.

She could not see the towns and cities or the mighty rivers of the North, but if she closed her eyes she could summon them to view. The grey, luminous mouth of the Tees, the yellow cranes of the Wear, and the bustle of the Tyne, the grey towers of Durham, the green parks of Sunderland, and Cleveland waiting to stir its great limbs at the promise of work.

Most of all, Belgate and its people. Not better or more friendly than southerners, but special people because they were her people. Inside her pocket her fingers closed around the piece of sea-coal she had carried up from the beach the night before. Solid and tangible, a talisman to take her safely along the sliding stream.

'It's time to go, Mam,' Martin said. 'Jim'll be waiting.' She turned away obediently. No need to stay and no need to look back. The kingdom of the North was in her heart and she would take it with her wherever she might go.

SIGNET

The Second Wife

Ellie has gone missing. Why?

Ellie is deeply in love with Richard, but two things stand in the way of her happiness. She is haunted by thoughts of Julia, Richard's first wife, and by another spectre – this time from her own past.

In a desperate bid to find Ellie, Richard enlists the help of Paul, her psychiatrist, and Terri, her best friend.

For Paul, entangled in a domestic turmoil of his own, finding Ellie becomes imperative when he realizes there is more at stake than Ellie's mental health.

For Terri – a talented journalist and herself a second wife, although her predecessor is very much alive – finding Ellie becomes a crusade to discover the secret that threatens her friend's marriage – and perhaps her life.

By the same author

None to Make You Cry

A woman's deepest love is for her children.

Helen, growing up in the North East of the 1960s, knows that the new mood of permissiveness will not extend to her. So she gives up the baby she has had in secret, and makes a new life in London.

Lilian, her sister, bound by the demands of her children and her coal-miner husband, envies Helen's freedom, little guessing the real reason for her flight.

Long-buried secrets surface again when the tragic death of Lilian's daughter draws Helen north for the funeral. It is then she realizes that she must become involved in the life of her son.

'What the reader needs is ... the detail of domestic life that so few authors can convincingly handle but which illuminates a novel when it is done with authority. Denise Robertson has this gift' – Philippa Gregory in the *Sunday Times*

and

Remember the Moment

THE BELOVED PEOPLE
Trilogy

Denise Robertson

'An intelligent, evocative saga … written with a strong historical sense and a fine eye for authenticity, this is big-hearted stuff in the best style'
– *Sunday Telegraph*

From the 1920s to the 1960s, *The Beloved People, Strength for the Morning* and *Towards Jerusalem* follow the hopes and heartaches of the people of the Durham mining village of Belgate. Through peace and prosperity, war and devastation, they are united by the forces of love and work and the struggle against poverty.

SIGNET

By the same author

The Stars Burn On

On New Year's Day 1980, Jenny and seven friends watch the dawn from a northern hill. On the brink of adulthood, confident of their futures, they vow to meet there again at the end of the decade. Just two weeks later, one of the group is dead. The others, irrevocably affected, go on to pursue careers in the law or media, and make new lives for themselves as husbands, wives and parents. Jenny, who establishes herself as a successful journalist in London, remains their linchpin – and only Jenny knows that the secret that binds them is a lie.

'A saga that'll keep you turning the pages ... told with perception and humour' – *Prima*

'Her prose has a fine flow, her knowledge of the region is deep and instinctive. Above all, her compassion and great understanding of life show in all she writes' – *Evening Chronicle*, Newcastle upon Tyne

and

The Anxious Heart